John Wycliffe, Thomas Arnold

Select English works of John Wyclif

Vol. 1

John Wycliffe, Thomas Arnold

Select English works of John Wyclif
Vol. 1

ISBN/EAN: 9783337282134

Printed in Europe, USA, Canada, Australia, Japan

Cover: Foto ©Andreas Hilbeck / pixelio.de

More available books at **www.hansebooks.com**

OF

JOHN WYCLIF

EDITED FROM ORIGINAL MSS.

BY

THOMAS ARNOLD, M.A.

OF UNIVERSITY COLLEGE, OXFORD

Vol. I

SERMONS ON THE GOSPELS

FOR

SUNDAYS AND FESTIVALS

Oxford

AT THE CLARENDON PRESS

M DCCC LXIX

INTRODUCTION.

The present edition of selected works of John Wyclif, English and Latin, was undertaken by the Delegates of the University Press at the earnest instance of the late Canon Shirley, who devoted the best part of ten years of a life, alas! too short, to the study of the works and the age of the English reformer.

At a meeting of the Delegates of the Press, held on the 23rd of March, 1866, a resolution was passed, and recorded in a minute, of which the material portion is as follows:—

'Dr. Shirley's proposal to prepare for publication selected English works of Wyclif in three volumes 8vo . . . . was accepted; and he was authorized to negotiate with Mr. T. Arnold . . . for the editing of the same under his own superintendence.'

Dr. Shirley intended, as general Editor, to have prefixed to the works an elaborate Introduction, in which he would have endeavoured to fix the exact theological position of the writer in reference both to his own and to later times, besides probably settling, so far as the means at our disposal allow, the chronology and authenticity of the immense mass of writings ascribed to Wyclif,—a subject which Bale left in utter confusion, and which Lewis has done very little to elucidate. Such minor matters as the critical collation of MSS., the preparation of a text for the press based on such collation, the verification of references, and the illustration of the text by occasional notes, he desired to commit to the hands of an assistant or assistants; and it was thus that he asked me to take a share in the work. I gladly consented,—having indeed already formed the opinion independently, after reading the *Fasciculi Zizaniorum* and Dr. Shirley's admirable Introduction to that strange miscellany,—that the principal works of the reformer, particularly his English works, ought long ere this to have been given to the public. Before, however, any material step had been taken towards the execution of his plans, this good man and ripe scholar was cut off by death. A greater share of the responsibility of the edition has, in consequence, been thrown upon me than was originally intended, or than, to say the truth, I feel myself quite competent to meet. I have however spared no pains to give to the reader a faithful and readable copy of those of the original works, which it has been resolved to print, and for this purpose I have collated, in whole or in part, a number of other MSS., preserved in various libraries, with the excellent Bodleian Codex, upon which the text of the following Sermons is based. I have also entered in the following pages, and shall enter more at length in the Introduction to the third volume, on the critical questions relating to the authenticity of the various works ascribed to Wyclif, so far as the discussion is necessary in order to justify the selection of his writings which has been made.

I desire to take this early opportunity of acknowledging the great and invaluable assistance that I have received in the task of editing from Professor Stubbs, whose learning and judgment, always most kindly and freely imparted, have signally lightened my labours, often directed me into the true path of investigation, and kept me from falling into many errors.

Wyclif wrote both in Latin and English; but his Latin works are far the most numerous and the most voluminous of the two. Ninety-six Latin works are enumerated in Dr. Shirley's *Catalogue* [a], and only sixty-five English. It is proposed in the following remarks to give some account of the English writings, to show what has been already done towards making them known, and to explain the grounds on which the selection resolved upon in the present work has been made.

[a] *Catalogue of the Original Works of John Wyclif.* Oxford, 1865.

English writings.—Of the sixty-five English works included in the *Catalogue*, there are a few which I have not yet had an opportunity to examine. The most important of these are Nos. 61 and 62, *De Officio Pastorali* and *De Papa*, the only MS. of which is in the library of Lord Ashburnham. Another is the tract *De Schismate*, No. 59, the only MS. of which is in the library of Trinity College, Dublin. Others are Nos. 58 and 60, short tracts contained in the same manuscript. There are five or six others, one of which, for reasons presently to be given, I do not believe to be authentic, while of the rest I will defer the examination to the Preface of the third volume.

I have only met with one English writing of Wyclif's, large or small, which was not included by Dr. Shirley in his *Catalogue*. This is the *Lincolniensis*, a short tract, the only copy of which, so far as appears, exists in a Bodleian manuscript (MS. Bodl. 647). I have no doubt that this, like most of the remaining contents of that MS., was written by Wyclif.

Spurious and doubtful writings.—For some time after I had begun to read the works which the *Catalogue* ascribes to Wyclif, I was strongly disposed to question the authenticity of a considerable number of them, for various reasons. With regard to some of these, farther inquiry has not removed my doubts, while in the case of others, that internal evidence on which I relied to establish for them the high probability, if not certainty, of a date subsequent to the death of Wyclif, has been proved by fuller investigation to be far less cogent than I had at first supposed. I will take these two classes of probably spurious and doubtful writings separately.

I. No. 1 in the *Catalogue* is marked 'Early English Sermons;' it is a collection of fifty-four sermons on the Sunday gospels, together with five others on great festivals. No one, except Dr. Vaughan, has ever ascribed these sermons to Wyclif; they exist only in two MSS., and the partial examination which I was able to make of them at Cambridge last year, convinced me that they were the production of a traveller in the well-worn track of homiletics, who possessed no spark of the erratic and daring spirit of our author.

Nos. 6–9 are Commentaries on the Gospels of Matthew, Luke, and John, and on the Apocalypse. Even if they were certainly authentic, those on the Gospels, at any rate, could not be considered as worth printing, because the substance of them is wholly taken from the writings of the Fathers, chiefly from SS. Chrysostom, Jerome, and Ambrose, from Theophylact, the Venerable Bede, and Aquinas. The Commentary on the Apocalypse is indeed original, but contains, so far as I have examined it, nothing very remarkable. But there is good ground for believing that no part of these Commentaries, not even the prologues and epilogues, is by Wyclif. This I will first endeavour to prove as regards the Commentaries on the Gospels.

In the prologue to the Commentary on Matthew occurs the following passage [b]:—

'For þis cause *a synful caytif* havyng compassion on lewed men declariþ þe gospel of Matthew to lewed men in Englische, wiþ exposicion of syntis and holy writ, and alleggiþ onely holy writ and olde doctours in his exposicion,' &c.

In the prologue to the Commentary on Luke (MS. Bodl. 143) we read,—

'Herfore *a caityf* lettid fro prechyng for a tyme for causis knowun of God writiþ þe gospel of Luk in Englysh wiþ a short exposicioun of olde and holy doctours, to þe pore men of his nacioun.' Farther on the writer again calls himself 'þis pore caitif;' and towards the end he breaks forth into fierce denunciations, as does also the writer of the Commentary on Matthew, of the 'ypocrisie, tirauntrie, and cursidnesse of Antecrist and his meynee,' by whom he evidently means the hierarchy.

Lastly, in the short prologue to the Commentary on John (MS. Bodl. 243) occurs this passage:—

'A symple creature of God, willinge to bere in party þe chargis of symple pore men, writiþ a schort glos in English on þe gospel of Joon,' alleging, as he tells us, his authors 'in general,' and remitting

[b] In the Bodleian MS. (Laud, 235); —the MS. at Trin. Coll. Cambr. (B. I. 38) is stated by Dr. Shirley to have a different prologue.

to 'þe grettur gloos writun on Joon where and in what bokis þes doctours seyen þes sentences.'

The strong similarity of style noticeable in these three prologues, particularly in the first and second, point to the conclusion that they and the glosses which they describe all proceeded from the same hand. If so, that hand was certainly not Wyclif's, for he was never 'lettid fro prechyng,' nor would he have been likely to describe himself as a 'caitif,' by which was then meant an abject, obscure, and despised person. One would be rather disposed to ascribe the authorship of these glosses to the same person who wrote a collection of tracts under the title of 'The Pore Caitif,' which Bale, Lewis, and Dr. Vaughan ascribed unquestioningly to Wyclif, but without cause, as Dr. Shirley was the first to show, since Bishop Pecock, a writer nearly contemporary, tells us that they were written by a mendicant friar 'pro suo defensorio [c].' And that the author belonged to a religious order, and therefore could not have been Wyclif, might with some plausibility be inferred from a passage near the end of the prologue to the Commentary on Matthew, where, in the course of an invective against the 'religiouse,' he says, 'In so myche, that if ony of siche religiouse, bounden to siche privat tradiciouns, wolde live as Crist and his postlis diden, and edifie truly Cristen soulis bi the gospel, the potestatis of singular novelries crien hym a cursed apostata and eretik districr of Cristendome.' There is a tone about these words, which certainly tends to make one believe that the writer was describing his own experience.

The Commentary on Luke is based on the 'Catena Aurea' of S. Thomas Aquinas, whom the compiler throughout the prologue calls 'Alquin.' That on St. John's gospel is also based on the Catena.

Bale, in his most inaccurate catalogue of the writings of Wyclif [d], describes the gloss on Matthew as a 'Translatio Clementis Lanthoniensis.' But the Commentary now in question is certainly no translation from Clement of Lanthony (a monk of the twelfth

[c] *Fasciculi Zizaniorum*, xiii. note 3.

[d] *Illustrium Britanniae Scriptorum Summarium.* Basle, 1559.

century), since its compiler quotes among his authorities Robert Grossetete, who flourished in the thirteenth. Nor again does it appear to be based on the Catena; for although there are fewer extracts on the whole, and those which coincide in the two works are usually given more fully in the Catena, yet particular extracts may be found which are fuller in the Commentary.

With regard to the Commentary on the Apocalypse, internal evidence is, I think, decisive against its being the work of Wyclif. The Introduction seems to me the work of a man of softer and less robust nature. In his interpretation of chap. xviii., the writer expounds the Scarlet Woman to signify Antichrist, characterized by idolatry, 'mammetrie,' covetousness and lechery; but the seven hills on which she sits are—not Rome, but—the seven deadly sins. As the kings under Antichrist fought against the Lamb, so the kings that now were fought against holy Church, and not only 'in bodily þingis but in goostly also, for þorow þe taliage þat þei maken þei bringen þe simple folk into synne.' This is far enough from the position of the man who thought that the secular power might freely resume Church property, and was bound to do so if it were misused; rather it reminds one of the state of things under Henry III. and Edward I. Again, the host that followed him that sat on the white horse, 'bitoknen hem þat willen fiȝte aȝen þe fend þorow lowness and wiþ conventise,'—i. e. in a conventual life; but Wyclif devoted all his powers during many years to the denunciation of the conventual life in all its forms. Again,—'As longe as Satanas is bounden, holy chirche regneþ, and is free to serve God, *and obedient to þe Prelatis.*' But it was the business of Wyclif's life to declaim against the prelates. Again,—'Þat þe folk schulen gon in his liȝt bitokneþ,' that towards the end of the world, 'þe religious of God schulen wexe more and more, and men schul forsake worldly blisse for hope of þe blisse above.' But such a prospect of the spread of monkery would have been to Wyclif a most dreary one. The reader will probably think that sufficient evidence has been adduced to prove that Wyclif was not the author of the Commentary on the Apocalypse.

No. 24, entitled 'A Short Rule of Life,' &c., is conceived in a beautiful spirit, but there is not a particle of evidence to connect it with Wyclif. Even the omnivorous Bale has not included it within the sweep of his catalogue. That it should be found in a MS. volume of tracts bequeathed by Archbishop Parker to Corpus Christi College, Cambridge, and loosely said by him to contain tracts by Wyclif, does not amount to evidence; for some of these compositions can be proved to be of different authorship, and the general statement of Archbishop Parker must not be taken for more than it is worth. Dr. Vaughan indeed says [c], after quoting a fine passage from this tract, inculcating the purest Christian virtues on different orders of men, 'The preacher whose counsels were of this description was not the man to become the agent of insurrection, after the fashion of John Ball and Wat Tyler, as some of his ingenuous opponents have insinuated.' This is quite true; but it would have been more to the purpose to prove that the tract is by Wyclif, instead of merely assuming it. So far as the evidence of style goes, I am myself greatly inclined to doubt its authenticity.

No. 48, a tract printed by Dr. Todd, in 1851, under the title 'Of Antecrist and his Meynee,' does not appear to be authentic. The style is narrower and more puritanic than that of Wyclif, and the allusions to the persecutions to which the writer and his party were subjected seem more suitable to a later time. Thus (p. cxlviii.) we are told that Antichrist 'harder al day punyschiþ, as al day now men may see.' Again, Antichrist and his followers 'kille treue men in her prison.' On the whole, this language suits a period subsequent to the constitutions of the archbishops Arundel and Chicheley better than the lifetime of the reformer; and as the evidence of style tends the other way, and there is not a tittle of external evidence attributing it to Wyclif, the tract not being included even in Bale's list, I think it may be safely struck out of the catalogue of the reformer's writings.

No. 47, 'Tractatus de Pseudo freris,' found in a single MS. at Dublin, is similarly destitute of all external evidence tending to asso-

[c] *Tracts and Treatises of John de Wycliffe*, p. 48.

ciate it with Wyclif; but as no previous writer has given any other than the most general description of it, and I have not yet been able to examine it myself, the question of its authenticity must be left in suspense. Nos. 51, 61, and 64 must be included in the same category; there is no external evidence in their favour, but from the only MSS. of them being either in private libraries or at Dublin, I have not yet been able to examine them.

It escaped Dr. Shirley's notice that Nos. 49 and 50 are merely extracts from No. 63, which will be considered in the next paragraph.

II. A considerable number of English tracts still remains, chiefly those contained in the well-known C. C. C. manuscript at Cambridge, with regard to which there is indeed some slight amount of external evidence connecting them with Wyclif, but that evidence is not strong enough to establish their authenticity, should the analysis of their contents lead to an opposite conclusion. I propose to enter upon the full examination of the claims of this class to rank among Wyclif's writings in the Introduction to the third or miscellaneous volume of the present collection. I did indeed at one time conceive myself to have found a test, the application of which would in many cases establish the non-authenticity of a treatise without further trouble. In this, however, deeper research has proved that I was mistaken; and as the point is one which bears upon the authenticity of a portion of the sermons in the present volume,—those for the Commune Sanctorum,—it must be treated of here.

Relying upon the *consensus* of all the ordinary English historians, including Lingard, I came to the study of the questions affecting the authenticity of writings ascribed to Wyclif with the preconceived belief, that the attempts of the English state and hierarchy to coerce heretical or erroneous opinions had not, previously to the enactment of the famous statute commonly called De Haeretico Comburendo, in 1401, proceeded to the length of inflicting capital punishment, either on the gibbet or at the stake, upon the holders of those opinions. The common impression certainly is,—and it was shared by myself,—that no one had suffered death in England for his religious opinions, by direct infliction at the hands of the magistrate [f], before William Sawtre, the first victim to the statute above mentioned. If then, in a tract, the style and handwriting of which showed it to belong either to the end of the fourteenth, or to the beginning of the fifteenth century, mention was made of death by burning or hanging as a fate ever impending over such as held the writer's opinions, the conclusion was ready, that the date of that tract must be subsequent to the passing of the statute of 1401, and that accordingly Wyclif could not have been its author. Tried by this test, the tracts numbered 12, 16, 18, 19, 29, 32, 33, 34, 38, and 63 (out of which all but the last, which is in the Bodleian, are found in the C. C. C. manuscript), since they all contain allusions to 'brennyng' as a punishment constantly impending over, or actually inflicted upon, the followers of Wyclif, would be proved to have been composed many years after the reformer's death [g].

But if this conclusion were to be considered irrefragable, it presently appeared that it would affect other writings, which tradition and common consent, and a fair amount of direct external evidence, had hitherto attributed to Wyclif. Such are the Homilies on the gospels contained in the offices of the Commune Sanctorum, forming the second division of Homilies in the present edition. In Sermon LXIV. (p. 201), in Sermon LXV. (p. 205), and again in Sermon LXVII. (p. 211), occur passages which it is difficult to understand in any other way than as testifying to the fact of a vigorous persecution of Lollards going on at the very time. The passages are subjoined in a foot-note [h]. It immediately became a pressing question,

[f] I use these words, because there is a case, mentioned by William of Newburgh in his history (lib. ii. cap. 13), where some thirty Paulician heretics, having entered England about the year 1163, were condemned at Oxford to be branded, whipped, and turned out of the city; after which, all persons being forbidden to harbour them or give them food, they 'misere perierunt.' For this reference I am indebted to Professor Stubbs.

[g] Wyclif died at Lutterworth in 1384.

[h] p. 201. 'oure prelatis . . . . stranglen and killen men, and spoilen hem of her goodis.'

p. 205. 'þis word counfortiþ symple men, þat ben clepid eretikes and enemyes to þe Chirche, for þei tellen Goddis lawe; for þei ben somynned and reprovyd many weies, and after put in prison, and brend or kild as worse þan þeves.'

p. 211. 'alle þese [popes and bishops, helped by secular lords] bitraien Cristen men to turment, and putten hem to deeþ for hoolding of Cristis lawe.'

whether, in the face of these passages, the authenticity of at least this portion of the Homilies could be maintained.

The first point to be ascertained was whether all the best MSS. contained the passages in question, or whether any omitted them, or showed marks of interpolation. The MSS. of the first class in which these sermons are contained are, besides Bodl. 788, upon which the text of this edition is based, two in the British Museum (Bib. Reg. 18 B. IX. and Cotton. Claud. D. VIII.) and one at Wrest Park (No. 11). I have not had an opportunity of collating the last-named MS., but a reference to those in the British Museum showed that in each of these passages they agreed word for word with Bodl. 788, and exhibited no trace of interpolation. It further appeared that in one of the homilies for the Proprium Sanctorum, a division which in all the copies is associated with that for the Commune Sanctorum, and indisputably formed part of the same work from the first, namely in Sermon CII. (p. 354), mention is made of Richard II. as then reigning. Now, on the supposition that no persecution proceeding to the length of capital punishment had taken place before 1401, how reconcile the mention of Richard, whose deposition and death happened in 1399, with the passages importing that such persecution was actually going on?

Being thus led to examine narrowly the grounds of the supposition above mentioned, I came upon certain facts which tended to throw doubt on their sufficiency to carry the conclusion based on them. Mr. Bond, keeper of the MSS. at the British Museum, was good enough to point out to me a passage in the Chronicle of Meaux, lately edited by him for the Master of the Rolls, which is much to the purpose of the present inquiry. Abbot Burton says (vol. ii. p. 323) that the Franciscans, or a section of them, opposed certain constitutions of Pope John XXII., who thereupon caused many of them to be condemned and burnt, some in France in 1318, others at various places in France, Spain, Italy, and Germany, in 1330; and that among the severities practised on this last occasion, 'in Angliâ, in quadam silva, *combusta sunt viri quinquaginta quinque, et mulieres octo*, ejusdem ordinis et erroris.' This is indefinite, certainly, but there seems no possibility of questioning its substantial truth; and if it be true, then men and women were burnt in England for heresy before 1401.

Again, though no chronicler records any actual execution in the fourteenth century, there is a passage in Walsingham which proves that it was threatened by at least one bishop, and, considering the imperfect nature of the communications between different parts of the country in that age, and the paucity of records, it would surely be hazardous to assert confidently, merely because the chroniclers are silent, that no such threat was ever carried into effect. Speaking of the Lollards in 1389, Walsingham, after blaming the culpable remissness of most of the other bishops, who instead of exterminating these pests went their ways, one to his farm, another to his merchandise, adds that the Bishop of Norwich, 'sit nomen ejus benedictum in secula!' set an edifying example of zeal for the faith, in that he swore that if any one of that perverse sect should presume to preach in his diocese, he should either be burnt or beheaded ('vel ignibus traderetur vel capite privaretur'). Walsingham adds that no Lollard coveted the honour of martyrdom, and that the diocese accordingly remained uncontaminated by their presence[1]. If the Bishop could threaten this, one may suppose that without any violation of law it could have been done. And in fact, if one reads the statute of 1401 carefully, it becomes plain that the legislature which enacted it was not thinking of introducing forms of punishment hitherto unknown to and unsanctioned by the law, but only regularizing and extending uniformly over the country a penal machinery already existing and legal. The remedy is to be applied, not *de novo*, but 'uberius et celerius' than has been hitherto possible;—and because experience proves that the bishops 'per suam jurisdictionem spiritualem dictos perfidos et perversos absque auxilio dictae majestatis regiae *sufficienter corrigere* nequeunt;' inasmuch as the Lollards, by passing from one diocese into another, can with so little difficulty evade the citations served upon them. In truth, to societies whose evolution for many centuries had been presided over by the Catholic Church, the crime

[1] Walsingham, *Historia*, vol. ii. p. 188: Rolls series.

of heresy appeared so tremendous that no punishment, however agonizing, could be commensurate with its turpitude; and when a provincial council, or even a diocesan court, had once declared the fact of heresy to be proved, and had handed over the culprit to the grasp of lay justice, the sheriff, or mayor, or bailiff, who received him, was little likely, unless there was a speedy and full retractation, to be incommoded by prayers or murmurs from the people that execution might be stayed. That such a monster should both in body and soul be as soon as possible got rid of, erased and annihilated off the face of the earth which he cumbered, was the shuddering desire of the pious and the superstitious alike; and for this, fire offered the readiest means; the miscreant might be reduced to ashes,—those ashes might be scattered to the winds; and while his soul commenced to endure its secular torments, his hateful presence would in no possible shape afflict Christian people more. The legislature, which ordained that obstinate heretics should be burned 'coram populo in eminenti loco,' was not afraid that any sympathy with them in their sufferings would be exhibited by the people. I have entered into these considerations simply in order to mitigate the *primâ facie* improbability that if any burnings or beheadings had taken place in the last twenty years of the fourteenth century, the chroniclers would have passed them over in silence. Things were changed in the sixteenth century, but at the time we are speaking of such a mode of dealing with heretics appeared to most men so obviously natural and right,—so much a matter of course,—that one can better understand how very severe punishments may have passed over absolutely without record.

On the whole, then, it appears that the mention of 'brennyng' in these tracts, and also in the sermons for the Commune Sanctorum, is not conclusive against their authenticity. There are, however, in the case of the tracts, or some of them, various other difficulties, the full consideration of which, as was said before, must be reserved for the Introduction to the miscellaneous volume.

THE HOMILIES.—To proceed to the contents of the present volumes. It was Dr. Shirley's intention, both on account of their intrinsic importance, and because, among all the longer English writings, there was the greatest weight of evidence in favour of their genuineness, to print the Homilies[k] first. This intention has been carried out, and the first two volumes of the present edition contain the entire collection,—Vol. I. giving the Sermons for the Sunday Gospels, and those for the Commune and Proprium Sanctorum, while Vol. II. contains the Sermons for the Ferial Gospels, and those for the Sunday Epistles. The original arrangement appears to have been, that the sermons for the Sunday epistles and gospels should be intermixed. This I infer, partly from the fact that such is the arrangement in a valuable MS. in the Bodleian (Douce 321), which, imperfect as it is, appears from the forms of the words to be somewhat more ancient than the manuscript I have printed from,—partly from the same arrangement being followed in one of the copies in the British Museum (Claudius, D. VIII.), and also in a curious MS. at Sidney Sussex College, Cambridge,—but chiefly from a discovery, made in the course of my editorial occupations on MS. Bodl. 788, that the copy from which the writer of that manuscript made his transcript, must also have had the sermons so arranged[l]. As, however, the majority of the MSS. adhere to the separate arrangement, and there is no reason to think that the two sets were written at the same time, or are in any way connected as to their contents, it seems upon the whole preferable to print them just as they stand in the MS. which is the basis of the edition.

The authenticity of these sermons, taken as a whole, cannot reasonably be questioned. Although, so far as I am aware, no one

[k] No. 2 in Dr. Shirley's *Catalogue*.

[l] At the bottom of page 62 of Bodl. 788, the scribe had arrived near the end of the *gospel* sermon for the Third Sunday in Lent. On turning the leaf, instead of the concluding portion of the gospel sermon, he has written down a portion of the *epistle* sermon for the *next* Sunday in Lent; nor did he discover his mistake till he had written about half a column; when at last he found out what he was doing, he drew a pen with red ink through the portion of the epistle sermon that he had written, and continued the transcript of the gospel sermon from the point where he had broken off. The conclusion is inevitable that the older copy which he was using contained the gospel and epistle sermons intermixed, so that parts of two sermons of each description would often appear on parallel columns, as may be seen to this day in Douce 321; such being the case, the scribe's eye on commencing a fresh page was caught by the wrong column, and thus the present appearance of the MS. is accounted for.

of the numerous and widely separated MSS. which contain them names Wyclif as the author in a handwriting contemporary with the copies themselves, yet they have all come down accompanied by the tradition of his authorship, and have never been ascribed to any one else. Again, the fact that the copies are so numerous attests their high popularity in the times before the invention of printing, and entirely accords with the statement of Leland[m], that even in his (Leland's) age, many of the reformer's writings, both in Latin and English, were religiously preserved and diligently read by certain persons, 'praesertim illa *vernacula* in plebis gratiam scripta.' Bale names the several divisions of the sermons in his catalogue, though not always in a way sufficient to identify them with certainty. For instance, his 'In Evangelia Dominicalia,' with *incipit*, 'Homo quidam erat dives,' might just as well refer to the spurious collection of sermons described on a previous page[n] as to those in the present collection. Again, the first words of his 'Sermones in Epistolas' do not tally with the opening of the first Epistle sermon in our present copies. But with regard to the sermons for the Commune and Proprium Sanctorum, and those on the Ferial Gospels, it may be held as certain that the works which he has catalogued are the same as those now printed. The authority of Bale indeed,—Bale, who sets down Wyclif's death in 1387, who takes him on a journey into Bohemia, who assigns to him a score of works which it is most certain he never wrote; moreover, who in his article on Chaucer, omits from the list of his works the *Canterbury Tales*, and includes Lydgate's *Falls of Princes*,—is, if uncorroborated, of almost no value. Happily in the present case the weight of internal evidence tends strongly in the same direction; the authoritative tone, the proneness to subtle and recondite distinctions, so completely in harmony with what we know of Wyclif's fame in the schools, the special hostility to the friars, the allusions to contemporary events, such as the crusade of Bishop Spencer, and the grant of papal indulgences to those who engaged in it (p. 136)—events which occurred in 1383, and therefore would have been naturally referred to in a

[m] *Commentarium de Scriptoribus Britannicis*, art. 'Wicoclivus.' [n] See p. iii.

series of sermons preached in his parish of Lutterworth during the last two years of his life, after he had been compelled to retire from Oxford by the Council of 1382,—lastly, a distinct reference at the end of Sermon XXX. (p. 79) to a Latin work by the writer, which, it can hardly be doubted, was the *De Veritate Scripturae*,—all these converging proofs, taken in connection with the unbroken tradition surrounding the MSS. which has been already referred to, appear to establish Wyclif in the authorship of these sermons beyond all reasonable doubt.

Assuming them, therefore, to be authentic, the questions which next present themselves for consideration relate, (1) to the form they bear, (2) to the nature of their contents.

1. Prefixed to the Sermons for the Commune and the Proprium Sanctorum, a few explanatory remarks will be found, from which the relation in which those sermons stand to the Sarum Missal, and to the general liturgical system of the Catholic Church in the fourteenth century, may be better comprehended. The collection of sermons for the Sunday gospels (which are for the most part the same as those in the English Prayer-book), needs no explanation. The originator of this style of sermon in the Western Church was Gregory the Great, whose forty Homilies, explanatory of the gospels read on various festivals, are most racy and profitable reading. Several passages in the opening sermons (see pp. 3, 6, 9) make it appear that Wyclif composed these homilies more as drafts, or skeleton sermons, which a preacher might take and fill in *ad libitum*, than as in themselves complete discourses. The curious MS. at Sidney Sussex College is a standing proof that he was sometimes taken at his word; in this MS. the sermon for the Sunday gospel is usually given entire, and followed by a few hortatory remarks enlarging upon Wyclif's hints; to these succeeds a short instruction based on a text taken from the epistle for the same Sunday [o].

[o] These instructions have been hitherto supposed (see Shirley's *Catalogue*, p. 33) to be identical with the 'Sermons on the Epistles' hereafter to be printed; but a minute examination showed that such was not the case; they appear to be original compositions, the work no doubt of the amplifier of the Gospel sermons.

2. To form a just estimate of the doctrinal and moral contents of these sermons, to realize and express the exact position which the writer, about whom so much windy declamation has gone forth during the last three centuries, occupied in face of the religious thought and life of his time,—this is a task for a theologian; and I am no theologian, but merely a literary editor. But I may be allowed to point out that the opportunity is now first afforded to the general reader of ascertaining Wyclif's opinions, not from four or five scattered sermons or tracts (some of which the learned editor, Dr. Todd, by clothing them in black letter, has left nearly as undecipherable to ordinary readers as if they were still in MS. [p]), not from pamphlets, such as those so largely analyzed by Lewis, Lebas, and Dr. Vaughan, of which a large proportion are of highly doubtful authenticity,—but from a large collection of sermons, which, if any of Wyclif's English works are so, may be deemed thoroughly genuine. As some assistance to those who wish to embark in this inquiry, it may be mentioned that in this first volume opinions on the following important doctrines and practices will be found at the places indicated:—on justification, at p. 350; on purgatory, at pp. 121, 321; on the sacraments, especially the Eucharist, *passim*, but see in particular pp. 119, 248, 265; on the privileges, graces, and power of Mary, at pp. 246, 257, 345, 356; on Antichrist, at p. 350; on private confession, at pp. 333, 351; and on clerical celibacy, at p. 364.

FORMATION OF THE TEXT.—The following are the MSS. which have been consulted, with a view to the production of a correct text of the Sermons:—

[p] Wycliffe's *Three Treatises on the Church*. Dublin, 1857.

Title of MS.	Distinguishing Letter.	Description.
Bodl. 788.	A.	This truly excellent MS. contains, in a small thick folio, the whole collection of genuine Homilies, numbered 2 in Shirley's *Catalogue*. As to its history, nothing whatever is known. Not a single leaf is missing, and although of course not free from errors, it is one of those unusually correct and serviceable copies which rejoice the heart of an editor. It is in the same handwriting from first to last, a handwriting probably of the last decade of the fourteenth century. It is on good but thin parchment, sparingly ornamented with blue and red flourishes and head-letters.
Univ. Library Cambr. Ii. 1.40.	B.	This MS., a small quarto, is in the University Library at Cambridge. It contains only the sermons for the Sunday gospels and epistles. It is on the finest vellum, and the handwriting is of a very superior description; here and there it is richly illuminated. One may feel certain that it was executed for some wealthy person, who desired that no expense should be spared. I was at first inclined to rate its value very highly, but the remarkable family likeness between it and A soon struck me, and at length I discovered a proof, amounting almost to a demonstration, that one must have been copied from the other. In the text of Sermon LIII., 'Si quis diligit me,' while the MS. Douce 321 refers to the right chapter, John xiv., A and B both fall into the *same* error, referring to John xviii. The balance of probability against the coincidence being accidental is of course enormously great; either then both MSS. must be copies from some earlier MS., now lost, which contained the error, or else one of them copied it from the other. But the former supposition is gratuitous and improbable; they have then copied each other, and of the two alternatives, it is more likely that B, a partial cópy, and a MS. *de luxe*, is copied from A, than A from B. The general conclusion is that B is of no value as an original authority; it has however the merit of not unfrequently correcting errors of inadvertence or carelessness in A.

Title of MS.	Distinguishing Letter.	Description.
Laud, 314.	C.	This is a small MS. of but little value, in the Bodleian Library, containing, besides the tract called *Vae Octuplex*, only the sermons for the Sunday gospels. The hand is apparently of a period past the middle of the fifteenth century.
Wrest Park, 11.	D.	This MS. is in the possession of Lady Cowper. It is a double-columned folio; at the foot of page 1 are the words 'Franciscus Comes Bedfordiae,' and the date '1566.' In respect of execution it is of a medium quality; the ornamentation is but slight, and the writing just mediocre. There are two changes of hand; in the first hand all the sermons are written except those for the Ferial gospels, the first portion of which is written in the second, and the remainder in the third hand. The first hand seems to be late fourteenth century; the third I should judge to be some fifty years later. So far as my examination extended, this appeared to be a good and serviceable MS.
Douce 321.	E.	In this MS., which is unfortunately much mutilated, the sermons are arranged in a peculiar order, those for the Sunday gospels and epistles being intermixed, while the Proprium Sanctorum precedes instead of following the Commune. It is a good-sized quarto, written on coarse parchment in a large bold hand, and very little ornamented. From the forms of the words ('schal,' 'gode,' 'pynyd,' &c., instead of 'shal,' 'good,' 'pyned,') it seems to be rather more ancient than Bodl. 788. Its readings are often different from, and not unfrequently superior to, those of Bodl. 788; between which and itself there is no more connexion or resemblance than must subsist between two MSS. of the same work, both good of their kind;—each must be regarded as an independent authority. It is this quality of its readings which makes this MS., for collating purposes, one of the utmost value. Not that it deserves to be ranked on the whole above Bodl. 788; not to speak of its mutilations, it is disfigured by a far greater number of carelessnesses, omissions, and other blunders than its rival. For it must be remem-

Title of MS.	Distinguishing Letter.	Description.
		bered, that since Bodl. 788 has been adopted as the basis of the printed text, every necessary correction of it for which support is found in any other MS. appears at the foot of the page, while the more numerous and more glaring errors of other MSS. are passed over *sub silentio*.
Baroness North.	F.	A MS. of medium quality, in the possession of Colonel North, containing only the sermons on the Sunday gospels. From the forms of the words, it appears to be intermediate in point of date between the complete copies already described and Laud, 314.
Bib. Reg. 18. B. ix.	G.	This MS. is in the British Museum. It is a good and carefully written text, having the sermons for the Sunday and Ferial gospels, and the Sunday epistles, arranged in order of the season, commencing with Advent Sunday; then follow the sermons for the Commune and Proprium Sanctorum. So far as I have been able to collate it, its readings differ little from those of Bodl. 788. The sermons in the last division appear to be defective,—twenty-eight only, against thirty-eight in Bodl. 788.
St. John's Coll. Camb. C. 8.	H.	The arrangement of the sermons in this MS., which is very imperfect, at least fifty-five sermons being wanting, is the same as that in G, of which I believe it to be a copy.
Cotton. Claud. D. VIII.	I.	This is a good MS., but imperfect at the beginning. The arrangement is nearly the same as that of the Douce MS. All the first portion of the volume containing it consists of a noble and apparently perfect copy of the 'Statutes, Charters, and Customs' of the university of Oxford.
Wrest Park, 32.	J.	This is a low class MS., somewhat dilapidated, in a hand of about the middle of the fifteenth century. It is inferior in every respect to the MS. at Wrest Park (D) already described.
Trin. Coll. Camb. B. 2. 17.	K.	A handsome folio, moderately ornamented. It is of the same class as Bodl. 788, the arrangement of which it exactly follows, down to the end of the Ferial sermons; the Epistle sermons are wanting. I think it is somewhat later than Bodl. 788, but my examination of it was not

Title of MS	Distinguishing Letter.	Description.
		long or searching enough to enable me to speak positively.
Wrest Park, 38.	L.	This is a still commoner and poorer copy than J; also decidedly of later date. Its contents correspond to those of K; i.e. it has all the sermons except those on the epistles.
Trin. Coll. Camb. B. 4. 20.	M.	This is a copy, poorly executed, and exhibiting several serious *lacunae*, of all the sermons except those on the Ferial gospels. The arrangement nearly corresponds to that of Bodl. 788.
Sidn. Suss. Coll. Camb. Δ. 4. 12.	N.	This is the remarkable MS. above referred to (p. xiv). It is in a rude handwriting, and upon coarse parchment, and conveys the impression of having been prepared by some poor parish priest for his own use.
Trin. Coll. Camb. B. 14. 38.	O.	A small volume, containing only the sermons on the Sunday epistles; the hand is rough and difficult, and not of an early date.
Harl. 1730.	P.	One of the Harleian MSS. in the British Museum, containing only the Epistle sermons, and ending defective in the sermon for the twenty-second Sunday after Trinity. So far as a brief examination enables me to speak, it appeared to be of no special value.
New Coll. Oxford, 95.	Q.	This MS. contains, besides a complete set of the sermons on the Ferial gospels, seven sermons on gospels belonging to the 'Proprium de Tempore,' but included by Wyclif under the head of Proprium Sanctorum. (See p. 295.) It also has one of the Sunday sermons, No. XXXI. The handwriting is of the first half of the fifteenth century.
C. C. C. Camb. 336.	R.	This MS. (wrongly described in Dr. Shirley's Catalogue) contains the sermons for the Commune Sanctorum, and most of those for the Proprium Sanctorum and the Ferial gospels. My examination of it was too hurried to permit of my forming a definite opinion as to its merits.
St. John's Coll. Camb. G. 22.	S.	This is the MS. containing the homilies criticised on p. iii. Besides these it contains a poor and late copy, much mutilated, of the sermons for the Sundays from Advent to Trinity.

The MS. Bodl. 788 has, as has been already stated, been adopted as the foundation of the text of the present edition,—being absolutely complete, singularly accurate, and probably older than, or equally old with, any of the others, except perhaps Douce 321. The arrangement of its contents has been adhered to in the printing, except that, in order not to break the series of sermons, the tracts *Vae Octuplex* and *Of Mynystris in the Chirche* (Nos. 4 and 5 of Shirley) which follow in the MS., one the Sunday gospel sermons, the other those for the Proprium Sanctorum, are reserved for the third volume. The orthography of the MS. is almost exactly reproduced, the characters þ and ȝ being retained throughout. The only deviations permitted are these: *v* is freely employed in the printing in place of *u* in the MS., wherever the sound appears to require it, because it is manifest that, except at the beginnings of words, the scribe employed the same characters for both sounds. He wrote *loue*, but it would be absurd to doubt that he pronounced *love*. Again, the character *i* is used in the MS. both for that sound and for the sound of *j*; it is always *iust*, *iniurie*, &c., instead of *just*, *injurie*; I have therefore printed *j* instead of *i* wherever the sound seemed to require it.

Like most of its class, the MS. Bodl. 788 contains the bare words of each sermon, and nothing more; there are no capital letters, no division into paragraphs, no punctuation. Passages quoted from Scripture are underlined with red ink. The editor is responsible for supplying the above-named defects, as well as for marginal analyses, biblical references, and the verse of the chapter from which each text is taken.

Of the transcript of the MS. the first part, down to p. 197, was made by the Rev. W. F. Cornish, of Lincoln College, the remainder by Mr. William Sorell; to both these gentlemen I am much indebted for the general fidelity and accuracy with which they performed their work.

In conclusion, I have much pleasure in taking this opportunity of returning sincere thanks to those whose assistance I have benefited by in preparing the present volumes;—to Professor Stubbs, of whose valuable aid I have already spoken; to the Rev. H. O. Coxe, Bodley's Librarian; the Rev. J. Mayor, the late, and Mr. Bradshaw, the present, Librarian of the Cambridge University Library; to Professor Dunne, of the Irish Catholic University, who kindly examined for me some MSS. in the Library of Trinity College, Dublin; to Mr. Bond, custodian of the MSS. at the British Museum; to the Rev. W. Macray, of the Bodleian Library; lastly, to Mr. Caldwell, Fellow of Corpus Christi College, Cambridge, and the Rev. J. J. Perowne, Fellow of the same College.

A complete Glossary will be subjoined to the last volume of the English works.

T. ARNOLD.

OXFORD, *October*, 1868.

CONTENTS.

EVANGELIA DOMINICALIA.

SERMON — PAGE

First Sunday after Trinity.
I. Homo quidam erat dives. *Luke* xvi. 19. 1

Second Sunday after Trinity.
II. Homo quidam fecit coenam magnam. *Luke* xiv. 16. . . 3

Third Sunday after Trinity.
III. Accesserunt ad Jesum publicani et peccatores. *Luke* xv. 1. 7

Fourth Sunday after Trinity.
IV. Estote misericordes. *Luke* vi. 36. 9

Fifth Sunday after Trinity.
V. Cum turbae irruerunt ad Jesum. *Luke* v. 1. . 12

Sixth Sunday after Trinity.
VI. Nisi habundaverit justitia vestra plus quam Pharisaeorum. *Matt.* v. 20. 14

Seventh Sunday after Trinity.
VII. Cum turba multa esset cum Jesu, nec haberent quod manducarent. *Mark* viii. 1. 17

Eighth Sunday after Trinity.
VIII. Attendite a falsis prophetis. *Matt.* vii. 15. 19

Ninth Sunday after Trinity.
IX. Homo quidam erat dives et habebat villicum. *Luke* xvi. 1. . 22

Tenth Sunday after Trinity.
X. Cum appropinquaret Jesus Hierusalem videns civitatem. *Luke* xix. 41. 24

Eleventh Sunday after Trinity.
XI. Dixit Jesus ad quosdam qui confidebant tanquam justi. *Luke* xviii. 9. 27

SERMON PAGE

Twelfth Sunday after Trinity.
XII. Exiens Jesus de finibus Tyri. *Mark* vii. 31. . . . 29

Thirteenth Sunday after Trinity.
XIII. Beati oculi qui vident quae vos videtis. *Luke* x. 23. . . 31

Fourteenth Sunday after Trinity.
XIV. Cum iret Jesus in Jerusalem, transibat. *Luke* xvii. 11. 34

Fifteenth Sunday after Trinity.
XV. Nemo potest duobus dominis servire. *Matt.* vi. 24. . . 36

Sixteenth Sunday after Trinity.
XVI. Ibat Jesus in civitatem quae vocata Naym. *Luke* vii. 11. 38

Seventeenth Sunday after Trinity.
XVII. Cum intrasset Jesus domum cujusdam. *Luke* xiv. 1. . . 41

Eighteenth Sunday after Trinity.
XVIII. Accesserunt ad Jesum Pharisei audientes. *Matt.* xxii. 34. 43

Nineteenth Sunday after Trinity.
XIX. Ascendens Jesus in naviculam. *Matt.* ix. 1. 46

Twentieth Sunday after Trinity.
XX. Loquebatur Jesus cum discipulis. *Matt.* xxii. 1. . . . 48

Twenty-first Sunday after Trinity.
XXI. Erat quidam regulus. *John* iv. 46. 51

Twenty-second Sunday after Trinity.
XXII. Simile est regnum coelorum homini. *Matt.* xviii. 23. . 54

Twenty-third Sunday after Trinity.
XXIII. Abeuntes Pharisaei. *Matt.* xxii. 15. 56

Twenty-fourth Sunday after Trinity.
XXIV. Loquente Jesu ad turbas, ecce princeps. *Matt.* ix. 18. 59

Twenty-fifth Sunday after Trinity.
XXV. Cum sublevasset oculos Jesus. *John* vi. 5. 62

First Sunday in Advent.
XXVI. Cum appropinquasset Jesus Jerosolumis. *Matt.* xxi. 1. . 65

Second Sunday in Advent.
XXVII. Erunt signa in sole. *Luke* xxi. 25. 68

Third Sunday in Advent.
XXVIII. Cum audiisset Joannes in vinculis. *Matt.* xi. 2. . . . 71

SERMON PAGE

Fourth Sunday in Advent.
XXIX. Miserunt Judaei ab Jerosolumis. *John* i. 19. . . . 74

Sunday within Octave of the Epiphany.
XXX. Vidit Johannes Jesum venientem ad se. *John* i. 29. 77

Octave of the Epiphany.
XXXI. Venit Jesus Galilea. *Matt.* iii. 13. 80

First Sunday after the Octave.
XXXII. Cum factus esset Jesus. *Luke* ii. 42. . . 83

Second Sunday after the Octave.
XXXIII. Nuptiae factae sunt in Cana Galileae. *John* ii. 1. . 86

Third Sunday after the Octave.
XXXIV. Cum descendisset Jesus de monte. *Matt.* viii. 1. . 89

Fourth Sunday after the Octave.
XXXV. Ascendente Jesu in naviculam. *Matt.* viii. 23. . 92

Fifth Sunday after the Octave.
XXXVI. Simile est regnum coelorum homini qui seminavit. *Matt.* xiii. 24. 95

Septuagesima Sunday.
XXXVII. Simile est regnum coelorum homini patrifamilias. *Matt.* xx. 1. 98

Sexagesima Sunday.
XXXVIII. Cum turba plurima. *Luke* viii. 4. 102

Quinquagesima Sunday.
XXXIX. Assumpsit Jesus duodecim discipulos. *Luke* xviii. 31. 106

First Sunday in Lent.
XL. Ductus est Jesus in desertum. *Matt.* iv. 1. . . . 109

Second Sunday in Lent.
XLI. Egressus Jesus secessit in partes Tyri. *Matt.* xv. 21. 113

Third Sunday in Lent.
XLII. Erat Jesus ejiciens demonium. *Luke* xi. 14. . . . 116

Fourth Sunday in Lent.
XLIII. Abiit Jesus trans mare. *John* vi. 1. 120

Fifth Sunday in Lent.
XLIV. Quis ex vobis arguet. *John* viii. 46. . . 124

SERMON | | PAGE

Palm Sunday.
XLV. Altera autem die quae est post parasceven. *Matt.* xxvii. 62. 128

Easter Day.
XLVI. Maria Magdalene. *Matt.* xxviii. 1. 131

First Sunday after Easter.
XLVII. Cum esset sero die una. *John* xx. 19. 134

Second Sunday after Easter.
XLVIII. Ego sum pastor bonus. *John* x. 11. 138

Third Sunday after Easter.
XLIX. Modicum et jam non videbitis me. *John* xvi. 16. . 141

Fourth Sunday after Easter.
L. Vado ad eum qui misit me. *John* xvi. 5. 144

Fifth Sunday after Easter.
LI. Amen, Amen, dico vobis, si quid petieritis. *John* xvi. 23. 148

Sixth Sunday after Easter.
LII. Cum venerit Paraclitus. *John* xv. 26. 151

Whit Sunday.
LIII. Si quis diligit me. *John* xiv. 23. 155

Trinity Sunday.
LIV. Erat homo ex Phariseeis Nychodeme. *John* iii. 1. . 158

COMMUNE SANCTORUM.

Vigil of an Apostle.
LV. Ego sum vitis vera. *John* xv. 1. 165

Common of an Apostle.
LVI. Hoc est preceptum meum. *John* xv. 12. 168

The same.
LVII. Haec mando vobis. *John* xv. 17. 172

Common of an Evangelist.
LVIII. Designavit Dominus Jesus. *Luke* x. 1. 175

Common of one Martyr.
LIX. Nisi granum frumenti. *John* xii. 24. 179

The same.
LX. Si quis vult venire post me. *Matt.* xvi. 24. . . . 182

SERMON | | PAGE

Common of one Martyr.

LXI. Qui vos audit, me audit. *Luke* x. 16. 185

The same.

LXII. Si quis venit ad me. *Luke* xiv. 26. . . . 189

The same.

LXIII. Nihil opertum quod non reveletur. *Matt.* x. 26. . 194

Common of one Martyr and Bishop.

LXIV. Circuibat Jesus civitates. *Matt.* ix. 35. . . 197

Common of many Martyrs.

LXV. Elevatis Jesus oculis. *Luke* vi. 20. 201

The same.

LXVI. Cum persequentur vos in una civitate. *Matt.* x. 23. . 206

The same.

LXVII. Ponite in cordibus vestris. *Luke* xxi. 14. . . . 209

The same.

LXVIII. Descendens Jesus de monte. *Luke* vi. 17. . 214

The same.

LXIX. Cum audieritis proelia. *Luke* xxi. 9. 218

The same.

LXX. Attendite a fermento Pharisaeorum. *Luke* xii. 1. . . 222

The same.

LXXI. Sedente Jesu super montem Olyveti. *Matt.* xxiv. 3. . 226

The same.

LXXII. Nolite arbitrari. *Matt.* x. 34. 231

The same.

LXXIII. Egressus Jesus de templo. *Matt.* xxiv. 1. . . 235

The same.

LXXIV. Dicebat Jesus turbis Judeorum. *Luke* xi. 29. . . 239

The same.

LXXV. Egrediente Jesu de templo. *Mark* xiii. 1. . . . 243

Common of a Confessor and Bishop.

LXXVI. Vigilate quia nescitis qua hora. *Matt.* xxiv. 42. . 248

The same.

LXXVII. Homo quidam peregre proficiscens. *Matt.* xxv. 14. 252

SERMON		PAGE
	Common of a Confessor and Bishop.	
LXXVIII.	Homo quidam nobilis abiit in regionem. *Luke* xix. 12.	257
	The same.	
LXXIX.	Videte, et vigilate, et orate. *Mark* xiii. 33. . . .	261
	Common of a Confessor and Doctor.	
LXXX.	Vos estis sal terre. *Matt.* v. 13.	266
	Common of a Confessor and Abbot.	
LXXXI.	Nemo accendit lucernam. *Luke* xi. 33.	271
	Common of many Confessors.	
LXXXII.	Sint lumbi vestri praecincti. *Luke* xii. 35. . .	275
	The same.	
LXXXIII.	Misit Jesus duodecim discipulos. *Matt.* x. 5. . . .	280
	Common of one Virgin and Martyr.	
LXXXIV.	Simile est regnum coelorum thesauro. *Matt.* xiii. 44.	284
	Common of a Virgin not a Martyr.	
LXXXV.	Simile est regnum coelorum decem virginibus. *Matt.* xxv. 1.	289

PROPRIUM SANCTORUM.

	Vigil of St. Andrew.	
LXXXVI.	Stabat Johannes. *John* i. 29.	295
	St. Andrew.	
LXXXVII.	Ambulans Jesus juxta Mare Galilee. *Matt.* iv. 18. .	301
	Octave of St. Andrew.	
LXXXVIII.	Postquam autem traditus est Johannes. *Mark* i. 14.	306
	Christmas Eve.	
LXXXIX.	Cum esset desponsata. *Matt.* i. 18. .	311
	Christmas Day.	
XC.	Exiit edictum a Cesare Augusto. *Luke* ii. 1. .	316
	St. Stephen's Day.	
XCI.	Ecce, ego mitto ad vos prophetas. *Matt.* xxiii. 34. .	322
	St. John the Evangelist's Day.	
XCII.	Dixit Jesus Petro. *John* xxi. 15. .	325

SERMON		PAGE
	The Holy Innocents.	
XCIII.	Angelus domini apparuit. *Matt.* ii. 13.	327
	Sixth day after Christmas.	
XCIV.	Erat Joseph et Maria. *Luke* ii. 33.	332
	New Year's Day.	
XCV.	Postquam consummati sunt. *Luke* ii. 21.	335
	Vigil of the Epiphany.	
XCVI.	Defuncto Herode. *Matt.* ii. 19.	337
	The Epiphany.	
XCVII.	Cum natus esset Jesus. *Matt.* ii. 1.	339
	The Conversion of St. Paul.	
XCVIII.	Ecce reliquimus omnia. *Matt.* xix. 27.	342
	Candlemas Day.	
XCIX.	Postquam impleti sunt dies. *Luke* ii. 22.	345
	St. Peter's Chair. (Feb. 22.)	
C.	Venit Jesus in partes Cesarie. *Matt.* xvi. 13.	347
	St. Matthias' Day.	
CI.	Confiteor tibi, Pater, Domine. *Matt.* xi. 25.	350
	Annunciation of the Blessed Virgin Mary.	
CII.	Missus est Angelus Gabriel a Deo. *Luke* i. 26.	353
	St. Philip and St. James.	
CIII.	Non turbetur cor vestrum. *John* xiv. 1.	357
	Ascension Day.	
CIV.	Recumbentibus undecem discipulis. *Mark* xvi. 14.	360
	Vigil of St. John the Baptist. (Midsummer Eve.)	
CV.	Fuit in diebus Herodis. *Luke* i. 5.	362
	St. John the Baptist. (Midsummer Day.)	
CVI.	Elizabeth impletum est tempus pariendi. *Luke* i. 57.	364
	Vigil of St. Peter and St. Paul.	
CVII.	Dixit Jesus Symoni Petro. *John* xxi. 15.	366
	Octave of St. John the Baptist.	
CVIII.	Dixit Zacarias. *Luke* i. 18.	367
	Translation of St. Martin. (July 5.)	
CIX.	Nolite timere, pusillus grex. *Luke* xii. 32.	370

SERMON | | PAGE

Octave of St. Peter and St. Paul.

CX. Jussit Jesus discipulos ascendere in naviculam. *Matt.* xiv. 22. 373

The Seven Brothers. (July 10.)

CXI. Loquente Jesu ad turbas. *Matt.* xii. 46. 375

St. James.

CXII. Accessit ad Jesum. *Matt.* xx. 20. 377

Vigil of the Assumption. (Aug. 14.)

CXIII. Loquente Jesu ad turbas. *Luke* xi. 27. 379

Assumption Day. (Aug. 15.)

CXIV. Intravit Jesus in quoddam castellum. *Luke* x. 38. . 382

St. Bartholomew.

CXV. Facta est contentio inter. *Luke* xxii. 24. 385

Beheading of St. John the Baptist. (Aug. 29.)

CXVI. Misit Herodes. *Mark* vi. 17. 387

Nativity of the Blessed Virgin Mary. (Sept. 8.)

CXVII. Liber generationis. *Matt.* i. 1. 390

Exaltation of the Cross, or 'Holy Rood Day in harvest.' (Sept. 14.)

CXVIII. Nunc judicium est mundi. *John* xii. 31. 392

Vigil of St. Matthew.

CXIX. Vidit Jesus publicanum. *Luke* v. 27. 395

St. Matthew.

CXX. Cum transiret Jesus. *Matt.* ix. 9. 397

Michaelmas Day.

CXXI. Accesserunt discipuli ad Jesum. *Matt.* xviii. 1. . . . 398

Vigil of All Saints. (All Hallow Eve.)

CXXII. Respiciens Jesus in discipulos. *John* xvii. 11. . . . 402

All Saints' Day.

CXXIII. Videns Jesus turbas ascendit. *Matt.* v. 1. . . . 406

EVANGELIA DOMINICALIA.

HERE BIGYNNEN

ÞE SONEDAI GOSPELIS,

EXPOWNED IN PARTIE.

Þe firste Sonedai Gospel after Trinite Sondai.

[SERMON I.]

Homo quidam erat dives.—Luyk xvi. [19.]

The parable of Dives and Lazarus.

Crist telliþ in þis parable how richessis ben perilouse, for liȝtli wole a riche man use hem unto moche lust. A parable is a word of stori, þat bi þat hydeþ a spiritual witt. Þe stori telleþ;—*Þere was a riche man* þat disuside his richesse in pride and in glotonye, for he was *cloþid in purpur and bise*, þat ben prescious cloþes boþe rede and white; and so he was an ypocrite, þat shewide him to þe world boþe austerne and clene, as worldly men done. And over þis, *ech daie was he fedd shynyngly*, boþ for shynyng of vessel and prescious food, *and þere was a pore man liynge at his ȝate þat was clepid Lazarus, full of sore biles; and he wolde be fillid by crummes þat felden fro þe riche mannes bord, but no man ȝaf him hem*[a], for avarise of þe lord, *but þe houndis of þe lord comen, and lickide his biles;* and þis signifieþ compassioun of riche mennes servantis, þat þey have of pore men; but þei ben lettid to helpe hem. *And it is maad* by Goddis wille *þat þis begger was deed; and was born by aungelis into Abrahams bosum; þis riche man was dede,*

[a] This additional clause is found in the Vulgate; 'et nemo illi dabat.'

but not solempnely to God, *and he was buried in helle*[a], in token þat he shulde ever dwelle there. Abrahames bosum is clepid a place of reste þat holy soulis restiden inne bifore Cristis ascensioun. And here may we see þat þat neiþer riche men ne pore, in þat þey ben sich, be blessid in hevene; sith Abraham þe riche man toke Lazarus into his bosum; but disuse of richesses and impacience of pore men ben dampned of Crist; and ellis not siche men; and þei ben not preisid of Crist but bi contrarie virtues. *Þis riche man lifte up hise iȝen in hise turmentis of helle, and siȝ Abrahame a ferre, and Lazarus in his lappe; and he criede, Fader Abraham, have mercy on me, and sende þe lazar hidir, wetynge his fyngres eende in water to colde my tonge, for Y am tormentid in þis flawme.* Þe manner of speche of holy writt is to undirstonde by names of bodi vertues of þe soule, þat dwellen for a tyme in siche bodies; and so, for þis riche man was boostful in speche and likerous in foode, he was tormentid in vertu of his tunge; and þus men in weye to blis, whanne þei traveilen in sutil and medeful werkes, þei swagen in a maner þe peyne of dampned men; for þei have slakyng of þer peyne in þat þat þey hopen to have fewer felowis in helle, to be peyned wiþ hem. *And Abraham seide to þe riche man*, dampnyd, *Sone, have mynde how þou haddist lust in this lyfe, and Lazar peyne, and þerefore*, bi rigt jugement of God, *he is now confortid and þou art now turmentid;* for he sufferide peyne paciently and þou toke þi lusts synfulli. And sum men þenken, for þis dampnid riche man clepid Abraham his fadir, and Abraham clepid him aȝen his sone, þat he was an Ebreu, and Abraham was his fadir; but *Abraham answeride him*, bi treuþe þat God tolde him, þat *þere was a myche void place stablid betwene hem, derke and unordynel, þat lettid dampned men to come to hem, al ȝif þei wolden, or hem come to dampned men:* for þei desiren it not, and ȝif sum seintis coveiten kyndely to comferte þer frendis, þey have stronger wille to confourme hem to Goddis wille, and men may neiþer falle fro hevene to helle, ne flee fro helle to hevene at þer owne wille. But *þe riche man preied Abraham to sende Lazar to his fadir hous, for*

[a] 'Sepultus est in inferno:' Vulg.

he hadde fyve breþeren, and he wolde þat þei weren warnid to amenden hem of her lyf; not for charite þat men dampned in helle have to lyvyng men or ellis to dampned men; for as seintis in hevene wanten envye, so dampned men failen in charité; but he dredde him of his peyne þat he shulde have by dampnyng of hise breþren; for he assentide to hem in þer wickide lyf. *But Abraham seide to him þat þei have Moyses and prophetis* in þer bokes þat þei writen, *heere þei hem* spedely, and kepe þei Goddis commandementis; *and þis riche dampned man seide to Abraham, Nay, Fadir Abraham, but if ony of dede men wende to hem and warne hem, þei shal do penaunce,* and flee þer dampnacioun. But Abraham seide aȝen, þat *ȝif þei heeren not Moyses and prophetis þat spaken by God, þei shall not trowe to dede men;* for þer wordes ben of lasse evydence, and it falliþ not to God to make a newe lawe and newe miraclis for ech man þat shal be dampned, as Crist wolde not come doun of þe crosse to conferme the fals Jewis.

Directions to preachers how to enlarge on the parable.

In[a] þis Gospel may preestis telle of fals pride of riche men, and of lustful lyf of myȝty men of þis worlde, and of longe peynes of helle, and joyful blis in hevene, and þus lengþe þer sermoun as þe tyme axiþ. And marke we how þis gospel telliþ þat þis riche man was not dampned for extorsioun or wrong þat he dide to his neiȝbore, but for he failide in werkes of mercy; and þus shulde we warne boþ o man and oþer how sum men shal be dampnyd more felly for raveyne, and sum shal be dampnyd more softly, for misusinge of Goddis goodis.

Þe secunde Sondai Gospel after Trynyte.

[SERMON II.]

Homo quidam fecit coenam magnam.—Luc. xiiii. [16.]

The parable of the bidden guests.

Þis gospel moveþ men bi witt of a parable to desire spedely to come to hevene. We shal undirstonde þat eche worde of

[a] The language of this concluding paragraph shows that these homilies were written rather with a view to publication than to delivery from the pulpit.

Goddis lawe is soþ, alȝates if some men undirstonde it falsely; for so þey undirstonden God, and ȝit þei maken him not fals; and so pryve undirstondinge of þis holy Gospel is alȝates soþ, and þe storye boþe. Þe Gospel telliþ þat *þere was a man þat makide a greet soper and clepide þereto many men.* Þis man is Jesus Crist, þat is boþe God and man; and þis grete soper is the grete mangery þat seintis in hevene shall eten of Goddis bord; and þis shall ever last wiþout irkyng or noye, for þere shal noþing faile þat seintis wolen desire. And, for þis shal be þe laste mete, it is well clepid a soper, for soper is þe laste mete þat man takiþ in þe daie. And for foure causis it is a greet soper, for þe Lord is grete þat makeþ þis soper, so þat no man but he may make siche a soper; also the peeple is grete and many þat sitteþ at þis soper; also þe mete is prescious þat þei soupen wiþ, siþ Crist is al maner of mete and drynke, þat þei be fed wiþ; also þe tyme of sittyng at þis soper is wiþouten eende. Þis lord clepiþ many to þis soper; for þere nys no man but ȝif he longe sum weie after blise; for ech man longiþ after good, and þe last good and best in which oonly man shulde reste is blisse. But þe gospel seiþ þat many men ben clepid, and fewe ben chosen, for alle men þat God ȝeveþ desiryng to blis ben clepide, but al oonly þese ben chosen, þat lasten in love of God to þer ending day, for to alle siche and oonly siche haþ God ordeyned blisse. *And he sente out his servauntis in houre of þis soper to seie to men clepid hereto to come, for now alle þingis ben redy.* Þe hour of þis soper is tyme of þe Incarnacion, for in þat tyme was heven first persid[a], and men sett first in hevene wiþ Crist. Þis servant sent out is the manheed of Crist, wiþ hise membris þat here lyveden wiþ him, as Joon Baptist and oþer apostlis and oþer trewe servauntis. Alle þingis were redy; for the Godhede and manhede of Crist was for þat time redy
Col. iii. 11. to fede seintes in hevene, and Crist, as Paul seiþ, is alle þingis in alle men þat shal be savyd, and riȝt so his lawe is þe first and þe laste and fully ynouȝ, after which shulde be noon other lawe. For Anticristis lawe, cloutid of many, is full of errors, and disseyveþ many men, as law of Sarasyns and of þese newe

[a] 'pierced' is used in the sense of penetrated, or forcibly entered.

ordris. And as þe gospel seiþ, *al siche men bygan togiþer for to excuse hem;* for al þese men and al oonli siche þat tellen more bi siche lawe þan bi Goddis lawe excusen hem to come þe riȝt weye to hevene. And as þere is þre maner of synne, so þre maner men excusiden hem fro þis soper. *Þe first seide þat he hadde bouȝt a toun and was nedid to go out and see it;* and þis bitokeneþ proude men, þat for worldly lordship wenden out fro þe weye of God, and occupien her wittes about worldely hey-nesse; and for þe first seide þat þis was nedeful, þerefore *he preide þe lordis messanger to have him excusid. Þe seconde seide, þat he hadde bouȝt fyve yockis of oxen, and he wente to assay hem, and þerefore he preide him to have him excusid.* Þes fyve yockis bitokenen plente of worldely goodis; for traveil and foure pro-fitis þat comen of oxen; and for þis bisynesse turneþ rundely in hemsilf þerefore it is well seide þat þere ben fyve yockis. And for siche worldely men ben yockid togiþere wiþ þe fend and þe world, þerefore the gospel clepiþ hem yockis. *Þe þridde man seide* þat he *hadde wedded a wyf, and þerefore myȝte not come.* Þis þridde bitokeneþ men þat ben overcomen wiþ fleishly synne, as glotonye and lecherie; and þes men more beestly excusen hem, not curteysly, as þese two first diden; but seien shortly, þay may not come. Þe first two men excusiden hem by þis, þat þey wolen be lordly to distroye Goddis enemyes, and þei wolen be riche to helpe pore men; but þe þridde, þat haþ his fleish as his wyf, maister of his soule, is an uncurtais fool; and þere-fore he answeride þus. *Þe servaunt turnide aȝen and tolde his lord þe answere of þese þre men;* for every creature seiþ to Crist fully himsilf. But þe lord was wrooþ wiþ excusacioun of þese beden foolis, *and bad his servaunt wende out into stretis* of þe citee, more and lasse, and brynge into þis feeste þis þre maner of men, pore feble men, pore blynde men, and pore lame men. Þese þre ben Goddis prisoneris, þat boþe God and man helpen wiþ almes. And it semeth þat þese and noon oþer shal come to hevene, for who shal come to hevene but if he be pore in spirit; who shal come to heven but ȝif he be feble in spirit and nedid to have mercy; who shall come to hevene but ȝif he bi liȝtned of his blindnesse; and who shal come to hevene, but he þat halteþ now hiȝe in vertues and now low in synnes?

Certis noon but þe lord of þis feeste; and to siche bodili pore men techeþ þis gospel men to do her almes; for we shall sue Crist, þat doiþ specialy his greet almes to þese þre men, and of þese þre maner of men many comen to heven. But Goddis servauntis boþe of men and aungelis seien after þis secounde maner of clepyng, *Lord, it is done as þou comandist, and ȝit þere is a voide place*, for men þat shulden soupe wiþ þee; for þis maner of clepyng of men to þe joie of hevene filleþ not hevene of men þat God haþ ordeyned[1] to blis, and herfore þe Lord of hevene in his þridde clepyng, þat shal be in tyme nyȝ þe daie of dome, *biddeþ his servantis go out into weyes and hegges and constreynen men to entre þat my hous be fillid.* For now in þe laste daies, whan preestis ben turnid to avarice, stonys shal crye and constreyne preestis þat maken hem a privat religioun as an hegge and oþer men þat suen hem in þe brode weye to helleward,—þese stoonys, þat ben myȝty men in þe worlde, shal constreyne boþe preestis and peple for to entre into hevene bi holding of Goddis lawe, for drede of takinge of her goodis and punishinge of her bodies shal constreyne hem by drede to kepe þis streyte wey to hevene. And so þe noumbre of men þat God haþ ordeyned to blisse mut nedis be fillid, maugre Anticrist. But *Crist seiþ to his Apostlis, þat noon of þe firste men þat God clepid to þe mete and wolde not come shal taiste his souper* in ye blisse of hevene. For God haþ ordeyned whiche men shal be saved and which shal be dampned, and boþ þese noumbres mote nede be fulfilled; and lordis for her profit moten nedes helpe herto, and Anticristis feynynge mote nedes be knowun.

Directions to preachers.

Here may men touche of alle manere of synne, and specialy of false preestis, traitors to God, þat shulden treuly clepe men to blise and telle hem ye wey of þe lawe of Crist, and make knowe to þe peple the cautelis of Anticrist.

[1] So in B; the Bodleian MS. has *ordeyneþ*.

Þe þridde Sonday Gospel after Trynyte Sonday.

[SERMON III.]

Accesserunt ad Jesum publicani et peccatores.—Luc. xv. [1.]

Prelates and monks are compared to the Scribes and Pharisees.

In þis gospel telliþ Crist two parablis of comfort, how his peple shal be saved alȝif preestis grutchen þere aȝen, boþe prelatis and religiouse, for her pryde and coveitise. Þe story of þis Gospel telliþ *how publicanis and sinful men weren comyng to Jesus* to here his lore; and he tretide hem graciously as a good lord; *but scribis and Phariseis gruchiden aȝens þis and blasfemiden aȝens Crist, and seiden, He ete wiþ hem* unlawfully; and þis dede may figure þingis þat falliþ now, siþ prelatis, as scribis, and religiouse, as Phariseis, grutchen aȝens trewe preestis, membris of Crist, þat communen wiþ commounes as publicanis and seculer lordis, as sinful men; and seien it falliþ not to hem to knowe Goddis lawe. For þei seien it is so hey, so sutil and so holy, þat al oonly scribis and Phariseis shulden speke of þis lawe. And þes seculer prelatis may wele be clepid scribis, for þei boþe more and lasse writen þe money þat þei pilen of þe peple more bisily þan þei prynten in her soulis þe knowyng of Goddis lawe. And þes religiouse ben Pharisees: for þei ben divydid fro þe comoun maner of lyvynge bi hir rotun rytys as Pharisees weren. Þre causis þere ben whi þis hevenly leche resseyvede freely þes synful men and eet wiþ hem,—ffirst, for he wolde converte hem to confusioun of proude prelatis þat lettiden þe fredom of Goddis lawes to have hir cours; by þis shulden þei mekely knowe þat heynes of state makiþ not a man evermore beter to God. Þe seconde cause is, þat Crist wolde ȝyve his preestis in tyme of grace lore and ensample to do wisely so, and to stonde for þe fredom of Goddis lawe. Þe þridde cause is,—for Crist wolde shewe his general lordship and savynge not oonly of Jewis but of heþene men in dyverse statis. Þese prelatis wolden fayn þat all Goddis lawe were hongynge on hem for to spuyle þe puple; for þanne

Exposition of the parables of the lost sheep and the lost piece of money.

wolde þei telle þis lawe, and put þereto fals undirstondinge, as þei myʒten have more wynnynge of þe puple.—¶ Þe first parable stondiþ in a question of Crist; he axiþ *which man of hem hadde an hundrid shepe* to kepe, and he were nedid to save hem ech on, *and he hadde lost oon of hem; ne wolde he not leeve fourescore and nyntene in a sikir deserte and go and seke þis lost sheep til þat he fond it; and when he hadde founden it, wolde leien it on his shuldris wiþ joie and whanne he comeþ hoom, he clepeþ togidre his frendis and neiʒboris, and seiþ to hem, Be ye gladde and þanke me, for Y have founde my sheep þat was perishid. Certis Y seie to you þat þere shal be joie in hevene upon oon synful man þat doiþ penaunce, ʒhe þo more þan upon foure score and nyntene riʒt-wise þat have no nede of penaunce.* Þis man is Jesus Crist þat was of þe Jewis, and he was herty and wyse and hadde in his kepynge þe aungelis confirmed in hevene, and wiþ hem mankynde. Nynty and nyne bitokeneþ þes aungelis, for þes nyne ordres þat ben knytted in Crist; and þis oo sheep is mankynde, þat acordiþ more to-gider þan þese nyne ordres of aungels. Þis oo sheep þat was lost perishide by synne of

Ps. cxix. 176.

Adam, as þe psalme seiþ. Hevene is clepid disert by many enchesouns, for it is selde visited of men, þat slowly comen þidir, and it is not tilid[1] as is erþe here wiþ us, and it is florishid wiþ goostly trees þat evermore ben grene, for grenesse in virtues may nevere faile in hevene. And þis is a sykyr place; for fendis tempten men not þere. Crist lefte þis aungel kynde dwellyng in hevene; for Crist toke not angels kynde but toke here mannis kynde, and bi his greet virtue he suffride peyne as oþer men þre and þritty ʒeer, and brouʒt mankynde to hevene, and bade þe aungelis his frendis, and man next him in manhede, rejoyeshe hem wiþ him, for he hadde saved mankynde þat was perishide. And bi þis aungels in hevene, mankynde, and feendis, shulde be gladde bi resoun; for þe more þat ben dampned þe more is fendis peyne, and þus is more joie in hevene of þis oo sheep, þan of nyne ordris of aungels þat neden noo penaunce, for þei synneden nevere. Þis o sheep þat is mankynde synede for þe more parte, and

[1] For 'tilled' (?) D has *tylud*; C *tillid*.

was quykid bi Crist, þat was oon wiþ his breþeren; and he, alȝif he myȝte not synnen, suffride peyne for his sheep. And more joie is in hevene of him and his membris þan of nyne ordris of angelis, for þei ben beter and lyveden more medefully as trewe knyȝtis of God. Þe seconde parable of Crist stondiþ in þis, þat *a wyse womman þat hadde ten dragmes, ȝif she hadde lost oon, she wolde liȝtne her lanterne, turne up hir house to seke þis lost dragme, and whan she hadde founden it*, she wolde make joie as it was seid bifore of him þat lost þe sheep.—¶ Þis womman is Jesus Crist, wysdom of þe fadir; þese ten dragmes ben his resonable creaturis, for þei ben maid alle to ymage and licnesse of þe Trinite. Þe tenþe dragme þat was lost is mankynde, þe lanterne þat was liȝtid is þe manhede of Crist, þe turning up of þis house is changinge of statis þat ben maid in þis world by manhede of Crist. For þe angel wolde not suffren Joon to knele and worshipe him, for his lord was Joones broþir, and þe aungelis weren hise servauntis; and so many þingis of þis world weren turnid up so down, siþ evry parte of þis worlde was beterid bi Cristis manhede.

Directions to preachers.

We may touche in þis gospel what spediþ men and what þing lettiþ men for to be saved, for men mote nede do penaunce in berynge of þis sheep, and have liȝt of þis lanterne for to fynde þis lost dragme.

Þe fourþe Sondai Gospel after Trynyte.

[SERMON IV.]

Estote misericordes.—Luc. vi. [36.]

The duty of showing mercy, and the sin of rash judgment.

Þis gospel moveþ men to mercy aȝen þe ypocrisye of þes false Pharisees, and Crist biddiþ first generally men to be *merciful as your fadir is merciful.* For whanne a general word is seid bi himsilf, it shal be taken for þe most famous. Þere ben many fadris, as fadir of kynde, and fadir of lore, but þe mooste propre fadir is he þat makiþ men of nouȝt, for he is fadir of mennis bodies, and fadir of her soulis, and in vertue

The clergy sellers of grace.

of him worchen all oþer fadris. And þis fadir shulden we sue in alle our werkes, for alȝif we may not atteyne to þis fadir, neþeles þo dedis ben nouȝtis þat ben not ensaumplid and wrouȝt by þis fadir. Þe mercy of þis fadir can we not telle fulli, for he is þe mooste worcher þat may be in þis world, and he cannot worche, but ȝif he medle mercy, for he wrouȝt by mercy whan he made þis worlde, siþ he dide good to angelis, and makide hem perfit, and brouȝte hem to heyer state wiþouten her disert. And so when he doiþ good to eny creature, he makiþ it perfit of his pure grace, siþ God Almiȝty, al witty, and al godely, cannot worche but ȝif he worche by mercy. Be we þan mercyful for goodnesse of God. Þe lest mercy of men is among clerkis: þat wolen not ȝyve goodis of grace but ȝif þei sillen hem, and þerefore þis synne is heresie before God, þe most and þe first þat parteþ men fro God, for þei weyen her wynnynges more þan þer God. And herfore all þat we done shulde be done in Goddis name, to wirchip of oure God, and profit of his church. Ȝhe ȝif we ben holden boþe to God and man by resoun of dette to do a good dede, loke þat þis reson be first hidde in our þouȝt, and so no man may excuse him fro werkes of mercy as no man may wante werkes of a good wille, for þat werke is þe first and heiest in man. First shulde a man have mercy of himsilf, and mercy of his modir, þat is Holy Chirche; and þan haþ he mercy of all his ende kyn[a]. Þe secound word of Crist *forbediþ fool jugement;* and resoun of þis stondiþ hereinne þat God may not folily juge ony man; and so as oure wille haþ nede to be cloþid wiþ mercy, so oure undirstondinge haþ nede to have riȝt jugement. For many men wenen to be merciful to ypocritis, and þei done harm to men to which þei wenen do profit; and many men wenen to juge þer breþeren, and ȝit þei jugen falsely and cruely of many; and eche man shulde tempere sich jugement aftir God, for God in his jugement may not faile for resoun. Þe þridde word bidditþ Cristen men *beware of foly dampnynge up peyne of þer dampnacion;* and al ȝif þis semeþ no comoun

The evils of rash judgment.

[a] *ende kyn.* There is no difference of reading in the MSS. The phrase seems to mean 'remoter kindred,' as 'ende-men' signifies 'borderers' in Anglo-Saxon.

synne among men, neþeles al maner of men synnen herynne; and prelatis, þat dampnen men in maner of þer cursyng. And ofte tymes þei witen not how þei ben to God; and by reputacion þat shulde be take of Goddis lawe þes men done well as God biddiþ hem do. Lordis jugen ofte tymes þat oþer men done amys, whan þei displesen hem in þir wronge wille; as we dampnen Clement[a] wiþ his fautours, and þei dampnen us, and o king dampniþ his adversarie, and he dampniþ him aȝen, and comounes dampnen proude men and oþers to be ypocrites. And comounly foly jugement is þing þat men knowen not, for þei leden not þer witt after Goddis lawe, for þei presumen as þe fende to kunne þat þei knowen not.—¶ Þe fourþe and þe fifþe word *biddiþ men forȝyve and ȝyve sum maner of goodis, and so shal God rewarde hem.* And not al oonly God, but seintis in hevene, shal rewarde men, after þat þey have done here to hem. For þese fyve dedis[1] alargid to alle men mut have sum men seintis in hevene. And þese seintis shulen reward men here in aboundance of foure þingis; first, þei shal rewarde men *in a good mesure*, for seintis in hevene done beter to men þan þei diden to hem here in þis lyf; and where men diden scarsely good to þir breþeren, seintis fillen trewe men wiþ all manere of goodis; and þis fillyng is not *voide but sadly replenchid*[2], and at þe laste *it is heepid* as myche as it wole take. And siche metyng of corn, of mele, or oþer þing, wolde be preisid among men fer þe largenesse of þe meter; and þis þing men have here in her bosum, but God filliþ þe substance. For certis *in sich mesure as men mesuren to* her breþeren shal *it be mesurid to hem* bi jugement of God. Ȝif þe mesure be good, þei shal have good aȝen, and ȝif þe mesure be unjust, þei shal have peyne aȝen. And, for defaute in al þis comiþ of ypocrisye of prelatis, þat shulden teche pleynly Goddis lawe and not þer erþly wynnynges, þerfore seiþ Crist in his parable, þat *ȝif þe blynde lede þe blynde boþe fallen in þe dike.* But for Crist shulde be oure maister, and

[1] After *dedis* D inserts *aren*. A and C agree with B. [2] *voydid but sadly replenyscbed*, D.

[a] This allusion fixes the date of the composition of these Sermons to a time between 1378 and 1394, in which latter year the anti-pope Clement VII died.

we shulden not strange from him, we shulden leeve þes ipocritis and sue þe lore of þis good maister, siþ he may not leve treuþe, ne faile in teching of truþe. And þus shulden men ben perfit, and flei the rote of falshede. And þes prelatis have of þere maistris comounly þis manere, *þat þei can see a mot in hir broþer' eye, but a beem in þer owen iȝe þenke þei not oon.* For þere witt is sett to spuyle and to accuse, and not for to helpe hem ne oþer men, and þerefore her coveitise blindiþ hem þus; but bi lore of Crist men shulden sei to hem, *Ypocrite, cast first þe beeme out of þin owne eye and þan maist þou poke beter þe mot fro þi broþir.*

Directions.

Here may men see þat sugettis shulden blame prelatis whan þey seen opynly greet defautes in hem, as defaute of Goddis lawe in keeping and teeching; for þis is a beeme bi which þe fende bindeþ his hous and þei shulden knowe þes as þei shulden fele the lore þereof.

Þe fyfþe Sondai Gospel after Trinite.

[SERMON V.]

Cum turbae irruerunt ad Jesum.—Luc. v. [1.]

Peter fishing in the Sea of Galilee.

Þe story of þis gospel telliþ good lore, how prelatis shulden teche folk under hem. Þe story is pleyn, how *Crist stood by þe river of Genazereþ, and fisheris comen doun to waishe þerynne þer nettes; and Crist wente up into a boot þat was Symonis, and preiede him to move it a litel fro þe lond, and he sate and tauȝte the peple out of the boot. And whanne Crist ceesside to speke, he seide to Symoun, Lede þe boot into þe hey see, and late out your nettis to takyng of fishe. And Simoun answerynge seid to him, Comandour, al þe nyȝt traveilinge token we nouȝt; but in þi word shal Y lose þe nett. And whan þei hadden done þis, þei token a plentenouse multitude of fishe, and þer nett was broken. But þei bekeneden to þer felowis þat weren in þe toþer boot, to come and helpe hem; and þei comen and filliden boþ botes of fishe, so þat wel nyȝ were þei boþe dreynt. And whanne Petre hadde seen þis wounder, he fell doun to Jesus knee, and seide, Lord, go fro me for Y am a synnful man.* For Petre held him not worþi to[1] be wiþ Crist, ne dwelle in his cumpanye: *for woundir came to hem alle in takynge of þes fishes. And so woundriden James and Joon, Zebedes sones, þat weren Symondis felowis. And Jesus seide to Symound, Fro þis tyme shalt þou be takynge men. And þei setten þer bootis to þe londe, and forsook al þat þei hadden, and sueden Crist.*—¶ Byfore we go to spiritual undirstonding of þis gospel, we shal wyte þat þe same Cristis disciple þat was first clepid Symoun, was clepid Petre after of Crist, for sadnesse of bileve þat he toke of Crist, which Crist is a corner stoon, and groundiþ al treuþe. Over þis we shal undirstonde þat þe apostlis were clepid of Crist in many degrees; first þei weren clepid and acceptid to be Cristis disciplis; and yet þei turneden aȝen, as Crist himsilf ordeynede, to lyve in þe world. After þei were clepid to see Cristis myraclis, and to be more homely wiþ him þan þei weren before; but yet þei turneden aȝen to þe worlde by tymes, and lyveden worldely lyf, to profit of folk þat þei dwelten wiþ. And on þis wyse Petre James and Joon wenten now to fishe. But þe þridde clepyng and þe moost was þis,—þat þe Apostlis forsoken holly þe world and worldly þingis, and turneden not aȝen to worldly lyf, as after þis miracle Petre and his felowis sueden Crist contynnely. It is noo nede to depe us in þis stori more þan þe gospel telliþ, as it is no nede to bisie us what hiȝt Tobies hound. Hold we us apaied on þe mesure þat God haþ ȝovun us, and dreeme we not aboute newe pointes þat þe gospel leveþ, for þis is a synne of curiouste, þat harmeþ more þan profitiþ. Þe story of þis gospel telliþ us goostly witt, boþ of lyf of þe churche and medeful werkis, and þis shulde we undirstonde, for it is more prescious. Two fishingis þat Petre fishide bitokeneþ two takingis of men unto Cristis religioun, and fro þe fend to God. In þis first fishinge was þe nette broken, to tokne þat many men ben convertid, and after breken Cristis religioun; but at þe seconde fishinge, after þe resurrectioun, whan þe nett was ful of many grete fishes, was not þe nett broken, as þe gospel seiþ; for þat bitokeneþ seintis þat God chesiþ to hevene. And so þese nettis þat fisheris fishen wiþ

Degrees of vocation to the apostleship.

Tobit vi. 1.

Mystical interpretation of the gospel.

[1] om. A.

bitokeneþ Goddis lawe, in whiche virtues and treuþes ben knyttid; and oþer propretees of nettis tellen propretes of Goddis lawe; and voide places betweene knottis bitokeneþ lyf of kynde, þat men han beside vertues. And foure cardynale virtues ben figurid bi knittyng of þe nett. Þe nett is brood in þe bigynnyng, and after streit in ende, to teche þat men, when þei ben turned first, lyven a brood worldely lyf; but afterward, whan þei ben depid in Goddis lawe, þei kepen hem streitlyer fro synnes. Þese fisheris of God shulden waishe þere nettis in þis ryver, for Cristis prechours shulden chevely[1] tellen Goddis lawe, and not medle wiþ mannis lawe, þat is trobly water; for mannis lawe conteyneþ sharpe stones and trees, bi which þe nette of God is broken and fishis wenden out to þe world. And þis bitokeneþ Genasareþ[a], þat is, an wounderful birþe, for þe birþe by whiche a man is borne of water and of þe Holy Goost is myche more wounderful þan mannis kyndely birþe. Summe nettis ben rotun, sum han hoolis, and sum ben unclene for defaute of waishing; and þus on þree maneres faileþ þe word of preching. And mater of þis nett and brekynge þereof ȝyven men greet mater to speke Goddis word, for vertues and vices and treuþis of þe gospel ben mater ynow to preche to þe peple.

Þe Sixte Sondai Gospel after Trinite.

[SERMON VI.]

Nisi habundaverit justitia vestra plus quam Pharisaeorum.— Matt. v. [20.]

It is seide in þe nexte[b] gospel what nettis preestis shulden have for to drawe men fro þe see of þis worlde to þe drye lond of þis lyf. Þis gospel telliþ of þe devylis nett, in which he

[1] *clenli*, B.

[a] Gennesaret is really a corruption of the older name, Chinnereth (Smith's Dict. Bible); but Wyclif appears to derive it from the Greek γεννάω or γένεσις.

[b] *nexte*. Meaning *the last*, proximus.

fishiþ and drawt men to helle. Cristis nett is knytt wiþ riȝt-wisenesse to God aboven men, to creatures bineþe men, and to aungels in oþer side of men; and þis clepiþ God fully riȝt-wisenesse, and feyned falsely riȝt-wisnesse of ypocritis clepiþ Crist not riȝt-wisnesse, alȝif ypocritis clepen it so, but of scribis and Pharisees, þat is to seie, unriȝt-wisnesse, feyned as it were riȝt-wisnesse, of scribis and Phariseis. And as Crist seiþ, *But ȝif your riȝt-wisness passe a point þe feyned riȝt-wisnesse of scribis and Phariseis, ȝe shal nevere come to hevene.* We may undirstonde by scribis and Phariseis men of þe fendis chirche, as we diden before; so þat scribis ben clepid seculer prelatis, and Phariseis ben clepid þese newe religious. Þes men maken hem a riȝt-wisnesse bi hemsilf as þei maken hem a lawe of Anticrist; and certis þis law may Crist never conferme; and so, as Poul seiþ, þes Anticristis disciplis heyen hem over Crist, boþ over his godhede and over his manhede. For riȝt-wisnesse generaly is fulfillinge of lawe, and so fulfillinge of Goddis lawe is verrei riȝt-wisnesse; and fulfillinge of mannis lawe is Anticristis riȝt-wisnesse. And so þre degrees ben in þe law of scribis; þe first and þe moost is in þe Popis welle; and as men of þe worlde seien, þere is welle of riþt-wisnesse; but þei gon ofte biside þe riȝt for þer roten ground; þei tristen on riȝt of mannis lawe, and gone ofte biside þe soþe. And ȝit þei excusen þis fals lawe, and seien it mut nede juge fals, for ellis it faillide in his cours, and riȝt of þe worlde were fordone. But þei þenken not how Crist forsoke to juge bi mannis lawe, teching þat eche jugement þat is not done by Goddis lawe, is jugement of þe fend, and we witen not where it be riȝt. And þat man is a fool þat jugiþ after ony law, and woot not wheþir he juge bi God, or ellis by jugement of þe fend; and ȝif men avysiden hem on þis resoun, noone shulde juge bi mannis lawe. And þis fals riȝt is more feyned in consistorie law and in chapitre lawe. For algatis þei supposen þat witnesse may not faile, or ellis þe juge may not faile þat jugiþ after fals witnesse; and of þis roten blasfemye comeþ many fals jugementis. Juge we bi riȝt conscience þat God telliþ or specifieþ and leve we mannis jugement, and suffre we fewe wrongis þat falle, for mo wrongis shulen be don for foli of mannis dome. Þe riȝt of þe Phariseis buriouneþ

Prelates and friars, like the Scribes and Pharisees, make for themselves a new righteousness and a new law, which Christ will not confirm.

2 Thess. ii. 4.

Consistory law.

to harme of þe Chirche, not oonly among hemsilf, þat holden al þing wel done þat is done bi þer ordre, alȝif it be a foly feyned by mannis witt, but how ever þei may gete good bi coloure of þis feyned ordre, þei clepen it hey riȝt-wisnenesse. For þe ground good and holy triste we to Cristis religioun, for þat is beter þan þes newe; for ellis we comen not to hevene, but shulen be dampned wiþ ypocritis. And witt of þese scribis is so myche sett in worldely goodis, þat þei clepen not riȝt-wisnesse but ȝif it be of worldely catel þat is geten by mannis lawe, alȝif Goddis lawe dampne it. And so þe fals Phariseis tauȝten men *þat Goddis lawe defendiþ*[1] *not but man-slauȝter or oþer sensible wrong*, and not oþir pryvey wrongs þat is worse roote hereof; and þis were blasfemye in God, to leeve þe worse and dampne þe beter. And herfore declariþ Crist þre manere of wickid ire.

Matt. v. 22. *Þe first maner of ire is whan a man is wraþþid wiþouten resoun, and sich is coupable aȝens God to be jugid to helle.* For þis unkyndely venym aȝen þe state of innocence is roote of malice wiþoute-forþ, þat in caas is lesse yvel; and for þis cause men usen whan þei drawen to þer deeþ to forȝeve men alle wrongis, and axe men mercy of here synne. *Þe secounde degree of þis ire is whanne a man haþ conseyved wraþþe and brekeþ out in scorneful wordis of his first conseyved ire.* Soþely ire may falle to men for to venge Goddis cause, and so may men scorne

1 Kin. xviii. 27. oþer, for þei folily synnen in God, as Hely[a] scornede þe preestis of Baal. But boþe þes ben perilous, and herfore he þat scorniþ þus *is coupable to falle in conseile*, where his foli shal be hardid, til þat he falle to more synne. *Þe þridde degree of þis ire is whan a man spekiþ folily, as he þat sclaundriþ a man or repreveþ him falsely; and þat man, as Crist seiþ, is coupable of þe fier of*

1 John iii. 15. *helle*, for his ire is turned to hate, and as Seint Joon seiþ, al siche been men sleeris, þat ben worþi to be dampned. And so shulden men kepen charite boþe in wille and in word, and not oonly spare strokis, as Fariseis falsely seiden. And herfore shulden irrous men axe mekely forȝyvenesse, for ȝif þei wanten charite al is yvel whatever þei do. And þerfore *if þou offre þi*

[1] *forfendiþ*, B and C.

[a] *Hely.* Elias.

gifte to God, þat þe scribis preisen myche, *and þou þenke þat þi broþir*, for þi synne, *haþ a cause aȝens þee, leeve þi offring at þe auter, and go first to be accordid wiþ him.* For meke offringe in mannis herte is betere þan offringe wiþoute-forþ. And ȝif þi broþir be ferre fro þee, Goddis lawe is so resonable, þat it suffisiþ þat þou go out of ire and be recounsilid in herte wiþ him, and in hool purpos to make aseeþ[1] as soone as þou goodly mayst. By þis lore may we see how ferre it is fro scole of Crist for to chide or to plede or to fiȝt as men now done.

Þe sevenþe Sondai Gospel aftir Trinite.

[SERMON VII.]

Cum turba multa esset cum Jesu, nec haberent quod manducarent.—Mark viii. [1.]

The miracle of the loaves and fishes.

For alle werkis of Crist ben good lore to Cristen men, to teche hem how þei shal lyve for to gete þe blisse of hevene, þerfore þis gospel of Crist telliþ how he bi boþe his kyndis did a miracle of mercy in fedynge of þe nedy folk. *Whan myche peple was wiþ Jesus, and þei hadden not to ete, he clepide his disciplis togidere and seide, Y have ruþ upon þe peple, for þei have sued me þree daies, and now þei han not for to ete, and if Y lete hem go fastinge home, þei shal faile in þe weye, for sum of hem comen fro ferre. And his disciplis seiden to him, Whereof myȝte a man fede þis folk here in þis waste place? And Crist axide hem, how many loves þat þei hadden, and þei seiden seven. And Crist commandide þe peple to sitte doun on þe erþe; and takynge þes sevene loves and doinge þankingis to God, he brak hem, and ȝaf hise disciplis to putt to þe puple, and þei ȝaven þis breed to þe puple. And þei hadden a fewe litil fishis, and hem he blesside and makide his disciplis ȝyve hem to þe peple. And þe peple eet, and was fulfillid; and ȝit þei gedriden seven berlepis*[a] *of relif þat*

[1] *aseeþ*, B; *asseþ*, D. See Glossary.

[a] That is, 'carrying-baskets,' from the A.S. 'beran,' to bear, and 'leap,' a basket. Both Wycliffite versions have 'leepis' at the same passage.

was laft. And þere was of þe puple, hungry and longe fastinge, as it were foure þousand, and Criste lefte hem, and lete hem go home. Þe gospel telliþ of siche two feestis þat Criste maade here in erþe. In þe first weren fyve þousaund fedde, and in þe toþir foure þousand, and þis was þe seconde feste, as seint Mark telliþ. And of greet witt weren þes two, as seintis beren witnesse[1]; for two is þe firste noumbre þat comeþ after oonheed, and herfore men clepen it a noumbre wiþouten fame; for it is þe first noumbre þat partiþ fro unite; and certis, if no man hadde partid from God bi synne, it hadde be noo nede to make siche feestis; for ech man shulde redely have mete whan him nedide, as beestis han gras[2] in plentenous pasture. And so bi þis bodili werk of merci of Crist ben we tauȝt to which men we shulden do sich almes; for Crist techiþ in þe gospel of Luke þat we shulde feden siche þat have greet nede, and if we feden oþir men, biside þe resoun of almes, þe fruyte of oure almes in þat is awey. And so curatis þat ben better occupied about spiritual nedis shulden for þer feblenesse, fer fro state of innocence, take bodily almes to perfourme þer office, ȝhe ȝif þei ben stronge in bodi in reward of oþer men; and þis title of almes is mooste acording to preestis; but in state of innocens shulde þis almes be awey; for men shulde have redily fruyt þat þai hadden nede of; and þis feblenesse of bodi is falle to men for synne. Crist þat was boþe God and man hadde not þis feblenes, for he myȝt have mete whan and wher he wolde; but we shal wite þat our Jesus Crist dide more miracle, and bad hise disciplis serve þe puple at þe mete, to teche us þat we ben mynystris and not autouris of miracle. And þus he quykide Lazarus, and made his apostolis efte to lose him, to teche þat he forȝeveþ þe synne, and his vikeris shewen it to þe puple. But þei assoilen on oþir weye, as prestis in þe olde lawe telden bi signis of the olde lawe þat men weren cleen of lepre. And ȝif þe Pope and his vikeris wolden studie wel þis mater, þei shulden leve to assoile men so largely in þis fourme, for our bileve techiþ us þat no viker assoileþe here, but in as myche as Crist assoileþ first him whom he assoileþ in virtue of Crist. We shal see moreover

Mystical interpretation of the miracle.

[1] This is the reading of B. A has *wittis*. [2] So in B; *gresse*, C; *grace*, A.

þat þe folke þat Crist fedde here weren fedde comounly, and not by maner of þis world, for to dampne riche mannis maneris þat feden hemsilf coostly, and ordeyne strange and likerous mete, and in greet multitude, and excuse hem herbi þat relif goiþ to pore men, for pore men myȝten many mo be beter fedde wiþ comoun metis; and so þis is a likerous pride, how-ever we gabben to God. But go we nere to þe witt þat þe gospel techiþ us, and we shall see þat eche preest shulde be viker of Crist, and take of him oyle of grace, and so in a maner be Crist, and fede þe puple goostly wiþ þe wordis of God; for neiþer Crist ne hise Apostlis hadden ay bodily mete to fede folk þus; and Crist techiþ us in þis þat goostly fode is beter þan þis, and in token herof þis secounde feste was algatis lasse, but goostly feeste shulde encreese, þat haþ fulli ende in hevene. Þese sevene loves ben sevene bokes of þe newe testament, and foure gospellis, and þerwiþ stories of þe Apostlis wisdom, of bokes of Poul, and Apocalips of Joon. Þese fewe litil fishes þat þei hadden to companage ben pistlis of reule of James and Petre and Joon and of Judas. Þe seven berlepis of relif ben alle þe sentences of seintis after, bi which þei feden trewe men by delyng of Goddis lawe. For many ben fedd by relif þat kouden not ete þis hole mete. Þe multitude of just men ben þes foure þousaund men, þat Crist grauntiþ her owne wille to go to þe house of hevene.

Þe eiȝtþe Sonedai Gospel aftir Trinite.

[SERMON VIII.]

Attendite a falsis prophetis.—Matt. vii. [15.]

Attack upon the Friars.

Þis gospel biddiþ Cristene men to *be ware wiþ false prophetis, þat comen in cloþing of sheep.* And þes wordis may be applyed unto fals freris; for soþe þis lore of Crist wolde he not ȝyve in tyme of grace, but if siche men weren for to come which þei shulden flee. And so, be þei freris or be þei oþer þat speken falsely in þer prechinge, oure good maister Crist bad þat we shulden be ware wiþ hem. Þei ben prophetis, in þat þei speken aferr of þe dai of dome, of blisse, and of peynes; and þus seiþ Crist þat he sendeþ prophetis to men þat ben of fals feiþ, and þei shal tormente hem. And it is noo doute þat ne siche men ben profetis, and þei ben false prophetis; if þei lyven þus þat þei shapen her lyf and her wordis boþe, more for ypocrisie and wynnynge of þe peple þan for worship of God or helþe of her soule. If þei fynden novelry in þer fals habitis, and ȝit lyven as yvel as oþir comoun men, who shulde drede of hem þat ne þei ben fals profetis? Al þer founden signes þei shewen oþir men, þat þei shulden crye þer holynesse over oþir Cristene men. But, Lord, whi shulden þei do þus? siþ holynes shulde be privy, and þei myȝten lyve as holy lyf wiþouten siche signes. Certis it semeþ no cause but if it be ypocrisie, þat þei shewen to þe peple þer holynes as Phariseis doen, and so to be more told by, and liȝtlyer to wynne goodis, for take awey þis eende, and her signes serven of nouȝt. And as Crist seiþ a good lore to knowe hem were, to *marke þer fruytis*, þat specialy comen of hem. Wel Y wote þat þe Churche profitide before freris camen in, and siþen han ben sowen many fals lores, boþe in þer religioun, and preisyng of scribis; as we seen of þe sacrid oost, of þe regginge of Crist, of lettris of þe breþheed, and oþir worldely lyvynge. Þe knowyng of siche signes shewiþ wel þer fruyte, how þei ben chargeous to þe peple, and fals in þer entent; for greet noumbre and costlewe housis and greet dispensis of þis world, wiþ reulynge of worldely causis, tellen what ende þei worchen fore. And herfore seiþ Crist, þat *þei ben wiþinne wolves of ravyne*[1]; wulves þei ben if þei loven more catel þan mennis soulis, and open þer mouþ to heveneward to feyne preestis power, þat neiþir þei can grounden in þe lawe of God, ne it may not falle to God himsilf, and bi þis power þei spuylen þe puple of þer goodis, and not assoilen hem freely for to save þer soulis. And bi þis fruyte may men knowe þe falshede of þes wolvys, for we shal wite as bileve þat who loveþ more mannis good þan he loveþ helþe of his soule, he is wulf and fendis child. And þis may men wel see by þes preestis'

False doctrines introduced by them.

Their covetousness.

[1] So in B. A has *rayne*.

bisynesse; and herfore seiþ Goddis word, þat *men gederen not of þornes grapis*, to glade men goostly wiþ, *ne gidere not figis of breris*, for as þes trees han not of kynde to brynge to men siche fruytis; so siche children of þe fend feden not men goostly, neiþir wiþ figis of bileve ne wiþ grapis of devocioun, but þei han more bisynes to spuyle fro men þer worldely goodis, as boþe þornes and bryres reven fro sheepe þer wolle. And þus *ech good tree* þat God haþ ordeyned to þe hous of heven, *bereþ here good fruyte* and *þe yvel tree beriþ venym;* for riȝt as Goddis children may not do but good þing, so children of þe fend may not do but harmful þing. For riȝt as fendis semen to do good, and it turneþ at þe ende to þer harm, so Goddis children semen to do yvel, but God turneþ it to þer good. And to þis witt seiþ þe word of Crist, *þat a good tree may not bere yvel fruyte, ne an yvel tree good fruyte.* For þei may not turne as þe wynd, for alle þingis þat shal come mut nedis come as we taken here; and so *eche tree* here in þis world *þat makiþ not þus good fruyte, shall be fellid and putt to þe fier* to brenne in helle wiþouten ende. And þus bi fruyte of preestis shulen ȝe knowe whos þei ben, and herby bewar wiþ hem, for condicions of her maistris. And *it sufficiþ not to seie, Lord, Lord*, but it nediþ to lyve wele to a mannes lyves ende; and so it sufficiþ not to preestis to seie, God be wiþ you, but þei mut seie wele in herte and wele in mouþe and lyve wele, for ellis a man shal not be saved ne broȝt to liknes of þe Trinite. Ne þis lore is not oonly constreyned to fals freris, but generaly to preestis, þat seien þat þei han care of mennis soulis; for worchyng bi riȝt lyf, endid after Goddis wille, makiþ a man Goddis child and come to þe blisse of hevene.

Men are justified by works.

Þe nynþe Sondai Gospel after Trinite Sonday.

[SERMON IX.]

Homo quidam erat dives et habebat villicum.—Luc. xvi. [1.]

The parable of the unjust steward.

Þis gospel telliþ how men shulde make hem frendis of worldely goodis, for reward þat þei shulden have aftir in hevene. Þe parable telliþ *how a man hadde a fermour*, as keper of a toun[a], *þat was defamyd to him as he hadde wastid his goodis;* but not al fulli, for he hadde spendid hem unwarly, but þe lord hadde þe worship. *Þis lord clepide þis fermour* and seide *þus to him, How heere Y þus of þee, þat þou wastist* my good? *Ȝife a rekenynge of þi baillyship, for þou maist be no longer in þis office. And þis servant seide wiþyne to himsilfe, What shal Y do? for my lord takiþ fro me þis office; delve may Y not,* and *me shameþ for to begge; but Y woot what Y shal do, þat whan Y am removed fro þis office, oþir tenauntis of þe lord shal resceyve me into þere housis,* for goodis þat Y shal do to hem: while Y am in þis office. And *he gaderide togidere alle þe dettours of his lord; and axide þe first how myche he ouȝt his lord; and he seide he ouȝte him an hundrid barels of oyle. And he seide to him, Take þi caucioun and sitte soone and wryte fifty barellis. And efte he seide to anoþir, How myche owist þou? And he seide he ouȝte an hundrid skippis of corn.* (Þis mesure of corn is more þan a quarter.) *And he badde him take his lettris,* bi which he was bounden, *and wryte foure score. And þe lord preiside þe bailly of wickidnes, for he hadde warly done; for children of þis worlde ben more ware þan children of liȝt in þer kynrede.* In þis parable we shulden wite þat Crist is þis lord, þat is kyng of kyngis and lord of lordis; þis bailly of þis

Interpretation of the parable.

[a] 'toun,' from the A.S. verb tynan, to hedge in or enclose, had originally pretty nearly the same meaning as the word 'clearing' has in our colonies now; it was the piece of land enclosed from the forest or moor and made habitable for men From a single clearing, it came to be applied to the whole cleared and enclosed land in any particular locality, and so to the principal collection of dwellings forming the homes of the cultivators of such land.

lord, or keper of his litil toun, is eche man of þis world, seme he never so greet, for emperoure or kyng is tenaunt to þis lord and keper of his litil toun, to regard of Cristis greet lordship. For Crist is lord of hevene and helle and al þis erþe, ȝhe lord of al þis world, wiþ goodis of it opyn and hidde, and no conquerrour myȝte ateyne to lordship of al þis erþe, for Alisaundre and Julius leften myche to conquere, and God wolde not þat þer lordship were more here in erþe, techinge us þat þe fend prince of þis world haþ but litil lordship of children of pryde, alȝif he be now partener wiþ Crist of mo servauntis of þe fend þan shal come to hevene. But Crist is chefe lord of þe fend and al his lymes, and þei mut nedis serve him oþir wele or yvel, doinge wel þat þei shulden do, or ellis suffringe peyne. And siþ Crist haþ lent ech man here al þat he haþ, and wole axe of þis streite rekenynge, how he dispendiþ it, to ech man of þis world may þis parable be applied; and whanne men dispenden not warly Goddis goodis, þanne þei ben defamyd to him as þei hadden wastid hem, but dispending of alle goodis mut sowne to Goddis worship. For alle men shulden knowe þat alle þes ben Goddis goodis, and he wole þat þei be spendid þus to profit of his Churche, and so spekyng of þis lord is movynge of mennys conscience, and þus God telliþ to men boþe more and lasse, how he knowiþ her traytery, whan þei done amys, and hou þei ben nedid to die from þis office, and hou þei ben nedid to God to rykene for þis servyse. And sum han drede how þei shal lyve after þis lyf, for after þer deeþ þei may not delve, or do medefulli to þer soule, and shameful þing it is to begge oþer of men þat here lyven, or of seintis in hevene, but as þei witen þat þei shulden helpe after þat men han her deserved while þei lyveden here in þis lyf. And so þis fermour grantide þre þingis þat men shulden knowe here in þis lyf. First he grantide þat aftir þis lyf he myȝt not wirche medefulli. Aftir he grantide þat he shulde shame to begge more þan he hadde disservyd. And so stronge beggers here on lyf, ben more unshameful þan ben soulis or in helle or in purgatorie, þat wolen not axe but þat þei han disservyd, for þei witen þat it were veyn to axe more of þer God. But þis baily turnede wisely him to a good conseil; þat while he lyvede here in erþe he shulde make men his frendis wiþ goodis of God þat he kepiþ, and þei shulde helpe him whan he is deed. And þus it perteyneþ to kingis first to do worship to God, and siþ to do riȝt to þer servauntis and so to alle men under hem. And þis discharge may baillies do wiþouten injurie to God; for sum men þenken þat þis bailly þat forȝafe fifty barels of oile and þerto twenty skippis of corn, dide wronge to his lord, and so þe lord preiside him not wele; but we shal wite þat þis lord is God, and þis bailly lord of þis world, and so God approveþ wele forȝyvynge of mannis rente; and wiþ graunte of þe cheef lord, baillyes may forȝyve þer dette; and so it were a medeful þinge to worldely lordis to forȝyve dette, and discharge þer pore tenantis of many chargis þat þei ben inne. And so as þis miȝte falle in dede, þat þis bailly was worldly wyse, so hevenly prudence myȝte falle to children of liȝt, but þe first prudence falliþ more comounly þan þe secounde unto men, for pryde and coveitise of goodis blyndiþ men to do almes, but herfore goodis of fortune ben clepid bi a fendis name, þingis of wickidnessis, for þei ben ofte unjustly delt. But conseil and bidding of Crist, þat is chefe lord of alle, is *þat men make hem frendis here of siche goodis of wickednesse.*

Þe tenþe Sondai aftir Trinite.

[SERMON X.]

Cum appropinquaret Jesus Hierusalem videns civitatem.—Luc. xix. [41.]

Þis[a] gospel telliþ generaly, what sorewe men shulden have for syne, siþ Crist, þat myȝte not do synne, wepte so ofte for synne. For we rede þat Crist wepte þries, and eche tyme he wepte for synne. And so telliþ our bileve in storye of þe gospel, *þat Jesus seynge Jerusalem wepte þeron*, for þe synne of

[a] In the margin of B here occurs the following note, in a late fifteenth century hand: 'Noat this specially of thee clergy the only hurt unto thee Churche of Christe.'

it, *and seide þat if þou knewe* þus synne, þou shuldist wepe as Y do nowe, *and certis in þis dai of þee þat shulde be comen in pees to þee*, if þou woldist receyve þis day and pees of it, as þou shuldist, *for alle þes þingis* þat þou shuldist cunne *ben now hidde fro þi iȝen. For daies shal come in þee*, for synne þat þou shalt do in me, and *þin enemyes schulen envyron þee as a palis al aboute, and parre þee in Jerusalem, as sheep ben parrid in a foold, and þei shal felle þee to þe erþe, and þi children þat ben in þee, and þei shal not leve in þee stoon liynge upon a stoon, þat þei ne shal be removed*, and þi wallis al distried, and þe cause of al þis shal be þé unkynde unknowynge *þat þou wolt not knowe þe tyme þat God* bi grace *haþ visitid þee.* Alle þes wordis weren shewide in dede, as Josephus makiþ mynde of hem, how Titus and Waspasian þe secounde and fourty ȝeer aftir þat Crist was steied to hevene, comen at solempnite of Paske, and ensegiden Jerusalem, and distrieden men and wallis uttirly þat þei founden þere. And þis is a pryvy synne wiþ which þe fend blindiþ men, þat þei sorewen not more for synne þan þei done for oþir harm; for þus wille is mysturned, and men failen to serve God. And herefore techiþ Crist hise apostlis þat þei shulden not be aferd for perelis þat shal come for to venge synne þat is done, but þe moste drede of alle shulde be to falle in synne, for þat is worse þan þe peyne þat God ordeyned to sue herof. And þus in foure affeccioums þat ben groundid in mannis wille stondiþ alle mannis synne þat he doiþ aȝens God, for if sorwe and joie of man and hope and drede were reulid wel, his wille were ordeyned unto God, to serve him as it shulde do. After þis telliþ þe storye how *Jesus wente into þe temple and caste out boþe bieris and selleris, and seide to hem þat it is writun, Myn hous shulde be an hous of preier, but ye have maad it a denne of þeves. And for a long tyme after he was eche day techinge in þe temple.* And in þis dede þat Crist dide, he techiþ his Chirche to bygynne for to purge his seintuarie, þat ben preests and clerks þerof, þat ben þe moost cause of synne, and siþ purge oþir partis, whan þe rote is distried.—¶ And þis telde Crists wending into þe temple after þes wordis, as ȝif he wolde seie in his worching, Þe cause of synne þat Y have told is wickednesse of preestis and clerkes, and herfore Y bigyne at þe temple, not to distric hem in her

Reformation must begin from the clergy.

persones, but to take from hem cause of her synne, and ordeyne þe Churche in temporal goodis as Y have ordeyned hem to lyve. And it is al oon to seie þat þese goodis ben þus sacrid and ȝyven to preestis þat no man may take hem fro þes preestis, and to seie þat Anticrist haþ so weddid þes goodis wiþ preestis þat noon may make þis dyvors; for preestis ben uncorrigible; but þes defamaciouns shulde preestis flee wiþ al þere myȝt, and preien þat þei weren amendid bi þe ordenance of Crist. For resoun shulde teche hem þat þei ben worse þan frentikes, and so þei hadden nede to be chastisid til þis passion were fro hem. For what man wolde bi resoun, kepyng a man in frenesie, ȝyve him a swerd or a knyf bi which he wolde slee himsilf? or who þat kepte a man in feveris, and wiste wele hou he shulde be reulid, and þat þis mete or þis wyne were contrarye to his helþe, wolde ȝyve him at his wille þis foode þat shulde anoye him? so, siþ preestis have goodis of men boþe of lordis and comouns, and þei disusen hem þus, þei myȝten and shulden by charite wiþdrawe þes brondis þat þus done harme to preestis, and in mesure and manere ȝyve þes goodis to preestis þat he himsilf haþ ordeyned him and hise to have siche goodis. And þis may bi charite be wiþdrawen by þe ȝyvers þerof, siþ no man may do yvel to men and not do good to þe same men, but if he be a quyke fend, þat we shulden not putte to seculers. And to þis ende shulden clerkes traveile and procure þat þis þing were done boþe for love of Goddis lawe and for love of clerkes and comouns, and ȝif þe fend by envie, þat is enemye to charite, seiþ þis þing may not be done by þe lawe þat now is sett, he seiþ þat Anticristis lawe, founden aȝens Goddis lawe, is strenger þan charite, and Anticrist strenger þan Crist. For þis ende shulden clerkes wepe and preie God þat his ordrenance[1] were kepte in his strengþe and Anticristis lawe putt abac.

Priests are incorrigible.

[1] *ordenaunce*, B.

Þe enleveneþe Sondi aftir Trinite.

[SERMON XI.]

Dixit Jesus ad quosdam qui confidebant tanquam justi.—Luc. xviii. [9.]

The parable of the Pharisee and the Publican.

Þis gospel telliþ in a parable how þat men shulden be meke and not justifie hemsilf and dispise oþir men, for þis is a spise of pride þat men clepen ypocrisie Þis parable telliþ þat *two men wente into the temple for to preye, þe toon was a Phariseie and þe toþir was a publican.* Þe *Pharise stood* as a proud man *and preiede þes þingis bi himsilf; God, Y þanke þee for Y am not as oþir men of þe world, robberis, unjust men, avoutrers, as þis publican*[1]; *Y fast twies in þe woke, and ȝyve tiþes of alle my goodis. And þe publican stood aferre, and wolde not lifte his iȝen to heven, but he smote upon his breest,* to figure true confessioun, *and seide, God be helplich to me þat am synful.* But Crists jugement seiþ þat, *þis publicane wente hoom, made riȝtful fro þis Pharise* for þe mekenesse þat he hadde, *for ech þat þus heiþ himsilf shal be made lowe,* bi peyne, *and he þat mekiþ him,* bi grace, *shal be heyed,* by mede of God. Of þis gospel may we wite how þe firste spice of pride, þat is ypocrisie, envenymeþ gretely þe churche, and, for þis ypocrisie is comounly amounge religiouse, þerfore biddiþ Crist his disciplis beware wiþ sour dow of Pharisees, and Crist himsilf expowneþ and seiþ, it is ypocrisie. Phariseis ben seid, as departid from oþir puple, and weren religiouse in Cristis tyme, as Saduceis and Esses. And al þes þree ordris of men Crist distried, and savyd þe persones, siþ boþe Poul and Nichodeme weren Phariseis, as Goddis lawe seiþ. And siþ al Cristis dedes ben ensaumples to trewe men, many men þenken þat þes newe sectis shulden be distried and þe persones saved, for þus ordeynede Crist maister best of alle; and Y clepe sectis newe mannes ordres, þat oon sueþ anoþir as he shulde sue Crist, and so eche secte smatchiþ[2] many synnes;

Application to the mendicant orders.

[1] So in B: *puplican*, A. [2] *smacchiþ*, B.

but if it be þat sect which Crist himsilf made, þat Goddis lawe clepiþ secte of Cristene men, for we shal bileve þat Crist may not do synne in ȝyvynge of his reule to lede Cristene men. And so þis secte is þe beste þat ony man may have, siþ Crist, almygty, alwitty, and alwilful, ordeyne þis sect covenable for eche man; but oþir newe sectis founden bi mannis witt mut nedis smatche synne for errour of þe fynder. And riȝt as þer weren þre suche sectis in Cristis tyme, so þer ben now monkes, chanouns, and freris; and dyvysyons in þes þree seien dyvysiouns in mennis wille. Al þes þree sectis mote nedis smatche errour, siþ þei grounden a perpetuel reule to all men of þes ordres þat þe gospel lefte by wisdom of Crist; and it were woundirful þat þes synful foolis shulde fynde a betere reule þan Crist himsilf fond. For who shulde make a reule to men þat he knoweþ not, ne haþ no maistrie of hem, ne techyng to kepen it? but o complexion and oon elde axiþ o manere of lyvynge and anoþir anoþir, þat þes patrons knewe not. And so oonly oure patron Crist, þat is boþe God and man, calengiþ as propre to himsilf to grounde siche ordres, and herfore seint Poul and Petre, wiþ oþir apostolis, fledden to grounde siche ordris for drede of blasfemye. And it were more suffrable to dwelle amonge Sarazynes or oþir paynym sectis as doen many Criste men þan to dwellen among sectis of þese newe religiouse. And þat þei seien, þat þei ben erberis betir þan comoun pasture, for erbis of vertue þat growen in hem, certis makinge of erberis in a comoun pasture wolde distrie þis pasture and lyf of þe comouns, boþe for dichyng and hegging and delvynge of tounes. And ȝif we marke alle siche erberis in Engelond, þat ben plantid of newe in comoun Cristis religioun, as þei spuylen þe remenaunt of temporal goodis, so, þat is more deel, þei spuyle hem of vertues, for alle Cristene men shulden be of oo wille, and variaunce in siche sectis makiþ variaunce in wille, and gendriþ discencioun and envye among men. And herfore ordeynede Crist but þree partis of þe Churche, ech to have nede and helpyng of oþir; but certis it is not þus of þese new religions. Of þis treuþe may be maad such a good resoun. It is a greet synne of two þingis to chese þe worse, whan a man may as freely have þe betere as þe worse; but þese new ordris ben worse þan þe sect of Crist, and it is more liȝt, more fre, and more perfit, þan ony oþir sect þat man may chese. And herfore it is a synful errour to chese siche sectis, siþ þe ordre of Crist wole betere occupie at þe fulle þan ony siche sect founden of men. And so siþ þese patrons han no leeve of God to make siche erberis in his comoun pasture, law of þis cheef lord shulde districe þes sectis, siþ Crist loveþ more his comounes þan þes newe erberis. And þus meneþ þe gospel þat þe þridde servaunt of God shal constreyne men to entre and soupe wiþ him in hevene, boþe men in comoun weyes and þes þat dwellen in heggis, and þus was Poul constreyned to crepe out of his hegge, and holde þe sect of Crist, forsakinge þe sect of Pharisees; and þus þis publican þat was a comoun laborer was beter þan þis Pharisee, as þis gospel seiþ.

Þe twelfþe Soneday Gospel aftir Trinite Sonday.

[SERMON XII.]

Exiens Jesus de finibus Tiry.—Mark vii. [31.]

Þis gospel telliþ a myracle of Crist to make men to love him and trowe in his power; how a deef man and a doumbe was helid of Crist. *Jesus wente oute of þe contree of Tirus* and he *cam by Sidoun to þe water of Galile, and he cam þourȝ a countree þat men clepen Decapolios*, which contre conteyneþ ten citees wiþynne him, *and men of þe contre brouȝten to him a deef man, and doumbe also, and preieden Crist to putte to him his hond*, for þei conseyveden þat bi þis shulde Crist fully hele hym. *And Crist toke þis syke man aside fro þis puple, and putte his fingres into boþe his eeres, and spittinge, wiþ his fyngir Crist touchide his tonge, and Crist lokynge into hevene wiþ a deulful chere seide to þis syke man, Be þi wittis opened; and anoon weren his eeres opened for to here, and þe bond of his tonge was opened for to speke ariȝt. And Crist bade þes men to publishe not þis myracle; but ever þe more þat he bad þus, ever þe more þei prechiden, and ever þe more þei woundriden, and seiden amonge hemsilf þat Crist hadde done*

The healing of the deaf and dumb man.

Four senses in which Holy Writ is to be understood.

alle þingis wele, for he made deefe to heere and doumbe men to speke. It is seid comounly þat holy writt haþ foure undirstondingis. Þe first undirstondinge is pleyne, bi letter of þe storye. Þe secounde undirstondinge is clepid witt allegoric, whan men undirstonden bi witt of þe lettre, what þing shal falle here bifore þe dai of dome. Þe þridde undirstondinge is clepid tropologik, and it techiþ how men shulden lyve here in vertues. Þe fourþe undirstondinge is clepid anagogike, and it telliþ how it shal be wiþ men þat ben in hevene. We shulde knowe þis secounde witt of þe gospel, for it is bileve of Cristene men in erþe; we shulden bileve þat mankynde felle fro þe staat of innocence for Adams synne and Eve, and Jesus, God and man, bouȝte mankynde fro þe fendis prisoun, as þis gospel telliþ. And so oure Jesus wente fro þe lond of Tirus, whan he wente fro þe bosim of þe fadir of hevene, for Tirus is makyng[a], and God made of noȝt boþe aungels and men and al þis brood worlde. He cam bi Sidon, þat is angel kynd, whan he grette oure Lady bi servise of angel, and þis angel Gabriel wiþ all oþirs stondinge heelden pees wiþ God, and leften þe firste synne, and Sidon is helþe or leevynge siche synne. But oure Lord Jesus wente out to þe water of Galile, for he took þe staat of man slydun from innocence; for Galile is a wheel[b] whirlinge or passinge; and so dide mankynde aftir þat it hadde synned. Crist came þurȝ þe cuntre þat hadde ten citees, for he cam bi alle men þat weren segid wiþ þe fend; and þes men ensegid þus ben al þes citees, and mankynde þus ensegid bryngiþ to Jesus hir kynde, þat was deef and dombe by þe synne of Adam, ffor þei leften to heeren God and herden þe fend, and trowiden to þe fendis lore, and lefte þe lore of God, and so weren þei deef to heere of God what þei shulden do. Jesus took mankynde þat þus was syke, not in ech persone but singulerly in oon, and Crist putt his fyngirs in eres of þis dombe man, whan he appliede his virtue, sutili worchinge, for to teche man how he wente fro God, and wiþ his spotle he touchide his tonge, whan he ȝaf him virtue to herye God riȝtli. And so Crist hadde sorewe of þes two synnes of

[a] Tzôr, the Hebrew name of Tyre, signifies a rock.

[b] Galil, whence Galilee is derived, means in Hebrew, circle, or circuit. (Smith's Dict. Bib.)

man, and bad þat þe bond of his witt shulde be opened. But Jesus bad þat þei shulden not preise him herfore bi his manhede, and for þis mekenesse þei preisiden him more bi his godhede, and seiden soþ þat he made alle þingis wele, for he made deef men to heeren and dombe men to speken. For men deefid in Goddis lore he made to heere what God spake in hem, boþ in mandementis and conseilis; and herbi þei lerneden to speke; and so þre miraclis did Crist togidere, in savynge of mankynde; he made men deef bi synne to heere what God spak in hem, and men dombe fro riȝt speche to speke opynly Goddis lawe, and so, biside þes virtues to heere and to speke, God moved mankynde to do as þei shulden; and so mai men see how myche þei ben to blame þat ben dombe and deef in þis manere of worching.

Þe þrittenþe Sonday Gospel aftir Trinite.

[SERMON XIII.]

Beati oculi qui vident quae vos videtis.—Luc. x. [23.]

The parable of the Good Samaritan.

Þis gospel telliþ bi a parable how eche man shulde love his even cristene; and, for siȝt pryntid in us of manheed of Crist techiþ þis lore graciously, þerfore bigynneþ Crist and seiþ on þis manere. *Blessid ben þe eyen*[1] *þat seen þat ȝe seen; for Y seie to ȝou, þat many kyngis and prophetis wolden se þat ȝe seen and siȝen hem not, and here wordis þat ȝe heeren, and herden hem not. And lo a wyse man of lawe roos and temptide Crist, and axide, Maistre, what shal Y do to have þe blisse of hevene?* For he wiste wele bi skile þat it was not ynouȝ to see þe manheed of Crist for to come to heven; for many þingis, as Scarioþ and bestis, siȝen Crist, þat weren not able to have blisse. *But Crist seide to þis legistre, What is writun in þe lawe? how redist þou? And he answeride and seide, þat þe lawe biddiþ þat a man shulde love þe Lord his God of al his herte and of al his soule, and of al his strengþis, and of al his mynd, and his neiȝbore as him silf.*

[1] *iȝen*, B; *eyne*, C.

And Crist seide to him þat he answeride riȝt; do he þis indede, and he shal lyve in blisse. But þis lawier wolde justifie himsilf, and þerfore he axide, who was his neiȝbore. And Crist tolde him a parable, þat was sutil in witt, for *Crist lokynge on him seide him þis parable*, how *a man wente doun fro Jerusalem into Jerico and felde in þefes handis, þat dispuyliden him and fastiden many sores on him and wenten and leften him halfe quyke. And it fell þat a preest passide þe same wey; and he siȝ him lye þus hirt, and wente awey and helpide him not. And a deken, whan he was niȝ þe place, and siȝ him sich, passide awey. But a Samaritan making his weie bi þat place cam bi side him, and siȝ his state, and hadde mercy on him; and he cam nyȝe, and bond his woundis, and helde in hem boþe oile and wyn, and put him upon his hors, and brouȝt him in to stable of a toun, and þere he did cure of him. And anoþir dai he toke two pens, and ȝaf hem to þe hosteler, and bade him have cure of him, and seide þus, What ever þou ȝyvest over, whan Y come aȝen Y shal pay þee.* And whan Crist hadde seide þis parable, he axide of þis man of lawe, *which of þese þree men semede him to be neiȝbore unto þis syke man þat þus fell into þeves handis. And he seide, þat þe þridde man, þat dide mercy on him. And Jesus seide to þis legistre, Go þou and do riȝt so.* Þis man of lawe þat is here nemed was neþir civilian ne canonistre, but he was man of Goddis lawe þat wolde lerne þe wey to hevene. And Crist supposiþ to þis wise man þat ech man is to oþir a neiȝbore as nyȝ as he may, siþ þei ben boþe of o kynde; but of neiȝborishep of place or dwellinge or of worldes ffrendship shulden men not recke here; but we shulden wite þat alle men þat God ordeyneþ to blis ben ful breþeren boþe of fadir and of modir, siþ God is þer fadir, and his Chirche is þer moder. And so techiþ Crist in þis parable, how ech shulde be to oþir neiȝbore in good wille, boþe for we came alle of Adam and Eve, and specialy for we came goostly of Crist and his Chirche and þei ben oure nexte and most fadir and modir. Þis man þat cam doun fro Jerusalem to Jericho is oure firste eldris, Adam and Eve, for þei camen fro siȝt of pees to state of slydyng, as þe moone. Þes þeves þat woundiden him ben þe fendis þat temptiden him, but þei lefte lyf in him, as God ordeynede him to blisse; but þei drowun fro þis man goodis of virtu and of

Interpretation of the parable.

kynde, and woundiden him boþe in bodi and soule, and lettiden him to live just lyf. Þis preest þat passide first bi mankynde and siȝ myscheffe þat it was inne, weren patriarkes, boþe bifore þe lawe, and in tyme þat God ȝaf law. Þe dekene þat passide bi þis weye weren prophetis and oþir seintis þat weren bineþe þes first seintis, as dekenes ben under preestis; and boþe þei knewen þat þei myȝten not helpe neiþer oþer men ne hemsilf fro þe synne þat þei fellen ynne bi tempting of þe fend. But þe þridde Samaritan, þat was Jesus, helpide mankynde, for he was an alien as anentis his godhede, and he was keper of man bi boþe two kyndis þat he hadde, and he myȝte not do synne, siþ he was boþe God and man, and hadde not personale beynge of mankynde as oþer men hadden, siþ he hadde a ful beynge bifore tyme þat he was man. He helde in oile to make woundis softe, and to dispose man to be hool; for he putte man in hope to come to hevene bi feiþ of Crist; and he putte in wyn þerwiþ, whan he spake sharpe wordis for to prik men fro synne. He put mankynde upon his hors, whan he made his own manhede to be oure broþer and to bere our syne; alȝif he ouȝte not for his synne; he brouȝte mankynde in to a stable, whan he helide men in þis Chirche; and þis is but a litil stable to regard of al þe Chirche; and he curide men in þis stable bi sacramentis and hevenly ȝiftes. And on oþir daie, after tyme þat he was deed, whiche was þe tyme of grace, and þe sunne was newe sprongen, he ȝaf two pens to þis keper, boþe of his godhede and of his manhede, to fede mankynde til þe daie of dome. And so þe keper of þis stable is alle þes men þat God haþ chosen to fede his Chirche wiþ his lawe, and Cristis godhede wiþ his manhede ben sufficient herfore, for þei ben wiþouten ende, as þes serkelis of two pens; and what ever þat prelatis traveilen unto spede of Cristis Chirche, Crist wole at þe daie of dome ȝelde hem graciously; and so ech trewe prelat þat helpiþ Crist to hele his Chirche, is trewe neiȝbore to þe Chirche and doiþ in part as Crist did.

Þe fourteneþe Sondai Gospel aftir Trinite.

[SERMON XIV.]

Cum iret Jesus in Jerusalem, transibat.—Luc. xvii. [11.]

The healing of the lepers.

Christ wole teche bi þis miracle in þis parable þat riȝt bileve is ground of mennes salvacioun. *Whan Jesus went to Jerusalem he went þurȝ Samarie and Galile, and whan he wente into a castel, ten meselis comen aȝens him, and þei stooden aferre and crieden on him as þei myȝten, and seiden, Jesus, comandour, have mercy on us. But whan Crist siȝ þes leprous men cryinge þus, and stondinge togidere afer*, lest þei blemyschiden oþer men, *he bad hem go and shewe hem to preestis*, as God bad in þe olde lawe, *and as þei wenten, þei weren heelid of her lepre. And oon of hem, whan he siȝ þat he was þus heelid bi miracle, turnede aȝen to Jesus wiþ a greet vois preisynge God, and he feld doun in his face bifore Cristis feet, and þankide him; and þis man þat þus cam aȝen was a Samaritan. And Jesus spake and seide þus* of þis dede þat was fallen, *Ne ben not ten maad clene, and where ben oþer nyne? Þere is noon founden þat cam aȝen, and þankiþ God, but þis alien. And Crist seide unto him, Rys and go whider þou wilt*, for *þi bileve haþ made þee saaf.*

Mystical interpretation of this miracle.

To þe witt of allegoric[1], bitokeneþ þis dede of Crist how he was wendinge to hevene, þat is clepide Jerusalem, and he passide by Samary and Galile, or he went to teche, þat he wolde save boþe heþene men and Jewis. For it is knowen of Samarie þat þei weren not of Jewis kynde but aliens þat dwelliden þere, fro þe time of conquest of þat lond. And ten kynredis of Israelis sones weren ever putt out, as now ben Jewis, and herfore þe Jewis loveden not þes Samaritanes, and to þe repreef of Crist þei clepide him a Samaritan, þat he grantide in a manere, and denyede þat he was ledd by þe fend. Cristis wendinge in to þe castel bitokeneþ his litil Chirche, þat is armed wiþ virtues as þe castel is kepte fro enemyes; ten leprous men ben alle þe synful þat mekeli axen forȝevenes of þer synnes. Þei stooden first fer fro Goddis folk; and siþ þei

[1] *allegorik*, B; *allegorie*, C.

wenten to Cristis preestis, and bifore þei comen to hem God assoilide hem of þer synnes; for God seiþ in þe psalme how man in purpos to leve his synne seide þat he wolde shryve him to God, and God forȝaf him his synne. And so Crist tauȝte bi þis dede þat assoilinge of men is not but ȝif God assoile bifore, as God himsilf assoilide þes leprous. And so preestis assoilen as Goddis vikeris, according to Goddis assoilinges, and ellis þei assoilen no more þan preestis of þe olde lawe heelide men of þer lepre, and þat myȝt þei not do. Þis alien þat cam aȝen to þanke God of his helþe, bitokeneþ trewe Cristene men þat dwellen in þis bileve; þes nyne þat ben many moo bitokeneþ men out of bileve, þat trowen þat it is ynouȝ þat her preest assoile hem, and specialy þe hey preest, how evere he erre in jugement, and how þei lyven bifore or after, þes men þat þus ben assoilid. And aȝens þis eresie shulde trewe preestis crye fast, for bi þis synne is synne hid, and assoilyng bouȝt and sold, as who so wolde bye an oxe or a cow, and myche more falsely. We shulden come aȝen to Crist, and confesse boþe his kyndis, and make covenaunt wiþ him to leve oure syn̄e from hennsforþ, and þenke how Crist bad þe woman go and wille no more do synne. For þis covenaunt, kept wiþ sorwe of synne and Goddis grace is ynow, alle ȝif men speken no more wiþ preestis; but speche wiþ hem is nedeful in þat þat þei techen men þis treuþe, and mennys ordenaunce may not reverse þis sentence; and þus we graunten þat ech þing þat Petre bonde or assoilid on erþe, or ony viker of Petre, in þat þat þei acorden wiþ God, is bounden or loosid in hevene, and ellis not, for ellis þei ben fals. And so ordenaunce of men in byndinge and assoilynge bryngiþ in many errours and lettiþ trewe prechinge. But Bede seiþ þat þes leprouse men bitokenen heritikes of many colours þat shulden stonde aferr fro men, and turne to Crist bi riȝt feiþ, and knowe þat Crist bi his word myȝte have mercy on hem; and aftirward algatis þei shulden be aliens fro Pharisees[a]. And so alle synful men shulden crye mekely wiþ þes leprous, þat Crist þat is boþe God and man shulde have mercy on þer synne, for he is lord wiþouten eende, and þei han yvel wraþþid him, and so her synne

Priestly absolution not efficacious unless the sin has been already absolved by God.

Sale of church pardons.

Beda's interpretation.

[a] The meaning seems to be, 'And even then, after having been healed, these lepers would still be counted aliens by the Pharisees.'

is so greet þat but if Crist of his power and of his grace forȝyve þis synne, it may never be forȝyven. And for þis þing seiþ þe Chirche in þer preyeris þat oure God makiþ moost his myȝt knowen in sparynge and havynge mercy; for ȝif Crist dide not so, no synful man myȝte be saved. But we shulde undirstonde þat as God is mercyful so he is riȝtful, and hatiþ men þat breken covenaunt; and þerfore holde we covenaunt to God, and disseyve we not oure silf, for God may not be disseyved, however preestis bigile us.

Þe fiftenþe Sondai Gospel aftir Trinyte.

[SERMON XV.]

Nemo potest duobus dominis servire.—Matt. vi. [24.]

No man can serve two masters.

Þis gospel techiþ men hou þei shulden be bisye for blisse and leve oþer worldely bisynesse þat lettiþ men fro þis. First seiþ Crist þis principle þat ech man shulde trowe, *þat no man may wel serve two fulle lordes, for oþir shal he hate þe toon and love þe toþir, or susteynen cause of þe toon and dispise þe toþir;* þus algatis he serveþ amys.—If he serve hem togidere, þe cause is more pleyn; and if he serve first þe toon and siþ þe toþir, oþer he serveþ amys þe toon or þe toþir. In alle þes resouns we shul suppose þat þe gospel spekiþ of siche lordis þat nouþir is wel servaunt to ouþir, as ben God and þe fend; for if þer ben two lordis and þat oon serve wel þat oþir, a man may serve wel to hem boþe, as we seen al daie; but þe gospel undirstondiþ of siche cheefe lordis þat han not above hem anoþir cheef lord. And so is þis world dyvydid in two maner of lordshipis þat ben Goddis and þe fendis, for alȝif þe fend have no propre lordship[a], neþeles he calengiþ to have greet lordshipe, and so

[a] Proper fiefs were those only which were held on condition of military service, in which case there was a mutual benefit. Improper fiefs were those held upon condition of various other kinds of service. The devil's lordship over man is not 'proper,' because he has no right to demand of man that he should fight his battles for him; nor is his forced service to God 'proper,' because it is attended by no benefit to himself. See Hallam's *Middle Ages*, I. 181.

maugre his he serveþ to God, and þis servise is unpropre, as is þe fendis lordship, siþ he serveþ not God to his owne mede but aȝens his wille he profitiþ to Cristis Chirche, and þus for generalite of lordship of Crist, he seiþ, who is not wiþ him is aȝens him, and þus seiþ Crist wel, *þat we may not serve God and richesse of þe worlde, for þei ben contraries;* for as we may not serve þe fend wiþ servise of God, so we may not serve þe world þat is þe fendis servant. But in al þis speche we shal speke of riȝt servise and of unpropre servise þat þe fend mystakiþ, and þan we may see how siche heed servise may not acorde to God and to þe world. For ȝif a man traveile for goodis of þis world, and haþ riȝt entent for to worshipe God, he serveþ not þe world, but it serveþ him. But it is ful hard to have siche riȝt entent, for sich entent mut be mesure of bisynesse, and noumbre of traveile, and weiȝt[1] of mannys wille, and herfor forbediþ Crist bisynesse of foode and hilyynge, for aboute þes two þingis shulden men sonnest be bysye, and Crist spekiþ of bisynesse most principal in man. And so trewe men witen welc þat ech man shulde cast al his bisynesse in God, as seint Petre biddiþ, and þus seiþ Crist, *þat we shulde not be bisye to oure lyf what we shulden ete, ne to oure bodi what we shulde be cloþid wiþ; for siþ lyf is more þan mete and mannis bodi more þan cloiþ, as God ȝyveþ man þes two, so wille he ordeyne for hem. Biholde ȝe þe foulis of þe eire, how þei sowen, neiþir repen, ne gederen not in to bernes, and ȝit God fediþ hem, and siþ ȝe ben more worþ þan þei,* God wole take more heed to you. For as ȝe bisien ȝou not of þe bodi, so shulden ȝe not bisien ȝou of hilyynge þerof. For what wolde it profite to man *to bisye him þus about his bodi, siþ he may not cast þerto a cubite,* over þat kynde ȝyveþ him. And þus siþ God bi kynde of man ordeyneþ for mannis bodi, he will ordeyne for þe lesse, how mannis bodi shulde be hilid. And ȝif þou seie þat many men bi þis shulde sterve for defaute of mete, wel Y wote bi my bileve þat no man shulde faile of mete unto harmynge of his soule, but ȝif his synne be cause þerof, and so þat it be good and just þat he faile þus of mete; and þus Y rede þat God bad foulis and pore folk fede his prophete, and fedde 1 Kings xvii.

[1] So in B; *wiȝte* in A, *weyȝt* in C.

him as best was to profite of his soule. *And of cloþis what ben ȝe bisye? loke ye to þe lylyes of þe felde, how þei growe and ben cled and þei traveilen not þereaboute, ne spynnen* for þer cloiþ, *and ȝit Salomon in al his glorie was not cled as oon of þes is*, for shap and coloure of lely flours is not made bi mannis crafte; and so, *ȝif þe hay of þe feld þat now is, and to-morewe is brent, is þus cled bi Goddis wit, myche more wolde he cloþe men*, þat he telliþ more by. And so litilnes of bileeve makiþ men þus to be bisy, for þei witen not what manere of þing is profitable for mannis soule, and so, *Be we not bisye what we shal ete or drynke or wiþ what þingis oure bodi shal be atired, ffor al sich þingis seken heþen men faste, and so seke we first þe kingdom of God and riȝtwysnesse of him, and all siche þingis shal be cast to us.* Aȝens þis lore synnen men of þe world, ȝhe preestis and clerkes and men of religioun, for þei bisien hem for atire and for foode also, þat profitith not to þer soule, þat God forfendiþ here; and, for breking of þis heste brekiþ þe ten comandmentis, and al men of þis world ben ful nyȝ to breke it, þerfore Crist and hise apostlis, and Baptist, and oþer prophetis kepten hem ferr fro þis peril, lest þei slydun þerinne. And Crist wiþ his disciplis wolde not be weddid wiþ habitis ne manere of penaunt[1] metis, lest þei weren to bisie for nouȝt, and hou evere we denyen þat we ben to bisye here, neþeles Goddis lawe, þat is Crist, shal rykene wiþ us and juge us at þe daie of dome, wher þis be soþ þat we seyen, and þan worship of þis worlde and curtais manere þat men axen shal not excuse us, but resoun shal be our juge.

Þe sixteenþ Sondai Gospel after Trinite.

[SERMON XVI.]

Ibat Jesus in civitatem quae vocatur Naym.—Lucae vii. [11.]

The raising of the widow's son at Naim.

Þis gospel telliþ of a myracle þat Crist dide of a deed bodi þat was þe secounde of þre þat Crist reiside fro deþ to lyf. And so telliþ þe gospel þat *Jesus wente in to a cite þat is clepid Naym*

[1] So in B; *penaut*, A; *poynant*, C; *penaunce*, E.

wiþ his disciplis and oþer puple. And whanne he cam nyȝ þe ȝate of þe citee, cam a cors þat was born to be biried, þat was a childe of a widowe, and myche puple of þe citee cam wiþ þis widowe and made sorewe. And whan Crist sawe þis widowe, he hadde mercy upon hir, and bad hir wepe not; but he went and touchide þe beere þat þei baren and þes men þat baren þe beere stooden stille to see the ende. And *Crist seide to þe dede bodi, ȝounge man, Y bidde þe aryse; And þe ȝounge man þat was deed sate up and bigan to speke, and Crist ȝaf him to his modir. Al þe puple hadde drede, and preisiden God, and saiden, þat a greet prophete roos amonge hem, and þat God hadde visitid his puple*, for this miracle þat þei seien. Þe gospel telliþ of þre dede bodies þat Crist reiside fro deþ to lyf. Þe firste was þe persones douȝter þat he reiside wiþin þe hous; þe secounde was þis widowes sone þat he quykede in þe ȝate; þe þridde was þe stynkyng careyne þat he quykide in þe grave. And þis bitokeneþ þree synnes þat God forȝeveþ in þis worlde. Þe firste bitokeneþ ful consense for to do aȝens God, but it comeþ not out in deede, as þe maide lay in þe hous. Þe secounde bitokeneþ þe secounde synne, whan a man to wickide wille putteþ to a wickide dede, but he comeþ not to custom as dide Lazarus þat was biried in a grave, and þis is þe ȝong man þat we speken of stonding in þe ȝate. Þe þridde synne addiþ to þes two a long custom to ligge in synne, and þis is Lazar þat foure daies lay stinkinge in his grave. Þe secounde is a widowes sone, for siche synners wanten God, and so þei, failinge of spouse, of þe Chirche may wel be clepid a widowe, but þei han sorwe of her synne, and oþir neiȝboris also. Crist biddiþ þe beere stoonde whan he ceessiþ men of her synne; and he touchiþ þe bodi, whane he ȝyveþ hem contricion, and he comandiþ it to arise, whanne he comandiþ medeful werkes, and þis man bigynneþ to speke, whanne he þankid God in grace, and Crist ȝyveþ him to his modir, whanne he makiþ him helpe his Chirche. And þus wente Crist into Naym, whanne he entride newe to his Chirche; for Naym is as myche to say as flowynge or movynge, for þe Chirche first flowide wiþ synne, and siþ was moved to God by bemes of þe Holy Goost, whan it hadde grace to come to him. Wiþ Crist wente his disciplis and a greet route of folk, for

Mystical interpretation of the miracle.

many weren helpers of God to bringe his Chirche to riȝt staat. Þe ȝate of þis citee is entree to religioun of Cristis Chirche, in which ȝate ben many ȝonge men, blynde and deed goostli, for þei knowen not Cristis religioun how it passiþ alle oþir. And so in þis ȝate ben two maneres of dede men. To summe lokiþ Crist, and quykeþ hem in grace, and ȝyveþ hem power and wille to come clene to his order. And wite þat al oþer ordris ben chargious to men as myche as þei adden to Cristis religioun, ffor noon addicioun is worþ but ȝif Goddis lawe grounde it. Sum men ben deed in þis ȝate þat Crist aquykeþ not, but lasten in her olde errours to her deþ dai; and ben þes þat taken a lyf ungroundid in Goddis lawe, and þes men lasten in her errour out of þe bondis of Goddis lawe, and ben born fro þe ȝate to be beried in helle. But þere is a privy quykenynge þat God doiþ neiȝ þe deeþ, þat we can not telle of, but if God wil shewe it us, and þerefore folis jugement shulde be fled in þis mater; and þus þes men þat baren þis beere to putt þis deed man in erþe, ben men þat consenten and procuren to wickidnesse. And so upon þes þree synnes God haþ mercy here, but upon þe ferþe synne God ceessiþ never to punnishe, for þei synnen to þe deeþ, and so aȝens the Hooly Goost, þat God mut needis punishe wiþouten ende, for þis synne may have noon eende in helle. In þis mater we shulden bewar of peril of ypocrisie, for many feynen hem in statis, and done reverse in her lyf, and ȝit þei seien þei ben perfiter þan weren þe first clerkis of Crist. And þus enemyes of Cristis religioun chalengen to be of his ordre, alȝif þey done even þe contrarie to name þat þei beren; as þe Pope shulde be moost meke man, moost servysable and most pore, as we ben tauȝt in Seint Petir þat was Pope next after Crist. And now men seyen þat þe Pope mote nedis reverse þis ordenaunce, and have more power for to do þingis þat touchen excellence, and þus bishopis þat shulden be clerkis and pore men, as apostlis weren, ben moost lordis of þis world, and reversen apostlis lyf. Sum tyme weren mounkes lewede men, as seintis in Jerusalem; and þanne þei kept hem silf fro synne as seynt Bernard beriþ witnesse; but now monkes ben turned unto lordis of þis worlde moost ydel in goddis travaile, and seyen þat þei ben betre monkes þan weren þe first

Attack on the hierarchy.

seintis. And so freris, þat weren breþeren in Crist, and not chargeous to þe Chirche, neiþir in noumbre ne in cloþing, ne in mete ne in housynge, ben even turned aȝen fro þe first lyf of hem, and ȝit bi þer ypocrisie þei blynden þe Chirche many ȝatis, and þus names of offices and names of virtues also ben changid bi ypocrisie, and cursed men reulen þe world.

Þe seventenþe Sondai aftir Trinite.

[SERMON XVII.]

Cum intrasset Jesus domum cujusdam.—Luc. xiv. [1.]

Þis gospel techiþ men how þei shal not by þer hiȝ staat hide þere synne, and disturble þe ordenaunce þat Crist haþ made. Þe story telliþ *hou Jesus entride in to a Pharisees hous on a Satirday to ete wiþ him, and þei aspieden to take him in defaute; and a syke man in dropesie was þer bifore Crist. And Jesus spake to wyse men of þe lawe, and to Pharisees, where it were leveful to hele in þe Sabot; and þei weren stille*, lest þat resoun wente aȝens hem; *but Crist toke þis syke man, and heelide him þanne bifore hem, and Crist axide hem þis demaunde, þat ȝif þer oxe or þer asse felle in þe diche, wolde þei not drawe him out in þer sabot daie;* and þei wisten wel þat þei shulden by bileve of þere owen lawe, *and þei myȝte not answere him to denye* þat he axide. And upon þis arguyde Crist þat myche more it were leveful to helpe in þe Sabot a man put in more peril, siþ þis work is more spirituel, and man is beter þan a beest. And, for þe synne of þese men stood in pryde of her statis, *Crist tolde hem a parable, techinge hem how þei shulden chese þe first statis;* þat God lovede moost, þat was moost meke statis, but þei chosen as proude men þe first statis to þe world. But Crist biddiþ in his parable, *Whan þou ert biden to þe feste, sitte not in þe first place, lest a more worshipful þan þou be beden to þe same feest, and þe lord of þe feste bidde þee, ȝive þis man stede, and put þee doun out of þi place, and þan shalt þou bygynne wiþ shame for to holde þe last place. And herfore whan þou art beden to a feste, sitte doun in þe last place,*

The healing of the man that had the dropsy.

so þat he þat haþ beden þee seie to þee for þi mekenesse, Frend stye more up; þanne shalt þou have worship and joie bifore hem þat sitten at þe feste. For ech man þat heieþ him by presumpcioun *shal be mekid* bi God, *and he þat mekiþ him* in his soule *shal be heyed* bi God. Þere we shal undirstonde þat Crist spekiþ not here of worldely feste, ne of place, for þanne his sentence were nouȝt; for þan strif shulde be for place, and oonli oon shulde do Cristis bidding, and so Crist shulde ordeyne discencioun wiþouten fruyt among men; and herfore shulde we undirstonde þat þis feste is þe laste soper, þat shal be in heven of seintis aftir þe day of dome; and þe last place at þis feeste shulde be mannis reputacioun, bi whiche he shulde not presume to be in heven bifore oþirs, but reste mekeli in þis þat he shal come to hevene. Eche man shal hope for to come to blisse; and if he lyve febly and make þis hope fals, himsilf is cause whi his hope is suche. Ffor þis fals hope, þat sum men do clepen dispeir, shulde have anoþir qualite, and it shulde not be sich, whan we witen þat we shulden hope for to come to hevene, after we maken comparisoun bytwene us and oþers; and many men for pryde hopen to passe oþers, and suche presumpcioun of hope is sittynge here in hey place. We shulden reste in þis hope þat we shal come to hevene, and leve sich veyne comparisouns, lest we setten us here to hey, and þis is þe last place þat þe gospel spekiþ of. And þus siche false presumpcioun of heynes of state, and aftir þis presumpcioun, of heyenesse in hevene, makiþ a man to come at þe laste to þe loweste place in þe world, þat is to seie, to depe helle, þat is þe myddil of þe world. And so spekiþ þe gospel on two weies of þe last place. The laste place here stondiþ in meke reputacioun, but þe last place at þe day of dome stondiþ in dampnacioun. And so knyttiþ Crist wel þe helynge of þis ydropesie, for as ydropesie is an yvel of fals gretenesse of mennys lymes, and comeþ of unkyndli watir bitwene þe fleish and þe skyn; so pride of worldly goodis, þat ben unstable as þe watir, makiþ a man in ydropesie, and falsely presume of himsilf; as many men in greet astaate and in ryches of þis worlde þenken þat þei shulden þus in heven be bifore oþir men. For, as þei supposen now, þei lyven to God aftir þer staat, and so þei profiten more in þis world þan done men under hem, and after þat þei profiten more, þei shal be heiȝer in hevene, and so þei seien, as þei shulden hope to come to hevene, so shulde þei hopen here to be heier in hevene. But siche proude men, and presumptuous of her staat, shulden traveil in virtues þat þei begilen not hem silf; and þerfore techiþ þe wise man, þat ever þe more þat þou be here, ever þe more meke þou shuldist be, in al manere of mekenes. And so, if þou be greet here, þou shuldist reste in þe last place, and suppose mekeli of þi silf wiþouten siche comparisoun. Ffor who is he þat may seie he serveþ God after his staat? and so statis here and statis in hevene, late or nevere acorden togidere, for fewe men here or noon serven God even to þer state; and so statis of men may cause þer dampnyng deep in helle, and for uneven service here in statis, may men ben ful lowe in hevene.

Þe lessoun of þis gospel is litil coud in þe Chirche, for lordis stryven wiþ hem silfe, and religiouse among hem silf, about heyenes of þer staat, and þe rote of al þis is pryde. And þei shulden wite þat states here ben harmful unto men, but ȝif men after her statis serven treuly to þer God; ffor falsnesse in statis makiþ men to be low or dampned.

The lesson of this gospel is against pride, both in the laity and the clergy.

ÞE EIȜTENÞE SONDAI AFTIR TRINITE.

[SERMON XVIII.]

Accesserunt ad Jesum Pharisei audientes.—MATT. xxii. [34.]

Þis gospel telliþ how Crist distroiede sectis, techinge us how we shulden traveile suying Crist in þis. Þe storye of þe gospel seiþ þat *whan þe Phariseis hadden herd þat Crist hadde stemned*[1] *Saduceis, on of þe Phariseis, þat was a doctour of lawe, temptide Crist on þis wise, and axide him þis question, Maister, which is a greet mandement in þe lawe? And Jesus seide to him þus, Þou*

[1] The reading of B is *stonyed*, i.e. astonished; C, *stoned*, a 'y' being inserted by a later hand; *stemnyde*, E. Both Wycliffite versions have 'put to silence.'

shalt love þi Lord God of al þi herte, in al þi soule, and in al þi mynde; þis is þe firste and þe moste mandement of alle. And þis mandement is þe first of þre of þe first table, ffor þre of þe first table techen to love God, and conteyneþ þre partis answeringe to þe Trinite. It is seid comounly þat in tyme of Crist weren þre sectis of religions, Pharises, Saduceis, and Esses, but of þe two first makiþ þis gospel mencioun. Þe firste was moost myȝty, and þerfor it lastide lengest; for aboundance of goodis, and long rotyng in þe sect, defenden þes sectis, and maken hard to distroie hem. But Crist distriede þes sectis and savede þe persones; as Poul and Nichodeme weren makid bi grace Cristen men. And herfore seiþ þis gospel, þat Crist stemned[1] Saduceis, not þat he distriede hem, siþ he lovede þer persones; and so Crist distriede þe errours of Phariseis, as he distriede þe errours of þe oþer two. Sum men þenken licly þat þis doctour þat here temptide Crist, dredde him of his sect þat Crist shulde distroien it, or ellis enfeblen it, as he distriede þe myddil sect, and þis is more licly þan þat þis doctour dide for veyn glorie or to be holden[2] wise or to lerne Goddis lawe. He clepide Crist reverently maister, ffor it is manere of ypocritis and of sophists to fage and to speke plesantli to men, but for yvel entent. But oure Pharisees to dai done wel wers, ffor þei putten abac goddis lawe and magnifien þer ordres; and þus þei failen in þe first mandement, and so in al oþer. And many men trowen not ne supposen þat þei ben men of holi Chirche, but supposen þat þei ben lymes of þe fend. But he loveþ God of al his herte þat loveþ him of al his witt; and he loveþ God in al his lyf þat loveþ him in al his werkes; for Cristen men lyven in God, and ben moved to al her werkes; for Crist is forme of god, and in Crist we lyven, as Poul seiþ. And herfore we shal not take þe word of oure God in veyn. Þe þridde part of þis mandement, answerynge to þe Holy Goost, biddiþ þee love þi God in al þi mynde, siþ he is mynde of þe Fadir, and of þe Sone, and love of hem two; for undirstonding in a man, and acte of him, þat is his lyf, and refleccioun of lyf, þat is mynd

The modern Pharisees are supposed by many to be limbs of the fiend.

[1] B here reads *stemnede*, in agreement with A; C has *stoned or stilled.*
[2] This is the reading of B; A has *bibolden; be boldun*, E.

and wille of soule, bitokeneþ to Cristene men her God, þat is þe Trinite. And herfore biddiþ Goddis lawe, have mynde to holde þin halidai. And þan we loven þis Trinite perfitli as we shulden, whan we loven it more þan ony oþir þing; and as many men þenken, ȝif þis Pharisee kepte þis, he shulde leve þis straunge sect, as shulden þes newe religions.—*Þe secounde mandement*, þat is sevene, *biddiþ þe love þi neiȝbore as þou lovest þisilfe*, and þat art þou tauȝt by kynde, *and in þese two mandements hongiþ al þe lawe and þe prophetis. And whan þe Farisees were gedrid, Crist axide* hem a questioun of þing þat þei shulden bileve, *What hem þouȝt of þe kynde of Crist*, and, *whos sone Crist is; and þei seiden, He is David sone; and Crist replied aȝens þis, how David clepide him his lord*, siþ Crist is David sone, and porer man þan David was. Þe psalm telliþ how David seide of þe Fadir and þe Sone, *Þe Lord*, þe Fadir, *seide to my Lord, Sitte up on my riȝt side as long as Y putt þi enemyes* in helle *a stool undir þi feet*. And siþ þis dampnyng shal be ever, God grantide here to Crist þat he shulde ever sitt in hevene on his Fadir riȝt hond; *Ffor ȝif David clepiþ him Lord, how is* pore Crist *David sone? And þei myȝte not here answere Crist, ne dursten not axe him more fro þat dai.*—And here convyctide Crist þes men of open untreuþe in hir bileve; and so mente privily þat þes sectis shulden be distried, siþ he shal reprove þe worlde of þe synne of untreuþe. And it semeþ to many men þat alle þes sectis synnen þus, for þei loven not hir God as þe gospel biddeþ here; for ȝif þei loveden wel God, þei shulden kepe þis word of him. Generaly þes newe sectis loven more þer owen ordre þan þei done þe ordre of Crist, which he ȝaf his owne persone; and þan þei loven her sect more þan þei loven þe sect of Crist. Þis sect of Crist by þat is lasse þat þei putten in þes newe sectis; siþ þei, kepinge Cristis secte, bi þat maken his sect more; and it is oon to love a þing and to willen þat þing good; but þei wolden þat al þis world were suget unto þer sect. And, Lord! if þat men wolden undirstonden, what it is to love a þing; and whanne men loven, loven þer god over al oþir þingis; þanne heresie of þes newe sectis, and oþir errours in þe worlde shulden be more knowen unto folk þan þei ben now for ypocrisie. Þes ypocritis seien þat þer sectis and al þe deedis þat þei done is groundid upon

The new sects love their own order more than the order of Christ.

Crist, and is Cristis religioun; and so þei have none newe ordris, but new customes, þat þei may leve; and so þei shulden seie bi resoun þat þer be not many ordris of freris, ne accepcions of persones to helpe or to punishe men; siþþe ech man of Cristis religioun is of alle manere ordre; and so lawe of apostataas and of oþir reulys þat þei have founden, shulden ben contrarye to hemsilf, as freris dedis reversen þis lawe.

Þe nyntenþe Sondai Gospel aftir Trinite.

[SERMON XIX.]

Ascendens Jesus in naviculam.—Matt. ix. [1.]

The miraculous cure of the paralytic.

Þis gospel telliþ of a miracle þat Crist dide before þe peple, and þerwiþ reprevyde þe scribis; and how he doiþ awei synne. Þe story telliþ *how Jesus steyȝe in to a boot, and cam to his citee*, and it is seid comounly þat *he rowide to Galilee, and cam in to Nazareþ, þat was citee of his birþe, and þere þey brouȝten him a syke man by palsie, liynge in a bedde. And Jesus seynge her bileve, seide unto þis syke man, Have trust, sone, þi synes ben now forȝeven þee. And sum scribis seiden wiþinne hemsilf, Jesus blasfemeþ in þis word. And whan Crist saw hir þouȝtis wiþinne, he seide, Whereto þei þouȝten þus yvel in her hertis?* And bi þis word he tauȝte hem þat he was God, for oonli God mai þis wise wite, what a man þenkiþ wiþynne. Crist axide hem, *Where is it liȝter, to seie, þi synnes ben forȝyven þee, or ellis to seie, rys and go?* as ȝif Crist wolde mene þis resoun, he þat haþ power to do þat oon, haþ power to do hem boþe. *And Jesus seide, For ȝe shulde wite þat Y have power to forȝyve synne, he seide to þe man in palasie, Rys and take þi bedde anoon and go hool in to þi hous. And he aroos and wente in to his hous* on þat manere þat Crist bad him, *and þe puple seynge þis þing dredden, and glorifieden God þat ȝaf siche power to men.* As to Jesus and his disciplis,

Mystical interpretation.

þis storye of Crist may betoken þe lyf þat Crist lyvede here; so þat þe takyng of his boot bitokeneþ his manheed, or þe bodi of his modir; for mannis bodi is liche a boot. In þis boot Crist wente over þe water of peynes of þis worlde, and wente not oonli into hevene, þat is propre citee of Crist, but into Nazareþ, in which Crist dide þis miracle. But boþe men and aungels offred to Crist mankynde, þat was smyten in palesie; for propirte of þis yvel palasie is a sikenesse groundid in synewis of a man, þe which sinowis ben unstable to move a man as þei shulden; and moistnes of þes senewis þat ben wrappid in moist þing is a cause of þis yvel, as philosophris seyen. Shaking in þe palesie is unstabilnesse of bileve; for eche article of þe trouþe shulde have a synowe for to lede it, and al þes articlis shulde come of Crist, þat is heed of holy Chirche. And, for þes þat offriden þis man ben o persone wiþ him, þerefore biddiþ þe gospel wel, þat Cristis sone shulde truste in him, and Crist forȝeveþ him first his synne of untreuþe þat he was inne, for untreuþe is þe first synne þat comeþ unto man, and it fel not to þis lord to ȝyve but a greet ȝyfte, siþ ech ȝyfte þat man ȝyveþ shulde answer to þe ȝyver. But scribis þat knowen not Cristis godhede seien þat Crist blasfemed in þis, for al oonli God may forȝyve synnes; but Crist techiþ þat he is God bi þe werkes þat he doiþ, for it is yliche[1] liȝt to do miraclis bi himsilf, and to forȝyve synnes, for noon but God may do þes þingis. And herfore Crist helide mankynde of his goostly palesie, and put bileve in oþir men þat Crist hadde power to do þus, and þus wente mankynde, þat God hadde ordeyned unto blisse, fro error of his olde synne into þe hous of Cristis Chirche.

Limits of priestly absolution.

But here men douten of þe letter, wher prelatis may forȝyve synne, and it semeþ þat þei may, for preestis may assoile of synne, and it is al oon to assoile men of synne and to forȝyve þe same synne. And it semeþ þat preestis mai not forȝyve synnes unto men, for þere is noo synne here but ȝif it be offence of God; but no man mai forȝeve þis but ȝif it be God him silfe. And so it semeþ þat oure prelatis may not here forȝyve synne. Soþ it is þat men mai here forȝyve trespas done to hem, and remitte mannis iniurie as much as in hem is, but not remitte uttirly synne done aȝens God. Here it is nede to undirstonde how preestis assoilen men of synne, and how preestis forȝyven synne,

[1] *ilich*, B; *eliche*, C.

for boþe ben conseyved wel and yvel: preestis may assoile of synne if þei acorden wiþ keies of Crist, and if þei discorden fro þes keies, þei feynen hem falsely to assoile. And so on two maneres men may be assoilid of her synnes; and first pryncipaly of God whan Goddis injurie is forȝoven; and þe secounde is assoiling by a turne þat preestis han; and if þis assoilinge be trewe, þei kepen þe boundis þat God ȝaf hem, and þis assoilinge han preestis as vikers of goddis wille. And þere lien many disseitis in suche absolucioun, for if þis assoilinge be trewe, it mut acorde wiþ Cristis assoilinge, and to such assoilinge is needful boþe witt and power. And so on two maneres may a man remitte or deny þe trespas þat is done to him, and so remitte synne; first remitte wronge of God, þat is propred unto God, or ellis dismitte wronge of his broþer in þat þat it is made aȝens him. And so remission is complete þat perteyneþ oonly to God, or ellis remissioun incomplete þat men shulden have generaly, for ellis Crist wolde not teche men to preie on þis maner, Forȝyve us, Lord, oure dettes of synne, as we forȝyven oure dettours. Ȝif ony man wolde telle more pleynly þis sentence bi Goddis lawe, Y wole mekeli assente þerto, ȝif þei grounden þat þei seien; and ȝif ony man prove þis fals or aȝens Goddis lawe þat Y have seid now here, Y wole revoken it mekeli, but wele Y marke þat þis gospel seiþ þat God ȝaf *sich* power to men, but þis gospel seiþ not þat God ȝaf *þis* power to men.

Þe twentiþe Sonday Gospel aftir Trinite.

[SERMON XX.]

Loquebatur Jesus cum discipulis.—Matt. xxii. [1.]

The parable of the marriage of the king's son.

Þis gospel telliþ in a parable what men shulde trowe of þis Chirche fro hennes to þe dai of dome, as it is touchid sumwhat bifore.

Jesus spake wiþ hise disciplis in parablis and seide þus. Þe rewme of hevene is maad liche unto a man þat is a kyng, þat made wedding to his sone; and sente his servauntis to clepe þes men þat weren beden to þe brydale; and, for þei wolden not come, he sente oþir servauntis and seide, Seie ȝe to men þat ben beden, Lo Y have made redy my mete, my boles and my volatils[1][a] *ben kild, and al oþir þingis ben redy; come ȝe faste to þe feste. But þei dispisiden his biddinge, and sum wente into his toun, and sum into his chaffaryynge, and token þis kyngis servauntis, and punishiden wiþ conteke*[2] *and killiden hem. And þe kyng, whan he say þis, was wrooþ, and sente his ostis, and loste þes mansleeris, and brente hir citee; and seide þan to his servauntis, Metis of þis bridale ben redy, but men clepid were not worthi; þerfore go ȝe to eendis of weies, and whomever ȝe finde clepe ye to þe mete. And þes servauntis wenten out, and gedriden men al þat þei founden boþe good and yvel, and þe bridale was fulfillid wiþ men sittinge at þe mete;* al ȝif þei weren not alle ful served. *Þe Kyng cam in to se his gistis, and saw þere oon wiþoute bride cloþis, and seide to him, Frend, how entredist þou hider wiþouten bride cloþis? and he was doumbe. And þan þe lord bade hise servauntis to bynde him boþe hondis and fete, and sende him into utter derknesse, þere shal be wepyng and gnastige of teeþ. For many ben clepid and fewe ben chosen.* Þe kyndom of hevene is þe Chirche, þat takiþ name of þe Heed, as þe gospel spekiþ comounly; and so þis rewme is liche a kyng; þat is þe Fadir in Trinite; and þis kynge made a mariage to Crist þat is his sone, and to þis Chirche þat is his spouse, and to damyselis þerof. For, as Salomon seiþ, foure degrees ben in þis Chirche; sum ben quenes, sum ben lemmannes, and sum damyselis; but oone is spouse þat conteyneþ alle þes þree, and þat is al holi Chirche. And þus þere ben many chirches, and a newe chirche wiþ Crist; ȝhe al þe chirche of men and aungels is newid bi þe Incarnacioun.—Þe servantis of þis spouse bidden men to þe feste, whan þei moven men to come to blisse bi þer just lyfe; and þes servantis weren prophetis and apostolis of Goddis two lawes; but þei weren clepid specialy whan Cristis birþe was shewid hem, for as it was seid bifore, þan alle þingis weren made redi; and many men in boþe

Interpretation of the parable.

[1] *volatiles*, E. [2] *contect*, B; *contec*, E; *conteke*, C; this is unquestionably the right reading; see Glossary.

[a] That is *poultry*, Fr. *volaille*.

þes tymes wolden not come þus to þis feste. After þes servantis he sent oþir, as men þat nexte sueden þe apostlis; and bolis and volatils weren slayn, and mete was redy to þis feste. Þe boles bitokenen þe olde fadris, as patriarkes and David, for þei diden bataillis of God, and turneden his enemyes wiþ her hornes, and ȝit þei kepten ful bisili þe grete mandementis of God. Þe volatils þat serven seyntis at þe secounde cours of þis feste ben seintis of þe newe lawe þat wiþ þes mandementis kepten Cristis conseilis; and ȝit men forsoken to come notwiþstondinge sample of þes seintis. And sum wenten aftir lordship of þis worlde, and sum after chaffare of þis worldely richesse; but sum slowen Cristis servauntis, as emperours of Rome and preestis. Þe king of hem was wrooþ herfore, and sente his oostis out to Jerusalem and slow þes sleeris of Crist, and brent þer citee, as Josephus telliþ. And þis dede done in Jerusalem þe two and fourty ȝeer after þe deeþ of Crist bitokeneþ þe vengeaunce of God for sleing of Cristis membris. And þus men þat stoonden bihynde, boþe in þe olde lawe and in þe newe, weren unworþi to fille þe nombre þat God ordeynede to be saved. And now in þes laste daies God bade hise servantis clepen men boþe good and yvel in to þe Chirche þat weren out of þe riȝt weye, and wenten bi weyes of errours þat weren hard for to wende; and so as Petir in his first fishinge toke two manere of fishes, sum dwelliden in þe nette, and sum borsten þe nette and wenten awey; so here in þis Chirche ben sum ordeyned to blisse and sum to peyne, al if þei lyven justly for a tyme. And so men seien comounly þat þere ben here two manere of chirches, holy Chirche or Chirche of God, þat on no manere may be dampned, and þe chirche of þe fend, þat for a time is good, and lastiþ not; and þis was nevere holy Chirche, ne part þerof.

But þe king aftir þis feste came in at þe dai of dome, for God shewiþ him þanne to alle, for he knowiþ alle mennes lyf; and þes þat wolden not laste in grace weren not cloþid in bride cloþis; and alle þes ben o man þat hadde noo witt to answere God. But, for þis man wiþ parts of him profitide to Cristis Chirche, and was of þe same kynde wiþ Crist, Crist clepiþ him frend, as he dide Judas; but alle þes men can not answere how þei entren in to þe Chirche, for it was told hem opynli þat þei ben traitours but if þei lasten, and ben more worþi to be dampned þan men þat nevere entriden þus. And so al siche men token peyne bi just jugement of God, þat þer willis shulden be bounden and þer profitable werkes, and shulden be cast in to helle, where men shulden wepe and gnaste wiþ teeþ; wepynge shal be sensible sorowe, and gnastynge shal be wantinge of blisse. Wherfore men shal moost grutche, siþ þei myȝt liȝtly have come to blisse, and aftir þis þei shal have noo wille neiþer to desire ne to wirche wel, and þus many men ben clepid, but few ben chosen to blisse.

ÞE OON AND TWENTIEÞ SONDAI GOSPEL AFTIR TRINITE.

[SERMON XXI.]

Erat quidam regulus.—JOH. iv. [46.]

The healing of the nobleman's son.

Þis gospel telliþ how a kyng, þat sum men seien was an heþene man, bilevede in Crist, and disserved to have a myracle of his sone. Þe story seiþ, *how in Galilee was dwelling a litil kyng, in þe citee of Capharnaum þat hadde a sone ful syke of þe feveris. And whanne he herde telle þat Jesus come fro Jude to Galilee, he came and mette him on þe wey, and preiede him come doun and hele his sone, for he was in point of deeþ. And Crist seide to þis kyng*, to amende his bileve, *ȝe bileven not in Jesus but if ȝe se signes and woundris;* as þis man bilevede not in þe godhede of Crist, for if he hadde, he shulde have trowide þat Crist myȝte have savyd his sone ȝif he hadde not bodily come to þis syke man and touchid him; but þis kyng had more herte of helþe of his sone þan he hadde to be helid of untreuþe þat he was inne, and þerfore he tolde not herby but axide eft Crist to hele his sone. And in þis forme of wordis[1] in which he shewide his untreuþe, *Lord, he seide, come doun bifore þat my sone die.* But Jesus, as wise lord and merciful, heelide his sone

[1] *wormes*, B; *wordis*, C and E.

in siche manere þat he myȝte wite þat he was boþe God and man; *Go, he seide, þi sone lyveþ.* And þerwiþ Crist tauȝte his soule boþe of his manhede and godhede, and ellis hadde not þis king trowid; but þis gospel seiþ þat he trowid, and al his hous; and upon þis treuþe *he wente homward and mette his men upon þe wey, þat tolden him þat his sone shulde lyve, for he is coverid of his yvel. And he axide whan his sone ferde beter, and þei seiden, þat ȝistirdai þe sevenþe houre þe feveres forsoke þe child. And þe fadir knewe* bi his mynde *þat it was þe same houre þat Crist seide, Þi sone lyveþ, and herfore bilevede he and al his hous* in Jesus Crist. And þerfore Jesus seide soþ, þat he and men liche to him trowen not but if þei se boþe signes and woundris; it was a signe of þe sike child þat he dide werkes of an hool man[a], but it was a greet woundir þat bi virtue of þe word of Crist a man so ferre shulde ben hool, for so Crist shewide þat he is virtue of Godhede, þat is everywhere; and þis virtue mut be God, þat dide þus þis myracle.

The inner sense of Scripture.

Þis stori seiþ us þis secounde witt þat God ȝyveþ to holy writt, þat þis litil kyng bitokeneþ a mannis witt bi synne slyden fro God, þat is but a litil king in regard of his maker; and his sone was syke on þe feveris, as weren þes heþene folke and þer affeccioúns þat comen of þer soulis; but þei hadden a kyndli wille to wite þe treuþe and stonde þereinne. Þis kyng cam fro Capharnaum, þat is, a feld of fatnesse[b]; for man fattid and alardid[1] wendiþ awey fro God. Þis mannis witt, whanne he herde þat Jesus cam to heþen men, and þat bitokeneþ Galilee, þat is, transmigracioun[c], mette wiþ Jesus in pleyn weie, and lefte his heþene possessioun, and preide God to heele his folke þat weren syke bi goostly fevere. But Crist sharpide þes mennis bileve, for feiþ is first nedeful to men, but undirstonding of man preide Crist come doun bi grace bifore mannis affeccioun die

[1] *alargid* in B and C; but A probably preserves the true reading; *largid*, E.

[a] The meaning seems to be, 'It was a *sign* that the sick child should be healed at all; it was a *wonder* that he should be healed though a great distance off.'

[b] Capharnaum, *i.e.* Kaphar-naoum, means 'hamlet of Nahum.' (Bib. Dict.)

[c] See p. 30, *note*.

aboute erþely goodis. But, for men trowiden þe godhede of Crist, þei weren hool of þis fevere, whan þei forsoken þis world and putte þer hope in hevenly goodis. Þes servauntis ben low virtues of þe soule, which, worching ioyfulli, tellen mannis witt and his wille þat þis sone is hool of fevere. Þis fevere bitokeneþ shakyng of man bi unkyndli distempoure of abundaunce of worldely goodis, þat ben unstable as þe water; and herfore seiþ Seint Jame þat he þat doutiþ in bileve is lyke to a flood of þe see þat wiþ wynde is born aboute.—Þat þes servauntis tolden þis king þat in þe sevenþe houre fevere forsoke þis childe, bitokeneþ a greet witt, as Robert of Lincoln shewiþ. First it bitokeneþ þat þis fevere goiþ awey fro mannis kynde bi seven ȝiftes of þe Holy Goost, þat ben undirstonden bi þes houres. And þis clerk dividiþ þe dai in two halves bi sixe houres, so þat al þe daie bitokeneþ liȝt of grace þat þat man is inne. Þe firste sixe houres bitokenen joy þat man haþ of worldely þing, and þis is bifore spiritual joy, as utter man is bifore spiritual. But in þe firste houre of þe secounde halve leveþ gostly fever man, for who so evere have worldely joie, ȝif he have grace on sum manere, ȝit he trembliþ in sum fevere aboute goodis of þe world; but anoon in þe sevenþe hour, þat is þe firste of þe secounde halfe, whan wille of worldely þingis is lefte, and spiritual þingis begynen to be loved, þan þis shakynge passiþ fro man, and goostli helþe comeþ to þe spirit. And so shadewis of liȝt of sunne fro þe sevenþe houre in to þe niȝt ever wexen more and more, and þat bitokeneþ goostli, þat vanite of þis world semeþ ay more to mannis spirit til he come to þe ende of þis lyf to lyf þat ay shal laste. And so þis man trowiþ in God, boþ wiþ undirstonding and wille, wiþ al þe maynè of his hous, whan al his wittis and alle his strengþis ben obeshinge to resoun, whan þis fever is þus passid. Of þis undirstondinge men may take moral witt how men shal lyve, and large þe mater as hem likeþ.

James i. 6.

Direction to preachers.

Þe two and twentiþe Sondai Gospel aftir Trinite.

[SERMON XXII.]

Simile est regnum caelorum homini.—Mat. xviii. [23.]

The parable of the indebted servant.

Þis gospel telliþ bi a parable how bi riȝt jugement of God men shulden be merciful.—*Þe kyngdom of hevene, seiþ Crist, is lyke to an erþeli kyng þat wolde ryken wiþ hise servauntis. And whanne he hadde bigun to rekoun, oon was offrid unto him þat owid him ten thousand besantis, and whan he hadde not to paye of, þe lord bad he shulde be soold, his wyf and his children and al þat he hadde, and þat þat he ouȝt þe lord shulde be algatis paid. Þis servant fell doun and praiede þe lord and seide, Have pacience in me, and Y shal quyte þee al. Þe lord hadde mercy on him, and forȝaf him al his dette. Þis servant went out and found oon of hise dettours, þat ouȝt him an hundred pens; and toke him and stranglide him, and bade him paie his dette. And þis servant felle doun and praiede him of pacience, and he shulde bi tyme ȝelde him al þat he ouȝte him. But þis man wolde not, but wente out and putte him in prisoun, til he hadde paied þe dette þat he ouȝte him. And oþir servauntis of þis man, whan þei seyen þis dede, mourneden ful myche, and tolden al þis to þe lord. And þe lord clepid him, and seide unto him, Wickide servant, al þi dette Y forȝaf þe, for þou preiedist me; ne bihoved þee not to have mercy on þi servant, as Y hadde mercy on þee? And þe lord was wroþ, and ȝaf him to turmentours, til he hadde paied al þe dette þat he ouȝte him. On þis manere, seiþ Crist, shal my Fadir of hevene do to you, but ȝif ye forȝyve, ech on to his broþir, of ȝour free herte* þe trespas þat he haþ done him.

Interpretation.

Þe kyngdom of hevene is holy Chirche, of men, þat now traveilen here; and þis Chirche bi his heed is lyke to a man kyng, for Crist, heed of þis Chirche, is boþe God and man. Þis kyng wolde ryken wiþ his servantis, for Crist haþ wille wiþouten ende to rykene wiþ men at þre tymes. First, Crist rykeneþ wiþ men whan he techiþ hem bi resoun how myche þei han hadde of him, and hou myche þei owen him; þe secounde tyme Crist rykeneþ wiþ men, whan in þe houre of mannis deeþ he telliþ hem at what point þes men shal ever justli stonde; þe þridde rekenyng is general, þat shal be at þe daie of dome, whan þis jugement generali shal be opynli done in dede. As anentis þe first rekenynge, Crist rekeneþ wiþ riche men of þis worlde, and shewiþ hem, how myche þei owen him, and shewiþ bi riȝtwisnesse of his lawe how þei and þeires shulden be sold, and so make aseeþ [a] bi peyne of þingis þat þei perfourmeden not in dede. But many sich men for a tyme have conpuncioun in herte, and preien God of his grace to have pacience in hem, and þei shal in þis lyf serve to Crist treuly. And so Crist forȝeveþ hem upon þis condicioun. But þei wenden out, and suen not Crist þer lord in mercy, but oppressen þer servauntis þat owen þem but a litil dette, and putten hem in prisoun, and þenken not on Goddis mercy; and oþir servantis of God boþe in þis lyf and in þe toþir tellen to God þis felnes, and preien him of venjance. No doute God is wrooþ at þis, and at two rekenyngis wiþ man, he resouneþ þis cruel man, and jugiþ him justli to peyne.

And þerefore Crist biddiþ, bi Luk, al men to be mercyful, for þer Fadir of heven þat shal juge hem is mercyful. But we shul undirstonde bi þis, þat þis mercy þat Crist axiþ is noþing aȝen resoun, and so bi þis just mercy men shulen sum tyme forȝyve, and sum tyme shulden þei punishe, but ever bi resoun of mercy. Þe resoun of mercy stondiþ in þis; þat men myȝten do cruely þei done justly for Goddis sake, to amendement of men; and men may mercyfully reprove men, and punishe hem, and take of hem þere just dettis for beterynge of þese dettours. On þis manere doþ God þat is ful of mercy, and seiþ þat he reproveþ and chastisiþ his wantoun children þat he loveþ; and þus Crist reprovede Pharisees, and punishide preestis wiþ oþir peple, and punishiþ mercifulli alle dampned men in helle, for it stondiþ not wiþ his riȝt þat he punishe but mercifulli. God ȝyveþ goodis of kynde bi grace to þes men þat he dampneþ, and if he punishide hem more, ȝit he medliþ mercy. But here men shulden be ware þat al þe goodis þat þei han ben goodis of her God, and þei nakide servantis of God; and þus shulden þei warly flee to take Luke vi. 36.

[a] By suffering pain, make amends for neglected duties.

þere owen venjance, but venge injurie of God, and entenden amendement. Þus Crist, mekist of all, suffride his owne injurie in two[1] temptaciouns of þe fend, but in þe þridde he saide, Go, Saþan, and reprovede him sharpli bi autorite of God.—Þus Moises, myldest man of alle, killide many þousand of his folk, for þei worshipiden a calfe, as þei shulden worshipe God. And þus in oure werkes of mercy lieþ myche discrecioun, for ofte tymes oure mercy axiþ to venge and to punishe men, and ellis justises of mannis lawe shulden nevere punishe men to þe deeþ, but ofte tymes þei done amys, and þei witen not whan þei done wele, and so religioun of preestis shulde leve sich jugementis.

Þe þre and twentiþe Sondai Gospel.

[SERMON XXIII.]

Abeuntes Pharisei.—Matt. xxii. [15.]

Paying tribute to Caesar.

Þe storye of þis gospel telliþ how þe Phariseeis casten to disseyve Crist bi wordis of ypocrisie. *And so þe Phariseeis wendinge out*, fro þe weye of treuþe, *maden a conseil bi hem silfe to take Jesus in speche*, and first þei spaken fagynge wordis, as ypocritis doen, but ȝit *þei senten her disciplis*, and comen not hemsilf, lest þei weren convictid bi wisdom of Crist. *Þei sente to Crist two* puplis, *Jewis and Erodians*, to witnesse aȝen him what ever he hadde seide, or aȝen þe Jewis, or aȝen þe emperoure. *Maister, þei seiden, we witen wel þat þou art sad trewe, and þe weie þat lediþ to God þou techist in treuþe*, (*and þou takist noon heede of man, but booldli techist þe soþe*,) *for þou reckest of no man* but puttist God bifore. And aftir þei axiden þis questioun of Crist, þat he shulde telle þat him þouȝt, and not bi oþer mennis witt, *where it where leveful to ȝyve taliage to þe emperour*. Hem þouȝte þat Crist shulde nedis seie ȝhe or nay; ȝif he seide ȝhe, he spake aȝen þe Jewis, for þei calengiden of

[1] So in B and C; A has *to*.

þer fadirys to be suget to no man; and ȝif he seide nay, he were aȝens þe emperoure, and so on ech side hem þouȝte þat Criste was take. But Crist shewide first þe purpos of þes ypocritis. Whan Jesus knewe þe wickidnesse of þes fals men, he clepide hem ypocritis, *and axide whereto þei temptiden him.* And efte Crist toke a meene weye, anoþir þan þei þouȝten on; *Shewe ȝe me, seide Crist, þe moneye of þe taliage; and þei shewiden him a peny. And Crist axide over, whos ymage is þis, and whos writing above? And þei seiden, it was þe emperours. And Crist* ȝaf hem þis answere, general and sutil, *Ȝyve ye to þe emperoure þat is his, and to God þat is His.* Bi which word it semeþ þat Crist approvede þe emperour and subieccion to him in þat þat he makiþ Goddis pees; and servise propre to God shulde be kepte to Him; and so Cristis wordis myȝte no man disprove.

The evils of hypocrisy, especially that of the 'orders.'

Here men may touche þe malice of ypocrisie, for þere is no wers synne, ne more general, ne more venymous; for it is more yvel þat it þus contrarieþ to treuþe, siþ an ypocrite feyneþ him holy, and he is a fals fend. And herfore reprovede Crist ypocrisy of ordris, for he wiste wel þat þei shulden after do more harm in þe world. Ffirst sich ypocritis lyen on hemsilfe, and seien þei done for holynesse what evere þat þei done, and so þei venymen first hem silf, and afterward oþer men. And it is more general þan many oþir synnes, for ech state of men is blemyshid wiþ þis synne, but first and moost, religions and clerkes, for þere is no spedy cause whi þei usen siche habitis but to devyde hem in holynesse fro þe common peple, siþ as medeful werkes myȝten þei done in seculer habitis, and more privily, as Crist biddiþ us be holy. And herfore Crist biddiþ to be war wiþ sour dow of Phariseis, siþ þere is no resoun to ypocrisy but to shewe menys synne[1], and to disseyve on ech side boþ þe ypocritis hem silfe and oþir men þat dwellen wiþ hem. And so her religioun serveþ to crye þat þei ben holy, and to make dyvysioun bitwixe hem and oþer men. And siþ liknes is cause of love amonge men, sich dyvysioun is cause of envye and hate. Goddis lawe and kynde techiþ þat ech beest loveþ beest like to him, and so experience techiþ þat oon ordre loveþ his broþir more þan a strange man

[1] So B and C; A reads *lyve.*

aȝen þe reule of charite. And sich gedring of lumpis bi sensible signes haþ not autorite of Crist but raþer repreving. For upon Good Friday Crist ordeynede him to be cloþid þries aȝens sich weddinge wiþ cloþis of colour and shap; and as Crist seiþ in reprof of siche sectis, Kynrede of hordom sekiþ siche signes; alle þe dedes þat þei done sownen to ypocrisie, and aȝens no men spake Crist sharplier.

Friars ought not to beg, nor have great houses.

And alȝif freris seien þat þei beggen for charite, whan þei have prechid for siche beggyng, and þat Crist beggid so, and bad hem begge þus, neþeles al þis speche is poudrid wiþ gabbinge, and, as ypocritis done, þei seken þer owen avantage and not þe worship of Crist, ne to profite of his Chirche. For if þei diden, þei wolden sue Cristis reule, and leve chargyng of þe puple boþe in noumbre and begging, and leve her heye housis þat þei propren unto hem, siþ Crist hadde no propre hous to reste in his heed. And as Macometis lawe takiþ myche of Cristis lawe, and meddliþ oþir lawis, and þere comeþ in venym, so doiþ Anticrist in þes newe sectis; and as þei bringen in breþeren bi falshede of lesyngis, so ben þer ordris groundid in falshede in ech side. And siche men mote needis disturble holy Chirche; and þus seculer clerkes ben ful of ypocrisie, boþ popis and bishopis and clerkes under hem. Crist forfendide to putte miraclis þat he had done to þe manhede of him for errour in bileve; but þe fend drediþ not to feyne absoluciouns and indulgencis wiþ oþir ȝiftis, þat God grantide nevere, to spuyle men of her money, and not for soule hele; for þan wolden þei ȝyve freely þes ȝiftis, as Crist ȝaf himsilf and bad oþirs do. And þus lower clerkes traveilen bi water and bi londe for to have benefices and propre possessions, more þan þei done for helþe of mannis soulis; and how ever þei speken, þei lyven al in ypocrisie; and þus whan men fiȝten, pleden, or chiden, charite is not þere ende, but pride and propre havynge. And þus it is of seculers þat ben weddid men; and so charite of men is blyndid bi ypocrisie, so þat no synne of þis world lettiþ now more charite; and so ypocrisie is more general synne, and more pryvy sin to begile men, and werst to distroien þe comoun peple, and al þis figureden Pharisees aȝens Jesus Crist.

Þe foure and twentiþe Sondai aftir Trinite.

[SERMON XXIV.]

Loquente Jesu ad turbas, ecce princeps[1].—Matt. ix. [18.]

Þis gospel telliþ of þe firste dede bodi þat Crist reiside to lyf, and how Crist helide a womman as he wente þidir. Þe storie telliþ þat, *as Crist spake to þe folk, a prince came to him and worshipide him wiþ honoure, and seide to him, Sire my douȝter is now deed, but come and putte þi hond on hir and she shal lyve,* bi vertue of þe. We shal undirstonde þat in tyme of Crist weren princes of preests, as princis of knyȝtis, as Nichodeme was a prince, and bishopis of Jerusalem weren clepid princes of preestis, and þis man here, þat was keper of a synagoge, as now ben persones; and þes men hadden comounly wyves and children, as preestis han wers now, for þei han out of wedloke. And *Jesus roos up, and suede þis prince, and his disciplis,* for he was redi to do good, and as he wente, *a syke womman by flix of blood þat lastide xii wynter came bihynde Jesus and seide to hir silf, If Y touche þe hemn of þe cote of Jesus, Y shal be safe for holynes of him. And Jesus turnede agen, and lokide on hir, and say her bileve, and saide þus to hir, Affie þe, douȝter, þi bileve haþ made þee saif. And þe womman was saved from þe same hour.* Þe gospel of Mattheu telliþ ferþer, *hou Crist came to þe hous of þis prince þat þe wenche lay deed inne; and whan Crist say mynystralis, and folk makinge nois, he badde hem go þenne, for þe wenche is not dede but slepiþ. And þei scorneden Crist,* for þei wenden þat he had errid. *And whan þe folk was cast out, Crist wente in to þe hous, and toke þe hond of þe wenche, and saide, Wenche, rys up. And þe wenche roos,* and dide werkes of lyf.

The healing of the woman with an issue of blood, and the raising of Jairus' daughter.

Clerical celibacy.

It is seid bifore[a] how þis firste bodi þat Crist reiside from deþ to life bitokeneþ siche men þat ben goostly deed, for ful concense to synne; but þei do not þe dede wiþout; and þat is bitokned þat þe wenche was in þe hous ȝit. Þis prince is mannis þouȝt, þat kyndly haþ sorewe þat þe spirit of it is þus fillid wiþ synne;

[1] So in B; A has *principes*.

[a] See p. 39.

and þus it preieþ to God þat þis dou3ter be quykened. And whan Crist entriþ to þe soule of þis maiden and moveþ wiþ his worchinge hond þe spirit of it, þan it riseþ to lyf and worchiþ by grace. And here men noten, how a ligginge man, þat shulde be areisid up, shulde bede his hond and þe reiser shulde take it, and so bi strengþe of hem boþe shulde þe man rise. Ech man in synne liþ[1] at þe erþe, and God helpiþ many men to rise up to grace, and if þei wirchen wiþ God to þis werke of lyfe, God wole make hem stonde, and comfort hem to wirche. Þis woman þat was heelid, as Crist wente to þis hous, of þe flix of blood þat she hadde twelve 3eere, is every persone of man combrid wiþ synne, where it be symple persone or gedrid of many; and þes twelve 3ere bitokenen double age of two kyndis of man bi which he dwelliþ in synne. But man may spende al þat he haþ aboute oþir fisicians[2] and gete him absolucions, 3he after þe daie of dome, and many indulgensis, wiþ lettris of fraternite, þat bihotiþ[3] him to come to hevene, as soone as he is deed, and 3it mai þe flixe of blood rennen wiþ al þis, and he may be depper in synne wiþ al þes dispensis. And herefore mekenesse of Crist is a special medicine, þat a man þenke hou he is in þe last place beden of Crist to soupe wiþ him in hevene. And þus þis cloþing of Crist ben seintis þat he cloþid, and þe last of þis cloþing is þe last place þat men shulden repute hem inne bi mekenesse of herte, and doing awey þes presumpciouns comen þei þus bihinden, and Crist bi siche mekenesse 3yveth hem grace to leve synne, and þis is beter þan medecynes þat fesicians sellen. And siche men ben confortid bi wordis of Crist, for Crist heliþ noone bodily but 3if he hele hem of synne, and þus ech storye of myraclis of Crist mai be moralisid to a good witt, ne is it no perel to varie in siche wittis, so þat men varien not fro þe treuþe, ne fro good lore, for þe Holy Goost, autor of þes wordis, ordeyneþ men to have al sich wittis, and he ordeyneþ þis tixt to move hem herto. Hou shulde sich sense be error in man? But siche wordis axen good jugement, for many heretikis seyen þat þei han witt of God, and 3it it mai be oon of þe fendis heresies.

Possible futility of church-pardons and dispensations.

Here men douten comonly whan men synnen dedely

[1] *liif*, B. [2] So in B; *fecicisians*, A: *fesicianes*, C. [3] *beten*, B; *bibeten*, C.

wiþinne in þer soule, and done noon yvel dedes wiþouten in þer bodi þat anoien men. And men moven over how resoun mai assente to ony synne of man, siþ ech synne is aȝens resoun; and ȝit sum men seien þat it is alon resoun and mannis spirit; and so ȝif mannis spirit assente, resoun assentiþ; for mannis spirit haþ al vertues in man honginge on him, and it mut nedelingis[1] do what ony of þes vertues doiþ. Here we shulen conseyve þat it is not nedeful here to wite which is dedely synne, and wite which is venial, but ech synne shulde a man flee, lest it be dedli to him. But clerkis seyen comounly þat man haþ two wittis, oon hongiþ on his bodi and haþ many partis; anoþir is aboven his bodi, þat dwelliþ wiþ his spirit, whan þe spirit and þe bodi ben departed atwynne, and þis vertue in a man is sum tyme clepid resoun. And so, as in þe first synne Eve temptide Adam, and Adam synnede not bifore he hadde assentid, so in ech synne in an hool man þe flesh temptiþ þe spirit, and it synneþ not bifore it have assentid[2] to lustis of þe flesh. And so power of þe spirit, þat sum men clepen resoun, assentiþ aȝen resoun to fleishli likingis, and so þe spirit is nedid to consente þus, but it is not constreyned, siþ it assentiþ freeli. And bi þis may we se hou argumentis gone awei bi equivocacion of wordis þat men speken, as a man haþ many wittis boþe fleishli and spiritualy, and so many maneres he assentiþ to a þinge. But sum foolis þer ben þat seien þat a man haþ no vertue of soule, but ȝif it be þe same soule, and þis errour bringiþ in oþir, and þus resoun of man is sum tyme clepid treuþe þat God causiþ wiþouten ende, ȝif a man die, and sum tyme vertue of man þat goiþ wiþ þe soule is clepid resoun of man to anoþir witt. Bi þis may men see sumwhat, how þei shulden answere to þe doutes þat ben maad, and to oþer also, for we shulde bileve þat men may be dampned for synne in her soule, ȝif þei worche not outward, for oryginal sin and actual[3] also, and þus mai men be saved for þouȝtis in þer hertis, al ȝif þei done not outward meritory werkes; and þus mai men done harm to oþers bi þouȝtis of herte, and profite also to hem, ȝif þei ben ferre from hem, and siþ spiritual harmynge or profite is myche more bodili profite.

Mortal and venial sin.

[1] *nedeli*; B; *nedely*, C. [2] So in B; A has *assentiþ*. [3] So in B and C; *accual*, A.

Þe fyve and twentiþ Sondai Gospel aftir Trinite.

[SERMON XXV.]

Cum sublevasset oculos Jesus.—Joh. vi. [5.]

The first miracle of the loaves and fishes.

Þis gospel telliþ a myracle how Crist fedde þe folk; and þis miracle techiþ men boþe good feiþ and vertues. It is seid bifore[a] how Crist fedde þe folk þus twyes, and of þe secounde fedynge it is seid bifore, and of þe first fedynge shulde we speke now. Þe gospel seiþ þus, þat þis miracle was don *whanne Jesus hadde cast up his eyen and seiȝ þat myche folk was comen to him, to here Goddis word, he saide to Philip, Whereof þei shulden bigge breed for to fede þis folk,* for he wiste þat þei hungriden. *Þis seide Crist to Philip for to tempte him, for he wiste ful wel what he hadde to do. And Philip seide to Crist, þat loves of two hundrid pens ne sufficiden not to hem, so þat ech on myȝte take a litil what of breed. But anoþir disciple, Andrew, Petris broþir, seide, þer was a child þat þere hadde fyve barly loves, and þerto two fishis, but what wolden þes be amonge so myche folke. And Jesus bade his apostlis to make þe men sitte doun to mete, for þere was much hay,* þat þei myȝte sitte on, *and þe men weren sette as it were fyve þousand. And Jesus tooke þan þes loves, and whan he hadde þanked God, he delide hem to þe sittinge men, and also of þe fishis as myche as þei wolden. And whan þei weren fillid, Crist seide to his disciplis, gedre ȝe þe relif þat lefte, þat it perishe not. And þei gedriden and filden twelve coffynes*[b] *of relif of fyve barly loves, þat weren lefte of þis folke þat eten. And þes men, whan þei hadden seen þe signe of þis myracle, saiden among hemsilfe, þat þis is a verrey prophete, þat is come in to þis world,* as prophetis bifore hadden told. We shal suppose of þis myracle þat it is dyverse fro þe toþir; for ellis Mark wolde not have told þes myraclis so dyversly and in diverse places, for þat oon hadde

[a] See Sermon VII.

[b] In this word, by which Wyclif (as well as both Wycliffite versions *in loco*) simply Englishes the *κοφίνους* of the original, we seem to have the source of the word 'coffin.'

þen be fals, and it hadde be superflue to þus have told þis tale; and herfor we shal suppose þat þes weren two myraclis þat weren do in þis maners as þe gospel telliþ. And we shal suppose over þat as Crist quykid þre men for a notable cause, who so koud[1] undirstonde it, so he made þes two festis, for a certeyn resoun. And it is seid comounly þat as þe noumbre of two is þe first þat comeþ from oonhede of noumbris, so þe two feestis bitokenen þat men for þer synne ben fallen in þis nede to be fedde þus. For, if man hadde stonde in þe staat of innocence, he shulde have had no nede to be fedde þus, for man shulde have feelid no peyne bifore þat he hadde synned, and so he shulde not have hungrid for defaute of mete. But, for he wente first bi synne from oonhede of God, þerfore he felde þus twyes in peyne for his synne. And God telliþ suche treuþes on diverse maneres, now for o cause, and now for anoþir; and þus bi þis resoun curatis of puplis, ȝif þei ben hooli in bodi, ben pore feble men. Þei ben pore men, ȝif þei kepen her ordre, for þei shulden sue Crist in poverte, nerrer þan oþir comounes, and þei ben feble, for þei have nede of sustenaunce þat þei shulde not have hadde in state of innocence; and þei mai not, as Crist, have mete where þei wolden; and þus for poverte and febilnes þei taken almes of comounes. Þes fyve loves ben fyve bokes of Moises, þat ben boþe streite and sharpe, as seint Petir seiþ. Þes two fishis ben two bokes, of Wisdom and of prophetis, þat ben sonel[2] to þes loves. And þis o child, þat haþ al þe mete, is þe child born to us, þat Ysay spekiþ of. Þis child makiþ his puple sitte don in mekenesse, þenkinge þat þei ben hey whos floure falliþ, but þe goostly food is proposid of Crist for to be tokned bi bodily foode. And fyve þousend of men fedde wiþ þis mete weren al þo in which Goddis grace was greene; for al þes moten meken hem, and be fed wiþ Goddis word; for ellis may no man come to hevene blis. And þus men þat ben fallen doun bi pryde of synne, shal bi mekenesse of þe centre be brouȝt unto hevene. For as lownesse of þe centre of þe world and þe erþe, is þe most lownesse þat God may make, so mekenes of Crist is þe mooste þat mai be, and

An allusion to the institution of 'Poor Priests.'

Acts xv. 10.

Isaiah ix. 6.

[1] *kowde*, B. [2] *souvil*, B; *sowle*, C.

in þis mekenesse mut a man grounde his toure, ȝif it shal teyne to hevene, for þe toure of þe gospel þat man shulde wille to rere is undirstonde comounly heynesse of vertues, of which vertues mekenes is ground, and charite þe heyeste parte, þat teyneþ unto hevene. After þis mete weren gedrid twelve cof-fynes, ffor holy doctours after þes maters weren more sutil in witt of holy writt þan aftirward ben doctours in witt of Goddis lawe. For siþ, men stonden in sophymes and crafte of worldely wynnynge, and lore of foure doctours is myche leid asleepe, naþeles þis relif shulde fede folk now, for neiþer þis hool mete ne relif þerof may rote or perishe, siþ it is treuþe of God. And so al þes twelve coffynes ben alle þe mo[1] sentencis þat first weren gedrid of witt of holy writt, but þe sevene lepis þat weren gedrid after weren fewere goode sentences þat weren take of Goddis lawe. And þis myracle of multipliynge of Goddis lawe bi so fewe prechours among so fele folk was more myracle þan bodili woundris, and þerfore holy men turneden to God, glorifien him, and holden hym þer kyng.

[1] *moo* in B.

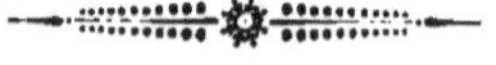

HERE BIGYNNEÞ

ADVENT BIFORE CRISTEMASSE.

ÞE FIRSTE SONDAI GOSPEL IN ADVENT.

[SERMON XXVI.]

Cum appropinquasset Jesus Jerosolumis.—MATT. xxi. [1.]

Þis Gospel telliþ of the secounde advent of Crist and it is noo drede it techiþ us vertues, siþ alle þe dedes of Crist tellen men how þei shulden do. Þe story telliþ *how Jesus cam to his passioun unto Jerusalem*, to teche þat he ordeynede himsilf for to suffre, for he myȝte have fledde þis passioun of him, ȝif he wolde himsilf not have suffrid þus. And so men seyen comounly þat þere ben þre adventis biside þe comoun advent þat Crist comeþ to mannis soule. In þe firste advent Crist cam to be man, and þis advent aboden seintis of þe olde lawe, and þis was no morynge but lassyng of God, ȝhe more lassyng þan to aungelis, as þe psalme seiþ, for God was made erþe whan he was maad man. Þe secounde advent is cominge to Cristis passioun; and of þis makiþ þe gospel mynde to daye. Þe þridde advent shal be whan Crist shal come to jugement at þe daie of dome, to juge boþe good and yvel. And in al þes þre adventis Crist visitide ever his sugetis to amende hem and not to spuyle hem; and wolde God þat preelatis[1] wolde þenke on þis now; þanne shulde þei not come in Anticristis name more to spuyle þer sugetis þan to amende hem. Þe first advent of Crist we bileven as passid, and þe þridde advent we abiden, þat is to come; but to þe secounde advent we shulden maken us redy to suffre in oure body for þe name of Crist.

The entry of Christ into Jerusalem.

Four different Advents.

Ps. viii. 5.

Crist cam to Beþfage[a], þat is a litil toun in þe foot, *of Olyvete*,

[1] *prelatis*, B.

[a] Bethphage is said to mean *house of unripe figs* (Smith's Bib. Dict.). Wyclif was apparently thinking of the Greek φάγω.

a myle fro Jerusalem, and þis toun was ȝovun to preestis for mete of her mouþis, for Beþfage is hous of mouþ, or ellis hous of etynge—and bi þis tauȝte Crist how he lyvede pore lyf and nedy for love of man, siþ he dwelte in siche þropis[1][a], and he tolde hou preestis eten hym by envie. *Þanne he sente two disciplis to Jerusalem,* þat was wallid, *and þerfore Crist clepiþ it a castel þat was aȝen holy Chirche*[2]. *Crist bad his disciplis to bringe him an asse and þe fole of þis asse þat þei shulden fynden al redy, and bad þat þei shulden lose hem and brynge hem to Crist; and ȝif ony seide ouȝt to hem, þei shulden seie, Þe Lord haþ nede of hem, and he shulde leve hem anoon. And þis was fild, as Crist seide bi prophete* longe bifore, *Telle ȝe to Syon þe douȝter of Jerusalem, Lo, þi kyng comeþ to þee, homely, sittynge upon asse and upon þe asse fole;* which asse was a drawyng beest. *And his disciplis wenten and diden as Jesus comandide hem.* For alle þes þingis moten nedis be riȝt as Crist hadde ordeyned hem, and bi þis myȝten þe disciplis knowe þat þis Lord was al witty. And *his disciplis puttiden her cloþis upon þes two beestis*, first upon þe fole, siþ upon þe asse, to teche us þat heþene men, þat weren wanton as foolis[3], shulden resseyve Crist and his lawes, and after Jewis as assis, for þei shal bere to þe ende of þe world þe wiȝte of þe olde lawe, as folt[4][b] assis beren chargis what so ever be leid on hem. *And his disciplis maden Crist to sitte upon þes boþe beestis.* But þre manere of folk cam out of Jerusalem and dide worship to Crist, for comounes lovede him riȝt wele. *Myche peple þat was riche spradden her cloþis in þe weye*, and porer *schreden branchis of trees and spradden hem in þe weye, and oþir*, boþe ȝong and olde, *comynge bifore and bihynde songen* þis song in worship of Crist; David Sone, *we preien, make us safe*[c]*:* þis we seien to David Sone, *Blessid be he þat is come þus to us in Goddis name!*

Sum men seien þat þes disciplis þat weren sent to Jerusalem ben herty preestis and worldely lordis þat shulde be boþe Cristis

[1] þorpes, C. [2] This clause is rightly not written as a quotation in C. [3] *folis*. B. [4] So in B and C; A has *foli*.

[a] *Þropis.* Þrop is given in Bosworth's Dictionary as an alternative form of þorp, village.

[b] Folt = foaled.

[c] 'Save, we pray,' is the correct translation of Hosanna.

disciplis, and brynge to Crist þis asse and hir fole to ryde to hevenly Jerusalem. And as Jerusalem was wallid aȝens Crist and his apostlis, so þes religious to daie ben wallid aȝens Cristen men. But þis wal is mennis fyndinge, hepid wiþouten charite, for it is no charite to leve þe ordre þat Crist ȝaf, and to take þes stynkinge ordres, and telle more prys bi þis resoun;—þis synful patroun bade do þus, þerefore we shulden do þus; þan bi þis,—Crist bad alle men do þus, þerfore þei shulden do þus. He þat synneþ in þis feiþ synneþ aȝen bileve; aȝen þe mandementis of þe first table, and so aȝen alle Goddis mandementis. And þus shulden Cristen men bringe to Crist boþ þis asse and hir fole þat ben bonden in Jerusalem bi sich fals religiouse; and so þis asse and hir fole ben comen to þes pryvat ordris, but not to alle Cristene men, al if þei ben betere and have more nede. Ȝit þes ȝoldes[a] founden of men helpen al þer breþeren in nede boþe of temporal goodis and laten hem dwelle in Cristis ordre, but þes sectis of newe ordris helpen not þus þer breþeren, for, be þei olde, be þei ȝonge, be þei nevere at siche meshese[1], þei wolen not helpe hem wiþ goodis for to lyven in Cristis ordre, but raþer emprisoun hem or punishe hem aȝens Goddis lawe. But bi þe reule of charite þei shulden selle þer hiȝe housis and alle þe meblis þat þei have, and helpe þer breþeren in nede, and lyven al aftir Cristis lawe. Þus Crist ȝaf boþe bodi and soule for relevynge of his enemyes, but how lasten siche religious, or in mercy or in charite, þat wolen not ȝyve þer ydel goodis for þe helping of þer breþeren? And þus hem wantiþ hiest love and ech degre of charite, for þei loven more þer ydel muk, þan þei done þer breþeren in God. Feyned lettris of fraternite[b] wolen þei ȝyve to symple men, but

Attack upon the Friars.

[1] *myschef*, B; *mischefe*, C.

[a] Besides the old Anglo-Saxon Guilds (on which see Pearson's *Early English History*, i. 271) there were the merchant guilds, and the art guilds. The last class is probably referred to in the text. A curious account of the organization of the guild of painters at Florence in 1319, by Jacopo di Casentino, will be found in Crowe's *Hist. of Painting in Italy*, ii. 2.

[b] Chaucer, whom nothing escaped, has noted this practice of giving 'letters of fraternity,' which however had been practised by the monks for centuries before the friars were heard of. In the Sompnour's Tale, Thomas, the farmer, asks the questing friar whether he is not his 'brother.'

> 'Ye, certes, quod the frere, trusteth wel;
> I took our dame *the letter*, under our seal.'

Among the Dominicans, and proto lordis and to men þat þei seyn þat þei loven more, wolen þei not profre siche lettris, lest her falsheed be perseyved. For siche lettris of chartris profiten not to men, but oþer to make men have riȝt, or ellis to defende her riȝt. Siche lettris maken no riȝt; ȝhe bi mannis lawe; and þis riȝt is not enpechid bifore þe dai of dome; and ȝif men shewen[a] þan þes lettris oþir to God or his lawe þei profite noþing to hem ne defenden hem aȝens God, and so þes lettris ben superflue, as ben þes ordris þat maken hem.

Þe seconde Sondai Gospel in Advent.

[SERMON XXVII.]

Erunt signa in sole.—Luc. xxi. [25.]

The signs before the second Advent.

Þis gospel telliþ derkely a prophecie of Crist; how it shal be in þis Chirche bifore þe dai of dome. Crist seiþ, *Þer shal be signes in þe sunne and moone and in þe sterres of hevene, and in þe erþe pressure of folk*, by movynge of heven. For þes þre partis of hevene, sunne and moone and sterris, shal move togidere boþe see and watris; for þei ben more redy to be moved by hevene þan oþir erþe or eir, for þei ben bitwene þes two, neiþir to hevy ne to þinne; but large in quantite and disposid to take liȝt of þes þre bodies of hevene *and to be confusid and to make noise.* And siþ of þis see and watir rysen wyndis and blowen on londis, it is no wounder ȝif oure eire be chaungid in qualitees; and siþ chaunginge of oure eire makiþ chaunginge in mennis bodies, it is no wounder ȝif mennis bodies be changid bi þis eire; and so maneres, þat suen þe chaunging of mannis complexioun, shal be changid in oure erþe þat men dwelle inne; and so, *men shal wexe drye, boþe be siche erþely eir, and bi drede of oþer signes þat shal come among men.* And þanne men shal fiȝte in erþ, o cuntree wiþ anoþir, for such changing in eir shal make changinge in mennis lyfe, and þus dede bodies

bably among the Franciscans also, these letters admitted to the brotherhood of the third order, and imparted to the persons admitted the benefit of all the masses, fasts, prayers, and other good works done or to be done throughout the order. For the 'formula admissionis,' see Ducange (Paris, 1843), article 'Fraternitas.'

[a] The reader will be reminded here of a passage in the *Paradise Lost*, Book iii. 485.

cast in þe water or erþe chaungen þe eir, and alle oure places þat we dwellen inne, oþerwise þan it shulde have be in þe state of innocens; for þanne our places undir þe mone shulde have be wiþouten siche medlinge; ffor hevene worchiþ kyndely, dyversely in dyvers maters. And after al þis shal men see Crist oure Lord come from hevene, and his angelis with him, to deme men þat dwellen here; *for þe vertues of hevene*, þat ben liȝts, shal be chaungid here, and al þe governaile of hevene shal be varied þus to men. And *þanne men shal see Crist comyng doun in a cloude wiþ greet power and maieste*, to men þat can rede þes signes; and Crist confortiþ his children, and biddiþ hem putte drede awey, *ffor comynge of siche signes* bitokeneþ þat þer blisse is neiȝe; and þerfore shulden þei *rere þer heedis*, and be gladde of þes signes, and nouȝt honge þere heedis doun as men hevyed wiþ þe erþe. For what man wolde not be gladde whan he shulde go out of prison, and be brouȝt to þe blisse of hevene and passe awey fro siche peyne. *And Crist seide to his disciplis þis similitude* in kynde. *See ȝe þe gardyn of fige trees and al oþer trees of fruyte; whan þei bryngen forþ fruyte* of hem, *ye witen wel þat somer is nyȝe.* (And somer is in sum contrees time to gedre fruyte of þe erþe.) *And so whan ȝe seen þes signes be made, wite ye þat youre bigginge is nyȝe.* For biginge is clepid here fruyte þat comeþ of þis bigginge, and Crist seiþ *soþely þat þe kynrede of his children shal not passe out of þis world bifore þat alle þes þingis be done. Hevene and erþe shal passe in chaunginge, but Cristis wordis shal not passe þus.* Wel we witen þe sunne stood and sum tyme it wente aȝen, but þus mai not sentence be chaungid of þe wordis of oure Lord; but þere is more stabilhede in wordis þat ben seid of Crist þan is in hevene or erþe, siþ Crist is above þes two, and comynge in þes tweyne is not nedeful but for þat Crist haþ ordeyned it.

Þes wordis of Crist may be undirstonden goostli, so þat þe sonne be Crist, God and man, and þe mone be holy Chirche, and þe sterres in hevene be seintis in þe worlde. Signes ben made in hem, for þei moven erþely men, and chaungen as þe see temporal goodis, and for siche chaunginge chaungen men in wille, and membris of þe fend ben drye fro grace and ben adredde for Crist, and sentence of his chirche. Ffor vertues of

Mystical interpretation.

hevene shal move Cristene men to vencushe þe fendes lymes, and to feren hem, al if þei for a tyme maken greet soune, and stynkyn wiþ synne, and froþyn wiþ lecherie. And þe more fishes swelewen þe lasse; and cours of þis moone moveþ worldely men, and wyndis of pryde wawen þes floodis, so þat it is perilous to shippis for to wandre, al ȝif þei ben born up wiþ þe crosse of Crist. But wele Y wote þat men þat ben chosen of God may flottre in þe see, but þei may not perishe; for al þing mut nede come þat God himsilf haþ ordeyned. And þus sad bileve of þis þridde Advent shulde stire men fro synne and drawe hem to vertues. Ffor ȝif þei shulden to morewe answere to a juge, and wynne greet rentis or ellis lese hem, þei wolde ful bisili shape for þer answere, and myche more ȝif þei shulden wynne or lese þer lyfe—Lord! siþ we ben certeyn of þe day of dome þat it shal come to us, and we wite not how soone, and þere we shal have jugement of hevenly lyfe, or ellis of deeþ of helle þat evermore shal laste, how bisie shulde we be to make us redy for þis! Certis defaute of bileve is cause of oure sleuþe; and þus shulden we fasten in us articlis of þe trouþe, for þei wolen be louse in us as nailes in a tree, and þerfore it is nedeful to knocke and make hem faste. For it is noo drede þat no man doiþ synne but ȝif he faile in bileve upon sum manere. Sum men wanten bileve, and nevere hadden bileve, as Paynemes and oþer men þat nevere weren turned to Crist. Sum failen in bileve, for þer bileve slepiþ, and oþer þingis wakeþ þat þei trowen more; and þus failiþ ech man þat is overcomen wiþ synne; for lust wakiþ in hem to whiche þe synne moveþ hem, and peyne and drede of his synne is leide asleepe; and þus failen in trouþe þe more part of men. We shulde þenke freishely on þe day of dome, and how no þing may þan lette Cristis jugement; ffor treuþe and resoun shal fulli go forþ þanne, and herfore seiþ þe gospel þat men þan nakid fro charite shal be þanne dombe, and not shal answere to Crist. And for þis cause prophetis of Goddis lawe clepen þe daie of dome þe daie of þe Lord, for in þat daie not[1] shal go aȝens him, but þei clepen daies bifore daies of men, for þe fend and his membris have now þer purpos, al ȝif þei shal þan bie it ful dere.

Matt. xxii. 12.

[1] *nout*, B and C.

Þe Þridde Sonday Gospel in Advent.

[SERMON XXVIII.]

Cum audiisset Joannes in vinculis.—Matt. xi. [2.]

John the Baptist sending messengers to Christ.

Þis gospel telliþ a storye of Joon Baptiste þat touchiþ al þree adventis of Crist, but specialy þe þridde, to whom serven two bifore. Baptist was in prison wiþ Heroude Antipas, for he reprovede his advoutre wiþ his broþer wyf. And *Joon bounden in prison herde of Cristis werkes*, and he made moche joie and preiside myche Crist, as oþer gospellis tellen, and specialy Jones gospel. Sum men in þe countre helden Joon more þan Crist, and Jones disciplis weren in þis errour; but ȝit þei trowiden þat þe greet prophete bihiȝt in þe lawe, þat þei clepiden Messias, was more þan Joon Baptist. *And herfore sente Baptiste two of his disciplis*, for to speke wiþ Crist and purge hem of þis errour. And Jon bade hem axe þus Crist on his bihalve, *Ert þou he þat is to come*, and to save mankynde, þat þe law spekiþ of? *or we abide anoþer?* We shal suppose þat Baptist was stable in his trouþe, and coveitide þat þe feiþ of Crist and love of Crist growide, and bifore þat he were deed, þat he trowide shulde come soone. For trewe men coveiten more þe honoure of God þan þer owen honour, for ellis þei weren unreasonable. And þus cast Joon þis weye to worship of Crist, and to þis entent of Joon Crist spake and wrouȝte in dede. *Go ȝe and telle aȝen to Joon what ye have herd and sen, Blynde seen, crokide gone, meselis ben heled, deefe heeren, dede rysen, pore men ben preisid of God*[a], *and blessid be he þat shal not be sclaundrid in me.*

And on two maneres men ben sclaundrid in Crist. Sum men bi worchinge putten errours in him, and þis manere of sclaundrynge is algatis yvel, siþ þei fallen in heresie þat þus trowen of Crist. Þes men ben sufferyngly sclaundrid in Crist þat fallen fro bileve þat þei shulden have of Crist. On þe

[a] This is a different mistranslation from that found in the Wycliffite versions, which is, 'pore men ben taken to prechynge of the gospel.'

þridde maner we seyen þat men ben sclaundrid whan þei ben defamyd of ony kyn þing þat þei have hem amys aboute ony siche þing; and þus many holy men weren sclaundrid of Crist. And so, of þes sevene myraclis, þe laste is þe moste; and alle þes sevene miraclis techen how we shulden love Crist; for we þat weren first blynde bi defaute of feiþ, sen aftir in oure soule what we shulden trowe; and so first crokid in medeful werkes, wandren after in holynesse of lyf; and so first leprous by heresyes of feiþ, ben after clensid of alle þes heresyes; deef men fro Goddis word, heeren his lawe; and dede men in soule bi custome of synne, rysen to spiritual lyf of þer soule; men þat weren pore bifore for þer holy werkes, ben seid good lyvers of him [1] þat may not erre. And it semeþ þat Jones disciplis saien summe of þes miraclis, or ellis hem alle, in feiþ þat Crist ȝaf hem.

And whan þei weren wente fro Crist, he preiside Joon Baptist, techinge þat men shulden not preise a man in his presence ne in presence of his, lest he were a faioure [a]. Crist preiside Baptiste, axinge of him þre þingis, so þat þe peple were nedid to graunte þat Joon was holy. *Whan ȝe seien Baptist in desert, what wente ȝe to see? sawe ȝe a reede wawinge wiþ þe wynde?* nay, suche men ben unstable for lovynge of worldely mukke, for Joon was stable in þe love of God, and so was he groundid in þe stone of riȝt-wisnesse. *Or what wente ȝe out to see* whan ye wente to see Joon? *wher ȝe wenten to see a man cled in softe cloþis? nay, lo, men þat ben cled þus drawen hem to kyngis hous*, and ben tenderly fedde wiþ metis þat plesen þe fleishe. For Joon Baptiste was contrarie to such men in boþe þes, siþ he dwelte in desert, and was fedde wiþouten foode þat was maad bi mannis crafte, and so þe world and his fleish overcame he perfitli, and it is no drede to us þe fende hadde þan noon holde in him. *But what went ȝe out to see? certis to see a prophete; ȝhe Y seie to you, Joon was more þan a prophete*, for Joon hadde office of God to se Crist, and waishe him, and to shewe hym at eye, þat is more þan prophetis office. *And he is of whom it is writun*, þat þe Fadir spekiþ to þe Sone,

[1] So in B; *hym*, C; A has *hem*.

[a] See Glossary.

Lo Y send myn angel, þat is myn owen messenger, *to fore þi face þat shal make redy þi weie tofore þee;* for Joon Baptiste movede men to trowe in Crist many gatis.

Here men may touche many synnes þat rengnen[1] amonge men, and specialy synne of clerkes þat lyven in lustis of foode and in lustis of atire contrarie to Joon Baptiste. And þus, as þe gospel seiþ, þei putten on Joon þat he hadde a fend, and was ladde in desert bi þis spirit þat susteynede him, and he lyvede not mannis lyfe, ne ȝaf ensaumple to sue him; and in Crist þei ben sclaundrid, and seiden he lyvede a lustful lyf and was frend to synful men, and þus shulden not men lyve. And þus þese newe religiouse fallen in heresie of Jewes, for neiþer þei make Baptist ne Jesus Crist þer patroun, but þei chesen hem a newe patroun and newe religioun; þei seien þat Baptist was to harde, and Cristis lyf was to large, but þei have founden a good mene and vertues to lyven inne. And þus boþe clerkes seculers and þese newe religiouse forsaken þes two weies and taken weie of þe fend; for þere is noon oþer weie but Cristis weie and þe fendis, siþ no man may lyve in vertues but ȝif þat he sue Crist, and no man may lyve in synne but ȝif þat he sue in þat þe fend. Boþe þes endes ben to blame, but more þes newe religiouse; ffor þes ypocritis leven Crist and Joon Baptist his prophete, and chesen hem a newe wey þat mut ofte tymes be cloutid and be dispensid wiþ bi Anticrist, as þe fend techiþ hem. Þe seculers ben lasse ypocritis, but þei lyven al amys, siþ þei dwellen wiþ kyngis and lordis for to geten hem benefices; and in þe mene tyme þei lyven in lustis, and leven þe state þat þei shulden kepe; and þus blynde men leden þe blynd, and boþe fallen in þe lake. For þere nys noon oþer wey but ouþer wende upward aftir Crist or ellis to wende doun aftir þe fend into þe deppest lake of alle[2]. Ȝhe, þes þat semen in þe heyer state suen Petir in his errour, and seien, Sire, God forbede þat þou lyve þus in þi membris, for witt and worship þat þou shouldist have. And certis al siche ben Saþanas, for þei wolen reverse Crist, or addinge to Cristis lawe, or ellis wiþdrawinge þat he bad.

The friars follow neither John the Baptist nor Christ.

[1] *regnen*, B; *regne*, C.

[2] B agrees with A; C reads *hel*, which must surely be right.

Þe fourþe Sundai in Advent.

[SERMON XXIX.]

Miserunt Judei ab Jerosolumis.—Joh. i. [19.]

John the Baptist bearing testimony to Christ.

Þis gospel telliþ of godhede and manhede of Crist, and of mekenesse of Baptiste, how myche þat he lovede Crist. *Þe Jewes senten fro Jerusalem preestis and dekenes unto Joon, for to wite what he was*, and how he groundide his newe lyf. Þese Jewes semeden hiȝe preestis of þe temple and Phariseis, and *þes þat weren sent to Joon weren of Pharisees*, for þei weren lasse of state and semeden of more religioun. *But Joon confesside unto hem and denyede not* treuþe, *and so he confessid first þat he was not Crist*, for it was most perilous to be holden Crist, and þerfore he putte first þe moost peril from him. And þus lowe preestis undir hiȝe preestis of þe temple, and dekenes þat boþe kouden[1] þe olde testament, and weren more lyk Jon in manere of religioun, and betere shulden enquere of his newe ordre, lest þe toon erride and supplantide þat oþer, weren sent to Joon to axe of his state. Þere was behiȝt a greet prophete in þe olde lawe þat þei clepiden Crist, and þis myȝte Joon have be holden, ȝif he wolde be proude. And here be we tauȝt to boste not of þis þat we ben membris of holi Chirche, and so selle our suffragies, for it is hid from us where we shal be savyd, and ȝif we shal not be savyd, we ben not membris þus, ne oure preier for þis is not worþ[2] to us silfe. And to gabbe þus in þis point is a greete synne, and to take mennis goodis bi sich a fals chaffare, for a worldely man wole not selle but þat he wote is his, and God haþ ordeyned þis privy þinge to be unknowe of us. For we shulde not þus boste ne disseyve oure neiȝbores, and þus to putte of Goddis ordenaunce were a greet synne.—*Þei axiden Joon þe secounde tyme, where he were Hely, and he seide he was not þis Hely* in persone. Þe Jewes hadden in þe olde lawe þat Helye was ravyshid, and lyveþ ȝit in a place, and shal come aȝen bifore þe daye of dome, and fiȝte wiþ Antecrist, and þus þei supposiden þat Baptist was he, speciali for solitary lyf and penaunce in etyng. And to þis entent denyede Joon þat he was Hely, but Crist seide þat Joon

2 Kings ii. 11; Mal. iv. 5.

[1] So in B and C; A reads *kouden boþe*. [2] *worþi*, B and C.

was Hely in figure, for riȝt as Hely figuride the firste advent of Crist, so Joon figuride þe þridde advent of him. And as sum men seien, þei boþe figuren þe day of dome; and þus þere nys no falshede in Crist ne in Baptist.—*Þei axiden* þe thridde tyme *where Joon were þe prophete, and he seide, Nay*, to þer undirstondinge, for name of prophete bi himsilf bitokeneþ þe more famous prophete. Crist seiþ þat Joon is a comoun prophete, and boþe þes weren soþe. And affter þes þree purgingis, *þei axiden of Joon who he was, þat þei myȝten answere to men þat hadde sent hem. And Jon seide mekely upon Ysay þe prophete, þat he was a vois of cryer in desert, to bidde men make redy þe weye of oure Lord.* For riȝt as a vois shewiþ þe word of mannis þoȝt, so Jon shewide þe word of þe Fadir; and clerkes knowen wele þat a vois or soun is substanciali þat þing þat souneþ; and alȝif Joon myȝte have seide þat he was criynge, neþeles he chees to speke more mekeli; for among alle þingis vois is a freel þing.

And þe messengeris axiden Joon, whereto he baptiside and brouȝt in a newe ordre, *siþ he was noon of þes þree. But Jon answeride hem þat he baptiside in water, and on myddis of hem stood þat þei knewen not;* and þat is þe greet prophete þat þei souȝten after, for he is boþe God and man to save mankynde. In þat þat he is God he is every where myddil, as he is þe myddil persone in þe holy Trinite; and in þat þat he is man, and heed of holy Chirche, he is myddil of alle men gedrid in his name. In vertu of þis man cam Joon þus, and baptiside in water to make redy bifore Crist, as a rude werke goiþ bifore a sutil. To þis prophete servede Joon, and dide him al worship in þat þat he was God. And, for he was þis man, *he is to come after Joon, al if he be Joonis pryour.* Ffor he was not made bifore Joon in tyme, neiþer bi his manhede neiþer bi his godhede, for Joon was man bifore þat Crist was man; and as nentis godhede, Crist was not made. And þei traveilen in veyn þat calculen þat Crist was conseyved bifore þe soule of Joon was knittid to his bodi, for Joon spekiþ of forþerhede of manhede of Crist bifore Joon in grace, and also in worþynes; and herfore seiþ Joon, þat *he is not worþ to louse*[1] *þe þuong*[2] *of Cristis shoo.* And þis men undirstonden þus, þat Baptist is not

[1] *loose*, B. [2] *þong*, B.

worþi to declare Cristis manhede; but, as me þinkiþ, it is beter and more suynge þis gospel to seie, þat Joon grauntiþ him not worþi to loose þe ordre of Crist, bi which Crist hadde ordeyned to be patroun of Cristene men. For þis ordre is a þuonge to bynde mennis willes togidere; and þus me þinkiþ þat freris chiden in veyn. Prechours[a] seyn þat Crist hadde hiȝe shone as þei have; ffor ellis wolde not Baptist mene þat Crist hadde þuongis of siche schone. Menours[b] seyn þat Crist wente barfote, or ellis was shood as þei ben, for ellis Magdalene shulde not have founde to þus have washid Cristis feet. But levynge þis chidynge, we supposen of oure Jesus þat he tok ful litil hede of such manere of wendinge, but he chargide myche þe wille of his religioun and affeccioun of his disciplis to be bounden fro worldely goodis. And þus freris, as Pharisees, clensen þe gnatte and swolewen þe camel; for þei dar, above Baptist, founde hem newe ordres, of reulis þat Crist chargide not, but ȝif it were to dampne hem; and coveitise of worldely goodis chargen þes ordres not, ȝif þei be gete[1] wiþ fals menes, which treuþe of Crist haþ dampnyd. *But þis was done in Beþanye beȝonde þe water of Jordan*, in þe lond of two kynredis[c]; and so men seyen þat þer ben two Beþanies in þat lond, oon biside Jerusalem where Lazarus was reisid to lyf, and anoþer biȝonde þe water *where Joon* hadde mater *to baptise men.* For Beþanie[d] sowneþ þes þre; it is hous of obedience and also hous of penaunce, and hous of Goddis ȝifte. Alle þes names accorden to Joon; but þei ben contrarie to alle þes newe ordris þat ben presumed aȝens Crist.

Hypocrisy of the Friars.

[1] *geten*, B, C.

[a] Fratres praedicantes, or Dominicans.

[b] Fratres minores, or Franciscans.

[c] 'Þe lond of two kynredis.' For a long time I was unable to satisfy myself as to the exact meaning of this phrase. There is nothing in the Commentaries of S. Austin, S. Jerome, and the Venerable Bede, nor in the Homilies of Pope Gregory, which throws the smallest light upon it. Upon turning however to the Commentary of Nicholas de Lyra, written in the early part of the fourteenth century, I found some words which, I think, solve the difficulty. Distinguishing this Bethany (Bethabara in the authorized version) from the one near Jerusalem, De Lyra describes it as lying beyond the Jordan, 'scilicet in sorte duarum tribuum et dimidiae;' i. e. Reuben and Gad, and the half-tribe of Manasseh. Wyclif probably meant to say the same thing, but inadvertently omitted mention of the half-tribe, of which indeed very slight notice is taken in the account (Numb. xxxii.) of the negotiation between Moses and the 'lynages' (Wycl. Ver.) of Reuben and Gad.

[d] Bethany signifies 'house of dates.' (Smith's Dict. Bible.)

Þe Sondai wiþinne octave of Twelfþe dai.

[SERMON XXX.]

Vidit Johannes Jesum venientem ad se.—Joh. i. [29.]

Þis gospel telliþ a witnesse, how Baptist witnesside of Crist, boþ of his godhede and eke of his manhede. Þe storye seiþ þus, *þat Joon say Jesus comynge to him and saide* þus of oure Lord, *Lo, þe loomb of God; lo him þat takiþ awey the synnes of þis world*, for he is boþe God and man. Crist is clepid Goddis lombe, for many resouns of þe lawe. In þe olde lawe weren þei wont to offre a lombe wiþouten wem, þe whiche shulde be of o ȝere, for þe synne of þe puple. Þus Crist, þat was wiþouten wem, and of o ȝeer in mannis elde was offrid in þe cros for þe synne of al þis worlde, and where siche lambren þat weren offrid felden sum tyme to þe preestis, þis lombe þat made ende of oþer felde[1] fulli to Goddis hond. And oþer lambren in a maner fordide þe synne of o cuntre, but þis lombe proprely fordide þe synne of alle þis worlde. And þus he was ende and figure of lambren of þe olde lawe, and þus shewiþ Baptist by his double spekynge þe manhede of Crist and his godhede; for oonly God myȝte þus fordo synne, siþ alle oþer lambren hadden wemmes, þat þei myȝten not hem silfe fordo. And so, al if preestis have power to relese synne as Cristis vikeris, neþeles þei have þis power in as myche as þei acorden wiþ Crist; so þat ȝif þer keies and Cristis wille be discording atwynne, þei feynen hem falsely to assoile, and þan þei neiþer loosen ne bynden; so þat in ech siche worchynge þe godhede of Crist mut first wirche. (The second testimony of John the Baptist to Christ.)

And herfore seiþ Baptist of Crist; *Þis is he þat Y seide of, After me is to comen a man, þe whiche is made bifore me, for he was* anoon *my priour.* For riȝt as Crist was a man, þe first tyme þat he was conseyved, so God made him þan priour of al his religioun; and he was abbot, as Poul seiþ, of þe best (Eph. i. 22; Col. i. 18.)

[1] *fel*, C.

ordre þat may be. *And first Y knewe hym not;* I wiste in soule þat he was born, but Y koude not wiþ bodily eye knowe him fro anoþer man. And þis falliþ comounly; but, *for to shewe hym in Israel, þerefore Y baptise þus in water. And Joon bare witnesse, and seide þat he sey a spirit come doun as a culver from hevene* and lefte oþer *and dwelte on him. But God, þat sente me to waishe wiþ water, he tauȝt me and seide þus, On whom þou seest þe spirit come down and dwellinge upon him, þat is he þat baptiseþ men in þe Holy Goost. And Y sey and bere witnesse þat þis is Goddis kyndely sone.*

We shal wite þat þis dowfe was a verre foule as oþer ben; and so it was not þe þridde persone in Trinite taken in oonhede of þis persone, as Goddis Sone toke his manhede; but for mekenesse of þe dowfe, and moo good propirtees þat she haþ, she bitokeneþ þe þridde persone; and þis persone is seid of hir, for Joon seiþ, The Spirit cam doun and dwelte long upon Crist;—and þis Spirit was þis dowfe. And so it semeþ þat þis dowfe was God; and so, al if þe two persones may be moved in creatures, neþeles þe Trinite may not be moved in his kynde. But it semeþ þat we may graunte þat þis dowfe was þe Holy Goost, as we granten þat þis persone was comynge doun in þis dowfe. And þus, as God seiþ in his lawe þat sevene oxen ben sevene ȝeer, and þat þe sacrid breed is verrely Goddis bodi, so it semeþ þat he seiþ, þat þis dowfe is þe Holy Goost. But clerkes witen þat þer ben two manere of seyngis, þat ben personel seynge, and habitudinel seynge. Þis dowfe myȝte not be God in his kynde, but bi sum habitude it signefieþ God, and þus bi autorite of God it is God. And if þou sey þat ech þinge bi þis shulde be God, as ech Goddis creature signefieþ his maker, as smoke kyndely signefieþ fier,
Col. iii. 11. and þus semeþ Poul to speke, whan he seiþ þat Crist shal be al þingis in al þingis to men þat undirstonden him; for after þe day of dome al þis worlde shal be a boke, and in ech part þerof shal be God writun, as God shal be in his kynde in ech part of þe world; and þus siþ God is bitokened first and moost in ech þinge, whi may men not graunten þat God is ech þinge? —in þis men mut undirstonde dyversite in wordis, and to what
The clergy should speak entent þes wordis ben undirstonden. And þus bi autorite of þe

lawe of God men shulden speke her wordis as Goddis lawe spekiþ, and strange not in speche from undirstondinge of þe puple, and algatis beware þat þe puple undirstonde wel, and so use comoun speche in þer owne persone; and ȝif þei speken in Cristis persone wordis of his lawe, loke þat þei declare hem, for drede of privy errours.

In a tongue understood by the people.

And scorne we þe argumentis þat foolis maken here, þat bi þe same skile shulde we speken þus, for God spekiþ þus in wordis of his lawe. Sich apes lickenes[1] passen beestis foly, for þei wolden brynge bi þis þat ech man were God. And so ȝyve we God leve to speke as him likeþ, al if we speken not ay so bi þe same autorite; þes wordis þat God spekiþ shulde we algatis graunt, and declare hem to trewe undirstondinge. And rekke we not of argumentis þat sophistis maken, þat we ben redargued, grantynge þat we denyen, for we granten þe sentence and not oonli þe wordis, for þe wordis passen awey anoon whan we have spoken hem. And as Aristotle seiþ[a], contradicioun is not oonly in wordis but boþe in wordis and sentence of wordis. And bi þis we seien þat Crist in speche is not contrarie to him silfe, ne o part of his lawe contrarie to anoþir. And þus ȝif we graunten þat Crist is al þingis, it sueþ not hereof þat Crist is an asse, ne þat Crist is ech þing, or what þat we wolen nempnen. For God seiþ þe tone and he seiþ nouȝt þe toþir. But we graunten þat Crist is boþe lombe and sheepe, for Goddis lawe grauntiþ boþe þes two of him; and so Crist is a lioun and a worm; and þus of many þingis þat holy writt telliþ. And it is ynow to seie for dyversite, þat God haþ special sentence of on and not so of anoþer. And þus þe comyn undirstondinge shulden we algatis holden, but ȝif Goddis wordis tauȝten us his propre sense. And siche stryfe in wordis is of noo profite, ne proveþ not þat Goddis word is ony wey fals. In þis mater we have ynow stryfen in Latyn[b] wiþ adversaries of Goddis lawe, þat seyen þat it is falsest of alle lawes in þis world þat ever God suffride.

Sophistical arguments.

[1] *apis licnessis*, B and C.

[a] Analyt. Prior. ii. 15.
[b] Wyclif probably refers here to the treatise *De Veritate Scripturae*.

Þe Gospel on octave of Twelfþe Dai, and it falliþ sumtyme on Sundai.

[SERMON XXXI.]

Venit Jesus Galilea.—Matt. iii. [13.]

The baptism of Christ.

Þis gospel telliþ how Crist tauȝte Baptist boþe bi word and myracle how he shulde be meke. Þe stôrye telliþ þat *Jesus cam fro Galilee to Jordan to Joon* Baptist, *to be baptisid of him.* And þis was greet mekenesse, þat þe Lord wolde come so fer to his servaunt, and to take of him baptym, *and Johan forfendide him*, for woundringe of þe dede, and seide *þat Y shal be baptisid of þee, and þou comest to me: to be* þus *baptisid. But Jesus answeride to Joon, and seide to him wiseli, Suffre now þis, for it falliþ to us to fulfille al riȝt.* It is opyn riȝt þat þe lasse be suget to þe more, and it is more privy riȝt þat þe evene obeishe to þe evene; but most privy riȝt of alle stondiþ in þis, þat þe hiȝeste of alle obeishe to his servaunt, as Crist priour of us alle obeishide to Baptist; and so was it sittinge Crist to teche þis mekenesse. And here schulen we wite, as men in comyn speche seien sum wordis rehersid hem of oþer, and sum wordis þei seien in her owne persone, (and þis may be varied after þre maneris; sum þing men seien, witinge þat it is soþ, affermynge þe sentence wiþouten ony condicioun, as trewe men seien þat God is in hevene; sum þing men seien, proposinge to fulfille it, but undirstonden, if God wole ȝyve hem grace, as men seyen þat þei shulen holde Goddis comandementis, and þus techiþ James, þat whan we speken of oure dedes þat we shulden do, we shulden undirstonde, 'if þat God wole;' but ȝit on þe þridde maner we supposen þat it shulde be þus, and neiþer we witen it ne trowen it;) and wiþ þis we undirstonden a condicioun, 'if God wole;' and þus spake Baptist whan he forfendide Crist to be baptisid of him, and herwiþ he heeld obedience. But over þis we shulde wite, þat þere is greet diversite bitwixe servise of a þing and obedience þerof, for God obeishide to mannis vois, and servede not to him; but in mannis persone þei rennen boþe togidere, for þe more obeishiþ to þe lesse, and eke serveþ to him, for þe more is erþ, and þe lesse is spirit, and so he is boþe more and lesse to his servaunt. And þus Crist fulfillide al manere of riȝtwisnesse, for riȝtwisnesse is comounly callid al manere of vertue, and so riȝtwisnesse is al manere of mekenesse.

And þus John suffride Crist to tak þis servise of him, and ȝit he seide soiþ in wordis þat he spake, for Johun was baptisid of Crist as he shulde, siþ he was baptisid of the Holy Goost; and werkes of þe Trinite ben undepartid wiþoutenforþ. And wiþ þis cam Crist to be baptisid in water of John, as he shulde for many enchesouns. First to teche þis moost degree of mekenesse. Siþ, for to halowe þe water of baptym, for vertue of touchinge of Crist streechide ful fer. Þe þridde cause is to ȝyve us ensaumple to take mekely baptem, siþ Crist was baptisid þus. And *herfore John leet Crist to be baptisid of him*, for Joon was tauȝt in his soule þat it was Goddis wille. And here takiþ men wel þat if a man avowe a þinge, and he wite after þat it were betere to leve it, þanne he shal leve it, and have sorewe of his foly biheste, but him nediþ not to go to Rome to perfourme þis medeful dede. And here manye ben disseyved in power of þer sovereynes; þei wenen þat hem nediþ to have leve of hem to do as þei shulden do; þis lore shulden men taken of þer prelatis above, and not traveilen in veyn, ne dispende more þan þei shulden. *And whan Jesus was þus baptisid, he wente anoon out of þe water*, to teche us þat in siche meenes we shulden not dwelle more þan nede is[1], and to confermen al þis þing, *hevenes weren opened*, to Crist, *and he siȝ þe spirit of God comynge down as a dowve and comynge upon Crist.* And þis þing þat he siȝ wiþ his eye was a dowfe, and þis þing þat he siþ wiþ his soule was God; and þus þe spirit of God cam doun in a dowve, *and þere was a vois comynge doun from hevene, and seide* in þe persone of þe Fadir, *Þis is my Sone*, ȝhe, *þat Y* kyndely *love, in whiche Y pleside to my silfe*, and þerfore, *heere ȝe him.*

For dispensation from foolish vows a visit to Rome is not necessary.

And so bi autorite of þe Fadir of hevene and eke bi autorite of þe Holy Goost, and also bi autorite of Goddis kyndeli Sone, was þe manhede of Crist here shewid wiþ his dedes. Bi autorite of Crist shulden Cristene men trowe, þat he is þe

[1] This clause is rightly written in B; in A and C it appears as a quotation.

best man, þe wiseste, and þe beste willid, þat mai be in þe world; siþ he is boþe God and man. And herof wole it sue þat Cristis owne ordre is beter þan ony newe ordre founde of synful men, for ellis hadde Crist failid in power, in witt, or in wille; and, for þis is aȝens bileve, þerfore þei feilen in feiþ þat trowen þat þes newe religious passen Cristis religioun. And herfore he ordeynede his ordre to stonde in vertues of mannis soule and not in sensible signes. And as þe holy Trinite approvede Crist here, so it approveþ þe ordre þat he made, and putte it in þes þree þingis, in obedience to God, in poverte, and chastite wel undirstonden. Men may undirstonden amys þis obedience to Crist, and trowe þat it stondiþ in doinge of ech þinge þat þi privat priour biddiþ þee do; and certis þanne þou puttest him to be unsynful above Crist, or ellis þat þou shuldist do his wille aȝens Crist. Certis Crist haþ no power to lyve as þis prelat doiþ, but if Crist hadde fredom to falle in synne, and þus þis pryour were more free þan Crist. And herfore shulde we trowe þat ech obedience to man is as myche worþ as it techiþ obedience to God; and if it faile herfro bi unobedience, men shulden leve þis as venym contrarie to obedience; for ech verry obedience is obedience to God, and men shulden more obeishe to God þan to ony creature. And so unobedience brouȝt yn bi þes newe ordres fouliþ many heepis of men bi foly of her prelatis. Soþeli in þes newe ordres men shulden obeishe to ech þing þat techiþ more obedience to God þan done siche prelatis. And it is not bileve þat þei techen betere obedience to God þan doiþ ony oþer lawe or þingis þat speken to þes ordris. And þis movede Poul and oþer Apostlis to holden hem to Cristis ordre, siþ þe abbot is betere, þe reule, and þe knyȝtis; and algatis it is more free to holde Goddis comandementis. For þis feyned obedience lettiþ ofte to serve Crist, and herfore men shulden lerne obedience, to aȝenstonde. Whan ony creature of God biddiþ þee do contrarie to þat þat þi prelat þiddiþ þee do bi expresse signes, and God bi his creature biddiþ þee do þe contrarie, þanne þou shuldist aȝenstonde þi prelate in þis, and obeishe to God in what signe þat he usiþ. On þis maner Petre and oþer apostlis seiden þat men moten more obeishe to God þan to man, and Goddis lawe seiþ þat

The order that Christ founded.

God obeishide to mannis vois; for to ech þing men shulden obeishe in þat þat it sowneþ obedience to God. And if þis bileve were kept wel, þis newe obedience shulde gone aweie.

Þe firste Sondai Gospel after octave of Twelfþe day.

[SERMON XXXII.]

Cum factus esset Jesus.—Luc. ii. [42.]

Jesus questioning with the Doctors.

Þis gospel telliþ a lore of Crist whan he was twelfe ȝeer olde, and þis lore is ful of myraclis as oþer dedis ben þat he dide. Þe story telliþ þat, *whan Jesus was maad of twelfe ȝeer olde he wente wiþ Joseph and Marye unto Jerusalem, as þei hadden custum at Paske for to make þis pilgrimage. And whan þe daies weren endid*, of makinge of þis pilgrimage, *his fadir and his modir wenten hoom, and Crist lefte aloone in þe citee. And his fadir and his modir wisten not þat Jesus was left bihynde*, for children hadden in free custom to chese wheþer þat þei wolden wende wiþ fadir or wiþ modir; and þus Joseph wende þat Crist hadde come wiþ his modir, and oure Lady supposide þat Crist hadde come wiþ Joseph. And among Jewis was þis religioun kept, þat men shulden go bi hemsilf, and wymen bi hemsilf; for þei kepten hem fro lecherie in siche pilgrimage; but now pilgrimage is mene for to do lecherie. And al þis ordeyned oure maister for to teche his Chirche to enfourme þe prelatis after general doinge[1][a], for errour in hem is more, and more harmful to þe Chirche. And whan þei weren met togidir, and wantiden þe child Jesus, *þei wenden þat he hade*[2] *ben in felowship wiþ sum kyn of his freendis, and þei wenten aȝen to* seke him amonge hem, *and oo dai þei wenten aȝen and fond him not* in þe wey. Þe þridde dale þei souȝten in þe citee, and þei fond him not, and *after þe þridde day þei fond him in þe temple, sittynge amonge doctours, heerynge and axinge hem.* No drede þat ne Crist kepte good order in his doinge, ffirst heerynge and after axinge

Dangers of the modern custom of pilgrimages.

[1] *doyngis*, C. [2] *badde*, B; *bad*, C.

[a] The meaning seems to be, 'in order to teach his Church so to fashion the mode of life of her prelates as that it may serve for a general example.'

wordis of þe lawe. *And alle þat herden him hadden wounder upon his wisdom and his answeris*, and seynge þe ȝouþe of þe childe *þei hadden wounder* of his dedis. *And his moder seide to him, Sone, whi didist þou þus to us? lo, þi fadir and Y boþe sorwynge have souȝt þee. And Crist seide unto hem, Wherto have ȝe souȝt me? ne wisten ȝe not þat Y moste be in þe nedis of my Fadir?* And here shulde prelatis lerne first to worshipe þer God, and to serve his Chirche, bifore þat þei bisieden hem aboute worldely werkes. For[1] ech man shulde serve God bifore þat he servede oþer þing, for his first entent shulde be to worship God whatever he dide; and þis mut nede be in Crist, for he did al þingis as he shulde. *But þei undirstooden not þe word þanne þat Crist spake here to hem.* And Crist wente doun wiþ hem fro Jerusalem to *Nazareþ, and he was suget unto hem*, in þingis þat þei baden him do. *And his moder kepte alle þes wordis, berynge hem in her herte. And Jesus profitide in wisdom, in age, and in grace boþe to God and to man.*

We shal wite þat oure Jesus, siþ he was þis manhede, and suget to oþer men, and growide[2] in wexinge and elde, he profitide in kunnynge which þat cam of his wittis; but he had cunnynge of godhede and blesside cunnynge of man, bi which he was in al his tyme yliche wiys and knewe al þing. Here may holy Chirche knowe boþ þe religioun of Crist and partis of þis religioun, as obedience and mekenesse. For Crist was suget to his lesse, and servede hem ful mekely, for Goddis lawe tauȝte him þat þei weren in spirit more þan Crist was bodily. And Goddis reule shulde suffice to men, al if þei cloutiden not newe reulis. For Crist tauȝte perfitli a ful reule for al Cristene men, and it is a foul pryde to cloute our errours to his wisdom, for olde cloiþ cloutid to newe makiþ more hole, as Crist seiþ. And we ben certeyne of oure bileve, þat Crist haþ mesurid his ordre in liȝtnesse and in fredom more þan oþer men kunnen shape. How shulden blynde foolis after amende þis reule þat Crist haþ ȝovun? And so God enformeþ men of þes pryvat ordres þat þre þingis of her ordres ben ydil and noyous; first þer clouting of þer reule, and siþ þer obedience, and after þer obligacioun to þer

Christ's obedience preferable to that imposed by monastic rule.

Matt. ix. 16.

[1] So B and C; A has 'And, for,' which gives no sense. [2] So B; *grouyd*, C; A has *growiþ*.

habitis and oþer uses. First, Cristis reule were fulli suffisant to alle men, and more free and more liȝt, and of more autorite. How myȝte þe fend for shame combre men wiþ sich cloutinge? And ȝif a man shulde wende aweie, it were noo nede to charge him wiþ þingis þat weren unprofitable ȝif he hadde ynowȝ bisyde. And so as God forfendiþ men to adde to his lawe, or for to drawe þerefro, for it is made in ful mesure, riȝt so we shulden holde his reule bi whiche he techiþ al Cristene men, neiþer adde to ne drawe þerfro, lest we peiren Goddis ordenaunce. And litil errour in þis bileve growiþ to more in longe tyme, and þis fendis blasfemye in God disturbliþ þe Chirche more and more. As anentis obedience, it is knowen þat Cristis obedience kept clene were sufficient to alle men here on lyf, and oþer obedience þat is cloutid doiþ harm manye weies. For it supposiþ þat þis prelate erriþ not in his commandementis, but ever more biddiþ his sugettis þe same þinge þat God biddiþ; and þus ech prelat shulde be yliche-wyse and evene wiþ God; and whan þei ben made prelatis bi synful menes as ofte falliþ, God shulde algatis ȝyve hem witt, and conferme hem in grace; for if þei myȝten after do synne, þei myȝten be proud in þer prelacie and reule þer sugettis amys aȝen þe comandementis of God. And þan were it profitable to wante siche blynde leders, siþ affiance in God and proving of his governaile myȝte not faile to men but ȝif þei shal faile first.—Lord! whi ordeynede not God siche ordris in þe olde lawe ne in state of innocense; but distryede newe þat weren mad? wher God be not as wise as he was in þe olde lawe, and ordeniþ[1] now for his spouse as tendirly as he dide þanne? And þus alle newe ordres ben ful of heresie. And as anentis þes newe habitis, certeinly þei ben of þe fend, but ȝif þere be sum nedeful cause byndynge men þus to hem, for ellis þei weren superflue, and not of God but of þe fend, siþ þei tarrien[2][a] mennis wittis and her kepynge fro Goddis werkes. But it is knowen þinge to men þat þes habitis profiten not to

[1] This is the reading of C; A and B have *ordeynede*, clearly the wrong tense. [2] *tauȝten*, C.

[a] Some words seem to have dropt out here, (though the MSS. consulted all concur in the reading given in the text,) which would have completed the sense, which is, that to attach more importance to the friar's habit than to counsels or commandments of God, is to do the devil's work.

werkes of vertues, but hiden þes ypocritis, siþ þei may wiþ siche habitis be quyke fendis in þis world. And ȝif þei profite bi ony caas, þei done harm ofter, as doiþ synne, and crien to men ypocrisie of siche ordris þat usen hem. And ȝif þes signes ben fals, þei maken men fals þat usen hem; and so algatis, siþ vertues myȝte be kepte wiþouten sich signes more pryvyly and sikirly, þei ben brouȝt in bi þe fende, and specialy, to charge hem more þan conseilis or mandementis of God. Ech man mut hav sum custom, but loke he wedde him not þerwiþ, ne bisye him not þat it be kepte of many men, for þei ben dyverse and axen dyverse costoms aftir þat God moveþ hym.

ÞE SECOUNDE SONDAY GOSPEL AFTIR OCTAVE OF TWELFÞE DAY.

[SERMON XXXIII.]

Nuptiae factae sunt in Chana Galilee.—JOH. ii. [1.]

The marriage at Cana in Galilee.

Þis gospel telliþ of þe first myracle þat Crist dide in presence of his disciplis. And þus telliþ þe story, *þat weddingis weren made in a litil dwellinge place in þe contre of Galile, and Jesus' moder was þere, wiþ Jesus and his disciplis.* For as men seyen comounly, Joon Evangelist was weddid here[a], and Crist was his cosyn, and Cristis modir was his aunte; and herfore þei weren homelyer in þis weddinge of Joon. Studie we not to what woman þis Joon was weddid, ne axe we not autorite to prove þat Joon was weddid now; ffor þat þe gospel seiþ here is ynow to Cristen feiþ. *And whan wyn failide, at þis feste, Jesus modir seide to him, Þei have noo wyn.* And herby þis Lady ment on curtays manere as she durst, þat Jesus shulde helpe þis feste of

[a] This myth, for it is nothing more, appears in its complete form in De Lyra (Biblia Sacra, Lugduni, 1589). 'Dicitur communiter quod istae nuptiae fuerunt Johannis Evangelistae a quibus eum Christus vocavit ante consummationem matrimonii per copulam carnis.' There is no trace of it in the works of St. Austin or St. Jerome, nor, according to Cave (*Antiq. Apostolicae*, p. 118), in any of 'the Fathers and best writers of the Church.' Bede (Prol. in Joh. Evang.) says, 'Hic est Joannes Evangelista . . . . qui virgo a Deo electus est; quem de nuptiis, volentem nubere, vocavit Deus.' But he does not identify these 'nuptiae' with the marriage at Cana.

wyn bi his myracle. But *Jesus answerede*, strangely, *What is þat to me and to þee, woman?* as if he seide, Y have not by my manhede of þee for to do siche myraclis, but þerto nediþ my godhede; but afterward shal tyme come whan Y shal offre my bodi þat Y hadde of þee, for savynge of mankynde. And herfore notiþ Austyn[a] how Jesus Crist clepiþ specialy in þes two places his moder, woman, and here he figuride his speche in his passioun. And to þis entent seiþ Crist, *þat his hour is not ȝit comen*, in which he shulde bi suffringe putte his bodi in werke. But his modir, supposinge ay good of hir sone, *seide to þe mynystris to do what ever he seide. And þere were at þe feste sixe water pottis sett, and ech of hem held a galoun or more.*—Þe Jewis hadden a custoum to washe hem ofte, for touching or seynge of þinge clene ynow, as Seint Mark meneþ in his gospel. Mark vii. 4. *Jesus bade þe servauntis fille þe pottis with watir, and þei filliden hem alle up to þe mouþe. And Jesus seide þan, Helde out now, and bere þe persoun:*—an architriclyn was he, þat was clepid to blesse þe feeste, and principal[1] in þe hous þat was of þre stages, as ȝif it were now a persone of a churche. *And þei baren to þis persoun þe wyn þat Jesus hadde made. And whan he hadde tastid þerof, and wiste not how it came, but þe servauntis wisten wel þat drowen þe water, he clepide þe spouse of þe hous, and seide to him þus, Þes men þat festen oþer putten first good wyn*, whan þer tast is freishe, for to juge þe goodnesse, *and after whan þei ben drunken and þer taist failiþ, þanne he puttiþ wers wyn*, but þou doist even þe contrarie, for, *þou hast kept good wyn unto þis tyme. Þis was þe bigynnynge of signes þat Jesus dide in Galile, and shewide his glorie*, bi doinge of þis myracle, *and his disciplis trowiden in him.*

Interpretation.

Þis wedding bitokeneþ love þat God hadde to his Chirche, how he wolde bicome man, and be newe weddid to it. And herfor was Crist not bigamus, ne brake not his matrimonye,

[1] So B; A and C have *principaly*.

[a] The interpretation throughout this sermon is generally founded on S. Austin's eighth Tractate *In Johannis Evangelium*. Compare the following passage: 'Miraculum autem quod facturus erat, secundum divinitatem facturus erat, non secundum infirmitatem; secundum quod Deus erat, non secundum quod infirmus natus erat. . . . . . Miraculum ergo exigebat mater, at ille tanquam non agnoscit viscera humana, operaturus facta divina, tanquam dicens, Quod de me facit miraculum, non tu genuisti; divinitatem meam non tu genuisti: sed quia genuisti infirmitatem meam, tunc te cognoscam, cum ipsa infirmitas pendebit in cruce.'

siþ þe same Chirche his wyf lastiþ ever more, but wiþ newe wenchis is Crist now weddid, and on newe maner he kepte his firste matrimonye; as, if a spouse of a wife were newe cled, herfore were not dyvors made bytwene hem. A newe weddinge wiþ membris of þis grete womman makiþ not divors, ne bryngiþ in no bigamye; as, if a wyf growide and hadde many partis þat she hadde not bifore, sche were not þerfore lefte. And þus Chana, þat is gelousnes[1], and Galilee, þat is a turnynge whele, bitokenen þe love of Crist þat he hadde to conforte his spouse in þis weie, and brynge her after to blisse in þe chaumbre of hevene.—Þe turnynge of þis water into good wyn techiþ hou Crist made his lawe more savery, as þe wyne was beter þan þe water bifore. And riȝt as o substaunce is first water and siþ wyne, riȝt so o lawe is first colde and siþ hote; and herfore seiþ Crist þat he came not to fordo þe lawe but to fulfille þe lawe, and make it more savery. And drede we not þes philosophris to graunte hem aptly þat þe same substaunce is first watir and siþ wyne, ne drede we not dyvynes þat axen in þis cas, what was maad newe of Crist in þis myracle; siþ qualite, as coloure or savoure of wyne, may not be by it silf. As Austyn seiþ[n], we shal wite þat myracle of Crist was wrouȝt here, so þat riȝt as water, þat first was in þe erþe, is drawen in to þe vyne tree, and siþ in to þe grapis, and by tyme defyed[2] til þat it be wyne, so Crist did þis chaunginge in a litil tyme; but more myracle was of beteringe of his lawe, and þe moste of alle, of swifte turnynge to it. Þes sixe water pottis þat helden þis colde water ben men of þe olde lawe þat kepten Goddis lawe. But þei weren sixe, for fro ȝeer to ȝeer þei kepten þis lawe þat was hard as stones, and made hem colde on oþer manere þan þe newe lawe; for it makiþ men liȝt, and hetiþ hem, and confortiþ hem, as wyn doiþ mannis bodi. As philosophris seyn, þes mesures of þes vessilis ben þe olde cerymonyes þat weren beden of God, and sum founden of Jewis, and al þes weren fillid of Crist. But, to anoþer witt, þis archytryclyn was

[1] *gelousnesse*, B and C. [2] *defied*, B, C.

[n] 'Sicut enim quod miserunt ministri in hydrias, in vinum conversum est opere Domini, sic et quod nubes fundunt, in vinum convertitur ejusdem opere Domini. Illud autem non miramur, quia omni anno fit; assiduitate amisit admirationem.' S. Aug. *loc. cit.*

þe manheed of Crist, for he made þis myracle bi his godhede. He was þe first þat tastide þis wyn and ȝaf it þes propreetes, boþe in him and oþers; and doinge of þis myracle passide mannis feestyng, for God puttiþ him silfe to be boþe mete and drynke to men þat he fediþ, and he is þe best. For worldely festyng is first savery to man, and siþ it is bittir as wermode[1] to hym; but goostly foode aȝenward first is unsavery, and siþ it is swete, whan men defien[a] it, for Goddis lawe savouriþ wele whan it is defoulid, as spicerye ȝyveþ smell whan it is powned, but dritte, ȝif stired more, is more unsavery, and þus þe ȝyvyng of þe lawe of God was ground and bigynnyng of Cristen mennis religioun. And þus þe disciplis of Crist, alle þat he haþ ordeyned for to come to hevene bi riȝt bileve, trowen in him bi vertue of þis wyne; and þus is Crist glorified in hevene and in erþe bi strengþe of his lawe þat he þus ȝaf.

Þridde Sondai Gospel after Octave of Twelfþ dai.

[SERMON XXXIV.]

Cum descendisset Jesus de monte.—Matt. viii. [1.]

Þis gospel telliþ of two myraclis þat Crist dide, and conteyneþ myche witt aboute þes two myraclis. Þe story telliþ how *Jesus cam doun of þe hille, whan he hadde ȝovun his lawe to his disciplis, and a myche peple suede him*, for devocioun þat þei hadden in his lawe, and eke in his wordis. *And lo, þere cam a mesel man, and loutide him and seide, Lord, ȝif þou wolt, þou maist hele me. And Crist seide he wold, and bade him be hole.* It is comounly supposid þat þis leprous man trowide þat Crist was boþe God and man, and so Crist myȝte hele him, but of his owne worþinesse affiede he not þis; and herfore he seide þat, ȝif Crist wolde, he myȝte hele him of his lepre, and þan was Crist God. And God wolde þat proude men and leprous heretikes wolden wel confesse þe feiþ, and þan shulden þei be hool. And *Crist stretchid out his hond, and touchide him, and seide, Y wole make*

The healing of the leper.

[1] *wormood*, B; *wormode*, C.

[a] The following passage from the first Wycliffite version (1 Sam. xxv. 37), throws light on the meaning of the text:—'Forsoþe eerli, whanne Naabal hadde *defied* þe wyn, his wyf shewide to him þes wordis.'

þee hoole, and able þee þerto; and þus doiþ God to whom he ȝyveþ grace. *And anoon was clensid þe lepre of þis man.* And þis hasty helynge bitokeneþ þis myracle; and þat Crist touchide þis leprouse techiþ us now þat þe manhede of Crist was instrument to his godhede, for to do myraclis þat he wolde weren do[1], and þat touchinge of leprouse men was leveful to men þat þus wolden helpe hem. But Crist myȝt not be blemyshid by touchinge of þis leprouse; and so tauȝte Crist his everlasting good wille, and tauȝte us to performe þe good wille that we have. *And after Crist bade him, See þat þou telle no man, but go and shewe him to þe preest, and offre þat ȝifte þat Moises bad in witnesse of siche helþe.*

Mystical interpretation of the miracle.

And so men seien, on þree maneris may þis word be undirstonden. First þat þis man shulde telle no man herof bifore þat he had offrid þat Crist bad him do. Þe secounde cause and betere is, þat Crist bad þis, to teche us to flee boost, and þanke of siche men to whiche we done good bi maner of mercy; and þus we shulden not telle þis, bi entent of mannis þank. Þe þridde weye seiþ, þat Crist bad þis negatife, to flee sclaundre of Goddis lawe and man, and flee bostinge of himsilfe, and conseyvynge of yvel of God. And, for þe olde lawe was þan ceesid, Crist bad fille þis lawe as autor þerof. And þus whan a man shewiþ by his holy lyf, actif lyf, þat is two dowfe bryddis, or contemplative lyf, þat is a paire of turturs, bi siche signes he shewiþ þat his synne is forȝovun, and þat unto preestis þat wel undirstonden þis. And þus synful men shulden conseile with preestis, and take of hem medecine to fle more synne.

Healing of the centurion's servant.

Þe secounde myracle techiþ how Crist helide an heþene man, for love of centurion þat kepte Capharnaum, þat was heed toun of þe contre of Galile. *Þis centurio tolde Crist þat his child lay in his hous syke on the palesie, and was yvel turmentid.* But Luke telliþ how þis knyȝt dide al þis by olde men of þe Jewis þat myche preisiden þis knyȝt, and seiden þat he was frend to hem, and bilde hem a synagoge. And Crist cam wiþ hem nyȝe to þis knyȝtis hous, and þis knyȝt seide þus unto Jesus Crist, *Lord, Y am not worþi þat þou entre under my roof, but seie oonly wiþ word, and my servant*

[1] *wer done*, C.

shal be hool. For Y am a man putt in þis place bi power of þe emperour, havynge under me knyȝtis, for to do myn office, *and Y seide to on, Go, and he goiþ, and Y seide to anoþer, Come, and he comeþ, and Y seide to my servaunt, Do þis, and he doiþ it.* And bi þis wolde þis knyȝt mene þat Crist hadde no nede to entre in to his hous to hele þis seke man, siþ Crist is God Almyȝty, under no power. Jesus *herynge þes wordis woundride* in hise wittis: al if he wist and ordeyned bifore þat þis knyȝt shulde þus trowe[1], and herfore *seide Crist to þe folk þat sueden him, Soþely Y seid to you, Y fond not so myche feiþ in al þe folk of Israel*, neiþer preestis ne comouns. Crist mente not of hise apostlis ne of his modir ne of his maynè, for þei weren take from Israel, as Crist was here a strange lord. And herfore bihetiþ Crist his Chirche þat shal be of heþene men, þat *many of þe este and west shal come and reste wiþ patriarkes in þe kyngdom of hevene*, where children of þis rewme shal be putt out, and cast into helle; *þere shal be wepynge*, þat is, sensible sorewe, *and gnastinge of teeþ*, þat is more, for it is peyne of harm of blisse, þat passiþ al sensible peyn. *And Jesus seide efte to þis knyȝt, Go, and þi servaunt shal be hool; for as þou trowist*, bi my grace, *be it done unto þee. And þe childe was maad hoole in þe same houre*, þat Crist spake þus. We shal wite þat feiþ is a ȝifte of God, and so God may not ȝyve it to man but ȝif he ȝyve it graciousely. And þus alle goodis þat men have been ȝiftes of God, and þus whan God rewardiþ a good werk of man, he corouneþ his owne ȝifte. And þis is of grace, for alle þingis ben of grace þat men have of wille of God; and Goddis goodnesse is firste cause why he ȝyveþ men þes goodis. And so it may not be þat God do good to men, but ȝif he do þes goodes freely bi his grace. And wiþ þis we shall graunte þat men disserven of God; for in grace þei maken hem worthi to have þis good of God; but we shal not undirstonde þat ech grace of God is a lump of þingis þat may be bi hymself, but grace is a manere in man bi which he is graciouse to God, and oþer grace on Goddis side is good wille of God. And for siche grace in God men resceyven grace in hem, and chiding of ydiotis, as was Pilagius and oþer, þat conseyven not

Interpretation.

The error of Pelagius.

[1] So in B; *towe*, A; *betrew*, C.

þat a þing may be but ȝif it be bi himsilf, as ben substancis, is for to scorne and to leve to foolis. For nyne kyndis of accidentis have contrary manere, siþ ech of hem is a manere of substance of a þing, and it may not be by himsilf, as heretikes dreemen. And herfore leeve we þis, and lerne we of þis knyȝt to be meke in herte in word and in dede, for he grauntide first þat he was under mannis power, and ȝit bi power of man he myȝt do many þingis; myche more shulden we knowe þat we ben undir Goddis power, and þat we may do noo þinge but by power of[1] God; and ȝif we disusen þis power, woo shal us be þerefore. And so þis rote of mekenesse shal gete oþer vertues to us, and grace of God to disserve mede of hevene and goodis of glorie, as it was in þe gentil knyȝte.

Þe fourþe Sonday Gospel after Octave of Twelfþe dai.

[SERMON XXXV.]

Ascendente Jesu in naviculam.—Matt. viii. [23.]

Christ stills the tempest.

Þis gospel telliþ a myracle þat Crist dide in þe water, and syche myraclis confermen þe feiþ of holy Chirche ful myche in rude men; al ȝif þei ben hard. And so doinge of myraclis in water and londe bitokneþ þat Crist shewide his woundris to dyverse men. Sum resseyveden hem not to hele of her soule, for þei weren unstable as water, and fordiden soone Cristis prente[2]; but oþer men weren stable as lond, þat helden þe prente þat Crist putt in hem, and bi þe ground of siche feiþ þei wenten fulli þe wey to hevene. Þe storye telliþ of Jesus þat he *stepide in to a boote, and his disciplis sueden him. And lo, þe water movede fast, so þat þe boot was hid with wawis, for þe wynd and þe water weren contrarye to hem:——Criste slepte* in þis tyme[3] in þe boot, as he hadde ordeyned. Þe *disciplis comen and wakiden him, and seide þus to Crist, Lord, save us, for we perishen. And Crist seide to hem, What dreden ȝe of litil feiþ? And Crist roos up anoon, and comandide to þe wyndis and þe water, and þei weren restid anoon. And al þe puple woundride*

[1] om. A. [2] *prynte*, B. [3] A and B include the words 'in þis' in the italics; C rightly excludes them.

herof, and saiden among hem selfe, What is he þis, for the wyndis and þe see obeishen to him?

Interpretation.

Siþe alle þe dedes þat Crist dide techen men how þei shulden do, þis restyng of Crist in þis boot bitokeneþ lore to be markid. We shulden be tymes reste, and preye to God in scilence[1], and heere of him heelful lore þat we shulden after teche þe puple. And þus shulde techers flee preisynge of þe peple, as Crist dide. And þis is a pryvy synne amonge men þat prechen to þe puple, and certis it is a greet synne, for God shulde have al hool þe þank. And þus þe sleping of Crist bitokeneþ his verre manhede, and makiþ his[2] myracle more, and to preye him hertlier in nede. And þus al oonli we dreden for defaute of feiþ in us, and Crist slepiþ not to us but for defaute of feiþ, for þe godhede may not slepe, and ȝit we speken unto him, Ryse, why slepist þou, Lord? and helpe us in þis nede. And þus on two maneres failiþ bileve in men. First, whan men wantiþ bileve, as þes þat trowiden not þat Crist was God; for ȝif þei hadden trowid þis hooli, þei shulde have trowid þat Crist myȝte slepinge have done þis myracle and myche more. On þe secounde manere failiþ bileve, whan it worchiþ not wele in dede, but is ydel as a slepynge man; and þan clerkes seyen it is in habite[a]. And þus may no man do synne but ȝif his bileve faile ouþer on oo manere or on oþer; for ȝif he hadde freishely bileve how foul his synne is, and hou myche it harmeþ him, he wolde not for al þis worlde do þis synne, but fleen it. And herfore preyden disciplis to alarge him[3] bileve, and Crist seide to Petre, Whi doutist þou of litil bileve? And Crist seide to a man þat he shulde trowe, for alle þingis ben possible to men þat bileve. And shortly no kyn vertue was preisid more of Crist þan was riȝt bileve, for it is ground of alle oþer; ne doute we not how bileve may now be lesse and now be more, siþ þan partis of bileve myȝten go awey and come newe, and þan þer weren dyverse bileves for dyversitee of parties. Siche doutes we shulden sende to þe scole of Oxenforde, and we shulden wite wel bi God þat dyverse feiþis in a man, now on[4] and now oþer,

Speculative doubts should be referred to the school of Oxford.

[1] *silence*, C. [2] *þis*, C. [3] *hem*, B; *hem in*, C. *Him* is the purer and older form for the dative plural of the third personal pronoun. [4] *oon*, B.

[a] That is, ἐν ἕξει, to use the language of Aristotle, not ἐν ἐνεργείᾳ.

make no feiþ in him, ȝhe, ȝif þe tyme be dyverse þat þis feiþ þus comeþ or goiþ. And þus may God encrese oure feiþ, and we by synne enfeblen oure feiþ; and Crist slepiþ ofte to us for siche slepynge of oure synne. For whan wyndis of mennis bost maken us to drede of worldely harmes, and flodis of tribulacioun comen to us, þei maken us dreden and crye on Crist to have helpe for failinge in our bileve. For we shulden trowe þat noo siche a cas myȝte anoy us but for synne, and ȝif it come for oure synne, it is just, and Goddis wille. Whi shulde we be þus distemprid for þing þat is nede to come? Love we God, and do we his wille, and drede we noo þing but hym. For defaute in oure bileve makiþ us to drede for siche þingis. For þes foure mannis affeccions, drede and sorewe, hope and joye, changen a mannis wille after þat he haþ vertues. And if he be rootid in synne þei chaungen myche in a man, for he haþ drede of þing of not[1], and after joye of worldely þingis, and also sorewe of losse of þinge þat were betere to him to want, and hope of þingis ferre fro his helpe, as is welfare of þis worlde. And alle þes techen þat his wille is not sette on hevenly þingis, ne his bileve groundid in God for defaute of good love, for ech man shulde drede more loss of Goddis love by synne þan he shulde drede losse of ony worldely þingis. For as bileve techeþ us loss of Goddis love were wers, whi shulde we not drede þis more, siþ it bringiþ more harm to us, and hope more helpe bi charite þan bi any mannis helpe? And þus cursiþ þe prophete him þat tristiþ þus in man. (Jer. xvii. 5.) And here may men have a myrroure to juge wher þei love God and where þei ben in charite, bi þe ordre þat þei shulden have ȝif þei loven God wel; þei shulde more have joie of him þan of ony erþelye þinge. And so of his loss, ȝif it come; ȝif þei lesen þe love of God bi þer synne, þat þei shulden knowe, þei shulde have more sorewe þerof þan of loss of oþer þing. And þis joye, wiþ þis loss, wolde make men to flee synne. Siþ many men with diligence fleen losse of worldely goodis, and kepen hem þat þei ben not dampned in siche los by mannis lawe, and drede not so myche to lese goodis of grace þat be beter, it is open þat charite is not ordynel in

[1] *nouȝt*, B.

hem. And þus of goodes of kynde, men drede myche to lesen hem, as reule of kynde techiþ us, and comoun experiens; and ȝif þei comen to us, we joien ful myche, as we witen well; but goodis of grace we putten bihynde, and þat fordoiþ oure charite. And ȝif we feynen falsehede in þes two þingis, boþe God and our bysynes shal be jugis aȝens us. Lord! wheþer traveilen we more, aboute goodis of þes two þingis or aboute goodis of grace? Oure owne traveil shal juge us; what preest bisieþ him more now for to sue Crist in vertues, þan for to gete a benefice, or for to gete worldely goodis? And þis techiþ þat he joieþ more of worldely goodis þan goodis of grace. How ever þat we stryven now, oure juge shal dampne us at þe laste. And bi þis same skile, hope and sorewe shal jugen us, for we casten more oure bisynes in hope of a worldely prowe þan we done in hope of hevene or hevenly blisse þat we shulden have; and þus we dreden more of loss of worldely goodis þat we hopen þus, þan we done of goodis of blisse; and þis reversiþ al oure lyf.

Þe fyfþe Sondai after octave of Twelfþe dai.

[SERMON XXXVI.]

Simile est regnum celorum homini qui seminavit.
Matt. xiii. [24.]

Crist in þis parable telliþ þe staat of his Chirche, and seiþ þat *þe kyndom of hevene is lyke to a man þat sew good seed in his felde.* Þe kyngdom of hevene telliþ boþe togidere, Crist and his maynè, but principali Crist. And herfore Crist is often clepid þe kyngdome of hevene, and þe Chirche, þat is his[1] wyfe, is o persone wiþ him. And þus þe kyngdome of hevene seiþ þis spouse and his[2] wyfe; but here is þis kyngdom take for Jesus Crist, þat is boþe God and man, and ordeyneþ wel for his Chirche. *Þis man sew first good seed in þe feld* of þis Chirche; for he puttide first good feiþ in herte of his servauntis, and þis seed is Goddis word, as Crist himsilf seiþ. Ffirst þis seed growide clene, and brouȝt

The parable of the tares.

[1] So in C; om. A, B. [2] *þis*, C.

forþ good fruyt, but þe fend had envye þat þis seed growide þus; and *þis man þat is enemye to Crist* and his Chirche *cam and sew tares whan men weren aslepe.* For bi dowynge of þe Chirche and necligence of prelatis is mannis lawe medlid wiþ Goddis lawe. And þes double mannis lawes, þe popis and þe emperours[a], letten Goddis lawe to growe, and gnaren þe Chirche, as tares gnaren corn, and letten it to þryve. And þe fend went awey, and ceesside sum what to tempte men, for he was sikir of þis tare þat it shulde myche lette þe Chirche. And þis is þe cautil of þe fend, to wiþdrawe his malice and shewe signes, as myraclis, whan he haþ sowen yvel seed, as if God were wel paied wiþ sowyng of siche seed. And as wete somers nurishen siche tares, so lustful lyf of men þat shulden florishe in vertues bryngiþ in siche lawes biside wordis of bileve. And þis lettiþ trewe men to telle Goddis lawe, and lettiþ þe Chirche to growe in feiþ and oþer vertues. And first, whan þe Chirche growid wiþ þis tare, ȝit it was hidd long after þe dowynge[b], but siþ was þis tare shewid, and Goddis lawe hidde. For many wete someres ben comen to þe Chirche, and so mannis lawe growiþ and Goddis lawe is lettid, and speciali bi lawes of þes newe ordres. But whan malice of þes lawes was knowun to trewe men, þanne þei and aungels spoken[1] to God and preyd Him þat þei myȝt gedre awey þes tares, so þat Goddis lawe myȝte renne freely as it first dide. But Crist denyeþ þis to hem, for harm þat myȝt come, for good corn myȝte be drawun up bifore þat it were rype, as trewe men in God myȝte be sone kild, ȝif þei shewiden to myche þis cause, of clennesse of Goddis lawe. But God haþ ordeyned his seed to growe til it be rype, as God haþ ordeyned his membris to helpe aȝens þe fendis lymes, as longe as it is good þat þe Chirche profite here bi hem. And þus ȝif sowynge of þe fend tarieþ here Cristis Chirche, and makiþ here Cristis corn ful þinne, and makiþ þicke þe fendis lymes, neþeles þis good corn groweþ more medefulli to þe Chirche, for þei have more lettinge, but wel is him þat may stonde. And herfor biddiþ Crist, *þat men shal suffre boþe þes*

Application of the parable to the present time.

[1] So in B; *spaken*, C; *speken*, A.

[a] The canon law and the civil law.

[b] The supposed endowment of the Church by Constantine under Pope Sylvester.

two growe til þet yme of repinge, and þan shal he sey to þe repers, Gidere ȝe first þes tares togidere, and bynde hem in knytchis to brenne, but gedere ȝe þe good corn to my berne. Tyme of þis repinge is clepid þe day of dome, or ellis tyme nyȝ it, and þes repers ben good angelis, þat gederen partis of Cristis Chirche; and þes good angels shal bynde Cristis enemyes in *knytchis;* and after þei shal brenne in helle bi þe ryȝtful dome of God, and trewe servauntis of Crist shall be gederid bi good aungelis and come to hevene as Goddis bern. And here supposen men, siþ it is nyȝe domes day, þat soone hereaftir shal be distryed boþ mannes lawe and her makers, and so, ȝif God wil, boþe ypocritis and trynauntis[1] shal be distryed, as þe Antipope wiþ his court, and þes newe religiouse. And þan shal Goddis lawe regne wiþ þe trewe partis of his Chirche; for, as þis gospel telliþ, þes tares shal be gedrid first; but at þe day of dome Cristis lymes shal first be comfortid; and so it semeþ þat Crist spekiþ here of tyme bifore þe day of dome, and þus he moveþ many men for to trete þis mater now. And prey we al devoutely þat God do here as him lykeþ, and stonde we stif in Goddis lawe, and preise we it bifore þis tare.

The anti-pope Clement and the friars compared to the tares.

Many men musen[2] of undirstondinge of þis gospel, and þenken þat it is foly to speke aȝens Anticrist, siþ treuþe of Goddis lawe telliþ þat he shal vencuschen Cristene men for a tyme, and we may see þis at eye. And þus telliþ þe gospel þat God[3] wole þat tare growe til þe day of dome among good corn, but who shulde reverse God and do aȝens his wille? Here shal we suppose comoun bileve and comoun distincciouns, þat ben said in Latyn, and þanne me þinkiþ þat we shulden preien þat Goddis wille be done, as it is in hevene, so here in erþe. And over þis we shulden stonde sadde in bileve of God, and lyve in vertues as Goddis lawe biddiþ us, and assenten not to synne of Anticrist þat regneþ now, but have sorewe þerfore, siþ Crist hadde sorewe for synne and wepte never but þries for synne, as Goddis lawe techiþ us, and resoun acordiþ herwiþ; siþ synne is moost yvel, and so we shulden more have sorewe for synne þan for ony

The opinion that it is folly to contend with Antichrist, as he is destined to triumph for a time.

[1] *tirauntis*, B; *tyrantis*, C. [2] *mosyn*, C. [3] So in C; om. A and B.

oþer yvel. And þus, ȝif we myȝte lette synne, we shulden be Goddis proctours, al if we dien þerfore, and profiten here no more. But lyve we wel, and God failiþ not to consaile us how we shal do, and þus assente we not to synne but profite we as God biddiþ us. And herby may we answere to þe fendis argument. Suppose we þat Anticrist shall vencushe trewe men for a tyme; but þis is in bodily victory and not in vencushing of treuþe; for þus he vencuschiþ no man, but ever is overcome him silf. And þus trewe men shal ever have mater for to fiȝte goostly, boþe wiþ þe fend and his membris, þat ben wickide men of þis world. And so wiþ þis undirstondinge fiȝte we wisely wiþ þis world, but algatis loke þat we be armed wiþ pacience and charite; and þan þe fiȝting of þe fend may no wey do us harm. And if þis skile shulde move men to performe Goddis wille, never shulde man fiȝte wiþ synne, for God wole þat synne profite. But what witen we wher tyme be come þat God wole þat þis tare be distryed? And herfore worche we wiseli, and fiȝte we aȝens þe fend, siþ þis stondiþ wiþ Goddis lawe and wiþ fillinge of Goddis wille.

Confuted.

Þe Gospel on Septuagesime Sonday.

[SERMON XXXVII.]

Simile est regnum celorum homini patrifamilias.—Matt. xx. [1.]

The parable of the labourers in the vineyard.

Þis gospel telliþ bi a parable how God haþ ordeyned for his Chirche fro þe bygynnynge of þe world, as longe as it dwelliþ here. *The kyngdom of hevene*, seiþ Crist, *is lyke to a good huseboonde*[a]*; þat wente first eerly to hire werkmen into his vyneȝerde.* Þis housbonde is God, and þis vyneȝerde is his Chirche, and at þe bygynnynge of þe world he hyred men to wirche þerynne, for alle þes men þat comen to hevene wirchen wel in þis Chirche; and *her hire is a peny þat þei taken*, for dai of hir lyf. And þis peny is hadde of men bi godhede and manhede of Crist. *And*

[a] *Bonde* in the Scandinavian dialects has the sense of peasant, or small proprietor.

aftir þis acorde made, he sente þes werkmen into his Chirche. And þis housbonde wente out in þe þridde houre of his day, and say oþer stondinge ydel in þe cheping to be hired, and þis fadir seide to hem, Go ȝe in to my vyneȝerde, and þat þing þat is riȝt Y shal ȝyve ȝou. Þes werkmen ben seintis þat God hadde ordeynede for to travaile in his Chirche after þe first age, and þei stoden ydel in þe way to heveneward bifore þat God hadde moved hem to traveile in his Chirche. And God bihiȝt þat he shulde ȝyve hem þat were riȝtful hem to have, and þat is þe blisse of hevene, þat falliþ to þis large lord. For it is uncerteyne to hem where þei shal perfourme þis travail, herfore he bihetiþ to hem to ȝyve hem þat were riȝtful. *And þei wenten forþ and wrouȝten wel,* werke of þis vyneȝerde; *and þus he dide in þe sixte houre and in þe nynþe houre also.* For God hirede laborers after þat his Chirche hadde nede, and so he bood[1] first oo our and siþ two to hire servauntis. *He wente forþ aboute þe enlevenþe hour, and fond oþer men stondinge, and seide to hem, Whi stonde ȝe here al dai ydel* fro traveil af þis vyneȝerde[2]? *And þei seiden to him, for no man hadde hirid hem; and he seide unto hem, And go ȝe in to my vyneȝerde.* He made noon oþer covenaunt wiþ hem, for two bifore weren ynow.

Þes fyve houres bitokenen boþe þe elde of þe Chirche from þe bigynnynge til þat Crist cam, and trewe men þat traveiliden þerinne. For it is seid comonly þat þe world haþ sixe eeldis. Þe first was from Adam to Noe; þe toþer from Noe to Abraham; þe þridde from Abraham to David; þe fourþe from tyme of David to passinge in to Babiloyne; and þe fyfte fro þat tyme til þe natyvyte of Crist. Þe sixte age is undirstonde from þennes til þe day of dome. Þan shal the liȝt of Crist go doun fro dwellinge in þis world, and shyne in þe toþer worlde by mene of þe day of dome, and for notablete[3] of Crist. He telliþ not hirynge for þis hour; and, for þis tyme is to come, and Goddis lawe is ful hereof, he telliþ not of þis sixte hiryng, but undirstondiþ it in oþer. Ne we shulde not knowe nowe þe quantite of þis age þat lastiþ fro Cristis ascencioun unto dai of jugement. Þe traveile in þis vyneȝerde stondiþ in þes þre þingis: firste, digge aboute þe vyne rotis, and dunge hem wel, and hile hem þanne.

The six ages of the church.

[1] *abode*, C. [2] So in C; A and B wrongly include the clause in the italics. [3] *notablite*, B; *notabilite*, C.

Þe secounde traveile in þis vyneȝerde is to kitte wel þe braunchis; and þe þridde traveile herof were to araile þes growynge vynes. Sum of þis perteyneþ to God and sum is done bi mannis traveile. God himsilf makiþ þes vynes, and plantiþ hem in his ȝerde; for God makiþ trewe men, and ȝyveþ hem witt to bryng good fruyte; and prechours ben helpours of God, and delven aboute bi bileve, but God ȝyveþ þe growynge, al ȝif men planten and watren. For þus dide Jeromye in þe olde testament; and þus also dide Poul in þe tyme of grace. And so þes laborers have nede to delve aboute þes rotis, lest yvel eerbis growen þere, and bastard braunchis wiþouten bileve. Þei ben dungid wiþ fyve wordis, þat seint Poul wolde teche þe puple; þe whiche sum men undirstonden hevene and helle and weies to hem; but þe first word and þe fifþe is þe holy Trinite. Whan þes fyve sentencis ben prechid, and declarid on good manere, þan þes vynes ben dungid, and wele hilid wiþ erþe. But wise men kitten þes branchis, whan þei wiþdrawun cursid men þat ben superflue in þe Chirche, and letten it to brynge forþ wyne. And to þis helpen myȝti men þat drawen fro clerkis worldely goodis þat þei have aȝen Goddis lawe, and done harm to his Chirche, but þei þat martiren Goddis servauntis, be þei knyȝtis, be þei preestis, þei be foxis þat ben aboute to distrie þis vyneȝerd. Þe railynge falliþ to prelatis and oþer vikeris of God, þat makiþ þe statis of men to stonde in þe bondis þat God haþ ordeyned; and ȝif wyndis or oþer weders putten doun þes statis to þe erþe, bi vertue and strengþe of prelatis shulde þes statis ben holden up. And so ech cristene man shulde helpe þis vyneȝerde; for growynge of coolwortis and oþer wedis maken malencolie and oþer synnes, and gladen men not, to wende to hevene, but maken hem hevy to falle to helle. *And whan evenynge was come, þe lord of þis vyneȝerde seide to his proctour, and bade hem clepe þes werkmen, and ȝyve hem her hire, bigynynge at þe last werkmen unto þe first laborers.*

Mystical interpretation.

Þe lord of þis vyneȝerde is þe godhede of Crist, and þe proctour herof may be clepid his manhede. Þis evenynge is þe day of dome, þat sum tyme is clepid myd nyȝt, and sum tyme clere dai, to dyverse men þerinne, as þe same tyme is clepid here day and here nyȝt, here faire tyme and hoot, and her foule wedir and coold. Clepynge of þes werkmen is clepynge to goddis dome, þat is þe laste trumpe þat seint Poul spekiþ of. Crist shal bigynne at men of þis last tyme, for men of þis last age shal be more blessid, and be first in worþynesse þan men of oþer ages, siþ þe manhede of Crist is in þe sixte age, and his modir wiþ apostlis shulen passe oþer in blisse, and so in oþer agis þe later hadden more grace, siþ Crist is þe emperoure, þat wendiþ ever alarginge. Þe sevenþe age is clepid of men þat slepen in purgatorye, and þe eiȝte age of blissed men in hevene, and in þes eiȝte agis endiþ al þis world.

1 Cor. xv. 52.

Sleep in purgatory.

And so al þes laborers toke ech one his peny. But men of þe first hour demeden þat þei shulden have more þan men of þe enlevenþe hour, *ffor þei travailiden first and longer. And þus þei grucchiden aȝen þe housebonde, and seiden to him; Þes comen in þe last houre, and þou madist hem evene to us, þat baren þe charge and þe hete of þe daie of traveile. But he answeride to oon of hem, and seide þus to him, Frend, Y do þee no wronge; for of a peny þou cordist wiþ me. Take þat is þine, and go ful paied, for Y wole ȝyve þis laste as myche as Y wole ȝyve þee. Where it is not leveful to me to*[1] *do wiþ my owne þing as Y wole? Wher þin eyen ben wickid for þat Y am good? Þus shal þe laste be firste, and þe first be last; for many ben clepid, but fewe of hem ben chosen.* Þis grutchinge of þes seintis is not stryvinge of hem, but woundringe in soule, as Seint Gregore[a] seiþ. And so þis demynge and grutching þat þis gospel spekiþ of is woundrynge in soule, and þankinge of Goddis grace, þat he ȝaf so myche joie to men for so litil traveile. For more joie þei myȝt not have, but fulli as myche as þei wolden. And so shal al witen wel þat God doiþ no wrong to hem, but þat he hiȝt hem graciously, he haþ fully ȝyven hem; ne noon of hem shulde grutchen aȝen goodnesse of þis just fadir, for he may ȝyve of his owne, more þan ony man may

[1] So in B and C; om. A.

[a] See the nineteenth Homily of Pope Gregory (Benedictine edition, Paris, 1705), vol. i. p. 1512. The labourers that murmured are interpreted to mean the saints under the old dispensation, who, though they had merited heaven by their good lives, yet obtained it not, till the descent of Christ into hell had set them free, and opened to them the gates of Paradise.

disserve bi mannis riȝtwisnesse, or evenhede[1] of ony chaffare[a]. And so God seiþ to ech seint þat he shulde take his mede by grace, and so go in to þe blisse of hevene where seintis shal ever dwelle in pees.

SEXAGESIME SONDAY GOSPEL.

[SERMON XXXVIII.]

Cum turba plurima.—Luc. viii. [4.]

The parable of the sower.

Þis gospel telliþ in a parable hou þat holy Chirche growide bi graciouse sowynge of Crist, and growinge of þis holy seed; and in tyme of Sexagesime men sowen bodili seed. Þe storye of þe gospel telliþ, *Whan myche puple was come to Crist, and þei hastiden of citeis to heere of him Goddis word, he seide bi a similitude; He wente out þat sowiþ ay to sowe his seed* in his lond; but on foure maneres felle his seed upon his lond. *Sum fellen bi side þe wey, and was defoulid, and foulis of heven ete it. And sum felle on a stone, and whan it was sprongen, it dryed up, for it hadde no moisture. Sum felle among þornes, and þornes growinge strangliden it. And sum felle in to good erþe, and þat sprong up, and made an hundrid fold fruyt. And Crist, seiyng þes wordis, cryede* and seide to þe puple, *He þat haþ eeres to heere, heere he,* and undirstonde þis witt. And evermore, as seintis seyen, whan God biddiþ men heere þus, his sentence is presciouse and shulde be markid wel of men. *And his disciplis axiden him what ment þis parable, and Crist seide unto hem, þat to hem was grauntid to knowe þe privyte of þe rewme of God, and to oþer men in parablis, þat þei, seynge* wiþouten forþ, *se not* wiþynne in her soule, *and þei heerynge* þe wordis of þe parable *undirstonden not* þe witt of þem.

Interpretation.

Crist seide *þat þis is* undirstonding of þis *parable. Þe seed is Goddis word*, þat felle to men on foure maneres.—Þis first seed is Goddis word, þat fell in sum biside þe wey; for sum ben

[1] *ony nede*, C.

[a] The meaning is, 'or according to the just understanding of any bargain.'

cumbrid wiþ þe fend, and so defoulid wiþ þe worlde þat þe erþe is not able to take þis seed and hilen it; *and herfore comeþ þe fend and takiþ* Goddis word fro þer hertis, for he puttiþ in her þouȝt strange þing fro þis seed and so he takiþ fro þer witt þe vertue of Goddis seed. And herfore it is perelous to dwelle þus biside þe weye, and be defoulid wiþ þe fend and wiþ sentence þat he wole teche. Þe fend takiþ fro men Goddis word þat þei trowe not in it; and for, bi suche trouþe, men may sunnest be saif, þe fend purposiþ to take awey Goddis word, last þat men trowen in it, and so be saaf. Þe fendis may dwelle in comoun weye, where God wole not sowe his seed, and pike awey þe seed biside, and aspie unsow place, and gedere þe seed þat is sowen. He haþ noo power of þis seed, but power of þe man by synne. And þus men out of bileve, þat ben hardid in þer untreuþe, maken a comoun weye and playne, where fendis and beestis may freely go; and on londis biside þis weye ben many voide places, for many semen in bileve, but feiþ is voided fro hem. *Þe secounde place of* þis lond þat Goddis seed is sowen ynne, is stony lond wiþ brood *stoonys*, upon which *þis seed falliþ*, and stones ben hard and erþe litil, *and for a tyme þei taken wiþ joie þe wordis of God* þat ben sowen, *but hem wantiþ rootis* of charite; and so þei turnen to þe world, for coveitise of worldely goodis. And þis seed wantiþ rotis of love to stonden in Goddis lawe, for þei loven more erþely goodis þan þe fruyt of bileve. For þis seed of Goddis word mut be rootid in charite, so þat neiþer poverte ne peyne ne manasse made of Antecrist make men falle fro Goddis lawe, for stabilnesse in þe roote. *Þe þridde lond* þat takiþ þis seed is ful of *þornes* and yvel weedis, and þes growen up wiþ þe corn, and distrye good seed; for siche ben ȝoven[1] to worldely lustis, and lustful þing lykeþ hem, as þingis þat plesen þe bodi, as mete and drynke, and ydlenesse, and leichery, wiþ worldely goodis þat susteynen bodily lustis. And þus it fareþ as Gregory seiþ[a]: al ȝif rychesse liken þe fleishe, neþeles þei ryven[2] þe soule, and maken it bisye aboute veyn þingis; and þus þei prycken and wounden þe soule, as þornes done harm to þe fleishe.

[1] So B; A has ȝyve. [2] *reyven*, C.

[a] S. Greg. *Homil. in Evang.* xv. § 3.

The good ground

1 John ii. 16; James iv. 1-5.

And þus þis lond is undisposid bi þree enemyes of a man, þe which be, þe fend, þe world, and þe fleishe wanton of a man. Of þes speken Joon and James, and Crist here in her[1] wordis; for þes þree letten Goddis word to bryng forþ fruyte in mannis soule. And þerefore, ȝif þou coveite in God þat his seed profite to þee, chastise wele þes þree enemyes þat letten Goddis seed to growe, and þan þou hast good land and wel disposid to take þis seed, and it bryngiþ in siche soulis fruyte to an hundrid fold; siþ goodis of blisse þat ben in hevene passen alle oure goodis here, as an hundrid done oon. And þes in substaunce ben þis seed, and þis lore is profitable to holi Chirche and makiþ it growe, and reisiþ it fro þe erþe to þe heynesse of hevene. Þis seed haþ many propertees þat fallen to bodily seed, for it is litil in quantite and þe vertue of it is hid, but Goddis grace mut quykene it, as liȝt of hevene quykeneþ oþer seed, and dewe of grace þat comeþ of God, wiþ þe hete of charite, norishen þis goostly seed, and maken it growe up to hevene. But as þe gospel of Joon seiþ, þe corn of whete falliþ in to erþe, and siþ it dieþ, and þan it groweþ many folde to myche corn. Þis whete corn is Cristis bodi, þat bicam man here in erþe, þat first was deed and siþ roos, and brouȝte of him many partis; and þus growide holi Chirche from oon to hir ful noumbre. But beestis and lymes of þe fend be myche to blame for þis fruyte, for þei letten it to growe many weies bi fendis cautelis, and sum, bifore þat it be rype, þei kitten[2] and[3] letten fruyte to come. And herfore *hey wardis* shulden be ware and do þer office in þe Chirche, for ellis þei ben traitours to God, in fals kepinge of his felds. And vertues of a soule, and specialy mannis pacience, ben as marle or dunge to men, and maken hem bryng forþ siche fruytis.

John xii. 24.

Questions raised and answered.

Aboute þis tixt may men doute, how þis seed may wexe drye, or faile in ony wyse, siþ it is Cristis word, and Crist seiþ þat hevene and erþe shal passe and faile, but not his word. But here we witen how treuþe of God may not faile in his substaunce, siþ it is kynde of God, þat nedely is ȝif ouȝt be; but þe fruyte þat it shulde make may faile in men by synne of hem. And þus þis seed haþ many names, and bi

[1] *his*, C. [2] om. E. [3] om. E.

many resouns is knowen, and bi diversite of resouns may men assoile þes doutes. But moreover þes men douten here, siþ God is sower of þis seed, and He is ful of witt and myȝt, whi sowiþ he in yvel lond? But here we shal undirstonde þat noo defaute may be in God; but as he ȝyveþ reyn and wedris to good men and to yvel, so he offrid his seed boþe to lond good and yvel; and al ȝif fruyte þat it shulde have perishe ofte for mannis synne, neþeles substaunce of þis seed may not faile, siþ it is God. And þus meneþ Anselme[a], þat þere is no treuþe but oone, for ech treuþe in his ground is þe first treuþe of alle. And leve we to ȝonge men scole tretynge of þis matere, but ȝit men douten what moveþ God to wiþdrawe his grace fro men, and to lette þis seed for to growe, as he shewiþ it in parablis. But here seiþ Poul þat no man shulde blame God for his good dede, siþ he doiþ bi his grace al þingis þat he doiþ, and wiþdrawiþ never his grace, but ȝif man unable him selfe; and þan bi riȝtwisnesse of God nediþ þis synner to be punishid. But sum men seyen þat alle þingis moten nedis come by God, and so what harmes comen in þis world, profiten unto þis world, eiþer[1] to make good þing beter, oþer to make good anewe[2], or ellis to preyse God and to joie for peyne þat is to men in helle. And so Crist telliþ in parablis his witt for many causis. First, for men unworþi to knowe it ben blyndid bi derke speche; moreover, for men þat medefulli traveilen for to knowe þis parable witt boþe shal traveile more medefulli and betere printe þe witt þus gate; and also, in siche parablis as myche philosophie is knowen as is nedeful for a man for to cunnen in þis weie. And so, ȝif God ordeyne þus, it is best þat it be so.

Rom. ix. 18-23.

[1] *euþer*, A; *for*, E; the reading in the text is that of B. [2] So in B; *onewe*, A; *of newe*, E; *of new*, C.

[a] 'Improprie hujus vel illius rei esse dicitur [veritas]; quoniam illa non in ipsis rebus, aut ex ipsis, aut per ipsas, in quibus esse dicitur, habet suum esse; sed cum res ipsae secundum illam sunt, quae semper praesto est his quae sunt sicut debent, tunc dicitur hujus vel illius rei veritas.' S. Anselm *Dialog. de Veritate*, ch. xiii. The heading of the chapter is 'Quod una sit veritas in omnibus veris.'

Quinquagesime Sonday Gospel.

[SERMON XXXIX.]

Assumpsit Jesus duodecim discipulos.—Luc. xviii. [31.]

Christ foretells his passion.

Þis gospel telliþ how Crist warnede his disciplis bifore of his passioun, to teche þat he ordeynede it, and suffride not aȝens his wille, but chees for love þat he hadde to man to suffre þus and bigge man. *Jesus toke his twelve disciplis, and seide þus* unto hem, *Loo, we steien to Jerusalem, and alle þingis þat ben writun bi prophetis of mannis sone shal be endid*, as þei nedis mote. Crist clepiþ himsilf mannis sone bleþeliche[1], for þis cause. Foure maneres þere ben of men þat ben brouȝt in to þis world. Þe first man was made of erþe, but Eve was made of man. Þe þridde man cam of hem two by comoun gendrure of man; but Crist worshipid[a] womans kynde, and cam bi myracle of Marye, so þat whan þat Crist clepiþ himsilf wommans sone, or his modir womman, he specifieþ his manhede. And so, ȝif prophetis and oþer men weren soþeli seid mannis sones, naþeles Crist was propreli sone of a persone of mankynde, for he was a virgyns sone, wiþoute man þat gate[2] Crist of hir. Þes forsfadris of whiche Crist cam, as Abraham, David, and oþer, gendriden not Crist of Marye, for she kepte ever her maydenheed. And so for worship of his modir, and of kynde of men and wommen, Crist wolde clepe him mannis sone, and specifie his manheed. Sixe þingis telliþ Crist to come in his passioun. First, *Crist shal be ȝovun to* Pilat and knyȝtis, to be slayn; and alle þes weren *heþene men*, and figuriden[3] þat þei shulden be turned. And ypocrisie of Jewis, whan þei feyneden unleveful to hem for to slee Jesus Crist, telliþ þat þei shulden be endured[b]. After Crist was many weies *scorned*, and aftir he was *tormentid*, and after he was *spitt upon;* and aftir þis turment *he was kild, and he roos on þe þridde day*, as it was shewid aftir in dede. But disciplis of *Jesus undirstoden not of þes sixe þingis;* for al ȝif þei herden þe voicis, þei undirstoden þan noon of þes, for it was unsemely to hem þat

[1] *bleliche*, B, C. E. [2] *gat*, B, C. [3] *figurid*, C.

[a] That is, dignified. [b] That is, hardened.

ony of þes þingis shulde falle; and so þei supposiden þat Crist spake mystily in þes wordis. *And whan Crist cam nyȝe Jerico, a blynde man sate bi þe weye and beggide*, for synne of þe puple þat wolde not helpe him wiþouten siche begginge, al ȝif Goddis lawe forfende siche beggers for to be. Whan þis blynde man herde þe puple *passinge* wiþ Crist in þe weye, *he axide what þat was; and þei seiden aȝen to him þat Jesus of Nazareþ passide þerbi. And he criede on him, and seide, Jesus, þat art David sone, have mercy on me. And men þat wenten bifore Crist blameden him, and bade him holde his pees; but he cryede myche more, David sone, have mercy on me.* And Jesus bleþeli dide mercy whan he was clepid David sone, for it was soþ bi Goddis heste; and David was woundirful meke, and figuride Crist specialy in many þingis þat felle to him. *And þus stood Jesus, and made þis man be brouȝt to him, and whanne he cam nye, Crist axide him, what he wolde þat Crist did to him. And he seide, Lord, þat Y see. And Jesus seide to him, Þan loke þou, þi bileve haþ made þee saaf. And he saw anoon, and suede Crist, heriyinge*[1] *God; and al þe puple, whan þei sawe þis, ȝaven loovynge*[2] *to God.*

The blind man restored to sight.

Mystical sense.

Þe goostly sence of þis gospel moveþ men to vertues, al if fleishely disciplis undirstonden þis not. A vertuous man must suffre of his kynde six maner of suffringis, as Crist dide here, and þan in siche pacience is þis man ordeyned to go to hevenly Jerusalem, as Crist wente here in erþe to bodili Jerusalem. A man shulde first be ȝovun to þes heþene fendis; and þei first scornen þis man, and tempten him bi his fleishe; and siþ þei puten him on þe cros to chastise his fleish as Poul dide, and siþ to die to þis world, and siþ to ryse spiritualy, for þus men shulden flee þer fleishe and ryse to God in þer goost. And ȝif þes wordis ben scorned of fleishly men and worldely, neþeles it shulde be þus, bi bileve þat men shulden have; and þus we shulden sue Crist, suffringe as he suffride, and we shulden wende bi Jerico, and speke wiþ þis blynde man, and do werkes of mercy to him goostly as Crist dide.—Jerico is þe mone[a], or smellynge þat men shulde have, for ech man in

1 Cor. ix. 27.

[1] So B, C, E; *beerynge*, A.

[2] *louyng*, E; *lowyng*, C.

[a] Jericho means "'place of fragrance,' from רוּחַ, *Ruach*, to breathe, הֵרִיחַ, to smell; older commentators derive it from יָרֵחַ, *Jareach*, the moon." (Smith's Dict. of the Bible.)

þis lyf shulde smelle Crist, and sue hym. And riȝt as þe mone is principale planete after þe sunne, so Cristis manhede is principal after his Godhede. And as fadris of þe olde lawe smelliden Crist in þer dedes, so myche more we shulden now smelle Crist in alle oure dedes, and þanne we shulden sue þis moone, and eende sikirly þis weie. For þis smelle is Crist, clepid plantinge of rose in Jerico, and his weye is smellinge of a ful felde þat God hadde blessid, and þis smel hadde Jacob and oþer fadris þat trowiden in Crist. Þis blynde man is mankynde þat was blyndid bi synne, and beggide boþe of God and man, for it was nedid herto. Ech man mote begge of God and axe of him his ech daies breed, and begge goostly werkis of mercy of his breþeren, for þei ben slowe to do þes werkes as þei ben holden to do bi þe lawe of God. And þes men sitten bi þe weye þat ben temptid of þe fend, þat takiþ of hem Goddis word, and makiþ hem pore in bileve. Þes men heeren þat Jesus passid bi þis wey in many membris, and þei cryen fast on him to helpe hem in þis nede; but Jesus biddiþ siche blynde men to be brouȝt to him in þer bileve; and þei axen first of Jesus, to see wel in riȝt bileve. And men þat ben worþi herto, seen anoon in þer bileve, suyinge Crist and lovynge God, for þan þei witen how þei shulden lyve. But þes men þat comen bifore blamen faste þis blynde man and letten him for to crye and axe helpe þus of Crist. For many comen not wiþ Jesus in þer lore þat þei techen, but comen bifore him, and seien þat þei ben betere þan he, and suen him not in þer lyf, but holden a lyf þat þei have founden. And þes men þat smellen Crist in his lyf, and his lawe, þei clepen hem ypocritis, and maken hem ceese to speke of Crist. But þes men þat saveren God bi suche wordis, speken more, and preien Crist to helpe hem to þe tyme þat þei ben dede, and ever þese[1] men smellen more of Jesus Crist, þat is þis rose. For good þing comfortiþ men, ȝhe more whan it is more defoulid. And þus þei seen and suen Crist to hevenly Jerusalem, and loven him in word and dede from þe tyme þat þei have þis siȝt.

[1] So in B; *þes*, C; *þis*, A.

Þe firste Sondai Gospel in cleene Lentun.

[SERMON XL.]

Ductus est Jesus in desertum.—Matth. iv. [1.]

Þis gospel tellib how Crist was temptid þre tymes of þe fend, and how he overcam þe fend, to teche us, how we shulde do. Þe storye tellib þat *Jesus was ladde of þe Holy Goost in to þe desert* sone after his fastynge, *to be temptid of þe fend.* For þe fend temptiþ men, whan he supposiþ þat þei ben moost feble. Þe fend supposid þis of Crist *whan he hadde fastid fourty daies*, and resouns of þe fend, where Crist was boþe God and man, marrid him so þat he wiste nevere where þis was soþ or fals. And þis coveitide he to wite, for þanne he wolde have lettid men to do Crist þus to þe deþ, lest he savyde mankynde. It was not pleyne to þe fend þat Crist was God for þis fastynge. For Moyses and Ely boþe fastiden fully fourty daies, and ȝit neiþer of hem was God, as þe fend wiste wel. But Jesus bi his manere of fastinge passide boþe Moyses and Hely. For Crist fastide fourty daies, and neiþer ete ne drank in þis tyme, and he was in quyke age, and listide wel to ete, and he was not occupied on oþerwise as þes two weren. Moyses was in þe mount wiþ God, and fed wiþ him in al þis tyme. Hely was an oold man, and fedde wiþ drede of þe kyng. But Jesus was a ȝonge man, and fourty daies lyvede wiþ beestis, and suffrid of God for to hungre more þan ony oþer dide. And so Crist passide boþe þes two and Joon Baptist wiþ hem, al ȝif he lyvede after comoun lyf to ȝyve ensaunple to his Chirche, but Baptiste lyvede more comounly peynful lyf þan dide Crist. The temptation of Christ.

Þe fend bigan to tempte first Crist at pryde and glotonye, for him þouȝt bi þes two he shulde sounest overcome Crist. *Þis tempter seide* þus to Crist, *ȝif þou be Goddis sone, sey þat þes stones be maad loves*, for þe fend wiste wele þat þis myȝte God liȝtly have do, for Crist dide more wounder whan he made þis world of not, and whan he fed so many folk wiþ fyve loves and fewe fishes, as þe fend wiste wele after, but ȝit þis was hidde The first temptation.

fro him. And here we witen þat oure philargis ben more foolis þan is þe fend; for þe fend wote wele þat God may liȝtly make stones loves, but oure philosophris seyen as foolis þat þis þing may no wey be. And so þe fend supposid of Crist, ȝif he were God, he shulde do þis, boþe for shewynge of his myȝt and for to[1] abate his hunger. But here answeride Crist to þe fend bi autorite of holy writt, and seide, *It is writun* þere inne *þat not oonly in breed lyveþ man, but in ech word þat comeþ of Goddis mouþ;* þat is, his vertue to speke to men in þer soule; and þis passiþ erþely breed. And so þe fend failide foule in þis temptacioun of Crist, for ȝif Crist wolde for pryde do þis myracle, and make þus breed of stoones, he wolde in comunalte[2] do þis dede, and not þus oonli in desert. And ȝif Crist myȝt þus make breed, he myȝt þus make boþe fleish and fishe, and þan Crist hadde noo nede þus to hungre aȝens his wille. And so þe fend was a fool whan he temptide Crist þus. But Crist answeride wisely, and for to ȝyve men ensaumple to answere bi Goddis lawe, and to love more it þan erþely þing.—A sophistre wolde denye þis resoun þat þe fend made to Crist, but he coude not teche þus þat Goddis word is more to love þan ony erþely mete, and so it shulde not be lefte þerfore. And þus ȝif we can answere covenably bi Goddis lawe whan þat we ben temptid of pryde, of glotonye or oþer synne, we may wel overcome þe fend and ech þing þat temptiþ us þus. For ȝif we love betere Goddis word þan ony mete þat we shulden ete, we shulden not leve Goddis word and chese þis mete aȝens resoun.

The second temptation.

Þe secounde temptacioun in which þe fend temptide Crist was done on þis manere, for to move Crist to pride. *Þe fend toke him in to þe holy citee*, and as men seien comounly, þe fend bare him over Jerusalem, as Crist were fleyng in þe eire, *and putte him above þe pynacle of þe temple:* þat sum men seyen weren þe aleis, and *seide to Crist, ȝif he were Goddis sone, þat he shulde make him silf go doun.* And herto aleggid þe fend to Crist þe psalme, þat he myȝte surely do þis, *for God bade his aungelis* of Crist *to kepe him in al his weies,*

[1] So in B and C; om., A. [2] *communete*, B.

lest he hurte his foot at þe stoone. And myche more Crist shulde not hirte him at þe eire, ne in his fallyng at þe erþe, ne at no þing þat Crist mette. And here men passen foly of þe fend. For he wolde alegge holy writt in temptacioun of Crist to prove him þat it were sykir; but Antecrist deyneþ not to alegge Goddis lawe for his power; but he seiþ þat if men denyen it þei shal be cursid, slayn, and brent [a]. But þus þe fend temptide not Crist, al ȝif he were of more power þan ben þes Antecristis disciplis to tempte Crist or Cristen men. But Crist answeride bi holy writt as þe fend aleggide it to him, and seide to þe fend þat it *was writun þat noon shulde tempte þe Lord his God.* But it were al oone to lepe doun þus and to tempte God. And so, siþ Crist chargide more Goddis word þan ony worship or mete, myche more he chargide þe synne þus for to tempte God.—Lord! what nede shulde Crist have to lepe doun þus fro þe pynacle, siþ he myȝte on oþer maner surely come doun bi þe aleis. And ȝif men perseyveden not þe heyng [1] of Crist to þe pynacle, ne berynge of him over þe citee, for mennys eyen as it is seide weren hid fro lokynge upon Crist, myche more men shulden not wite hou Crist cam doun to þe erþe. For lesse it is to come doun from an hey place þan to come þider. And þus feilide foly of þe fend to tempte Crist þus to pryde. But here men douten comounly what it is to tempte God, and it is seid comounly þat ech man temptiþ God þat chesiþ þe werse weye, and leveþ þe beter þat he shulde knowe. And so no man may do synne but ȝif he tempte God in a manere, for God dide no wronge to man ȝif he dampnede man for synne, were it never so liȝt synne, and ȝif his temptynge were never so stronge. And þus þenken many men, þat who ever entre a newe religioun þat was not first ordeyned of Crist, he temptiþ God and synneþ gretely. For two weyes ben putte to him. Þe toon is religioun of Crist of whiche he shulde be sure bi feiþ þat it is þe best þat may be, and þe toþir is new founden of synful servauntis of Crist, þat men shulden wite is not so good as Cristis ordre

Those tempt God who enter a new 're-ligioun.'

[1] *byeng*, B, C.

[a] This passage alone would prove that there had been question among the bishops of resorting to the *ultima ratio* of fire and faggot, many years before the enactment of the statute of 1401.

more liȝt. And so þis man temptiþ God þat chesiþ þus þis newe ordre, and þis synne is comoun now among men for chesing of state. For who ever chesiþ him a state to lyve inne, and to serve God, but ȝif he trowe þat þis state be betere to him and more siker, þat man in þis temptiþ God, and þis man mut putte awey þe worlde, þe fend, and his fleishe, þat þei disseyven him not in chesynge of siche state.

The third temptation.

Þe þridde temptinge of þe fend made to Crist is þus told. *Þe fend toke Crist in to an hill þat was ful hiȝ, and shewide hym al þe rewmes of þis world and þe joye of hem, and seide to Crist, Al þise shal Y ȝyve þee, ȝif þou falle and loute me. And þan seide Jesus to þe fend, Go awey, Saþanas, ffor it is writun in Goddis lawe, þe Lord þi God þou shalt worshipe, and to him oone þou shal*[1] *serve þus.* And here men marken how þat Crist was pacient in two temptyngis bifore, but in þe þridde he myȝte not suffre þat ne he spake sharpely to þe fend. And in þis be we tauȝt to suffre mekely oure owne wronge, but aȝen wrong of God we shulden be wood to venge it. For þus dide Crist and[2] Moyses and oþer men þat sueden him. And þus in þree temptaciouns oure Lord Jesus overcam þe fend by þe wisdom of God, and autorite of holy wrytte. And ȝif we marken wel þes þre, we may not be temptid of yvel spirit, but ȝif we have lore to overcome him, ȝif we studien wel þis gospel. And after þes þre victories *þis greet fend lefte Crist, and good aungelis comen to him and serveden to him as to þer God.* And[3] sum men seien þat þis fend was Saþanas, þe moost of alle, þat siþ was bonden in helle a þousand ȝeer, as seint Joon seiþ, for as men seyen comounly whan a fend is þus vencushid, he haþ no power to tempte þat man, and specialy of þat synne. And þus delyveride Crist þis world of þis fend and his felowis, þat þei anoiden[4] lasse his Chirche after bi þis þousand ȝeer.

Apoc. xx. 2.

[1] *schalt*, B, C. [2] So B and C; A has *to*. [3] So B and C; A has *As*. [4] *anoieden*, B; *anoyden*, E.

Þe secounde Sondai in Lenten.

[SERMON XLI.]

Egressus Jesus secessit in partes Tyri.—Matt. xv. [21.]

Þis gospel telliþ a myracle of Crist to stire men to hope mercy, al ȝif þei ben synful. Þe story telliþ *how Jesus wente oute of Jude and fel in þe contrees of Tiry and Sidon*, þat were countres occupied wiþ heþene men, and nyȝe to Jude. And hem visitide Crist, and lo, *a womman of Canaan wente out of hir coostis, and cryede upon Crist, and saide þus to him, Lord, have mercy on me, David sone, my douȝtir is yvel traveilid of a fend.* And Crist to contynue devocioun of þis womman, *answeride not first a word to hir.* And here may we lerne to contynue oure good werke, al ȝif God graunt not oure wille at þe bigynnyng; for God wole have oure herte devoute to him wiþouten ende, here and in hevene. Þe *disciplis cam to Crist and spake þus to him, Leve þis womman, for sche crieþ after us. But Crist answeride and seide* þus comounly[1] [a], *Y am not sent but to þe perishid sheep of þe hous of Israel*, wher þis woman be siche[2]. *And bi þis þis womman came and loutide Crist, and seide, Lord, help me, and Crist answeride and seide, It is not good to take þe breed þat falliþ to children and ȝyve it to houndis* to ete fro þes children. *And þis womman answeride* knowinge Cristis speche, *and grauntide þat it were good;* as if she wolde mene þus; siþ þou clepist me an hound, and Y suffre mykely, ȝyve þou sum mete of children to þis hound, *for whelpis eten of crummes þat fallen fro lordis boordis. And Jesus answeride to her*, and wiste hir entent[3], *and seide, O womman, grete is þi feiþ; be it done to þee, riȝt as þou wilt. And hir douȝter was heelid riȝt in þat hour.*

The healing of the daughter of the woman of Canaan.

Here men douten comounly, where Crist mysseide þis womman or scornede hir, or putt on hir þat she was an hound.

The use of scornful or ironical language sanctioned in Scripture.

[1] So rightly in E; A and B include the words in the italics. [2] So rightly in B, C, and E. The clause is included in the italics in A. [3] So rightly C; clause included in the italics in A and B.

[a] *comounly* is equivalent to 'in general terms.'

Or ellis al þes wordis of Crist shulde be take axingly.—Here we shal bileve þat Crist dide alle gatis evene as he shulde do, and þus ȝif Crist scornede hir, þat Y dar not seye, scornynge was leveful, as holy writt proveþ. For Hely þe prophete bade priestis of Baal þat þei shulde strongely crye, leste þer god slepte, or spake wiþ oþer men, þat he myȝte not here hem. And þus scorneþ Poul spekynge to Corynþios, Where Y dide lasse to you þan oþer apostlis diden, but þat Y toke not of ȝou, forȝyve ȝe me þis wronge. And so ofte in Goddis lawe is scornynge wel ment, as ȝif it were leveful done on good manere. But it is seide comounly þat þre þingis ben hard to men, to scorne men medefully, or medefulli plete wiþ men, or ellis for to fiȝt wiþ man, bi þe weye of charite. But al þis may be done, as wise men þenken. But for þei ben perelous, many men supposen þat Crist uside hem never, but wente þe kyngis hye weye. And so Crist axide[1] bi manere of questioun where it were not good to take children mete and ȝyve it unto houndis, as who seiþ, Telle þou, and þus heþene men weren clepid houndis of Goddis folc, for properte of houndis acordinge to heþene men. But þis womman mekely grauntide siþ question, and þus men clepid houndis may bicome Goddis children as it bifel of many heþene, þat weren convertid to Crist and made Cristene. men. And þus Crist preiside þis womman by hir greete feiþ, and wiþ þis bodili myracle made hir soule hole, and figuride þat heþene folk shulden be turned to him, and of men þat weren first houndis shulden be maad by grace his children. And so þe word of Crist[2], þat he was not sent but to þe seke children of Jacobis hous, was sooþ to þis entent, þat he was sent to hele þes. For what man it be þat Crist convertiþ and saveþ him in hevene, he is Israelis sone, for he supplantiþ þe fend as Jacob dide Esau, and he is maad a man þat seeþ God bi feiþ. And Crist is clepid þus boþ Jacob and Israel, and oþer holy fadris þat figureden Crist, and þus men ben maad by grace of þe hous of Jacob.

1 Kings xviii. 27.

2 Cor. xii. 13.

Mystical sense.

But it were to wite þe moral sense of þese wordis, siþ þis kernel is more swete þan sense of þe storye. Tyrus and

[1] So B and E; *axid*, C; *axinge*, A. [2] A and B insert here the word *shewiþ*, which makes the sentence ungrammatical; E and C have it not.

Sidoun weren of þe lond of biheest, nye þe hill of Libanye, but Israel sufficide not to cast hem out of þis lond, and so heþene folk dwelten þere til þat Crist came[a]. And so þis paynym womman is þe substans of mennis soule, þat is moved of God to preye for hir douȝtir heele. For boþe vertues of þis soule and werkes þerof ben drecchid[1] of þe fend and lyven unmedefully. And suche a soule wendiþ out of þe coostis of Chanaan, ffor it forsakiþ þe paynym life þat it was before inne, and it sekeþ not oonly Crist in þe hous but upon þe weye, and cryeþ on him keneli[2] whan by contemplacioun it is devoute in God. And in doinge of werkes it preieþ to him þat it do fully to plesaunce of God. And interpretacioun of Canaan acordiþ, siþ Canaan is chaungid or chaunging[b], and a soule þat is first heþene and þus turned to Crist is chaungid by myracle more þan ony body. And Crist norishiþ and scharpiþ þe preier of siche soulis til þat þei ben worþi to have grace of him. And so þes soulis knowun þat þei ben seke sheepe of þe hous of Israel þat have nede of confort. And þei seien þat siche whelpis shulden ete trenchours of lordis, and knowe how God haþ fed his children, and so do bi hem. For it is liȝt to God to make of siche whelpis hool sheepe of Jacobis hous, and þus converte her soulis. And þus bi greetnesse of feiþ enfourmed wiþ charite ben siche soulis maad hool, and turned unto Goddis children. And riȝt as in Cristis tyme, and after bi hise apostlis, he turnede many heþene men to Cristis religioun, so now in tyme of Antecrist ben Cristene men maad heþene, and reversen Cristis lawe, his lore and his werkes. As now men seyen þat þei shulden, bi lore of þer feiþ, werre upon Cristen men, and turnen hem to þe pope, and slee þer persones, þer wyves, and þer children, and reve hem þer goodis, and þus chastise hem. But certis þis came nevere of chastyment of Crist, siþ Crist seiþ he cam not to lese lyves, but save hem. And herfore þis is chastyment of þe felle fend, and nevere chastyment of Crist, þat uside pacience and myraclis. For Crist techiþ in his lawes þat al þat we shulden

An allusion apparently to the crusade of Bishop Spencer.

[1] *dretchid*, E. [2] So B; *kenely*, C, E; A has *keneely*.

[a] This sentence is almost literally translated from De Lyra.

[b] See Excursus at the end of the volume.

wille þat men diden skilfulli to us, we shulden do to hem. But what man wolde by skile be þus chastisid of his broþer, for mannis obedience þat he doutiþ to be a fend? Crist axide not siche obedience to be done to him, but who so wolde wiþ good wille obeishe to him wiþouten ȝifte, Crist wolde take hem to grace; but þes men taken to tirantrie. But, as þe sixte sermoun seiþ[a], scribis and pharisees seiden þat man-sleynge was forfendid, but neiþer yre ne yvel word. But Crist diffineþ þus, þat who so is wroþ to his broþer is worþi of jugement, to be dampnyd in helle; and who so wiþ þis ire spekeþ wordis of scorne, he is worþi to be dampned bi counseile of þe Trinite. And whoso wiþ þis wraþe spekiþ folily wordis of sclaundre, he is worþi to be punishid wiþ þe fier of helle. Myche more ȝif preestis now wiþouten cause of bileve sleen[1] many þousand men, þei ben worþi to be dampnyd—Croiserye ne assoilinge feyned now of prelatis, shal not at þe daie of dome reverse Cristis sentens. And take we hede to þes þree þat Crist chargiþ bi ordre: wraþe, and scorneful speche, and foli speche of sclaundre; and to þes þree Crist shapiþ jugement, conseil, and þe fier of helle. It is hard to be dampned bi jugement of Cristis manhede, but it is hardere to be dampnyd bi conseile of þe Trinite, but it is hardest to be putt bi þes to þe fier of helle. Lord! ȝif God punishe þus wille and mannis wordis, myche more shal he punishe wille, word, and wickide dede.

Þe þridde Sonday Gospel in Lenten.

[SERMON XLII.]

Erat Jesus ejiciens demonium.—Luc. xi. [14.]

The miracle of casting out a dumb devil.

Þis gospel telliþ how Jesus bi a myracle and witty wordis enformeþ his Chirche to flee synne and perel þerof. Þe storye telliþ *how Jesus was castynge out a fend of a man and þis fend was doumbe.* For he made þis man dombe. *And whan he*

[1] So B and E; A has *slen.*

[a] See page 16, supra.

hadde cast out þis fend, þis man dombe bifore spake and the puple woundride herof for gretnesse of þe myracle. But þe enemyes of Crist, as weren scribis and pharisees, whan þei myȝten not denye þis dede, for it was open to þe puple, þei enterpretiden it amys; and *seiden þat Crist dide suche woundris in þe power of a fend,* to whom he servede bisily. *And þis fend was clepid of hem Belsabub, a*[1] *prince of oþer.* And þes men þat defameden Crist þus weren preestis or pharisees; *but oþer men* bi lasse envye[2] *axiden of Crist a signe of hevene,* to conferme þat he dide þis bi þe vertue of God. *But Crist when he knew þere þouȝtis,* þat þei weren turned þus fro treuþe, bi many resouns proved hem þat þei weren fals in þouȝt and word. And first he seide þus to hem, *Ech rewme dividid in him silfe shal be desolatid, and hous shal falle upon hous; and þus ȝif Saþanas be dividid in him silfe as ȝe seien, how shal his rewme stonde* stably wiþouten eende? For siþ ȝe seien þat Y cast out a fend bi anoþer, nedis o fend mut be contrarye to anoþer. Þe first word þat Crist toke is soþ by open resoun, for þe strengþe of a rewme comeþ of acord of þe partis of it, and ȝif oon contrarieþ anoþer, nedis þe strengþe is enfeblid. And ȝif þe partis mut ever laste and oon wite anoþeris state, þat rewme mut nede be desolate, al ȝif þes partis shal laste ay; for on hous of a more myȝti prince shal falle upon anoþer hous, and bi fiȝtynge amonge hem shal al þe rewme be feblid, siþ þes partis, ful acordid, shulden helpe þis rewme and make it strong. And riȝt as a ruynous hous falliþ on anoþer and brekeþ it, so o maynè of a rewme falliþ on anoþer and enfebliþ it. And so shulde it be of þe fendis, ȝif o prince contraried anoþer. And so ȝif Saþanas, prince of fendis, be þus dividid in him silfe, how shulde his rewme be strengþid by dedes þat Crist doiþ? but myche more Cristis rewme, þat is strengþid aȝens the fend, shulde have anoþer prince contrarie to Saþanas. Also, ȝif *Y cast out a fend in vertue of Belsabub, ȝour children,* þat ben my postlis, *in whos name shulden þei cast out fendis?* Certis not in my name, for þan Y were a wickide man, and siþ þei done þus comounly in my name, þat is Jesus, *þei shal juge ȝou as fals* in þis interpre-

Interpretation.

[1] om. E. [2] Words rightly excluded from the italics by E, but included by A, B, C.

tacioun. *But certis ȝif Crist cast out þus þe fendis in special werk of God*, þe rewme of God, þat is his Chirche, is *comen*[1] *amounge hem.* And so þe heed of þis Chirche, contrarye to Saþanas, is comyn among hem, in whos vertue þes dedis ben done. And so bi chasynge of þes fendis done bi Crist in þis manere, myȝte þei wele wite þat Crist was evene contrary to þe fendis, and þan Crist was a spirit þat was nedis boþe God and man.

Christ vanquishing the evil one.

Also ȝif a strong man wel armed kepe his castel, alle þingis þat he haþ þerynne ben surely kept in pees: and ȝif oon stronger þan he com on him and vencushe him, he wole take awey his armes in which he affiede him. And siþ þis is done to fendis, as ȝe may se bi þer dedis, ȝe mut graunt þat a prince more strong þan þe fend is comen. Þis strong man is þe fend; his armes ben his cautelis; his castel ben his lymes þat he dwelliþ inne. Þe strenger is Crist þat comeþ upon þe fend; þat vencushide þe hede fend, in his þre temptaciouns, and ofte tymes he cast out fendis of men. Al þe cautelis of þe fend toke Crist awey, and kyndely vertues of men þat þe fend spuylide Crist delte graciousely aȝen, as þe gospel telliþ. And as Matheu seiþ, Crist toke awey þe vesselis of men þus segid wiþ fendis, whan he dide awey her synnes, þat weren ful of venym to ȝyve men to drynke, and þe poweris of þe soule Crist fillid wiþ vertues. Also, þe generalte of lordship of Crist shewiþ þat þe fendis ben contrary to him; *for whoever is not wiþ Crist, he is aȝens him*, as whoever is not wiþ trouþe holdiþ wiþ falsehede; *and who ever gederiþ not wiþ Crist, scateriþ of his good.* And siþ þe fend is not wiþ Crist, he mut nedis be aȝens him; and herfore comaundide Crist þe fendis þat he caste out þat þei shulden not speke to witnesse his Godhede, for þes weren fals witnessis to prove siche treuþe. And here supposiþ Crist þat he is treuþe, and þat þe fend is fadir of lesyngis, and þat his lordship haþ noon enemye but falshede. And þanne is þe resoun pleyne bi his general lordship and bi his contrarite of þe fende þat was ofte shewid.

The last state worse than the first.

And after þes fyve resouns Crist telliþ a sharpe sentence of malis of þe fend and how þat it is endid. *Whan an unclene spirit*

[1] So B and E; A has *comoun*.

is went out from a man, he waundriþ bi drye placis and sekiþ him reste; and whan he findiþ noon, he seiþ to him silfe, Y shal turne aȝen to þat house þat Y cam of. And whan he comeþ to þat house, he fyndiþ it ydel, clensid wiþ besemes[1], *and shynyngely arrayed. Þan he goiþ and takib wiþ him sevene oþer spiritis worse þan him silfe, and þei, entrid in to þe man, dwellen in him, and þus þe laste of þis man ben worse þan he was bifore.* Þis unclene spirit is þe heed fend, and þis man ensegid bi him is þe kynrede of þe Jewis, of whom Crist shulde come, and þerfore he assailide it; but patriarkes and holy fadris fouȝten wele aȝen þe fend, þat him þouȝte he hadde not þere a plesinge place to dwelle inne. And so he wente to heþene folc þat weren wiþouten grace, and ȝit he likide not wiþ hem for þer kyndely resoun. And þanne þe fend seide to him silfe þat he wolde go aȝen to generacioun of Crist and perverte it more. And in tyme þat preestis regneden, he entride to aspie it, and he fond it ydel from kepyng of Goddis lawe, and occupied wiþ mannis lawe þat sownede unto coveitise. And bi þis þei swepten comynalte of men and maden hem bare and colde as floures ben maad. But housis of preestis weren worldely arayed, and þei kepten as sacramentis many of her fynding, and bi þes þe fend þouȝt þat he shulde overcome hem. And he gidere to him al manere of fendis, and dwelte wiþ þis peple, and made hem worst men; for þei growiden ever in malice, til þei hadden killid Crist. And þus, seiþ Crist, shal be to þis worste kynrede, siþ ende of mennis wickidnesse was to slee Crist. And so, it is lickely[2] þat þe Chirche fariþ now bi sleynge of treuþe þat is Goddis lawe, so þat men in erþe, clepid Cristen men, passen in malis[3] Jewis and Sarasynes. And rote of þis malice is coveitise of preestis, and levynge of Goddis lawe, and hiȝyng of mannis lawe. Bi þis is þe comynalte of puple maad pore, and swepte as þe pament from hilyyng of stree, and coldid in charite, boþe þei and preestis. But housis of preestis ben worldely arayed, and þis aray is hid from partynge of comounes. And þis is wey of Antecrist, and ende of þe last yvel. And soone after þis lyfe shal come þe daie of dome, but bifore, ȝif God wole,

New sacraments.

[1] *besemys*, B; *besomes*, E. [2] *licli*, B; *licly*, E. [3] *malice*, E.

The Church in peril.

the Chirche shal be mendid. And þis is þe moost perelous harme þat þe Chirche hadde ever, for cautelis of Antecrist disseyven many men. *And whan Jesus saide þes wordis, a womman of þe puple heyed*[1] *her vois and seide þus to Crist, Blessid be þe wombe þat bare þee in to þis world, and blessid be þe tetis þat þou hast soukid. But Crist blessid more þes men þat heeren Goddis word and kepe it* wiþouten lesyng, as oure Lady dide; ffor þis bi himsilfe makiþ a man blessid. And it is lickely þat þis womman undirstood Cristis wordis, and herfore she blesside þe moder þat bare sich a child.

Þe fourþe Sonday Gospel in Lenten.

[SERMON XLIII.]

Abiit Jesus trans mare.—John vi. [1.]

The miracle of the loaves and fishes.

Þis gospel telliþ þe first feste þat Crist made to þe puple, bi multipliynge of mete, as þre gospelis tellen. Þe story telliþ þat *Jesus wente over þe water of Galile þat is clepid Tiberiadis*, and many oþer names, for contres and touns þat it ȝede bitwene. *And a greet multitude suede Crist here, for þat þei seien þe signes þat Crist dide on syke men. And Jesus whan he cam over* þis water of Galile, *he wente in to an hill and sate þere wiþ hise disciplis. And Paske was ful nyȝe, a greet feste among Jewis. And whan Jesus cast up his eiȝen, and saw a ful grete multitude was comen to him, he seide unto Philip, Wherof shal we bigge looves, þat þes men ete. And þis seide Crist to tempte Philip, for he wist what he was to do. And Philip seide to Crist þat looves of two hundrid pens suffiden not to hem, þat ech man take a litil what. And oon of Cristis disciplis, Andrew, Petris broþer, seide to Crist, þer was a child þat hadde fyve barly loves and two fishes, but what ben þes among so many men? And Jesus seide to hem, to make hem sitte doun to þe mete, for þere was myche hay in þe same place; and so þei sate*

[1] So B. C. E; *heid*, A.

to þe mete, as fyve þousand men. And Jesus toke þes fyve looves, and ȝaf þankynge to God, and delide among þes sittinge men, and also of þe fishis as myche as þei wolden. And whan þei weren fillid, Crist seide to his disciplis, Gedre ȝe þat ben lafte relefes þat þei perishe not. And so þei gedriden and filliden twelve cofynes of relyf of fyve barly loves and two fishis þat weren lefte of hem þat hadden ete. And þes men, whan þei hadde seen þe signe þat Crist hadde done, þei seiden þus of him, þis is a verre prophete þat is come in to þis world.

Þis bodily fode bi whiche Crist fedde þe folc, bitokeneþ goostly foode bi whiche he fedeþ mankynde. His passynge over þis water with his disciplis, is passyng over worldely perilis to take Goddis lore. Cristis sittinge in þis hille is rysyng to spiritual lyf, and Cristis lokyng on þe peple is goostly mercy do[1] to hem, and steiynge in to þe hille of Jesus wiþ his disciplis is takynge of goostly lyf for to lerne Cristis lawe. Axinge of Philip, þat was made to shewe þe myracle þe more, and for to have beter in mynde, is fillinge of Goddis word in dede. Þes fyve looves þat Andrew shewide ben harde lyfe þat men moten lyve bifore þei kunne Cristis lore; and two fishes ben þenkinge of God and hevene. Sittinge doun in þe hey, is meke þouȝt of mennis freelte. And so Andreu undirstood more þan Philip þat God þat multiplied mete, as þe lawe telliþ, by Helyse, myȝt liȝtly multiplie þis mete and so fede al þis peple. But wiþouten myracle myȝte not so myche puple be fedde of Crist. And þes fyve þousend of men, wiþouten wommen and children, ben þe noumbre þat shal be savyd bi þis spiritual foode; for fyve is a round nombre þat turneþ wiþouten eende in to him silfe. And so not al þat ben fed þus shal come to þe blisse of hevene. Þe twelfe coffynes of relyfes, ben alle þe seintis gloses þat be gedrid of Goddis lawe to fede þe puple afterward. And goostly lore haþ properte to be multiplied in men; for of o lore comeþ anoþer, and al is þe same treuþe. And bi þis fode men þanken God, and seien þat Crist is þat grete prophete þat is to come in to þis world, and fille it of hevenly lore. For of oþer myraclis of

Mystical interpretation.

2 Kings iv. 43.

[1] *done*, E, C; *to do*, B.

Crist þis myracle is oon of þe most, þat so fewe disciplis of hise filliden þe world in so short tyme wiþ þe same gospel of Crist; and he it was þat dide þis myracle.

Difficulties stated and solved.

And here men moven þre doutis. First, how Criste absentide him fro Jerusalem at þis Paske, siþ Baptiste hertely reprovede Heroud, and Crist was more hardy þan Joon for to suffre passioun for þe love of mankynde. But here we trowen þat Jesus, siþ he was boþe God and man, dide alle his dedis at point devys, and myȝte no wey be amendid. And þus he absentide him now to prophite[1] more to his Chirche, for his tyme was not come to die at þe Paske, þat he hadde ordeyned. For, as men seyen comounly, Crist moste passe þis secounde Paske, and in þe þridde Paske die gladly for mankynde. And so Crist suffride more freely þan Baptist or oþer martiris. But he was more nedid bi wisdom to suffre as him silfe had cast, and so, as Crist himsilfe hadde ordeyned, Baptist shulde die bifore, and so go to purgatorye and be taken out bi Crist. And þus Crist ȝaf ensaumple to us to fle deþ, whan he moveþ us, as al his lyf was ensaumple to teche men how þei shal lyve. Þe secounde doute is axid here, whi Crist wolde not take þe rewme of Judee þat was owid to him, siþ þe puple preferide him anoon, aftir þis myracle þat Crist had fedd þus þe folk. But here men seyen, as to þe first, þat it were a manere of biggynge to have þe rewme for suche a feste, and of puple þat was so symple. Also, al ȝif Crist was kyng, he wolde not þus regne worldely, ne him was owid no siche rewme, siþ God wolde not þat it were so. Also Crist ordeynede him silfe to lyve wiþouten wronge of ony man, and so he wolde not regne þus wiþouten þe emperour's leve, þat men shulden wite þat his lyfe no weye reversid þe emperour. And so witnessis þat accusiden him in tyme of his deeþ weren opynly fals. And þus as oure Lord forsoke to be preisid of þe fendis, so he forsoke now to take þe rewme þus of þis puple.—Þe þridde doute þat sueþ þes two is, how Crist myȝte disserven in suffringe of his passioun, siþ he was nedid to suffre þus. But here we witen, as Crist was nedid to suffre and die as he hadde ordeyned, so he was

[1] *profite*, B, C, E.

nedid to have blis for þis wilful passioun, siþ al þis passioun of Crist was more wilful þan any oþer my3t be. And for myche wilfulnesse was his passioun more medeful. And here þes blynde heretikes wanten witt as ydiotis, whan þei seien þat Petre synnede not in smytynge of Malcus ere, but 3af ensaumple to preestis to fi3t. And þus Crist lettid him to fi3t more; for hadde Petre and oþer apostlis fou3ten þus, þanne þei hadden lettid þe passioun of Crist and savyng of mankynde. But here þes blynde heretikes, þat ben unable to conseyve sutilte of holy writt, shulden first lerne þer owen wordis. Soþ it is þat al þingis mut nedis come as God hath ordeyned, and so ech dede of Crist muste nedis be done as he dide it. And þus 3if men shulden not sue Crist here, for he muste nedis suffre, no Cristen man shulde sue Crist in no þing þat he dide. For alle þe þingis þat Crist dide musten nedely comen as þei came, and so siche heritikes musten nede suen Antecrist and be dampnyd wiþ him, for defaute of her bileve. And 3if þei seien þat þis is fals, þat al þing mut þus nedely come, Lord! hou dremeden þes foolis þanne þat 3if Petre hadde fou3te forþ, þanne Crist shulde not have suffrid deeþ, ne have bou3t mankynd! Certis þes idiotis can not shewe hou þis shulde suen of ony treuþe, but 3if þei supposen here, þat þus it mut nedis be. And 3if we shulde herfore lette to take ensaumple to sue Crist, we shulden lette evermore to sue Crist and take his lore. But siþ Crist reprovyde Petre and saide a cause general, þat who ever smytiþ þus wiþ sworde, he shal perishe bi Goddis word, it is knowun þing þat Petre synnede in þis fy3tynge; and myche[1] more shulden preestis fi3t not for a cause of lasse value.

Whether St. Peter sinned in using the sword.

[1] So E; om. A, B, C.

þE FIFþE SONDAY GOSPEL IN LENT.

[SERMON XLIV.]

Quis ex vobis arguet.—JOHN viii. [46.]

Christ without sin.

Þis gospel techiþ bileve by hie wordis þat Crist spake, and hou men shulden lyve þere after, and trowen in Crist and suen him. First axiþ Crist *þat who of hem shal reprove him of synne;* and he wolde mene þat noon myȝte. And so Crist myȝte not do synne, for ȝif he myȝte have synned, þe Jewis myȝten have reproved him of synne, as þei enforsiden many gatis, but þei traveiliden in veyn. And here we undirstonden reprofe for matere þat is trewe for cause þerof. As false peny is noo peny, so fals reprofe is no repreefe, for ech þing mut have treuþe in þat þat it haþ beyng. And in þis word Crist wolde mene þat he was boþe God and man, for ȝif he hadde not be God, he myȝte have synned as aungelis diden. And it were liȝt for to synne in veyn glory or in gabbyng, for ech gabbing is synne, and Crist gabbid, or he was God. And after þis bileve of Crist, proveþ he þat þei shulden trowe him. For siþ he seiþ but treuthe to hem, as he may noo gatis synne, þei shulden trowe unto þat treuþe, siþ þat God knowiþ al treuþe. And herfore seiþ þe word of Crist, *þat ȝif he seiþ treuþe, whi trowen þei not to him.* But as Crist soþely takiþ, *he þat is on Goddis syde, he heeriþ Goddis wordis,* or bodily or spiritualy; siþ no man may be but ȝif he heere treuþe or o tyme or oþer. And so þes hey preestis of Jewis *heeren not þus Goddis wordis, for þei ben not on Goddis halfe;* and þanne þei ben wiþ þe fend.

His answer to the Jews.

But þes Jewis conceyveden þes wordis how þei weren sharply seid to hem, and þei hadden no wey to answere ne to replie aȝens him. And herfore þei bigan to chide and accusiden Crist wiþouten cause. And two þingis þei putten on him, *first þat he was a Samaritane,* and[1] *siþ þat he hadde a fend,* þat was felowe and helpe to him. But Crist lefte answere to þe first, and þe secounde he denyede; and so he grauntide in a manere þat he

[1] om. B, C.

was a Samaritan, siþ he was keper of mankynde, as he telliþ in a parable. Þat man is seid to have a fend whom þe fend disseyveþ, as he is seid to have an heed þat is hedid bi þis hede; and so of oþer relatives as clerkes knowen in manere of speche. And after þis answere Crist telliþ how he doiþ treuþe and þei done falshede aȝen, *for he doiþ worship to his Fadir and þei unworshipiden him; he sekiþ not his owne glorye, but his Fadir sekiþ and jugiþ.* And þis is þe maner of speche þat Crist usiþ ofte, þat he bi his manhede doiþ not suche þing, whan he bi þis kynde doiþ not principalli þis þing. For Crist seiþ to þis entent þat his lore is not his, ne þe word þat ȝe herde is not his, but his Fadris. And on þis manere semeþ Ambrose [a] to graunten þat þe sacred breed is not after breed but Goddis body, for it is not after principaly breed but Goddis bodi, in maner as Austin seiþ [b]. But siþ al werkes of þe Trinite may not be departid, al þe þree persones seken glorie of Crist. But þe manhede of Crist is herto an instrument; and as þe ax hewiþ not, but þe wriȝt bi his crafte, riȝt so Crist sekiþ not his owne glorie. But Crist to shewe boþe his kyndis *doubliþ* þis *amen*, and telliþ þat *he seiþ soþeli to hem*; þat *who ever kepiþ his word shal not taste deeþ wiþouten eend.* For he bi comoun speche kepiþ a þing, þat wiþouten lesyng kepiþ þe same þing, and þus whoever kepiþ ony word of Crist, he shal never have þe deþ þat ever shal laste.

An allusion to the doctrine of the Eucharistic presence.

But here þe Jewis knewen not þe manere of Cristis speche, and replieden aȝen him and *seiden, Now we witen wele þat þou*

[a] S. Ambros. *De Fide*, lib. iv., cap. 5. 'Nos autem quotienscunque sacramenta sumimus, quae per sacrae orationis mysterium in carnem transfigurantur et sanguinem, mortem domini annunciamus.'

[b] I have examined scores of passages in the works of St. Austin, but have not found one which exactly corresponds to the reference in the text, so as to imply that the sacramental bread, after consecration, while it became *principally* the body of Christ, yet continued in a certain sense to be bread. For this is clearly the meaning of Wyclif's words, and this was in fact the main point of his controversy with the friars on the Eucharistic mystery; in which he quarrelled with their definition of the consecrated species as an 'accident without a subject' for this very reason, that it utterly denied the co-presence of *bread* in any sense, after consecration. It is therefore a point of much interest to ascertain whether St. Austin's works really contain any passage which would justify the reference in the text; in other words, which would support Wyclif's favourite theory of consubstantiation; and I shall be glad if this note should be the means of directing the attention of theological students to the search. (See note on p. 379, Serm. 112.)

hast a fend þat lediþ þe in þi dedis. *Abraham was deed, and oþer holy prophetes, and þou seist, whoever kepiþ my word shal nevere die. Lord! wher þou be more þan oure fadir Abraham þat is deed, and prophetis also; whom makist þou þee?* wher þou be more þan ony of þese seintis? Here may we see þe folye of þes Jewis, for þei koud not knowe dyversite of þes wordis; who þat lyveþ þus, he shal not taaste þe longe deþ; and who so lyveþ þus shal never taste deþ. But Jesus lefte þis foly and spake to þe purpos; *ȝif Y glorifie þus my silfe, my glorie is not, but Y have a Fadir þat þus glorifieþ me; and ȝe seyen þat he is ȝour God; but ȝe have not knowe him; but Y have knowe him, and ȝif Y sey nay, Y shal be like to you, a lyer. Abraham ȝoure fadir hadde grete joie to se my daie, and he sey it and hadde joie.* But here þe Jewis knewen not þe maner of riȝt speche of Crist, for þei knewen not how Crist clepide God syngulerly his Fadir. For þan bi riȝt speche God was his Fadir bi kynde. God is oure alþer fadir[1] but who ever of us seiþ, God is my fadir, he blasfemeþ in God. Þis man is my fadir, ȝif þat Y have properte in gendrure of him bifore oþer men. And þus þes foolis replieden aȝen þe wordis of Crist, *and seiden; Þou hast not ȝit fifty ȝeer in age and ȝit þou menest in þi speche þat þou hast seen Abraham.* And, for þe first blyndenesse þat þei weren to blame fore, Crist spake more derkely to hem þan he dide bifore, *and seide, Soþely, soþely,* to showe his two kyndis, *Bifore þat Abraham shulde be, Y am.* And herfore þei weren depid in worse synne of dede, *whan þei token up stonys* to stone Crist to deeþ. *But Jesus hidde him and wente out of þe temple,* as it was liȝt to hym to hiden him among many; for boþe he myȝt stoppe her siȝt, and shewen him in dyverse formes. And here he tauȝt his disciplis in dede for to flee, but he tauȝt hem nevere for to fyȝte bodily. And siche blessid cowardise makiþ Goddis children, for Crist seiþ þat in þer pacience þei shal have þer lyf in pees. But þe fend techiþ his children to be hardy heere, and fiȝte wiþouten hevenly cause, and þus þei lesen þer lyf; for techingis þus contrarye leden to contrarye eendis.

Christ's declaring his divinity.

But we þat ben in bileve over þes blynde Jewis shulden

[1] *aller-fadur.* C. See Glossary.

knowe þes wordis of Crist þat he seid to hem, Biforn þat Abraham shulde be, Y am. But as we witen bi oure bileve þat þes wordis ben ful of witt, so we witen þat in hem Crist shewide his godhede. For we witen wel þat þis word, Y am, bitokeneþ þe godhede, for godhede may not be chaungid, neiþer from ȝonge to elde, ne from worse to beter; for it is ever oon, and a þousand ȝeer ben to him as ȝisterday; and, shortly, al þing þat was or ever shal be hereafter is present unto him, ffor streeching of his longe beying. And herfore telliþ God to Moyses þat he þat is, is his name, and þis is a memorial to God wiþouten ende. But over þis we shulden wite whan Abraham shulde be. And certis, siþ þat God wiste, ȝhe[1], bifore he made þis world, þat Abraham shulde be, þanne it was soþ, and herfore seyen clerkes þat ech creature haþ beyng in his sample[a] þat is wiþouten eende. And so, þat Abraham shulde be, is treuþe wiþouten eende, but ȝit bifore þis treuþe, is God þat knowiþ it. And so þis word, bifore, bitokeneþ forþerhede of beyng, and not forþerhede of tyme, siþ al þis was wiþouten ende. And so to blaberynge in þis speche mennis voicis ben not sufficient, but sum glymerynge we have in oure soule of þis treuþe, and betere knowen it in oure herte þan we can speke it in vois. And blessid be þe Holy Goost þat sette siche wordis in his lawe, þat alle men here in erþe can unneþe undirstonde hem. For Y am certeyn ȝif þou be never so wyse ne olde, unneþe þou wolt afferme þis shorte word of Crist, whan he seiþ þat, Bifore þat Abraham shulde be, Y am. And here tellen seintis cause of þis derknesse. First we shulden wel witen þat autour of þis gospel is more witty in himsilf þan we alle can conseyve.

[1] So B and E; ȝ*e*, A.

[a] The belief that the ideas, or original patterns (exemplaria—'samples'), of all things and persons exist from eternity in the divine mind, borrowed by the schoolmen from the Platonic philosophy, is defined and adopted in the *Summa* of St. Thomas. The following extract is from the first Article of Quaestio xv., Prima Pars. 'Dicendum quod necesse est ponere in mente divina ideas. Idea autem Graece, Latine forma dicitur. Unde per ideas intelliguntur formae aliarum rerum praeter ipsas res existentes. Forma autem alicujus rei praeter ipsam existens ad duo esse potest; vel ut sit exemplar ejus cujus dicitur forma; vel ut sit principium cognitionis ipsius.' Again (Art. ii.) quoting St. Austin, he says, 'Ideae sunt principales quaedam formae, vel rationes rerum stabiles atque incommutabiles; quia ipsae formatae non sunt, ac per hoc aeternae.'

Also he wole þat his preestis traveilen fast in his lawe, and kepen hem medefully from oþer occupaciouns; for noon of us haþ matere to say þat he can alle Goddis lawe, and so he haþ no more to lerne þerynne. Also we shulden trowe þat alle mennys wordis may not come to þe witt þat is in Goddis wordis; for we witen þai nouȝt in hem is seid wiþouten chesoun, but in ech Goddis word is more witt þan we knowe.

Þe Gospel on Palm Sonday.

[SERMON XLV.][a]

Altera autem die quae est post parasceven.—Matt. xxvii. [62.]

We suffisen not here to telle pleynly þis gospel, but þe ende þerof makiþ mynde of oure bileve, how, after þe tyme þat Crist hadde suffrid deeþ, þe nexte day after, þat is þe holy Satirday, þes men þat hadden kild Crist gideren to gidere. For þe gospel telliþ þat *princes of prestis and þe Phariseis comen to gidire to Pilate*, and þes two folk, as hie preestis of þe temple and þes religiouse, diden Crist to deþ. And herfore telliþ Matheu how þes two dredden more þat þe name of Crist shulde growe among men, and so þer defamyng shulde growe, and þei shulden be distryed. And certis as þese two maner of folk diden Crist to þe deþ, so þei ben now cheveteynes to distrien his lawe; for þei letten þat þei may þe treuþe of þe gospel. And noo woundir is; for þei in þer lyvynge reversen þe lyf of Crist, and ben weddid to contrarye lyf. And siþ þe gospel telliþ dampnynge of siche men, and hou þat men shulden flee hem as heretikes and fals prophetis, þei dreden þat þer gile by þis shulde be knowe. And herfore þei seien þat Goddis lawe is fals, but ȝif þei glosen it after þat þei wolen; and þus þer glose shulde be trowid as bileve of cristene men, but þe tixt of Goddis lawe is perelous to trowe. *Þes two manere of folk comen to gidere to Pilate on þe next Satirday aftir* þei hadden kild Crist, and þus seiden to him,

Prelates and friars again compared to the high priests and the Pharisees.

[a] The style of this sermon rises occasionally to real eloquence.

Sire, we þenken on þat þis gilour[1] *saide whan he was on lyve, þat he shulde ryse after þre daies; þerfore commaunde his sepulcre to be kept til þe þridde day, lest his disciplis comen and stelen his body, and feynen to þe peple þat he is risen fro deþ; and so þe laste errour shal be worse þan was þe former.* And þes pagyn playen þei þat hiden þe treuþe of Goddis lawe. And *Pilat seide to hem, ȝour silf have þe kepyng; goþ forþ and kepiþ it as ye can,* for þis is not myn office. And þus seyn þes two folk to princes of þe world, þat þes heretikes ben fals men aȝens holy religioun, and þei casten to distrye lordshipis and rewmes; and þerfore comaunden hem to be dede or lette hem to speke. But lordis seien aȝen þat þei shulde knowe þe lawe þat holy Chirche haþ, to punishe siche heretikes; and þerfore þei shulden go forþ and punishe hem bi þer lawe. And bi siche execucioun of fals prelatis and freris, is Goddis lawe quenchid and Antecristis arerid. But God wolde þat þese lordis passiden Pilat in þis point, and knewen þe treuþe of Goddis lawe in þer modir tunge, and have þes two folk suspect, for þer cursid lyvynge and hydyng of Goddis law fro knowyng of seculers. For bi þis cautel of þe fend ben many trewe men quenchid. For þei wolen juge for heretikes al þat speken aȝens hem, ȝhe, ȝif þei tellen Goddis lawe, and shewe synnes of þes two folke. *And þei wenten forþ, and kepten wiþ knyȝtis þe sepulcre of Crist, markynge þe stoon* þat was putt at þe dore in siȝt of þe keper, to marke þer diligence. And þus done oure heye preestis and oure newe religiouse. Þei dredden hem þat Goddis law shal quyken after þis, and herfore þei maken statutis, stable as a stoon; and þei geten graunt of knyȝtis to confermen hem. And þis þei marken wel, wiþ witnesse of lordis, lest þat treuþe of Goddis law, hid in þe sepulcre, brest out to knowyng of þe comoun peple. O Crist! þi lawe is hid ȝit; whan wilt þou sende þin aungel to remove þe stone, and shewe þi treuþe to þi folk? Wel Y wote þat knyȝtis tooken gold in þis case, to helpe þat þi lawe be hid, and þin ordenaunce ceesse, but wel Y wote þat it shal be knowen at þe day of dome, or bifore whan þe likeþ aȝen al þi enemyes.

An allusion to the new translation of the Bible.

Here shulden men marke þe passioun of Crist, and prynten in þer herte sumwhat to shewe it, for it was most wilful

The voluntariness of Christ's Passion.

[1] *gylour*, E.

passioun þat ever was, and most hard passioun þat ever man suffride. It was þus wilful and so moost medeful. And herfore tolde Crist þe forme of his passioun to his xii disciplis, whan he wente to Jerusalem; and herfore Crist, þat[1] hidde him bifore to come to þe citee, came[2] now for to suffre, to shewe his free wille. And herfore he seiþ at his soper here, Wiþ desire Y have coveitid to ete þis Paske wiþ you. For desire of his godhede and desire of his manhede movede him to ete þus and to suffre after. But al þis was mene and figure of his last soper þat he etiþ in hevene wiþ men þat he haþ chosen. And þus siþ noo contrariete was in Cristis resoun, to suffre þis passioun, and his witt was moost clene, no þing þat man dide was to him more willeful. And siþ Crist suffride þus for synne of his breþeren, þei shulden suffre þancfulli for þer own synne. Crist axiþ not greet peyne in his breþeren, but þat þei have sorewe for þere synne, and purpos[3] to forsaken it; and þis is cause whi þat God wolde have his passioun þus rehersid, for profit of his breþeren and not for his owne. Þis peyne of Cristis passioun passid al oþer, for he was moost tendir man and in his myddil age, and God leet bi myracle Cristis wyttis suffre, for ellis he myȝte bi joye have hadde noo sorewe. But alle circumstauncis þat shulden make peyne hard, weren in Cristis passioun to make it more medeful. Þe place was most solempne and þe day also; þe houre was most knowun to Jewes and to heþen men; and þe dispit was moost: for men þat moost shulden love Crist ordeyneden þis moost foule deeþ, aȝen Cristis moost kyndnesse. And we shal bileve þat Crist suffride not in no manere but for certeyn enchesoun; for he, boþe God and man, þat made al þingis in noumbre, shope his passioun to answere to byggynge of mannys synne. And so sevene wordis þat Crist spake on þe cross answeren woundirfully to alle synnes of men; and shortly, no þing þat Crist ever dide was done but for greet cause and profit of men. Suche causes shulde we studie, and prenten hem in oure mynde, for wyte wel þat al þis was done for profit of Cristen men. And þus trowe we not þes heretikes þat ben foolis out of bileve, þat seien we may not sue Crist, and namely in his passioun, for Crist was nedid to suffren here al þat he

The pain of Christ's Passion.

[1] om. E. [2] *and cam*, E. [3] So B. E. C; *in purpos*, A.

suffride. Certis þes founede[1] heretikes shulden wel wite þat al þing mut nede come as God haþ ordeyned. And so sue we Crist afer in his blessid passioun, and gedre devout mynd of him, and kepe us aferre fro synne.

Þe Gospel on Eestir Day.

[SERMON XLVI.]

Maria Magdalene.—Matt. xxviii. [1.]

The two Marys at the sepulchre.

Þis gospel telliþ hou þes holy wymmen comen to bileve þat Crist was rysen fro deþ. Sum men seien þat here weren but two Maries, þat was Marie Magdalene, and Marie James modir; and þis secounde Marye was boþe our ladyes sister and Salomens dauȝter. But sum men seien þat þere weren þree. But it is ynow to us to trowen þat þei weren two, and leve to knowynge of God ȝif þere weren moo. *Þes two Maries bouȝten hem at even oynementis*, for it was leveful to wirchen at even in þe Sabotis. *And eerly on þe Sonnenday þei comen to þe sepulcre of Crist, at þe sunne rysynge, and seiden to gidere, Who shal turne to us þe stone fro dore of þe sepulcre? And þei lokiden þerto, and siȝen it turned awey, for soþe it was ful grete;* and passide þes wommans power to removen it fro þe dore, by castynge of þe Pharisees; for þei seiden þat Cristis disciplis wolden come and stelen his bodi. And so þis stone was removed bi service of aungelis, for disciplis of Crist dredden hem ȝit to walken. *And þes wymmen comen in to þe sepulcre of Crist, and þei seien an angel of God in forme of a ȝonge man sittynge on þe riȝt side and hild*[2] *wiþ a whiȝt stole. And þei woundriden of þe siȝt, but þe aungel seide to hem, Wole ȝe not drede*, for Y knowe youre purpos, *ȝe seken Jesus of Nazareþ þat was done on þe cros, but he is rysen to lyve, and is not now here.* For *here is þe stede voide, where þei hadden putt him. But go ȝe and seie ȝe to Christis disciplis, and algatis to Petir, þat Crist shal go bifore ȝou to þe contre of Galile. And þere shal ȝe see him as he saide* ȝou bifore; and he may not lye.

Ech word of þis gospel bereþ grete mysterye. First Crist

[1] *founyd*, B; *fond*, C; *foltid*, E. [2] *bilyd*, E.

Christ manifested ten times between the Resurrection and the Ascension.

apperide to þes holy wommen, fer to graunt a privylegie to womman's kynde. For it is seid comounly þat Crist apperide ten tymes from hour of his rysynge to his steiynge into hevene. First Crist apperide unto Marye Magdalene, and made her sterre of þe see, to ȝyve liȝt to men, and to put hir fro dispeire of hir first synnes. We denyen not þat ne Crist bifore þis apperide to his modir, hou þat he wolde, or in body or in soule, for she was ever sad in feiþ. Þe comynge of þes two Maries, þat was þe secounde shewynge þat Crist shewide him on lyve þat þe gospel telliþ, techiþ hou Crist wolde shewyn him unto many statis, and hou men shulde be disposid to have the siȝt of Crist. Þis eerly comynge with liȝt of þe sunne is redy comynge in grace for to serve Crist, and ȝit þe making redy on þe nyȝt bifore is done of Crist, but not in siche grace. The musing of þese wommen as þei wenten by þe wey, bitokeneþ bisy þouȝt how men shal come to serve Crist. But lore of good aungelis opneþ to men þis lessoun, for þe stoone of unbileve is first ful grete in synful men. Þis entrynge to þe sepulcre is comynge to þe service of Crist. Þis aungel þat techiþ men treuþe is good aungel of God þat sittiþ on þe riȝt side, to teche men þe wey to hevene, and to sitten on Cristis riȝt hond on þe daie of dome. Þe whitnesse of þis stole is clenesse of victorye þat siche men have of þer goostly enemyes. And as Gregory notiþ[a], þe face of þis aungel semed as liȝtnynge, and his cloþis whiȝt as snow; for Crist and his aungelis ben dredeful to wickide men, and plesyng to good men. Ȝhe, to þe day of dome þis aungel confortiþ men, and riȝtiþ þer purpos, and telliþ hem how now Crist is sittynge in hevene, for his staat here in erþe is fulli performed. And office of suche men is aftirward enjoyned hem, þat þei shulden parte wiþ þer breþeren goostly werkes of mercy, not oonly wiþ comounnes[1] but also wiþ prelatis. Þe goynge bifore of Crist to þe contre of Galile is, goinge bifore of Crist to hevene. Þere he shal shewen him to men as he haþ hiȝt to hem ofte in þe gospel.

[1] *comyns*, E.

[a] S. Greg. *In Evang.* Hom. xxi. 'In fulgure etenim terror timoris est, in nive autem blandimentum candoris. Quia verò omnipotens Deus et terribilis peccatoribus, et blandus est justis, recte testis resurrectionis ejus Angelus et in fulgure vultus et in candore habitus demonstratur; ut de ipsâ suâ specie et terreret reprobos, et mulceret pios.'

Here after þis witt men may large þis gospel, and trete what mater þat þei wenen shulde profite to þe puple; but it is comounly told of þe sacrament of þe auter, and how men shal disposen hem now to take þis sacrament. And it is seid comounly, þat as þes holy wymmen hadde lefte þer former synne, and taken þer freishe devocioun; so men shulden come to þe chirche to take þis holy sacrament, and þus come wiþ þes hooly wymmen wiþ liȝt of þe sunne. And þus men shulden cloþen hem wiþ þes þre vertues, bileve, hope, and charite, to resceyve þis sacrament. Bileve is first nedeful; and algatis of þis breed, hou it is Goddis body by vertue of Cristis wordis. And so it is kyndely breed, as Poul seiþ [a], but it is sacramentally verre Goddis bodi. And herfore seiþ Austyn [b], þat þing is breed þat þi iȝen tellen þee and þat þou seest wiþ hem. For it was not trowid bifore þe fend was losid [c], þat þis worþi sacrament was accident wiþouten suget. And ȝit dwellen trewe men in þe old bileve, and laten freris foulen hem silfe in þer newe heresie. For we trowen þat þere is beter þing þan Goddis bodi, siþ þe holy trinite is in eche place. But oure bileve is sette upon þis point; what is þis sacrid hoost, and not what þing is þere. Þe secound vertue þat shulde cloþe trewe men is þe vertue of hope, þat is ful nedeful; how men shulde hope bi þer lyfe here, and first, wiþ þe grace of God, for to come to hevene. And to þis entent men taken now þis sacrament, so þat bi takynge herof þer mynde be freschid in hem to þenken

This gospel commonly applied to the sacrament of the altar.

[a] I do not know to what passage the writer refers.

[b] I am indebted to the kind assistance of Professor Stubbs for the discovery of the passage in the works of St. Augustine to which the text probably refers, though some force appears necessary to make the words of the saint bear the meaning which Wyclif imposes on them. The passage is in a remarkable sermon, No. 272 (vol. v., p. 1104 of the Benedictine edition), addressed 'ad Infantes' on their due reception of the Eucharist. The impression left by the entire sermon might certainly, to a mind already prepossessed, accord with the view of the Eucharist taken by Wyclif; on the other hand, the language is quite compatible with the view taken by his opponents, the friars. The words most to the purpose are these: 'Ista, fratres, ideo dicuntur sacramenta, quia in eis aliud videtur, aliud intelligitur. Quod videtur, speciem habet corporalem; quod intelligitur, fructum habet spiritalem.'

[c] It had become a popular belief by this time, among the spiritual Franciscans and the various revolutionary sects, that since the year 1000 A.D. the devil, after his millennary captivity (Apoc. xx. 2), had been let loose from the bottomless pit 'to deceive the nations.'

on kyndenes of Crist to maken hem clene in soule. And herfore seiþ Poul þat he þat wantiþ þis ende, etiþ and drynkeiþ his judgement, for he jugiþ not þe worþines of Goddis bodi, ne worshipiþ his ordenaunce. Þe þridde vertue nedeful for to take þis sacrament is vertue of charite; for þat is ever nedeful, siþ no man comeþ to Cristis fest but ȝif he have þis cloþing. And þus, as Austyn declariþ[a], foure poyntis þat falliþ[1] to makinge of breed techen us þis charite, and algatis to have it now. For ellis we greggen[2] our synne in etynge of þis breed. And ȝif we have þis cloþinge, takinge þis mete in figure, it shal brynge us to hevene, þere to ete Goddis body goostly wiþouten ende; and þat is mennis blisse.

1 Cor. xi. 29.

ÞE FIRSTE SONDAI GOSPEL AFTIR EESTIR.

[SERMON XLVII.]

Cum esset sero die una.—JOHN XX. [19.]

The fifth appearing of Christ after his resurrection.

Þis gospel telliþ of þe fifþe apperynge, þat was þe last, and late done upon Paske daie, and þis is told wiþ oþer to conferme bileve of þe Chirche. As þe secounde apperynge was to þe holy wommen, so þe first apperynge was alone to Marye Magdalene, as telliþ þe gospel of Joon in þe same capitle. Þe þridde tyme Crist apperide to Petir as Seint Luke telliþ in eende of his gospel; and þis was, as sum men seyen, whan Petre and Joon comen fro þe sepulcre, and Petre went bi himsilfe woundrynge and musinge. Þe fourþe apperynge was maad to two disciplis þat wenten to Emawus, and Crist soupid wiþ hem. Of þis telliþ þe eende of Seint Lukes gospel. Þe fifþe apperynge was þis þat oure gospel telliþ of, and þis was last of fyve, þat Crist

[1] *fallen*, B, C, E. [2] *agreggen*, E.

[a] I have to thank Professor Stubbs for this reference also. In Serm. 272, already quoted, and also in Serm. 227, the various processes that enter into the making of bread are compared to the spiritual operations which combine to make the perfect Christian. But in Serm. 229, these processes are distinctly set down as *four:* threshing, which answers to conversion by preaching; grinding, which represents the discipline of fasting and exorcism; mixing with water, which is Baptism; and baking, which corresponds to the flames kindled in souls by the Holy Ghost.

shewide on Paske daye. And on þat dai sevene niȝt Crist apperyde þe sixte tyme, and of þes two apperingis telliþ þis gospel.

Þe storye seiþ, *whan it was late, þe first day of þe woke* þat came nexte after þe Frydaye þat God was done to deþ on, and þat was in þe Sonenday next after þe Sabot. But it was late, *and þe disciplis weren gedrid þere,* to conforte hem to gidere, *and for drede þat þei hadde of Jewes* þat weren her enemyes: *þer ȝatis weren fast shitt, for drede* of þe same folk; *Jesus cam,* not lettinge *þat þe ȝatis weren shitt* þus, *and stood in þe myddis of his disciplis, and seide þus unto hem; Pees be to ȝou, for Y am* alyve, *wole ȝe not drede* þe while ȝe have siche a keper. *And he shewide to hem his hondis and his side, and þe disciplis hadden joie*[1] *whan þei hadden seen þus þe Lord.* For sorewe of his deþ and drede of Jewis weren clenly putt awey bi siȝt of þis lord. And *Christ seide aȝen, Pees be to ȝou,* to tellen hem þe ful pees þat þei shulden have þerafter boþe in bodi and soule, for þere medeful pacience. And þei shulden not grutche for þis short pursuynge, for Crist telliþ þat, *as his Fadir sent him so he sendiþ hem,* to suffre tribulaciouns; and þei shulden holden hem paied of sich form of sendinge. And whan he hadde seid þus, *he blew on hem and seide, Take ȝe þe Holy Goost,* for herby ȝe shulen be stronge by power and by witt, þat ȝe shal have by him.

Here we shal wite þat Crist blew not bi childhode upon his apostlis but bi greet witt; for herby Crist tauȝt þat þe Holy Goost comeþ boþe of þe Fadir and þe Sone, as wyne of erþe and water. And comyng forþ of þis Gost is not nativite, but sutil inspiringe of þes two persones, and herfore þei ben clepid o principle of þis Gost. And holy writt grauntiþ þat þe Sone sendiþ þis Goost, and herfore Crist grauntiþ þis privylegie to his disciplis, *þat whos synnes þat þei forȝyven, þei ben forȝovun to hem,* and *whos synnes þat þei wiþolden, þei ben holden to hem.* And boste men not for þis privylegie grauntid to þe apostlis, for it is undirstonden in as myche as siche apostlis acorden wiþ þe keies of þe chirche above. And herfore shulden siche bostours ben certeyne at

Double procession of the Holy Ghost.

[1] So in E; A wrongly excludes the words 'and —— joie' from the italics.

þe firste þat þei ben verrey vikers of þe holy apostlis. And siþ God enspiriþ[1] hem and ȝyveþ hem witt and power to bynden and to lousen as Crist him silfe doiþ, or ellis hem wantiþ þis power, and þanne þei shulde not boste þat þei have siche power, so þei myȝte not pleynher shewen hem to have no siche power þan fer to bargayn herwiþ, and boste hem to have siche power. For þanne þei ben noon of hem to whom Crist ȝaf þis power; for ȝif þer weren two popis, the toon aȝens þe toþir, and þe toon looside alle þat þe toþer boond, it were not for to dreme wheþer of hem did soþely, but wheþer more suede Goddis doynge and resoun. And siþ God may not folde fro riȝt and resoun, it is knowen bi Goddis lawe þat no pope assoiliþ but in as myche as Crist assoiliþ first[a]. And herfore Seint Petre and oþer Cristis apostlis asoilliden not þus, ne ȝyve siche indulgencis; for þei diden never siche dedis but whan God enspiride hem. And so no þing is falser þan ypocritis to boste þus, and ȝif men loke to resoun þei may wele se þat many siche feynyngis ben of þe fendis scole. For ellis myȝte a pope assoile men boþe of peyne and blame[b], for þei killen þer evene cristene[c], and ever while þei done so; and ȝif þei ceessen fro sich killing, þer assoilinge shal ceesse. But what men wolden triste to siche assoilinge? Wel we witen

[1] So in B and C; *enspireþ*, E; A has *enspirit*.

[a] This position recalls one of the twenty four conclusions, condemned by the 'earth-quake' synod of 1382: 'That no prelate ought to excommunicate any one, unless he first know that he is excommunicated by God.' Lewis's *Wyclif*, p. 108.

[b] The ordinary indulgence absolved *poena sed non culpa*. In theory, the guilt of sins, and the *eternal* punishment due to them, were remitted in the sacrament of penance; it was the *temporal* punishment only, the *poena*, which the indulgence professed to remit, in whole or in part. But it is well known that, during the fourteenth and fifteenth centuries, a great laxity prevailed, if not in the actual wording of indulgences, at any rate in the language of those to whom their distribution was entrusted. The form was probably observed strictly enough all along; so that the preacher's words must be taken with some allowance. In turning over the pages of the Bullarium, I observe, under the year 1515, only two years before the first public appearance of Luther, the formal grant by Leo X of two indulgences, and in both cases the form of words is; — [Indulgemus] 'quod quilibet Christi fidelis . . . . . . plenariam omnium peccatorum suorum, *de quibus corde contritus, atque ore confessus fuerit*, indulgentiam et remissionem consequatur.'

[c] The allusion is to Bishop Spencer's crusade. When it was over, and men should cease to kill their fellow-Christians, then the papal indulgence, or 'assoilinge,' would also cease.

þat God is moost lord of al oþer, and no man may do synne, but ȝif he synne aȝens him, and no synne may be forȝovun but ȝif God first forȝyve it. And so it is propre to God to forȝyve þus offence, and ȝif a man forȝyve siche synne, þat is bi power of viker; and siche power haþ he not, but ȝif God shewe it him. For ellis myȝte he graunte pardoun for longe after þe day of dome to men þat God wole have dampnyd, for a newe founde praier, and heien it for mannis love more þan þe Pater Noster: as men seien þat a pope haþ grauntid two þousand ȝeer to ech man þat is contrite and confessid of his synne, þat seiþ þis orisoun 'Domine Jesu Christe' bitwene þe sacringe of þe masse and þe þridde Agnus Dei. And þan it were ydil to traveile for ony pardoun, siþ a man myȝte at home gete him fourty þousand ȝeer bi noone. And so þat man þat shal be dampned, þat is confessid and contrite, and seiþ þus ofte þis praier, shulde have many þousand ȝeer in helle after þe daie of dome. Triste we to þe old bileve þat Crist assoiliþ as he wole, and þis forme is hid to men as oþer treuþis þat God wole hide.

Thomas oon of þe twelve þat is clepid Didimus was not wiþ þes ten whan Jesus came and dide þus; and oþer disciplis tolden him hou þat þei saien þe Lord. But he seide unto hem, But ȝif Y see in his hondis picching[1] *of þe naillis, and putt my fynger in þe place þat Crist was ynaillid in, and put my hond in his syde where he was persid wiþ þe spere, Y shal nevere trowen þat oure Jesus is rysen. And on þe Sonday nexte after, weren þes disciplis inne and Thomas wiþ hem;* and Crist shewide him as bifore. *For he came whan þe ȝatis weren closid and stood amyddis, and saide, as he saide bifore, Pees be to you. And after he seide to Thomas,* þat he sente after to Inde, *Putt in here þi finger and se my hondis and putt hidir þin hond and putt in to my side, and wole þou not be untrewful but trewe in bileve. Thomas answeride and seide to Crist, My Lord and my God. And Jesus seide to him þan, For þou say me þus, Thomas, þou bilevidst in me; but blessid ben þo þat saien not þis, and trowen* as þou doist. *Many oþer signes dide Crist in siȝt of his disciplis, but þes few ben writun in þis book for þis ende, þat ȝe bileve þat Jesus is Goddis sone, and þat ȝe for þis bileve have blisse in his name. Amen.*

[1] *pitchyng*, E.

Þe secounde Sonday Gospel aftir Eestir.

[SERMON XLVIII.]

Ego sum pastor bonus.—John x. [11.]

Christ the good shepherd.

Christ telliþ in þis gospel þe maners of a good herde, so þat herbi we may witen how oure herdis failen now. And defaute of siche heerdis is moost peril in þe Chirche; ffor, as riȝt office of hem shulde moost bringe men to heven, so defaute of þis office drawiþ men moost to helle. Crist telliþ of him silf, *how he is a good herde*, for he is þe beste herde þat mankynde may have. For he is good bi him silf and may no wey faile, for he is boþe God and man; and God may no wey synne. And þus we have þe mesure to knowe a good herd and an yvel, for þe more þat an herd is lyke to Crist, he is þe beter, and þe more þat he strangiþ from him, he is þe worse in þis office. And efte whan Crist haþ ȝyve þe mesure for to knowe good herdis, he telliþ þe heieste proprete þat falliþ to a good herde: *a good herde*, as Crist seiþ, *puttiþ his lyf for his sheep;* for more charite may noon have þan to putte his lyfe for his frendis, and ȝif he worchiþ wysely[1], for to bring þes sheep to hevene. For þus þe herde haþ moost peyne and þe sheep moost profit.

The Pope compared to Antichrist,

Þus we may see, who is good herde and who failiþ in þis office; for as Crist puttiþ wisely his owen lif for his sheep, so Antecrist puttiþ proudly many lifes for his foule lyfe. As, ȝif þe fend ledde þe pope to kille many þousend men to holde his worldely state, he suede Antecristis maneres. And siþ þis propirte of herde groundiþ charite in men, eche man shulde have herof algatis more or lesse; as he is ferre fro þis maner þat wole not ȝyve his worldely goodis to his sheep or his breþeren, whan þei have grete nede þerto, for sich goodis ben worse þan mannis lyfe. And þus semen oure religious to be exempte fro charite; ffor nede a man nevere so myche to have helpe

[1] om. E.

of siche goodis, ȝee, alȝif þei have stoonys or oþer jewelis þat harmen hem, but þei wolen not ȝyve siche goodis ne value of hem to helpe þer breþeren, ne ceesse to anoye hem silf in bilding of hye housis, ne to gaderen sich veyn goodis, ȝif it do harm to þer breþeren. Sich averous men ben ferre fro maneres of a good herde, and so thes newe religious þat þe fend haþ tollid inne, bi colour to helpe þer former heerdis, harmen hem many weies, and letten þis office in þe chirche. For trewe prechinge and worldely goodis ben spuylid bi siche religiouse; and herfore techiþ Crist to flee hem, for þei ben ravyshinge wolvys. Sum wole, as breris, tere wolle of sheepe and make hem coold in charite, and sum wole sturdly, as þornes, sleye sheep of Holy Chirche, and þus is our moder shent for defaute of mennys help. And more mede myȝt no man have þan to helpe þis sory wydewe; for princis of preestis and Pharisees þat calliden Crist a giloure have crocchid[1] to hem þe chesynge of many heerdis in þe Chirche. And þei ben tauȝt by Antecrist to chese hise herdis and not Cristis, and þus failiþ Christis Chirche. Lord! siþ heerdis shulden passe þer sheep as men passen bletyng sheep, how shulde Cristis Chirche fare, ȝif þes heerdis weren turned to woolvys! But Crist seiþ þat þus it fareþ among þe heerdis of þe Chirche, þat many of hem *ben hired hynes and not heerdis over þe sheep, for þe sheep ben not þer owun*. And so þei loven to litil þe sheep, for ȝif þei have þere temporal hire, þei recken not how þer flok fare. And þus done alle þes curatours, þat tellen more by worldely wynnynge þan by vertues of þer sugettis or soule hele to come to hevene. Siche ben not heerdis of sheep, but of dunge and wolle of hem, and þes shal not have in hevene joie of þer sheep þat þei kepen. Siche hynen *seen þe wolvys comynge* to flokkis þat þei shulde kepe, and *þei fleen* for drede of not[2], and þes wolvys *ravyshen þe sheep and scateren hem*, for þis eende þat þei þanne may souner perishe. And þus moved Poul to found none ordre, for Christis ordre is ynouȝ, and þanne shulde alle Cristen men be more surely in o flok. Lord! ȝif cowardise of siche hynen be þus dampned of Crist, how myche more shulden wolvys be

the friars to wolves.

[1] *crochid*, B, C, E. [2] *nouȝt*, B, E.

dampnyd þat ben putt to kepe Cristis sheep. But Crist seiþ a clene cause *whi þes hired hynen* fleen þus. *For he is an hyred hyne, and þe sheep perteynen not to him*, but þe dung of siche sheep, and þis dung suffisiþ to hem, howevere þe sheep faren. Sum ben wolves wiþouten forþ, and sum ben wolves wiþinne, and þes ben more perilous[1], for homely enemyes ben þe worste. Yvel wolvys ben religiouse, þat Crist seiþ in Mathew's gospel, ben wolvys ravyshinge, alȝif þei comen in sheepis cloþis; for bi þis ypocrisye þei disseyven sonner þe sheep. And alȝif þer dwellyng be wiþouten parishens of þes sheep, and þei ben strange and newe brouȝt in by þe fend, ȝit þei forȝiten not to come and visite þe sheep. But comounly whan þei comen, þei comen moost for to spuyle; and þus done generaly boþ freris and monkes and chanouns. But þei ben wolvys wiþinne þat seien þat þei have cure of soulis, and ravyshen goodis of þes sheep, and feden hem not goostli, but raþer moven hem to synne, and waken not in heerdis office.

Three functions proper to a good shepherd.

But Crist seiþ he is a good heerde, and knowiþ his sheep, and þei him. For þe office þat falliþ to heerdis makiþ him known among hem, *as my Fadir knowiþ me, and Y aȝen knowe my Fadir.* So seiþ Crist, *Y putt my lyf to kepe my sheep* aȝen wolvys. And as þis knowynge myȝt not quenche bitwene Crist and his Fadir, so shulden þes heerdis waken upon þer sheep; and þei shulden knowen him not by bodili feestis ne oþer synnes þat he doiþ, but by þree offices of heerdis þat Crist haþ lymytid to hem. It falliþ to a good herde to lede his sheep in hole pasturis, and whan his sheep ben hirt or stabbid, to hele hem and to grese hem; and whan oþer yvel beestis assailen hem, þan helpe hem. And herto shulde he putte his lyfe to save his sheepe fro siche beestis. Þe pasture is Goddis lawe, þat ever more is greene in treuþe, and rotun pasture ben oþer lawes and oþer fablis wiþouten ground. And cowardise of siche heerdis þat dar not defende Goddis lawe witnessiþ þat þei failen in two offices suyng after; for he þat dar not for worldes drede defende þe lawe of his God, how shulde he defende his sheep for love þat he haþ to hem? And ȝif þei bryngen in newe lawes contrarie

[1] So B; *perilouse*, E; A has *perolous*.

to Goddis lawe, how shulden þei not failen after in oþer offices þat þei shulden have? But Crist þat is heed of herdis *seiþ, þat he haþ oþer sheep þat ben not ȝite of þis flok, and hem mut he brynge togidere, and teche hem to knowe his vois. And so shal þere be oo flok, and oon herde over hem alle.* Þes sheep ben heþene men or Jewes þat Crist wole converte, ffor al þes shal make o flok, þe which flok is holy Chirche; but ferre fro þis undirstondinge, þat alle men shal be convertid.

Þe Þridde Sondai Gospel after Eestir.

[SERMON XLIX.]

Modicum et jam non videbitis me.—Joon xvi. [16.]

Here telliþ Crist to his Chirche how þer wille shulde be temprid, for variynge of þer heed after his resureccioun. He seiþ ferst to his apostlis *þat þer is ny a litil tyme and þei shal not see him*, for he shal be deed and buried; for þes wordis of Crist weren seid þe nexte Þursday bifore his deeþ; and aftir Crist seiþ to his disciplis, *þat þere shulde sue a more tyme and þan þei shulden see Crist*, and ofte tymes be confortid by him. And þat was fro rysynge of Crist to þe tyme þat he steye to hevene. But for Crist haþ lymytid tyme þat he shuld come to his Fadir, Crist seiþ þis time shal be litil, *for he goiþ to his Fadir.* For boþe Cristis liynge in þe sepulcre and his dwellinge here in erþe was litil tyme as God limitide, to answere to his ascencioun. *And sum of disciplis of Crist saiden togidere, What is þis þat Crist seiþ to us, a litil and efte ȝe shal se me, for Y go to my Fadir. And þei seiden, What is þis litil, for we witen nevere what he meneþ. And Jesus wiste þat his disciplis wolden axe him* of þis unknowun þinge[1], *and he seide þus to hem; Of þis ȝe axen among you, þat Y seide, a litil tyme shulde come, and þan ȝe shal not se me, and siþ a litil but more tyme, and þan ȝe shal see me. Forsoþe, fforsoþe, Y seie to you, þat ȝe shal boþe grete and wepe, but þe world*

[1] So E; A and B wrongly italicise the word.

þanne shal joie, and þan shal ȝe be soreuful, but ȝoure sorewe shal turne to joie. And þis was soþ of þe apostlis aftir þe rysyng of Crist, ffor first þei maden more sorewe, and siþ lasse, and siþ joie. And worldely men contrarieden hem, þat first hadden joie and siþ sorewe, for þei joieden of apostlis sorewe and sorewiden of apostlis joie. And efte Crist telliþ a kyndely saumple, to prynte þis word more in þer herte.

A womman, seiþ Crist, *whan she travailiþ wiþ child, haþ sorewe* of hir peyne, *but aftir whan she is delyverid, she haþ joie of hir child, and forȝetiþ her former sorewe, for man is bore in to þe world. And þerfore ȝe have sorewe now, but efte Y shal see you, and youre herte shal have joie, and no man shal take fro ȝou ȝour joie.* Þis womman, to Cristis entent, is oure modir holy Chirche, and every party þerof þat is also holy Chirche. And as long as we lyven here, we ben travelynge of child, to brynge oure soule to surete fro bisie sorewe of þis world, and so to brynge forþ þe hole man to blisse boþe in bodi and soule. And whan we comen to þis state we þenken not of oure former sorewe to oure anoye or to oure mornynge, for joie of ende þat sueþ; but we þenken in oure herte þat for þis peyne þat we have now, we shal have myche joie whan we ben ful made in þe world. And þat shal nevere be done fully bifore þat we come to blisse, for we mornen til þat tyme. For we may liȝtly perishe fro lyfe, but þanne a man is fully made, whan he is corouned in blisse, for þanne he is certeyne to lyve evere in blis withouten peyne.

Four endowments of the glorified body: Clerkis seien þat whan a man is brouȝt þus to Goddis chambre, þan he is fully spousid with God, and dowid, boþe in bodi and in soule, of foure doweris of þe bodi. Crist toke ernes[1] here in þis world, for whan he cam out of his modir he brak not þe cloister of hir, but, as þe sunne comeþ þorouȝ þe glas, so Crist cam fro his modir wombe. And þis morwȝyve[2] is clepid of clerkes, dower of bodily sutilte, and ofte usid Crist þis dower
1. subtilty. fro þat tyme þat he was rysen. Þe secounde dower of þe bodi
2. agility. is clepid agilite, þat is swiftnesse þerof and to moven hou a man wole; and þis dower usid Crist whan he wente upon þe water, and specialy at þat tyme þat he stied in to heven. Þe

[1] *ernys*, C. [2] *morwe-ȝyve*, B: *morcw-ȝyfe*, E.; *more ȝif*, C.

þridde dower of þe bodi is incorruptibilite, þat þe body may not die ne be broke bi no þing; and þis dower knew þe fend whan he aleggide to Crist þat he shulde not hurte his foot, ȝif he lepte doun fro þe temple. And by vertue of þis dower þe knyȝtis broken not Cristis þies, ne, whan he cam in at þe ȝatis þe bordis broken not his bodi. Þe fourþe dower and þe laste is cleryng of mannis bodi, whan it shyneþ briȝt in hevene as þe sunne or oþer sterres; and þis dower toke Crist to him in tyme of his transfiguringe. And herfore seide Petre þanne, þat good was hem to be þere, for þis is þe heiest dower þat falliþ unto mannis body. 3. incorruptibility. 4. transparency.

And after þes foure doweris fallen foure unto þe soule. Þe first and þe moste dower answeriþ to þe last of þe bodi, þat a soule blessid in hevene haþ clere knowyng of alle þingis, þat is or was or ever shal be. And siþ a man haþ delite to see a pley here in erþe, or a lord, or þing of wounder, and þerwiþ fediþ his bodi, myche more þis clere siȝt of God and alle his creaturis shulden fulli fede þe blessid soule, and þereafter blisse þe bodi. And herfor seiþ oure Jesus, in the gospel of Seint Joon, þat þis is lyf wiþouten ende, to knowe þe Fadir and his Sone. For þan men knowen in þis myrour al creaturis þat may be; and þis clere siȝt is more joyeful þan ony tunge may telle here. Þe secounde dower of þe soule is vertue to kepe ful knowynge, so þat knowyng of oo þing contrarieþ not to anoþer. And riȝt as bodi shal ever last, for acorde of alle his partis, so mannis wittis shal ever last for lokynge in þe first myrour; and so man forȝiteþ not in hevene þingis þat he sum tyme knewe. Þe þridde dower of þe soule is redynesse for to knowe al þingis þat man wole, hou ofte þat he wole þenke on hem; for ȝif he traveilid in þis þouȝt ony þing aȝens his wille, he were not fully in blisse, ne wiþouten anoyous peyne. And neþeles we bileven þat seintis have what þei wolen have, and þei wolen noo þing þat is yvel. And þus men grounden many blyssis, but al ben brouȝt to þes foure þat we can rekene in seintis. As þe fourþe dowery of man in blis, answeryng to þe first of þe bodi, is sutilte of mannis soule, þat it takiþ al kyn treuþe, and herby is [not][1] undisposid to cast out oo treuþe by Four endowments of the soul: 1. knowledge, John xvii. 3. 2. capacity. 3. nimbleness. 4. subtilty.

[1] The 'not,' which spoils the sense, is rightly omitted in E.

anoþer; but as many blessid bodies ben togidere in o place, so many blessid knowyngis ben togidere in oo soule. Surete of siche goodis may not faile to þes seintis, siþ þei seen clerely in God how it is nede al þis to be. And so þei witen how þei have al þe joie þat þei wolen, siþ hem wantiþ no kyn þing þat þei shulden desire to have.

Þe fourþe Sondai Gospel aftir Eestir.

[SERMON L.]

Vado ad eum qui misit me.—John xvi. [5.]

Christ foretells his ascension.

Þis gospel of Joon telliþ hie pryvete of þing þat is to come bifore þe day of dome. And, for Cristis assencioun is neyȝ, þerfore Crist telliþ a word of his assencioun þat his apostlis shulden trowe. Crist, to whom al þing þat shal be is present, seiþ upon þe Þursday þat he shulde die on þe morow: *Y go to him þat haþ sent me* to þe erþe, and þat is a myche office, to bye þe chirche of men. And for my steiyng is so opyn, as[1] it is hid bifore tyme, *noon of ȝou axiþ me whidir þat Y go, but ȝit, for Y have spoke þes þingis unto ȝou,* ȝe trowen not[2] but liȝtly þat þei ben soþe, and so oonhed[3][a], *sorow haþ now fillid ȝoure hertis,* for Y have told ȝou how þat Y shal suffre, hou Y shal be reproved, and how Y shal die, and how Y shal aftir be absentid fro ȝou; and how Y shal dwelle in hevene til Y come to þe last day to juge þe world to joye or to peyne. And þes wordis shulden make frendis to mourne among hem silf, but *Y seie ȝou treuþe, it spediþ to ȝou þat Y go, for ȝif Y go not, þe Holy Goost shal not come to ȝou, and ȝif Y shal go, Y shal sende him to ȝou. And whan he shal come he shal reprove þe world of synne, of riȝtwisnese, and also of jugement.*

[1] *and*, E. [2] *now*, E. [3] *oon bid*, B; *unbid*, E; *on bid*, C.

[a] The variations of the MSS. and the fact of their all including the words 'and so oonhed' in the italics, show that the scribes themselves did not understand this passage. I have restored the words to Wyclif, and explain the passage thus; 'You readily believe that my words are true, and so unity;' i. e. harmonious and self-consistent.

But þis shal be undirstonde thus — God shal reprove þis world *of synne of untreuþe, for þei trowiden not in me.* And þis is þe first synne, and moost unkynde þat þei myȝten do to God; ffor siþ Crist came to þis world and by-cam our broþer to bye us, and algatis to profite to mankynde, and he is so opyn treuþe shewid þus unto man, þis is a greet synne to trowe not here to Crist. For in synnynge in þis feiþ unkynde men untrowen to his Fadir and to Crist and also to þe Holy Goost, for þis holy Trinite witnessiþ þis journey. And as bileve is first vertue and ground of al oþer, so unbileve is þe first synne of alle oþer, and þerfore synne take[1] by himsilf is take for þis moost famous. Of þis synne shal the Gost repreve men of þis world.

The world reproved of unbelief,

Secoundly shal þis Goost *repreve men of riȝtwisnesse* þat þei shulden have to Crist and unkyndely wanten it. For sich a messanger should be worshipid of alle men, and heried, for sich a message, siþ it was so profitable. And so þe world shal be dampned for wanting of þis riȝtwisnesse, and specialy, *for siche a persone goiþ aȝen to his Fadir.* And þat shewiþ þat Crist is þe secounde persone in Trinite, and so bi his godhede evene wiþ his Fadir, and bi his manheed lasse, but even in kynde wiþ his breþeren. And þus riȝt wole axe þat þis persone were worshipid.

of unrighteousness,

Þe þridde tyme shal þis *Goost reprove men of þis world, for þei jugide folily* þat Crist was led by a fend. And ȝit þe most hie fend, *prince of þis worlde, is now juged* to helle, for he temptide þus Crist and dide him unworshipe.

of rash judgment.

Ȝit, seiþ Crist, *Y have many þingis to seie to ȝou, but ȝe may not bere hem now; but þe spirit of treuþe shal come to ȝou, and teche you alle treuþe,* and make ȝou strong to bere treuþe to suffryng of deeþ. Þerfore þis good maister shal here bygynne for to teche þe boke of lyfe, and he shal nevere ende to teche, til þat his disciplis comen to hevene; and þere þei shal clerely knowe eche treuþe þat men can telle. *He shal not speke of himsilf,* wiþouten ony cause bifore, *but al þingis þat he shal here* of the Fadir and of þe Sone *shal he speke* and telle

The teaching of the Holy Ghost.

[1] *taken*. E.

ȝou, and ȝe shal after teche his Chirche. *And þingis þat here after ben to come shal þis Goost telle ȝou.* For þe apostlis knewun here al þat now is nede to knowe, for in þis mesure ledde God hem, and movede hem to do his dedis. He chargide hem not wiþ ydel witt þat herfore þei shulden be proud, but alle þat nedide hem to kunne, þei kouden þat redely. *Þis Goost shal clarifie me, for he shal take of myne and shewe ȝou* þe treuþe þat Y am and þat Y have. And so in knowing of þis treuþe þe apostlis shal wele knowe Crist, how bi his godhede he is ever wiþ þe Fadir, and anentis his manhede, he is evere in kynde wiþ his breþeren. But in grace of oonhede he passiþ alle oþer men þat may be, siþ no man may be God but he, and welle of grace as he is. And herfore Crist declariþ him silf, and seiþ, *þat alle þat his Fadir haþ ben*[1] *hise, and herfore he seide þat þe Goost shal take of his and shewe to his disciplis*, as ben þe apostlis and oþer after.

The double procession of the Holy Ghost.

And in þese heye wordis of witt, Crist techiþ how he wiþ his Fadir is þe same God in kynde, and bryngiþ forþ þe Holy Goost. For ellis þe Fadir hadde þis Goost, and Crist hadde not þis same Goost, and so not al þat þe Fadir haþ had Crist as verre God. But siþ þis word of Crist is soþ, it shewiþ openly þat Crist is God and of him wiþ his Fadir comeþ forþ þe Holy Goost. Þis Holy Goost may not be made, but ever comeþ forþ of þes two, as ȝif þe shynynge of þe sonne come forþ evere of liȝt and briȝtnesse. But, for þis sentence is myche hid fro witt of þe comoun peple, þerfore shulde preestis shapen of þe wordis of þis gospel, what myȝt profite to his puple after undirstondinge of hem.

Explanation of verse 7.

And we shulden marke þis word of Crist whan he seiþ to his disciplis, but ȝif he go fro hem to hevene, he shal not sende to hem þe Holy Goost; and many men musen of þes wordis, siþ Crist was every where almyȝty, and so he myȝt as wele in erþe as in hevene sende hem þis Goost. Lord! what nedid Crist to stye and speke wiþ mouþ wiþ þis Goost. Sich wordis shewen men ful rude to conseyve þis mater, and þerfore it were nede to hem to knowe witt of þes wordis. We shal trowe þat Cristis

[1] *is*, E.

disciplis loveden him here to fleishly, and þei musten be purgid here of þis love bi þe Holy Goost; and þes þingis myȝt best be done whan manhede of Crist was fro hem. And þus for rudenesse of apostlis, Crist seiþ þat it spediþ þat he go fro hem, but he dwelliþ bi his godhede and his vertue ever wiþ hem. And herfore he seiþ anoþer tyme, þat he is al daies wiþ hem unto þe eende of þis world, bi Godhede and vertue of his manhede. And þus whan Crist was went to hevene, his apostlis weren clere in love, and leften þe love of erþely þingis, and þouȝten clenly of hevenly þingis.

The evil of endowments and the sufficiency of tithes.

And of þis witt taken sum men þat it falliþ not to Cristis viker ne to preestis of holy Chirche to have rentis here in erþe. But Jesus shulde be her rente, as he seiþ ofte in the olde lawe; and þer bodily sustynaunce þei shulden have of Goddis parte, as of dymes and offryngis and oþer almes taken in mesure; þe which by þer holy lyf þei abliden hem[a] to take þus. Lord! siþ þe bodi of Crist undisposid þe apostlis to take þis Goost, myche more shulde worldely lordship unable men now to take þis Goost. And siþ þei have now o Goost, it is lycly bi þer dedis þat þei have a wickide Goost þat lediþ hem an yvel wey. And in þes wordis we may see hou religiouse þat ben to day, drawen more to þer abite and to þer stynkynge ordenaunce, þan Crist wolde þat his apostlis chargiden þanne[1 b] presence of his bodi. And herfore Crist sent his apostlis aloone, scaterynge into þe world, and certis þei weren more able now þan whan he sent hem two and two; for now þei weren rype by þe Holy Goost more sadly þan þei weren bifore. But oure freris þat ben syke ben closid now in cloistre togidere, mo þan twelve of Cristis apostlis; and þis semeþ by þe fendis cautel, þat ȝif on blec[2] not his broþer, anoþer worse shulde fylen[3] hem. And herfore sum freris have witt to holde hem ferre fro siche a lumpe and avente hem in þe world; and þan shulden þei have good goost, for þus did Crist wiþ his disciplis, and him þei shulden suen in lyf.

[1] om. C; *þe*, E; *þanne*, B. [2] *blekke*, B, C; *blecke*, E. [3] *defoule*, B.

[a] *abliden hem*, that is, qualified themselves.

[b] Unless *þanne* is to be taken as representing the old form of the A. S. masc. sing. accus. *þone*, the reading of the Douce MS., *þe*, is preferable.

Þe fyfþe Sondai Gospel after Eestir.

[SERMON LI.]

Amen, Amen, dico vobis, si quid petieritis.—John xvi. [23.]

Praying in the name of Christ.

Crist telliþ in þis gospel hou his disciplis shulden be helpid by vertue of her preier, whan he was styed in to hevene. And first he seiþ a general word, and takiþ boþe his kyndis to witnes, þat, *ȝif þei axen ouȝt þe Fadir of hevene in his name, he shal ȝyve it hem.* But, as Crist seiþ, *unto þat tyme his disciplis axiden not in his name, and herfor aftirward shulden þei axen þat þere joie were ful, and þei shulden take.* Al þe hardnesse of þis mater is to cunne perfitly to axe in Cristis name, for he shal have þat axiþ þus. But siþ oure Jesus is treuþe and helþe of men þat trowun in him, þat man axiþ in Cristis name, þat axiþ in treuþe his soule helþe. Crist is moost lord of al, and þerfore he wole have dispit, but ȝif men axen him a greet þing; ffor ellis his lordship and þat axing acorden not to his name. And so, ȝif þou wilt axe in Cristis name, axe þe blisse þat evere shal laste; and siþ Crist is treuþe and resoun, loke þi axinge be resonable, and þan maist þou be sure to have þe þing þat þou axist þus. And herfore Crist in þis gospel biddiþ us to axe oure ful joie, and þan shal we have it, if þat we axen it in resoun; for no man haþ but half joie, but ȝif he be ful of blisse. And þis greet lord wole not be axid but þis blisse, or menes þerto; and ȝif man axe þus in resoun þat he be worþi to have it, he shal have it wiþouten doute whan best tyme were þat he hadde it; and he shal have on þe best manere þe þing þat he axiþ þus.

Men who go to war cannot rightly use the Pater noster.

And herfore þe seven axingis þat Crist techiþ in þe Pater noster meneþ[1] þis forme of axinge; and algatis to axe in charite; and þerfore men þat lyven in werre ben unable to have þer axinge: but þei axen þer owne dampnynge in þe fifte peticioun, for þer þei axen þat God forȝyve hem þer dettis þat þei owen to hym, riȝt as þei forȝyven men þat ben dettours unto hem. And

[1] So in B; *menen*, E, C; *moveþ*, A.

here we shal undirstonde þat ech man is dettour to God, and ech man owiþ to eche oþer to do him good in charite. And so failynge to love God of al þin herte and alle þi wille, þou rennest in grete dette boþe aȝens God and man. And so in þis fifte axing þes men þat werren now-a-daies, axen him as þei wolden mene,—forȝyve us for we ben even wiþ þee, or ellis take venjaunce in ire of us, as we taken vengeaunce of oure breþeren. And þis is noo good praier, but more axinge of Goddis venjaunce; and for þis cause many men ben unherd in þer praier, and turned in to more yvel for þere unskilful praier. And siche men weren better to leve þan to preien on sich maner. For many men preien for venjaunce and for worldis prosperite, and in þe ire of God he ȝyveþ hem þat þei axen; but it were beter to hem to preye not þus, ne to have þes þingis. And þus men of contrarie londis preien God in grete processiouns; and for unworþinesse of her preier hem were beter to sitten at home. And, for men witen not for what þing þei shulden preie God in siche causis, þerfore good lyvynge profitiþ more, and þe Holy Goost axiþ þan for hem. And who ever stere[1] men to yvel lyfe, ȝif[2] þei ben freris þat crien heye, God heereþ hem not to good, but raþer to take venjaunce on hem. For Crist seiþ, þat not ech man þat seiþ to him Lord, Lord, shal come in to þe blis of hevene, but he þat eendiþ in riȝt lyf, for he preieþ in þe name of þe Trinite. And þus Ȝebedeus sones preieden for good, but in yvel manere. And so algatis ryȝt lyf is þe beste in mannis preier, for siche lyfe preieþ beter to God þan hie voicis of ypocritis.

Good life better than imperfect prayers.

And after seiþ Crist to his apostlis, *þat þes þingis he seide bifore to hem in proverbis* and mystily; *but now is come tyme whan he shal not speke* þus *unto hem in proverbis, but apertly of his Fadir he shal telle hem* as best is. *In þat daie shal Cristen men axe in Cristis name* unto þer blisse. And now he *seiþ unto hem þat he shal preie his Fadir of*[3] *hem,* for þei shal be mateer to Crist and make his rewme. Wherfore he preieþ, *þat þe Fadir love þes apostlis* and oþer men þat suen him, *for þei loveden Jesus Crist and trowiden þat he cam fro God;* ȝhe, þat Crist bi his manhede

[1] *stireþ*, E. [2] *alȝif*, E. [3] *for*, E.

came of God in his godhede. *Crist cam fro þe Fadir and cam in to þe world,* and now whan Crist haþ done his message, *he forsakiþ aȝen þe world,* and goiþ bi manhede *to his Fadir.* And Cristis disciplis seiden to him, *Lo, now þou spekist opynly, and þou seist now noo proverbe; and þerfore we witen wele þat þou knowist alle þingis, and it is to þe no nede þat ony man axe þe ouȝt,* for þou wost bifore þe axinge, what men shulde axen and what þingis leve. *In þis we trowen þat þou come fro God* as his owne sone.

And þis bileve is ground to men to have of God what þat hem nediþ, and to wite what is best to hem, al ȝif it displese to þe world. But, as men þat ben in feveris desire not þat were best for hem, so men here in synne coveiten not best þing for hem. For þe world seide þat þe apostlis weren foolis and forsaken of God, and so it wolde seie todaie of men þat lyveden lyke to hem, for worldis joie and eerþely good plesiþ to hem, wiþ meenes þerto, and þei saveron[1] not hevenly good ne riȝt suyng after Crist. And þis jugement now in þe world is open witnesse aȝens men, þat þei be not hoole in soule, but turned amys to worldely þingis. For as a mouþ of a syke man distempered fro good mete, moveþ him for to coveite þingis contrarie to his helþe, so it is of mannis soule þat savoureþ not Goddis lawe. And as wanting of appetit is a signe dedly to man, so wanting of Goddis witt is signe of his secounde deeþ. And jugement þat now regneþ of worldely prosperite is token of men þat þei ben foolis and saveren not of Goddis lawe. For þe world seiþ comounly þat ȝif a man have worldely blisse and þe world leiȝe[2] to him in killynge of his enemyes, þan God loveþ him and doiþ miraclis for his sake. But, Lord! where is oure bileve þat we shulde trowe in love of God, þat it stondiþ not in þis but raþer hate of God! And, as Gregori seiþ[a], as a bole þat shal be kild goiþ in corn at his wille, and is not pyned[3] ne traveilid wiþ oþer beestis; so a lyme of þe fend is left fro þe grace of God, to figure his dampnacioun, and suffrid

[1] *saveren*, E. [2] *joye*, C. [3] So in B; *pynyd*, E; *pynde*, C; A has *pyndid*.

[a] I have been unable to verify this reference.

to do myche harme here, to large his peyne aftirward. We shulden leve þes sensible signes and take ensample of holy men, as of Crist and of his apostlis; hou þei hadden not her blisse here. But here Crist ordeynede peynes and hate of þe world and pursuyng to men þat he moost lovede, to teche us þat come after hem. And þus signes of paciens and pursuynge in þis erþe shulde be tokens of Goddis love and not signes of Antecrist.

Þe sixte Sondai Gospel after Eestir.

[SERMON LII.]

Cum venerit Paraclitus.—John xv. [26.]

The mission of the Comforter.

Crist telliþ his disciplis of comyng of þe Confortour, þe which is þe Holy Goost, and what lyf þei shal after lede. And ech man shulde cunne here þis lore, for þan he may be soulis leche, and wite, bi signes of his life, wher his soule be seke or hoole. Lord! siþ a fisician lerneþ diligentli his signes, in veyne, in pows[1], and oþer þingis, wher a mannis bodi be hool; how myche more shulde he knowe sich signes þat tellen helþe of mannis soule, and how he haþ him to God. Alȝif siche þingis ben pryve and passen worldly witt of men, neþeles þe Holy Goost telliþ men sum of siche signes, and makiþ hem more certeyne þan men can juge of bodily helþe. And, for we shulden kyndely desire for to knowe þe soulis state, þerfore þe Holy Goost, þat techiþ us to knowe þes signes, is clepid a confourtour of men, passinge oþer confortours. And as a mannis soule is beter þan þe bodi, and endeles good passiþ temporal good, so þis knowynge of þe soule passiþ oþer mannis cunnynge.

Crist seiþ þus to his disciplis, *Whan þis confortour shal come þat Y shal sende ȝou of þe Fadir, Goost of treuþe þat comeþ forþ of him, he shal also bere witnesse of me; and ȝe shal also bere*

[1] *pouse*, E; *powse*, C.

witnesse, for ȝe ben wiþ me alwey fro þe bigynnynge of my prechinge. But here may Grekes be moved to trowe þat þe Holy Goost comeþ not forþ but of þe Fadir and not of Crist þat is his sone; for þe toon seiþ Crist, and in þis gospel leveþ þe toþer. And it semeþ to sum men, ȝif þis were treuþe þat shulde be trowid, God wolde liȝtly telle þis treuþe as he telliþ oþer þat we trowen; and ellis it were presumpcioun to charge þe Chirche wiþ þis truþe, siþ neiþer autorite of God, ne resoun, techiþ þat þis is soþ; and al bileve nedeful to men is tolde hem in þe lawe of God. Here me þinkiþ þat Latynes synneden sum what in þis poynt, for many oþer pointis weren now more nedeful to þe Chirche; as it were more nedeful to wite, where al þis Chirche hange in power of þe pope, as it is seid comounly, and where men þat shal be savyd ben nedid here to shryve hem to preestis, and þus of many degrees þat þe pope haþ liȝtly ordeyned. But me þinkiþ þat it is soþ þat þis Goost comeþ boþe of þe Fadir and of þe Sone, and þes persones ben o cause of him; and me þinkiþ, to noon entent shulde Crist seye, he sendiþ þis Goost, or þat þis Goost is his, but ȝif þis Goost come of him. And to þis þat Grekes seien, þat Crist leveþ þis word, certis so doiþ he many oþer for certein cause, and ȝit we trowen hem; as Crist seiþ his lore is not his, for it is principaly his Fadris; and ȝit we trowen þat it is his, but þe welle is in his Fadir. So we trowen þat þe wille bi which þe Fadir loveþ þe Sone comeþ of witt þat is þe Sone, but principaly of Goddis power. And in þis word Crist techiþ us to do algatis worship to God. And þus þes Grekes may not prove þat we trowen fals in þis bileve, or þat Crist lefte þis treuþe, wiþouten cause to telle it þus; for bi þis þat Crist seiþ, þe Holy Goost came of his Fadir, and leveþ þus þe comynge of him, he stoppiþ þe pride of þe Chirche and techiþ men to worshipe God. But whan he seiþ þat he sendiþ þe Holy Goost to his disciplis, and alle þat his Fadir haþ ben his, he techiþ clerely þat þis Goost comeþ of him; and oþer wise shulde Crist not speke.

And þus Latyns ben to blame, for þei leven nedeful treuþe, and depen hem in oþer treuþe, þat is now not so nedeful. And þus seien sum men þat þe bishop of Rome, þat þei clepen heed of þe Chirche, and þerto pope, and Cristis viker, doiþ more harme to þe

The doctrine of the double procession, a doubtful point: other points more need to be determined; e.g. the authority of the Pope, and the duty of private confession.

On the overgrown authority of the Popes

Chirche of Crist þan doiþ viker of Thomas in Inde[a], or viker of Poul in Grees, or þe Soudan of Babilon. For þe rote of which he came, þat is dowynge of þe Chirche and heyng of þe emperoure, is not ful holy ground, but envenymed wiþ synne. But þis venym first was litil, and hid by cautells of þe fend, but now it is growen to myche and to hard to amende. Soþ it is þat ech apostle was obedient to ech oþer, as Petre obeishid unto Poul whan he reprovede hym; and þus þenken sum men þat þei shulden obeishe to þe pope, but no more þan Crist biddiþ, no more þan to oþer preestis, but ȝif he teche bettre Goddis wille and more profitiþ[1] to men; and so of alle his ordenaunce, but ȝif it be groundid in Goddis lawe, sette no more prys þerby þan bi lawe of þe emperoure. Men shulden seie myche in þis matere, and oþer men shulden do in dede; but men wolden holde hem heretikes, as þe fendis lymes diden Crist. And so þicke ben his membris þat who so holdiþ wiþ Cristis lawe, he shal be schent many weyes and algatis wiþ lesyngis.

And þis telliþ Crist bifore unto his postlis, to make hem stronge and arme hem aȝens siche persecuciouns. *Þes þingis, seiþ he, Y spake to you, þat ȝe be not sclaundrid.* He is sclaundrid þat is lettid by word or by dede, so þat his riȝt wille falle doun fro his witt; and so ȝif a man be pursued and suffre it paciently, he is not sclaundrid, al ȝif men synnen aȝens him. Þe first pursuyt aȝens Crist shal be of false preestis, not al oonly lettyng þe membris of Crist to reule þe puple in chirchis, as curatis shulden do, but putte hem out of chirche as cursid men or heretikes. And herfore seiþ Crist þat þei shal make ȝou *wiþout synagogis.* But ȝit shal more woodnesse come after þis, for þei procuren þe puple, boþe more and lasse, to kille Cristis disciplis for hope of grete mede. And herfore Crist seiþ certeyn of þis

Persecution.

[1] *profite*, E.

[a] The tradition of the visit of the apostle Thomas to India is of later origin than the time of Eusebius, being first mentioned by writers of the close of the fourth, and beginning of the fifth century, such as Gregory Nazianzen, St. Ambrose, and St. Jerome. The Christians found in Malabar by St. Francis Xavier certainly called themselves 'Christians of St. Thomas;' but this is supposed by many to have arisen from a confusion between the apostle and a Nestorian missionary. (Dean Stanley, article 'Thomas;' Smith's *Bibl. Dict.;* Kitto's *Cyclopædia.*)

mater, *þat hour is come þat ech man þat killiþ þus good men, shal juge him to do to God medeful obedience.* And to þis ende procuren freris, Antecristis disciplis, þat wel ny3e it is þus now among Cristene men. Sum men be sumnyd to Rome and þere putt in prisoun, and sum ben cryed as heretikes among þe comoun peple; and over þis, as men seien, freris killen þer owen breþeren, and procuren men of þe world to kille men þat seien hem treuþe. And oo drede lettiþ hem þat þei stirte not to more woodnesse, for þei defenden þat it is leveful and medeful, preestis for to fi3t in cause þat þei feynen Goddis; and so 3if þer parte be stronger þan seculers, þei may move þes preestis to fi3t a3ens þes gentilmen. And as þei have robbid hem of temporal goodis, so þei wole pryve hem of swerde as unable, and seie þat sich fi3ting shulde best falle to preestis. Þus hadden preestis þis swerd bifore þat Crist cam, and þei drowun so ferre out of religioun of God til þat þei hadden kild Crist, heed of holy Chirche.

The wiles of the evil one.

Alle men shulden be ware of cautelis of þe fend, for he slepiþ not, castynge fals weies, and al þes done fendis lymes; *for þei knowen not þe Fadir and his sone* bi propertees of hem. Þe fend blyndiþ hem so in worldly purpos, þat þei knowen not strengþe of God ne wisdom of his bidding; for feiþ failiþ unto hem þat þei loken not aferre, but þing þat is ny3e þer eye, as beestis wiþouten resoun. *Alle þis haþ Crist spoke to his disciplis þat whan tyme comeþ of hem, þei shulden þan have mynde þat he haþ seid hem þes perelis to come.* And þe Holy Goost moveþ ever sum men to studie Goddis lawe and have mynde of þis witt; and so love of Goddis lawe and sadde savoure þerynne, is token to men þat þei ben Goddis children, but 3it of þer ende þei ben uncerteyn.

Þe Gospel on Witt Sondai.

[SERMON LIII.]

Si quis diligit me.—John xiv.[1] [23.]

In þis gospel moveþ Crist his children to love, for charite is þe best cloiþ þat ony man may have; and herfore seiþ Goddis lawe þat love is stronge as deeþ, for love moveþ men to suffre deeþ gladly, in Goddis cause. And where deþ is þe moste þing þat man drediþ here, þis love passiþ kynde and makiþ men to coveite siche deeþ; and þis wille is not harmful but glorious to men, siþ bi siche love men brennen as coolis[2], and turnen in to Goddis cloþis as angelis of hevene. First seiþ Crist þus, *ȝif ony man love him, he shulde kepe his word*, for þat is þe same treuþe; and siþ God is kynde aȝen to men þat loven him þus, Crist seiþ þat *his Fadir shal love him aȝen;* and ȝif his Fadir love a man, þe two oþer persones loveþ[a] him, and al siche love of God mut nedis be evermore. And þe manhede of Crist worchiþ þus bi þis love; *it shal brynge wiþ Crist siche membris of him to hevene*, and so to clere siȝt of þe holy Trinite. *And so Crist wiþ his membris shal make þere þer dwellinge* wiþouten ony ende, bi love of þe Holy Goost; for scintis in hevene may not passe þis ende, for þan þei weren foolis chesynge a worse eende.

Christ moves his children to love.

For Crist wolde shewen oonhede to loven him and to kepen his wordis; þerfore he seiþ efte, *He þat loveþ him not, he kepiþ not hise wordis.* And herfore Crist, discryvynge a man þat loveþ him, seiþ þus after in þe same gospel, *He þat haþ my comandementis and kepiþ hem in his lyfe, he is þat ilke þat loveþ me wel*[3]. Here may we wite where a man love God, for ȝif he loveþ God, he loveþ his lawe and wordis

which is the same thing as to keep his commandments.

[1] So in E; both A and B have *xviii*, erroneously. [2] *colis*, B. [3] So E and B; A and C give no marks of quotation.

[a] This is the old plural present indicative of the Southern dialect, proceeding directly from the West Saxon form *lufiað*.

What these commandments are,

the Holy Ghost teaches us,

through the peace of Christ.

of þe gospel, for alle þei comen to oon; and ȝif he loveþ not Goddis lawe he loveþ not his God. And herfore ech man þat loveþ not Goddis word, þat he wolde not die þerfore to defende it, he loveþ not his God as he shulde love him; for it is al oone to love God and to love his word, and as myche as þou lovest God, shuldist þou love his word. But for love of þi God, þou shuldist lese þi lyfe, and so þou shouldist lese þi lyfe for defence of Cristis word; and in cowardise of þis love ben many men smyttid, but knyȝtis bi þer ordre shulden be redy in þis love. But, for Crist haþ seid þat men shulden kepe hise wordis, many men myȝten muse what þing ben þese wordis. But Crist seiþ þat alle þes wordis ben treuþes, as ten treuþis of þe comandementis, and alle ben wiþouten ende; and so he þat kepiþ not þe wordis of Crist, he kepiþ not his o word *þe which þei have herd, and þis o word which þei have herd is not Cristis, but his Fadris.* For it is Cristis persone, and Crist is not Cristis sone, but þe Sone of þe Fadir; and þus we may see worþinesse of Goddis word. Wordis of God ben many by diversite of resoun, but al þei rennen to gidere in o myddil poynte, and so þei ben alle Goddis word, þat is him silfe. And, for þes wordis ben mysty and derke to þe puple, þerfor ȝyveþ Crist hem a confort in þis matere, and seiþ, *þat he haþ spoke þes þingis unto hem dwellynge wiþ hem,* and þei ben ȝit mysty; *but þe Confortour þat is þe Holy Goost, þe which þe Fadir shal sende in þe name of Crist, shal teche hem alle þingis* þat ben now hid to hem. And þus it falliþ unto men to know rudely first a þing and generaly, as philosophris speken, and after shulden þei knowe more sutilly þe same þing; and þus Crist bi his manheed told first mysty wordis, and siþ bi his fynger shewide sutilte of hem. And ȝit þis Holi Goost shal have order of þis lore, *for first he shal move mennis eris* in sensible voicis, and siþ he shal be slyden ynne and *teche mennis þouȝtis,* in alle þat Crist haþ spoke bifore, in general wordis. Þei ne shal ceese anoon to lerne more sutilly, but ever in þis lyf þei wexen more rype til þat þei comen to hevene, and þere knowe al fulli.

And, for pees of mannis soule disposiþ him to lerne, þerfore Crist byhotiþ his children þis pees, and seiþ þus, *Pees Y leve to you; and my pees Y ȝyve ȝou.* Crist wiste þat him silfe shulde soone passe fro his children; ffor on þe Þursdaie at niȝt he seide to hem þes wordis, and on þe morewe at noon he died for þer love; and herfor he bihiȝt hem þat he shulde leve hem pees. But Crist specifieþ þis general pees, whanne he seiþ þat he ȝyveþ hem his own pees; and þis shal be first wiþ pursuynge of body, but it shal grow after to moost ful pees. And herfore seiþ Crist *þat not as þe world ȝyveþ, he ȝyveþ hem*, but on contrary maner. Þe world ȝyveþ þingis þat now ben likyng, but bi processe of tyme þei wexen more bitter, and so þei turnen to peyne and sorewe, þat first weren likynge; and so pees of þis worlde is ever more decresynge, but pees of God growiþ unto ful pees.

We are commanded to be hopeful and of good courage.

And bi þes wordis of witt Crist confortiþ his children, and biddiþ hem, þat *þer herte be not disturblid ne drede;* for who ever troweþ fully þis sentence þat is seid, and hopiþ fully þat he were of nombre of þes children, he were an untrewe man ȝif þat he drede þus. Apostlis dredden hem of perelis þat weren nyȝe, but þei failiden not of þis treuþe, þat þei ne shulde have a good ende, and what þingis þat felle to hem, it shulde falle to hem for þe betere. And so as þe worlde is sikir of þing neyȝe it, and in doute of þing ferre, so in contrary manere ben Cristis children sikir of þer ferre eende, but of þer nyȝe menes ben þei sum tyme in drede. And grounde of þis sentence is Cristen mennis bileve, and herfore seide Crist, *ȝe herden how Y seide to ȝou, Y go and Y come to ȝou;* and he þat trowiþ fully þes witty wordis of Crist he shulde not drede him of þis for seid sentence, for Crist seiþ, as God to whom al þing is present, Y go and Y come to you, for certeinte herof. And as Crist was certeyne of his deeþ and his steiyng up and of his comynge aȝen at þe daye of dome, so shulden his children be certeyn of his forseid sentence. And ȝit Crist moveþ his children to have joie of his goyng, and þis was a point for which þei mourneden moost; and Crist seiþ þus to hem to abate þer mournynge, *Certis, ȝif ye loveden me, ȝe shulden have joie for Y go to my Fadir, siþ he is more þan Y;* for þus bi manheed Y shulde encreese in bliss, and he þat joieþ not herfore, he loveþ not Crist. And it is told bifore hou ech man shulde love him; *And now Y seide to you, bifore it is falle, þat whan it done, ȝe trowen* in my witt;

and so shulde þei trowe to alle þing þat he hadde seid, for þus he is God þat can wel al þing. And Crist, teching his children to marke beter his wordis, seiþ, *þat he shal speke now but fewe þingis unto hem*, but þei shulde have moost enemyte here of þe heed fend þat Crist haþ overcome; and þerfore he telliþ hem, *þat prynce of þis worlde is come* for to tempte Crist, *and he haþ not in him;* and þus in þis overcomynge shulde þei not drede þe fend. *But al þis is done þat þe worlde knowe þat Y love þe Fadir;* and so shulde ȝe do, for alle þingis þat Y do shulden be ensaumple to you. And *herfor Y do as my Fadir comandide me*, for wel Y woot in þis may I not faile. And al þis sentence of þe gospel of Joon is fully perteynynge to comynge of þe Holy Goost, and so redyng of þis gospel was wel ordeyned for þis day.

Þe Gospel on þe Trinite Soneday.

[SERMON LIV.]

Erat homo ex Phariseeis Nychodeme.—John iii. [1.]

The visit of Nicodemus.

Þis gospel undir a story telliþ of þe Trinite, and boþe þes ben harde, as comounly is Jones gospel. Þe storye telliþ *þat þer was a man of Pharisees þat hiȝte Nichodeme, and was prince of þe Jewis; he cam to Jesus on a nyȝt and seide þus to him; Rabi we witen wel þat þou art come fro God;* and raby is as myche as maister in Englishe. And Nichodeme tolde þe cause whi he trowide þis, *for no man may make*, he seide, *þes signes þat þou makist, but ȝif God be wiþ him*, and so he comeþ fro God. *And Jesus answeride Nychodeme, and seide* þus *to him*, bi my double kynde Y seie to þee, *but ȝif a man be born aȝen, he may not se Goddis rewme.* And þes wordis weren woundirful to Nichodeme, *and þerfore he axide where a man myȝte be bore whan he were an old man, wher he myȝte crepe in to his moder wombe* for tyme þat he was olde *and be born aȝen.*

Þis Nichodeme cam in þe nyȝt, þat figuride his ignoraunce, but to þe literal witt, he dredde him for his breþeren, to come apertly in þe day, and speke wiþ Jesus Crist; and boþe þes undirstondingis shope þe Holy Goost. And so þis goostly birþe þat Nichodeme mut first have bitokeneþ þe Fadir of hevene þat bryngeþ forþ two oþer persones; and so Nichodeme to litil knewe þis persone of God, and for þis unknowinge he axide þis questioun. For he seide not þat Crist was kyndely Goddis Sone, ne þat he was Goddis word and so God him silfe; and so þis Nichodeme hadde nede to be cristened in feiþ, and so Crist lovede his persone, alȝif he hatide his ordre, for Crist savyde his persone and distryede his ordre. And þus Crist lovede Poul, þat seiþ he was a Pharisee; but þe more part of Pharisees weren fals and heretikes. And þis nativite shewiþ Crist in þes wordis; *Forsoþ, forsoþ, Y seie to þee, but ȝif man be born of watir and þe Holy Goost he may not entre in to Goddis rewme.* And þus bi þis baptym, þis water and þe Holy Goost, Crist tolde him þe Trinite ȝif he koud conseyve it. Þis baptym seiþ þe Trinite, in whos name it is mad; þis water is þe waishinge þat ranne of Cristis herte; and so baptym and water and þe Holy Goost tellen Nichodeme þe Trinitee, and þerwiþ þe sacrament, for Crist is compendious in spekynge of his wordis.

But Crist makiþ distynccioun of two manere of birþis, and seiþ þat *þing born of fleishe is fleish* in his kynde, *and þing þat is born of spirit is spirit* on sum manere; and *þerfore, wounder þou not þat Y seide to þee, ȝe moten be born aȝen,* and bi Goost made children of holy Chirche, and so in spirit maad Goddis children, and so his spouse shal be your moder. Þis gendrure of þis Goost is boþe free and wilful, and herfor Crist seiþ to Nichodeme, þat *þe spirit breþiþ wher he wole, and þou herest his vois* bi which he moveþ þee. And on þis maner þe Spirit of oure Lord haþ fillid þis world wiþ witt of oure feiþ, and þat þing þat holdiþ alle haþ science of vois. And herfore at Wit-Sonday whan þis Goost apperide was a greet soun, and tungis of fier, to telle þat men shulden speke on hiȝt[1] to þer breþeren, and þei shulden have charite, þe which seiþ þe Holy Goost. And alle ȝif we knowen þe vois of þis Goost, neþeles we witen not whennes þat it comeþ ne whidir þat it goiþ, to men þat ben

[1] *beyȝt*, E; *beiȝþe*, B; *beiȝe*, C.

biside us; for we knowen not þe ordenaunce of God, whi he enspireþ þes men, and to what ende, or wheþer he shal save þis man or wende awey from him. *And so ech man þat is born of þis spirit* is unknowun to oþer by many hid resoun, and so ech man is sumwhat knowun and sumwhat unknowun for wisdome of þis spirit.

But *Nichodeme answerede and seide here to Jesus, How may þes þingis be done? And Crist seide to him;* In þe lond of Israel ben manye blynde maisters, *for þou art maister in Israel, and ȝit þou unknowist þes þingis:* and so it is noo wounder ȝif þis lond be mysled, ffor ȝif þe blynde leden þe blynde, þei fallen boþe into þe lake. And neþeles Y teche hem as myche as þei ben worþi; and so seiþ Crist to Nichodeme, *Soþely, soþely, Y seie to þee*, defaute is not in me, in teching of þes puple, but in untrewe hardnesse of it; for, *þing þat we knowun, we tellen to hem*, and *þat we have sene* in Godhede, *we witnessen, and ȝe taken not oure witnesse*, for ȝoure unkynde hardnesse. And þerfore ȝe knowen not þe gendrure of þe firste persone. *Ȝif Y seide to ȝou erþely þingis and ȝe trowen hem not, how, ȝif Y seide to you hevenly þingis, shal ȝe trowen hem?* Crist tolde here of bodily birþe, and ofte tymes of erþely treuþe, but þei trowiden him not for þer fole hard herte; but neþeles Crist telliþ þis man knowinge of þe secounde persone, and in an article of bileve, þat is, his ascensioun; and *no man, seiþ Crist, steieþ in to hevene but he þat cam doun fro hevene, mannis sone þat is in hevene.* And in þes wordis myȝt Nichodeme undirstonde boþe þe godhede of Crist and þerto his manhede, and so shulde he knowe wel þe secounde persone of God. By þat þat Crist steied þus, and þus is mannis sone, miȝt he knowe his manhede bifore oþer manhedis; for alȝif oþer men steieden a litil in þis eire, neþeles no man steieþ in to hevene þus but Crist. And so noon oþer man comeþ to hevene but ȝif he be Cristis membre, and be drawun bi þe Trinite in to þis hey place. And þus seiþ Crist soþ, þat no man steieþ in to hevene, but him silf aloone; and seiþ þere ben foure manere of bryngingis forþ of man, and þe fourþe and þe laste, apropred unto Crist, is þat man comeþ clene of womman wiþout man. Crist clepiþ him wel here a sone of mankynde; and þus bi þes two wordis myȝt he knowe Cristis manhede. And by oþer two wordis myȝt he knowe Cristis godhede; first by þat he seiþ þat þis man cam doun bifore fro hevene, and þis myȝt nevere be but ȝif Crist were God or[a] he were man. Þe secounde word þat shewiþ þe godhede of þis persone, is, þat Crist seiþ þat he is mannis sone þat is in hevene, ȝhe, after þat he bycam man; ffor þus is Crist[1] two kyndes godhede for evermore, and evermore[2] in hevene drawynge to him whom him likeþ. And þus Crist techiþ wel ynouȝ to knowe þe secounde person, boþ in godhede and in manhede, as myche as he shulde þan knowe him.

Christ teaches Nicodemus the complete doctrine of the Trinity.

But to telle þe þridde persone, in pointis of bileve, Crist telliþ to Nichodeme, *As Moyses heied þe addre in desert* to hele þe puple by lokynge on him, *so mut mannis sone be hyed* in þe cros, *þat ech man þat trowiþ in him, perishe not* in helle, *but have lyf wiþouten eende*, þat is blisse of hevene. Here mut we knowe þe storye of þe olde lawe hou þe puple was hirt by stynging of addres, and Moses preied God to telle him sum medecyne; and God bade him take an addre of bras, and hong hym hye on a tree to þe puple to loke on, and he þat lokid on þis addre shulde be helid of þis yvel. And al þis was figure of hanging of Crist, for Crist was in forme of addris of venym, but he hadde no venym in his owene persone, as þe addre of bras hadde no venym in him. But as riȝt lokynge on þis addre of bras savyde þe puple fro venym of serpentis, so riȝt lokynge bi ful bileve in Crist saveþ his puple fro synne of þe fendis. And þe fende was þe first addre þat ever noyed man, and Crist was hongid in tre, as þis addre hongide in tree. But it were to wite over, hou þis story perteyneþ to þe Holy Goost, siþ al þis was done in Crist; but we shal wel wite þat ech of þes þre persones is in ech oþer, as ech bitokeneþ oþer. And siþ þat Crist seiþ þat no man haþ more love þan for to put his lyf for his frendis, þis blesside hanginge of Crist in þe crosse is þat hye charite þat God lovede man inne, and þis charite is þe Holy Goost; and þus was Nichodeme tauȝt þe feiþ of þe Trinite, and in þis feiþ many oþer articlis, and þus is þis gospel approprid to þis feste.

[1] *Crist is*, B, C. [2] So E; A, B, C, om. *and evermore*.

[a] *or* = 'before that.'

Þere ben many witnessis and resouns to þe Trinite, but þis manere of lore is more plentenouse and more profitable to men; and herfore Crist seiþ it þus; and þus eche man shulde reule al his lyfe after þis holy Trinite, for ellis he must faile. Loke first þat he be groundid in stable bigynning, and siþ þat he procede in gracious mene, and siþ þat he ende in fulnesse of charite, and þan his lyfe is ensaumplid aftir þe Trinite.

COMMUNE SANCTORUM.

[THE sermons which follow, on the gospels of the office of the Commune Sanctorum, are thirty-one in number. The order of the feasts, and the gospels themselves, appear to have been taken by the writer from the Sarum missal. Every separate office included in that missal is dealt with by the writer of the sermons except those for 'Many Virgins' and 'Holy Women not Virgins;' and for this omission there is an obvious reason, viz. that the gospels for those offices are the same as those for 'One Virgin not Martyr,' and 'One Virgin and Martyr,' and had therefore already formed the subjects of sermons. With one exception, all the gospels correspond with those in the Sarum missal. This exception is in the office for 'One Apostle.' Two gospels for this office are treated of by the writer, *Hoc est praeceptum*, (John xv. 12) and *Haec mando vobis*, (John xv. 17). The latter one of these gospels alone is given in the Sarum missal. But the *Hoc est praeceptum* is the gospel for the 'Vigil of an Apostle' in the present *Roman* missal.

Although of course there is a general agreement, the office of the Commune Sanctorum in the Sarum missal differs considerably from that of the present Roman missal. In one direction it is fuller, in another not so full. It is fuller, in that it has a greater number of distinct offices or masses, there being twenty-nine in the Sarum, and only twenty-four (including that for the anniversary of the Dedication of a Church) in the Roman. It is less full, because, though it has more offices for several of the feasts, certain festivals are not represented in it at all, e.g. those of 'One Martyr not a Bishop,' and of a 'Martyr not Virgin.'

Out of the thirty-one gospels treated of by the writer, twenty-one are also found in the Commune Sanctorum of the Roman missal, and ten are different.]

HERE BIGYNNEÞ ÞE

COMOUN SANCTORUM,

ÞE SECUNDE PART OF ÞIS BOOK.

ÞE GOSPEL IN VIGIL OF APOSTLE.

[SERMON LV.]

Ego sum vitis vera.—JOON XV. [1.]

As comune þing is betere and bifore oþer þingis, so þis gospel þat is red in comun story shulden men knowe sum what, and speciali preestis, for it is a foul þing þat prestis speken as pies, and knowun not her owne vois more þan doumbe beestis, and speciali whanne þei reden bileve of holi Chirche, for þes men ben to ferre to preche þis to þe peple. Þis gospel of Joon tellid a parable of Crist, bi which he tauȝte his disciplis for to dwelle in him, and for to love him, for ellis þei ben nouȝt. Crist seiþ þus: *I am a verri vyne and my Fadir is tylyer* of þis vyneȝerde. For Crist bi hise twoo kyndis is a good herde; as anentis his godhede, he is þe same tilier wiþ his Fadir, and as anentis his manhede he is heed of holi Chirche. And for þis seiþ Crist þat, *ech braunche þat is in him, and beriþ not fruyt, his Fadir shal take awey*, for keper of a vyneȝerde falliþ þus to clense it, and algatis kepe þe vynes þat þei beren grapis. And, for alle þe Fadir dedis doiþ also þe Sone, þerfore seiþ Crist þat *ech braunche of þe Chirche þat beriþ fruyt, his Fadir shal purge þat it bere more fruyt;* and so doiþ Crist, for he sendiþ water of wisdom to hise braunchis, and herof comeþ grapis to preche to

The parable of the true vine.

þe peple and gladen hem in Goddis lawe. Sum men ben braunchis of þis vyne, þat dwellen in holy Chirche, and ȝit þei ben not þerof, al if þei lyve of þis vyne, and ben siche þat gaderen gredili Cristis patrimonye, as dymes and offringis and rentis, þat þei seien weren ȝovun to Crist; and wiþ þis þei done not þer office to quykene oþer branchis; and þes ben moost noious branchis þat ben plauntid in þis vyne, for þei maken most oþer men to rote and drye and falle fro þis vyne in to þe fier of helle. For no men ben of holi Chirche, al if þei ben þer-inne, but þese men þat beren fruyt and han love wiþouten eende.

Necessity of union with Christ.

After seiþ Crist to his disciplis, *Now ȝe ben clene for þat word þat Y seide to ȝou, Dwelle ȝe in me and Y dwelle in ȝou.* Boþe goode men and ivel moten be on sum manere in Crist, siþ he is God þat susteyneþ al þing; but men shulden be in him bi grace and take moisture of his lore, and so profite to oþer braunchis þat growen in þis vyne, and þus þei shulden take moisture of lore of þis tree, or ellis þei ben not of þis tree, al if her kynde be susteyned in it, but þei growen in kynde to make of a fier in helle. And þis vyne dwelliþ not in a man as for his membre, but if he helpe þis man to make here a good ende, and die in charitee to God and to his Chirche. And so, al if ech man shulde hope þat he be lyme of holi Chirche, neþeles he shulde suppose þis bineþe bileve and wiþ a drede, but if God tellde him specialy what eende þat he shal have. And þis triacle haþ God ordeyned aȝens preestis and ypocritis, þat þei shulden not disceyve þe puple, bostinge þat þei ben of holi Chirche, for, be þei popis, be þei bishopis, or oþer preestis more or lasse, þei bosten and hewen above her heed, if þei ben proud of þis title. And herfore God, þat loveþ þat ech man shulde be meke, hidiþ þis point from ech man þat he woot wole not holde mekenesse. And to conferme þis mekenesse, seiþ Crist after in þis gospel, *As a sioun mai not bere fruyt but if it stonde stable in þe vyne, so no Cristene man mai bere fruyte but if he be dwellinge in Crist.* And herfore seiþ Crist bi Matheu, þat a good tree mai not make yvel fruyte ne an yvel tree good fruyt, al if mennis jugement faile in þis, for þese þat God woot þat shal be saved, al if þei synnen for a tyme, neþeles her synful lyf shal turne to hem to fruyt of hevene. And so þese men þat shal be dampned, al if þei done good for a tyme, ȝit þei han an yvel maner þat quenchiþ þe goode þat þei done. And so it is unknowun to men who dwelliþ þus in God; but ech man shal do good, supposinge þat he dwelliþ in God. And herfore rehersiþ Crist, as he haþ seid to his apostlis, *I am a vyne, and ȝe þe braunchis, and so þat man þat dwelliþ in me and I in him, he beriþ moche fruyte*, and upon þis shulden ȝe þenken, for ȝe moun do nouȝt wiþouten me. And so shulden we lerne þat vynes ben trees þat profiten not to mennis work but in beryng of her fruyt. So shulden preestis in þis worlde shapen her lyf to Cristis Chirche, not to be enheritid here, ne to be riche, ne to fiȝte, but to teche Cristis lore boþe in her lyf and in her word. And þus shulde ech man do, but sum more and sum lesse.

And aftir seiþ Crist, as here is seid, *þat who þat dwelliþ not in him shal be sent out, as a kitt braunche, and so he shal drye and siþ be cast in to þe fier, and þere he brenneþ* wiþouten ende in þe fier þat evere shal laste. For fendis of helle shulen *gadere him* boþe in bodi and in soule, and witnesse aȝens him how he servede hem aȝens God. And over þis bihetiþ Crist þis privylege to his braunchis, *þat if þei dwellen in him and hise wordis dwellen in hem*, bi bryngynge[1] forþ of hevenly fruyte, *whatevere þei wolen þei shulen axe and it shal be done to hem*. Þese hiȝe wordis þat Crist seiþ here, tellen witt hid to men. For many þenken þat summe ben fulli lymes of þe fend, and ȝit þei enden holi men and comen to hevene for her good lyf; and summe ben now holi men, as ancris[2] heremytes and freris, and efte þei ben apostataas and dien enemyes of Crist. Al þis is hid þing, for if siche men semen to do yvel, and summe siche semen to do good, as ben many ypocritis, neþeles þe ende is hid of which þei shulden take her name. And so God hidiþ þe qualite of siche workes of men here, for men shulden not dampne hem ne preise hem to liȝtli. And þus men maken hem over wise in jugement of holi Chirche, and in demynge of mennis lyf, þat þis goiþ to hevene and þis to helle, for God haþ kept to him þe knowinge of an ende, þat makiþ al. Þou maist knowe þat þis man is oþer a bishop or in sich office,

The final destinies of individual men are hidden from us.

[1] So rightly E; A includes the words in the italics.

[2] *ankeris*, E.

but wheþer he shal wende to hevene, God haþ hid þe knowinge fro þee; and siþ after þat he is man of holi Chirche or a lyme of þe fend, it is wel seid þou maist not see þis point of þi bileve, which ben lymes of holi Chirche, but þou shalt trowe þe general. And so þat þing þat þou trowist here, þou seest not here wiþ þi iȝen, but þou trowist it above hope, and bilevest it bineþ science. And þus þese wordis þat Crist seiþ shulden move men to lyve wel, and be meke, and leve pride of hiȝenesse of her staat. And wolde God þat men lerneden þis lessoun þat clepen hem men of holi Chirche, and bi colour of þis fendis synne spoilen men þat be undir hem; and in þis raveyn þei shewen wel, þat þei ben not of holi Chirche.

Þe Gospel in þe dai of Apostle.

[SERMON LVI.]

Hoc est preceptum meum.—John xv. [12.].

No perfect standard of bodily health, but Christ the perfect standard of charity.

Þis gospel techiþ Cristis apostlis, and in hem al Cristis Chirche, how þei shulden holde charite ech man to oþer. Crist seiþ, *Þis is my comandement, þat ȝe love togidere, after þat forme þat Y have loved ȝou. More love þan þis haþ no man, þan þat he put his lyfe for love of hise frendis.* And þus, as fisik[1] techiþ, þei shal þenke on a man þat is fulli hool wiþynne and wiþoute, and bi mesure of such a man þei shulden mesure mennis helþe; and whanne men axen, where is he þat is on þis wise hool, þei seien, þere is noon siche, but siche oon þei ymagynen; and after mesure of þis helþe þei heelen him þat þei delen wiþ. But blessid be oure science, and auctour þerof, for we seien þat þere is a love in þe heed of þe Chirche þat is moost in dede of alle loves þat mai be, and after þis love shulden alle oþer be mesurid. But, for fisik shameþ to sette sich a mesure þat þei knowen not, ne witen not where[2] it be, herfore þei seien þat þer ben two helþis, oon to riȝtwisnesse and anoþer

[1] *phisic*, E. [2] *wheþer*, E.

to weiȝte. Þe firste helþe shulde stonde in a mannis membris, and in his compleccioun, in humouris, and in elementis, which in suche acord ben knettid to gider, þat noon of þese mai be contrarie to anoþer; and siþ no man is siik but[1] bi sich contrarite, þis man þat þei speken of mai nevere more be siik. But hoolnesse of weiȝte mai falle to a man; and þat is nevere more wiþouten greet sykenesse, al ȝif it be hid by governynge of fisike. He is hool in weiȝte þat haþ of ech element as moche as he mai worche, wiþ dedes þat fallen to men, and on þis wise moun þei maken men hool. But blessid be oure mesure, þat Crist puttiþ in charite, for þat is moost rial and ground of al oþer; and no man mai be saaf but if he knowe þis mesure, and þis mesure helpe him to gendre in him charite; and þus shulden men in dede practise in þis science, for veyn speche þerof profitiþ not, but harmeþ. Þis love was shewid in Crist, whanne he putte his lyf for love of his breþeren, and brouȝte summe out of helle, and savede oþer þerfro; and herfore seiþ Crist, for practisinge of þis love and ensaumple þerof, *þat þei shulden love togidere as he haþ loved hem*[2]; and þanne þei ben al hool.

The test of the love of Christians is obedience.

And herfore moten we nedis lerne þe bileve of þe passioun of Crist, and of his deþ suwynge, siþ after forme of þis love we shulden love togidere; and wantinge of þis love is cause of ech synne and of ech harm þat falliþ in þe Chirche; and þerfore men shulden enforce hem more to lerne þis love. And herfore traveilide Poul in techinge of charite, and telde sixteen condiciouns, þat shulden folowe it. And as many men seien þat þei ben hool in bodi, many men seien þat þei ben in charite, and loven God over al þing, and her neiȝbore as hem silf, but ȝit þei gabben opynli, as her lyf shewiþ. Þis lore þat Cristis scole axiþ loveþ none gabbingis, but þat þei do in dede as her mouþ confessiþ. And, for Crist haþ teeld þat þis hiȝe charite techiþ a man to putte his lyf for love of hise frendis, and þis love is oonli in persone of Crist, he telliþ how hise apostlis and oþer men ben hise frendis. *Ȝe ben* þanne, seiþ Crist, *frendis of me* þat han þis love, *if ȝe done* sadli *þe þingis þat I bidde ȝou.* And so it is of oþer men þat doen as þese apostlis, for þei ben

1 Cor. xiii.

[1] om. A; perperam. [2] So E; no italics in A.

mesure after Crist to oþer men þat suen hem. And certeyn þei ben not frendis to Crist þat han not þis love, but oonli þei þat han þis love; and siþ þis frenship axiþ þat boþe frendis loven togidir, and þat þe love be shewid in dede, as philosophris seien, if we ben frendis to Crist, it is þus in dede bitwixe him and us.

The apostles friends of Christ.

And Crist seiþ efte þis word of love, *Now shal Y not clepe ȝou servauntis, for þe servaunt woot not* in þat[a] *what his lord doiþ.* And þus men seien comounly þat þer ben two manere of servauntis, servaunt of condicioun, and servaunt of mynysterie. And servaunt of mynysterie may ben on two maneris. Sum men be oonli servauntis of greet service outward, and sum ben servauntis of þes two, boþe of privy counceilis and to do siche service. And on þis wise þe apostlis weren servauntis of Jesus Crist, as þey graunten comounly in bigynnynge of her epistlis; but on þe former manere weren not apostlis now servauntis, for Crist tauȝte hem his privyte and lymytide hem to worþi werkes. And þus spekiþ Crist here; and herfore wolde not þe aungel take worshipe of Joon, as seiþ þe book of pryvytees, but þe angel seiþ to him þat he was his servaunt, and hise breþeren boþe, siþ Crist was man in hevene, and he hadde ordeyned so hiȝe place for hise apostlis, and telden[1] hem privytees unknowun to angels. And bi þis equivocacioun moun men liȝtli acorden to Cristis lawe; for, as clerkes witen wel ynowȝ, contradiccioun is not oonly in wordis. And þus seiþ Crist, *þat he seiþ hise apostlis to be hise frendis from henneforþ, for alle, he seiþ, þat Y have herd of my Fadir I have maad knowun unto ȝou.* And þis is soþ, siþ Cristis apostlis knewen comunly þe book of lyf, and weren in lernynge of þis book, til þat þei knewen aboven aungels; and apostlis wisten þanne truþis þat weren hid from aungels. And cheef cause of þis frendship stondiþ in Crist and not in hem, for *þei chesiden not Crist her maistir, but he chees hem* unto þis office, and ȝaf to hem vertue for to do al þe service þat he shope hem to.

Apoc. xxii. 9.

The threefold office of the Apostles.

Crist ordeynede þree þingis to be fillid bi hise apostlis, first þat þei shulden go forth in to þe world and preche his gospel,

[1] *teelde*, E.

[a] *in þat* seems to mean, *quâ* servant.

and þat þis shulde be fruytous to þus converte so myche peple, and siþ þat þis fruyt dwelle, boþe in þis worlde and in þe toþer. And þes þree ben grete myraclis amonge alle þo þat Crist dide, for it passiþ mannis work to make fruyt þus to laste in heven. Men moun worche bi mannis craft figuris and hid qualitees; but þis is more wiþouten mesure, þus to fordo synne, and bringe in blis; and þus seiþ Robert Grosthed[a] þat þis craft passiþ alkemmye[1], for it makiþ soulis hoole, þat ben betere þan sunne or moone.

And þes þingis myȝten not ben do[2] but bi special helpe of God; and þus telliþ Crist to his apostlis, *þat what evere þei axen his Fadir in his name, he shal ȝyve to hem*, for þe love of him. And bi þis was shewide þe frendship bitwixe Crist and hise apostlis, and here moun we knowe treuþe[3] þat is nedeful for þis gospel, how þes men ben frendis to Crist þat shulen be saved bi his vertue. And, as it semeþ, oonli þes men weren saved bi Cristis deþ, and oonli for þes men Crist putte his lyf and bouȝte hem; but wel Y woot þat Crist ȝaf ynowȝ to save moo men, if þei wolden take his medicine and ablen hem to vertue of it. And here we moun not putte foli to marchaundiȝe þat Crist made, siþ savynge of his Chirche is betere þan was lyf þat Crist lefte, for þis deþ was a meene to betere lyf; and al was Cristis. And þus Crist was not peirid by his deþ, but sum wey beterid, siþ he loste not[4] substaunce, but gat o betere habitude. But leve we þis, and speke of love, þat it profite to þe peple; for siþ þer is no rewme, ne state of men, ne persone here, þat he ne failiþ in holdinge of þis love of Crist,—for ellis shulden men not þus synne,—alle we failen in þis love þat Crist haþ beden to his Chirche; for siþ every man in erþe is neiȝbore to ech oþer, how shewe we in our lyf ful love to alle þes neiȝboris?

[1] *alkemye*, E. [2] *done*, E. [3] *þe treuþe*, E. [4] *no*, E.

[a] I cannot find this passage in the *Opuscula* of Grossetete printed in the Appendix to Brown's *Fasciculus*; it is probably in one or other of his many writings which exist at present only in manuscript.

Þe Gospel on þe day of oon Apostle.

[SERMON LVII.]

Haec mando vobis.—John xv. [17.]

The precept of Christian love, its compass and scope.

Þis gospel telliþ sharpli, as Crist doiþ ofte bi Joon, how men shulden love togidere and putte awei þe lettingis, for þe bigynnynge and þe eendinge of Goddis lawe is love. Crist bigynneþ þus and comandeþ hise disciplis; *Þese þingis I bidde to ȝou þat ȝe love togidere.* No þing is more beden of God þan þis love; and þerfor, what man leveþ it, he despisiþ God; but al were for to know þe craft of þis love, for it is oon to love a þing, and to wille good to þat þing. Ech þing shulde be loved after þat it is good, and so God shulde be moost loved, and betere men more þan worse men. And we shulden for Goddis love love yvel men and yvel comunes, and for his love be bisie to ȝyve hem mater to be betere, and as myche as in us is, to do good to ech man, sum to make betere and sum to make lesse yvel; but oo firstnesse of love shulde we have to us silf, and to oure fadir and oure modir, savynge ordre of Goddis lawe. Þe firste lettinge of þis love þat Crist telliþ here, is hate of þis world to men þat kepen þis love, for þe world is so blyndid þat it clepiþ hate, love, and love it clepiþ hate, for it erriþ in bileve. Al oure love shulde stonde in þe love of God, to kepe his lawe and move oþere to kepe it; but many, for defaulte of feiþ, holden þis a fooly[1], for gooddis of þis world fallen not to siche men.

Repinings, how to be corrected.

And herfore seiþ Crist, *If þe world hate you,* ȝe *shulden wele wite þat it hatide me bifore;* and þis worþinesse of Crist þat suffride þus for man, shulde move trewe men in God to suffre for Crist. If þou grutche aȝens poverte, and coveite worldeli worshipe, wite þou þat Crist bifore was porer þan þou, siþ he hadde not bi his manhede place to reste his heed ynne. If þou grutchist þat þi sugetis wolen not ȝyve þee goodis, þenke how Cristis sugettis wolden neiþer ȝyve him mete ne herberwe; and ȝit herfore he curside hem not, but dide hem moche good. And if þou grutche þat þe world doiþ þee ony

[1] *foly.* E.

injurie, and þou profitist to þe world aȝen in love and mekenesse; þenke how Crist bifore þee profitide þus more to þe worlde; and ȝit Crist suffride more wronge of hise sugettis þan þou maist. And þus if þou woldist þenke on Crist, how he suffride for love of man, it were þe beste ensaumple þat þou shuldist have to suffre, and to cese þi grutching; for, as Austyn seiþ[a], no man in þis world mai synne but levyng þat Crist tauȝte, or grutche aȝens þing þat he suffride.

The world hates the elect; application of this to the friars.

And for þis, seiþ Crist after, *If ȝe weren of þe world, þe worlde wolde love þat is his;* for þis lawe lastiþ in good and yvel, þat o man loveþ lyk to hym, ȝhe, if þei shulen be dampned for þis, as o synful loveþ anoþer for þe likenesse of her synne; and ȝit þei shulen boþe in helle suffre harm for þis likenesse. And þus it is no kynne[1] wounder if lymes of þe fend haten lymes of Crist, for þei ben so myche contrarie here, and after þe dai of dome; and þis meveþ many men to hate þes newe religiouse, for þis newe dyversite quenchiþ love and makiþ hate. Ȝhe, ȝit þei han sum fendis manere, þat þei haten her owne breþeren, and turmenten hem, for þei holden wiþ Goddis lawe aȝens heris[2b]; and certis þei loven to litil oþirs, but feynen, to spoile hem of her goodis. And þus seiþ Crist to hise disciplis þat, *for þei ben not of þis world, but he haþ chosen hem of þis world, herfor þe world hatiþ hem.* And if þou lernest of þe world to hate þus, þi love is quenchid, but if þou hatist bi Cristis lawe men of þis world for þis synne, and wiþdrawist hem fro þe world, þanne þou lovest þese men in God. For þe world is takun here, for men overcomen bi þe world, þat loven more worldeli þingis þan Goddis lawe, or good of vertues. And of þis world seiþ Crist, þat it hatiþ hise disciplis.

What it is to overcome the world.

And, for þis lore passith oþer in profit and in holynesse, þerfore biddiþ Crist hem *to þenke on his word þat he haþ seid*

[1] *kyn*, E. [2] *beres*, E.

[a] The reference is probably to the treatise *De Urbis Excidio*, the concluding chapter of which especially, in a strain of eloquent and tender reproof, exhorts the Christian people of Rome, just after the sack of the city by the Goths, not to repine on account of their terrible sufferings, remembering the unapproachable circumstances of the passion of their Redeemer.

[b] *aȝens heris*; i.e. against *theirs*,—the friars' law.

here to hem, for þanne þei overcomen þis world; and herfore seiþ Joon evangelist, Breþeren, what man is he þat overcomeþ þe world? Certis noon, but if he trowe þat Jesus is Goddis Sone. If we holden þis ground in feiþ þat Crist is verri God and man, and over þis trowe wel his lyf, and alle hise wordis þat he seiþ, we shal overcomun þis world and alle þe helpers of þe fend. For, as Crist seiþ soþeli, *þer is no servaunt more þan his lord is;* and so Crist is more boþe in vertue and in worþinesse þan ony oþer man mai be; and siþ Crist suffride þus and tauȝte Cristene men þis lore, what man shulde we trowe or sue in oure lyf but Crist? And neiþer þe world ne þe fend mai in þis harme a man; and so confortiþ Crist hise membris bi two knyttingis of treuþe, *If men* of þis world *have pursued Crist, þane þei shulen pursue hise membris; and if þei han kept hise wordis, þei shulen kepe hise disciplis wordis.* And þis is liȝt for to knowe; for al þat shal be moot nedis be; for it is more hard to fendis to pursue þe persone of Crist þan to pursue hise membris, and þus þe liȝter wolen þei do. But oo confort lieþ here, þat as Crist convertide summe þat weren men of þe world, so shulen hise disciplis do. And þus þei shulen not worche in veyn to kepe his lawe as he biddiþ, for ech man þat shal worche mote have an hope of sum good ende, for dispeire of sich an ende wolde lette a man for to worche.

Sin is engendered by unbelief.

But þe blyndenesse of þe worlde þat turmentiþ Crist wiþ hise lymes, is unknowinge in bileve[1], *þat þei knowe not Cristis Fadir.* For if þei knewe wel Cristis Fadir, þanne after þei shulden knowe his Sone, and þat þese two ben o God; but who wolde stryve aȝens þis God? And so defaute of bileve, and uncunnynge þat men have, gendren al yvel dedes; and þus ech synner is a fool; and if men knewen Goddis power and his witt in þes two persones, how he mai not forȝete synne to punishe it whanne it is tyme, þanne shulden men dreden to synne, for knowinge of þes two persones. But þis feiþ is oþer weie in wakyng[2] or in slepynge. But Crist reproveþ þis unbileve, and seiþ, *if he hadde not comen and spoke not þus wiþ hem, þis synne shulde not þei have hadde.* For siþ Crist moste nedis have come in his manhede as he cam,

[1] The words *þat—bileve* are excluded from the Italics in E.
[2] *oþer awey in wantyng*, E.

and alle þe dedes þat he dide, have do to men as he dide to hem, þis greet synne shulde not have be, of unkynde untreuþe of Jewes. For þis was gret unkyndnesse, to þis manere trete þere broþer, þat algatis mekeli dide so grete kyndness aȝen; and it was an opyn untreuþe, to þis manere hate her God; but now þese Jewes han noon excusinge of þis synne. And herfore seiþ Crist þus, *þat what man þat hatiþ him, he hatiþ also his Fadir*, for þei ben boþe oo þing. And, for in ech kynde of þingis is oon first, þat mesuriþ alle oþere þat ben in þat kynde, þerfore in maner of synnes moote be oon first of alle oþer synnes, and marke alle þe oþer, and þat is þe synne of preestis aȝens Jesus Crist. And herfore seiþ Crist þat, *if he hadde not do werkes in hem, þat noon oþer man dide, þei hadden not hadde þis synne, but now þei siȝen þis feiþ, and ȝit þei hatiden boþe me and my Fadir.* But þis synne was not done wiþouten grete cause, siþ God suffriþ noo synne wiþouten avauntage þat it doiþ. And so was *verified þe writinge in her owne lawe, þat þe Jewes hadden wilfulli Crist in hate.*

On dai of oon Evangelist.

[SERMON LVIII.]

Designavit Dominus Jesus.—Luc. x. [1.]

Þis gospel telliþ how Crist sente lesse disciplis to preche to þe peple, and ordeyne for þe apostlis; and þes wordis helpen moche for prechinge of simple preestis, for grete apostlis figuren bishopis, and lesse disciplis lesse preestis. But þese *disciplis weren two and seventy* in noumbre; and so many, as men seien, weren langagis aftir making of Babiloyne[a]; and alle Cristis

The mission of the seventy-two disciples.

[a] This very precise calculation appears to be taken from the *De Civitate Dei* of St. Augustine, who, (Lib. xvi. cap. 3-9), reckoning the posterity of Shem at 27, that of Ham at 31, and that of Japhet at 15, (Gen. x.) considers that the human race, after the flood, was divided into 73, or rather, as he undertakes to prove by a particular argument, into 72 nations. Till the building of the tower of Babel, these nations had all one common language; but after the dispersion which followed as a penal infliction upon that event, there came to be as many languages as there were nations.

disciplis traveiliden to bringe to oon men of þe Chirche, so þat þer shulde be oon heerde and oon flok. Þis noumbre of Cristis disciplis *sente he, two and two bifore his face, into ech place þat he was to come to,* for to preche and to teche, as weren citees and comune places. And here moun Cristene men se þe falshede of þese freris, how þei letten symple prestis to preche þe gospel to þe folk. For as þei feynen falsely, noon of Cristis disciplis hadde leve to preche til þat Petir hadde ȝovun him leve, and bi þis same skile, noo preest shulde preche to þe peple, but if he hadde leve of þe bishop or leve of þe pope. Þis gospel telliþ þe falsnesse of þes freris lesynge, for Crist sente þese disciplis to preche comunly to þe peple, wiþouten lettre or axinge of leve of Seint Petir; and as Petir shulde not graunte þis leve in Cristis presence, so preestis in Cristis presence have leve of Crist, whanne þei ben preestis, to preche treuli þe gospel. And if þei prechen þus treuli þe gospel as Crist biddiþ hem, Crist is amyddis hem, and þe peple þat þei techen. And alȝif prelatis shulden examyne prestis þat prechen þus, neþeles it were more nede to examyne þes freris, þat feynen hem to be preestis, for þei comen in of worse ground, and ben more suspect of heresie.

Poor priests forbidden to preach the gospel, while friars are free to preach fables.

Lord! what resoun shulde dryve herto, to lette trewe preestis to preche þe gospel freeli, wiþouten ony let, or ony fablis or flaterynge, and ȝyve leve to þese freris to preche fablis and heresies, and aftirward to spoile þe peple, and selle hem her false sermouns. Certis þe peple shulde not suffre siche falshede of Antecrist. Also Poul, Cristis apostle, techiþ in bokes of oure bileve, how God wolde þat he prechide to þe peple wiþouten sich axing; for fro þe tyme þat he was convertid, þree ȝeer after, he preechide fast, and axide noo leve of Petir herto, for he hadde leve of Jesus Crist. Siche novelries of pseudo freris shulden prelatis and alle men aȝen stonden, lest her falshede growide more and largerly[1] envenymede þe Chirche. Þus shulden preestis preche þe peple freeli Cristis gospel, and leve freris fablis and her begginge, for þanne þei preche wiþ Cristis leve; and herof shulden prelatis be feyn, siþ þei synnen moche on

Gal. i. 18; ii. 7, 8.

[1] *largerely*. E.

oþer sidis, but if þei ben Antecristis preestis and shapen to quenche Cristis lawe. But þe peple comunli trowide in Crist and lovede him, and þus þei obeschen[1] to þis tyme, boþe to Crist and his lawe.

Yet their mission, authority, and rule of life, are clear.

And Crist shewide þe cause and þe nede of þis prechinge, *for he seide, Ripe corn is moche, and fewe workmen aboute it.* But for þis work is medeful, and Crist sovereynli performyde it, þerfore he techiþ his disciplis, to *preie þe lord of þis ripe corn to sende hise workmen þerto.* And here Crist techiþ opinli þat men shulden not bie þis office, ne take no mede of þe peple to traveile þus in Cristis name, for þanne þei puttiden upon Crist þat he sillide prechyng of his word, and ȝaf leve to do symonye; and boþe þes ben blasfemyes. But Crist stiride his men to go, and telliþ[2] hem þe peril bifore, but he moveþ hem privyly for greet mede to traveile þus; *Go ȝe,* seiþ Crist, *for Y sende ȝou as lambren among wolves.* And so we have mandement of Crist, and autorite to go, and foorme of þis perilous goinge, þat makiþ it more medeful. But Crist ȝyveþ his prechours[3] foorme how þei shal lyve in þis work; *Nyle ȝe, he seiþ, bere sachil ne scrippe, ne hosis, ne shoon, ne greete men bi þe weie,* ne do þing þat shulde lette þis work. If ony siche helpe to þis work, Crist wolde not þat þei leften it. And þus seiþ Crist þat, *In to what hous ȝe entren, ȝe shal first seie, Pees be to þis hous; and if þere be child of pees, ȝoure pees shal reste upon him, and ellis it shal turne aȝen to ȝou,* and so ȝoure work shal not be idil. But if ypocritis worchen here, al ȝif þei seien sich wordis, þe housis and þe peple ben worse, þat þese false men comen among; for Crist doiþ þese vertues, in whos name þese prechours speken, and if þei ben þe fendis lymes, comunly þei moven to synne. But Crist wolde not þat hise workmen wenten aboute wiþouten fruyt, and þerfore he biddiþ hem *dwelle in þe same hous* upon resoun; but þei shulden be not idil þere, ne curious in mete and drynke, but þe peple shulde gladly fede hem, and þei shulden homly take þat þei founden, and þei shulden take no newe reule bi which þe peple were chargid. And neiþer part shulde grutche here to do þus as Crist techiþ,

[1] So E; A has *oblisshen.* [2] So E; A has *telle.* [3] *preciouse,* E.

for it shulde turne wiþoute charge to mede of boþe partis; and good lyf of sich workmen shulden move þe peple to do hem good, and devocioun of þe peple should preie hem to take her goodis. But gredynesse and avarice letten here þes two partis; and al if boþe þes synnes letten moche fro Cristis work, neþeles coveitise of preestis is more perilous in þis caas; for avarice of þe peple mai be helpid on many maners, oþer to turne to oþer peple, or to traveile as Poul dide, or to suffre wilfulli hunger, and þrist if it falle; but coveitise of wickide preestis blemyshiþ hem and þe peple, for comunly þei shapen her wordis aftir þe ende þat þei coveiten.

Various characteristics of true preachers; not possessed by the friars.

And here þenken many men þat siche prechours shulden be war þat þey come not wiþ myche peple ne many hors to preche þus, but be paied of comun diete, and þerwiþ redi to traveile, for þei shulden be noo cause of synne, neþer of hem ne of þe peple. And here it semeþ to many men þat þese newe ordris of freris shulden eiþer leve her multitude, or traveile wiþ her hondis, and if þei diden boþe þes two discretely, it were þe betere. Ne take þei not of Cristis lyf to traveile not, as Crist did not, for neiþer þey can ne moun be occupied ellis as Crist was; but raþer þei shulden take of Poul and oþer apostlis for to traveile, and leve her newe tradiciouns, as Petir dide, wiþ oþer apostlis, and profitiden more þan þes men done. We shulden þenke how Petir lyvede whanne Cornelious sente after him, how symply he was fed and herborid, and how he answeride; but now freris reversen Petir and multiplien newe lawes [1] and persones of þeir ordris, havynge more þan Petir hadde. And herwiþ þei seien to men þat þei passen bishopis and popis, and certis þei seien here þe soþe, if þei menen passinge in synne, for unleveful excesse is passinge to þes freris. And so as þei varien in abitis, so þei ben speckid in her ordris, for as þe sect of Sarasynes [2], þei han sum good and sum yvele.

[1] So E; *lawyes*, A. [2] *Sarascenes*, E.

IN DAI OF OON MARTIR.

[SERMON LIX.]

Nisi granum frumenti.—JOHN xii. [24.]

Þis gospel moveþ men bi wordis of Crist to martirdom. And first Crist spekiþ þus bi symylitude in kynde. *But if þe corn of whete fallinge in erþe be deed, ellis it dwelliþ aloone wiþoute fruyt*, þat springiþ þerof, *and if it be deed* in erþe, *moche fruyt springiþ þerof;* and thus it is of Cristis lyf, that licneþ him to whete corn. It is knowun þing in kynde, and in sentence þat clerkis tellen, þat þe whete corn whan it is sowun and wel hilid wiþ erþe, it takiþ not a newe foorme, but if þe elde passe awei; and siþ it lyvede sum tyme, it must nedis þanne be deed. And if þis corn be þus deed, it bringiþ forþ myche fruyte, for it growiþ bi vertue of hevene first to gras and after to corn, and of oo corn comeþ an eere, and in oo eere ben many cornes. So it is in holi Chirche of Crist, and corn þat comeþ of him. Crist is bi sum proprete oo wheet corn among alle, and Crist mote nedis die, and after growe in hise apostlis, and bi hem growiþ Crist in myche multitude of corn. And how ever clerkes speken þat þe same vertue is in þe seed þat is after in þe fruyt, and passiþ from o fruyt to anoþer, we bileven þat in gendrure of holi Chirche it is þus;—þe vertue of þe firste corn, þat is Crist, of whom comeþ þe Chirche, dwelliþ in ech corn þat comeþ in part of þis Chirche. But þis vertue is not an accident wiþouten a suget, siþ þis suget is þe secounde persone of God, þat is in ech lyme of þe Chirche, and bringiþ wiþ him a grace þat clerkes clepen predestynynge. And so, al ȝif Crist was bifore his manhed hed of þis Chirche, neþeles bi his manhede þis corn hadde newe purginge and colour.

Interpretation of the gospel.

After þis mysty speche, knyttiþ Crist anoþer word which semeþ woundirful in heerynge of many men. *He þat loveþ hys lyf*, seiþ Crist, *he shal lese it*, and aȝen, *he þat hatiþ his lyf in þis world, he kepiþ it to lyf wiþouten eende.* A man is

The true following of Christ.

seid to love his lyf, þat loveþ it more þan oþer þing; and he is said to hate his lyf, þat puttiþ oþer love bifore it; for þe first is a passinge love, and þe toþer a maner of hate; and bi þis manere of speche many gospellis moun be knowun, for it is a suynge þing to love a þing and to hate it þus. But in þe þridde word of þis gospel spekiþ Crist more speciali, how þes wordis longen to him, as to ground of good religioun. First Crist seiþ, *If ony man serve to Crist, sue he him;* and here he techiþ þat no man mai mynystre to Crist, but if he sue him; and þus moun we se how feyntli we serve to Crist, for now we leven þe weie of Crist and bowun[1] bi a wrong weie, and now we gone ever abak to synne þat we han first done. And so fewe men or noon suen Crist wiþouten defaute, for we speken of suynge in vertues, and not of suynge of bodili weie. And þis suynge stondiþ most in ordynal love of man, and herfore spekiþ þe gospel of love, and of hate next bifore.

The reward of such following.

But over þis, Crist seiþ þat, *Where he is, his mynystre shal be*, and þis is seid suyngli to þe word þat is seid bifore; for it semeþ of þat word þat it is hard to serve Crist, and herfore telliþ Crist þe meede þat men shulden have þat serven him; for he þat may not lye bihetiþ þat his servaunt shal be þere, boþe in blis and in place, where Christ is wiþouten eende. And siþ Crist is in hevene and in blis bi boþe hise kyndis, þis biheest shulde move men to sue Crist, al ȝif it be hard, for þe mede of þis suynge passiþ gretli þe traveile herfore; for Crist mai not rewarde men but if he ȝeve hem over her traveil; as he mai not ȝyve a þing, but ȝif he ȝyve it graciousely; for as he is al grace, so he mediþ and ponishiþ bi grace. But þe laste word here shulde move a trewe man to serve Crist, for he seiþ, *If ony man serve me, my Fadir shal worshipe him.* And þis worship mai not be, but if it make þis man Goddis sone, and so eir[2] of God, and ȝyve him goodis of all his rewme; and þanne he is maad worshipful, as we maken worship unto kyngis. And so alle eiris of Crist ben moche more þan erþeli kyngis.

Objections answered.

In þis shorte gospel ben doutis, boþe of conscience and

[1] *bowen*, E. [2] *beyr*, E.

of oþer. First philosophris douten, where seed leesiþ his forme, whanne it is maad a newe þing, as þe gospel spekiþ here; and sum men þenken nay, for siþe þe same quantite or qualite, or vertue, þat was first in seed, leveþ aftir in þe fruyte, as a child is ofte lyk to his fadir or to his modir, or ellis to his eelde fadir, aftir þat þe vertue lastiþ,—and siþ alle þese ben accidentis, þat mai not dwelle wiþouten suget, —it semeþ þat þe same bodi is first seed and after fruyte, and þus it mai ofte change fro seed to fruyte and aȝen. Here many, clepid filosophris, glaveren dyversely; but in þis mater Goddis lawe spekiþ þus, as diden eelde clerkis, þat þe substaunce of a bodi is bifore þat it be seed, and now fruyte and now seed, and now quyk and now deed. And þus many formes moun be togidere in oo þing, and speciali whanne þe partis of þat þing ben medlid togidere; and þus þe substaunce of a bodi is now of oo kynde and now of anoþer. And so boþe þese accidentis, qualite and quantite, moun dwelle in þe same substaunce, al if it be chaungid in kindis, and þus þis same þing þat is now a whete corn shal be deed and turne to gras, and after to many cornes. But variance in wordis in þis mater falliþ to clerkes, and shewinge of equivocacioun[1], þe which is more redi in Latyn; but it is ynow to us to putte, þat þe same substance is now quyk and now deed, and now seed and now fruyte; and so þat substaunce þat is now a whete corn mut nedis die bifore þat it be maad gras, and siþ be maad an hool eer. And þus spekiþ holi writt and no man can disproven it. Errour of freris in þis mater is not here to reherce, for it is ynowȝ to telle how þei erren in bileve.

Two kinds of martyrdom.

The secounde doute in þis mater is of suynge of Crist. It semeþ þat no man sueþ him but if he be martrid as was Crist, and siþ no man mai be saved but if he sue Crist in lyf, it semeþ þat no man shal be saved but if he be martrid. Here men seien truli, þat þere ben two martirdoms, martirdome in bodi and martirdome in wille. Martirdome in bodi nediþ not ech man to have, for many men ben seintis þat dien confessours. Generali to speke, þat man is

[1] So E: A has *equyvacioun*.

a martir þat is killid in charite and þus goiþ to hevene, be he killid of just men or ellis of þe fendis lymes. Þis secounde manere of martirdom shulde ech man have, siþ ech man shulde more love his soule þan his bodi, and algatis he shulde more love God and his lawe; and who evere loveþ þus, is redi to suffre deþ of his bodi for love of his God. And fewe seintis, or noon, ben here on lyve þat ne þei maken hem martirs for þe love of God; for to chastise her fleishe þey shorten her lyf. But Y speke not here of martirdom of glotouns, for þei shorten her lyf for love of her fleish, and taken to myche fode, wherfore þei dien sunner; but þe firste men fasten for love of her God, and to have pees of her fleish þat ellis wolde be wantoun. But siþ men knowun not evenly þe mesure þat wolde lengþe her lyf, þes men ben not mensleeris, for bi sich chesinge of þe betere, þei lesen wysely þe worse; and so done bi Goddis heeste þes bodily martris. And þus men shulden not folili slee hem silf, neþer in fastinge ne in etinge ne in cause defending, but stonde for truþe if her deeþ sue, willinge to maynteyne truþe, and mekeli to suffre deeþ, but not folily desire it.

OF OON MARTIR.

[SERMON LX.]

Si quis vult venire post me.—MATT. xvi. [24.]

What it involved in taking up the Cross and following Christ.

Þis gospel techiþ as þe former doiþ, how a man shulde ordeyne him for to suffre martirdom. First seiþ Crist þat, *who ever wole come after him, he mut denye him silf and take his crosse and sue Crist.* Þat man denyeþ him silf þat loveþ him silf lasse þan he loveþ his God or lawe of his God. For þis principle of love moten men suppose, whanne þer ben two þingis put in a mannis chois, and he mut nede leve þe toon for takinge of þe toþer. Þat þing þat he leveþ, he loveþ þanne þe lesse, and þis clepiþ Crist denyynge of þat þing, and in anoþer place, hate of his lyf; and þus shulden alle men renounsen her goodis, for goodis moven men to love hem in ordre, and if men tellen to þese goodis þat her love passe[1] resoun, þanne þei tellen aȝen[a] her answere to þes goodis. But þis synne is in men and not in goodis, and þis tellinge aȝen is renounsinge of hem; as if a man be temptid to love an erþeli þing more þan his God, for fals undirstondinge bi which he can not weye þe riȝt weiȝte of love, þanne he forsakiþ his God, for love of þis erþeli þing. And if he staunche þis love, and seie to þis þing þat he wole not love it so myche, for þe love of God, þanne he renounsiþ to it, þat here he wole forsake it. Þe secounde word þat Crist seiþ, þat men shulden take her crosse, biddiþ þat men shulden make hem redi to suffre for Goddis love; for þe crosse bitokeneþ passioun in Goddis lawe, and þis purpos is nedeful Cristen men to have. And þe þridde word þat Crist techiþ here, þat whanne a man haþ þes two he shulde sue Crist, ech man shulde have in mynde and do it in dede; for he sueþ Crist, þat moveþ himsilf to holde Goddis heestis; for þis weie wente Crist and failide in no tyme to do his Fadris wille. And þis word answeriþ to þe Holi Goost, as two wordis bifore menen þe Fadir and þe Sone, for þe name of God þat is al myȝti answeriþ bi proprete to þe firste persone, and man shal denye himsilf for þis name; and so whanne we preien to God in oure Pater noster, we seien first to þe Fadir, Halowid be þi name. Þe crosse bitokeneþ þe persone of Crist, for he was done on þe crosse for love of mankynde, and shape him evermore to suffre bi comun counceil. And here aȝen þis Trinite synnen many men; as, he þat bi mannis lawe is clepid to an office, in which he mai not kepe him silf in charite, and answeriþ for þis name and takiþ on him þis office, þis man synneþ aȝens Goddis name, and denyeþ not him silf for love of God.

But after Crist ȝyveþ a reule to kepe þes þree þingis, and seiþ, *Who so wole make his lyf saaf, mut nedis lesen it*, lyvynge in þis world, *but he þat lesiþ his lyf for þe love of Crist shal fynde it*, in þe toþer world. Þat man lesiþ his lyf, þat puttiþ it

[1] *passiþ*, E.

[a] 'telle aȝen' is meant as the literal rendering of 're-nuntiare.'

bihinde and þe love of God bifore, whanne þe caas comeþ, and so it is al oon a man for to lese his lyf and denye himsilf, or ellis to hate himsilf; and who þat leesiþ not his lyf here on þis manere, he failiþ in charite and in þe firste mandement. But siþ a mannis lyf is ordeyned of God evermore to be, it is not lost to God, but he, for whom þis lyf is lost, kepiþ it wele and ȝyveþ it him in blis in þe toþer world. And who wolde not chaffre þus wiþ his owne lyf? Clerkis witen wele how a mannis soule and a mannis lyfe ben boþe oon in a manere, for lyf is þe firste acte þat comeþ of a mannis soule, and of siche actis taken þingis names, as clerkis clepen angels undirstondingis[a]. And þus spekiþ þe gospel of a mannis lyf, and Crist provede bi resoun þat men shulden chaffare þus, *For what profitiþ it to a man, if he wynne al þis world, if he suffre þerbi peiringe of his soule; or what chaunginge shal a man ȝyve for his soule.* Siþ a mannis soule is persone of þis man, he shulde ȝyve al his catel for savynge of þis soule; and siþ a mannis bodi is worse þan his soule, ech man shulde more love his soule þan his bodi. And so he shulde hate his bodi for love of þis soule, and speciali siþ sich chaffare shulde turne him to betere. And ground of þis speche stondiþ in þis bileve, *For Crist is to come fro hevene in his glorie* at þe dai of doome *wiþ hise aungelis* to juge ech man, *and þanne shal he ȝyve to ech man after hise workes.* And siþ þis lore[1] of Crist deserveþ hevene blis, he is a greet fool þat wole not chaffare here. Defaute of bileve lettiþ algatis þis chaffare.

The Transfiguration predicted.

And for þis sentence is hard for to trowe, þerfore telliþ Crist of his glorifiyng, how he shal shewe him here glorious in his bodi, so þat bi þis shewyng here in þis lyf, þei ben more stablid in þis to trowe in Crist. *Soþeli,* seiþ Crist, *Y seie to ȝou, þere be sum of men þat stonden here, þat shulen not taaste deþ, til þei seen me comyng in my rewme* in blis of my bodi. And for þis was done in þe kynde of Cristis bodi, þerfore he clepiþ him here sone of a man; and þis was done in dede, as Matheu telliþ after, for Petir, Johun, and James

[1] So both A and E; but the sense evidently requires *love*.

[a] Or 'intelligences;' a translation of the Latin *intelligentiae*.

weren here wiþ Crist, and his face shynede as sunne, and Moises and Helye apperiden to him. And þus Crist cam in his rewme, or þese disciplis weren dede; and þis was a greet skile to move hem to trowe in Crist, and to traveile bisily to gete sich a blisse, for sich a bodili lyf were wel chaungid for þis lyf. And herefore seid Petir, It is good to us to be here and þerefore make we here þree tabernaclis. And þus who so trowiþ wele bi love of þe gospel, he shal trowe to Cristis lore and lyve þerafter. Ne drede we þes sophists þat Crist seide here fals, whanne he seide þat he cam here in his[1] rewme, for as part of þe Chirche is treuli clepid þe Chirche, so part of Cristis rewme is treuli clepid his rewme. And siþ many aungels comen wiþ þes þree men, and Crist cam to þes apostlis in dowers[2] of his bodi, it was soþeli seid þat he cam here in his rewme. For men here þat shulen be saaf as weren Cristis apostlis, ben clepid his rewme in þe Pater noster; whi not þes seintis in which Crist cam here?

IN DAI OF O MARTIR.

[SERMON LXI.]

Qui vos audit, me audit.—LUC. x. [16.]

True preachers have authority direct from Christ.

Þis gospel telliþ a lore of Crist, how he tauȝte his disciplis, to holde hem in mekenesse, and to flee veyn glorie, þat is a fendis synne. Þe gospel telliþ how lasse disciplis, þat weren two and seventy, comen aȝen to Crist wiþ joie, and seiden, as þe gospel telliþ after, and we shulen reherce. Crist ȝyveþ autorite first to hise disciplis, and spekiþ to hise membris as þes þat shulen be saved, and seiþ; *He þat heeriþ ȝou*, in þat *he heeriþ me* and *he þat dispisiþ ȝou*, in þat *he dispisiþ me;* for whanne a messanger spekiþ in name of a man, he þat heeriþ him or dispisiþ him þus, heeriþ or dispisiþ him in whos name he spekiþ. And bi þis cause shulden men worshipe prechours,

[1] So E; A has þis. [2] *doweris*, E.

and dispisen hem[1] þat prechen fablis or lesingis, for þei comen in þe fendis name, as her work shewiþ. And þus if prechours holden hem prechinge in Cristis name, þei han ful autorite more þan prelatis moun ȝyve hem; and if a man preche aȝens Cristis biddinge, as in falshede, or for begginge, or for worldeli wynnynge, þe autorite þat he haþ comeþ of þe fend, for þe fend is his maistir, in whos name he prechiþ, and þis is þe autour þat lettiþ prechinge to profite. But Crist telliþ over, how hard it is to dispise him, for, *who ever dispisiþ Crist, dispisiþ him þat sente Crist*, and so he dispisiþ þe Fadir and al þe Trinite. And þus telliþ Luke þat after þis autorite ȝyven to Cristis disciplis, *two and seventi turneden aȝen, and hadden* unskilful *joie, and seiden* to Crist; *Lord, ȝhe, þe fendis ben suget to us in þe name of þee.* But Crist shewide þat he was God, and answeride to þes disciplis, not to þe wordis þat þei spaken, but to þe caas þat þei weren inne, and it is propre to God to wite þus synne of þe soule.

On the nature of thunder.

Crist seiþ to þes disciplis þat he saiȝ Saþanas fallinge fro hevene, as þe þunder floon falliþ fro þe cloude. It is knowun to clerkes of þree þingis in þe þundir, þe liȝtning and þe noise and þe þundir stoon. Þe liȝtninge is first in brekinge of cloudis, as if two stoones on a nyȝt weren knockid togider, and þis noise is maad of þis hard hurtling; but liȝt is more swift þan heeryng in perseyvyng, as sowne comeþ softe, but liȝt comeþ soone; and þis is cause whi þat liȝt is perseyved bifore soun, and þus comeþ mannis liȝt bifore mannis heering. But þe þridde propirte þat falliþ sum tyme in þundir is as it were a whirlewynd led aboute among cloudis, and comynge to þe erþe and doinge þere woundris; and þes men þat knowen þe worchinge of þe elementis, how manere of saltis and poudir fleeþ fier, and worchiþ woundir bi craft in mevynge of curranntis, woundren lesse of þis þundir floon. Sum tyme, it cleveþ grete okes in sundir, and sum tyme it meveþ grete stones fro her place; sum tyme it moltiþ þe swerd in þe sheþe, and ȝit þe sheþe is al hool, and many oþere woundirs; and al þis is maad bi a sutil mater þat is moved fro þe cloudis bi

[1] So E; om. A.

kynde of þe elementis. And þus seiþ Crist, þat Saþanas bi pryde, and kynde of Goddis justice, fel sudenili fro hevene, and in þis fallinge he dide woundris, more þan þis þundir floon, and he was stinkynge wiþ synne, as þis blast stinkiþ sum tyme. And þis fal of þe fend sai Crist bi his Godhede; and al þis was of pride, þat God myȝte not suffre more, þat ne þe[1] angel in hevene was dryvun þus in to helle. How myche shulden men drede pryde, þat God wole þus punishe, and have no vein glorie þat þei ben Cristis aungels, and don woundris in his name in casting out of fendis! And to be war wiþ þis pride spekiþ Crist þus þese wordis, for Crist knewe wel her pryde þat þei hadden in her hertis, and to remove þis pride spak Crist to her hertis.

Four predominant passions in the soul.

For as it is ofte seid, þer ben foure passiouns in a mannis soule, in which stondiþ synne or mede after þei ben reulid. And þes foure ben þes, joie and sorewe, hope and drede of þingis þat shulen come. Summe han joie of sich manere hiȝenesse, and summe han joie of synne or richesse of þe world, and sum men han sorewe of oþer mennis welfare or lesinge of worldeli goodis, for þei loven hem to myche, and sum men han hope of welfare of þis world, and dreden of fallinge þerfro; but men shulden have sorewe for her synne and oþer mennis. And þus Crist wepte þries, and ever more for synne, for synne is worse þan ony peyne mai be; and siþ þe worsnesse of þing is matere of sorewe, man shulde have more sorewe for synne þan for ony oþer þing, and more joie of hevenli blis þan ony worldeli welfare or hiȝynge of mannis staat, were it nevere so myche. And herfore seiþ Crist, *Lo, I have ȝovun ȝou power to defoule upon neddris*[2], for many seintis, as Margarete[a], hadde power of God to defoule þe fendis þat weren

[1] om. E. [2] *adderis*, E.

[a] St. Margaret, whose legend makes her a native of Antioch in the fourth or fifth century, was so popular a saint in England from the eleventh century, that no less than 238 parish churches are said to be dedicated in her honour. According to the more popular version of her story here alluded to, the foul fiend, in the form of a dragon, visited her in the prison into which the persecuting governor of Antioch had thrown her, and swallowed her up; but immediately burst asunder, so that the holy virgin came forth unhurt. A good general account of her may be found in Mrs. Jameson's *Sacred and Legendary Art*. See also

in forme of dragouns, and sette her feet upon hem, and heeld hem aȝens her wille. And þis was grete peyne to þes proude fendis; and sich manere of power hadde Cristis disciplis upon fendis, for þei castiden hem out of placis þat þei wolden dwelle inne, and made hem to dwelle in placis þat þei wolden not dwelle inne, and sich subjeccioun is noious to proude spiritis. But Crist badde his disciplis, joie not þus for suche power. And þus, to speke goostli, þis power to defoule eddris, and to defoule scorpiouns, is power to overcome þe fendis whanne þei tempten men to synne bi stingginge of her venym; and herfore seiþ Crist, *þat he haþ ȝovun hem power upon al power of her enemye and he shal not noie hem. But neþeles, joie ȝe not in þis þing* to vein glorie, *þat spiritis ben suget to ȝou*[1], for þis mai falle to dampned men, as many men moun reise þe fend, and make him worche woundris, and ȝit in alle þes dedis þei moun be fendis as he is; for bi vertue of Crist þes fendis ben þus suget, and þes names han vertue to make þe fend drede kindeli. But Crist techiþ hise disciplis to *joie more of þis, þat her names ben writun in hevene*, for to come to blisse. Of þis shulde þei have more joie, and holde hem in mekenes. And Crist telliþ not þis to men as he dide to þes disciplis, but if he kepe hem in vertues and bringe hem to hevene, for ellis Crist tauȝte hem to joie of þingis þat weren fals. And þus it semeþ þat þese disciplis weren confermyd in manere, and ȝit God leet hem falle, to teche his Chirche to flee pride; and þus Crist leet Petir falle ofte, after þat he was apostle, and þat, to teche prelatis after, to joie not to myche of her staat, for sich boost is fendis synne, þat stynkiþ foule bifore God, and it is maad in feyned power to loose men and bynde. Men shulden loke þat þei weren certeyn þat God wolde worche þus wiþ hem, bifore þei spaken of þis power, and of þe dedis of þat to men, and þanne wiþ grete mekenes, to moven men to þanke God; for liynge in sich a caas smatchide a myche more synne, þan was in þes disciplis þat Crist reprevyde so sharpli. For þei seiden

[1] This passage is rightly marked as a quotation in E, but not in A.

Seinte Marherete The Meiden ant Martyr (a version of the legend in old English prose of the thirteenth century), among the publications of the Early English Text Society.

soþ and herieden God, and in þes boþe failen prelatis, for þei for pride feynen falseli and coveitise of wordeli goodis, to do þing þat þei moun not do; and þis is a greet synne, for it were synne to a pore man to defoule a kingis cloþis, moche more synne were it to men to putte falsehede upon treuþe. For þis is a foul blasfemye, þat is a foul synne of alle oþere; as, if a man putte on God falshede þat he myȝte not have, he dispiside in þis his God more þan þe fende durste ever do. It is no drede alle þes popis þat seien þat þey graunten sich pardons, seien opinly ynowȝ þat God grauntiþ hem bifore, and if God knowe hem unworþi to have siche pardon of him, þes popis blasfemen in God more þan evere þe Apostlis dursten. And þus shulden prelatis be war to graunt no þing in þe name of God but if þei weren sikir bifore þat Goddis justice grauntide it, and þis myȝte þei not knowe but if þei hadden revelacioun; and if oure prelatis abiden ever sich revelacioun, þey shulden disseyve fewe men or noon in grauntinge of suche pardons; but as Petir held his pees in grauntinge of siche þingis, so shulden þei holden þer pees, siþ þei ben lasse worþ þan Petir, and þe comun peple shulde not trowe hem in siche casis.

Papal indulgences.

IN DAI OF OON MARTIR.

[SERMON LXII.]

Si quis venit ad me.—LUC. xiiii. [26.]

Þis gospel telliþ men how þei shulen dispose hem to be disciplis of Crist, and certis ellis þei shulen not come to hevene; for be he knyȝt, be he clerk, but if he be Cristis disciple þenke he not to come to hevene; and so it were good to lerne þis lore. Crist seiþ at þe bigynnynge, *If ony man come to him and hate not þes seven þingis, he mai not be Cristis disciple*, and so he mai not be saved, for ech man þat sueþ Crist is disciple of Crist; and þus knyȝttis in Cristis tyme weren his privy disciplis, as Joseph of Armaþie, and centurio also, and Nichodeme, and oþer moo, as þe gospel telliþ us. First mut a man *hate his*

Conditions annexed to the discipleship of Christ.

fadir and siþ *hate his modir;* þe þridde tyme mut a man *hate his wyf* and þe fourþe tyme *hise children;* þe fifþe tyme he shulde *hate his breþeren* and þe sixte tyme *his sisters;* þe sevente tyme moost of alle he moste hate *his owne lyf.* First men shulden wite here what were to hate in þis gospel, for Crist moveþ algatis to love, and no tyme to envye; but here it is seid bifore þat þis hating is denying, and þis is, lovynge in ordre as þe þing shulde be loved. And so þes sevene þingis shulden be loved, but lasse þan Crist or his lawe; and þus puttinge bihinde of love, is hating þat Crist spekiþ of.

Objections answered.

But ȝit sophistris replien here and seien þat many men comen to Crist þat han not þes sevene þingis, and no man hatiþ but þing þat is. But here men moten lerne to speke to þat witt þat Goddis lawe spekiþ. Here fewe men or noon comen to ordre of Crist, but if þei have fadir and modir oþer next or fer. Sum men have fadir and modir þat geten hem into þis world, and sum men han eldris bifore þat gaten sich fadirs and modirs, and alle þes ben clepid fadir in Goddis lawe þat is trewe. Adam and Eve hadde noon sich fadris, but þei hadden erþe and erþeli þing, and þes myȝten be clepid here modirs, and her fadir was mannis kynde; and as þei mosten nede be saved, so God was her fadir. And siþ ech word þat Crist seiþ is trewe to his entent, and he seiþ þat who evere doiþ þe wille of his Fadir in hevene, he is his broþer and his sister, and his modir also, no man wantiþ here þes frendis, al if þei wanten sich for a tyme; and if mennis eldris ben dede, þanne þei han suche for sum tyme[1]. And mannis fleishe is his wyf, and her workes ben hise children; and so ech haþ such a wyf, and sich children of his wyf; and so siche sevene þingis ben longinge to ech man, and alle þes sevene shulden men love lasse þan þei loven Crist her God. And þis is þe reule of Crist, þat passiþ alle þes newe ordris, and who evere loveþ not Crist more þan alle þes sevene wantiþ charite, and brekiþ alle Goddis hestis. And þis is veyn religioun, and so, as we seiden bifore, *who ever beriþ not his crosse and comeþ* in lyvynge *after Crist,*

Against the new orders.

[1] *a tyme*, E.

mai not wiþ þis *be his disciple.* And þis is liȝt for to prove, for man shulde hate his own lyf, and so suffre for Cristis sake, and ellis he brekiþ Cristis ordre; and þes newe religiouse moten nedis breke þis reule of Crist, for þei loven more þes newe ordris þan þei done reule of þe gospel. And þus þei feynen ofte tyme to stonde wiþ lawe of þe gospel; and if men axen whi þei done so, þei seien þat ellis here ordre were loste, but God cursiþ alle sich ordris þat neden men to hate her God.

The parable of the unfinished tower.

And to printe þis in mennis hertis Crist telliþ two hard parablis. First he seiþ, þat, *Ech of hem þat wolde make an*[1] *nedeful tour, shulde sitte first and acounte dispensis nedeful herefore þat he have to make þis tour, lest he faile aftirward whanne he haþ sett þe foundement, and alle men þat seen þis bigynen for to scorne him; and seien, þis man bigan to bilde but he myȝte not make an ende.* Þis tour is ful nedeful to ech man þat shal be saved. Þis toure is gedringe of vertues, and þe ground is mekenesse, grounded in Crist, þat is mene persone of God; and as no þing mai be lower þan is the myddil of þe world, so no man mai meker be þan is Crist, þat is þis ground. And siþ þis tour mute reche to hevene, men moten nedis take þis ground; and herfore seiþ Poul, þat no man mai sette oþer ground þan is sett, þe which ground is Jesus Crist, for no man is meke but in his vertue. Þe hiȝest part of þis tour is briteysing[2] of charite þat lastiþ into hevene, for charite falliþ not doun, but lastiþ boþe in þis worlde and after þe dai of dome. Oþer vertues put in ordre maken þe myddil of þis tour; and þus we shulde avise us what staat or religioun were most acordinge to þis makinge, and reste þerinne, and make þis toure. And bileve techiþ us þat þe staat of Cristis sect is moost certein and nedeful to men, þat wolen arere þis tour, for no man mai arere it, but if he be of Cristis ordre. And þus boþe aungels good and yvel scornen men þat kepen þis ground, and after wenden fro Cristis ordre, to newe ordris þat ben worse, for bi þis weye mai no man eende[3] þe laste bretais[4] of þis tour. Þis tour is algatis sure to men þat putten hem wel upon þis ground, and holden hem wel þeron, and reulen hem bi þe firste reule, þat þei baggen not þerfro;

1 Cor. iii. 11.

[1] *a*, E. [2] *britasyng*, E. [3] for *eende*, E reads *wende but ȝif he have*.
[4] *britayse*, E.

for none enemyes mai anoie þat man þat bildiþ þus his tour, for þe fend and oþer enemyes moun not meve aȝens þis ground. And þus a man in þis tour drediþ not arwis ne dartis, but arwis of Goddis Word overcomen enemyes þat ben wiþoute. Traveil þat men hav in vertues, ben dispensis to make þis toure, and suyng after Cristis lyf, as many gospels techen bifore, is þe hiȝinge of þis toure, and growinge into charite. And þus shulde ech man chese his staat, and do þe traveil þat falliþ to vertues, and algatis reule his wal[1] after Crist and his lawe; and if he have endeles lastinge here, he mai not faile of þis makinge.

The parable of the two kings.

But, for it falliþ to a werriour sum tyme to go[2] out and fiȝte, þe secounde parable of Crist telliþ of þis fiȝtinge, and seiþ: *What king shulde wende to do batel aȝens anoþer kyng, þat he ne wolde sitte bifore and þenke wiseli, wheþer he myȝte wiþ ten þousynd fiȝte wiþ him þat cam aȝens him wiþ twenti þousand; ellis whilis he lediþ afer his oost, þe lesse kyng preieþ him of pees.* Dyvers men undirstonden þis text to dyvers wittis bineþe bileve, but we weren wont to telle it þat ech man shulde be a kynge and governe þe rewme of his soule bi keping of ten comandementis; and good keping of þes ten þousynd is ynowȝ to ech man. Þe toþer kyng wiþ twenti þousend, is comunli seide þe fend, for Joob seiþ þat he is kyng upon alle children of pride, and he doubliþ ten þousynd of werriours aȝens Crist; for he passiþ fro unyte, as doiþ þe noumbre of two, and aȝens ech comandement he haþ cautil of double entent. And if þese ten þousynd ben alle þo þat helpen Goddis part, and þes twenti þousynd alle þo þat loven doublenesse to helpe þe fend, it semeþ not aȝens Goddis witt, siþ his wordis ben plentenouse. If þis first king wexe coward and traitour to his God, and love richesse of þe world and worldeli frendship of men, and lustis of his bodi, and pees fro pursueris here, he sendiþ message to þis fend, and many tokenes of cowardise, and preieþ him of his pees, and he wole serve unto him; and þus failen many men from hardynesse in Goddis cause and bicomen þe fendis servauntis, for þei scien þe world axiþ þis, and so, þat þat her enemye axiþ, þei graunten to him cowardli.

Job xli. 34.

[1] *walle*, E. [2] So E; *goene*, A.

Oþer wittis of þese wordis for shortnesse we leven here. But Crist seiþ in þe ende oo word of greet hardynesse; *Þus ech of ȝou þat renounsiþ not to alle þingis þat he haþ, mai not be my disciple.* For þanne he telliþ aȝen to þe fend, to þe world, and to his fleish, þat his hiȝeste charite is stabli sett in God, and he loveþ noon oþer þingis but in ordre of þis love; and þus þe world, þat haþ lest[1] colour, is overcome bi Goddis clerk, and þe fend, wiþ mannis fleishe, ben also overcomun wiþ þis word[2]. For if a man have no desire ne no lust regnynge in him, þat ne he telliþ þe same tale how he moost loveþ his God, alle his enemes ben discumfitid bi þe first þousynd of his oost. And here men seien soþeli þat men renounsen on many maneres; as Crist wiþ hise apostlis forsoke þis world wiþ lastinge havynge, for he hadde no more of þis world but as him nedide to his lyf; and þus shulden preestis do, þat entren in to Cristis ordre, for ellis goode and yvele wole scorne hem of her folie. But ech man þat shal be saved, renounsiþ alle þese worldeli goodis, whan he leveþ alle hem bihynde to love more God and his lawe. But þis is þe fouleste synne þat falliþ here to ony preest, to love more þese newe ordres þan to love Cristis lawe. Bi þis þe fend overcomeþ manye wiþ þe dart of ypocrisie, whanne he makiþ hise servauntis, þat ben oblishid to serve him, to seme holi to þe peple, and seme hooli to lyve so. And herfore Crist lyvede comun lyf, and hise apostlis after him, and weren not weddid wiþ þese newe signes, as now þes ypocritis ben. And herfore Crist, to purge his Chirche, distriede þes þree sectis, Phariseis, Saduceis, and Essees also, but þe fend bi his cautel haþ brouȝt inne now oþer þree, as monkes, chanouns, and freris, and many braunchis of hem. And sich fals religioun, bi þe lawe of Antecrist, is bitwixe prelatis now and preestis þat ben her sugettis, but reule of Cristis lawe wolde[3] þat alle men shulden renounsen to hem obedience or oþer service but as þei shulden obeishe to Crist.

Against monks, canons, and friars.

[1] *lost*, E. [2] *world*, E. [3] So E; *wolden*, A.

Þe Gospel on feeste of oon Martir.

[SERMON LXIII.]

Nihil opertum quod non reveletur.—Matt. x. [26.]

Þis gospel confortiþ martirs, and telliþ hid syne þat is in þes newe ordris, biside þe ordre of Crist. Crist seiþ þat, *nouȝt is hilid, þat ne it shal be shewid and no þing is so pryvy, þat ne it shal be knowun.* Þes wordis ben of bileve, for alle þingis ben knowun of God, and þat myrrour shewiþ forþ þe moost pryvy þing in þis world; and at þe dai of dome, whanne bokis shulen ben opin, þe whiche bokis ben mennis soulis, and conscience of hem, þanne shulen boþe gode and yvele knowe mennis þouȝtis and her werkes. And herfore shulden alle men hardeli stonde bi treuþe, and speciali bi Goddis lawe, for þerinne liyþ no shame; and herfore biddiþ Crist þat, *þat he haþ seid in derknes, þei shulden seie eft in liȝt*, more comounli and more clereli, boþe in lyf and in word. And þis reule of Cristis ordre shulden men kepe, but algatis preestis, and to þis entent biddiþ Crist þat þat þei have herd in her eere, þei shulden preche opinli upon platrowes of housis, for þus shulde þe comunte of men betere undirstonde; and þus wole Crist, þat alle þingis þat God spekiþ to eeres of soule, shulden þese heereris speke forþ, and drede no worldeli muk in housis. And þanne men prechen aboven hilingis, lyvynge comun lyf as briddis, and taken noon heede to worldeli goodis þat ben closid wiþinne housis. But, for sich prechinge axiþ hardynesse and martirdom, þerfore Crist confortiþ hise to drede not sleynge of bodi; *Nyle ȝe*, seiþ Crist, *drede þese men þat sleen þe bodi, and mai not after slee þe soule*, ne lette God to quyke þat þing þat þei killen, and to make þat betere; *but raþere drede him þat haþ power to leese boþe þe bodi and soule into helle* for evermore, for to dwelle þere in peyne. Ne ben not two sparowis sold for þe leste moneie in chaffaringe,—for, as Luk telliþ, fyve ben sold for two ferþingis,—and ȝit God ordeyneþ for alle þes foulis. And siþ þes foulis ben

The true rule for preachers.

litil of prys and uncerteyn in þeir mevynge, and ȝit God ordeyneþ for hem whanne ever þei liȝten upon þe erþe, more God shulde ordeyne for ech man, þat haþ a soule to Goddis ymage; and speciali for such men þat serven truli to her God more þan ony foul may, for þei ben not able to serve þus. And siþ God ordeyneþ þus for foulis, oþer men moten graunten God unwise, or moche more he shulde ordeyne for men, þat ben hise trewe servauntis. And þis resoun þat Crist makiþ moveþ trewe men þat han witt, to be hardi in Goddis cause, and for him to suffre martirdom; and no man can avoide þat oþer men shulden þus suffre, or ellis be untrewe to God, as ben þes heretikes. And þus seiþ Crist of Goddis wisdom, þat alle þe heeris of hise disciplis ben noumbrid to Goddis knowinge, and noon of hem mai fulli perishe; and siþ þes heeris of mennes heedis ben leste worþi of ony part of man, and noon of þese mai perishe þus, how shulden betere partis perishe? And þus ben martirs confortid to putte her bodies for Goddis lawe, for no part of her bodi mai þus perishe to harme of hem; and myche more soulis of siche men, and alle vertues of her soule, mai not perishe fro hem, for þe soule mai not be quenchid. And nedli after þe soule moten sue þe vertues þerof, as aftir a mannis bodi suen quantite and figure; and no drede, as God wole ordeyne, whanne he restoriþ a mannis bodi, noumbre and quantite and figure þat is moost acordinge to þis bodi, moche more God ordeyneþ to the soule vertues þat it shulde have.

And trewe we not to foolis here þat seien þat þis ben accidentis which God mai putte bi hem silf, and freeli take þes fro men, so þat neiþer in bodi ne in soule man hadde ony siche accidentis; as who seide, men moun be, al if þei hangen not on God, for siche a dependence of men is accident unto hem. Þese foolis moten lerne predicamentis and ten kyndis of þingis, and þanne þei moun se her foli, and folie of heresie þat groundiþ hem. And of þis concludiþ Crist treuli to hise apostlis, þat þei shulden not wille to drede, siþ þei ben betere þan many sparewis; and oure bileve techiþ us þat God kepiþ þingis after her valu, for if ony þing be betere, God makiþ it to be betere.

And so Crist spekiþ here a word þat shulde move men to

Auricular, as opposed to open, confession.

stonde wiþ him; *Ech man þat shal knowelich*[1] *me bifore men* bi boþe my kyndis, *I shal knoweliche þat man bifore my Fadir*, to þat mannis worshipe. Here we shulen undirstonde, þat confessioun, þat Crist nameþ here, is not rownynge in preestis eere, to telle him synne þat we han done, but it is grauntinge of treuþe, þe which is apertly seid, wiþ redines to suffre þerfore, what ever man denyeþ it. And so þat man confessiþ Crist þat grauntiþ þat he is God and man, and al þing þat wole sue herof; and þese ben ful many truþis, for al þe gospel þat Crist seiþ, such a man mut confesse, and al þat sueþ of þe gospel, and þis displesiþ to sinful men. And certis a man confessiþ not Crist, þat he is boþe God and man, but if he confesse of Crist þat he may no weie synne, ne gabbe, ne bere fals witnesse of no word þat Crist haþ seid. And so ech word of Goddis lawe is trewe, siþ Crist witnessiþ it, and ech treuþe þat is þerinne; and so ech prest confessiþ Crist bifore men, þat tellen[2] to hem þat Crist is boþe God and man; and þus Crist seiþ and mai not lie. Certis if a man seie þus, and faile not for cowardise to telle Goddis lawe to men þat synnen, he puttiþ him wel to martirdome; and every sich man, seiþ Crist, he shal confesse to his Fadir. And þanne Crist wole confesse þis man to be trewe in Goddis cause, and worþi to have mede after worþinesse of his traveile, and to be crownyd wiþouten eende in hevene bifore þis greet lord, þat falliþ not to ȝyve such servauntis but if he ȝyve hem blisse of hevene; for gretnesse of siche a lord rewardiþ not lesse his knyȝtis. O Lord, if a man þat traveiliþ in werre wiþ a capteyne, wolde telle myche[a] þat þis capteyne wroot of him to his kyng and seide þat he were a good werriour, and worþili and hardili traveilide in þe kingis cause, and herefore þis erþeli kyng shulde have him and hise comendid; how mouche more were it worþ þat þe persone of Jesus Crist comendide bi his owne word a trewe servaunt unto God, and telde þat God shulde þenke on him and ȝyve him blisse wiþouten ende! And as confessioun of treuþe is to be loved of Goddis knyȝtis, so confessioun of cowardise is to drede of men in erþe; and þus

[1] *knowleche*, E. [2] *telliþ*, E.

[a] That is, 'would esteem it a great gain.'

defaute of bileve lettiþ men to traveile in Goddis cause. But wordis of þis gospel ben yvel undirstonden of manye, þat, bi logik þat þei han, graunten þat alle þe heeres of seintis be knowen wel of God, but God woot not how many þei ben, for noon heeris ben þes alle, siþ þanne þei weren wiþouten noumbre, and ech greet þing in erþe were maad of partis indevysible. And siche errours þat men han in logik and in kyndeli science, bryngen men yn, as heretikes, to graunte after many fals þingis. Soþ it is þat God knowiþ alle þe partis of a man, and how many þes partis ben, for þei ben fewe to Goddis witt; and so ech þing þat God contynneþ[1] is maad of partis indyvysible, and o gretter þing haþ mo siche. But þis is hid to mennis knowyng, but after þei shal wite it wel, whanne God shal shew it hem in hevene.

Of o Martir and Bishop.

[SERMON LXIV.]

Circuibat Jesus civitates.—Mathew ix. [35.]

Þis gospel telliþ of þe office þat shulde falle to Cristis disciplis. And so it telliþ how prestis shulde now, boþe more and lasse, occupie hem in þe Church in servise of God. And first, Jesus dide in dede þe lore þat he tauȝte. Þe gospel seiþ how, *Jesus wente aboute in þe cuntre*, boþ to more places and lesse, *as citees and castellis*, to teche us to profete generali to men, and not to lette to preche to a peple for þei be few, and oure fame shulde be litil, for we shulden traveile for God, of whom we shulde hope oure þank. Castels ben undirstonden litil touns, but wallid, as Jerusalem is clepid a cite bi Mathew; and sich grete castels ben clepid citees. And no drede Crist wente to smale uplondishe touns, as to Bethfage and to Cana in Galile; for Crist went to þese places, where he wiste to do

How Christ preached his gospel,

[1] *conteyneþ*, E.

good and he traveilide not for wynnynge of moneie; for he was not smyttid wiþ pryde ne wiþ coveityse. He cheese him places to teche in þe peple þat were moost able, as synagogis among Jewis. For synagogis weren among hem as churchis ben among us; and Crist was not lettid þanne bi feyned jurisdiccioun, to preche among þe folk, al if he wraþþide þe prelatis; for þis use in iurisdiccioun was not ȝit brouȝt in by cautel of þe fend, as it now is, to lette trewe prechinge. Crist prechide not fables, *but þe Gospel of God, þat was good tiþingis of þe kyngdom of hevene.* And Crist was not occupied al oonli in þis prechinge, but in heeling of syke men, and men þat were in languishe. For two men hav nede of bodili heele. Sum men hav sykenesse or hurtinge in her bodi þat men moun see at iȝe, and þis is clepid sykenesse. Sum men have languishe, and þat on two maneris; as sum men ben syke wiþinneforþ, but þis sykenesse is hid to men, as men þat ben in fevers or oþer sykenesse of herte; and sum men ben syke bi sorewe of herte, and of discounfort of þingis þat fallen hem. And þese men were in languishe, and ofte weren heelid by Crist; and if we hav not virtue to hele þese two sykenessis, ȝit we moun have wille to do þat is in us, and conforte and preie for men þat we delen wiþ.

and sent his apostles to preach it,

And Crist ceeside not here to do good to men, but he ordeynede hise disciplis many, to traveile among men, þat þe people weren not alle traveilid in heering of oo man. For, as þe gospel telliþ, *Crist saie þe peple traveilid in þis, and hadde mercy on hem, for þei weren traveilid and ligginge as sheep wiþouten heerde; and þanne he seide to hise disciplis, Þere is myche ripe corn and fewe workmen þereaboute, and þerfore preie ȝe God to move his prechours,* boþ in bodi and in soule, *to traveile among þe puple*, as gospelleris shulden. *Crist bade hem wende forþ and preche to þe peple þat þe kyngdom of hevene shal come*, al if hem þenke þat it dwelle longe; for many peplis shal turne to God fro þeir synful lyf, and afterward come to hevene whanne þat þei be dede. Ȝhe, þe dai of dome comeþ ful fast, siþ no tyme mai come faster þan þis dai comeþ. For, as clerkis seien, tyme passiþ as swiftly as ony tyme mai passe, or come into þis world.

And herfore Crist ȝiveþ power to hise disciplis of þis office, to heele speciali foure manere of siikenessis. First, he ȝyveþ hem power to heele men wiþynne forþ; but þe moste power in þis was of her wordis, þat Crist wrouȝte wiþ hem, and heelide þe peple in soule; and, for Crist wolde not þat his power were idil, þerefore he biddiþ hem *heele siike men*. After he biddiþ þese disciplis *reise up dede men;* þat mai be undirstondun upon two maneres. For þese disciplis hadden power to reise up dede men in bodi, and to quykene bi Goddis grace dede men in soul; and þis virtue is more, siþ þe soule is betere þan þe bodi. Þe þridde tyme Crist ȝyveþ hem power *to hele mesele men;* and boþ siche syknessis and ordres of hem shulde be more to charge in soule of a man, þan þei shulde be of a mannis bodi. Meselrie is comunli figure of heresie, or of ony oþer synne þat fouleþ men wiþoutenforþ, for þus done bodili meselis to men þat dwelle among hem; and herfore in þe eelde lawe shoulden meselis stond afer. And al if many synnes defoulen men biside hem, neþeles heresies done myche harme. And þerfore men shulde bisili distrie sich heresies; as a greet heresie is, in dowinge of þe Church wiþ lordship of þe world, as it is now dowid. And breeþ of þis heresie fouliþ many clerkes, for it is seied in oþer placis þat Goddis lawe forbediþ sich lordship to clerkes, for alle þei shulden lyve in mekenesse and povertie. And to distroie þis heresie shulden lordis traveilen bisili, for þis myȝten þei do liȝtly and leve fulli to draw awei her owne goodis, by which þei harmen clerkes. For it were inowȝ to us to have offringis and dymes, siþ Crist and hise apostlis holden hem paied on lesse. Þe fourþe and þe laste dede þat Crist bad hise disciplis do was, *to caste out fendis þat dwelliden in men*. And as God ȝaf hem power to cast hem out bodili, so he ȝaf hem power to caste hem out of þe soul, whanne he ȝaf virtue to his wordis to converte þe peple, and of a soule þat first was nest of þe fend, to make a nest of God, to dwelle by grace and by virtues.

giving them a fourfold commission of healing.

The present endowment of the church amounts to a heresy.

How to cure it.

And after þes foure vertues Crist telleþ hem a maner þat þei shulen algatis kepe in worchinge of Goddis work. For Crist seiþ þus: *Ȝe token* of God *freely*, and *þerfore ȝyve freeli* youre traveile to þe peple; and þanne shal it be medeful, and ellis is it symonye. And here is begginge of prechours forfendid of God, siþ it is an hid sillinge[1] of prechinge of Goddis word. And for it is a privy synne, covered wiþ ypocrisie, þis synne is the more and foulir before God; and herfore techeþ Poul, to be siker of þis syne, þat preestis shulden be paied wiþ mete and wiþ hilinge. It is leefful us to take þese two, þat ben nedeful[2] to þis service of God, and þere wiseli ceesse. But freris and preestis þat gadren hem tresure, and maken riche churchis and housis wiþ oþer gere, and algatis fynden a peple superflue and charginge, passyn Goddis lawe bi a cursid ground, for Seint Poul biddiþ þat he þat traveiliþ not, shulde not ete by colour of þis office. And preisynge of preier þat is now brouȝt in, is a foule synne among many preestis.

The mendicancy of friars is indirect simony.

2 Thess. iii. 10.

And Christ telliþ after how hise disciplis shulen bere hem among yvel peple þat þei traveilen among, and so moun þei liȝtlyer dele wiþ good peple. Christ seiþ, *I send ȝou as sheep among wolves, and þerfore loke ye be prudent as neddris*[3], *and symple as dowves*, for warnesse of þes two is ynowȝ to ȝou to dwelle among men. And it is comunli seid þat wolves be beestis of raveyne, and yvele for to daunte fro spoilinge of meke beestis; and whanne þei bigynen to ȝoule, þei turnen her snowte to hevene ward. And so pseudo-clerkes, for her greet covertise, spuylen symple men as wolves doone sheepe; and Crist clepiþ trewe men in God sheep for many enchesouns; and as þe wolf wiþ ȝoulinge makiþ sheep to flokke for drede, so prelatis bi cursinges maken men to gadere hem and ȝyve þese prelatis goodis þat þei wolen have. And ȝit þei hav anoþer cautel þat þese ypocritis usen: þei seien þat þei wolen ȝyven suffragies goostli to menis soulis þat passen al þis worldis good; and to coloure al þis ypocrisie þei turnen her snowte to hevene, and seien þat God haþ ȝovun hem power to ȝyve pardone as þei wolen. And here þei ȝoulen comunli, and blasfemen in God, and where Crist biddiþ hem be sheep dwellinge amonge wolves, oure prelatis, by þe fendis lore, ben turned to þe contrarie, whan þei stranglen and killen men and

Bad priests are like wolves among sheep.

[1] *sellyng*. E. [2] *leveful*. E. [3] *eddres*. E.

spoilen hem of her goodis[a]. And occupiyng þat Crist bad hise prestis traveile inne is put al bihynde, and fendis service is putt before; and þus flokkis of sheep ben maid of lewyde men, and flokkis of wolves ben maid of preestis.

But Crist biddiþ hise disciplis be prudent as eddris. An eddre haþ þis witt; whanne charmeris come to take him, þe toon of hise eeris he clappiþ to þe erþe, and wiþ þe eende of his tail he stoppiþ þe toþer. And so Goddis children, whanne þei be temptid to synne, þei þenken mekeli how freel þei ben maid of þe erþe, and wiþ greet þouȝt of her deþ, þat shal come, þei witen not whanne, and drede of her jugement lest þei ben demyd to helle, þei stoppen her oþer eere and kepen hem wel fro synne. And þus þei hav prudence, þat God haþ ȝovun to serpentis. And symplenesse of douves stondeþ in þis; þei hav no clawis to fiȝte as oþer foulis, but whanne þei ben assailid of foulis of raveyne, þei tristen not to her owne strengþe, but fallen on stones, and þese haukis dreden þanne to smyte at hem, lest þei frushen[1] her owne brest at þe hard stoone. So Cristis disciplis knowen mekeli her freelti, and liȝten on þe corner stoon, þat is Jesus Crist; and þanne fendis of helle dreden hem to swippen[2] at[3] hem, lest þei harmen hem silf at þe stoone of hurtinge. And þus Cristis disciplis ben goostli dowves. But þis lore is forȝete[4], and þe fendis lore take[5].

Christian prudence,

and innocence.

IN FEESTIS OF MANY MARTIRIS.

[SERMON LXV.]

Elevatis Jesus oculis.—LUKE vi. [20.]

ÞIS gospel telleþ foure confortis of martiris, in whiche þei shulden have joie for pursuynge of Crist. Þe gospel telliþ how, *Jesus lifte up hise iȝen on hise disciplis*, and seide þus;

The joys of martyrs.

[1] *flusche*, E. [2] *assayle*, E. [3] om. E. [4] *forȝetun*, E. [5] *taken*, E.

[a] The bearing of this passage on the authorship and date of these sermons has been already discussed in the Introduction.

Blessid be pore men in spirit, for ȝe, þat þus be pore men, *han þus certeinli þe kyngdome of hevene.* Þis poverte is a virtue þat men shulden first sue Crist inne, and it is hard for to use, and þerfore telleþ Crist þus þe meede. And þese men þat hav þis virtue, as weren Cristis apostlis, hadden here þe rewme of hevene, for þei hadden here Crist; and Crist, heed of þis rewme, is ofte tymes clepid þis rewme; for he is þe moste jewel of al þis rewme, in which ech part of þis rewme is many weies conteyned. And þus he mai by many causis be clepid al þis rewme. In þat he is God, he is ende of al þing, and in him we lyven, we moven, and we ben; and for him, as ende, we done alle our dedis. For in virtue of him al his Chirche worcheþ, and by þis moun men se wher men ben lymes of Holy Churche; for þanne þei ben groundid in his lyf, and his worchinge. And if þei ben in stait or werkes ungroundid[1] in Cristis lyf, it is licly to men þat þei ben Antichristis disciplis; for Crist seiþ and mai not lye, þat, Who is not wiþ me, he is aȝens me; and so he is wiþ Anticrist. And so if stait of þese freris be not groundid in Crist, and þei gabben many maneres upon þe lyf of Crist, as inugginge, and asoilinge, and oþer feyned lesyngis; þanne it is a tokene þat þei ben not of holy Chirche, but Saþanas children whos dedis þei done. For if þei ben more bisie aboute worldeli goodis, þan þei ben of dedis þat vertu techiþ to do, þanne þei ben wiþ Mammon, and he lediþ hem. For worldeli goodis, þe which Crist clepid Mammona of wickidnesse, ben moost souȝt of sich men. And so þis fend lediþ hem, and siþ uneven departinge of suche worldeli goodis makiþ dissencioun, ȝhe, þe mooste þat here is, it semeþ þat sich freris ben cause of þis dissencioun. But þei have goodis in comun unevenly departid; ȝhe, more þan hem nedide ech man to have ynowȝ; and þus þis nest of Mammon genderiþ many strives, and ȝit þe fend techiþ hem to seie þat þei have nouȝt, but ben more pore in spirit þan weren Crist and hise apostlis. But certis þis is not poverte of which Crist spekiþ here, siþ Crist spekeþ here of poverte in spirit, to mekeli holde men in havynge of wordli goodis, as moche as nediþ to sus-

Attack on the friars.

[1] *þat ben not groundid*, E.

teyne her office. And he þat forsakeþ þus for þe love of Crist worldeli richesse, and fame þat comeþ to þe world for havynge of siche goodis, is a pore man in spirit, as Crist spekiþ here. For þanne he synneþ not in havynge of goodis for to make feestis, ne to make riche housis, ne noo costli ornamentis þat fallen to men, but it is inowȝ to him to hav foode and hilinge. And al his bisynesse is to helpe Cristis Chirche, and he disseyveþ not men in multitude of coventis, but lokiþ how fewe prestis moun profite to Cristis Chirche, and how he mai holde þe office þat Crist haþ bedun in his lawe; for his desire stondeþ in þe kyngdome of hevene. And þus ben vertues knyttid oon wiþ anoþer, and algatis in preestis, þat hiȝer suen Crist. And, for suche poverte bringiþ ofte tymes in hunger, þerfor in þe secounde blyss seiþ Crist[1], *þat þei ben blessid now.* And it is no drede Crist spekiþ of sich hunger þat is vertuousli take[2], after þe Trinite; for a þeef mai hunger aȝens his wille in prisoun, and a werriour mai hunger for an yvel ende; but loke who haþ power to robbe mennis goodis, and ȝit he spareþ upon resouns, for þe love of God, and þat man hungriþ as Crist spekiþ here. And þus alle þese comunes of þes newe religiouse, þat[3] wasten Goddis goodis, for fame of þe world, or love of her belye, synnen aȝens þis virtue; and þei shulden hungre now to deþ, as done þese martirs, or þei wastiden þus þese pore mennis goodis. And if þei han greet wille to do þis for Goddis sake, þei han now a maner of blis, delitinge in Goddis lawe; and it is no drede þes men shulen be fillid, whanne þei shulen have full joie in pleyn filling of Goddis wille. For after þe day of dome noþing shall displese hem, for þei shulen wel wite þat God ordeyneþ al þings þanne, riȝt as it shulde be, by resoun of Goddis wille. And þis ordenaunce is so faire and so plesinge to seintis, þat þei shulden be fulfillid in wille of her soule, and þat shal be inowȝ to hem to boþe her kyndis. For þanne þei shulen have no hunger of þing þat þei desiren, for þei shulen be fulfillid in bodi and in soule, and þus trowen seintis þat hungre endiþ here.

Þe þridde blisse is seid to þe same entent. *Blessid be ȝe þat*

[1] So E; A includes 'seiþ Crist' in the italics. [2] *taken*, E. [3] So in E; om. A.

wepen now, for ȝe shulen leiȝe. It is knowen þat whoso lastiþ fulli in Goddis lawe he mut nedis wepe here, for enemyes to Crist; for suche Goddis proctours shulen be pursued, for reprevyng of synners þat ben Goddis enemyes, and he is a coward aȝens God þat spekiþ not boldly aȝens synne. And herfore Joon Baptist and Cristis apostlis token ensaumple of Crist to þus repreve synne; and þus þei wepten for pursuyte, and algatis for synne, siþ Crist in all hise þre wepingis wepte for oþer mennis synne. For he loveþ nowȝt wel Crist and his Modir þat sorowiþ not for her injurie, and despite þat is done to him. And sich men of charite shall leiȝe at ȝe dai of dome, for Salomon seiþ, þe Churche shall leiȝe in þe last dai; and sich gostli gladness is clepid here leiȝyng[1], for bodili leiȝyng is fer fro þis purpos. And of þese þree pursuyngis þat comen to þe Chirche, þe firste is leste of alle, þe secound is myddil, and þe þridde is moost; and þus it is of þe[2] þree rewardis.

Prov. i. 26.

Persecution of Christ's servants.

Þe fourþ word þat Crist seiþ conteyneþ þre pursuingis; *ȝe shulen be blessid,* seiþ Crist, *whanne men shulen hate ȝou, and whanne þei shulen departe ȝou, and after repreve ȝou.* Cristis servantis on many maneris ben departid here. Worldeli men fleen hem, and leven hem by hemsilf; þei ben cursid of Anticrist, and put out of chirchis, and þei ben partid in prisouns fro oþer men of þe world. And in alle þes statis þei suffren reproves, and if þei ben certeyn, bi lore of her bileve, þat þei suffren in all þis fro cause of her God, þei moun be blessid and joiful for hope of þe ende, as a syk man gladli wole suffre peyne whanne he hopiþ þerbi to come aftir to hele. And joie þat seintis shulen have whanne þei suffren þus is a manere of blisse þat þei han here, for it is more joie þan all þese worldli lustis. And, as Crist telliþ, þese þat stonden in Cristis cause, *han her names cast out* as cursid men and heretikes, for her enemyes ben so blynde, and so depe in her synne, þat þei clepen good, yvel, and yvel, good. But woo be to suche. And Crist biddiþ his servantis *to joie þat dai in her herte, and shewe a glad countynaunce,* to men þat ben about hem, *for certis her mede is moche in þe blisse of hevene.* And þis word coun-

[1] *leyȝinge*, E. [2] om. E.

fortiþ symple men, þat been clepid eretikes, and enemyes to þe Chirch, for þei tellen Goddis lawe; for þei ben somynned and reprovyd many weies, and after put in prison, and brend[1] or kild as worse þan þeves[a]. And maistris of þis pursuyng ben preestis more and less, and moost pryvy freris wiþ lesingis þat þei feynen, as Crist was pursued wiþ Caiphas and oþer preestis, but privyli wiþ Pharisees þat weren hise falsseste[2] enemyes. And þis gospel is confort to alle þat ben þus pursued.

But certis as tradiciouns maid biside Goddis lawe, of preestis and of scribis and of Phariseis, blyndiden hem in Goddis lawe and made it dispisid, so it is now of Goddis lawe by newe mennis lawis, as decretals and decres. And þe Sixte, wiþ Clementyns[b], done myche harm to Goddis lawe, and enfeblen bileve. And þus done þese newe reulis of þese þree ordris, as þei harmen rewmes and cuntreis þat þei dwellen inne. But remedie agens þis is used of many men, to dispise all þese lawis whanne þei ben aleggid, and seien unto men þat aleggen hem, þat falsehede is more suspect for witnesse of siche lawis, siþ Goddis lawe telliþ al truþe þat is nedeful to men. In þis laste pursuyng of our modyr, þat is greet and perilous, haþ Anticrist moche part aȝens Jesus Crist, and feyneþ bi ipocrisie þat he haþ þe riȝt part. And defaute of bileve is ground of all þis errour.

[1] *brent*, E. [2] *falseest*, E.

[a] See note on p. 201.

[b] The compilation of the Sixth Book of the Decretals was made by order of Boniface VIII. and promulgated by him in 1297. It is entitled Sextus, or the Sixth, as following and being supplementary to the five books of Decretals published by Gregory IX, in 1234, (on which see Milman's *Latin Christianity*, vi. 163):—

Gregorii noni post libros quinque, vocatur
Sextus; nomen habeus ordinis a numero *.

The Clementines were first published by Clement V at the Council of Vienne in 1312; they were afterwards given out in a fully digested form by John XXII in 1316. They treat of various points of canon law and church discipline, and are supplementary to the Sextus.

* These lines are in a fine copy of the Sextus in the Bodleian Library, edited by Giles Perrin, 1572.

Þe Gospe[l] of many Martris.

[SERMON LXVI.]

Cum persequentur vos in una civitate.—Math. x. [23.]

How the true patience of Christ's martyrs is to be shown in the present struggle between Christ and Antichrist.

Þis gospel telliþ a medicine of Crist, how hise martirs shulen do in tyme of her pursuynge. Crist biddiþ hise disciplis to flee from her enemyes; for vertuous pacience and sich manere cowardice ben armes to Cristene men to overcome her enemyes. For hope of our victorie is in Jesus Crist, and þerfor we trustyn in him þat he doeþ þe dedis. And so[1] Crist and Anticrist striven togidere, and oon seiþ þat he haþ þe just part and þe hooli; and þe toþer reversiþ him and seiþ þat he haþ Cristis part. And as anentis Cristis lawe þat men shulden grounde hem inne, Anticrist haþ foundun þis cautel, to seie þat it is myche fals. And if men seien þat Goddis lawe mut nedis be soþ to Goddis entent, þei graunten þat þis is soþ, but þe entent lieþ in hem. So, as princes of prestis, and Phariseis joyned wiþ hem, wolen interprete Goddis lawe, aff hem shal it be taken; and so her exposicioun is more in auctorite þan is text of Goddis lawe; for by þe firste, men shulen be demyd. And by þe cautel of þe fend þese ben maid myȝti to þe world, and by ȝiftis þat þei ȝyven to seculer men, and to sum clerkis, þei hav many comunes wiþ hem, and of all manere of men, and crien þat þus seiþ holi Churche, to which we shulden algatis trowe, and do worshipe to it, and reve it nouȝt but ȝyve it more. And þus is Cristis cause feld doun for a tyme, but ȝit þere ben many men stondinge þerewiþ, as þei doren. And þis reule han many men to juge wel in þis mater; if a man lyve riȝt lyf boþe to God and to man, and have for him text of Goddis lawe, and witt þat sowneþ to charite, and symplenesse in lyvynge, wiþ forsakinge of worldeli liif, it is tokene þat þis man haþ þe riȝt part of Jesus Crist. For Anticrist drawiþ evere to pryde and

[1] So E; A reads *for*, which gives neither sense nor syntax.

to coveitise; and herbi moun men knowe what man holdiþ wiþ Anticrist. But beware with ypocrisie, for þat bigiliþ many men to trowe þat men ben Cristis children, alȝif þei ben þe fendis lymes. And so bi loore þat Crist techiþ men shulden trowe to sich mennis workes more þan to her wordis, for þei speken ofte in striif, and Poul seiþ þat he and hise breþeren have noon custum to speke þus. 1 Cor. xi. 16.

Þe first biddinge þat Crist biddiþ here stondiþ in þese wordis, þat we shulen kepe. *And whanne many enemyes shulen pursue you fro oon citee*, þat ȝe have dwelt inne, *fle ȝe into anoþer;* but ever wiþ discrecioun, for if þis were ever kept no men nedide to be martris, for þei myȝt fle fro toun to toun, and nevere countre wiþ her enemyes; and þus Crist wiþ hise disciplis hadde do agens his owne lore. And here men studien wiþ rulis, whanne þei shulden flee þus, and whanne þei shulden stonde and suffre. In boþe þese tauȝte Crist, and it is no doute to men þat ofte it profitiþ on boþe sidis to fleen from oo toun to anoþer, for bi þis fleinge ofte tymes hav boþe þe partis space to turne to Crist and profite, more þan þei shulden to suffre deþ, abidinge in oo place. And here Y can[1] not grounde of God, þat we shulden fle oure enemyes, riȝt whanne þei folowen us and seen us in mennys presence, for þis were yvel cowardice, to feere men þat saien þis fliȝt; but Crist spekiþ here, as we þinkiþ, of hid removynge before. And þus Crist fledde ofte tymes, and hidde him among þe peple. And if þou axe whanne men shulden flee, and whanne stonde in Goddis cause, certis sum tyme men ben constreyned to come, and to answere for Crist; and so, if we lyven good lyf and lette not þe love of Crist, he shal teche us for to flee and to answere as we shulden.

But algatis be we war þat we confesse not falsehede, and denye not Cristis lawe, for no cais þat mai falle. If we undirstonden not þe witt, graunte we þe forme of þe wordis, and confesse we þe truþe of hem, al if we witen not which it is. And þus faile we not God in liif, and he wole not faile us in loore; for þus he biholiþ þat we shal have in

[1] *kan*. E.

sich hour what we shulden speke. But here it is good to us, if we ben in myche pees, to knowe and love Goddis lawe, for bi þis we moun betir lyve, and wite how we shulen answere men whanne we ben opposid of fendis. But ȝit men miȝten replie here þat Cristis lore were not ynowȝ, for men myȝten liȝtli take a citee where alle weren enemyes and noon trewe men. But lyve we wel, and Crist wole teche to what a citee we shulen go; and herfore seiþ Crist after, *Soþli, I seie to ȝou, ȝe shulen not ende þe citees of Israele til þat mannis sone come, at þe laste dai of Jugement.* A flok of treue men is citee of Israele, for þese men seen God, and ben redi to helpe hise lymes, whanne þei be þus pursued, and suffre Cristis disciplis to traveile, and lette Anticristis bi her power; and such flokkis shulen not faile, boþe to worche and to helpe. And in þe dai of dome it shal be no nede to axe help, for þanne shal Cristis baner be rerid, and alle hise enemyes shulen lurke.

Persecution of the writer's party.

And herfore seiþ Crist after, *Þer is no disciple aboue his maistir ne servant aboue his Lord.* But þus was Crist himsilf pursued, and þis forme kepte Crist, in fleyinge and in answerynge. *And it is ynowȝ to þe disciple þat he be as his maistir, and to servaunt þat he be as his Lord.* In þis þing and bi þis weie shulden Cristis servauntis kepe mekenesse and hope in God, and wite wel bi her bileve þat þei moun not do wiþouten him. And herfore seiþ Crist: *If þei clepiden þe good Lord Belzabub, moche more þei shulden dorre*[1] *mysseie þe servantis of þe Lord.* And oþer pursuytis and bodili deþ shulen sue aftir, siþ Crist hadde hem, and þerfore Crist telliþ ofte, how hise shal be sikir of þese. And þerfore Cristis armure is good to ech to Cristen man to hav, for it noieþ not hevely, neþer in pees ne in werre, and it makiþ Cristen men hardi aȝens þe fend and alle hise lymes. And herfore seiþ Crist to hise; *Þerfore drede ȝe hem not;* for we have betere ground þan þei, and more helpe þan þei have; but oure helpe is spiritual, hid to þis world and for[2] þe toþer. And þis lore is nedeful now in þis world, for Anticrist; for he haþ turned hise clerkes to coveitise and worldli love, and so blindid þe peple and derkid þe lawe of Crist, þat hise servantis ben

[1] *dore*. E; meaning *dare*.

[2] *fro*. E.

þikke, and fewe ben on Cristis side. And algatis þei dispisen þat men shulden knowe Cristis liif, for bi his liif and his loore shulde help rise on his side, and prestis shulden shame of her lyves, and speciali þes hiȝe prestis, for þei reversen Crist boþe in word and dede. And herfore oo greet Bishop of Engelond, as men seien, is yvel paied þat Goddis lawe is writun in Englis, to lewide men; and he pursueþ a preest, for he writiþ to[1] men[2] þis Englishe, and somoniþ him and traveiliþ him, þat it is hard to him to rowte[3]. And þus he pursueþ anoþer preest bi þe helpe of Phariseis, for he prechide Cristis gospel freeli wiþouten fablis. O[4] men þat ben on Cristis half, helpe ȝe now aȝens Anticrist! for þe perilous tyme is comen þat Crist and Poul telden bifore. Butt oo confort is of knyȝttis, þat þei savoren myche þe gospel and han wille to rede in Englishe þe gospel of Cristis liif. For aftirward, if God wole, þis lordship shal be taken from preestis; and so þe staaff þat makiþ hem hardi aȝens Crist and his lawe. For þree sectis fiȝten here, aȝens Cristene mennis secte. Þe firste is þe pope and cardinals, bi fals lawe þat þei han made; þe secounde is emperours[5] bishopis, whiche dispisen[6] Cristis lawe; þe þridde is þes Pharisees, possessioners and beggeris. Alle þes þree, Goddis enemyes, traveilen in ypocrisie, and in worldli coveitise, and idilnesse in Goddis lawe. Crist helpe his Chirche from þese fendis, for þei fiȝten perilously.

There is a great bishop who is displeased that God's law should be written in English.

Þe Gospel of many Martris.

[SERMON LXVII.]

Ponite in cordibus vestris.—Luc. xxi[7]. [14.]

Þis gospel telliþ, as oþer bifore, how Crist helpiþ his martris, whan þe fend and hise lymis pursuen hem for Cristis lawe. For Christ suffride for þis lawe al þe peyne þat he suffride, and hise martris aftir him suffriden for þis same law. Crist tauȝte

Christ's help to his martyrs.

[1] om. E. [2] om. E. [3] *route*, E. [4] So in E; A has *oo*.
[5] So E; *emperour*, A. [6] *dispensen*, E. [7] So in E: *xix*. A. perperam.

opinli his lawe to þe peple, and þe hiȝe preestis of þe temple, wiþ Scribis and Phariseis, þouȝten þat þis was aȝens hem; and þus þei weren aȝens him; and speciali, for Cristis wordis weren aȝens þese þre mennis pride, and aȝens her coveitise, in which þei disseyveden þe peple, but not bi so opyn blasfemye as prelatis use to daie. For þei seien, þat þei han power of Crist to assoile alle men þat helpen in her cause, for to gete þis worldli worshipe, to assoile men of peyne and synne[a], boþe in þis world and in þe toþir, and so whanne þei dien, flee to hevene wiþouten peyne. And þus durst not þe fend feyne for þe tyme þat Crist was here; and siche blynde leden blynde men, and maken falle boþe in þe lake. And þus þis is a perilous tyme, for many men ben dryvun to helle, and þat is more perilouse þan ony deeþ þat þe[1] bodi haþ here, and þe peril is þus more for feynynge of ypocrisie; and we moun not see þis peril, ne fele it in þis liif. And many witnessis ben aȝens þis, and seien þat it is fals; but, as þei seien, we han þe fals part, and þei han þe goode religion. And so þis is more perilous þan sectis departid fro Crist, as Jewis or Sarasines, or oþer heþene men; for þese worchen bi ypocrisie and ben myȝti heretikes, and medlid among trewe men, and þus her fiȝting is feller.

Plenary indulgences granted to those who fight against the Antipope.

But neþeles Crist supposiþ þat hise disciplis shulden sue him, and lyven wel after his lawe, and þei shulen be sure ynowȝ, for þanne God shal fiȝte for hem aȝens enemyes of Crist. And herfore bigynniþ Crist and biddiþ hem, *putte in þeir hertis, not to þenke bifore wiþ bisinesse, how þei shulen answere* to her enemyes, for Crist shal answere þanne for hem, *and ȝyve hem þanne mouþ and witt, to which alle her adversaries moun not aȝenstonde ne aȝenseie.* And siþ þei ben not þo þat speken, but þe Holi Goost spekiþ in hem, it is soþ þat God himself shal answere for his part. It is seid ofte tymes, þat maner of speche of Goddis lawe is to denye þe instrument, and to graunte þe principal, and þus seiþ Crist þat þei speken not but þe Hooli Goost in hem. But Crist prophecieþ of betraying þat hise shal hav: *ȝe shulen be betrayed, he seiþ, of your owne eldris,*

[1] So in E; om. A.

[a] See page 136, note.

of ȝoure breþeren, and ȝoure cosyns, and ȝoure owne frendis. Þis lettre was verified of martiris of Crist, for alle þes foure consentiden to deþ of þese martiris, for þei þouȝten obeishe to God in killinge of Cristene men. And as Cristis lawe seiþ þat sevene þingis shulden be hatid for Crist, as fadir and modir, wyves and children, breþeren and sistren, and mennis owne liif, so feynede þe fend þat þese foure frendis shal be hatid of man, for þe love of Anticrist. And þus many fadris killiden her owne children, for þei confessiden Crist; and þus, as we supposen, þe Jewis diden. And to speken generali of Anticristis scole, þese popis ben fadris, and her churches ben modirs, þese bishopis ben breþeren, and oþer prelatis ben cosyns; seculer men for muk ben to þese prelatis, frendis, and alle þese betraien Cristene men to turment, and putten hem to deeþ for holdinge of Cristis lawe. And þis is more perilous for her fals feyning, for þei seien þat her Chirche mai no weie faile þat haþ lastid so longe in truþe and in holinesse. And þus as Crist was pursued and kild of þese foure folk, so bi cautels of Anticrist ben men kild to dai. And ȝit þe pope is clepid holyeste fadir, and þe bishopis hise breþeren, and abbotis his cosyns, and seculers ben frendis þat helpen to þis pursuyte; and þese foure goostli frendis ben most perilous. And Crist telliþ hise disciplis how *þei shulen be hatid of alle* worldli *men, for þe name of him;* and þus ben men hatid now bi lesengis of freris, for þei holdin þe gospel and lawis of Crist. But Crist comforteþ hise and telleþ hem þat no part of her bodi shal perishe at þe daie of dome; *so þat an heere of her*[1] *heed shal not þanne perishe.* And armer to fiȝte wiþ in Criste[2] men is pacience, for wiþ þis fouȝte Crist, and alle hise gloriouse lymes; *and in þis pacience* bihetiþ Crist to hise, þat þei shulen hav her soulis in pees, as Crist hadde his soule.

The hierarchy and many of the laity united in persecuting Christian men.

And here moven many men, siþ Cristis lawe is opyn, and his part is knowun good, and Anticristis wickid, and many devoute men holden wiþ Crist, what moveþ Cristene men to move hem not to fiȝtinge? For siþ þe fend haþ but þree partis for his side, Cristene men myȝte soone meve to fle þes þree partis.

Armed resistance not advisable.

[1] om. E. [2] *Cristen*, E.

For popis and bishopis and prestis of her sort, and þese new religiouse, possessioneris and beggeris, and seculer men þat ben disseyved wiþ hem, ben þe moste enemyes to Crist and his lawe. Whi wolen not holi seculers risen aȝens þese þree, siþ þei moven seculers to fiȝte aȝens her enemyes? Here men þenken þat Cristene men shulden algatis loven pees, and not procure to fiȝte; for Crist is a pesible kyng, and he seiþ in his gospel þat in oure greet pacience we shulen have oure victorie; and Crist shal fiȝte for us. But many men þenken þat seculer men shulden helpe here, not to fiȝte bodili aȝens Cristis enemyes, but wiþdrawe her conceil and consent fro þes þree folk; and þis dede were sure before God and man.

He appeals to the laity.

And siþ þese false freris camen last into þe Churche, it semeþ þat at hem shulden men begynne to practise, for þei semen leste groundid or rotid in malice, al if her malice be sharpest, as fevere of a daie. Þe rote of possessioners semeþ harder to overcome, for þei ben rotid in richessis and frendship of þe world; but liȝtli miȝten trewe men discomfite þese freris, not but wiþdraw her defence and consente to hem; and þese fendis shulden faile, as þei began wiþouten ground. And here moun men liȝtli se wheþer seculers ben trewe men, for þei confessen communli þat þei loven Crist moost, and wolen stonde bi his lawe, and also bi his ordenaunce, for to suffre deþ, but þei failen in þes wordis. Hem nediþ neþer to fiȝte ne dispende ne traveile, but consent not wiþ þes fendis, ne defende hem aȝens Crist, and þei shulden soone be destryed among hemsilf. Wel Y woot þat begging holdiþ hem up, and oþer lesingis upon Crist and his Churche. Comune not wiþ hem, ne ȝyve hem noon almesse, bifoore þei hav declarid þese[1] gabbingis aȝens bileve, and liȝtli shulde be an ende of þese false prophetis. Her preieris, and her massis, and oþer false signes, ben signes þat þei chaffaren wiþ disseyvynge þe peple. But dwelle we in þis bileve, and tell hem boldli þat þei witen never[2] wher þei ben fendis; and if þese ypocritis ben fendis, her preiris doiþ harm, ȝhe, boþ to hemsilf and to oþer men; and no man þat hadde witt shulde chaffare wiþ her preiris. And herfore biddiþ Crist

[1] *þe*. E. [2] *not*, E.

flee from false prophetis þat come in cloþing of sheep, but þei ben wolves wiþ men, and her comyng is moost to ravyshe bi ypocrisie.

The doctrine of friars concerning the Eucharist.

As anentis her massis, a man þat hadde Cristis hert shulde seie hem soþeli, þat he wolde not truste þerynne, but if þei purgiden hem of heresie, of which þei ben suspect. It was taken as bileve, longe bifore þat freris cam ynne, þat þe sacrid ost þat men seen at i3e is verrili Goddis bodi, bi vertue of hise wordis. Freris seien þat þis is fals, but it is an accident wiþouten ony suget, and þei gilen þe peple. If a man charge Goddis lawe more þan fals in name of sich lyeris in þe world, þat doiþ myche harm. Comune he not wiþ hem, ne 3yve hem no goodis, before he have asaied wheþer þei ben here heretikes; and seie he, þat Crist takiþ not service of man but if he 3yve betere a3en, and þus shulden prestis done; and herfore, but if þe frere bringe under his comune seel, what is þe sacrid oost, þei wolen not comune wiþ him. For, as Seint Joon seiþ, who- (2 John, 11.) ever gretiþ an heretike shal hav of his synne, what man ever he be. And þus, if a trewe man love more Crist þan þe worldis fame, he mai li3tli wiþ worship avoide sich fals freris. And certis þis dede were unsuspect boþe to God and man. For if þei hav a ri3t bileve, þei shulden telle it for charite, and if her bileve were fals, þei shulden wille þat it were distroied. And algatis þei witen wel, þat þei varien in bileve fro þe gospel and comun peple, and many weies disseyve men. For þei tellen not what is þat, but þat þis is Goddis bodi. But þese idiotis shulen wite, þat boþe þere and everywhere is betere þing þan Goddis bodi, for þe holi Trinitie is in ech place. And so men axen what is þat, þat þe prest sacriþ, and aftur brekiþ, and þat men worshipen as Goddis bodi, but not accident wiþouten suget. And þus defaute of ri3t bileve, practisid among þes freris, shulden dampne hem as heretikes, and take hem in her owne falshede.

And so, bi alle oþer signes þat þei feynen in religioun, aspie how þes freris camen inne, and by whos auctorite; for if þei camen not in bi Crist, þat is dore of his Churche, þei ben þeves and heretikes, and stien up by þe roof. And þis proof were not costli, ne chargious, ne shameful; and for levyng of siche proofe synnen men ful grevousely boþe aȝens Crist and his Churche, ȝhe, aȝens freris þat men þenken þei helpen. And þis shulden alle men do in dede, and stire oþer men þerto, sum bi love, sum bi drede; and þus shulden oure bileve be shewid, and rotyn heresie, hid now, shulde come to proof wiþ false lesingis. And here moun men wel assaie wheþer clerkes and knyȝtis wiþ her comunes love God as þei confessen, and doren stonde bi his lawe; for he þat is necligent in so litil þing for to do, wolde soon be necligent in harder þing of more charge.

Þe Gospel of many Martris.

[SERMON LXVIII.]

Descendens Jesus de monte.—Luc. vi. [17.]

How Christ deals with those that love him.

Þis Gospel telliþ, as we hav seid, how þe peple lovede Crist, and how Crist ȝafe hem loore þat was betir þan al þis world. And so Crist, as a good knyȝt, stood now in hil, and now in pleyn, now in water, and now in erþe, to telle þat he was Lord of alle. But here he stood in the pleyn feld, for þer men miȝten betere heere him; and þus he techiþ, þat he loveþ all men þat holden his lawe, be þei clerkis, be þei kniȝtis, or laborers þat maynteynen tilþe. *And þus Crist cam doun of þe hill, and stood in a feldi place, and to him cam dyverse folkis, as sum men þat weren hise disciplis, and a great multitude of* oþer *folk* fro fyve places. Sum men camen fro fer countrees of þe lond *of Jude*, and sum camen *fro Jerusalem*, and sum camen *fro þe see*, and sum men *fro þe lond of Tire*, and sum fro þe lond *of Sidon*.

Five causes why men followed Christ.

And men seien comunli þat men sueden Crist for fyve causis. Sum men camen to sue Crist, to lerne of him Goddis lawe; and þus sueden þe apostlis Crist þat speciali sueden him, and oþer trewe men, bi riȝt entent to be informed in Goddis lawe, and speciali at þis tyme; for now ȝaf Crist his lawe, and so he ordeynede many folk to here alweie þis newe lawe. Þe secounde cause þat men sueden Crist for, was to be heelid of

Crist. For alle manere of sykenessis of men he helid wiþouten hire; and so seiþ þe gospel here þat many folkis camen to Crist, *to heere him, and to be helid of syknesse* þat þei were inne. Þe þridde cause whi folk sueden him was for to se wondris of Crist, as men traveilen in fer weie to se pleics[1] in þe world; and more woundris þan Crist dide was not seen bifore ne aftir. Þe fourþe cause whi sum folk cam to Crist was cumpanye, þat oþer men cam to Crist, oþer for oo cause or for oþer. And þus þei camen to se Crist for sum cause þat here is seid. Þe fifte cause, and þe worste, þat sum men camen to here Crist was to take him in wordis, as ofte tymes camen hise enemyes, as Pharisees and oþer servauntis of hiȝe preestis of þe temple.

And þus seiþ þe gospel here;—*þat men travelid of þe fendis weren heelid, and al þe peple covetide to touche Crist, for vertue wente out of him, and helide alle men. And Crist cast up hise iȝen in hise disciplis*, and seide foure wordis, as it is told bifore in þe firste sermoun of martirs[a]. First seiþ Crist, *Blessid be þe*[2] *pore men, for ȝoure is þe kyngdom of God;* and comunli such men þat ben pore of goodis here, ben also pore in soule, as seiþ þe gospel of Matheu. For sum men ben proude in her herte of fair chirchis and hiȝe steplis, and sum of faire ȝate housis, and sum men of hiȝe kycchynes[3]; and so if pryde were fulli layd doun, few or noon wolden hav sich housis. And if all þe good were weied þat comeþ of sich costli þing, it were but pure fantasie, and worldli pryde þat comeþ þerof. And if we þenken how Crist was pore, more þan ony of us mai be, we shulden not bolue for richesse of þe world, for no good þat comeþ þerof. And so we shulen understonde þese þree wordis þat come after;—*Blessid be ȝe þat hungren now, for ȝe shulen aftir be fillid. Blessid be ȝe þat wepen now, for ȝe shulen leiȝe aftir; and blessid shulen ȝe be whanne þat men shulen hate ȝou, and whanne þei departen ȝou fro Cristene men þat þei loven, and whanne þei shulen reprove ȝou, and caste out ȝour name as ivel, for ȝe holden wiþ Cristis lawe*, al if it displese to þe world. *In þat dai joie*

[1] *for to see pleyes*, E. [2] *ȝe*, E. [3] *kychynes*, E.

[a] See Sermon LXV, p. 201.

ȝe wiþine, and make ȝe glad countynaunce wiþouten, *for lo ȝoure neede is moche in hevene ;* and by þis weie ȝe deserven it.

Against monks and canons.

As it is seid bifore, God haþ many enemyes þat feynen bi her professioun þat þei ben pore as was Crist, and ȝit þei han worldi goodis, boþ meblis and unmeblis, and þei disturblen Cristis ordre, and contreis þat þei dwellen ynne, as monkis and chanouns wiþ her degrees, and oþer possessioneris. Crist techeþ hem to be pore for love of him, but wilfulli; and þei crepen ynne to be riche, bi falsenesse of ipocrisie; and þus ben lordis and rewmes poorid, to whos stait shulde[1] richesse falle; and ȝit boþ prelatis and lordis and oþer folk ben so blyndid, þat þei holden up þis fendis cause and cursen trewe men þat letten it. And it is oon to do þus, and to curse Cristene men, for þei holden on Cristis side aȝens þe fend, and his helpe; for he haþ so blyndid men bi unbileve of Goddis lawe, þat dedis þat ben aȝens it ben holden good and nedeful: as twelve lawis ben aleggid how God ordeyneþ clerkes to lyve, and confirmede hem bi his Sone, and bi liif of hise apostlis, and ȝit men seien þei ben acursid, þat traveilen to kepe þese lawis. But as þei feynen, þei han prelatis, and þe hiȝeste is þe pope; and but if men have leve of hem no man shulde take þes goodis aweie. And heron ben lawis ordeyned and cursingis wiþouten nombre, and lordis ben undermyned wiþ sutiltees of the fend; and but if God send a gretter[2] grace, þis heresie wole not be amendid, but if some conquest come, or þe laste dai of dome.

Bi many causis moveþ the fend to holde þis cause aȝens aȝens Crist, for herbi he haþ foundun pley in clerkis, knyȝtis, and in comunes; for clerkis herbi ben proude and worldli, and leve þe office þat God haþ bedun clerkis do to profite of his churche. For herbi clerkis ben oþer lewid or occupied aboute þe world, so þat prechynge and techinge ben aweie for þe more part; and þes prelatis above seen þat bi þe same skile þei shulden wante her worldli richesse, as wantide boþ Crist and Petir, and herfore for to flee þis eende þei maken meenes in weie bifore. And siþ averise[3] drieþ more, þes

[1] So E; *shulden*, A. [2] *grete*, E. [3] *averice*, E.

prelatis ben þus coveitous, and seculer lordis boþe, for lordship is taken fro hem. And þus þe pore comuns bien[1] þe trespas of Goddis lawe, but not so myche as þes two oþer; for þei bien it more in helle. Þe fend traveileþ bisili to holde þis nest aȝens Crist, and ypocrisie of preestis is þe beste mene þat he haþ; and þus officeris of Cristis hous ben so turned in her service, þat if[2] Peter were now alyve, and saie how preestis weren occupied, he wolde seie þei weren not prestis of Crist, but proctours of Anticrist. But, for þe fend dredिþ him þat Cristene men shulden knowe þis wille, to[3] fordo þis fendis falsehede, and turne aȝen to Cristis lawe, and algatis þat Cristis preestis shulden lyv in povertie as he dide, he haþ cast anoþer weie to preise preiyinge of sich preestis, and telle þat it is more worþ þan al þe lordship of þis world boþe to lordis and to her eldris, and specialy at mydnyȝt, as þese religiouse preien. But here men speken aȝen þe fend, and seien he blyndiþ here but foolis, for men wilen þat God loveþ more just liif þan siche preier, and it is a fendis folie to chaunge office of Cristis servauntis. Crist haþ ordeyned hise preestis boþe to teche and preche hise gospel, and not for to preie þus, and to be hid in sich closettis; and þus a liif of oo just man, þat held wel Goddis lawe, were worthi many such preieris as now ben procurid folily. And if þe fend alegge þe Psalm, þat Daviþ[4] roos at mydnyȝt to confesse to his God; whi Ps. cxix. 55.
shulden not we now do so? But here we axen þe fendis clerk, siþ Crist dwellide at nyȝt in his preier, and in þe dai tauȝte þe peple, and dide hise workes privyly for to flee ypocrisie, why shulden not preestis now do þus? and siþ þe same Psalm seiþ, Lord how Y have loved þi lawe, al þe dai it is my þouȝt, Ps. cxix. 97.
whi shulde we not holde þis more? siþ it is moche betere þan to rise at mydnyȝt. And if Baal preest feynen þat þanne God mai here wele, and þanne lordis of þe worldlyven in lustes in hers bedde, and good it is þat God be sued ech hour of sum men; wite þei wele þat God lokiþ betere to goode dedis þan to sich preieris. But neþeles devoute men þat be disposed to preie þanne, God forbede þat þei shulden be lettid; but make we

[1] *byen*, E. [2] *ȝif*, E. [3] *and*, E. [4] *Davyt*, E.

no general reule to undispose men on þe dai, whanne þei shulden do workes of liȝt. Wel I woot þat þeves usen to worche on nyȝt and slepe on þe dai, and so usen þese neue þeves þat comen in abov þe dore; for Crist koude have tauȝt þis preier if it hadde more plesid him, as he koude hav tauȝte to preie, and lefte to preche his gospel to men. And siþ sich religiouse moun not preie God for hemsilf to come to hevene, for þei shulen be dampned, how moche wole God here sich fendis preier for oþer men! However þe fend seiþ here, þe office þat Crist haþ ordeyned of hise servantis in his hous is þe beste of alle oþer.

Þe Gospel on feeste of many Martris.

[SERMON LXIX.]

Cum audieritis proelia.—Luc. xxi. [9.]

The signs which shall precede the Day of Judgment.

Þis gospel telliþ to Cristis martris, what peril shal falle on his house boþ bifore and aftir here, er[1] þe dai of dome come. And þus shulden martris be confortid bi witt and ordenance of Crist, and suffre wiþ good wille, riȝt as þis Lord haþ ordeyned; for certis he ordeyneþ for þe beste, to his worship and to his Churche.

First spekiþ Crist to hise disciplis; and biddiþ hem, *þat þei shulden not be adred, whanne þei shulden here batels and contekes wiþ men*[2]*; for þes þingis moten nedis be, but ȝit is not anoon ende.* And þanne Crist seide to hem of sevene perils þat shulden come. Þe first peril of þese sevene is, þat oo *folk shulden rise aȝens* anoþer, as Cristene men fiȝten wiþ Sarasynes, and oo secte wiþ anoþer; and þus boþe eldir men and ȝonger hatiden divisioun in þe peple, for suche divisioun is cause of bateilis and strives among men; ne it is not oo peple, but for oonhede of lord and lawes. And þus alle Cristene men shulden holde of Crist and his

Seven perils to the Churches: The first peril.

[1] *or*, E.

[2] *wiþynne*, E.

lawe, and obeisshe to hise bailies, in as myche as Crist biddiþ obeishe to hem.

The secounde harm þat shal come to Cristis Chirche for synne of men, is, *þat oo rewme shal rise aȝens anoþer* for wantinge of charite, and cause hereof shall be defaute of keping of Cristis ordenaunce. For Crist ordeynede his Chirche to stonde in sich an evene mesure, þat ech part shulde profite to oþer, and noon reverse oþer in liif; as partis of mannis bodi þat is hoole fiȝten not togidir, but raþer oon helpiþ anoþer, and kepiþ it fro many harmis. And þus partyng of lordships among preestis must nedis make fiȝtinge: and so sectis þat soutren þe peple oþer weie þan Crist ordeynede, as þese newe religiouse, moten disturble helþe of rewmes.

The second peril.

Þe þridde peril þat Crist telliþ here, *is grete erþe-denes*[1] *bi places;* for as þe erþ-denes, as clerkis seien, comeþ of wyndis closid wiþinne þe erþe, so wyndis closid in proude preestis, and oþer men of þe world, ben figurid by erþe-dene. And þei distrien countreis and citees, for prelatis more and lesse here bosten more þan Goddis lawe techiþ, and þese wyndis be algatis closid wiþinne þe boundis of Goddis lawe, for þei ben evene as grete as Goddis lawe wole suffren hem. And as it wole close hem or ponishen[2] hem, so it is; and whanne þei ben aventid, bi conquest or oþer manere, Goddis lawe lymyteþ how þes wyndis shulen passe aweie.

The third peril.

Þe fourþe and þe fifþe peril, shal *be pestilencis and hungris,* for as distempour of þe eir shal sle men and unable þe erþe, so distempour of wyndis of pride shal lette preching of Cristis word, and þanne comeþ pestilence of soule worse þan pestilence of bodi, as hungre of Goddis lawe is worse þan bodili hungre. And siþ hevene worchiþ in erþe, after þat erþe is disposid, þere mut come into erþe pestilence and hungre. Pestilence shal come of distempour of elementis, and of oþer medlid bodies þat ben unkyndeli temprid; for þe fumes of þese blowun wiþ þe wyndis, and drawun in to man,

The fourth and fifth perils.

[1] *erþedones*, E. [2] *punysche*, E.

distemperen his bodi, and maken hise humours and alle hise lymes to wante her kyndeli tempour; and þus comeþ pestilence, boþe to man and beste. And siþ corn and oþer fruytis ben nurished by þis eir, and þis is so distemperid bi causes þat ben bifore seid, þe blewinge[1] of þes fruytis mut faile for þis same cause, and so hungre mut come for defaute of sich fruyte. But Crist spekiþ more here of spiritual veniaunce þat is more to drede þan bodili peynes.

The sixth and seventh perils.

And so þe sixte and þe sevenþe perils þat Crist telliþ ben, *feringis fro hevene and oþer grete signes;* and as þes muten come bi kynde for variance of þe erþe, so mut oo synne bifore bringe in anoþer synne, and þus shal Goddis veniaunce[2] be varied after þes synnes. As it is distempour, þat erþeli men shal calengen here to be evene wiþ Crist, and do more þingis þan he wole do,—so after siche signes moten come to men peyneful wondris, as it is an hidouse þing þat men contrarien to Crist boþe in word and in dede, and, ledinge of oþer peple, seien þat þei moun do wiþ þis as myche as þe manhede of Crist, and wiþ þis senden out signes to witnesse þis blasfemye. Þese ben more hidous signes þan bodili comynge fro hevene. But Crist telliþ to hise disciplis *þat bifore alle þes sevene, þe ferventeste enemyes*[3] *to Crist shal caste hondis upon hem, and pursue hem, and ȝyve hem in to hondis of false preestis;* and þei shulen putte hem in to feyned holdis, and punishe hem many weies, and after þei shulen drawe hem to kyngis and to justices, þat ben myȝti in þis world. And þus for Crist shulen þei be ponished; and liche to þis falliþ now by ponishing of Anticrist. But Crist seiþ to hise disciplis *þat it shal falle in to hem into witnesse,* þat þei ben on þe trewe side, *þat þei shulen have clere answere, to which alle her adversaries shal not moun*[4] *aȝenstonde;* and þis shal be Goddis loore comynge to hem so privyli. And Crist seiþ as he dide bifore how he shal ȝyve hem alle þis wisdom, to þe witt þat is seid bifore.

An invective against the prelates.

And here men noten comunli how prelatis weren disposid by Crist to take of him wisdom, to cunne reule his Churche; and so oþer Cristis bileve faileþ, or prelatis be undisposid now to take

[1] *blowyng*, E. [2] *vengeaunce*, E. [3] *þe moste enemy*, E. [4] *mowe*, E.

wisdom of Crist to reule his Churche wel. And siþ a prelat mai not do, but if he hav keies of þe Churche, þe which ben power and science to dispence Goddis tresour, it semeþ þat prelatis now failen in boþe þes. For bi mannis traveile þei hav not passingli geten þis witt, siþ þei hav ben occupied in þe world, and ben simple of lettrure of Cristis lawe, and of inspiringe bi Goddis grace. It semeþ þat siche prelatis ben ful fer to take of God suche liȝtnynge of Goddis cunnynge, fer þei ben ful of worldeli witt in worldeli occupacioun, and herbi unclene in þouȝt, to take siche wisdom of God. And dedis of þes men, wiþ fruytis of her liif, shewen þat þei ben not ful cunnynge in wisdom of Goddis lawe, and so þei ben untrewe dispenders of tresour þat þei feynen of God. And siþ a wastour of worldeli goodis shulde be blamyd of God and man, how myche a wastour of betere goodis is more for to blame; and moche more if a prelate feyne by ypocrisie þat he haþ power and witt, ȝovun of God to reule his Chirche, and doiþ al amys[1] in þis, and sueþ not God ne his lawe. Certis, syche an ypocrite addiþ first a lesinge, and bi his feyned traitorie he lediþ amys Cristis sheep; and if wastinge of Goddis goodis be worse, þat þe goodis be betere, þis is worse wiþouten mesure þan wastinge of erþeli goodis. And ȝit men þat shulden be martris ben so smytun wiþ cowardise, þat þei deren not speke a word for riȝt bileve in þis matere; but þei constreynen men as bestis to bileve a falshede, þat þis prelate haþ power and witt of God to do þus. And whoever denyeþ þis he cursiþ hem, and pursueþ hem.

Their presumptuous claims.

First þei begynnen wiþ þis:—þat he is hede of holi Chirche; and of þis þei bringen forþ more, þat God mut comune wiþ him his tresour; and where God haþ ordeyned to hide, wheþer men shal be saved or dampned, þese ypocritis seien þei witen wel þat þei ben heed of hooli Chirche, and þanne þei shulen be saif, and wite of Goddis privytees, which man he wole have saif, and how longe þis shal be in peyne. And so he woot[2] bi Goddis lore whanne þe dai of dome shal be, for he mai not for shame graunte pardon after þe dai of dome; for after þis daie ben but two places in which pardone mai be feyned, and in ne-

[1] So in E, A has *almys*. [2] *wote*, E.

especially with regard to indulgences.

þer moun suche prelatis pardoun profite to men þat þer ben. And whanne þei graunten many þousynd wynter of such pardone, oþer þei witen, þat þis tyme shal be bifore þis dai, or ellis þis pardoun shal serve of nouȝt. Sich ben many blasfeme lesingis feyned of popis and oþer prelatis; and whoso reversiþ hem in Crist he mai be martir if he dair; and betir cause of martirdom fynde we noon to Goddis servauntis. For as meynteyning of bileve is a cause of martirdome, so mayntenyng of þing not bileve shulde be reversid of Cristen men, for ellis miȝte al bileve be changid, eeld[1] put out, and newe brouȝt inne. For þei seien þis is bileve, þat þis is heed of holi Chirche, and what þing þat he feyneþ is performed of Crist. And more perilous heresie was never feyned of þe fend.

On dai of many Martris.

[SERMON LXX.]

Attendite a fermento Pharisaeorum.—Luc. xii. [1.]

The sin of hypocrisy,

Þis gospel telliþ, as oþer hav don, how men shulen be confortid bi Crist, and stonde in his feiþ to deþ, for good þat shal come þerof. *Fle ȝe*, seiþ Crist, *fro þe synne of Pharisees, þat is ypocrisie.* For among oþer synnes þat þe comuns be blyndid bi, þis is oon of þe moste þat rengneþ[2] in prestis, boþe among prelatis and al maner religious. For as Crist likiþ moost in good werk and wilful, so þe fend likiþ moost in yvel werk and wilful. For as þe first mut nede be good, so þe toþer mut nede be yvel. And so men seien þat ypocrisie is fals feyninge of holynesse, and falliþ whanne evere a man feyneþ þat he haþ spiritual good of God, and he haþ not þis good, but synne for his fals feyninge. And al if many spiritual goodis ben feyned of ypocritis, neþeles holynesse and witt ben feyned more comunli; and bi þese two ben folk disseyved, in þing þat touchiþ soulis helþe. And, for þis

[1] *olde*, E.   [2] *regneþ*, E.

þing mai not be seen, and power of God is feyned to prelatis, þerfore þis synne is more hid, and more privyly disseyveþ þe peple. And so þe fend cast a long tyme to marre men in bileve, and bi þis errour bringe aftir[1] inne more synnes to blynde þe peple.

And siþ Crist is holi treuþe, and ypocrisie is fals feyning, it semeþ þat þis ypocrisie is moost synne aȝens Crist. And so as lordis weren bifore tormentours of þe fend, so þes prestis and Pharisees ben tormentours of Anticrist, and more falseli disseyven þe peple, and more turmenten Cristis servantis. And herfore Crist biddiþ fle þis synne of Pharisees. Crist biddiþ attende his lawe, þat is, bisili to perceyve it; and he biddiþ attende from false prophetes; and þat telliþ two þingis, þat is, to perceyve Goddis lawe, and flee from falshede feyned þerof. For we supposen þat in Goddis law is al treuþe þat is needful, and if þis feyned þing of ypocritis were nedeful to Cristene men, he wolde telle þat, as he doiþ oþer, but now he leveþ þat ypocritis seien. And, for ypocritis ben cautellous for to take men in wordis, þerfore Crist biddiþ flee hem, and calliþ her synne sour dowȝ[2]; and riȝt as sour dowȝ shendiþ þe dowȝ þat it to longe dwelliþ wiþ, so synne of þese Pharisees shendiþ men þat consenten to it. And wisdom of water þat is feyned, stablid to hem bi longe tyme, confermeþ þis synne to men, and makeþ hem bileve amys[a]; and herfore biddiþ Poul to clense out þis old synne þat þei be new springinge of flour, as þei ben clene in þe newe lawe. Crist ordeynede in his law alle hise children to be free, and flee rites[3] of Pharisees þat cumbren þe folk before. Loke we þat þis be not knodyn[4] wiþ us, but holde we us in þe whete flour, þat tauȝte us fulli Goddis lawe, and þe weie to come to hevene. Cunne we wel Goddis lawe, and loke wher Fariseis grounden hem in it; and if þei done not, flee we her sentence as heresie or fendis glewe[5]. And, for we shulden

as exemplified in the modern Pharisees,

1 Cor. v. 7.

[1] om. E. [2] *dowȝ*, E. [3] *riȝtis*, E. [4] *knoden*, E. [5] *gleu*, E.

[a] The meaning seems to be:—as 'sour douȝ,' or leaven, is made from a mixture of pure flour with water, and, if left too long with fresh dough, spoils it,—so the doctrine of the hypocrites, being compounded, partly of Christian truth, partly of an unsound philosophy of their own invention ('wisdom of water þat is feyned'), if it has established itself firmly and for a long time in men's minds, makes them 'bileve amys.'

must be shunned.

examyne it bi þe flour of Goddis lawe, þerfore Crist biddiþ flee fro it whanne we witen þat it is ungroundid. And so men hav tauȝt comunli þat men shulden not holde al gold þat shyneþ as gold, for many þingis ben fourboshid ful falseli. And so, but if Goddis lawe telle a feiþ, trowe it not, but fle it as falshede, and dispise þe techeris of it. And on þis wise spekiþ Crist to fle þis synne of Pharises, for it is not ynowȝ men to be spoiled þus of her goodis; but worse it is to be spoilid of bileve and oþer vertues. And if þis synne be now hid in soulis of ypocritis, neþeles it shal be knowun at þe laste jugement of Crist; for he seiþ, *þat nowȝt is hilid þat ne it shal be shewid* þanne, *and noþing is privy now þat ne it shal be knowun* þanne. Alle false castis and her ententis, shulen be knowun þanne to þe world; and so riȝt truþis of Cristis disciplis shulen be seid þanne in liȝt, al if þei doren not seien hem now opinli unto þe world.

And for sich cowardise in synne, þat many servantis speken in drede, Crist seiþ to his disciplis, *þat what þei hav seid in derknessis shal be seid þanne in liȝt, and þat þei rowned*[1] *in erre*[2] *in beddis, shal be prechid upon housis.* And þus, as Crist haþ seid bifore, he hirtiþ[3] and confortiþ hise frendis, *to be not aferd of þese men þat mai oonli slee her bodi, and hav no more to ponishe hem*, neiþer in bodi ne in soule. For deed bodi feeliþ noo soore, and þe soule goiþ whidir is Goddis wille; for enemyes moun not cacche þe soule and ponishe it, as þe bodi. And þus seiþ Crist, þat *he shal shewe hem what lord þei shulen drede. Drede þe Lord of bodi and soule, þat after he haþ slawe*[4] *þe bodi, haþ power to sende boþe þe bodi and þe soule in to helle.* So, seiþ Crist, *Y seie to ȝou, drede ȝe þis Lord þat haþ þis powir. Ne ben not fyve sparewis sold for* a weiȝte of *two ferþingis; and oon of hem* so lytil of priis *is not*[5] *forȝeten to fore ȝoure*[6] *Fadir?* Moche more God wole þenke upon hise owne childre here, þat tellen opynli his treuþe, and susteynen his lawe to men. And for surete of þis feiþ, Crist seiþ, as he seide bifore, þat *þe heeris of ȝoure heed alle ben noumbrid unto God;* and þerfore Crist biddiþ hem not drede, *for þei ben betere þan many sparewis.*

[1] *þan rownyd*, E. [2] *eren*, E. [3] *hertiþ*, E. [4] *slowen*, E. [5] So in E; in A, the word, after being written, has been cancelled. [6] *oure*, E.

And þus I seie to you, seiþ Crist, *þat ech man þat confessiþ me bifore men*, ȝhe, if he die, *I shal confesse him bifore Goddis aungelis*, how he was trewe servant to God.

On the limits of the right of the Pope to legislate for the Church.

And here men douten comunli of bileve of Cristene men; it semeþ þat þe pope mai ordeyne lawe even wiþ Goddis lawe, siþ he ponishiþ more for his lawe, þan he ponishiþ for Goddis lawe, and oþer he doeþ wrong in þis, or his lawe is betere þan þe firste. But who dar seie þat he doiþ wrong in such ponishinge for lawis? Also þe pope mai ordeyne sum lawe, as done Princis of þis worlde; but whi mai he not make as many as him likiþ to profite to þe Chirche?—what ert þou þat settist a mark þat he mai make þese, and no moo? For bi þis same skill he was longe siþen at his mesure, and þus shulden[1] him faile power now to reule þe Chirche bi his lawe. Also, ellis we diden amys in singinge, and in service seiynge, and so in al þat we doen, siþ we taken þis of þe pope; and þus in lower prelat moten we graunten siche power, for ellis failide obedience, and alle þes ordris þat ben newe. Here men seien þat popis and bishopis and oþer men mai make lawis, so þat þei acorden wiþ Goddis lawe, and sumwise ben in Goddis lawe, for þus þei techen Goddis lawe more opinli þan it was tauȝt bifore. But, for boþe errour and pride suen ofte tymes to þis dede, þerfore seintis after Crist helden hem paied on Cristis lawis; for if þei weren executid, þei weren sufficient and ynowȝ. But newe turnyng of Anticrist to newe office in þe Chirche, mut nede bringe in newe lawis, and putte Cristis lawe abak; and þus seiþ þe Psalm of Anticrist, þat God shal putte a maker of lawe, and reule hem after her coveitise biside þe lawe þat Crist haþ ordeyned. Ps. cix. 6?

Christ's law is best, and is sufficient.

And þis mai ben opynli seen in benefices departid to men, and newe ordris þat now ben maad, to greet chargis of Cristis Chirche. But folk shulde knowe þat þei ben men, and holden hem paied of Cristis boundis; for if þei ben reulid by resoun, Cristis lawe is best, and ynowȝ, and oþer lawis men shulden not take, but as braunchis of Goddis lawe. And herfore biddiþ bileve to men, neþer adde to, ne draw fro;

[1] *schulde*, E.

and if þei done, God cursiþ hem, and in þis cursing hav many men ben depid bi long tyme. And þus is ordenance of Crist put abak, and newe brouȝt inne. Ne it falliþ not to us to justifie þes newe officis, ne to defende þat þei ben leueful, alle þe dedis þat prelatis done; for it is ynowȝ to us to cunne and declare Goddis lawe, and shewe þat it were ynowȝ, if oþer lawis weren aweie; and so amende by Goddis lawe þe ordris þat weren maad by Crist, and not for synne of þes ordris to bringe in newe ordris to hem. For alle moten lyve on þe peple [a]; and þe secounde ben þe worse, siþ betere were bi Cristis lawe to amende men of his ordre, þan to putte more unstable ordris, and algatis worse to þe Chirche. But litil errour bringiþ inne more, and at þe laste goiþ al doun; and herfore boundis of Cristis ordenaunce shulde be holde of alle men. And it falliþ not to us to assoile þese fresshe resouns, þat þus þe Chirche doiþ amys in many þingis þat it defendiþ.

In Dai of many Martris.

[SERMON LXXI.]

Sedente Jesu super montem Olyveti.—Matthew xxiv. [3.]

In þis gospel telliþ Crist how hise membris shulen be pursued, and what perils þei shal be inne for holdinge wiþ him and his lawe. Þe gospel telliþ first, *how Jesus sat on þe Mounte*

[a] *alle moten lyve on þe peple.*] There was a growing feeling in England towards the end of the fourteenth century, that the monastic and mendicant fraternities were becoming so numerous as to form a serious burden on the industry of the country. Besides direct statements to that effect, such as the passage in the text, and others that might be gathered from the *Vision of Piers Plowman*, there is an exquisite piece of irony in Chaucer's *Canterbury Tales*, which really says the same thing, though in such forms as became the tender and tolerant genius of the large-minded poet. In the prologue to her tale, the Wife of Bath, after saying that England was once 'fulfilled of faerie,' adds,—

I speke of many hundred yeres ago;
But now can no man see non elves mo;
For now the grete charitee and prayeres
Of limitoures and other holy freres,
That serchen every land and every streme,
As thikke as motes in the sunne-beme,
Blissing halles, chambres, kichenes, and boures,
Citees and burghes, castles high and toures,
Thropes and bernes, shepenes and dairies,
This makith that ther ben no faeries:
For ther as wont to walken was an elf,
Ther walketh now the limitour himself,
In undermeles and in morweninges,
And sayth his matines and his holy thinges,
As he goth in his limitatioun.

of Olyvete, and he wiþ hise disciplis spaken of þe makinge of þe temple, and how al þis shulde be districd, and how þe dai of dome shulde come, and of many þingis þat shulden be, as þe gospel telliþ bifore.

The sin of unchastened curiosity.

And þus telliþ þis gospel, *how Cristis disciplis comen privyli; and axiden him* of þese þingis, and what tyme þei shulden falle, *and bi what signes men shulden wite þat Crist shulde come to þe jugement.* For bi þis myȝten þei knowe *whanne þis world shulde be eendid.* But Jesus answeride and seide to hem þingis þat weren betere for hem to cunne; and bi þis answere moun we se how curiouste of science or unskilful coveitise of cunnynge, is to dampne. For riȝt as coveitise of man is yvel sett for erþeli goodis, so coveitise of cunnynge, þat profitiþ not to come to blisse. For man mai disuse cunnynge to his harm, as Poul seiþ, but if men coveiten to plese God and profite in charite. And in suche comune desiris mai not a man synne; but, as comun þing is ofte soþe, whanne þe singuler is fals, so it falliþ ofte tyme of comun witt and comune wille. And þus techiþ Crist here men, to knowe treuþe for her profit.

1 Cor. viii. 1.

which makes the canon law more prized than the law of Christ.

And þis is a comun synne among men now on lyve, for þei tellen more priis bi lawe, civile or canoun, to cunne hem or oþer jappis[1], þan to cunne Goddis lawe; and for sich wrong cunnyng comeþ harm to many men. And many prelatis, for coveitise setten her wille on sich cunnyng, for þei ben out of bileve, and coveiten more worldli muk þan Goddis worship, or hevenli bliss. And þis is a grevous synne, boþe among prelatis and comuns, for þis synne makiþ hem rude and unable to Goddis lawe, and unable in wille and maneres to lyve wel as Godd[2] biddiþ. And herfore seien sum men, þat þe pope and his lawe ben cursid for sum part, for þei loven not Cristis lawe, but avaunsen and loven men þat holde wiþ his rotun lawe. For as men loven Jesus Crist, so shulden men love his lawe. But Poul seiþ, If ony man love not Crist, cursid be he; and þis cursinge is more þan any oþer prelatis cursinge. And for þis cursing seien sum men þat

1 Cor. xvi. 22.

[1] *japis*, E. [2] *God*, E.

þe pope is more ypocrite, for he makiþ him Cristis felowe, and seiþ he is 'moost holi fadir.' But Crist wole þat þis fole wite not wheþer he be a fend or not; and þis is moost ypocrisie, and moost aȝens skile. For what cause shulde meve þe pope to make him clepid moost blessid fadir, siþ neþer truþe ne leve of God moveþ þat he is ouȝt blessid? But to morewe, whanne he is deed, ceessiþ þis ypocritis name, for he hiriþ his name, and þe hire goeþ wiþ his deþ; neþeles, if he were blessid, he shulde be more blessid after his deþ. Alle þe ypocritis in Cristis tyme dursten not speke so greet blasfemye, and of þis ypocrisie ben many oþer falshedis coloured.

The 'false Christs' of the gospel paralleled in the present hierarchy.

But Crist seiþ to hise disciplis, þat þei shulden loke þat noon disceyveden hem; and speciali in bileve for þis knowing is more nedeful, and þis peril shulde be beter fled for þe word þat Crist seiþ aftir: *Many shulen come in my name, and seie þat, I am Crist, for ȝe shulen heere batels and opynyons of batels.* For now in tyme of oure popis ben many opynyouns of batels, siþ ech lond haþ opynyoun to fiȝt for his pope; and pseudo clerkes and freris seien þat preestis shulden fiȝten sounest. And sich disseit was not herd siþ þe tyme þat Crist was born, and certeinli it haþ ben gaderid of eelde synne of many popis. Crist is a comune name to preestis þat ben anointid of God, but Crist takun by himsilf bitokeneþ oon passinge oþer, as þe pope passiþ oþere preestis, boþe in witt and power, and algatis in holynesse, as he makiþ men to seie. But Crist seiþ *þat such Cristis shulen disseyven many men;* and no prophecie is soþer, ne more to note of trewe men, siþ þis disseit of Anticrist is moost perilous of oþer.

But *Crist confortiþ hise disciplis,* and biddiþ hem *loke þat þei be not troublid; for þese þing moten be, but not ȝit is þe eende.* For of þis rote of striif, shal folk fiȝte aȝens folk, as Sarasynis aȝens Latyns, þat clepen hem Cristene men; *and rewme shal fiȝte aȝens rewme,* as we seen now at iȝe. And pride of þis cursid rote is cause of þis fiȝtinge, for if þe empire were hool, and lordshipes of oþer rewmes, so þat þei weren not cursidli partid among clerkes,—þanne wolde God move seculers to lyve in pees, as he haþ bedun hem. But siþ God seiþ in his lawe, þat hise preestis shulden not be lordis, þe pope and hise holden þis lordship a3ens þe law and wille of God, and more opinli my3te no fend a3entonde God and his ordenance. But Joob axiþ, who ever a3enstood God, and hadde pees in him silf? And of þes harmes comen aftir *pestilencis and hungris*, as it is seid, and *alle þes bigynyngis of sorewis*, þat shal be boþe here and in helle. *Þanne shulen þei put 3ou to turmente*, and oþer þat wolen stonde wiþ truþe. *And after þei shulen slee 3ou, and 3e shulen be in hate to alle folk for my name.* And herfore haþ þe fend ordeyned to sende currours of hise lesingis to diverse rewmes and men, and move hem by hise tiþingis; and þus ben rewmes troublid, and men sclaundrid and disseyved. And herfore seiþ Crist, *þat þanne many shulen be sclaundrid, and shal bitraie hem togidir; and oon shal hate anoþer, and many pseudo profetis shulen rise and shulen disceyve manye.* And þis semeþ to many men to be seid of false freris. And, *for wickednesse shal be plentenous* boþe bifore and þanne, *þe charite of many men shal þanne wexe cold; but he þat lastiþ to þe eende shal be saif* bi God. Job ix.

And here it semeþ to many men, þat Crist spak of þis tyme, in which þes two popis fi3ten þus togidir; for siþ Crist is al witti, and loveþ wel his Chirche, and telliþ in Apocalips of many lesse perils, whi shulde he not tell of þis þat is so perilous? And clerkis hav a rule, þat a word seid bi himsilf shulde be understonden for þe more famous. Wel Y woot þat many preestis hav comen in Cristis name, and ech seide þat, I am Crist, but noon oþer as þe pope; and herfore seiþ Crist in þe same chapiter, þat þere shal be þanne greet tribulacioun, what maner was never fro þe begynynge of þe world to now, and shal not be after. For bodili turment is now ful greet, whanne oo pope sendiþ bishopis and many men to sle many men, wymen, and children, and for þe toþer pope comen many a3ens hem; and cause of þis fi3tinge is a fendis cause, for no man of erþe woot wheþer of þes popis be a fend to be dampnyd in helle, or ellis þei boþe. And bileve techiþ us þat Crist reprovide Petir, for he wolde save his liif, þat was beter þan þes boþe, and made him put up his swerd, and suffride pacientli, whanne he mi3te wiþ a word have vencusid

May not the words of the gospel be a prophecy of the present schism?

hem alle. And Crist techiþ bi word þe maner of a good herde, how he puttiþ his owne liif for his sheep; and so of bileve he is Anticrist þat puttiþ many þousynd lyves for his owne foule liif. And however Anticrist speke here, it is opynli Cristis lawe þat men shulden not fiȝte þus, ne for sich a cause; for ȝif þe pope shal be dampned, as God woot wheþer þei boþ shal, þanne men fiȝten for falshede in cause of a fend; and sich a cause was never herd so opynli aȝens treuþe.

The danger to souls from the present state of things is the greatest of all.

But gretter tribulacioun is in dampnynge of soulis, which ben in false bileve of þes ypocritis; for boþe sitten in Goddis temple and seien þei ben Cristis vikeris and hav more power þan even Crist hadde. For Crist had no power to graunte sich asoiling, and lyve on siche maner, as þes popis done. And so in many pointis þes popis feynen falseli þat þei passen in power oure Lord Jesus Crist. But Crist biddiþ his children to trowe not here neþer þe ferþer ne þe nerrer, but reste in oolde bileve. And not oonli where men fiȝten is þis persecucion, but in fer cuntreis bitwixe contrarie parties. And so, if men tellen Goddis lawe opinli in þis matter, how men shulden not fiȝte þus, but reste in old bileve, þe fend haþ many proctours to pursue siche men; and so, siþ consente is evene wiþ þe dede, þe more part of men is partener in þis dede. Many oþere wordis seiþ Crist in þis chapitre which mai be applied to þis tribulacion; but oo word of confort telliþ Crist here, þat þe daies shal be abreggid of þis fel pursuynge, for men þat ben chosen unto blisse of hevene. Oþer men þat have tyme to expowne þis chapitle[1], and ben tauȝte of God, and meved for to telle it, and speciali ȝif þei seen þe dede acorde wiþ þe speche, mai telle more of Cristis wordis here. But holde we us in bileve, of which we ben certein.

[1] *capitle*, E.

Þe Gospel of many Martris.

[SERMON LXXII.]

Nolite arbitrari.—Matt. x. [34.]

In what sense Christ came not to send peace but a sword.

Þis gospel techiþ men how þei shal riȝtfulli love God, and makiþ martirs hardi to suffre for Cristis sake. And, for many ben cowardis to suffre in Cristis cause, and seien þat it is wisdom to lyve here in pees, and entermete not[1] of þingis þat wolen greve men, þerfore biddiþ Crist his children *not to juge þat he cam to sende sich pees here in erþe. He cam not to sende sich pees but swerd.* Þis swerd semeþ to many men not material swerd, or bodili fiȝtinge, þat Crist techiþ here, but wise wordis boþe of repreef[2] and pacience, and suffringe for truþe, ȝif þat deeþ falle; for comunli in holy writt is swerd clepid word. And þis is a swerd sharpe on boþe sidis, boþe to kerve awey synne, and to nurishe virtues, for sich a swerd of wordis kerveþ and departiþ, and so plantiþ love, and puttiþ out cowardise. And for witt of þis gospel shulden men first undirstonde, þat boþ pees and discord is on two maneres. First is veri pees bitwixe God and man; þe secounde is acord bitwixe man and his enemye. As, if þe fend and þi fleish and þe world acorde togidir, sich acord is clepid pees, al ȝif it be aȝens God; and þus on two maneres is taken striif or discord. Þis secounde is clepid pees, likyng to þe fleish, and ȝit it is to a man venymous discord. And of þis pees spekiþ Crist, þat he cam not to sende it, but discord and fiȝting aȝens sich pees. And þus seiþ Crist *þat he cam to parte a man aȝens his fadir.* For he techiþ how a soule shulde more love God þan ouȝte ellis; and so love þat man shulde hav to God shulde passe love and lawe of kinde, for al siche kyndeli love shulde serve to þe love of God. *And so Crist cam to parte þe douȝter aȝens her modir;* and þat he doiþ whanne fleishli wille holdiþ wiþ God aȝens þe fleish, as

[1] *entermete men not*, E. [2] *reproue*, E.

þei þat taken worldli fode ever in resoun, to serve God, and not to lustli fede þe fleish, for likyng þat is þerinne. Þe þridde tyme seiþ Crist, *he cam to departe þe housebondis broþer aȝens his wyves sister;* and þat is done whan love of manhede of Crist puttiþ awei fleishli workis. And þus not oonli fleishli fadir but goostli fadir shulde be left, whanne þei ben aȝens God, for þat love shulde be kyng. Ȝhe, ȝif þi pope or þi bishop or þi persoun bidde þee do þat God biddiþ þee not do, leve hem þanne and holde wiþ God. And we mai not seie to þes, þat þei mai not erre, ne be aȝens mannis soule, siþ þei ben put to reule it;—certis so ben many þingis put bi kynde to helpe and reule, and ȝit yvel custom of mannis enemy mai turne hem to anoie þe soule, much more þes þree fadris[a] þat ben more strange fro[1] man. And þus seiþ Crist, þat mannis enemyes ben his owne homely; for more enemyes haþ no man þan is lust þat sueþ his fleishe, and moche more þes þree fadris, þat shulden helpe man to hele of soule. For ech þing þat lettiþ þis hele, and bringiþ in siknes of soule, is enemy to þis man, ȝhe, more þan he þat sleeþ his bodi.

Human authority and affection to be despised if they clash with the law and love of Christ.

And to shewe þat al þis reule stondiþ in skilful love of God, seiþ Crist moreover, *þat whoso loveþ his fadir or modir more þan Crist, he is not worþi of him,* for he is not worþi to have Crist in hevene, boþe God and broþer. And so bi reule þat Crist ȝyveþ here, boþe fleishli fadir and modir shulde be lesse loved þan Crist, and if þei stireden aȝens Crist þei shulden be left, and dispisid, and moche more þes oþer fadirs þat ben more strange to men. As, ȝif þi pope or þi bishop or þi persoun bidde þee fiȝte or ȝyve him of þi goodis aȝens þe resoun þat Crist haþ ȝovun, dispise hem utterli, and holde þe reule þat Crist techiþ; and ever flee þis heresie, þat þes fadirs mai not erre here. And to þis witt seiþ Crist after, *þat he þat loveþ his sone or douȝter more þan Crist, is not worþi of him;* and þis is soþ of fleishli children and of workes þat þe soule doiþ, for summe ben workes of þe soule, and summe workes of þe fleishe. And ofte tymes in boþe þes erriþ a man fro þe reule of treuþ, as ofte tymes is a mannis soule occupied to

[1] *to*, E.

[a] Namely, a man's pope, bishop, and parish priest.

lerne and teche worldli lawis; and God biddiþ þat his law shulde be tauȝt bifore þese. And þes men loven more her sones, þan þei loven Jesus Crist;—for it is oon to love him, and in dede to love his lawe; and so whoso loveþ better goode gobetis, or lustli[1] workes þan he loveþ dedis of Crist, he loveþ more his owne douȝter þan he loveþ þis holi abbot. And þus, he brekiþ his ordre for defaute of skilful love.

We must take up the cross.

And, for þis love is shewid in dede, and speciali in mannis suffringe, þerfore seiþ Crist afterward, þat *he þat takiþ not his crosse, and sueþ him, is not worþi of him.* It is seid ofte tymes bifore, þat þis cros þat Crist spekiþ of is redynesse of mannis wille to suffre for Cristis sake, boþe to dispise alle erþeli þingis þat stretchiþ doun to þe erþe, þat is þe stok of þis crosse, and to dispise alle frendshipis boþe of kyn and of þe worlde,—and þes ben clepid two armis of þis crosse. And þanne mannis love lokiþ freeli to hise Jesu above him; and defaute of þis cros bringiþ men alle maner of synne. And þis is cause whi men now ben not martirs as þei weren wont; for a man shulde weie[2] þis love, and loke þat he hadde þis crosse, and suede Crist in wille and dede, redi to suffre for his sake:—but what clerk wole not now leeve þe treuþe of Goddis lawe, ouþer for love of his fleish, or for love of þe world. And cause of þis defaute in love is scatering of mannis love; for men loven cloutid ordris, and þat lettiþ moche love of Crist; and sum men loven worldli worschippis, and worldly[3] lordshipis þat bringen hem inne; and sum men loven worldli goodis, boþe for worshipis[4] of þe world and for lustis of her fleish. And sich shenden Cristis ordre. And herfore Crist forbede his preestis siche lordshipis, and siche goodis, for he woolde þat her love were hooli gaderid in him. And ech man, boþ knyȝt and clerk, shulde be bisi to kepe þis lawe, and make oþer to kepen it; or ellis þei loven not Jesus Crist. And what man þat haþ þis cros, and seeþ Cristis lawe reversid, shulde putte him forþ for love of Crist, and fiȝte wiþ swerd of wise wordis, and telle to men, as Joon Baptist, þat it is not leveful to lyve þus? And siþ ech

Absence of a spirit of martyrdom.

Causes of this.

[1] *lusty*, E. [2] *weyȝe*, E. [3] So E; A om. *worschippis and worldly*. [4] *worschip*, E.

man shulde fiȝte þus wiþ him þat doiþ aȝens Goddis lawe, sich a synner wolde þenke anoon þat he moste do oon of þes two; or to sle siche a man, þat meveþ þus aȝens his wille, or ellis to amenden his lyf, as it is tauȝt bi Cristis lawe. And þus shulden sum men ben martris, and sum mennis lyf be amendid. But charite of manye is woxen cold, and þat makiþ þe Chirche bareyne; for litil fruyt growiþ in wynter, for coldnesse þat is þanne.

The messengers of Christ are to be received and helped.

And þus seiþ Crist afterward, þat, *Who þat haþ founden his liif shal lese it, and he þat leseþ his lyf for me, shal* afterwarde fynde it in blis. Þis sentence seiþ Crist ofte to meve hise martiris to sue him, for no man myȝte lerne here better chaffare or merchandise. For lese þi liif here for God in þe tyme þat is now present, and þou shalt trowe to fynde þy liif aftirward in blisse of hevene. And bileve mot grounden þis dede; for, as Poul seiþ, bi þis wrouȝten martiris. And þus failen now in men, feiþ, hope, and charite. And, for men shulden not forsake to holden þis reule þat Crist ȝeveþ here, for drede of worldli sustynance, þat þe world shulde faile hem, herfore seiþ Crist to hise disciplis, *þat, who ever resseyveþ hem resseyveþ him and his Fadir þat haþ sent him, and who resseyveþ a prophete in þe name of a profete shal resseyve mede of a profete.* And so it is of oþer vertues. *And he þat resseyveþ a just man, in þe name of þe first juste man, he shal take mede of þis juste man; and who ever ȝeve oo of þe leste of þes in name of disciple of Crist, ȝhe, a drauȝt of cold water, soþeli Crist seiþ to us, þat he shal not lese his mede.* And þis vertue of Cristis wordis shulde meve men to helpe goode preestis, and to ȝyve hem of worldeli þingis, to done her office þat Crist biddiþ; for Crist mai not faile in wordis ne in dedis þat he haþ ordeyned. For ouþer defaute is in þe prestis, or her peyne is profitable; as sum maken a newe reule to charge þe peple in noumbre and spensis. And þes men moten nedis falle[1] in peyne of her former synne; and þus cam in begginge and lying and failing of trewe preching. And to þes men shulden noon ȝyve goodis in name of Crist, as he biddiþ here, for þei reversen Crist as his enemyes, and traveilen not in name of him.

Heb. xi. 32-40.

[1] *fayle*, E.

þE GOSPEL OF MANY MARTRIS.

[SERMON LXXIII.]

Egressus Jesus de Templo.—MATT. xxiv. [1.]

Christ foretells the destruction of Jerusalem.

Þis gospel telliþ, as oþer bifore, how men shulden lyve in þis world, and suffre persecucioun þat mut nedis ſalle here. Þe story telliþ, *þat Jesu wente out of þe temple, and his disciplis camen after him, to shewe him þe makyng of þe temple;* for it was fallinge to his wordis þat he hadde seid bifore to þe peple, to wite, what Crist ſelide of þis makyng of þe temple. *But Crist answeride and seid to hem; Se ȝe alle þes. Soþeli, Y seie to ȝou þat here shal not be a stoon lefte upon anoþer undistryed.* And þis þing was fulfillid, wiþinne fifty ȝeer after, for þe secunde and forty yeer after þat Crist was steied to hevene cam two princis of Rome, Titus and Vaspasian, and ensegiden þe citee, whan it was ful of men at þe feste of Paske, as Crist tolde bifore bi Luke. And þis oost envyrounede þis citee on ech side, and lettide þe peple to go out, and slewe þe folk, and at þe laste toke þe cite; and þanne was þe temple distroied, and al þe citee was turnid, so þat þe mount of Calvarie was sette fer wiþinne þe citee, whan it was bifore wiþouten. And so was not a stoon left upon anoþer undistroied, for all þe citee and þe temple weren turned to make newe citee. And bi þes wordis men taken þat Crist tolde litil by þe temple, or ony siche workes of crafte þat passen þe state of innocence; for clene liif wiþouten siche is beter to Crist þan siche churchis. Alle siche profiten not, but in as moche as þei helpen þe peple to heere Goddis word, and betere þere to preie God; and þis is comunli betere don in þe eire under hevene, but ofte tyme, in reyny wedir, chirchis don good on halidai. And þus curiouste of foolis is ungroundid by Goddis lawe. *And whanne Crist sat on þe hill of Olyvete, þe disciplis comen and axiden Crist, to telle hem whanne þis shulde be, and whanne shulden be þe daie of dome.* But Crist tolde hem of sounere perils, þat was betere hem to knowe, and lefte þis þing hid to hem, as it is told bifore.

Three things hidden from men.

And so men seien þat þree þingis wole God have hid to men. God wole þat tyme of deþ be comunli unknowun to men, and whanne þe daie of dome shal be. For men shulden ever more wake, and kepe hem from peril of synne, siþ þei witen never whanne God hall come; so þat whanne he come he fynde hem redi to take þe jugement of God. For servauntis shulden biden þe Lord, and not þe Lord abide hise servauntis; but whanne ful tyme is comen to God, þanne falliþ him to make amende. And siþ God wole þat his tyme be hid, þei synnen gretli þat traveilen here to knowe þis tyme, and leven oþer þing þat God wole þat men knowen and done; and þus, as it is seid bifore, popis ben gretli to blame þat menen þat þei shulden knowe þis dai, bi fool[1] graunting þat þei graunten[a]. Þe þridde þing þat God wole have hid to men is privyte of his ordenance, wheþer God have ordeyned to save þes men, or ellis to dampne hem for her synne. And cause of þis is as bifore, for men shulden ever be redi to God, and ever serve þis Lord in drede, lest he dampne men at þe laste. And þus many men synnen in God aȝens his firste comandement, þat wolen not rise out of her synne, but dwelle þerinne, and chese[2] a tyme; for Crist seiþ to false men þat he is Lord, ȝhe of tyme.

We have knowledge enough to guide our lives.

And þus seiþ Crist, *þat of þat daie no man knoweþ in þis liif, but aloonli þe Fadir of Hevene*[3], and two oþer persones of þe Fadir; for þing proprid to þe Godhede is þus aproprid to þe Fadir. And herbi it is not denyed to þe two Persones aftir. But ȝif it acorde to þe Fadir, in as moche as He is God, it mut nedis acorde to þe Sone, and also to þe Hooli Goost, siþ þei ben þe same God. But it falliþ not þus to aungels, ne to ony oþer creature, for in þat þat þei ben, þei ben divers from her God. And þus, whan þe Fadir haþ ony þing in þat þat he is God, þe Sone and þe Holi Goost hav comunli þis same þing, siþ it is comune and propre to hem for to be þe same God. And

[1] *foole*, E. [2] *chesen hem*, E. [3] So E; no italics in A.

[a] No indulgence could conceivably be of any avail, except in the interval between death and the day of judgment; the writer means therefore, that by granting indulgences for specified terms of years, the popes did in effect assert the possession of a knowledge respecting the time of the day of judgment which Scripture expressly denies to all men.

þus þe general undirstonding of þe laste dai of dome shulde be knowe unto men, and special knowinge shulde be hid, and whanne and how it shal be. And þerfore Cristen men ben apaied in knowing of Goddis lawe, for þat is ynowȝ to hem, and þerafter þei shulden lyve. And ȝif þei ben idil from þis knowinge, God wole axe ful streite acountis. So ȝif a lord al witty as God ȝaf a man al þat he hadde, in noumbre and mesure and in weiȝte, to serve þis lord after þes goodis, þis lord wolde seie to þis servant, þat axide more þan were ȝnowȝ: Servant, holdist þou me a fool? how usist þou þat þat þou hast? ne have Y not ȝove þee ȝnowȝ of cunynge nedeful to þee? And moche cuninge hast þou hid, and puttist it not in werk; and þou shuldist wite þat þee were better to worche after þis cuninge þan for to have newe cunninge, and þus to be idil wiþ þis. God is þis lord þat mesuriþ man bi cuninge þat he ȝyveþ to him, and wole þat man worche after þis cuninge; and þus shal man occupie him, and not aboute newe cunnynge, and leve þe work þat he shulde do. And þus synnede[1] oure firste fadris, bi byheste þat þe fend hiȝte hem, þat þei shulden not die to ete þus, but be as Goddis, knowing good and yvel; and þus synneþ ech man þat is slow in Goddis service, for he leeveþ to putte in work þe witt þat God haþ ȝovun him, and languishiþ after a newe cunninge þat comeþ of his idilnesse; and þis is a sinful ende, þat mote nede bring in peyne. And so we synnen comunli here bi þe firste synne of þe fend, and aȝens þe witt of God, as ȝif we wolden be al cunnynge. Þenke what witt þou hast of God, in which þou art now ydil, and putt wiseli þat witt in work, and holde þee paied of Goddis grace; for ellis þou takist þis grace in veyn, and runnest in dett aȝens þi God.

Abuse of indulgences.

And þis is a comune synne in prelatis, boþe more and lasse; for God haþ ȝovun hem witt in mesure, how þei shulden profite to his Chirche, and þei disusen ofte þis tresour, and languishen after witt as fendis; for þe presumen and tempten God, and graunten pardoun for longe tyme, and þei witen never where God haþ ordeyned þat þis pardon mai stonde bi him. And þus if men wolden wel examyne dedis ungroundid in holi writt, þei

[1] *synneden*, E.

shulden shame of þes dedis, how þei ben aȝens God. Trowe we not, þat Petre wiste how he shulde spende Goddis tresour, and how he shulde after, wiþ Goddis goodis, do profite unto his Chirche? Who dar putt on Petre þis synne, þat he was necligent in þis, þat he sparide Goddis tresour, þe which popis profiten wiseli now? And þis shulden alle men, but algatis prelatis, overse her astait and her liif, wheþer it be acordinge to Goddis lawe or after customes of þe fend, and contynue þing wel don, and mende þat is amys. And siche a rekenyng shulde a man make ech dai wiþ him silf, for þis is a comun word þat many seintis have in mouþ;—ech tyme þat God haþ ȝovun þee, God wole axe ful sharpli how þou hast dispendid it; wel in his service, or amys. And þis rekenyng shulde ech man drede, but speciali þes hiȝe preestis; for her office is more perilous, and more medeful ȝif it be wel. Þerfore is nede hem to wite what dedis þat þei shulden do, and algatis faile not in her work, for peril þat wole come þerof; siþ synne of hem turneþ to harm of many sheep þat þei shulden kepe.

The pastoral office three-fold.

And however þat men feynen her office, it is toold in Cristis lawe, how þei shulden be occupied in þre officis of sheepherdis. Þei shulden wiseli lede her sheep in sound pasture of Goddis lawe, and þe sheep þat weren scabbid heelen, and stablen in good liif, and algatis putte her liif to save her sheep aȝens wolves. And þes herdis shulden flee sich tyme, in which þeeves sleen þe sheep, and coveiten more þe wole of hem, and þe donge, wiþ oþer goodis, þan þei coveiten her soule helþe; for þis is a wolvis entent, and ȝif þei taken þus þe office of herde, þei ben wolves at þe bigynynge. And so þis tyme is wasted to hem, in which þei traveilen, for her hie stait, or for coveitise of richesse or ony oþer þing oþer þan Goddis worship, or oþer þan profite of her sheep bi þe reulis of Goddis lawe. And þus if þei hiden Goddis lawe, and hiȝen her owne lawe for þis eende, þei lesen her tyme to þer dampnynge, and to harmyng of her sheep. Sich þing shulden þes herdis þenken; for þei moten nedis reken wiþ God, siþ tyme is a preciouse tresour, þat God ȝeveþ to dispende wel. And tyme shal comen whanne we dien, þat we hadden lever to have a dai þan al þe worship or richesse þat hav fallen us in þis world. And þanne our jugement shall be hool, and wille a þing after þat it is good. Siche oversiȝt of oure lyf, and speciali of hiȝe prelatis, helpiþ þis Chirche, and makiþ hem to drede God and serve him[1].

Of many Martris.

[SERMON LXXIV.]

Dicebat Jesus turbis[2] *Judeorum.*—Luc. xi. [29.]

The kindred of God's children and the kindred of the devil's children.

Þis gospel telliþ what prelatis shulden do, and whereof þei shal be reproved. And þis wole bringe in martirdom, boþe in o man and in anoþer. And þus is told of martirdom þe begynnynge and þe ende. Crist spake here to princis of prestis and to þe comuns of Jewis, for in boþe þes was þe kynrede which slowȝ þes martirs. Þer ben two kynredis þat Crist spekiþ ofte of, þe kynrede of Goddis children, and kynrede of fendis children; and at þe bigynnynge of þis world bigan þes two kynredis. Þe firste kynrede of martirs bigan in a man at Abel; þe secounde kynrede toke bigynnynge at Cayn; and þes two kynredis shal not faile bifore þe dai of dome come. Þe laste seint þat shal lyve here shal be of þe firste kynrede, and þe laste þat shal be dampned shal be of þe toþer kynrede; and þes kynredis ben scatirid among many folke, ne þei gone not bi lyne of blood, but bi medling[3] bi lynes of kynde. But þe firste kynrede hadde bigynnynge bifore þe toþer, for it bigan at Adam, siþ Adam is saved. Þe toþer began at Adames sone, þat slowȝ þe firste martir. But, for Adam was not martir, þus slayn for Goddis love, and martirs ben þe moste and beste þat ben in þis kynrede, þerfore it is marked to begynne at Abel; for þe toþer kynrede was sum maner cause of þis forþer. And, as many men supposen, aboute þe daie of dome shal þis firste longe lyve here, whanne þe toþer shal be aweie; for bi vertue of Crist, þat is begynnynge and endinge, shal men þikke turne to him, and leeve þe fend wiþ hise workes.

[1] *serven him wel*, E. [2] So in E; A has *turbas*. [3] For *bi medling* E reads *ben medlid*.

But leve we now þis mater, and sue we þe storie of þe gospel. Crist grette þis kynrede and seide; *Woo be to ȝou þat maken þe graves of prophetis, and ȝoure fadris killiden hem. Certis ȝe beren witnesse þat ȝe consenten to her workes;* for al ȝif þei killiden hem and ȝe maken faire her sepulcris, neþeles ȝe wolen kille Crist, þat is heed of martiris. And bi þis polishing, ȝe tellen ȝour ipocrisie, bi which ȝe florishen ȝoure synne in killinge of martiris; for, as Crist seiþ to þis kyn, þei demen in þis to obeishe to God. And Caiphas þat ȝaf ȝou conceil seide, it helpiþ o man to die[1]
John xvi. 2. for þe folk; but al if þese wordis weren soþ, ȝit þis ypocrite seide hem falseli; and so þis kynrede bi her ypocrisie telde how þei wolden kille Crist. And þus seiþ Crist here; *Ȝoure fadris killiden þes prophetis, and ȝe bilden her sepulcris,* as who seide, we wolen amende; but as Crist seiþ bi Matheu, þei þenken þei wolen fille þe mesure of þat þat her fadirs bigan, in killinge of þe heed of prophetis. And herfore telliþ Crist to hem, how þe wisdom of God seide of þis kyn; *I shal sende to hem prophetis and apostlis, and of þese shal þei boþe pursue and kille.* Þe Jewis killiden not alle þe apostlis, for Joon was not þus killid, but þei killiden James, and pursueden oþer in oþer contreis: *so þat þe blood of alle prophetis, fro þe begynnynge of þe world, be souȝt of þis kynrede,* siþ þis haþ done hem alle to deþ, *fro þe blood of juste Abel unto þe blood of Zacharie, which þis kynrede killiden, bitwixe þe auter and þe temple.* It is no nede to trete which was þis Zacharie[a], and which Barachie was his fadir, and whanne þis martirdom was done; for siþ o persone haþ mony names, and Crist takiþ sum tyme þe witt of þe name, it is noo drede þat ne Crist seiþ soþ here, as nediþ us to knowe it. And, for þese prestis shulden printe betir þes wordis in her soulis, þerfore Crist rehersiþ to hem, and seiþ on þis maner; *Ȝhe, I seie to ȝou, þis blood shal be souȝte of þis kynrede.* For alȝif þis kynrede hadde two divers

[1] *þat o man dye,* E.

[a] 'There has been much dispute who this Zacharias was. From the time of Origen, who relates that the father of John the Baptist was killed in the temple, many of the Greek Fathers have maintained that this is the person to whom our Lord alludes; but there can be little or no doubt that the allusion is to Zacharias, the son of Jehoiada (2 Chron. xxiv. 20, 21).' Smith's Bib. Dict. Article 'Zacharias.'

partis:—þe firste slew martiris from Abel unto þis Zacharie, þe secunde slouȝ martiris fro Zacharie to þe laste;—neþeles boþe alle þes killeris and martiris þat ben killid maken two kynredis, and ech helpeþ oþer. For as seintis taken part and helpe of oþer seintis, so shrewis taken part and harm of her felowis.

And Crist gretiþ hem after, for þo þat holden hem wise men, and seiþ; *Woo be to ȝou, wise men of þe lawe, þat token aweie þe keie of cunnynge, and ȝe entriden not inne; and oþer men þat entriden ȝe have forfendid.* And here streyneþ þe pope, what þing is þis keie; and he wole algatis have þat it is not cunnyng, for often tymes mony oþer þan popis han moch more cunnyng, and ȝit han not þes keies. And herfore he feyneþ þat þes keies ben poweris, boþ upon clerkis and eke upon seculers;—power of jurisdiccion, and power to assoile and bynde. But many men þenken here þat þei shulden more trowe to Crist þan to many Pope Joonis[1], for he is suspect here. Crist clepiþ þis cunnyng here, þe keie of cunnyng, and alle þe fendis in helle shulden not move[2] to denye Crist. Þes feyned poweris mai not be proved ne perceyved in dede; and þerfore ben þei feynid, and by cautelis of ypocritis is þe folk bigilid. And þus trewe men seien here, þat þer ben two keies: þe firste is keie of cunnynge, and þe toþer keie of power. Þese keies hadden Peter and many oþer apostlis; but Peter hadde prerogatif bifore hise oþer breþeren. Þis cunnyng was not speculatif, of gemetrie, ne oþer sciencis, but practik, put in dede, how men shulde lyve by Goddis lawe. And after þis science cam power to bynde and unbinde; and to whom God grauntiþ þe first he grauntiþ þe secounde. And oonhede of þes keies was not oonli ȝovun to Peter, siþ hevene was open to oþer folk in cuntreis þat Peter cam not inne, bi keies þat Crist ȝaf to oþer apostlis. And so þese feynede keies ben keies of helle, ȝif þei open helle gatis to children of pride; and ȝif þis pope hav cunnynge to þis work, he is maister of þes keies. For God wole ȝeve cunnyng to teche his weie to hevene to whom ever him likiþ; and he is Petris viker, alȝif neiþer fendis ne cardinalis putten him in his trone.

Exaggerated papal pretensions.

[1] *Popis Jons*, E. [2] So E; *mowe*, A.

Whanne Crist seide þese treuþis unto þes hie prestis, Phariseis and men of lawe stoden gretli aȝens him, and stoppiden his mouþ wiþ many false wordis, and lettiden Crist to speke more, as a man þat spak blasfemye. And herfore þes lawyeris, for þes wordis of Crist, layen in awayte more to do Crist to þe deþ. And God wote where þe court wolde þus shape for men, þat seiden sharpli to hem þis sentence of þe gospel; and if þei done, þei ben þanne of þe secounde kynrede. For þis kynrede lepiþ from oo folk to anoþer; for it is now among Jewis and now among heþen men, and now comeþ aȝen, as þe fend hopiþ victorie, and failing of Goddis lawe, and growinge of mannis lawe. For noþing is beter post to likyng of þe fend. And siþ þis kynrede is now moost among prestis, as it was in Cristis tyme, trewe men shulden speke to hem sharpli as Crist dide. For þe fend haþ hem moost helperis in þis cause, and makeris of martiris bi pursuynge and sleynge. And ȝif þei senden men to hevene, þat is on wrong maner; but þei senden men evene to helle, as to her owne hous, for þei have exilid Goddis lawe, bi which þei shulden worche, and brouȝt in þe fendis lawe bi which þei rengnen.

And after seiþ Crist, how þes lawyeris *aspieden how þei myȝten take ouȝt of Cristis mouþ for to accuse him*, and so do him to deeþ; and þus þese ypocritis feyneden to fulfille her law. And þus it is to daie of þes hiȝe prestis; for þei hav newe lawis maad biside Goddis lawe to dampne men to deþ as open heretikes. And to do þis dede þei counseiliden not wiþ Goddis lawe, but wiþ foundun[1] heresies þat hemsilf holden, þat þei mai not synne ne erre in siche jugementis. But þei jugen for heretikes al maner of sich men þat seien þat þei shulden sue Crist, and leeve her worldli liif. Ȝif þei leven Cristis liif, and ȝeven hem þus to lordship, þei ben þe fendis children and open Anticristis; for þei mai not be Cristis children, but ȝif þei suen him, and holden hem in his boundis, and go not out by newe lawes, and speciali holde hem in mekeness and poverte. And here we mai assaie where þei doren be martiris.

[1] *founden*, E.

IN FEESTIS OF MANY MARTRIS.

[SERMON LXXV.]

Egrediente Jesu de Templo.—MARK xiii. [1.]

Christ foretells the destruction of Jerusalem.

Þis gospel telliþ, as oþer bifore[a], how Crist mesuride his disciplis, boþe in wit and wille, to suffre for his love. Þis gospel telliþ, as oþer bifore, *how Jesus wente out of þe temple, and oon of his disciplis seide to him; Maister, loke what stoones and makingis* ben of þis grete temple. *And Jesus answeride and seide to him:—Seest þou þese grete bildingis. Þer shal not be a stoon lefte upon a stoon, þat ne it shal be distried. And whanne Crist satt upon þe Mounte of Olyves, aȝen þe temple, his disciplis axiden him, þes foure bi hem silf, Peter and Joon and James and Andrew:—Telle þou us whanne þes þingis shal be don, and what tokene shal be, whanne alle þes shal bigynne to have an ende. And Jesus answeringe, bigan to seie to hem; See ȝe first þat no man disseyve ȝou; for many shal come in my name, and seie þat Y am he* þat governeþ holi Chirche, *and þei shal disseyve many. But whanne ȝe shal here bateilis, and opynyons of batels, drede ȝe not,* but be ȝe sadde in bileve.

Rumours of wars between the adherents of the rival popes.

Moo opynyons of batels, herden we never; for men wiþ þe oo pope seien þat it is needful to fiȝte wiþ men þat holden wiþ þat oþer, and þei wiþ þe toþer pope have contrarious opynyons. And ȝit men wiþ oure pope hav þis opynyoun; þat prelatis and prestis shulden fiȝte aȝens þe toþer pope, and men þat holdiþ wiþ him, but if þei converte hem. Sum of us have þis opynyoun; þat preestis shulden not fiȝte, but move men bi resoun and Goddis lawe to treuþe, and preie mekeli for men þat þei do after Goddis wille; and þat it is not bileve þat oþer þis, or þis, be Pope; for ȝif he shal not be saif, he is noo part of holi Chirche. And so þis is no cause to Cristen men to fiȝte inne; but raþer shulde boþe þes popis go mekeli to þe emperour, and renounse al her lordship þat þei have of seculers; and siþ

[a] See Sermon LXXIII.

lyve a pore liif as Peter and Poul diden, and algatis move no men, ne counseille hem, for to fiȝte þus. And in þis opynyoun resten many meke prestis. In[1] oþer pointis of þis mater ben an hundred opynyouns among clerkes, and lewide men, and alle ben of bateiles.

Interpretation of the gospel.

And after, seiþ Crist, þat alle þes moten ben, but ȝit is noo eende, to make þe dai of dome. *Folk shal rise aȝens folk*, as Sarasins aȝens Latyns; *rewme aȝens rewme*, as Inglond[2] aȝens Franche[3]; *and erþe-dene*[4] *shal be, bi placis, and hungris*, as men hav feelid[a]. *Þes ben bigynnynge of sorewis; and þerfore loke wel ȝou silf, for þei shall bitraie ȝou in her counceilis, and in her sinagogis shal ȝe be betyn; and bifore kyngis and justices shal ȝe stonde, for me, in witnes to hem. And in alle folk moot first be prechid þe gospel.* And þis ordeynede Crist of his grete wisdom; for bifore þei hadden killid þes hooli apostlis, þer was no maner of folk, Grekis ne Latyns, ne barbares, þat ne þei hadden þe gospel of Crist prechid unto hem. *And whan þei shal lede ȝou, and bitraie ȝou to jugis, þenke ȝe not bifore bisili, what ȝe shal speke; but what shal be ȝovun ȝou in þat hour, speke ȝe þat, for þat seiþ God. For ȝe ben not spekinge, but þe Holi Goost*, siþ ȝe ben hise instrumentis, and he spekiþ first;—*O*[5] *broþer shal bitraie his broþer in to his deþ, and þe fadir shal bitraie his sone, and þe sones shal rise aȝens her fadris, and do hem to deeþ. And ȝe shal be in hate to alle men for my name; but he þat lastiþ to þe eende he shal be saf.*

Þe lettre of þis gospel is told bifore, and so it is ynowȝ here

[1] So E; om. A. [2] *Englonde*, E. [3] *Fraunce*, E. [4] *erþedone*, E. [5] *one*, E.

[a] This passage might be expected to supply the means of fixing the date of the composition of these sermons, but I have not found it so. In Professor Rogers' valuable *History of Agriculture and Prices in England* (i. 217), I find it stated that in the fourteenth century, 'the following are years of famine, the average price of wheat having risen above 10s. the quarter:—1315, 1318, 1321, 1351, 1369.' Again,—'It rose above 9s. in 1294 and 1370:' 'above 8s. in 1293, 1314, 1350, 1363, 1367, 1374, 1390.' In the years 1381–1386, within which these sermons must have been composed if Wyclif was their author, the price of wheat was remarkably low. These statistics refer to the southern and midland counties, and are thoroughly reliable. Either then, if Wyclif wrote the sermon, the reference must have been to a time of scarcity as far back as 1374; or, if we suppose the scarcity of 1390 to be pointed at, Wyclif was not the author of the sermon.

to telle pleyne storie. Here men moven li3tli, siþ Crist tolde alle þes perils, it semeþ þat þei mut nedis be; but who my3te þanne lette hem? Here men seien comunli, þat al þing mut nedis be, and 3it men moten nedis a3ensstonde many of þes; and so þei moten nedis have mede of siche a3enstondinge. For as we moten nedis preie for þingis þat nedis moten be, as shewen þree þe firste axingis of þe Pater noster; so we moten nedis enforse a3ens þingis þat nedis moten be. And of sich enforsinge mote nedis come mede; for ellis shulden no men lette yvel to come; and mede in a3enstonding, and conseillinge to goode, weren al aweye bi þis lewide resoun. And, for alle þes ben false, and many oþer þat suen, enforse we a3ens yvel, and preie we for goode, al3if God have ordeyned þat þei moten nedis come. And, for men shulden do þus, þerfore haþ God ordeyned, þat comynge of many sich þingis ben unknowen to men.

A predestinarian objection answered.

But here men douten over þis, of ordre of þis help to þe Chirche; but here seien Cristene men, þat no man shulde doute to helpe þe Chirche, but alle men shulden help it here, ech man on his maner; siþ God tellip us bi his lawe þat þis is his wille. Seculer lordis shulden helpe here principali, for many causis. Oon, for God haþ 3ovun hem swerd for to helpe his Chirche bi strengþe, and strengþe wiþ mennis drede is nedeful to do þis dede. Also lordis of þis worlde ben þo, to whiche þis harm is don, who shulde stonde more for þis cause, þan lordis þat hav lost þis lordship. Also, þat man þat haþ synned shulde algatis make aseeþ; but þe generacion of lordis bi folie brou3t in þis wrong, and herfore it falliþ to hem to make aseeþ for þis synne. And þus shulde kny3tis knowe, how þei shulden stonde for Goddis cause, and not al oonli kille men in mennis cause, as boucheris. Þei shulden have shame how þei ben hardi in cause of þe world and of þe fend, but in þe cause of God þei ben boþ cowardis and foolis. And neþeles þis lord doiþ worship and profite to kny3ttis þat serven him, and þei mai not denye þis, þat ne for blyndenesse and cowardise holdiþ þe fend a3ens God þis lordship þat þei shulden have.

Church-reform

But over þis, men have doute what ordre men shulden have, and where men shulden begynne to worche, in iust restoringe of þes goodis. But here men seien, siþ þis wrong is brood sprad in Cristendom, and Goddis oost shulde be myȝti to do þis dede aȝens þe fend, in many placis shulden men worche on þis weie to helpen her modir. But siþ þe nest and heed hereof is at Rome, where it bigan, it semeþ to many men þat at Rome shulde þis riȝtting bigynne; and so shulde þis heed be stoppid to feyne censuris aȝens God, and fere foolis bi cursingis for þei fulfillen Goddis lawe; and wiþ þis boþe lordis and comuns mai lette freris to harmen þe Chirche. And þus were Goddis word soþ whanne he spekiþ to þe fend, and seiþ, a woman shal disquatte[1] his heed. And Marie helpe[2] þe Chirche þat it be so. For ȝif richesse and worldli lordship weren taken aweie from prelatis and preestis, moche of þe fendis pride were abatid in þes clerkes; and Goddis name were not dispisid ech dai as it is now, but his lawe shulde be betere holde, and Anticristis jugementis shulde ceesse.

should begin at Rome.

But ȝit men douten wheþer þei shulden fiȝten in þis cause aȝens her enemyes;—speciali, siþ Crist movede two princis of Rome for to fiȝte, Titus and Vaspasian, þat distroieden Jerusalem. Here men þenken, þat Cristene men shulden not fiȝte but if Crist bad hem; for Crist seide þat his yoke is softe and his charge liȝt to bere. And so neiþer bodili swerd neþer oþer armes, ne fiȝtinge shulde be here usid of Cristene men; ne oþer lawe but Goddis lawe, and lordis drede, and manassing to clerkis þat wolden aȝenstonde. And to bindinge and prisoninge of hem shulde alle maner of men helpe; but bi Goddis grace þis shulde not falle, siþ clerkis shulde helpe here in Goddis cause, and feyn[3] to be dischargid of erþeli goodis, þat þei beren now. And þanne þei shulden go liȝt to hevene, and drawe þe world after hem; þer þei doppen now to helle, and drawen many men wiþ hem. Freris shulden help in þis cause, siþ þei ben groundid in poverte, and þei have but temporal goodis[a], þe which ben knytt to her hertis. And shortly alle maner of men, ȝhe, prestis boþe more and lesse, shulden helpe here in Goddis cause, for love þat þei shulden love her modir.

Spiritual arms alone should be used to heal the schism.

[1] *disquate*, E. [2] *helpe Marie*, E. [3] *fayn*, E.

[a] As opposed to lands or lordships.

But now þei clepen good, yvel, and harm, profit, and bondage, fredom; but þanne shulden þei wel witen how al þat helpiþ to hevene is good, and al þat shulde be by Goddis lawe were free and helpli[1] to þis ende.

And þus þe lord preisiþ his baili, for he forȝaf to his tenaunte fifty barels of oile. And so þis ȝifte was riȝtful, siþ þis lord is God himsilf; and þis tenaunte is kynde of clerkis, for þei shulden ȝeve devocioun, and be paied of litil corn[a]. For, as Poul techiþ, þei shulden holde hem paied wiþ bodili fode and hileyng. And þus shulden preestis preche to lordis, to holde hem paied of worldli goodis, and sette her wille in hevenli goodis, which wille shulde make hem liȝt to hevene. But þe fend haþ stranglid þese houndis wiþ talwe[2], þat þei mai not berke. And þus siþ seculer men shulden be moo þan prestis shulden be, and prestis shulden have, by titil of almesse, her sustenance of þe peple, wiþdrawing of her service aȝen shulde move to wiþdraw þes goodis. And whoever aȝenstondiþ þis sentence is unlawful aȝens God.

The pope should be obeyed, as far as consistent with the laws of God.

And so men shulden graunte in dede to obeishe to þe pope, as þe peple obeishide to Petre, and as Goddis lawe wole axe; but it were to myche to pass þis, for þanne men obeishiden to þe fend, siþ Goddis lawe shulde be reule, and teche how God wole þat men obeishe. And siþ þe freris accusen þe court, in matter of þe sacrid oost, and saien þat it techiþ þat þis oost is not Goddis bodi, but accident wiþouten suget þat alle men knowen not, men shulden axe þis treuþe of þis court wiþ good grounding[b]. And ȝif þis court faile in þis, þei failen in

[1] *helpiþ*, E. [2] *talow*, E.

[a] Does this mean,—the clergy should be content to retain for themselves 'litil corn,' or temporal riches, just as the debtor in the parable retained only twenty for his own profit out of the hundred measures of wheat that he had to render to his lord, but they should rejoice in being permitted to keep an abundant measure (fifty out of a hundred barrels) of 'oile,' or devotion? See Serm. LXXXV.

[b] The general drift of this remarkable passage seems to be as follows. The friars,—after the synod of 1382, which had been promoted, and indeed ordered, by 'the Court,' or, as we should say now, by the Government,—and after the sending down of letters patent into all the counties (see Lewis, p. 106), appointing inquisitors, who would be in many or most instances friars, to search out heretical writings and their fautors,—might well say that the Court taught their doctrine concerning the Eucharist, and condemned that of Wyclif. This is called by the writer, *accusing* the Court of teaching the said doctrine; because,

The doctrine of the Eucharist.

moost þat þei shulden do; for þei shulden teche men bileve þe which is ground of Cristis ordre. But Crist seiþ wiþ many seintis, þat þis oost is Goddis bodi, al if it be breed in his kynde, as Poul techiþ ofte tymes. Þus shulden rewmes stoppe first fruytes, and avaunsing of Cardinalis, wiþ oþer spoilingis of þis court, bi þe which rewmes and peplis ben chargid. And ȝif men seie þat rewmes mai not defenden hem fro sich spoiling, certis þanne þei ben to feble to defende hem from oþer enemyes; and ȝif cowardise lette hem, bi feynynge of Anticrist, þanne þei ben to unstable for defaute of bileve. For neþer God ne man mai noie, and moche more alle fendis of helle, but ȝif þe law of Holi Writt accuse men[1] aȝens God.

Þe Gospel of oon Confessor and Bishop.

[SERMON LXXVI.]

Vigilate, quia nescitis qua hora.—Matt. xxiv. [42.]

The duty of watchfulness.

Þese gospellis ben passid þat fallen to þes martiris, and now comen gospelis þat fallen to confessouris. And so þis gospel techiþ a wisdom of Crist, how men þat have cure shulden kepe þer sheep; and þis lore perteyneþ to moo þan to preestis, but þei shulden kepe passingli þe lore þat Crist techiþ here. Crist biddiþ first þat hise servantis *wake, for þei witen never whanne þe Lord is to come. And it is knowen* to men þat Crist spekiþ here of wakinge fro synne, for þat is þe best wakynge, and þis beste Lord spekiþ of beste þing; for as creaturis tellen a man his God, so þingis of kynde tellen men how þei shulden serve God. It is knowen to clerkis þat man haþ fyve wittis, and stopping of þese wittis bringiþ in sleep to man; and þanne man is half

[1] *hem*, E.

as he goes on to say, Christ and many of the saints unmistakably taught *his* doctrine. He proceeds to suggest, apparently in the hope of setting himself right with the Court by appealing to its self-interest, that the existing hierarchy was terribly burdensome both to Court and nation, and that to 'stoppe first fruytis,' and other ecclesiastical exactions, would be greatly to the advantage of the state. The advice was not acted upon till the year 1534.

deed, and unable for to worche or to defende himsilf aȝens enemys þat wolen harmyn[1] him. Þese wittis ben clepid siȝte and heering, smelling and taist, wiþ groping; and alle þes shulden be fed wiþ God, þat mai never faile fro mannis witt. But stopping of love wiþ worldli þingis lettiþ mannis heed to perceyve God; and so, as clerkis seien, þes fyve wittis comen of a vertue wiþinne in þe heed, and ȝif a man bi sleep be lettid in þis virtue, ouþer bi fumes, or drunkenes, or oþer cause, þes fyve wittis ben stoppid and wanten her worching. And letting of þese fyve wittis is clepid mannis sleep. But al þat man haþ is ȝovun to him of God, for to serve his God, ouþer worching or suffring; and ȝif he leve þis service, þanne he slepiþ goostli. And wit wiþinne in mannis heed, þat is God himself, mut move his out-wittis to worche as þei shulden; and so al þat lettiþ man to be moved þus of God bringiþ in sleep of synne, and lettiþ him to wake. And so erþeli fumes comyng fro þe stomak ben grete cause of þis sleep, and lettiþ[2] helping of God; for God dwelliþ not wiþ man bisi aboute erþeli þingis. But worching of a mannis soule aboute siche þingis makiþ worldli fumes lette[3] a mannis resoun to knowe hevenli goodis, and wake wiþ hise wittis; for sich a man loveþ more goodis of þis world þanne he loveþ his God, for on hem his wille is more sett.

And þerfore clepiþ Poul þese averouse men, serveris of maw- *Eph. v. 5.* mettis, and brekeris of Goddis heestis; and alle wittis of sich men slepen fro Goddis service. We shulden wake to resoun, and *Sins of sight.* knowe þat our siȝte is ȝovun us of God, to serven him and oure soules; and ȝif we failen hereof, for synne þat we ben inne, we misusen oure siȝte, and slepen wiþ it. Siȝte is ȝovun to man as hiest out-witt, for to sue his profite, and flee þing þat harmeþ him; and þingis þat ben bifore him, þe which he shulde do, shulde a man wel knowe, and take to him þe profitable. And þus, as Crist techiþ, men synnen in siȝte of wymmen, for he þat seeþ a woman for to coveite her, he haþ in þat done lecherie in his herte. For, as Crist techiþ, þe rote of a man's synne is wiþinne in his herte bifore þat it be in dede, and herfore men shulden flee cause þat þus bringiþ synne to mannis herte. Þe

[1] *harmen*, E. [2] om. E. [3] *and lettiþ*, E.

synne of siȝt is not þus oonli in lecherie of fleish, but it is also in coveitise of worldli goodis; as whanne þou seest erþeli þing, and coveitist to hav it, aȝens þe wille of þi God, þou synnest
1 John ii. 16.
þanne in þi siȝte. And þus seiþ Seint Joon, þat in coveitise of iȝen is understonden al coveitise of oþer wittis aȝens resoun. Ne a man synneþ not in siȝt, al oonli on þes two maneres, but whanne he is idil in his siȝt, and aspieþ not his profit; as sum men loken to veyn plaies, and many siȝtis of worldli þingis, þe which profiten not to her soule, but raþer doiþ hem harm. And siȝt is þe first witt stoppid whanne a man slepiþ. Soþeli we shulden ever loke upon God, as we mai here seen him bi mirrour, in a derknes of þingis þat he haþ maad; ȝhe, boþe niȝt and dai, slepinge and wakinge, shulde we þus þenke on God and his lawe.

Sins of hearing.

Þe secounde uttir witt is heeringe of man, þat is brouȝt many weies in to sleping of synne. For God haþ ȝovun us þis virtue for to heeren him, and so to heeren pees and charite þat he spekiþ in us; but men ben now redi to heeren of unpees, batailis, and strives, and chidingis of neiȝboris; and cause of sich heeringe is assent to siche þingis, for litil worldli wynning and lesyng of pees. And bi sich heeringe men mai knowe whos children þei ben. We shulden witen þat heeryng
Rom. x. 17.
was graunted to man for to cunne his bileve, as Seint Poul seiþ; and so bileve is of heering, and heering is by Cristis word. And for þis, Crist wole þat men preche þe gospel; and for þis haþ kynde ordeyned þat heering shulde be in a sercle, bifore men, and bihinde men, and on[1] ech side of men, as bileve is of treuþis, bifore us, and bihinde us. And to oure bileve shulde we shape oure heering. And þis is o defaute þat men have in heeringe, þat þei wolen gladli heere fablis, and falschedis, and slaundris of her neiȝbouris, al ȝif þei knowen hem false. But al ȝif sich telleris ben moche for to blame, neþeles sich heereris ben hatid of God. For kynde haþ ȝovun to men to heeren voicis in þe eire, and not in erþe bineþen us, where voices comen not; in tokne þat we shulden ȝyve oure wittis to trowe þing þat mai be in eire, þat is aboven us, which

[1] So E; *oon*, A.

þing profitiþ to oure soule. And if we heeren sich falsenes þat we wite profitiþ not, we shulden not heeren but wiþ peyne, and trowe not þerto, and algatis fle sich men þat tellen sich talis; for God haþ ȝovun us heeringe to heeren his workes, þat ben moo and sutiler þan þis witt wole suffise to.

The cure of the deaf and dumb man.

And herfore þe gospel telliþ how Crist dide a miracle, and heelide a deef man and domb upon þis manere: Crist toke him aside fro þe comune peple, and putte his fyngris in his eeris, and wiþ his spitting touchide his tonge, and ȝaf him þanne vertue to heeren and to speke. God here techiþ man for to fle fablis þat ben in comune peple, and take hede to him. Þe sutil workes of God ben hise smale fyngris, þat men shulden heer and trowe, and þerwiþ fede þer wittis, and wiþ sich savery treuþis occupien her speechis. And þus mai we þenke how we ben deffe and dumbe; but we shulden wiþ þes two wittis wake to oure God, for he wole have rekenynge, boþe in oure deþ and at þe daie of dome, how we have dispendid vertues þat he haþ ȝovun us.

And siþ we witen not whanne þis rekenynge shal falle, it is a greet wisdom to wake aȝens þis tyme; and herfore seiþ Crist, *Þis þing wite we wel, þat ȝif þe hosebonde wiste whanne þe þeef were to come, certis he wolde wake, and suffre him not to myne his hous*[a]. Þis þeef is þe fend, joyned to man, to tempte him, and to harme him al þat he can, and speciali in tyme þat þis man shulde die; for if he take þeefli virtues fro þis man in hour of hise deeþ, he doiþ þise þefte moost. And ȝif he have maistrie to sle siche a man, he chesiþ sich a tyme whanne he is moost unredi; and þanne he is ful bisie to bringe in þe worste synne, for þanne his ful victorie is endid in þat man. And here men douten comunli, what hour men shal dien, wheþer God shal take hem in her beste tyme. But here we shal wite, þat alle þo þat shal be saif waken in hour of her deþ, and over comen þe fend, and suffren him not þanne to undirmyne her hous. And so þes men dien, whanne þei ben moost ripe. But ȝif þe fend lede hem þanne as his owne servantis, and þei shal be dampned, he waitiþ him a tyme whanne he trowiþ best

[a] In the first Wycliffite version—'suffre not his hous to be undirmynyd.'

to overcome þes men; and so þes men dien in her worste tyme, for in tyme þat þei have þe synne þat evermore shal laste. And þat is þe worste yvel, þat God mai suffre to be; for God mote nedis punishe þis synne in helle wiþouten ende. And for þis peril of þis þeef shulden men waken warli; but, for þis harm of þis þeef is not but bi Goddis jugement, þerfore seiþ Crist to warn alle men; *And þerfore be ȝe redi, for in þat hour þat ȝe hopen not Crist is to come.* For, as it is ofte seid, deeþ is þe þridde þing [a] þat God wole have unknowun to man, for he shulde ever be redi.

The faithful servant.

And, for ech man shulde gouerne alle his wittis, and make hem serve to hise profit, as a man doiþ his meyne, þerfore seiþ Crist þus: *Who, trowest þou, is a trewe servant, þat þe Lord haþ put to be upon his meynè, þat he ȝyve hem mete in good tyme to ete?* Þis Lord is God himsilf, and we ben hise servantis; þis meynè of þis Lord ben alle oure wittis, which we ȝeven mete for to serve God, whanne we leden hem bi resoun to profite to oure soule. *Blessid be þat servant, þat whanne his Lord is comen, he haþ foundun him doinge so unto þis meynè; soþeli Y seie to ȝou, þat he shal putte him upon alle hise goodis, and make him his eire.* Þat man þat doiþ þus shal come to hevene, and þere shal he be Cristis eire, and ful lord of Cristis heritage; and þis lordshipe shal serven to alle Cristis children.

Þe Gospel of oon Confessour and Bishop.

[SERMON LXXVII.]

Homo quidam peregre proficiscens.—Matt. xxv. [14.]

The parable of the talents.

Þis gospel telliþ a parable þat Crist tauȝte his disciplis, and, in hem, alle Cristene men, how þei shulden chaffare here. And þis parable telliþ þe resoun whi men shulden wiseli chaffare þus:—*A man, seiþ Crist, goinge a pilgrimage, clepide hise servantis, and ȝaf hem his goodis. And oon he ȝaf fyve besauntis,*

[a] See p. 236.

and two to anoþer, and to anoþer von, ech on after his owne virtue. And whanne he hadde delid þus, he wente anoon his pilgrimage. And of þes þree servantis, þe first, þat hadde fyve besauntis, wente and wrouȝte in hem, and gat oþer fyve; þe secounde, þat hadde two besauntis, wan oþer two; but he þat took oon, wente and dalf[1] *in þe erþe, and hidde þe monie of his lord wiþouten encreese. And after long tyme cam þe lord of þese servantis and rekenede wiþ hem. And þe firste, þat hadde fyve besauntis, cam to þe lord and offride him oþer fyve, and seide; Lord þou ȝavest me fyve besauntis, lo I have geten over*[2] *oþer fyve. And his lord seide to him; Wel be þe, good servaunt and trewe; for þou was trewe of litil, upon many þingis Y shal putte þee; entre in to þe joie of þi lord. Þe secounde cam nyȝe þat hadde two besauntis, and seide; Lord þou ȝavest me two besauntis, lo, oþer two have Y wonne ouer. And his lord seide to him; Wel be þee, good servaunt and trewe; for þou was trewe of fewe þingis, Y shall putte þee upon many þingis; entre into joie of þi lord.*

Interpretation of the parable.

Þis o man þat wente þus in þilgrimage is comunli seid, oure Lord Jesus Crist, for he is o man among alle oþere. His wendinge on pilgrimage is taken on two maners; comunli it is takun for his steyng in to hevene, for dwellinge in hevene is strange to mannis fleish. Þe secounde maner of pilgrimage of þis o man is clepid dwellinge in þis world bi manheed of Crist; for þis was strange pilgrimage to Cristis Godhede. And algatis in þis pilgrimage clepide Crist hise servantis, and ȝaf hem his goodis to profite wiþal. But þese þre manere goodis ȝovun to þes þree servantis, is comunli understonden upon two maneres, as doctouris varien in þese two pilgrimagis. For as a man is two þingis, þe spirit and þe bodi, so Crist is two kyndis, þe Godhede and þe manhede. As anentis his Godhede, his waundringe here, is pilgrimage; and as anentis his manhede, his steynge to hevene is pilgrimage. And he clepide hise servantis bi a long cleping, fro þe bigynnynge of þe world to þe laste dai, but at þis dai of dome he makiþ a ful rekenyng. And siþ Cristis Godhede is everywhere, he mai wel clepe þese servantis, and ȝyve hem his goodis, siþ þei have nouȝt but of

[1] *dalve it*, E. [2] om. E.

The explanation of St. Gregory.

God. It semeþ þat Gregory meneþ þus þes þree partingis of þes goodis [a]. Sum men have of God her fyve outwittis wiþ her purtenaunce; and þes ben þe firste men þat have þese fyve besauntis. Þe secounde men wiþ two besauntis, ben siche trewe men þat passen not in þese wittis, but have good undirstonding, and þerwiþ riȝtful workes. After þis understondinge, þe þridde servant is wickid men wiþ sutil undirstonding, gaderid of her wittis wiþouten and wiþinne-forþ; but þei failen juste workes answeringe to þese wittis. And þes men delven her wittis in undirstondinge of þis worlde, and profiten not to heveneward, ne to þe Chirche, ne to hem silf.

Another explanation.

Þe secounde undirstondinge of þis parable of Crist is more sutil and traveilous, and acording wiþ þe text, as boþe þes undirstondingis may be aplied to þe text. Þese fyve besauntis of þe firste man ben fyve maner of goodis þat God ȝeveþ to sum men, þat he wole have saved. Goodis of grace ben þe firste, þat Austin telliþ moche bi [b], and fallen to sich men þat lyven to Goddis worship and to profite of her soulis; for þei have ever goodis of grace in all oþer þat þei have. Goodis of kynde ben goodis of vertues, boþe bodili and goostli, bi which a man worchiþ to disserve þe blisse of hevene. Þe þridde ben goodis of fortune þe which God ȝyveþ to men, to serven him and to wynne hem blisse, bi wise delyng of þes goodis; and þus weren Job and Abraham riche, wiþ seintis of þe newe lawe. Þe fourþe manere of goodis þat God ȝeveþ here to men, ben goodis of good fame, þat God grauntiþ in þis world; for sum men have alle þes þree goodis and þerwiþ a good fame, þat þei serven wel to God, and to profit of his Chirche. Þe fifte goodis, ben sparkelis of glorie, þat sum men have here in þis world; þe which ben joie of hevenli blisse þat þei hopen fulli to have, and blisse[1] hem on

[1] *blessen*, E.

[a] S. Greg. *In Evang.* Homil. ix.: 'Quinque ergo talentis donum quinque sensuum, id est exteriorum scientia exprimitur. Duobus vero, intellectus et operatio designatur. Unius autem talenti nomine, intellectus tantummodo designatur.'

[b] It would be idle to seek to illustrate the statement in the text by passages from the works of the great doctor of grace, seeing that hardly a treatise of any length came from his marvellous pen in which the doctrine of the necessity of prevenient grace in order to good works is not more or less enforced.

sum manere [a], þe while þei lyven here on erþe. Þes men ben þe firste servant, þat profitiþ in þes fyve besauntis. Þe secounde servaunt wiþ two besauntis is undirstonden alle siche men þat have in plentee goodis of kynde and goodis of grace, and worchen wiþ hem. Þe þridde servant wiþ o besaunt is undirstonden alle sich men þat have in plente goodis of kynde, and profiten not wiþ þes goodis, for worldli occupacions letten to disserve hem blisse. And þes men delven in þe erþe, and hiden þe goodis þat God haþ ȝovun hem. And to þes þree men, and no moo, partiþ God here hise goodis. Þese two firste worchen wiþ God wiþ witt and wille þat þei have, and turnen al her lyvynge here to worship of God, and profite to his Chirche; and herfore þei maken hem worþi to take fulle goodis at þe dai of dome. And so doublyng of her workes is merite þat þei have added, bi which God makiþ hem able for to have þe blisse of hevene; and alle þese goodis þat men have here ben but litil to hevenli goodis, for þere men shal have fulli alle þe goodis of hevene and erþe.

And God shal grete his trewe servantis þus at þe daie of dome, whanne he shal seie; Come ȝee þat ben blessid, my Fadris children, and take ȝe now þe rewme of hevene, þat was maad redi to ȝou fro þe bigynnynge of þe world. For ever God is making redi þe blis þat hise seintis shal have; and alle þe goodis þat we have here ben now but fewe and litil, to regarde of þe goodis þat we shal have in hevenli blis. For ȝif man shal come to þis joie, he shal have al þat he wole, and as fulli as he wole, and on what manere þat he wole; but here we languishen for oþer havyng þat us falliþ to have in hevene.

The goods of fortune preferred by most men to all the other four

And here men seien þat goodis of fortune ben þe leste of þes fyve, siþ a man wolde skilfulli ȝyve alle þes goodis for his helþe, and heelþe of bodi is good of kinde wiþ oþer partis þat man haþ. And siþ a man shulde chaffare here, and lese all þes goodis of kynde for to wynne him goodis of grace, goodis of grace ben algatis beter. And siþ mannis

[a] De Lyra's explanation does not differ much from this. He interprets the five talents to mean, the goods of nature, those of grace, those of knowledge, those of power, and those of wealth. *Bibl. Sac.* vol. v.

fame, þat is his name writun in þe book of liif, is betere þanne alle þes oþer, and þerof man shulde more joie, þese fourþe goodis ben betere þan þe goodis told bifore. And siþ a man travailiþ here for to gete þe fifte[1] good, it moot nedis be beter þan þei, siþ it is eende of alle bifore. And in travaile aboute þese goodis, and algatis in priis[2] of hem, stondiþ al þe mede in þis liif, and al unþank of peyne of helle; for now þis worlde haþ blindid men aȝens her witt and her resoun, þat goodis of fortune, þat ben lest, ben moost told bi of þes fyve. And for þes, and worldli name, men fiȝten and traveilen hugeli; but al if þes ben goode in kynde, neþeles havynge of hem profitiþ not to man here, but for vertues and goodis of blisse. And ofte it falliþ, þat þis havyng þat philosophris tellen leest bi, harmeþ to man in oþer goodis, for unskilful love of hem; and so in love of mannis soule, wiseli weyed as it shulde be, stondiþ al þe mede of man, þat he haþ here in erþe. Loke þat he love moost his God, siþ he is þe beste þing þat mai be, and siþ, he love[3] him silf, and aungelis wiþ[4] neiȝboris, as þei ben goode. But in þis love, man shal have ordre; as kynde haþ tauȝte him for to love first himsilf, and oþer in kynde after þat þei ben nere to him. And in anoþer ordre of love, betere and ferþere, shal man love more; but þis craft of good love is turned now up so doun, for þis world and worldli goodis passen now in weiȝte of love. And herfore þes worldli men chaffaren aboute worldli goodis, and her traveile wiþ þer bisynesse techen þat þei loven moost þes goodis. And certis þei failen in craft of love, and comen not to þe goode of blisse; and bi þis cause haþ Crist ordeyned his prestis to be not worldli, but to lyve in povert of þis world, and in peyne of her bodi. For þus dide Crist wiþ hise disciplis, and tauȝte us to sue him. And bi þis cause men supposen þat many prelatis of þis Chirche hiden Goddis tresour in þe erþe, to her owne dampnacion; and so at þe daie of dome, God shal not seie, Wel be þee, but God shal seie, austernli; Of þi mouþ Y juge þee, for þou shuldest have þis cunnynge, and lyve þerafter bi þy state[5]. And þus diden þes confessouris, and so þei camen to joie of hevene;

because their love is ill directed.

The last end of the new crusaders.

[1] *fyveþe*, E. [2] *pris*, E. [3] So E; A has *loveþ*. [4] *and*, E.
[5] So E; A reads, *love þerafter bi þe state*, which is nonsense.

and þus þese martiris of þese werres, siþ þei ben þe fendis servantis, ben in martirdom of helle þat shal lasten wiþouten ende. And her techeris more and lesse ben not confessouris of Crist but confessouris of þe fend, whos lawe þei holden and techen.

Þe Gospel of o Confessor and Bishop.

[SERMON LXXVIII.]

Homo quidam nobilis abiit in regionem.—Luc. xix. [12.]

The parable of the ten pounds.

Þis gospel telliþ how men shulden lyve, as þe nexte bifore dide in a lyche parable, and knyttiþ þerto many treuþis. And it mai falle ful wel þat Crist in dyvers tymes seide dyvers parablis, þe which weren of liche sentencis. Crist seiþ þat, *o noble man wente out into a fer contre for to take to him a rewme, and turne aȝen*, whan he hadde do. Doctouris seien comunli þat þis nobleman is Crist, þat wente out of þe Godhede, and bicam man heere in erþe, for to gete him a rewme of þe Churche of trewe men. But Crist lefte not to be God, al if he made his manhede wiþouten; and þus he styede aȝen to hevene, whanne he hadde made þis marchandiȝe[1]. And þis is a noble man, as þis regioun is ferre; for nobler man þan is Crist mai noon be in þis world, siþ speciali God is his Fadir, and his modir is wiþouten synne, and þis child is God and man. But where mai be a nobler man? And as moche as Crist made him lasse, as fer fro Godhede is þis regioun. And here taken many men, how Crist þat is þis noble man was porest man here in erþe, and suffride for us many peynes. And noblei of oure prelatis shulde not lette hem to be pore, siþ þei ben sinful wiþ her eldris, and mai not come to Cristis noblei. And siþ al þat Crist suffride here, he suffride for love of his lawe, he loveþ to litil Crist or his lawe þat grutchiþ aȝens þis poverte. And false glosis seid in þis mater maken prestis synne more grevous, for it is a moche synne a preest to seie Ps. cvi. 6.

[1] *marchaundise*, E.

þat he is Cristis viker, and by auctorite of Crist reuliþ fulli his liif, and ȝit he gabbiþ upon Crist and bi blasfemye bigiliþ þe peple.

Þis *noble man clepide ten servantis*, þat ben alle þe kynde of men, *and ȝaf hem ten besauntis*, þat weren delid among hem; and *bad hem chaffare wiþ þis moneie til þat he come aȝen.* Þes ten besauntis ben alle þe goodis þat Crist ȝaf here to mankynde, and her chaffaryng wiþ þes is her profitable worching; and Crist at þe dai of dome wole axe rekenyng of alle þes. It is no charge to us now to wite how moche þis moneie is, for moneie changiþ ofte in priis, after þat þe prince wole ordeyne. Þe *citisenis of þis noble man* weren hiȝe prestis of þe temple, wiþ scribis and Phariseis; and al þis peple *hatide Crist and senten message after him*, now bi prestis, now bi dekenes, now bi knyȝtis of Heroude, and ever to take Crist in wordis to fynde hem cause to dampne him. And, for þei myȝten not bi her lawe, þei feyneden many gabbingis. And ever þei meneden and seiden in dede, *þat þei wolden not þat Crist rengnede on hem;* and neþeles Crist is hiȝest king and regneþ upon al þis world. And cause of þis rebellioun was þe lore of Cristis lawe, for he tauȝt poverte and mekenesse, and lore to bringe men to hevene; and al þis displeside hem, for þei weren þe fendis children. And þus have cardinalis pursued þe pope[a], and many sugettis her prelatis, and many prelatis pursuen trewe men þat grutchen aȝens her lordship; and alle þes seien in dede þat þei wolen not þat Crist rengne over hem. And for þer message is fals, and failiþ þe ground of truþe, þerfore seiþ God þat þei senden[1] a message bihinde him, for þis[2] is feyned vanite, for to putte treuþe bihinde[3]. *But it is maad*, longe after at tyme of þe dai of dome, þat *Crist cam* aȝen, whanne he had gaderid al his rewme, for þanne shal holi Chirche be hool, and ever dwelle wiþ her kyng. And for hool cumyng of þis rewme we preien in our Pater nosters.

[1] *senten*, E. [2] *and for* þis, A; E om. *and*. [3] om. E.

[a] *pursued the Pope.* This seems to be an allusion to the rejection of Urban after his election by the majority of the Cardinals in 1378. The 'persecution of their prelates by subjects' may possibly refer to the rising of the Commons in 1381 and the murder of Archbishop Sudbury.

Whanne þis kyng shal come aȝen for to juge alle maner men, *he shal bidde clepe hise servantis, to whom he ȝaf bifore his moneie, þat þei shewen how þei hadde chaffarid* wiþ goodis, þat þei hadde take[1] of God[2]. *Þe juste servant come and seide; Lord, þi besaunt haþ getcn ten. And þe kyng seide to him, Wel be þee, goode servaunte; for þou was*[3] *trewe in litil, þou shalt ben havynge power upon ten citees.* Þes ten citees ben alle þe goodis þat seintis shal have in hevene. *And þe toþer servaunt cam, and seide; Lord, þi besant haþ maad fyve. And þe kyng seide to him, And be þou upon fyve citees. And þe þridde wickede servant came, and seide to þe lord; Sire, lo here þi besaunt, put aȝen in a sudarie. For Y drede þee herfore, þat þou art austerne*[4] *man þat takist þing þat þou puttist not, and repest þat þou hast not sowun. Þe king seiþ to him, Of þi owne mouþ Y juge þee, wickide servaunt. Þou seiest, þou wistist þat Y was an austerne man, taking þing þat Y putte not þere, and reping þat Y have not sowun; and whi ȝavest þou not my moneie to þe table*, to be occurid[5], *and Y shulde have axid after my moneie, wiþ oker þerof.*

Þer ben sum men þat lyven here in swete and bisynesse, and casten hem not for to profiten wiþ goodis þat God haþ lent hem for to wynne þe blisse of hevene, as God haþ bodyn hem to do. And þes ben þe þridde servant þat shewiþ Goddis moneie in a cloiþ; for goodis of kynde shal man bringe to Goddis dome, mawgrey[6] his. And his liif in þis world is money wlappid in sweting cloiþ. But God jugiþ sich men of her owne conscience, siþ ech man shulde wite, þat God, over goodis þat he ȝyveþ, axiþ profite of mennis workes; but to men, and noon to him. And so, siþ God puttiþ in chaffare þing to profite bi mennis traveile, men shulden traveile fast þerwiþ for to profite to hem silf; and so God repiþ many þingis þat he sue[7] not bi him silve, for he helpiþ man to worche, and al þe profit he ȝeveþ to man. And þus seiþ Austin[a] þat Goddis oker is leueful and gracious, for God

[1] *taken*, E. [2] So E; A wrongly includes the words *wiþ—God* in the italics. [3] *wast*, E. [4] *an austerne*, E. [5] *to be ocurid*, E, and excludes rightly from the italics; A includes. [6] *magrey*, E. [7] *sewe*, E.

[a] S. Aug. *Enarratio In Psalm. XXXVI.* 'Attende quid facit foenerator. Minus vult dare certe, et plus accipere: hoc fac et tu; da

okuriþ not wiþ man, but ȝif God make þe encrees; and al þe vantage of þis okir, God kepiþ to man and not to him. And so man ȝyveþ Goddis moneie for to drawe at þe table, whanne he puttiþ Goddis ȝyftis to wynne him þe blisse of hevene; and þanne þis kyng haþ encrees to his worship, and mannis profite.

And so seiþ Jesus Crist to aungels þat stonden biside; *Take þis besaunt fro þis þef, and ȝyve it him þat haþ ten besauntis. And þes seintis seiden to Crist, Lord, he haþ ten besauntis.* For evry þing seiþ himsilf, and ech þing seiþ oþer to God; and þus telliþ Cristis jugement to men, þat Crist wole not bigile. For soþe Y seie to ȝou; to ech þat haþ shal it be ȝovun, and bi þis ȝifte shal he have plente; but from him þat haþ not, þat þat he haþ shal be taken awey. For þis is trewe sentence of seintis, þat just men þat han hevene, han alle worldli þingis bi resoun of her Lord: and so alle unjuste men, þat God ȝyveþ helle for her service, have not justli, al ȝif þei semen to have moche. And ȝif þou axe who shal take aweie goodis fro þese uniuste men, siþ þei ben comunli myȝte, and no man dar take fro hem; Crist answeriþ here and mai not gabbe, þis just man to whom God ȝeveþ hevene takiþ fro þis uniuste man þat þat him semeþ to have; and not bi his owne autorite, ne bi strengþe of him silf, but bi autorite of God, and bi vertue of his lawe. And al ȝif worldli men semen to have myche goodis, ȝit þis is a false havynge, for it is unjuste to God; and siþ God is chief lord, þat jugiþ men þus to have and þus to wante bi his lawe, no man shulde aȝen-seie þis. And uniust occupacion, clepid havynge to þis world, is soþeli noon havynge, but holding of oþer mennis goodis[a]. And sum men þat shal be saif, al if þei semen now pore, neþeles þei have now hevene, and alle goodis of þis world: but þis havyng is now hid, and ȝit unknowen to men, for Goddis riȝt is not ȝit put in possessioun. Þis trewe sentence of seintis is now

The property of wicked men is not truly their own

modica, accipe magna. Vide quam late crescat foenus tuum. Da temporalia, accipe aeterna: da terram, accipe coelum. Et cui dabo, forte dicis? Ipse Dominus procedit quem foeneres, qui tibi jubebat ne foenerares.'

[a] This favourite opinion of Wyclif's, that mortal sin invalidates the right to hold property or lordship, both as regards laymen and as regards ecclesiastics, is set forth at large in his *De Dominio Civili* and other treatises. Among the twenty-four propositions condemned by the Synod of 1382 (Lewis, p. 108), was the assertion 'that a civil lord is no lord, a bishop no bishop, a prelate no prelate, whilst he is in mortal sin.'

scorned bi mannis lawe; neþeles seintis have now alle þing þat þei wolen have. And as philosophris seien, havyng is on many maneres. And herfore þis gospel seiþ þat unjust man haþ not sich þing, and þe gospel of Mathew seiþ þat him semeþ to have it; for if man robbe oþer mannis goodis, and waste hem at his wille, neþeles he haþ hem not, but occupieþ þingis þat ben not his.

But Crist spekiþ at þe dai of dome of false prestis, þat weren his enemyes, to angelis and seintis in hevene; þat þei shulden bringe hem bifore hem, and sle hem in his presence, for þei shal be dampned by Goddis jugement. And þis dampnyng to helle is a manere of sleying more noyous þan bodili sleying. And seintis shal here juge wiþ God. And þe storie of þe gospel telliþ, how Crist, whanne he hadde seid þes wordis, wente bifore oþer men and stieden[1] into Jerusalem. And þis bitokeneþ þat þis sentence, al if it be scorned here in erþe, ȝit it is kept saf in hevene, and is above mannis power.

Of oon Confessor and Bishop.

[SERMON LXXIX.]

Videte, et vigilate, et orate.—Mark xiii. [33.]

Þis gospel gaderiþ shortli þe sentence bifore seid, and telliþ how men shal wake, and speciali bishopis. First Crist biddiþ þree þingis þat[2] hav hem in ordre; first, he biddiþ *þat we shal see*, and after þat *we shal wake*, and þe þridde tyme þat *we shal preie*, to contynue þes two. Þe firste is needful to prelatis; for riȝt as þe witt of siȝt shewiþ a man moost wakinge among oþer wittis, so siȝt of Goddis lawe makiþ a man moost wake to God. For þis lawe is bileve, þat man shulde moost stodie inne. Crist biddiþ þat man shulde see, not vanitees of þe world, ne unstable mannis lawe, for boþe þes siȝtis don harm to men, but lawe of Crist þat is book of liif, and Goddis word, Jesus

Clear vision, watchfulness, prayer; virtues specially episcopal.

[1] *styȝede*, E. [2] So E; A has *þan*.

Crist. And so here we ben bodun to eendyn oure firste witt at God. For þe secounde witt, seiþ David, þat he shal heere what God spekiþ in him; for he is certeyn of bileve þat God spekiþ pees to his peple. And so ȝif bullis bidden werre, to kille men for unknowun cause, it is oþer not Goddis bidding, or þe folk is þe fendis peple. Of þe þridde witt seiþ Poul, þat he and his felowis ben good smel of Crist to God, for þei suen Crist in lyvynge. Of þe fourþe witt seiþ þe Psalme; Taste ȝe and understonde, how þat þe Lord is swete, and oþer worldli þingis ben bittere; for al ȝif þei semen swete first, þe laste of hem is bittere as wormod. For þe fifte witt, seiþ Crist; Take my ȝoke upon ȝou, and lerne of me þes two lessouns, þat Y am mylde and meke of hert; for my ȝoke is swete and softe, and my charge is liȝt ynowȝ, siþ it drawiþ men upward, and puttiþ not down to helle. And so shulde we wake wel, and reste þes fyve wittis in God; for if a man have al bileve þat Goddis lawe techiþ ouwher [1], but ȝif he wake in charite, al siȝt of þis man is nouȝt. And þerfore biddiþ þe secound word þat we shulen algatis wake to God. And, for we mai not laste in þis, but ȝif God contynue his grace, þerfore þe þridde word biddiþ þat for þis grace we shulden preie. But, for þe secounde word of wakinge is ful nedeful here to men, and wakinge is loosing of wittis, to perseyve þings present, and it is told of siȝt and heering [a], of oþer þree wittis were to speke.

Ps. lxxxv. 8.

2 Cor. ii. 15.

Ps. xxxiv. 8.

The nature of Christian *savour*.

And first of smelling of a man, more spiritual þan oþer two, as þe nose is more hiȝer in þe heed þan is þe tunge. It is speche of holi writt, þat name þat man haþ in þis lyf to þe jugement of God is smeling of þat man; and so sum men ben good smelling and sum men stinking to God. And þus seiþ Poul, for he was certeyn þat þei sueden Crist in lyvynge, þat þei weren a good odour of Crist to God for her liif; for as we shulden be membris of Crist, so we shulden be odours of Crist. And so we shulden sue Crist here in al oure manere of lyvynge; and ȝif we lyven a contrarie lyf, and go fro Crist spirituali, we ben stinking bifore God bi synne and ypocrisie, for þat synne stinkiþ

[1] *owȝwhere*, E.

[a] See Sermon LXXVI.

moost bifore God of alle oþer. And so, ȝif þat hiȝe prelatis taken þe fame of good name, and gon fro þe weie of Crist, no man stynkiþ more þan þei. And herfore ofte God heeriþ not þe preier of þe comune peple, for þe liif of her prelate is so stinking bifore God. And þus spekiþ Goddis lawe, þat God smellide brent tiþes, for devocioun of hem þat offriden smellide wel unto God; and þus preieþ David þat his preier stretche to God as incense. But stinke unto men, as Goddis children stonke to Pharao, is not moche for to flee, but stinkinge to Goddis jugement; and þus wake we in þis witt þat al oure liif smelle wel to God, for alle þat slepyn in synne ben stynkinge bifore God. Gen. viii. 21; compare Ez. xx. 40, 41. Ps. cxli. 2.

Þe secounde witt of þes þree, is tastinge of mannis tonge; and bi mannis speche mai we wite who tastiþ of Goddis sweetnesse, for þat man haþ delite to speke of God and his lawe. And oþer men ben in feveris, and tasten not of Goddis word, but it semeþ bitter to hem, for her tast is turned amys; and þes moten be goostli heelid, as þei heelen men of feveris. And deedli signe of sich syk men is þat hem wantiþ appetit of Goddis word, þat shulde be her food and lyf, as Goddis lawe techiþ. And herfore techiþ Seint Petre, þat ȝif ony man speke, loke þat he speke Goddis wordis; and bi þis tokene he is hool. Here mai we see how mannis lawis hav distemperid kynde of men, and turned hem into swyn þat þei savere not Goddis word. Taste. 1 Peter iv. 11.

Þe þridde witt is felynge, þat is everywhere in þe bodi, boþe above and beneþe, for it is so nedeful; and herfore haþ kynde ordeyned his instrument bi al þe bodi, al ȝif it take roote of þe herte, in which is jugement of taist. And it is ful nedeful to fede mennis bodi in mesure, for þe bodi serveþ to þe soule, and is horse to it in many goode workes. And þus all þes þree wittis ben more fleishli þan þes oþer two, and moven man unevenli to glotonye and lecherie; and herfore þe fend temptiþ algatis bi þis þridde witt, as he temptide Adam and Eve to ete of þing þat God forbad. And ȝif we þenken on þat state, and how we shulden ever sue God, and how exces and defaute in þe feding of oure fleish, whanne it passiþ good resoun, smacchiþ synne aȝens God, it is ful hard in þis liif to kepe Feeling.

us fro synne of taist; but as his instrument is everywhere as a nett in mannis bodi, so þe fend haþ many wilis, to make man slepe bi þis witt. And neþeles þis wakiþ last, among oþer wittis of man. And so þe fend, bi þis witt, bringiþ deeþ of oþer wittis, and makiþ a man falle fro God in dedeli synne, and fele not, al ȝif his wittis semen opyn to jugement of oþer men. And þis is þe fallinge yvel, in which mennis iȝen ben sum tym opyn, and ȝit þei mai no more see, þan an ymage þat haþ noo witt. For her nerves of charite, bi which þei shulden love God moost, failen in her herte, and þere þei shulde moove her lymes to serve God. And þus we shulde wake to God in þre wittis of our soule.

Responsibility of Christian ministers.

Þe resoun þat Crist telliþ whi we shulden wake þus is told bifore bi Mathew, how we witen never whanne þe Lord comeþ. *For ȝe witen never*, seiþ Crist, *whanne is tyme* for to wake; *as a man þat wente in pilgrimage lefte his house, and ȝaf power to his servantis of ech work* of his hous, *and bad his porter wake wele.* Þis man þat wente in pilgrimage is Jesus Crist, boþe God and man, and lefte þe goodis of his Chirche in mannis hondis after him. And so alle þe goodis of þis world haþ he put in mennes hondis, but speciali in prelatis hondis; whom he biddiþ kepe his Chirche, and speciali soulis, þat þei shulden kepe and teche hem bi Goddis lawe. And siþ Cristis Chirche is men þat shal after be saf in hevene, and þes men hav here al þis world, and moche more þis grete prelatis, þes shulden kepe alle Goddis workes, and algatis wake in charite. For þei shulden be fisheris to God, and open and shette þe dore of hevene bi þe keies þat God haþ ȝovun, oonli to profite to þe Chirche. And þus it semeþ to manye þat no man shulde take prelacie ne cure of soulis but in greet drede, lest þei weren unable to God and sich men þat shulden be dampned; and þe sheep shulden be savyd. For þanne her care of prelacie doiþ hem moche harm of soule, algatis ȝif þei taken sich cure for wynnynge or worldli worship; for God ȝyveþ men cure ynouȝ, and speciali unto his prestis, to whiche he ȝyveþ power and wit to govern his Chirche after his lawe; whereto shulde men take more care, siþ þis is hard and mouche ynowȝ. Þus Petre and oþer apostlis token care of

Cristis Chirche, and not bi chesing of man and jurisdiccioun þat is now usid.

But it is drede now þat prestis kepen dritt and vanite, and to þis is her entent; and herto þei shapen lawis. For þe lawe þat Crist haþ ȝovun, and þe chesinge þat he haþ chosen, were ynowȝ to governe his Chirche wiþouten lawis now maad. And office for to preche þe gospel, wiþ few oþer sacramentis, weren service liȝt and ynowȝ to siche preestis for to kepe; and þis diden Petre and Poule and oþer apostlis everychon. Þei stryven not for mannis choise, ne for jurisdiccioun, for ȝit was not þe Churche dowid, for to take þes worldli goodis, but for to take mede of Crist for good kepinge of his Chirche. And not al oonli siche preestis have keping of Cristis Chirche, but kingis and princis of þis world, as Ysidere beriþ witnesse [a]. And so ech man þat God ȝyveþ power and witt for to knowe his wille, shulden, after her power and witt, profite to Cristis Churche; for God wole þis streitli at domes dai of alle siche men. For God haþ ȝovun þese men siche power to serve God þus in erþe; and to profite to her modir holi Churche þat þei shulde helpe. And þis bond is streite ynowȝ, al ȝif man made noon oþer bond, for þis bindiþ ech man to profite to his modir. What nede is it to make newe bondis, þe which done more harm þan good, and man can neiþer kytte ne loose, but if God telle hem speciali.

Kings and princes are keepers of Christ's Church as well as priests.

And herfore biddiþ Crist men wake, and speciali for þis

[a] I am again indebted to the kindness of Professor Stubbs for pointing out to me the curious passage to which the text probably refers. It is in the *Sententiae* of Isidore, Bishop of Seville, lib. iii. cap. li, and is so interesting in itself, that I quote it at some length:—'Principes seculi nonnunquam intra Ecclesiam potestatis adeptae culmina tenent: ut per eandem potestatem disciplinam Ecclesiasticam muniant. Ceterum intra Ecclesiam potestates necessariae non essent, nisi ut, quod non praevalet sacerdos efficere per doctrinae sermonem, potestas hoc imperet per disciplinae terrorem. Saepe per regnum terrenum celeste regnum proficit, ut qui intra Ecclesiam positi contra fidem et disciplinam Ecclesiae agunt, rigore principum conterantur; ipsamque disciplinam quam Ecclesiae humilitas exercere non praevalet, cervicibus superborum potestas principalis imponat; et ut venerationem mereatur, virtute potestatis impertiat. — Cognoscant principes saeculi Deo debere se rationem reddere propter Ecclesiam, quam a Christo tuendam suscipiunt. Nam, sive augeatur pax et disciplina Ecclesiae per fideles principes, sive solvatur; ille ab eis rationem exiget, qui eorum potestati suam Ecclesiam credidit.'

Christ's exceeding love for his Church.

cause:—*for þei witen not whanne þe lord of þis house shal come*, in tyme of mennis deþ, ne in tyme of his laste dome. And þanne he shal speke in þis cause moost sharpli of alle oþer. For þis cause he chargiþ moost; siþ he loveþ more his Chirche þan ony persone þerof, and bad alle to worshipe þis modir boþe in þe olde lawe and in þe newe. And, for God shal come privyli to þes two jugementis at unknowinge of men, þerfore he is seid to come *on þe nyȝt*. A nyȝt is partid in foure houres; as *evenynge and mydnyȝt, cockis crowinge and morewnynge;* and alle þes houres ben unknowun. For if we departe our lif to our deþ in foure houris, or tyme to þe laste dome in four houris, evene to hemsilf, we witen never how nyȝ or ferre is þe comynge of þis Lord. And algatis, ȝif we wole be saved, we moten waken fro synne, so þat we be not foundun þanne on deed sleep. For þe trumpe shal waken us, ouþer to blisse or to peyne. And þis Lord shal dampne alle þo þat he shal þanne fynde sleping; for ech man þat shal be saved shal be clene at þe dai of dome. And þus Crist spekiþ generali, to printe þis love in alle mennis hertis; *þat þing þat Y seie to ȝou, Y seie to alle,—wake ȝe.*

Þe Gospel of oon Confessor and Doctour.

[SERMON LXXX.]

Vos estis[1] *sal terre.*—Matt. v. [13.]

The salt of the earth.

Þis gospel is seid of Crist, as it semeþ to many men, to alle þo þat he ȝyveþ witt to profite to his Churche. But it is seid speciali to bishopis, and to confessouris, and to techeris of Goddis lawe, for to alle þes God ȝyveþ salt. And Crist telliþ to alle siche what office þat þei shal have, and whanne þei faile in her office, and what wise þei shal be punished. First seiþ Crist to þes servantis: *ȝe ben salt of þe erþe. And ȝif þe salt vanishe awey, in what þing shal þe erþe be saltid? Þis salt is not worþ after but to be casten out and be defoulid of men,* þat shulden

[1] So E; *Vos qui estis*, A.

take hede to þis salt. Þis salt of þe erþe ben techeris þe whiche bi þe lawe of Crist speken sharpli to men, and tellen hem þer defautis. Þis þei done to erþeli men whanne God rubbiþ by hem his lawe. We shal first wite þe kynde of salt, and siþ what properties it haþ. And bi þis mai we wite where men þat comen as apostlis done þe office of her stat, or ellis þei failen of her office. Clerkis seien þat salt is maad of gravel and of water, wiþ hete of þe sonne or of fier, and maad hard wiþ blast of þe wynd. And by Aristotlis reule it is dissolved bi þe contrarie [a]. And so cold þing and moist dissolvyþ salt, siþ hote þing and drie makiþ it hard. Þes disciplis ben made salt, þat sum tyme weren unstable as gravel, bi þe water of baptem, and hete of charite, and wynd of þe Holi Goost, to savore men as salt doiþ. And þes ben maad whittere þan snow fro þe blaknes of her synne. And kynde of water saddid in hem bitokeneþ þe stable witt of God. And þus, for Goddis lawe commandiþ in offringe to be devocion and hete of charite, þerwiþ Goddis lawe biddiþ, in figure of þis, in ech offringe to be salt offrid. And þus shulden doctours teche þe peple how þei shulden lyv to God, and how þei shulden do here almes. For ȝif coveitouse men rubben to hem, þei ben not salt but cold water.

The composition of salt.

Many propirteis ben of salt, and to telle few here is ynowȝ. O propirte of salt is þat it makiþ fleish drie and kepiþ it fro rotting and fro stinkinge and fro wormes. So prestis, bi Goddis wordis, shulden have hem to fleishli men. Þei shulden drie hem from lecherie, and kepe hem from yvel conscience, and fro stynking of synne, and þanne þei hav þe kynde of salt. And þus salt makiþ mete savory, and salt makiþ þe erþe bareyne, and salt heliþ fleishli woundis whanne it is stoppid in hem. Bi þes þre propirtees of salt shulden doctours worchen in fleishli men, and avoide hem fro ivel workis, and make hem bareyne fro fleishli dedis. And þei shulden savore Goddis wordis, and declare hem bi resoun, and pronounce hem to þe peple, as þes wordis wolden plese to hem. And þus depe woundis in man þat weren groundid

The properties of salt.

[a] οὐδὲν δοκεῖ ἅμα τὰ ἐναντία ἐπιδέχεσθαι. *Categ.* 6, 18; compare *Topicorum*, ii. 7, 4.

in old synne shulden be heelid bi virtue of God. And þanne men kepten þe kynde of salt, and failing in ony of þes wolde make failinge in oure salt.

And þus mai men wite wher bishopis or oþer prechours to þe peple failen in þis kynde of salt, or ellis done treuli her office. Crist techiþ þat ȝif þei faillen þei shal be cast out, and defoulid of men, and to þes two ben þei worþi. And þis shal be at þe last dome, whanne þese false men shal be cast out into þe fier of helle and to be defoulid of many men. But, as many þenken, sich men shulden be punishid here, and be put out of her office and be defoulid of oþer men. Þus þe wise kyng

1 Kings ii. 26. Salomon tretede þe hiȝe preest of his fadir. For siþ lordis shulden reule Cristis Chirche, and þes don so moche harm þerto, a greet charite were it in lordis to put doun þes Goddis enemyes, and bi forme of Goddis lawe to maken hem serve in her office. And þis is oon þe moste defaute þat rengneþ now in þe Chirche. Þese prelatis þat shulden be salt and

Col iv. 6. make Goddis lawe savory—for, as Seint Poul techiþ, oure word shulde be savorid wiþ salt—þei ben now fresh brotel[1] and stinkinge, and turnid al fro þe kynde of salt, and wiþ stinkinge wordis and lawe þei maken Goddis lawe unsavery.

Wealth the cause of the corruption of the clergy.

And goodis put in preestis possessioun is rote of al þis synne; for þei wolden ellis be stable as salt and savoren her word and stonde þerbi, and suffre for Goddis lawe deþ, and districe þe fendis lawe. But now þei ben fresh as foolis and wanten witt

Matt. xxiv. 12. and charite. And herfore þe charite of many wexiþ cold, as Crist haþ told.

Light and its properties.

Þe secound word of þis gospel seiþ to þes Cristis disciplis: *ȝe ben liȝt of þe world.* And foure propirtees ben in liȝt, þat shulden acorde to þese techeris; and þanne Crist seiþ soþ of hem as he dide of his apostlis. Þe first propirte of liȝt stondiþ in þis þing, þat among bodili qualitees liȝt is more spiritual. Þe secounde propirte of liȝt stondiþ in þis þing, þat among bodili formes liȝt is moost general, for it bringiþ forþ alle þing þat groweþ here in erþe. Þe þridde propirte of liȝt stondiþ in þis, þat in al his worchinge it worchiþ bi ordre; for

[1] *britil*, E.

reule of þe[1] hiȝe kynd ledip liȝt ever. Þe fourþ propirte of liȝt stondiþ in þis, þat among oþer qualitees it confortiþ more man; for a man kyndeli hidousiþ derknesse and is gladid bi liȝt as oure witt telliþ. As anentis þe firste propirte prelatis shulde be spiritual, and holden hem paied of litil bodili goodis; for so dide Crist and Baptist and oþer apostlis; but now þei axen worldli fare in fode and aray. As anentis þe secounde propirtee, prelatis shulden be comun and profite to alle men, and acorde wiþ hem in goode, and be to alle alle þingis, as Seint Poul was. For he shulde grutche aȝens nouȝt but þat þat smacchiþ synne. After þe þridde propirte prelatis shulden worche wiseli, now prechinge, now preiynge, now wel lyvynge. And what liif ever þei lyveden shulde[2] profite to þe Chirche, and wher þei myȝten more profite, more þei shulden worche. After þe fourþe propirte a prelat shulde ȝyve confort to lyve after Crist, and fle derkenes of synne, and nevere speke of peyne but for þis entent, to make men fle synne and ȝyve hem to virtues. And al þe lif of prelatis shulde sowne counfort to þe peple. And shortli, noþing falliþ to þe reule of preestis þat it ne is ensamplid in propirtees of liȝt. Liȝt worchiþ redili, and boþe in fair and in foule, and takiþ not but beyng of þe place to which it profitiþ. And þus shulde prestis be liȝt of þis world, and gendre witt and charite among men þat þei delen wiþ.

The clergy should be the city set on a hill.

Þe þridde tyme lickeneþ Crist his clerkes to *a cite*, and seiþ, *þat it may not be hid whanne it is sett on a hill.* Prelatis shulde be a citee and take fleying of þe contre whanne þei ben pursued of her goostli enemyes. Liȝt and al maner of fode shulde þis cite hav, þat ȝif it failide in þe contre þere shulden men fynde it. Al maner of marchaundise shulde it have to selle, and store þe contre wiþouten ony charging; for goostli þing encresiþ whanne it is more usid. And so as Ysaye techiþ, þei shulden not chaffere wiþ moneie; but as þei token freeli of God so shulden þei ȝyve freeli. This cite shulde be sett upon an hill, þe which hil is Jesus Crist, þat is hied over oþer hillis as Ysay telliþ. For Crist is fondement and hill and dore bi many resouns. And no man shulde take þis state but in virtu of Crist, lest he be a smoky hill, wyndi, and of yvel wedris. Is. 1. 1.

[1] om. E. [2] So E; *shulden*, A.

And like the candle set on a candlestick.

Þe fourþe liknesse of Crist is of *a liȝt lanterne þat men putte on a candelsticke in a derk hous, þat men þat comen in see soone liȝt.* And, for sich prelatis ben not liȝt in kynde, þerfore þei ben likned of Crist to a lanterne; and wyndis of þis world shulden not quenche her liȝt. Þe candilsticke þat þei ben inne shulde be Cristis lawe. And so, ȝif a prelate implie him wiþ seculer nedis, he crepiþ undir a bushel and failiþ of his liȝtyng. *Þis hous is* holi Chirche, to which prelatis shulde profite wiþouten envie for taking of her liȝt. And herfore biddiþ Crist to his disciplis, *þat her liȝt shal shyne in presence of men, þat þei see her goode workes, and so þanke God of hevene.* And here mai we see how dowing of þe Chirche is not tauȝt of Crist, but evene þe contrarie of it. For bi þis prestis ben hid under þe bushel, and þe peple seeþ not þer postlis workes, but workes of þe world. And þei glorifie not God bi hem, but preisen þe emperour. And wise men holden him a fool, for he derkide þus þe Chirche. And, for men myȝten seien þat Crist cam to unbinde þe lawe, and so office of his preestis shulden chaunge fro þe olde lawe, as Anticristis prestis serven now to þe world,—herfore seiþ Crist, *þat men shulden not gesse þat he cam to louse þe lawe, but for to fulfille it.* And so as preestis in þe olde lawe weren bisee aboute her bestis, so prestis in Cristis lawe shulden be more spiritual, and liȝtne folk bi þe gospel, and bicome profetis. But þe fend haþ turned þis work al to worldli liif, alȝif disciplis of þis worlde shulden have here her blisse. And for filling of þis law Crist seiþ þus: *Soþeli, Y seie to ȝou, til þat hevene and erþe passe aweie, an i ne a title shal not passe fro þe lawe bifore alle þingis ben doone.* And þis word of Crist is aȝens lawe of Anticrist, for Crist spekiþ here of þe old lawe of God, and wole þat, as longe tyme as hevene goiþ aboute, and peple dwelliþ here in erþe by chaunging of men, þe leste mandement of God, [is][1] undirstonden bi leste lettre[a], ne þe leste counseil, or þe witt of ceremonie, shall not passe fro Goddis lawe til þe dai of dome come. For alȝif Anticrist have brouȝt a lawe þat lettiþ þe use[2] of Goddis lawe, ȝit þe treuþe

[1] om. E; rightly. [2] So E; *uss*, A.

[a] Yōdh, or iōta, the smallest letter in the Hebrew alphabet.

of Goddis lawe and þe dette to usen it lastiþ evermore and bindiþ men ful harde. And it is not liȝt to unbinde oon of Goddis heestis; for Crist bihetiþ here; *Þat who ever doiþ þus he shal be clepid leste in þis Chirche wanderinge*, siþ þe Chirche above jugiþ him in þis Chirche and not of þe Chirche, but to be dampned in helle. And þis cleping of þe Chirche above mut nedelingis stonde; but defending and teching of þe lawe of God makiþ a man clepid of him grete in þe blisse of hevene.

Of oon Confessour and Abbot.

[SERMON LXXXI.]

Nemo accendit lucernam.—Luc. xi. [33.]

How Christian men are to keep themselves in the state of salvation.

Þis gospel techiþ how ech confessour shulde kepe him, and speciali abotis and þes newe religiouse. But, as it semeþ to juste men, Crist telliþ litil bi þes ordris, but telliþ ech man of his Chirche how he[1] shal profite þerto, and how he shal kepe himself in state of salvacioun. First spekiþ Crist in figuratife speche, and seiþ þat, *no man liȝtiþ a lanterne* in derknesse, *and puttiþ it* in oon of þes two infamous[2] places; *neþer in hid place*[3] *ne undir a bushel.* Ech man shulde be a lanterne liȝtid of God. Þe bodi of þis lanterne is mannis bodi; þe hornes of þis lanterne ben spiritis in man, and þe remanent of his bodi, as fleish and boon, ben oþer tres[4] in which þis horn is picchid. Þe liȝt in þis lanterne is mannis soule, and liȝtnynge wiþinneforþ is witt þat God ȝeveþ man. Þat man puttiþ his lanterne in hidd place or undir a bushel, þat lyveþ in worldli bisynes and not profiteþ to þe Chirche. For God haþ ȝovun him soule and witt, to liȝt men here in erþe þat ben in derknes of synne, as ech man shulde liȝte to oþere; for ech man haþ sum knowing þat failiþ to anoþer man; and so ech man shulde be lanterne to liȝtne sum men of Goddis hous; and herfore ȝeveþ God

[1] So E; *we*, A. [2] *famous*, E [3] *placis*, E. [4] *trees*, E.

þis liȝt to liȝte sum men in þis world. And þanne þe liȝt failiþ in þis lanterne whanne þe man is deed in bodi. And ȝif he be deed in good workes þis lanterne is deed in a man. But riȝt as lanterne wantiþ of himsilf liȝt to shyne wiþinne or wiþout, so mannis bodi wantiþ of himsilf liȝt of liif and of witt.

And so God biddiþ þis lanterne to be put *on hye on a candilsticke to ȝeve men liȝt in Goddis hous*, and algatis to liȝt þis hous. And so þis candilsticke may be state þat God approveþ to þis ende,
Apoc. i. 20. as sevene candilstickis of gold ben sevene statis of bishopis.
The religious inutility of cloistered orders. And, as many men þenken, alle þes newe religious ben hid bi mannis ordenaunce to bere liȝt to Cristis Chirche; for ȝif a man be closid in a cloistre, what profitiþ he, bi Cristis ordenance, to make liȝt to his broþer þat feliþ not of his profit? And þus closing of þes cloistres, or hiȝe housis, þat men hav foundun, is biside Cristis lawe, foundun of prince of þis erþe. And so alle þes ben yvel hid fro profit of holi Chirche.

The single eye. And þus spekiþ Crist generali to Cristen men, and seiþ, *Þe lanterne of þi bodi is þin iȝe*. And þat is on double manere; for sum men hav *a simple iȝe, and þat eiȝe liȝtiþ al þe bodi; and ȝif þin eye be wayward, ȝhe, þi bodi shal be derk*. Here is þe lanterne clepid, þe liȝt þat shulde be in þis lanterne; for þis liȝt is þe ende wherfore God haþ maad þis lanterne. And ȝif þis liȝt be of riȝt entent þanne is þin iȝe simple; as men þat wolen profite to Cristis Chirche, after Goddis lawe, hav a riȝt eiȝe and a simple, even after Goddis wille. And so a simple þing is seid wiþouten folding fro þis riȝt. And þe liȝt of charite shyneþ in
1 Cor. xiii. 5. siche a lanterne; for as Poul seiþ :—Charite sekiþ not his owne wynnyng, but how it myȝte best profite to many men of þe Chirche. But he haþ a blynd eyȝe turned aweyward from God þat sekiþ more his owne wynnyng þan profit of Cristis Chirche; and in þis angle of þis eiȝe is derknesse fro charite. And þes men wanten liȝt of God, þat shulden shyne riȝtli bi hem. And but ȝif Goddis grace worche bi hem, þei ben derke as to merite. And so seiþ Crist, þat simple iȝe makiþ al þe bodi shynyng, and iȝe þat is turned amys makiþ þe bodi al derk. And þe bodi may be clepid þe multitude of mannis workes, or mannis liif, þat is medeful or sinful bi sich ententis; for bi þes man haþ charite or wantiþ charite in his workes. And herby

mannis lyf is medeful or dampnable bi Goddis lawe. And þus þe charite of Crist stretchiþ riȝtli wiþouten angle, to profit of Cristis Chirche, and not to profit of him silf. And þus Poul souȝte many mennis profit, and not his owne worldli wynnyng; for sich entent is algatis derk, and liȝt of God goiþ not þerby. 1 Cor. x. 33.

And herfore biddiþ Crist to us *þat we shulde see þat liȝt in us be not derknesse*, bi yvel entent; for þanne it is an yvel liȝt. No man is here in erþe þat ne God ȝeveþ him sum liȝt: as sum knowing and sum entent in coveiting of sum good. And ȝif þis liȝt be riȝtful, wiþouten angle of crokidnesse, þanne Goddis grace shyneþ wiþ him, and ellis his liȝt is derknesse; for sich crokidnesse bringiþ aȝen derknesse of mannis liif. *And so, ȝif al þi bodi be al shynynge, havynge noo part of derknesse, it shal be shynyng al, and it shal liȝtne þee as a lanterne of shynyng.* Þes wordis semen superflu and seid of Crist wiþouten witt. But it is aȝens bileve to trowe þus of Cristis wordis; and þerfore we shal undirstonde þat þer ben two goodnessis in workes; goodnesse in kynde of workes, and goodnesse in vertues. Þe firste mai be wiþouten þe secounde, but þe secounde is þe betere; as ȝif a man bi ypocrisie ȝyve good to nedi men, þan his ȝyvyng is good and his work is ful of liȝt; but it haþ oonli liȝt of kynde and not liȝt of vertues. And þis techiþ Crist us: þat ȝif al þe bodi of oure workes be shynyng bi liȝt in kynde, and hav noo part of derknesse, neiþer in kynde ne in vertues, þanne it shal be al liȝt bi double liȝt of kynde and vertues. And þis secounde liȝt of vertues men shulden moche telle bi, and fle derknes in vertues, al ȝif þei have liȝt in kinde. For God lokiþ to þis secounde liȝt, and blessiþ men in hevene þerfore; and for þe first liȝt of kynde a man mai be depe dampned in helle: as ȝif þou bi ypocrisie do good to þi neiȝbore, and die in þis ypocrisie, þou shalt be depe dampned in helle; and for þis good þat þou didist þou shalt be dampned wiþouten ende. And ȝif þou ponishe a man of þe Chirche, for double love þat þou hast, boþe to þe Chirche and to þis man, al if þou erre in þis man, supposing þat he be yvel, and he be good to siȝt of God, and God excusiþ þi ignoraunce for derkness hid to þee; ȝit þou maist be saif in hevene for þis yvel werk in his

Objective goodness and subjective goodness.

kynde, and goodnesse þat it haþ in vertues[a]. And þerfore loke to þis godenesse. And þus seiþ Crist: þat ȝif þi workes ben alle ful of liȝt of kynde, and þei have noo derkness of vertues, þanne þei shal be algatis liȝt, and liȝten þee as lanterne of shynyng. And þus þou shuldist riȝte þi iȝe, and alȝatis from derknes of vertues. And ȝif þou have þes two liȝtis, it makiþ more shynyng to þee. But algatis have þis secounde liȝt; for wiþouten it is noȝt medeful. And herfore seiþ Crist here, þat þis bodi of þi workes shal liȝte þee as a lanterne of shynyng bi Goddis grace. And þus, ȝif we studien wel, þes wordis of Crist, þat semen unsavery, and rehersid wiþouten witt, ben ful of witt þat men shulde knowe; siþ mannis entente shulde be reulid bi riȝtnes of his vertues, and man shulde also be bisie to done his workes good in kynde. But riȝtnes of þis oþer entent is algatis nedeful to man, siþ mannis entent moot nedis be reulid bi þe lawe of God, þat he do bi charite alle hise workes þat he doiþ. And so blyndenesse of þe first liȝt takiþ man in excusing; but blyndnesse of þe secounde liȝt mai no way be excusid. But boþe þes blyndenessis shulden be fled; siþ þe firste bringiþ in þe toþer.

Application to the friars.

And blyndenes of þes newe ordris makiþ many men to be dampned; siþ þe state of preestis þat Crist ordeyned was liȝt and esi for to knowe, but þe fend marieþ[1] manye wiþ newe statis þat he brouȝt inne; and he mooveþ hem to speke aȝens þe lore þat Crist haþ tauȝt. And, for þes derke wordis of Crist maken many men to muse, men seken divers weies to undirstonde Cristis wordis:—as sum men seien þat Crist techiþ here, þat ȝif alle workes of þi liif be, at þi deþ, shynynge by grace, þei shal be shynyng after in hevene, and liȝte þee as a lanterne of briȝtnes; for men shal after be briȝt in hevene, moche more þanne we wenyn[2] here. How ever Crist undirstood, we bileve þes wordis ben soþ, and ful of resoun and witt, and knowun to hem þat he wole shewe it.

[1] *marriþ*, E. [2] *wenen*, E.

[a] 'In kynde,' that is, objectively, the persecution of an innocent man is an evil work; but 'in vertues,' or subjectively, and by virtue of your pure intention, it may be a good work, and may help to make you 'saif in hevene.'

þE GOSPEL ON FEESTIS OF MANY CONFESSOURS.

[SERMON LXXXII.]

Sint lumbi vestri praecincti.—LUC. xii. [35.]

Þis gospel techiþ alle men how þat þei shulden lyve to Crist, but speciali prelatis, þat shulden be li3t to þe peple. And so, for confessours kepten þis lore in her liif bifore oþer men, þerfore þe Chirche rediþ þis gospel whanne men seien of confessouris. First Crist biddiþ to his disciplis, *þat her lendis be girdid bifore, and lanternes brennynge in her hondis, as þei shulden bide her Lord whanne he comeþ a3en fro bridalis.* Þes lendis þat Crist spekiþ of ben þe fleishli kynde joyned wiþ þe soule. And þes lendis helpen þe spirit upon two maneres; and for þes two maneris þei ben clepid lendis. Þis fleish serveþ to þe soule, suffringe as it shulde suffre, and doinge as it shulde do, whanne it is tau3t wel of þe soule. And þus seiþ Poul [a], þat Crist was in Abrahams lendis. And so Crist techiþ here chastite, as Gregory seiþ [b];—but not oonli chastite but alle fleishli vertues. Þes lendis ben girded bifore, whanne man, by discrescioun, drawiþ from his fleish þe norishment þerof; or chastiseþ it, on oþer manere, bifore it falle in synne. Brennynge lanternes ben medeful workes þat men have in her vertue, bi whiche þei shulden worche; and, for þes workes comen boþe of bodi and of soule, þerfore þei ben clepid of Crist two lanternes, and þei ben in oure hondis whanne we worchen wiþ hem. For it is not ynow3 to kepe us fro synnes, but if we worken gode workes bi þes two lanternes. The saintly life.

But for þes bridalis, we shal wite þat þei ben taken on many maneres; first for þe weddingis þat Crist is joyned wiþ þe soule; after for þe dwellinge þat Crist dwelliþ wiþ þe soule; The lord's return from the wedding.

[a] Compare Hebrews vii. 10, Gal. iii. 17. The writer of the sermon appears to have misunderstood the first of these passages.

[b] S. Greg. Homilia xiii. 'Lumbos enim praecingimus, cum carnis luxuriam per continentiam coarctamus.'

and þe þridde for þe goostli fode þat soulis ben fed wiþ Crist in blisse. And so þei ben þree weddingis þat Crist is weddid here; first whanne he toke mankynde, and made it oo persone wiþ him; after whanne he takiþ his Chirche, and makiþ it oo spouse wiþ him; þe þridde wedding is particuler, whanne Crist takiþ oo soule to him. And so Crist is seid to turne aȝen fro bridalis on two maneris. First, whanne a man is deed þat Crist haþ ordeyned to come to blisse, Crist turneþ aȝen to his soule from dwelling wiþ þe Chirche in hevene. But Crist leveþ not þis Chirche, but on new manere dwelliþ wiþ þis soule. But þanne he must have dwelt bifore, or ellis þis soule cam not bi þis state. And so we shulden be liche to men þat abiden þe comynge of Crist, in tyme of deþ, or þe dai of dome. And þis abiding shulde alle men marke, for þis comyng is uncertein, and þis tyme is perilous; siþ þis drauȝt mot be wel drawen ȝif oure liif shal ouȝte profite. And so to þes comyngis of Crist shulde ech man make him redi; siþ Crist shal come and knocke at doris, and entre to hem þat ben wakinge, and redi to resseyve Crist wiþouten sleping in synne. And þis openyng shal be doon anoon, as liȝtnyng of sonne[1] is in þe eir. And so Crist knockiþ at oure doris whanne he techiþ us signes of deþ, or signe of þe dai of dome; but þe laste knockyng is sudeyne. Ȝif a man be redi bifore to dwellen wiþ Crist wiþouten ende, þanne he openeþ to Crist, siþ þis openyng is redynesse. And þus seiþ Crist ful soþli, *þat þes servauntis ben blessid whiche, whanne þe Lord comeþ, he findeþ þus wakinge. Soþeli, Y seie to ȝou, þat þis Lord shal girde him, and make hem sitte to mete, and passe and mynystre to hem.* Þe sitting to mete of seintis, is confermyng of hem in blisse; þe passing of þis Lord bi hem is his shewing to oon and oþer. And al ȝif þis shewing be togidere, ȝit her taking is divers; and her diversite is signefied bi þis passing of Crist. Þis service is liȝt to Crist, for it is but Cristis shewing of his Godhede, and his manhede, in which seintis shal be fed.

Opening to him.

And ȝif þis Lord come in þe secounde vigile, and eke in þe þridde, and fynde sich redynesse in þes servantis, ful blessid ben þes servantis, siþ þei anoon ben blessid of God. Þes þre vigiles þat Crist telliþ

The meaning of the three watches;

[1] *sunne*, E.

of here, ben þre wakingis fro synne, and algatis fro þe laste synne þat is þe worste yvel þat mai be; and so we preien in þe Pater noster God to delyvere us fro þis yvel. Þes vigiles ben clepid þre, for þe Holy Trinite, for þouȝt of resoun of him, shulde make men to wake wel. And so ech tyme þat man lyveþ here is departid in þree parties, and tyme to þe dai of dome is also departid in þree; and, for þe quantite of þes þree is uncertein to man, þerfore he shulde ever wake, and þanne he wakiþ þes þree vigilis. Þe first þree haþ ech seint, bifore þe soule go fro þe bodi; þe toþer þre haþ þe Chirche, bifore þe dai of dome come. And so unknowing of þes tymes, and knowinge how men shulden ever wake, profitiþ unto Goddis children, as done alle þingis. As Poul seiþ [a], bi þat þat we knowun not þe quantite of þes þre tymes, shulden we ever more be in drede and ever wake out of synne.

And þis lore techiþ Crist in a parable to his children. *Þis þing he seiþ, wite we*[1] *wel þat ȝif þe housebonde wiste what tyme þe*[2] *þeef wolde come*, and stele his goodis, *he wolde wake warli, and suffre not þis þeef þus to breken his hous*, and spoylen him. It is touchid bifore [b] how þis þeef is þe fend, þat doiþ al his diligence to tempte man whanne he shal die. For ech man and a fend ben couplid togider in a liste and fiȝten boþe niȝt and dai, and algatis whanne þe fend hopiþ to overcome. And so whanne þe nyȝt of synne blindiþ men to knowun hemsilf, þanne is tyme to þe fend to fiȝte fastist[3] wiþ his make; for riȝt as nestis in a sunne beem ben wel perceyved wiþ filþe of man, so synnes ben wel perceyved of a man þat is in grace. Þis þeef worchiþ ever bi disseitis, and fiȝtiþ bleþeliest[4] on nyȝtis; and in tyme of mannis deþ he enforsiþ moost to overcome, for þis victorie shal ever laste, on wheþer side þat it falle. Þis housebondis hous is his bodi, þat his soule is kept ynne; and undirmynyng of þis hous mai be don on two maneres. First, whanne þe fend supposiþ þat a man shal die here, he gaderiþ togidere mannis spiritis, and temptiþ him to mony synnes, as to ire and lecherie, and algatis to dis-

and of the thief.

[1] ȝe, E. [2] So E; om. A. [3] *fast*, E. [4] So E; *blelyerst*, A.

[a] The passage referred to is not in any of the Pauline epistles, but in 1 Pet. i. 17. [b] See Sermon LXXVI, p. 251.

Spiritual safe-guards.

peire. But blesse we us wiþ þe Trinite, and þenken on him in þis cais; and aȝens þe firste synne þenke we mekeli on Goddis power, how God is stronger þan þe fend, and wiþouten him mai we nouȝt do. And sich þouȝt of þe Fadir of Hevene shulde overcome þe fend in hour of deþ. Aȝens þe secounde synne of þe fend we shulden þenke on God þe Sone, how kyndeli he is spouse to us, and bouȝte us wiþ his precious blood, and how he mai not parte fro us, but ȝif oure unkyndenesse be in cause; how fair and good a spouse is Crist, and how foul is þe fend; and bi sich þouȝtis Crist wolde ȝeve vertue to men to overcome þe fend, whanne he temptiþ man in hour of deþ to þenke on lecherie. Aȝens dispeir we shulden þenke on goodnesse of þe Holy Goost, how oure good God may not leeve us, but ȝif oure folie be in cause; and ȝif we hav synned nevere so moche, and nevere so longe have leien in synne, axe we God mercy in oure þouȝte, and have we sorewe for þis synne, and God is redi to forȝeve it, how ever þat preestis failen.—For þe fend may be awey fro mannis soule, but not God; and þe mercy of God is more þan is envie of þe fend, and goodnesse of God is more þan is hate of þe fend. What shulde move men to dispeire, siþ þei may so liȝtli be saif?

The hour of death.

And noþing is more in mannis power þan is þouȝt of his soule, but we mote have alone drede to oure God in þis hour; siþ we witen þat olde synne may be so hard þanne in oure soule, þat we shal not be þanne in power to aȝenstonde tempting of þe fend. For as a ȝerde mai growe so greet, and be so stiff in his strengþe, þat men shal not wriþe it, þouȝ þei wolde never so fayn, so synne may growe in man, and be so strong in tyme of deþ, þat riȝtwisnes of God wole lette man to obeie þanne þus to God. Þis drede of God shulde we have, and algatis in hour of deþ; and þis is a good defence aȝens þe fend and dispeir. But þis mote be alone drede, and hope in þe love of God; how þat God haþ more love þan þe fend haþ envye; for Goddis love is wiþouten ende, but þis envie is foul and feble; and þis envie mai not do but in vertue of Goddis love; for love þat God loveþ riȝtwisnesse makiþ overcomyng in þis hour. Lord! siþ good God ȝeveþ us strengþe to love him, and to hope in him, and þe fend mai not lette to þenke on þis ȝifte of God, what man shulde dispeire of God, in our[1] þat God departiþ þe soule? God suffriþ þe fend to have power to haste a man to his deþ, but gode God wole nevere suffre þat ne man mai freli þenke on him; and ȝif þis power be for barrid[2], synne of man is þe cause, and resouns of þe fend ben blindid in þis matere. Þe fend puttiþ to us grete synnes þat we have done in work and þouȝt, and for gretenesse of þes synnes Goddis riȝtwisnes haþ hardid us. But þis foole shal wel wite how þat we wolen answere here. We graunte mekeli þat we have synned in þouȝt, and word, and in dede; but we wite þat Goddis grace is moche more þan al oure synne. And þis fool knowiþ not how þat God haþ mekid us now, for we felen þe grace of God, how we hopen in his goodnesse, and sorowen for oure synne. And þis þe fend knowiþ not, but ȝit þe fend argueþ þus: algatis sum man mote be dampned; but who shulde be dampned, but þou, þat þus hast ben unkynde to God? Here we answeren to þe fool, þat he takiþ a þing þat is soþ, but how can þis fend prove þat Goddis riȝt wole have me dampned? siþ Y have hope in my soule, þat is hid to þe fend. And wel Y woot þe fend knowiþ not þis pryvy ordenaunce of God, as he knewe not his owne dampnyng, how God shope it to blis of seintis. But ȝit þe fend argueþ þat alle þingis þat shal come mut nedis come bi þe ordenance of God, and þus þe fend mote have of me a glorious victorie. But here we answere to þis fend, and graunte him þat he takiþ; and so he mut nedis be dampned for folie þat he is inne; for he travailiþ bisili to have victorie of us, but ȝit we hopen þat he shal faile, bi sparclis of grace þat we felen. And wel we witen as bileve, ȝif þe fend overcome us, it shal not be glorious to him, but more to his dampnacioun; for ever þe more harm þat he doiþ, ever þe worse shal he be punishid. And so men þat shal be dampned wiþ him shal be ever peyneful to him, for he shal ever forþinken þat he dide so myche yvel. And so þe fend, concludid in insolible, shal ever forþinke and like togidere. What man þat knowiþ þis foolis castis shulde be overcomen wiþ þis fend, siþ oure good God is so nyȝe, and his mercy is so greet, and folie of þis proude fend in bostinge of þingis þat he knowiþ not is so stynkinge bifore God, and so knowun to Goddis children?

Reflections against despair.

[1] *houre*, E. [2] *forbarrid*, E.

Þe Gospel on feestis of many Confessours.

[SERMON LXXXIII.]

Misit Jesus duodecim discipulos.—Matt. x. [5.]

The mission of the Apostles and their successors.

Þis gospel tellip how preestis shulden traveile in Goddis cause, and how kynde þat þei shulden be boþe to God and to þe peple. For wordis seid to Cristis disciplis shulden teche us preestis how we shulden do, siþ we shulden be vikeris of hem; and ellis Crist bindiþ us bi no lore. And þus a prest dampneþ himsilf þat seiþ þat Crist spekiþ not here to him; for he seiþ in a maner þat he is þe fendis child. And for his unkyndnes Crist wolde not bidde him do Goddis work, but do as yvel as he mai; and Crist þerafter shal dampne him; and þis man beriþ upon him mater of his dispeiring. And þis shulde moove prestis alle to fille þe wordis þat Crist bad; for if þei dispisen þes wordis, þei mai dispeire as fendis children. And þus boþe bishopis and freris beren her dispeir wiþ hem, and þis will not be shaken of, but ȝif þei leven her olde synne, and suen þe love of Crist þat he techiþ in þis gospel.

Þis gospel tellip how, *Jesus sente hise twelve disciplis, and comandide hem: Go ȝe not out* aȝens my bidding *in to weie of heþene men, and entre ȝe not into citees,* þe which ben *of Samaritans.* Þese wordis moten be wel undirstondun to þe witt þat God spekiþ hem; for Crist himsilve wente ofte tymes to Gentilis and Samaritans; and he biddiþ at his departing þat þei shulden teche alle folk; and þus þes Gentile folk weren turned, many moo þan weren of Jewis. And herfore seien holi men þat Crist tauȝte ordre in preching, how men shulde first go to her kyn, and first moove hem to turne to God; and ȝif God telde hem unablite[1] of her kyn, þei shulden speke to oþer. And to þis entente dide Crist, and tauȝte hise apostlis to do. And so men seien comunli þat Crist here forbed goinge

[1] þe inablite, E.

in to þe weie of Gentile folk; but he forbed not to go to hem; but Crist biddiþ *raþer go to þe sheep þat perischiden*[1] *of þe hous of Israel.* And it semeþ þat þes sheep þen þo men þat shal be saif; for all þes ben of Goddis hous, and men þat seen God in hevene. And alle þes weren in point to perishe bifore Cristis treuþe was teld to hem. To þes folk shulden men preche; for Cristis word wole florishe in hem, and mede and worship is in hevene to men þat prechen to þis peple. *Crist bad hem go and preche þis:—þat þe kingdom of hevene shulde neiȝe.* And þis is soþ; for Crist shal come to his laste jugement, and rekene sharpli wiþ hise, boþ wiþ servauntis good and yvele. And Crist is ofte clepid in þe gospel þe kingedom of hevene, for he is heed. And þis bileve, among oþer, shulde meve men to turne to Crist. For love of þis gode Lord and drede of his ponishinge shulde be two sporis to Cristene men for to drawe in Cristis ȝok; but wanting of bileve makiþ many men dolle[2] in þis.

Five rules for preachers.

And fyve maneres enjoyneþ Crist to his prechours for to kepe. First, þat *þei shal hele sike men*, oþer of bodili sykenesse, or þerwiþ of goostli sekenesse. Boþe þes hadde Cristis apostlis, but we have unneþe þe toon; for we have greet grace of God ȝif we heele men fro synne. And we failen in þis craft whanne we bosten of oure power, and leven Cristis lore, or[3] to lyve or to preche. Þe secound manere þat we shulden have shulde be, *to reisen up deed men;* and þis mai be on two maneris. As it was seid of þe firste, algatis we shulden traveile to reise up men deed bi synne; for þis is more þan þe firste, and eende wherfore þe firste is good. And ȝif we don oure diligence þat God haþ ȝovun us power to, we mai liȝtli do þes two; for synne is þicke sowen in londe. Þe þridde cure þat we shulden do, we shulden *hele leprouse men.* And siþ lepre is heresie, a synne bi þe whiche men ben defoulid, we have power to do þis wondir, ȝif we worchen after oure power; and oo lepre left unheelid mai enblemisshe many folk. And þus we shulden be diligent to worche þis wondir in þe Chirche; for o leprous mai foule a flok, and a flok mai foule a more[a]. Þe fourþe work þat

[1] So E; *perichiden*, A. [2] *dul*, E. [3] *oþer*, E.

[a] A tainted flock may taint a whole moor.

preestis shulden do shulde be, þat *þei shulden caste out fendis*. And þis we done on betere manere ȝif we casten out synnes fro men; for ech synne haþ a fend, þat goiþ whanne þis synne goiþ. But þe fend on two maneres is in diverse men. In sum men he is to tempte hem, al if he be not in her soule: In sum men he is incorporate, as in men þat have synne; and in þes soulis þe fend dwelliþ, as who shulde dwelle in his house. Þe fifte manere þat prestis shulden have shulde be þankful[a] traveilinge; for ȝif þei wolen have þank of God, þei shulden here fle symonie, and neiþer sille her preching ne oþer workes þat þei done. And þis forgeten many men, boþe more prestis and lesse; for popis wolen have þe firste fruytis for benefices þat þei ȝyven, and bishopis an hundrid shillingis for halewynge of oo Chirche[b]; and lordis wolen have longe service for o Chirche þat þei ȝyven, and þis is worþ ȝeer bi ȝeer moche rente or moche moneie. And howevere we speken, God woot wel how þis chaffaringe is maad, pryvyli or apertli; for God knowiþ al kyn þingis, and God biddiþ us do þes dedis and hope noȝte here for hem; for ȝif we hopen to be here rewardid oure hope perishiþ to have blisse.

Attack upon the friars.

And wiþ þis synne ben freris bleckid þat shapen to preche wynnyng here; and herfore þei prechen þe peple fablis and falshede to plesen hem. And in tokene of þis chaffare, þei beggen after þat þei have prechid; as who seiþ, ȝyve me þi moneie, þat Y am worþi bi my preching. And þis chaffare is sellinge of preching, however þat it be florishid. Soþeli preestis mai medefulli, after þer sermouns, ete wiþ folk; but not calenge for her sermouns, neiþer bi dette ne bi custome. And herfore seien many preestis, þat no men þat have cure shal lyve but on Goddis part, as on dymes and on offringis; and so bi clene

Tithes and offerings sufficient for the support of the clergy.

[a] That is, gratuitous.

[b] This, if ever really exacted, must have been an excessive charge. Originally, the bishop was to receive nothing for consecrating a church; but by degrees the custom crept in of allowing a reasonable 'procuration,' not for the consecration itself, but for the expenses of travelling, lodging, &c., which it entailed on the bishop. The amount of this procuration varied, says Gibson, in different dioceses. He had collected scarcely any information on the subject, beyond the single fact that in the time of Archbishop Warham (circa 1530) the sum of £10 was paid for the consecration of three churches in the diocese of Bath and Wells, or at the rate of £3 6s. 8d. for each consecration. (*Codex*, Tit. ix, cap. 1.)

titil of almes shulden þei have goodis þat þei have. For þus lyvede Crist, hiȝest pope. What art þou þat wole not lyve þus? wolt þou be gretter þan Crist þat is Lord of al þis world? Also þis manere is more meedeful to men þat shulden fynde þes preestis, and more meke and lesse worldli to prestis þat shulden be susteyned. And so it is on boþ sidis more vertuous[1] þan þes rentis now. And þanne God, wiþouten doute, biddiþ þat þis manere be kept. Who drediþ[a] þat ne it is more mede man to ȝeve wel his charite þan to ȝyven his worldeli dette which he oweþ bi worldli lawe? And who drediþ þat ne it is more meke to be paied on Goddis part þan to calenge bi worldis titil more þan Goddis lawe axiþ? For þis were neer to Poulis reule, þat preestis shulden be paied of foode and hiliyng wiþouten more worldli richesse; and þanne our titil myȝte be groundid; and oþer is feyned of þe fend. Also men myȝten bi conscience ȝyve good men, and take fro truauntis[2] betere þan þei now done. And so þis were Goddis wille, bi what resoun shulde he have dymes and offringis of þe peple þat lyveþ in lustis and in ydilnes, and profitiþ not to þis peple? Certis þis were a fendis lawe, to ȝyve Goddis part to sich men. And so comunes weren excludid of false ȝyvynge to alyens; as to popis, and cardinals, and siche Antecristis disciplis. Þei weren also excusid of ȝifte to persouns þat ben lordis clerkis, þat lyven unclerkliche; and þei weren excludid wel of þes Chirches þat ben aproprid to ȝyve Goddis part to men which ben of þe fendis covent[b]. And cursinge noieþ not to man, but ȝif he lyve aȝens resoun. Freris wolen have anoþer titil, and plete and fiȝte for siche goodis; but þis is Goddis lawe, however þe fend termyne. And þus curatis shulden not selle no kyn service þat þei done; but do freeli, and taken aȝen almes þat men wolen ȝyve hem; and never more curse, ne plete for sich almes of þe peple, but flee sich lawis þat techen þis, as þei weren lawis of Anticrist. And þus preestis shulden lyve clenli bi Goddis lawe, as þei diden first. And þus men shulden

[1] So E; *vertues*, A. [2] *tirauntis*, E.

[a] 'who drediþ' means 'who can doubt:' compare the expression, so constantly occurring in these sermons,—'it is no drede.'

[b] That is, parishes, the tithes of which were impropriated to monastic communities, which then served the cures from their abbey or priory.

wiþdrawen her hond fro freris þat beggen whanne þei have prechid; for þei ben coupable bi consente þat ȝeven hem on þis manere. For al þis chaunging shulde be free, þat man shulde do bi Goddis titil.

What may properly be given to priests.

And þus seiþ þe gospel here, *Siþ we token freeli of God we shulden freeli ȝyve to men,* for hope of more mede in hevene. But here þe peple shulde be tauȝt how þei shulden freeli ȝyve þingis þat ben nedeful to preestis, for tyme þat þei shulden serve hem; for þus ȝeveþ God to his servauntis þing nedeful to his service, and man ȝeveþ to his bodi þing nedeful to serve

1 Cor. ix. 11.

him. And herfore Poul seiþ it is litil ȝif we taken þing nedeful to us. But first, er[1] men done symony, þei shulden travaile wiþ her hondis, or go to anoþer peple, or raþer sterve in her bodi. But þis wolde falle late or never, but ȝif oure synne be in cause. And þus men þenken þat prestis mai take almes of her parishis, and go to scole, and gadere hem lore to teche hem efte þe wey to hevene; but þis is fer fro dwelling of lordis[2], or from oþer unhoneste liif, or from wendinge to Rome to gete a fattere benefice. Myche þing shulden men knowe here þat is hid bi þe fend, and lettiþ service of Cristis Chirche þat he ordeynede to be done.

Þe Gospel on Feestis of oon Virgyn and Martir.

[SERMON LXXXIV.]

Simile est regnum caelorum thesauro.—Matt. xiii. [44.]

The parables of the hidden treasure, the pearl of great price, and the net cast into the sea.

Þis gospel, in þre parablis, spekiþ of virgines; and here men reden it, whanne þei seien of a virgyn þat was virgin and martir, as was þe heed of virginis. Þese þree parablis ben þe laste of sevene þat Crist seide togidere in þe gospel of Mathew. For

Ps. lxxviii. 2.

God spake ofte in parablis; as David prophecicde of him, and seiþ, in Cristis persone, Y shal opene my mouþ in parablis and shal speke in proposiciouns þat weren beyng and hidd at

[1] *or*, E. [2] *wiþ lordis*, E; which seems the better reading.

þe bigynnynge of þe world. Parablis on good manere tellen many faire treuþis; and þus, for many causis, Crist spake ofte in parablis.

The hidden treasure.

Þe first parable of þes þree is seid þus of Crist; *Þe rewme of hevene is like to tresour hid in þe feld, þe which, whanne a man findiþ, hidiþ*[1], *and for joie þerof goiþ and selliþ al þat he haþ, and goiþ and bieþ þat feld.* Þe rewme of hevene is ofte taken for heed of þis rewme, þat is Jesus Crist, for he is in manere al þis rewme, siþ Crist is in manere ech part of himsilf. And so þe rewme of hevene, of which Crist spekiþ here, is Goddis word, oure Lord Jesus Crist. Þis feld is undirstonden þe feiþ of Holi Writt, and Goddis word is hid everywhere in þis feld; for every part of Holi Writt telliþ Goddis word,—þe olde law in figure, and þe gospel expressly. Man findiþ þis tresour, whanne he takiþ þe feiþ of Goddis Sone of hevene, þat is ȝit hid; for bileve is a þing hid to men þat bileven, siþ bileve is a þing þat men kyndeli seen not. And so siȝte of bileve, þat is an hid siȝte, is ofte tymes clepid no siȝte, but treuþe. He hidiþ þis tresour founden in þis feld þat kepiþ Holi Writt in forme of her wordis, and kepiþ þe witt of it in his soule; for no man shulde presume to amende Holi Writt, but kepe it in þe fourme þat God himsilf haþ ȝovun it. He goiþ for joie and silliþ alle his goodis to bigge þis feld, and after to traveile þerinnne. He haþ first joie of þis foundun tresour, for man haþ moche joie of his riȝt bileve. He silliþ al þat he haþ, þat renounsiþ al his erþeli goodis, and ȝeveþ him to þouȝt and studie of Hooli Writt. And þus he biggiþ þis feld for erþeli substaunce, as prestis, þat wolen be pore for to be Cristis disciplis, and occupien her wittis in wordis of þe gospel. And alȝif þis be wisdom to jugement of God, it is holden foli to men of þe world; but jugement of God mai no wey faile, and jugement of þe world is algatis fals and failinge. And so þis chaffare of þis feeld is wiys[2] and profitable; for rotis of bileve hid in þis feld springen out into erbis and wel-smellinge flouris. And þis susteyneþ þe Chirche here, and bringiþ it to blis; and oþer worldli profitees ben nouȝt to þis profite. And þus shulden

[1] So both A and E. The Wycliffite versions render, 'whiche a man þat findiþ hidiþ.' [2] *wise*, E.

bishopis and prelatis chaffaren, and studie in Holi Writt, and leeve worldli richesses, and þanne þei miȝten be doctours and disciplis of Crist.

The pearl of great price.

Þe secounde parable of Crist is seid in þes wordis; *Eft soone þe rewme of hevene is liche to a man marchaund þat souȝte good margaritees, and whanne he hadde foundun oon presciouse margarite, he wente out and selde al þat he hadde, and bouȝte þis margarite.* Þe rewme of hevene is clepid here þe Chirche, waundringe after Crist; for Crist, heed of al þe Chirche, bigan þe newe Testament; and fadirs of þis lawe, wiþ vertues of Crist, mai be clepid here þe kyngdom of hevene. Þis man þat chaffareþ here is clepid ech man þat comiþ to Goddis lawe and lyveþ þerafter. Þes margaritees ben treuþis foundun in Goddis law: Þis o margarite is Goddis word, treuþe of alle treuþis, oure Lord Jesus Crist, and þe same tresour þat was bifore foundun. Clerkis seien þat margarites ben prescious stones foundun in þe see wiþinne shellefishe; and þei ben on two maneres: sum hoolid[1] and sum hool. And margaritis ben a cordial medecine, and þei maken faire mennis atire, and conforten mennis hertis. Þis oo margarite is oure Lord Jesus Crist, foundun in tribulacioun of see of þis world; and oþer margarites ben lymes of Crist, foundun in shellis of smale se[2] fishes. Þe manheed of Crist is a margarite þat worshipiþ his Chirche and confortiþ mennis hertis. Þe shelle of þis fishe is bodi of Crist, þat was stable and stef[3] in all his temptaciouns. And he wiþ his martiris weren hoolid margarites. And so Crist, bi his two kyndis, is o margarite, holid and unholid; for Cristis Godheed miȝte not be hoolid; but his manheed was hoolid, as shewen his fyve woundis. And to bigge þis margarite many seintis han traveiled in þe state of grace, and bicamen ful herty; for þis medecine of margarites haþ confortid alle martiris, and made hem herty for to die for þe love of treuþe. Confessouris and virgynes ben maad faire bi þis margarite, and ech state of men þat shal be saaf in hevene. Alle þes men sellen her goodis, as we have seid bifore, and bien þis

Is. lv. 1.

margarite wiþouten any chaunging. For, as Ysay seiþ, sich

[1] *holide*, E. [2] *see*, E. [3] *stiffe*, E.

men bien, wiþouten silver and wiþout chaunging, boþ wyn and mylk. For men þat chaffaren wiþ God and bien hem hevene lesen not þat þei ȝyven, but hav alle þingis betere þat[1] þei hadden bifore, and bi a stabler titel.

The net cast into the sea.

Þe þridde parable þat Crist telliþ is told in þes wordis: *Est soone þe rewme of hevene is liche to a net sent in to þe see, and gaderinge in him alle maner of fishe; þe which net, whanne it was fillid, þei þat ledden it out,* [*and*][a] *sitting bi þe brinke, chesiden good fishes in to her vessilis, and senten out yvel fishes. So shal it be in eendinge of þis world; angels shal wende out and shal departe yvel men fro juste men, and shal sende yvel men in to þe chymeney of fier; þer shal be wepinge and gnashing of teþ*[2]. *And after Crist axiþ hem where þei undirstonden alle þes þingis, and þei seiden, ȝhe. And Crist seide to hem, Þerfore, ech tauȝt writere in þe rewme of hevene is liche to an housebonde man þat bringiþ forþ of his tresour boþe newe þingis and olde.*

Þis rewme of hevene is þis fiȝtinge Chirche, sent into þe see of þis world. And þis Chirche haþ lawis knyttide togidere; and in þe myddis þerof is Crist, a blessid worm[b], þat alle men coveiten kyndeli. And so alle maner of men ben gaderid into Cristis Chirche; but on two maners ben men in þis Chirche. Sum men ben in þis Chirche, and eke of þis Chirche; and þes men mai not wende out of þis nette. And oþer men ben oonli in þis Chirche and not of þis Chirche, and þes men wenden out; and in figure herof, Petre fisshide twyes; firste bifore Cristis deþ, and þanne his net was broken; and eft after Cristis deþ, and toke many grete fishes; and alȝif þei weren so many, þe net was not broken. For alle þes men þat God haþ ordeyned to hevene, mai not wend out of þe nett þat is of Goddis lawis, siþ þei moten holde hem in þe bondis of þe ten comandementis. And so Crist takiþ in his Chirche two manere of juste men. Sum men þat he ordeyneþ ever to be in blisse, and þes mai not

[1] *þan*, E. [2] *teeþ*, E.

[a] The construction requires the omission of the conjunction, which however is found both in A and E. The earlier Wycliffite version renders, 'men ledynge out, and sittynge bysidis þe brynke, chesiden, &c.'

[b] The 'worm' must signify here the bait that is put in the net to attract the fish.

be dampned for strengþe of Goddis ordenaunce. And sum men ben in Cristis Chirche juste for a tyme, þat fallen fro Cristis Chirche for her owne folie, siþ þei breken Goddis heestis, and lasten ever þus unkynde. But þes fishes gon not but wilfulli out of Goddis net. But þis net is nevere ful bifore þat men ben in þe Chirche, as many as God wole have saved, wiþ oþer þat he wole have dampned. Aungels of hevene ben þo þat sitten on þe banke and drawun þis nett in þe see of þis world, and bringen hem to Crist at þe daie of doom. And so þis fishinge lastiþ in tyme of boþe lawis; but þes angels departen yvel men fro juste men; and bringen juste men to hevene, and senden yvel men to helle. And þus dwellingis in hevene for dyverse holi men ben diverse vesselis into which þei ben takun. And þe chemyney of fier is þe fier of helle; for alle sich manere of fier, glowing of þikke mater, shal be closid in helle at þe daie of dome. And how þis shal be fillid þe gospel telliþ after. Þe weping þat shal be in helle is sorewe þat dampned men shal have; and gnashing of her teeþ is harm of her lesing; and þis is more peyne þan þe firste is.

The duties of bishops.

Alle þes þingis undirstonden Cristis disciplis; for oure good maistre tauȝte hem more speciali. And herfore ech bishop and ech curate in þe Chirche shulde cunne þis lessoun, to teche it to þe peple. For at þe dai of dome þes uncunnynge prelatis þat can not þis lore shal be unknowun for to come to blisse; and þerfore we shulden ouþer denye for to be prelatis, or, ȝif we ben prelatis, we shulden cunne Goddis lawe, and preche it to þe peple, ȝif we wolen come to hevene. And þus seiþ Crist of sich goode prelatis, þat herfore ech writere, tauȝt þus of God, is liche to an housebonde man þat ordeyneþ for his hous; siþ a prelate shulde more ordeyne for goostli fode þan an housebonde shulde ordeyne for bodili fode to his folk. And as þis ordeyning is betere, for þe soule passiþ þe bodi, so þis defaute of goostli foode is more dampnable bifore God. And þes prelatis ben not writeris þat ben tauȝt of God, for neiþer þei ben writun in þe book of liif, neiþer þei can write vertues in mannis soule. And so þes doumbe men ben not writeris in þe rewme of hevene, but raþer doumbe foolis in þe rewme of helle; for as þe fend is a king, so he haþ a rewme;

and alle men þat shal be dampned mai be clepid þe rewme of helle. And þes ben rewme of þe fend, siþ he is þer alþer-kyng. But, as a good housebonde serveþ his meynè wiþ olde fruyte and wiþ newe, þat ben of two ȝeris, so a good prelate, þat shulde teche his peple, shulde cunne two Goddis lawis, and how þei acorden togider, and teche his peple, and knowe two weies [1], to go þe weye of hevene, and flee þe weie of helle, and cast out now þe ritis of þe olde lawe. But mandementis of þe olde lawe ben evermore newe; and, in tokene herof, a bishop haþ a mytre þat haþ two hornes, oon behinde and anoþer bifore; and þes two hornes bitokenen þat þei cunnen two Goddis lawis; and ȝif þei tokene falsly, he is a fals prelate, and an horned devyl to be dampned in helle.

Symbolical meaning of the bishop's mitre.

Of a Virgyn and not Martir.

[SERMON LXXXV.]

Simile est regnum coelorum decem virginibus.—Matt. xxv. [1.]

Þis laste sermoun of þe Comoun is red in two manere of festis:—in feste of o virgine, not martir, and in festis of many virgins;—and it telliþ þe state of þe Chirche, boþe now, and at þe daie of dome; and speciali bi þis part þat shulde quyke þe toþer half. For, riȝt as a man is maad boþe of bodi and of soule, so þis Chirche shulde be maad of actyves and contemplatyves. And, for þis spiritual part shulde be more worþi þan þe toþer, as þe soule is betere þan þe bodi, þerfore it haþ name of al þe Chirche. Crist seiþ þus at þe bigynnynge:—*Þe rewme of hevene is like to ten virginis, þe which token her lampis, and wente [2] out aȝens þe spouse and his wyf; but fyve of hem were foolis, and fyve of hem weren ware. But þe fyve foolis token her lampis, but þei token not oile wiþ hem: þes oþer fyve war virginis token oile in her vesselis wiþ her lampis.*

The parable of the ten virgins.

Þis rewme of hevene is þis Chirche: þes ten virginis ben þei

Interpretation.

[1] *and teche his puple two weyes*, E. [2] *wenten*, E.

þat ben spiritual, as ben prestis, and religious, and many oþer in þe Chirche; for as þe soule shulde quykene þe bodi, so þes shulden quykene þe actyve part. But þes ten virginis ben partid in two, in fyve foolis and fyve wise. Alle þei ben virgyns herfore, for þei ben chast of bodi, and kepen hem from outward synnes þat mai be knowun to siȝte of men. And boþe þes partis ben in fyve; for þe wise shal be in hevene evere in a sercle of blisse, as fyve is noumbre in a sercle[a]; and þe toþer fyve foolis shal be dampned in helle wiþouten eende. And as a sercle haþ noon eende, so shal not peyne of þes ypocritis. And þus telliþ Crist fair, how boþe þes partis ben fyve. Þis oile is riȝt devocioun[b], þat alle þes virgyns shulden have. Þes vesselis of þe virginis ben þe poweris of her soulis; for riȝt as a vessel holdiþ oile, so þe power of þe soule shulde holde riȝt devocioun in alle þe workes þat man doiþ. And riȝt as oile makiþ þe bodi soft, and ever more fletiþ above, so

[a] *Fyve is noumbre in a sercle.* On the mysterious virtues and significance supposed by the ancients to reside in the number five, the reader may, if he cares to do so, consult the treatise in Plutarch's *Moralia*, Περὶ τοῦ Ει τοῦ ἐν Δέλφοις, and Sir Thomas Browne's *Garden of Cyrus*. The relation of five to the circle, and also to the sphere, is arrived at in two or three ways. Plutarch ascribes to Plato the opinion that if there are more worlds than the one which we inhabit, there must be *five*, neither more nor less; and that, even if there be only one, that one may be considered as compounded out of five subordinate worlds,—the four elements, and the sky, or fifth essence, 'to which alone,' he says, 'amongst all bodies, the property of revolving in a circle naturally appertains.' The apparent revolution of the celestial sphere round the earth is evidently intended. Again, Sir Thomas Browne, in noticing the singular frequency of the quinary arrangement in nature, observes (it is a thing indeed which many have observed independently) upon the very large number of flowers which have *five* petals, as if that was the simplest and most fundamental division of a circle into sectors. 'Five-leaved flowers are commonly disposed circularly about the stylus, according to the higher geometry of nature, dividing a circle by five radii, which concur not to make diameters, as in quadrilateral and sexangular intersections.' (*Garden of Cyrus*, p. 526, ed. Bohn.) The next paragraph begins,—'Now the number of five is remarkable in every circle,' but as I cannot understand the reasoning which follows, I forbear to quote it In a curious statement quoted by the editor of Browne from Mr. Colebrooke, it is clearly shown that the simplest distribution of groups of objects round a central and interior group is a *quinary* arrangement, while at the same time, when the groups come to be multiplied indefinitely, it is necessarily spheroidal. The reader will remember also the quinary grouping of animals by Mr. Macleay, once so famous, and the remarkable vindication of the theory in the *Vestiges of the Natural History of the Creation*.

[b] See p. 247, note A.

devocioun of men makiþ hem soft in her traveile, and makiþ hem ever more liȝt to bisie hem for hevenli blisse. Þes lampis ben goode workes in kynde, þat boþ þes partis of virgins done; but þes lampis brennen not ne shynen bifore God, but ȝif þei have riȝt devocioun in þe workes þat þei done. And as oile haþ moche of þe eir and of þe fier, wel medlid wiþ water, so men of riȝt devocioun han mouche of hevenli þouȝtis, and also myche of charite. And her tribulacioun semeþ litil, and herbi ben þei liȝt and glad to go þis litil wey. And þus Crist, heed of þe Chirche, was glad here to renne his[1] wey; for he hadde greet desire to suffre peyne for mannis kynde. And so of his oile shulden we take part in goinge of oure traveilous weie. Þes fyve foolis hadden lampis, but þei hadden noon oile wiþ hem; for many men in þis lyf, boþe oon and oþer, don myche good; but hem wantiþ riȝt devocioun, bi which þei shulden go liȝt to hevene. For al oure traveile here in erþe shulde be don for þis ende; to meete wiþ Crist and his Chirche riȝtli at þe dai of dome. And þe Chirche þat comeþ from hevene wiþ Crist at þe dai of dome is clepid þe wif of Jesus Crist; for þei ben weddid ever togidere.

The indevotion and worldliness of the clergy, from the Pope downwards.

It were for to telle here how devocioun wantiþ in clerkis; as popis taken þer stat here for a foule devocioun, to be worshipid in þis world and have moche of worldli lordshipe. And so done þes cardinalis and þes bishopis also. Curatis taken benefices for þe same cause, but lesse; and preestis taken her ordris for devocioun of ten mark[a]; religious possessioneris

[1] *þis*, E.

[a] *for devocioun of ten mark.*] This sounds like a phrase in common use at the time, as if one were to say now that a curate took orders for his £100 a year. The passage is of some importance, as showing that, in spite of the efforts both of the court and the bishops to keep down the salaries of priests, the average rate of pay to a working priest, (the passage has nothing to do with the *parsons* of livings,) in the reign of Richard II, was ten marks, or £6 13*s.* 4*d.* per annum. It may be as well to take this opportunity of putting together a few particulars respecting the salaries of non-beneficed clerks in England between the thirteenth and fifteenth centuries.

A constitution of Stephen Langton, dated in 1222, thus regulates the pay of vicars perpetual:—

'Statuimus, ut vicario perpetuo ad minus reditus quinque Marcarum assignentur, qui scilicet pro quinque Marcis solet dari ad Firmam; nisi forte in illis partibus Walliae sit....' where the parish is too poor to afford so high a stipend.

Five marks then were esteemed a competent salary in the early part of the reign of Henry III. Nearly a

for devocioun of her bely; and many freris taken her stait to lyve lustli in þis world, for ellis þei shulden be laborers, and lyve hard lyf in lewid stait. And so devocioun of clerkis, fro þe firste to þe laste, is studie of avarice, and no trewe devocioun; and so freris, in her statis, wanten riȝt devocioun; for þei taken not her degres, neiþer in scole, ne in office, for riȝt devocioun to renne þe weie þat Crist haþ tauȝt. And þei wolen not be confessours,—speciali of lordis and ladies,—for þe devocioun þat þei have for to make her soulis clene, but for devocioun of worldli likyng, þat þei taken wiþ þes folk, (for þus þei ben exempt from cloistre and from risyng at mydnyȝt, and fro fastinge in her fraitour[1] [a], and oþer workes of obedience,) and

[1] *freytor*, E.

century and a half later the standard had varied but very little. In a constitution of 1362 Archbishop Islep ordains that a priest simply celebrating 'annals,' or masses by the year, for the repose of departed souls, shall be satisfied with five marks a year, but that if he have also cure of souls, he shall receive six marks. Following up this constitution, the act of 36 Edw. III (1363) prohibits under penalties any layman from paying more than five marks a year to a priest residing in his house, and having no cure of souls.

The next fifty years witness a rapid change in the value of money. Archbishop Sudbury orders that the stipends which Islep had fixed at five and six marks, shall for the same duties, 'on account of the changed times,' be raised to seven and eight marks respectively. But these were doubtless the minimum rates, and in practice more was usually given. There is even distinct evidence that *ten marks* was a customary rate of salary for a priest to ask. The act of 2 Henry V (1414), after reciting the act of Edw. III previously mentioned and setting forth that the priests 'which now be' will not serve but for twelve marks, *or ten marks by year at the least*, to the great damage of the king's liege people, enacts that seven and eight marks shall be the legal salaries, unless by special license of the ordinary; nine marks not to be exceeded even in that case.

But the changing times soon rendered this statute ineffectual, if it was not ineffectual from the outset. A constitution of Archbishop Chichely, dated in 1415, ordains that all through the province of Canterbury the stipends of needy vicars shall be augmented as a general rule to at least *twelve marks* a year, if the parish revenues equal that amount.

The above particulars are found in Gibson's *Codex Juris Ecclesiastici Anglicani*, pp. 748, 755, 938-9.

In the province of York the rates appear to have been lower. From the *Testamenta Eboracensia*, published by the Surtees Society (vol. ii, p. 118) it appears that at York, in the middle of the fifteenth century, the customary payment in respect of a single mass was fourpence. Thus in a will dated in 1446 we find—'Lego ad quindecim missas pro animâ meâ in ecclesia Sti Nicholai apud Novum Castrum super Tinam Vs.' And the ordinary annual payment at the same period, to a priest celebrating masses for the repose of souls, was in Yorkshire seven marks.

In preparing this note I have been greatly assisted by Professor Stubbs.

[a] *Fraitour*, or *freytour*, is a corruption of refectorium, in old French,

lustis, þat þei have wiþ ladies, oþer þan þei shulden have at hom. And þus þes laste folk semen virginis; but þei ben foule putis. And assaie her wordis and her lyves, and þanne þou maist betre wite. Defaute in[1] oile of[2] oþer beggers þat ben walkinge in þis world mai men see þat take hede, and of oþer pore men boþe, as trowauntis can feynen hem sike and defourme hem in bodi; and þis is foul ypocrisie and no riȝt devocioun. So it is to drede to many þat ben pore and lyven chast, þat þei shal, at þe dai of dome, wante oile in her lampis.

But whanne þis spouse made dwelling, alle þes virgines napten and slepten. Bi which wordis God undirstondiþ many faire wittis. And goode napping of þes fyve wyse virginis is short deþ þat þei have here to tyme of þe dai of dome. For þis deþ is clepid slepinge; but þes foolis slepen ever bi slepe of everlasting synne. And so þes ten al togidir slepten and nappiden on þis manere; but foolis slepten þis longe sleep, a part here and a part in helle. And þus dwelling of þis spouse is abidinge to þe dai of dome. *Certis at mydniȝt was maad a crie: Lo! þe spouse comeþ, go ȝe out aȝens him. Þanne risen up alle þe virgyns, and maden þer lampis fair. And þes foole virginis seiden to þes wise virgyns; Ȝyve ȝe to us of ȝoure oile, for oure lampis ben quenchid. And þes wise virgyns answeriden and seiden, Lest it suffice not to us and to ȝou, go ȝe raþer to hem þat sellen oile, and bie ȝe oile to ȝou silf. And while þei wenten to bie oile, þe spouse cam. And þes virgyns þat weren redi entriden[3] in wiþ þe spouse; and anoon þe ȝate was shut.*

Interpretation continued.

Þis myddil of þe nyȝt is þe tyme þat Crist shal come to þe laste dome. For certein enchesoun þis tyme is nyȝt; for it is derk and unknowun to men whanne it shal be, and wheþer þei shal go þanne to hevene or to helle. And it is þe myddel for þis enchesoun. It is after þe derknesse, þat goiþ bifore þis jugement,

[1] *of*, E. [2] *in*, E. [3] So E; *entride*, A.

refreitor. It means the dining-hall of a monastery. In later times the word was further corrupted to *Frater-house*. Thus Davies, in his *Ancient Rites and Monuments of the Church of Durham* (1672), says, 'In the south alley of the cloisters is a fair large hall, called the *Frater-House*, finely wainscoted on the north and south sides, as also on the west.' See Halliwell's *Glossary*. Bénoit, in his Chronicle of the Dukes of Normandy, l. 10998, writes,—'Cloistre i fist faire e dormor, Celier, quisine, e *refreitor*.'

and bifore þe derknes þat ever shal be in helle. Þis crie is warnynge of aungels, þat shal be to þis daie, þat Poul clepid þe laste trompe, and sum, Gabrielis horn. Þanne shal it be seid in sentence: Lo, now comeþ þe spouse of holi Chirche; go ȝe aȝens him. And þis bidding of God shal not be aȝenseid. And þus men þat shal be savyd and dampned, shal rise aȝens þis daie of dome, and make hem redi to answere of dedis þat þei have done. And þanne her conscience shal be open of alle þe lyves þat þei have led. And þus shal þes foolis wite þat hem failide devocioun, and herfore þei shal be dampned, but ȝif þei can excuse hem. Þe axing of þes foolis of men þat shal be saif, is a privy wishinge of þes founed virgyns, þat þei taken part of devocioun of seintis; and wel mai þes be foolis þat þanne have siche desiris. But þes men þat now dremen an accident wiþouten suget mai falle aborde wiþ þese foolis, and axe þis as possible. Þe answere of þes wise virginis telliþ treuþe to þes foolis, how devocioun þat þei have sufficiþ not for hem boþe; and þerfore shulden þei go to seintis, þat sellen in weye devocioun. But þat tyme is passid now; and so moten nedis þei dispeire. And in tyme þat þei þenken þus, how þei shulden have lyved riȝtfulli, and have had devocioun in good workes þat þei diden, comeþ Crist to þe dome, and takiþ to heven just men. Alle þes þingis have ordre of kynde, al if þei hav not ordre of tyme. *At þe laste comen þes founed virgyns, and seien to Crist in þis wise: Lord, Lord, opene to us. And Crist answeriþ unto hem: Soþeli, I seie to ȝou, I knowe ȝou not:* Goiþ forþ ȝour weie. *And þerfore, wake ȝe, seiþ Crist, for ȝe knowun not þe daie, ne þe hour.* Þis comyng of þes fool virgins, after þat seintis ben in blisse, is grutchinge of her conscience aȝens Goddis jugement; and criyng of openyng of Crist is languishing to come to hevene. But answere þat Crist ȝeveþ aȝen, is stabling of her peyne in helle; for þei shal þanne be certein þat her double peyne in helle moot nedis be, bi Cristis jugement, for her wickid lyving here. And so her double criyng þanne is her unfamous conscience; for þanne hem shal wante fame, boþe of þis world and of þe toþer. And þus, as Crist concludiþ ofte, alle manere of men shulde wake, siþ þei knowen not þe daie of dome, ne hour in which þei shal be deed.

PROPRIUM SANCTORUM.

[Bishop Bale, in the later edition of his Summarium, dated Basle, 1559, thus enters the following series of sermons for the Proprium Sanctorum on his list of Wyclif's works:—

In Evangelia festivalia, lib. I. 'Hoc Evangelium historicè narrat.'

The writer, whether Wyclif or not, composed the thirty-eight[a] sermons which follow upon gospels which he took, partly from the Proprium de Tempore, partly from the Proprium Sanctorum or Sanctorale, of the Sarum Missal. The title 'Proprium Sanctorum' is not therefore strictly appropriate. Those on gospels taken from the 'Proper of the Season' are ten in number, and are numbered in the present edition LXXXIX to XCVII and CIV. The offices for the first nine of the festivals thus included in the writer's plan, stand all in close juxtaposition in the Sarum Missal, except that the office for St. Thomas of Canterbury (Thomas à Becket,) comes between those for the Holy Innocents and the Sixth Day after Christmas, and St. Sylvester precedes the Circumcision. The omission of St. Thomas' feast by the writer is perhaps significant, and may be taken as the first premonitory symptom of the storm raised against the Archbishop's memory, and against the popular devotion to him, in the reign of Henry VIII.]

Þe Gospel on Seint Andreus Evyn.

[SERMON LXXXVI.]

Stabat Johannes.—John i. [29.]

Þis gospel telliþ in storie, how Crist gederide his disciplis, and seiþ, þat *Joon stood and two of Joones disciplis, and Joon biheld Jesus wandringe, and seide* þus of him: *Lo, þe lombe of God.* Joon Baptist was bifore Crist to make þe weie redi to John sending disciples to Christ.

[a] By an error of the scribe these sermons are numbered as thirty-seven only in MS. Bodl. 788, the same number being assigned to sermons CIV and CV; and the mistake is repeated in Dr. Shirley's Catalogue.

him; and al his entent was to hiȝe Crist and his ordre. And þus whanne he clepide Crist þe lombe of God, he tolde þe innocence of Crist, and how he shulde die for man. And þis was figurid in sleying of þe Pask lombe. For as þe Pask lombe was offrid of oo ȝeer wiþouten wemm, so Crist was offrid at Pask to bie his Chirche, of þe firste preest; and þis preest is boþe God and man. And þus Crist is þe lomb of God; and as a lomb haþ no kyndeli gendrure, but it is clene wiþouten scabbe, so Crist was evermore a virgyn, and clene wiþouten ony synne. *And two disciplis of Joon herden him speke, and sueden Jesus. And Jesus turnede aȝen and saw hem suyng him, and seide to hem: What seke ȝe? And þei seiden to Crist, Maistre, where dwellist þou? And Crist seide to hem, þat þei shulden come and see. Þei comen and sawen where Crist shulde dwelle, and dwelliden wiþ him þat dai; and it was as þe tenþe hour. And oon of þe two disciplis was Andreu, Symondis broþer, þat*[1] *herden þeir maistir Joon* speke þus, *and sueden Crist for good entent.*

Comparison between the behaviour of John the Baptist and the friars.

Soþli Joon Baptist hadde disciplis, to make hem redi to Cristis ordre. And þis priour grutchide not, but was fayne þat þei wenten to Crist; for he synneþ hugeli þat of two goodis chesiþ þe worse. And wolde God þat oure newe ordris wolden wel undirstonde þis storie. Þanne þei shulden preise Crist and his ordre, and be mekeli his disciplis, and make þer disciplis redi to come to Cristis ordre, and grutche not for þei wenten out fre from hem to Cristis ordre. For certis Baptistis ordre was betre þan ben alle þes newe ordris, and he grutchide not but was ful fayn þat þei ȝeden fro him to Crist. And so shulden alle þes privat patrons be fayn of þer disciplis whanne þei wenten fro þer ordre, and camen freli to Cristis ordre; for Cristis ordre is betere þan is hern, as we taken here of bileve. And þus alle þes synnen gretli, þat taken þis worse and leven þe betere. And it is a fendis envie, on þis manere to harme þer breþren, and algatis, for a pride bifore, to hie aȝen Crist þer rotun ordre. And ȝif þou seie þat þis skile wente forþ[2], ȝif Crist were dwelling here in erþe, and gedride to him[3] disciplis as he

[1] So E: A has *and.* [2] *forþe wente*, E. [3] *hym*, E.

dide in Baptist tyme; but now Crist is went to hevene, and men gaderen to hem disciplis; certis þis feyned skile wolde distrie alle þes ordris. For þer patroun, as þei seien, is went to hevene, and dwelliþ wiþ Crist. And ȝif þer ordre dwelliþ aftir, muchil more shulde Cristis ordre, siþ Crist is ever wiþ his disciplis oþerwise þan þes patrouns mai. And where þou seiest þat þes ordris gederen disciplis unto Cristis ordre, certis þanne þei erren foulli, to cloute þus to Cristis reule; as, if men varieden þus fro þer reule, þei wolden seie þei broken þer ordre, siþ þes ordris acorden more togidere, þan ony of þes and Cristis[1] ordre, þat is comoun to Cristyn men, and was bifore þes ordris bigan. Lord! siþ þes ordris wolden bere hevy þat men wenten to anoþer ordre, how shulden not Crist and hise bere hevy þat men wenten out of Cristis ordre? and moche more[2] ȝif fendis lettiden to come aȝen freeli to Crist. Þis synne wole Crist juge, þat is weie, treuþe, and liif, how men letten to wenden his weie. And errour wole not excuse, siþ Poul wende he hadde do wel plesing God whanne he blasfemyde. Acts xxvi. 9. Þis prisonyng in þes ordris, þat letten men to go freeli out of hem to Cristis ordre, is worse þan ony oþer sect, and liik to þe fendis ordre, þat lettiþ men to go from him. For fro Crist mai men go freeli unto þe fend; but þis condicioun of þe feend, foundun in þes[3] newe ordris, is sprongen to popis and to kyngis boþe, þat consenten and helpen herto.

Þis Andreu fond first his broþer, þat is seid Symound, and seide to him: We han foundun Messi[4], *þe which is þe grete Crist.* It was comun in þe olde lawe þat a greet profete shulde come of þe kynrede of Jewis, and bringe hem to ful freedom; and þis was clepid Messias, and Crist bi o witt. *And Andrew ledde Petre to Jesus; and Jesus biheld Petre, and seide, þou art Symont, þe sone of Johanna: Þou shalt be callid*[5] *Petre,* and be maad capteyn of apostlis, for vertues þat Y see in þee. *On þe morewe wolde Crist go out into Galile, and fond Philip, and seide, Sue me. Þis Philip was of Beþsaida, þat was citee of Andreu and Petre. And Philip fond Nathanael, and seide to him* on þis manere: *Him þat Moises haþ writun in þe lawe and*

[1] So E: A has *Anticristis*, which gives no sense. [2] So in E; om. A.
[3] So E; A has *þis*. [4] *Messy*, E. [5] *clepid*, E.

prophetis, we han founden, Jesus, Josepis sone, of Naȝareþ. And Nathanael seide to Philip, Of Naȝareþ mai sum good be? And Philip seide to Nathanael þat he shulde come and se Jesus. Jesus saw Nathanael comyng to him, and seide of him: Lo, verili, a man of Israel in whom is noo gile. And Nathanael seide to Crist: Wher-of hast þou knowe me? Jesus answeride and seide to him, Bifore þat Philip clepide þee, whanne þou was undir þe fige tree, Y saw þee. And here Crist techiþ his Godhed in a maner bi his speche þat he seiþ here. Nathanael was a wise man, and þerfor spak more sutilli. For as Poul seiþ, we speken wisdom among wise men. Crist telliþ here to Nathanael how he saw him undir þe fige tree. Þat mote be bi his Godhede; for bodili siȝt cam not þanne. And þus þat Crist knewe þe hert of Nathanael was bi his Godhede. And þus Crist telliþ, but privyly, whereof he knewe Nathanael,—for of his Godhede he knewe him, as Crist mente in hise wordis. *And Nathanael answeride and seide to Crist: Maister, þou art Goddis sone, and þou art king of Israel. Jesus answeride and seide to him, For Y seide to þee þat Y saw þee undir þe fige tree, þou bilevest; þerfore þou shall se more þan þese. And Crist seide to þes men* togider, *Soþeli, I seie to ȝou, ȝe shal se hevene open, and aungels of God steynge up and comynge doun upon me*, al if Y be, *mannis sone.*

Christ teaches his divinity.

1 Cor. ii. 6.

In þis story mai we see many treuþis þat we shulden trowe. First, how proctours of Crist shulden gete disciplis to him bi skilful mevyng[1] of Goddis lawe, þat þei miȝten freeli come to Crist, and not bi chaffaryng of erþeli þingis, as þese newe ordris chaffaren. Men þat comen to þes dowid ordris [and][2] bringen þer cloþing wiþ hem, boþe for her bedde and bak; for richesse lettiþ to ȝyve hem þese; and over þis þei moten bringe boþe a cuppe and spone to drynke and ete þeir potage; for on þes þingis is þer þouȝt. In þes ordris of þese beggaris þei have contrarie maner; for þei, al ful of disseit, not wiþouten gile as Naþanael, wiþ divers and litil ȝiftis, and false wordis, disseyven children. For þei abiden not to ful age, as weren Andrew, Peter, and Philip; but bifore men have discrecioun in þeir childhode þei ben þus begilid. And so þe first part of þes ordris telliþ

[1] *movyng*, E. [2] om. E; rightly.

how þei shal ever be nedi, and þat oþer latter part telliþ how þei shal ever be bigilid; but on neiþer of þes maners chees Crist his disciplis; but þes men likli ben oblishid unto fendis—to þe fend þat is Mammon, and to þe fadir of lesingis. And boþe þes ben fendis, as ben alle þat shal be dampned. But here þes ordris fagen, and seien, we knowun not þes entrees, for þes ordris wiþ possessiouns bi þis cause taken men wiþ goodis, þat þe worlde shulde knowe þat þei take not beggers, but riche, as þei shal ever be. Þe freris seien, þei taken in children, for þei ben moost innocentis, and liȝt to norishe in Goddis lawe, as þei ben at þe bigynnyng. But neiþer of þes grounden hem in Goddis lawe bi þer dedes. Þe firste word of þe firste ordre techiþ how he partiþ wiþ þe toþer patroun, and þe toþer partiþ wiþ him in synne, as seintis parten in good. Soþli þes possessioners maken in þer professioun þat þei professen povert, chastite, and obedience to Crist, and at þe bigynnynge þei moten nedes professen þe contrarie. And in tokene of þe firste, þat þei han renounsid[1] povert, and ben oblishid to worldli richesse, þei bringen her cuppe and her spone, in tokene þat to drynke and pulment þei ben oblishid bifore oþer; and boþe þes ben no povert to sue Crist, but þe contrarie. Þes freris, þat oblishen þer breþren bi falshed and oþer giles, maken þer protestacioun þat þei forsaken after treuþe; and in reule of þe fadir of lesingis þei wolen drawe to þe deþ dai. And ȝif disseit of ȝong men bi Goddis lawe shulde be dampned, muche more disseit of children þat wanten discrescioun, but han þer eldris for þer keperis; for þei wittis wanten kyndeli[a]. And siþ God seiþ in his lawe, þat whoso steliþ a man, he shal be kild bi Goddis lawe, it semeþ þat alle þes benperis shulden be kild of God by skile; for siþ þefte is taking of oþer mennis þingis, aȝens þe wille of þe lord, it semeþ þat þis takyng of children, þat freris shulden have bi noo lawe, is taking of oþer mennis þingis, for taking of fadirs þing and modirs. And þis tresour is moost presciouse and ful costli to þes fadirs. And where it be aȝens þeir wille, examine hem, and þei shal telle. And þes children comen in bi þefte, and þei ben þeves in al her lyf, to

Hypocrisy of the regulars.

Ex. xxi. 16.

[1] So E; *renounsiþ*, A.

[a] That is, are naturally deficient.

caste how þei shal cleke to freris alle þe goodis þat þei mai geten, ouþer of þer frendis or of oþer, bi what menis þat þei can caste. And þes ordris folwen more to fendis þan don þe firste ordris of Mammon.

Why Nathanael was not chosen to be an apostle.

Over þis, men douten comunly, whi Crist chees not Nathanael, siþ he was witty and good to be Cristis apostle. But here men seien comunli þat þer ben many chesingis of Crist. Crist chesiþ sum to his disciplis for to come afterward to blis. And þus men supposen þat Crist ches þis Nathanael; for Crist preiside him ful myche, and algatis of[1] virtu of treuþe. And þus Crist haþ many disciplis þat ben hid, as Nathanael, as was Joseph and Nicodeme and oþer, til þe daie of dome; for ever Cristis ordre shal laste, and tellen here oþer þer defautes. But þis Nathanael was to wiis to be chosen Cristis apostle, for Crist wolde shewe bi miracle, bi rude[2] men to turne þe world. And þus he wolde make up of fisheris and oþer comunes his apostlis, and make hem passe in witt and wisdom alle oþer men of þis world.

Why some apostles were left for a time in the world.

But ȝit men douten comunli how Crist chees here þes þree apostlis, and toke hem[3] not anoon wiþ him, but lete hem wende into þe world and lyve comun lyf as laborers, as it was tauȝt in Petre and oþer. But here we trowen þat Crist dide þus to confounde þes cloistreris; for Crist wiste wel þat þei shulden come and disseyve muche of þis world, and seie þat it falliþ not to hem to labore, ne dwelle out of þer cloistre, siþ þei passen oþer men in newe signes þat þei han founden. And to distrie þis ypocrisie dide autor of religioun þis:—he chees not þes disciplis unto cloistre þat he dwelte inne, but into place removable, as was Moises tabernacle. And þis is better ordre here; siþ here we have noo citee dwellinge, but here we seken þe blisse of hevene. And þus wente Crist on þe morewe in to þe contre of Galile. But men seien comunli þat Crist clepide ofte his disciplis: first, to be homely wiþ him, and leve sumwhat of worldli curis; after, whanne þei weren more ripe, to suen him boþe dai and niȝt, and siþ, after his resurreccioun, to don þer hiȝe apostlis workes. And þus was Poul chosun to be apostle after þe

[1] *in*, E. [2] *bustouse*. E. [3] So E; om. A.

assencioun of Crist; and anoon he wente and prechide and dide as hiȝest apostle shulde do. And algatis we ben tauȝt bi Crist to flee prisonyng of men as þeves. But ȝif þei wolen dwelle wiþ Crist, þei shulden freeli do þer werkes, and avente hem in þis world, and be not weddid wiþ erþeli þingis. Soþ it is þat Crist sum tyme constreynede men, shewinge his Godhede; as Crist smot Poul doun, and turnede his herte to love of him. But he wolde þat his ordre stood in pacience, mekenesse, and charite, and speciali to turne þe world fro richessis and lustis of bodi: but þes newe religious reversen Crist in alle þes þingis.

Þe Gospel on Seynt Andreus Day.

[SERMON LXXXVII.]

Ambulans Jesus juxta mare Galilee.—Matt. iv. [18.]

Þis gospel of Mathew telliþ how Crist clepide foure apostlis: Petre and Andrew, James and Joon, fro craft of þer fishing. And so seiþ Mathew þat *Crist wandride bi þe water of Galile.* Ebreus clepen ech water a see; and so ech ryver is a see. And þis ryver of Galile likide Crist ofte to wende[1] biside it. Crist saw þes foure breþeren þat weren fisheris in þis water. *First he saw Symound Petre, and Andreu þat was his broþer, putting þer nett into þe water; for þei weren fisheris. And he seide to hem, Come after me, and Y shal make ȝou to be maad fisheris of men.* Crist spak ofte bi his manhede, and dide worship to his Fadir; as here Crist bad þes two disciplis þat þei shulden come after him, —neiþer go bifore him ne come aside in þer lyvyng,—but as þei sawen þer maistre lyve, so shulden þei sue him in þeir lyf. And herfore Crist reprovede Petre, as þe gospel telliþ after, and seide; Go bihinde me, Sathanas, for þou savorist not Goddis þingis. Crist clepide not þes two apostlis to his chaumbre to ete applis; but in þe comun feld, he clepide hem fro worldli traveil, and tolde hem

The calling of Peter and Andrew and the two sons of Zebedee.

[1] *go*, E.

The gospel in every part true and self-consistent.

of a betere traveile, in which þei shulden take men. *And þes two anoon leften þer nettis, and þer boot, and sueden Crist.* Mathew telliþ not how fer þes apostlis sueden Crist; but oo þing we trowen as bileve,—þat no gospel contrarieþ to oþer, and no part of þe gospel is fals; but ech part acordiþ to oþer. We trowen also þat Jesus Crist mevede þes men, boþe wiþinne and wiþoute, and shewide his vertue in þer soulis, and made hem bowe to his bidding. But God forbede þat we shulden trowe, for men wolen not bowe to us, þat we shulden clepe hem worldli, contrarie to Cristis cleping, or ellis grounde a newe ordre, as we wolden passe Crist. For if we wolen holde Cristis ordre, we moten nedeli sue Crist. And þus it semeþ[a] to many men þat patrouns of þes newe ordris gon bifore Crist, as Sathanas; and leeven and dispisen his ordre.

And Jesus goinge forþ þennes, saw oþere two breþeren, James and Joon, whiche weren Zebedees children; and wiþ þis fadir in þe boot, beetinge þer nettis to take fishe. And Crist clepide þes two breþeren; *and þei anoon leften þer nettis, and þer fadir, and sueden him;* for þes two disciplis weren meevyd of Crist, as oþer two, and it semeþ þei loveden more Crist, for þei leften more þer fadir; and þus þei weren worþi of Crist, siþ þei loveden him so muche. For Crist seiþ, whosoever loveþ ony man more þan him, he is not worþi of him, and so not worþi of hevenli blis. It is told ofte bifore of alle þes newe ordris, how þei ben not groundid in Crist, ne in ony dedis þat he dide. Þei done sumwhat þat is good, and many þingis amys; and so stondiþ þer cloutid reule, boþe in good and in yvel; and þus is Macometis lawe and conjourisons maad. And shortli, noon yvel is suffrid, but ȝif it be groundid in good.

Attack on the friars.

Papal appointments to bishoprics and benefices discussed.

But it were to wite over, wheþer þese chesingis þat preestis maken, and þis dowyng þat þei have, ben groundid in Goddis lawe. And trewe men witen wel þat boþe þes reversen Crist. As anentis þis chesing, foolis maken þis resoun. Crist chees him apostlis, and prelatis shulde sue Crist, and speciali popis

[a] Two leaves of the MS. E (Douce 321) are here wanting; the hiatus, beginning at this point, extends to the words 'muche in gloterie,' inclusive, on p. 306. The text is therefore solely dependent on A, up to that point.

and bishopis; whi shulden not þei chese curatis? for ellis shulden officeris perishe, and, bi defaute of hem, Goddis hous. And þus þes two þingis wolen sue: þat oþer popis shulden not sue Crist, or ellis þei shulden chese prelatis, as þe popis lawe techiþ. Þe secounde þing þat sueþ here is foule inconvenient, þat þe pope, Cristis viker, þat haþ his Chirche for to kepe, shulde lete þe Chirche perishe for defaute of siche chesinge. And it is fittinge þat þe pope, þat haþ more witt and autorite, shulde ordeyne for þis chesing, siþ he is heed of holy Chirche. Here we shal suppose, first, þat we speken in þis mater, as if þe pope hadde not ʒit ordeyned lawis of sich eleccioun, but how Goddis lawe and resoun wolde teche for to worche here; and þanne many men þenken þat þis eleccioun shulde not be, siþ it mai not be groundid in resoun ne in Goddis lawe. And to þe resoun þat is maad for þe contrarie part, we shal suppose þat ech man, but algatis þe pope, shulde sue Crist. But ʒit, for dignite of Crist, men shulden ever putte him bifore, and ʒyve to Crist a worþines þat mai oonli acorde to him, for ellis Crist were not abbot over alle oþer men, and maister over alle hise breþeren, as he is boþe God and man. And þus ech oþer preest shulde mekeli sue Crist, and neiþer go evene wiþ Crist, ne bifore him, as dide Petre, and þerfore he was clepide Saþanas, and beden go bihynde Crist. And þus a perel in þe Chirche, þat Poul tauʒte for to come, is, þat Anticrist hiʒe him above Crist, boþe God and man. And þus we graunten þat Crist chese to him apostlis and oþer disciplis, oþerwise þan þe Pope of Rome mai or can chese him servauntis; siþ Crist was boþe God and man, and knewe alle þingis þat shulde be, and wiste fulli what was best, and wrouʒte ever wiþoute defaute. And þus seiþ þe gospel bifore, þat disciplis sawun where Crist shulde dwelle; for alle þingis þat Crist dide he shulde do so for þe beste. And þus ʒif Crist chees disciplis, þe pope shulde not þerfore chese þus; for þe pope mai not be evene wiþ Crist, in witt, ne in autorite; but he shulde sue Crist here as diden Cristis apostlis bifore. Goddis lawe telliþ, whanne þei chosen Mathi as þe twelfþe postle of Crist in þe stede of Scarioth, þei kepten þis ordre in þis eleccioun: þei chosen two, þe whiche þei wisten moost able to be apostle, and moo þei wolden have

2 Thess. ii. 4.

chosen ȝif þei hadden knowe siche moo; but, for þei knewun not þe beter of Joseph and Mathi, þei putten it in Goddis jugement wheþer of þes two Crist wolde have; and preieden ful devouteli, siþ Crist knewe þe hertis of men, þat Crist shulde shewe wheþer of þes two he hadde chosen, bi casting of lottis. And siþ Petre and oþer apostlis weren in þis chesinge, and þei weren moo, and more witti, þan þe Pope of Rome, it semeþ þat he shulde after hem make his more eleccions. Apostlis chosen preestis in contres þat þei wenten bi, and maden hem dwellinge curatis; and þei hadden myche goodis. But apostlis weren algatis pore men and overseeris; for þis poverte was perfeccioun þat felde more to hem. For Crist, her alþer maister, was moost pore man. But oþer fourme of chesinge can we not grounde in Goddis lawe. And siþ Crist, God and man, chees so fewe men in þis office, and þe pope chesiþ so many, wiþoute siȝt in Godhede, it semeþ þat he is hied over Crist, and so over al þat is seid God. For certis Crist myȝte not make al þes eleccions; siþ Crist ne myȝte not chese, but þat he saw þe Godhede chese. But popis chesyn, for moneie or for preier of princis, many men þat ben unable to bere haly water in chirchis[a]. Lord! siþ Crist myȝte not do þis,—and þis þei taken for excellence,—how sich men hien hem not above Crist and al þat is God! for certeinli Crist myȝte not make siche eleccions. Þes men suen not Crist, as diden Peter and oþer apostlis, but algatis gon bifore Crist. And so Crist clepide hem Saþanas; siþ Crist acceptiþ not persones, but takiþ ech man as he is worþi, sum men goode and sum men fendis, after þat þei suen Crist. And þus it semeþ to many men, ȝif þe Pope wolde be Cristis disciple, he shulde leeve þes eleccions, or use hem as Petre dide. Wel Y woot þat Crist forsook to juge in temporal goodis; and þis jugement, evyl done, is myche worse to þe juge. And þus apostlis makinge preestis hadden

The Pope's proceedings appear to identify him with Antichrist.

[a] 'men þat ben unable to bere haly water in chirchis.'] This may either mean *laymen*, — men who are not qualified to discharge even the humblest ecclesiastical function,—or, as I am more inclined to believe, clerks, so ignorant and incompetent as to be unfit even for the duty of an acolyte in carrying the Aspersorium with holy water, for the priest to use in the ceremony of the Asperges. *To bere* is the expression, not *to use*, for the act of sprinkling could only be performed by a priest. See Ferraris' *Bibliotheca*, articles *Aspersorium*, *Aqua Benedicta*, *Ordo*.

shewing of God; for ellis þei hadden do folili in þingis þat þei knewen not. And ȝif þe pope lefte þis þing for peril þat lieþ þerinne, holi Chirche shulde not perishe, but profite more þan it doiþ now. For þanne weren bishopis ful apostlis and pore men as þei weren first, and not chargious to þe peple, but doinge þingis þat felde to hem. And so, wiþouten sich signes, miȝte þe chirche be wel governed. And þus is þis resoun assoilid þat was first maad for þe pope, þat he mot nede, for Cristis love, and for love of his Chirche, be þus occupied, for prelacie þat holi Chirche must nedis have. Certis þis is a false ground and mychel harm comeþ þerof. But whanne o blinde lediþ a blynde, þei fallen boþe in þe lake. And þus seien men, þat coveitise of worshipis and worldli goodis blinden prestis bi symonye, þat al þe chirche fariþ þe worse. And þus mai men see here. If þes prelatis wolden sue Crist, and putte his Chirche out of peril, þei shulden leve þis, as Crist dide. But boþe þis chesing of þe pope, and oþer þing þat bringiþ[a] herto, is brouȝt in bi þe fend, and not bi Cristis autorite. For certis Crist miȝte not himsilf make þes eleccioums. But as þei seien, þe pope mai make a lewid man, for money, a greet bishop on his chirche; but þis is chirch of wickide men.

And þus alle þes popis lawes, biside þe lawis þat Crist made, and alle þe dedis þat he doiþ þat ben not groundid in Cristis liif, ben ful venym to þe chirche,—ȝif a man durste seie þus,—and popis lawis beren no strengþe aȝens men þat holden þis. Lord, what vertue is in þis lawe!—þat ȝif two han þe popis grace, at o tyme, in oo cuntre, where many benefices mai falle, he þat presentiþ first his grace, he shal be sped bifore þe toþer. It haþ fallen ofte tymes, and so mai it falle hereafter, þat two men have grace at oo tyme of oo collacioun, and þe more unable man, þat loveþ more worldli good, presentiþ first his grace to patrons,—for Scarioth slepiþ not,—and þanne, bi vertue of þis lawe, shal þis fend be putt bifore, and þis good man putt bihynde. But þis is yvel fruyt of lawe; and God myȝte not make þis lawe, for God myȝte not do amys. How mai ony viker of Crist sue Crist in doinge þus? But certis he goiþ bifore

a That is, contributeth.

Crist, or ellis on oþer side weie. What woot þe pope þe stat of contreis of many hundrid myle from him? And wordis of false coveitouse men shulden not in þis lede þe pope; but he shulde lyve as Crist haþ tauȝt, and not þus blyndeli lede þe Chirche. Of þis comen a þousand errours, þat siche prelatis fallen ynne. Þei seien þat þei mai not synne in þis state, as Crist myȝte not; for Crist haþ hiȝt to his Chirche, þat he shal never faile to it; and þus þe pope is God in erþe, and þe moste blessid fadir. Sich heresies ben sowen, þat a man þat lovede Crist, shulde, for to suffre deeþ, aȝens stonde þes heresies; for it were all oon to seie þus, and to putt Anticrist above Crist.

On eiȝteþ day of Seynt Andreu[a].

[SERMON LXXXVIII.]

Postquam autem traditus est Johannes.—Mark i. [14.]

The necessity of penance.

Þis gospel telliþ, as oþer bifore, of chesing of Cristis Apostlis. And it semeþ þat Crist prechide first whanne Baptist was taken to prisoun. And ȝif Crist prechide privyli bifore Baptist was enprisound, þat was in anoþer manere; for Crist wolde ȝeve Baptiste his time. *After þe tyme þat Joon was traied in to þe prisoun of Eroude cam Jesus in to Galile, prechinge þe gospel of Goddis rewme; and seide, þat tyme is fulfillid, and þe rewme of God shal come.* Matheu telliþ how Crist bigan to preche fro þe tyme þat Joon was taken, and toke þe same word for his teme þat Baptist toke whanne he prechide:—Do ȝe penaunce, for þe rewme of God shal come. It is knowen of Goddis lawe, how mannis kynde was exilid for synne of our firste fadir þat stood muche in gloterie[b]; and so resoun of God axide þat comyng aȝen of þis rewme shulde be gete bi penaunce contrarie to gloterie. And herfore Crist, oure first fadir in

[a] There is an office for the octave of St. Andrew's Day in the Sarum missal, and from it the writer took the gospel here preached upon. The Roman missal has no office for the day.

[b] See note on p. 302.

spiritual gendrure, tauȝte us for to do penaunce contrarie to Adam's lore; and Baptist, þat was Cristis spouse[a], tauȝte bifore þe same lessoun. And, for Goddis kingdom is to come, and not wiþouten sich penaunce, ech man þat wole have hevene shulde be aboute to do sich penance. And þus þe cause of Crist is pleyn to men þat wole undirstonde it. And þis forþinking is not ynowȝ, but ȝif trouþe be joyned þerwiþ. And herfore seiþ Markus[1] Gospel:—*Forþenke ȝe and trowe ȝe to þe gospel.* Penaunce disposiþ a man to take byleeve over a beest, and þanne bileve ordeyneþ him to be groundid in oþer vertues.

Calling of Simon Peter and Andrew.

And Jesus wendinge forþer biside þe see of Galile, saw Symount, and Andreu his broþer, castinge her nettis in to þe water; for þes two weren fisheris. And Jesus seide to hem, Come ȝe after me and Y shal make ȝou to be maad fisheris of men; for my Fadir shal make þis. *And anoon þei leften þer nettis and sueden him*, as his disciplis.

Reasons for our Lord's supposed preference of fishermen to hunters.

It is noo drede Crist movede þes men, bi his Godhede, in þer soule, and disposide hem to religioun fro þe tyme þat he ȝaf hem witt; for siche men wolde Crist have to grounden men in Goddis lawe. But here men douten comunli whi Crist lovede þus fisheris, and hunteris he lovede but litil, as Lameth and Esau. But here shulden we bileve þat Crist acceptiþ noo persones; but after þat he makiþ hem good, he loviþ hem more or lesse. And so fisheris weren betere men, and þerfore Crist lovede hem more. But ȝit stondiþ þe doute moved, whi Crist made not hunteris betere men þan fisheris, siþ it is more gentil craft. Here is no greet questioun; for God mai worche as he wole. But ȝit men seien here, þat fishing is þe porer craft, and more acording to men, and neer þe state of innocence; and þerfore Crist lovede it þe more. Soþeli men hunten in Lenten, and gentil men,—to have þer game, whanne þei have noon oþer

[1] *Markis*, E.

[a] St. Gregory (Homil. xx.), in commenting on the text, 'He that hath the bride is the bridegroom,' says, 'ac si [Johannes] diceret: ego sponsus non sum, sed amicus sponsi sum.' But our author, possibly from imperfectly remembering the passage, calls John the Baptist the *spouse* of our Lord, a title of dignity which I cannot find was ever conferred upon him by any of the Fathers or Doctors of the Church.

avauntage, alȝif þer travaile be bisie and muche. But not so comunli falliþ þis in fishing. And fishis ben ner þe elementis, and not so like to mannis fleish; and þerfore men holden an ordre to ete fishe and leve fleish; and þus fishe is neer to mete þat man shulde have in Paradise, and sleying of fishe is ferþer from sleying of men þan is sleying of erþeli beestis, which fleish heweris usen. And God wolde þat man hadde orrour of sleying of his broþer; but now men usen a newe craft[a] to slee men comunli, more þan þis craft was usid fro þe tyme þat God was born; and seien, þat preestis shulden usen þis craft betere and more meedefulli þan shulde seculer men, as preestis shulden be lordis over hem. And þis lore is tauȝt bi freris bi myche merit feyned þerto. But what men þei shulden kille, oþer þer breþeren or aliens, þei holden ȝit in þeir purs; alȝif þei practisen on þer breþeren. But þis peple is wyde scaterid,—sum in Engelond, and sum wiþoute. And þes moo freris wiþouten seien þat men shulden moost kille English; and so lesse errour at bigynnynge growiþ to mykil and perilous.

Church endowment and its evils.

But leve we þis doute here, and trete we of þe Chirche dowyng; for bi þis mo men travailen bi symonie. For many, bi þe fendis cast, loven to be hye prelatis, for lordship and richesse, more þan to quykene þe Chirche after þe poverte of Crist. And we supposen, as declarid bi twelve lawis of þe two testamentis, þat preestis and clerkis shulden be pore, as Crist was wiþ hise Apostlis. And in tokene of þis poverte, þes freris ben pore, as þei seien; and ȝit þei passen Scarioth in averice and worldli goodis. And herfore þes blasfemes seien þat begging is medeful, and þat Crist tauȝte hem to begge. And þus þes traitours ben maad riche. Men have proved ofte tymes þat preestis shulden not þus be riche, ne þus be dowid in temporal lordship. Bi men of resoun, or of Goddis half, it is knowun þing ynowȝ þat sum tyme weren preestis pore, and þanne þei shulden, bi Cristis lawe, profite to þe Chirche after þer power; but dowing makiþ hem lesse of power, and þei profiten not more þan þei mai. And so bi þis dowyng þei ben more holden, and

[a] *a newe craft.* This seems to refer to the recent introduction of gunpowder, the invention or the re-discovery of a friar, Roger Bacon, into the art of war.

lesse done. Þat þei ben more holden bi þis dowynge is liȝt to prove bi mannis lawe; for siche a rente or benefice mot axe sum reward aȝen, but no reward is more fittinge þan spiritual office of preestis. And þat dowyng makiþ hem lesse of power mai men shewe bi þis maner. Þei have no more of kyndeli witt þan preestis hadden bifore þe dowynge; and siþ þes wittis ben moche occupied about dowing and worldli þingis, þei have lesse witt to be occupied aboute God and hevenli þingis. And no man of witt haþ drede þat ne þe world and worldli þingis distracten a man fro God and his service in spiritual þingis. And so it semeþ þat prestis moten nede oþer seie þat þei weren ydil bifore þe dowing, or, bi dowing, þei ben more unablid for to serve God, and to profite to his Chirche, and helpe goostli to ony man. And here it semeþ þat þes prestis ben moche[1] unholden to seculer lordis bi þe dowyng þat þei have take; for þei ben harmed so myche þerbi. And so folie on boþe partis bringiþ in harm in ech side; for no man doiþ aȝens God, but ȝif he have harm anoon. And it is knowun bi Goddis lawe þat traveile bi Cristis ordenance disposiþ a man to have grace, and to be more loved of Crist. And ȝif preestis lyveden as Crist ordeynede, þei shulden more encrese in vertues, and profite more to hem and to þe Chirche þan þei done reversynge Crist. And no man þat witt haþ wole seie, þat Crist ȝeveþ preestis more grace, for þei ben unkynde to Crist and leven þe ordenance þat he ȝaf hem. And over þis, it is knowen, þat he þat loveþ his God more shulde more profite to Cristis Chirche, and betere love his neiȝbour. But bileve techiþ us þat God biddiþ men to love him of al þer herte, of al þer liif, of al þer mynde, and of al þer strengþe; so þat, after þe ȝiftes of God, a man is holden more to serve him. And so, siþ prestis shulden not be idil, but do good after þeir power, þei shulden profite to þe Chirche bifore dowyng, as þei myȝten. But bi double folie, brouȝt in boþe in clerkes and worldli lordis, prestis ben of lesse power, boþe to serve God and his Chirche. And noo drede God axiþ acountis of þis foltish chaffering.

An objection answered.

But here þe fend techiþ his clerkis to seke after feyned an-

[1] om. E.

sweris. And þei seien, first, þat bi þis dowyng þei ben in quiet and in pees, and so þei serven God betere, as þei bi resoun ben more holden. And þus þei ben holden in scole to lerne philosophris lore, oþer weie þan þei shulden be, ȝif þis dowing wantide hem. Here Cristen men shulden wite þat þe fend medliþ soþfastnes wiþ falshede to bigile þe folk, and turne hem fro Cristis lore. Soþeli men lernen of gentil craft[a] bi occasioun of dowing, but not so muche as done þese beggers; for fadir of lesingis mai more in hem. Cristene men shulde lerne Goddis lawe, and holden hem paied þerof; and in þis mesure, and in þis nombre, and in þis weiȝte, shulden þei lyven here, and abiden lore in hevene þat men shulden have over þis. For þis lore þat Crist tauȝte ys ynowȝ for þis liif. And ȝif men lyven after him, þei shal have lore as þei have nede; and þus þis dowing makiþ lore þat doiþ harm to Cristis Chirche, boþe lore of vanite, and þerto lore of mennis lawis. Crist ȝaf lore, þe which he lovede, þat he wolde teche Cristen men; and oþer lore, and more, over þis, wolde Crist þat were suspendid. But ȝit men replien, and seien, þat bi þis dowyng prestis ben many; and so, in multitude of clerkis, doiþ þis dowing muche profit; for clerkes wolden not be so many but ȝif þis dowyng were here. God techiþ trewe men to graunte þat dowyng and feyned begging makiþ to multiplie prestis more þan God himsilf haþ ordeyned; for God coude ordeyne noo kyn þing, but in mesure, noumbre and weiȝte. God wolde not þat alle weren preestis, ne alle knyȝtis, ne alle laboreris; but of alle þes þree partis, God wolde make his Chirche in mesure. And ȝif þou seist þat men faylen witt to ateyne[1] to Goddis noumbre, lyve men wel, and God wole teche how muchel shulde be noumbre of preestis. For defaute of Goddis lawe makiþ defaute in þis noumbre. Lerne men wel Goddis lawe, and it shal teche mesure in þis, if men prechen wel þis lawe, and hiden it not fro þe peple. Wel I rede in Goddis lawe, whanne God wolde have myche travaile in beryng of þe tabernacle and sacrificis of many beestis, he wolde have, of twelve kynredis, but o kynrede of Levy, to serve his folk for preestis

Earthly learning unnecessary, if we have the lore of Christ.

Another objection.

[1] *atteyne*, E.

[a] *gentil craft* appears to mean what we call secular knowledge.

and dekenes. And ȝit he wiþdrowȝ many of hem and unablide hem to serve God þus for sykenesse þat he sente hem. And to alle þes preestis and dekenes God lymitide but dymes and offringis. Lord! ȝif Cristene men wolden be paied of þe mesure of Goddis ordenance, and have þe twelfþe part of[1] clerkis[a], and ȝyve her dymes and offringis to hem and hyris[2] to lyve bi, ȝit it were now ynowȝ, siþ Apostlis wiþ lesse goodis profitiden more to Cristis Chirche. And þus wiþdrawe we kyngis clerkis and clerkis þat ben in lordis housis, and algatis þese religious þat ben to charge of Cristis Chirche; and passe we not þanne þe tenþe part, to dowe clerkis over oure God, and he wole teche us, bi riȝt liif, in what noumbre we shulden have clerkis.

ÞIS IS ÞE GOSPEL ÞAT IS RAD ON CRISTEMASSE EVYN.

[SERMON LXXXIX.]

Cum esset desponsata.—MATT. i. [18.]

Þis gospel telliþ of Cristis birþe, how his modir was pore womman, and seiþ; *Whanne Joseph was weddid to Marie*, þe which Marie was Jesus modir[3], *bifore þat þei shulden com togidere, she was founden* of her housebonde, *havynge of þe Holi Goost;* for Joseph perseyved wel þat oure Ladi was wiþ childe. Here holy doctours seien þat Joseph was weddid wiþ Marie, and, bifore þei shulden go to bedde, Marie was gret of þe angel, and conseyved, of þe Holi Goost, Jesus oure Savyour. Soþeli þe Holi Trinite made þis concepcioun; but siþ charite is proprid to þe Holi Goost, and moost charite was, þat God wolde make himsilf man, it is soþ þat Crist was conseyved of þe Holi Goost. And bi þis þe two oþer Persones ben not excludid, but includid. Crist was conseyved in oure Ladi of her clene blood wiþouten

The nativity of Christ.

[1] om. E. [2] *beris*, E. [3] So in E; A includes the whole clause, except the word *Marie*, in the quotation.

[a] That is, 'if but a twelfth part of the population, as was the case among the Jews, devoted themselves to the service of the altar.'

man, and hadde anoon mannis forme, and growide in hir as oþer done. And þus Joseph, bi lyȝt touching, or ellis bi þe lore of God, perceyvide þat she was wiþ childe, and wolde not disseyve oure Ladi. And seintis selen þat Crist was conceyved after þis weddinge; for Crist wolde be conseyved in wedlok of his fadir and modir; and ellis myȝten þe Jewis forsake Crist as unlawful, and not þe greet bihiȝte prophete. And so Joseph shulde have oure Ladi more unsuspect, and more love Crist, and betere kepe him as his lawful sone, and serve him, and nurishe him. And so we ben more certified of maidenhed of oure Ladi; for Joseph, ȝif he wiste[1] hir have knowe man bifore, for repreef he wolde have told it. And, for *Joseph was a just man* and loved of God, *God tolde him bi an angel þat he shulde not drede to take Marie to his wif.* Ech word of þis gospel shulde be take bi his sentence. And so, siþ Joseph was a just man, God myȝte not faile to him, how he shulde do in þingis þat weren hid to him. It is seid comunli, bi processe of Lukes gospel, þat oure Ladi, fro þat she was grett of Gabriel, as Luk telliþ, wente to Elizabeth, and dwelte wiþ her a long tyme, and in al þis tyme Crist growide in her wombe. And whanne she cam hoom to Joseph, he myȝte betere knowe hir wiþ childe; but Joseph wiste, bi Goddis lawe, þat ȝif oure Ladi were corrupt in þis caas, she shulde be punishid; but he coude not prove þis, and so he wolde not defame oure Ladi, ne put hir up to mannis jugement; siþ he trowide þat oure Ladi myȝte conceyve þus bi þe Hooli Goost. Not þat þe seed of þe Holi Goost was put in to oure Ladi, but þat God, of hir blood, gedride in place of hir wombe; and wiþouten oþer seed, God formede þis bodi, and ȝaf it soule. And þus, bi þe aungel's lore, Joseph was afer enfourmed, and not of alle þingis togidre, but now a litel, and now a litil; and þus he shulde betere lyve bi feiþ, and hope, and charite; for bi whiles he shulde be confortid bi speche of þis aungel, al ȝif he apperide to Joseph for þe tyme þat Joseph slepte. And þis is a beter siȝt þan ben comune dreemes of men. And Joseph was clepid Daviþis sone, for he shulde þenke þat Crist was bihiȝt for to come of Daviþis kynde; and

[1] *hadde wiste*, E.

so myȝte he muse, and þenke how Marie myȝte þus be wiþ childe. And he hadde noon occasioun to have Marie suspect, for þis tyme, and þes wordis of þe aungel, moveden Joseph to þis treuþe: *for þat þat is born in her is of the Holi Goost.* Wel he wiste þat ech man is maad of þe Holi Goost, but þis aungel mente sumwhat ellis; for ellis his speche hadde be veyn. And so Joseph undirstood þat Marie hadde conceyved bi myracle; and to þis witt he was disposid, but not to no[1] more ȝit.

Þe aungel seide þat Marie shulde bere a child, and he shulde clepe his name Jesus, as Gabriel hadde seid bifore. And siþ Jesus is savyour, bi þis Joseph þouȝte more; and speciali, siþ þis aungel seide, þat *þis Jesus shulde save his peple fro þer synnes.* And þat is moche; for þanne he shulde boþe have a peple, and shulde save it fro synne, þat oonli God mai do. A man mai save fro bodili perilis, but oonli God mai save fro synne; and speciali fro þe laste synne, þat makiþ a man be dampned in helle.

Poverty the proper state of ecclesiastics.

Here men douten comounli, siþ alle men shulden sue Crist, how preestis shulde not have peple þat were suget to hem. And siþ þe peple shulde serve to prestis and do hem worldli worshipis, it semeþ þat for worship of God men shulden þus ȝyve hem rentis, and þus encreese hooli Chirche in devocioun of dowyng. Here we graunten, as we seiden next[a], þat ech man after Crist shulde sue him, ferþer or nerer, or ellis he comeþ never to hevene. And herfore Crist ledde comun lyf, neiþer to large ne to streit, þe which liif myȝte be ensaumple to alle men of þis world. But ȝit Baptist, ne ony oþer, myȝte not passe Crist in o vertue; for Cristis fasting was betere þan ony oþer fastyng myȝte be, and his passioun was more as his charite was gretter. But siþ Crist dide al þing so þat he myȝte not be amendid, he myȝte not take worldli lordship to þe worship of his Chirche, for, if he hadde, he hadde fuylide[2] his stait, and fordone him and his Chirche. And þis wisten apostlis wel, and dwelten þerfor in þer povert. And þus pore staat of men is liker to staat of innocence þan is rich worldli staat, seme it

[1] om. E. [2] So E; A has *foilid.*

[a] See page 310.

nevere so glorious. And þus þe pope, takinge dowing,—were it Silvester or oþer,—foulide[1] þe Chirche and dide it harm oþer weie þan Crist myȝte do. And so it is not bileve þat ne þis pope synnede myche. But men supposen þat he hadde sorewe in his ende for þis synne; and so we supposen now, þat bi grace þat Crist ȝaf him, he is a seint now in hevene, as oþer men þat token þis dowyng. But oþer apostlis, bi oure bileve, passen in heven sich staat; for it is bineþe bileve þat þes popis ben in hevene, siþ bileve of holi writt seiþ not þat þei ben seintis. And so for blyndenes of þis world þei token to worship þat was shame. And Crist myȝte not have do þus, for Crist myȝte not have synned. And þus, where ypocritis seien þat þis dowing doiþ worship, it doiþ myche shame to men, ȝif riȝt bileve coude conceyve it. For shame of synne is þe moste þat ech man shulde eschewe, for it bringiþ to þe moste shame, þat shal be at þe daie of dome. Wel Y woot þat fendis lymes wolen argue aȝens þis sentence, and disprove oure wordis here; but jugement of þe firste treuþe, and his liif, wiþ his reule, techiþ us sumwhat here how þis is Goddis treuþe. And sich lordship of preestis, wiþ oþer synnes þat comen after, may distroie rewmes here, and do harm to al þe Chirche. For, siþ sich lordship is rote of batailis and divisiouns, it mai falle bi þis synne þat prestis taken fiȝting fro lordis; and so þes lordis shulden lyve as vikeris, and þes prestis shulden lyve as knyȝtis. And þus myȝte Cristis religioun be reversid for þe more part. And prelatis, boþe more and lesse, mai assente to þis sentence, and freris mai falle wiþ hem, and chide bi wordis þat it is soþ; as it falliþ in þis tyme þat prestis fiȝting is preisid, ȝhe, for a feyned cause, þat noon in þis world can grounde. And after þis synne mai falle, þat ladies ben taken privyly, and afterward apertli, fro þer hosebondis, bi preestis. And þis wey may fiȝting falle wiþinne rewmes and distrye hem; for preestis mai coveiten to myche of rewmes, and chef lordship of hem. God shilde us fro sich perils; for ȝif þei fallen in oure tyme, many helpers shulden þei have of Anticristis clerkis þat darken now. For Goddis lawe seiþ þus; þat þei ben cursid of him þat bowen

[1] So E; A has *foilide*.

fro Goddis comandementis; and þis cursing is more to charge, for þis Lord mai not erre. And herfore alle men shulden defende Goddis lawe on þer manere; for litil errour in þis lawe wole growe to a greet harme.

Crist axiþ here mekenes and poverte, wiþ verri pees; and algatis in hise preestis þat ben hier in degree; and ever þe hiȝere þat þei ben, þe more þei shulde have of þes vertues. And ȝif þou seie, þat þes richessis ben goode, and Cristis prestis ben more worþi; whi shulde not þei have þes goodis passinge bifore oþer men? many sich blynde resouns ben maad bi Anticristis clerkis; as sum men arguen for þeves, þat þei ben more hardi men, whi shulden þei not have þe goodis þat þei robben fro oþer men? Speciali, siþ bi Goddis lawe alle þingis shulden be comune. But here men seien, þat þeves ben hardi but to do synful dedes, and þei ben þe moste cowardis in doinge of dedes of vertue. And as a corde is a good þing, and þe tree is a good þing, but ȝit þe hanging on þe galewis is harmful to þis þef; so worldli goodis ben good, but mysuse of hem is yvel. For God haþ put alle þingis in mesure, and passyng þerof is foul and yvel; as many creaturis ben good, and habitude of hem is yvel. And Goddis lawe techiþ þis ordre, and which of þis is better þan oþer. Certis, worldli richesse is good, but not so good as ben vertues; and cloþis of þe ordris ben good, but not so good as ordre in soule. Goddis lawe techiþ in what ordre hise servantis shulde use his goodis; and mesure of þis ordre is betere þan is havynge of þes goodis. And þus we graunten þat preestis shulden have peple þat were suget to hem, but first suget to Cristis lawe; and þus þei shulden have þis peple for þe traveile and þe service þat þei shulden do to þis peple. But Crist haþ in anoþer manere peple, and alle goodis of þis world; for he is boþe God and man, þat mai faile in noþing.

Þe Gospels of þe firste masse and þe secunde on Cristemasse Morwenyng ben ex[pounded][1] in oon sermoun togidere, as it sueþ.

[SERMON XC.]

Exiit edictum a Cesare Augusto.—Luc. ii. [1.]

The Nativity.

Þis dai men singen þree massis in worship of þe Trinite; but þe þridde and þe moste is of þe manhede of Crist, þe which is boþe God and man for þe love of mankynde. Þe gospil of þe firste masse, and of þe secounde also, tellen what þingis bifellen in þe birþe of þis child. Þe Emperour of Rome was þanne in his flouris, and in pees on ech side, as þis autour of pees ordeynede. Men seien þat þis emperour was clepid Octavian; and in þe two and fourtiþe ȝeer, whanne he was in moost pees, was Crist born, God and man, in þe lond undir þis emperour. Men scien also, þat þis Cesare was moost in generalte and larges, and pees of his lordship; for more generali þan oþer hadde he lordship of þis world. Of Julius he took þis name to be clepid Cesare; and August he was clepid, for he alargide[a] þe empire. *Þis emperour sente a comandement* to al þe peple of his empire, to *discryve alle his londis*, þat was wel nyȝ al *þis world. And he bigan at Sirie*, for it was myddil of his empire. And so Syryne[2] [b], þat was þere cheef undur þe emperour, bigan to make þis discripcion, and gaderide tribute to þe emperour. And þus myȝte þe emperour wite what peple he hadde in his empire, and what þei myȝten helpe him in tyme of nede, in men and moneie. And þus he devidide þis rewme in þree partis, þat men shulden come in nyne ȝeer to Rome, and bringe tribute for her lond. But al þis is passid now; for þe pope and his covent haþ[3] so put doun þe em-

[1] Restored conjecturally; the MS. (A) has only the letters *e x*, followed by the long stroke of a *p*. [2] *Siryne*, E. [3] *han*, E.

[a] 'Augustus,' as if from *augeo*.
[b] In the authorized version, 'Cyrenius governor of Syria.'

perour[a], þat litil rewmes tellen li3t by him. And so dukes, and eerlis, and lesse, wolen fi3te wiþ him, and dispise him. *And so wente alle of Jude*, þat was ny Sirye, *to make þer profession* in her owne citee. Ech man hadde an heed toun þat was next to his dwelling, and þat was clepid his citee; and sum men clepen it cheping toun[b].

And Joseph wente fro Nazareth þat was a toun in Galile in to þe toun of Bedleem þat was sett in Judee. For boþ Joseph and oure Ladi weren þe hous of Daviþ; and þe cite of Beedleem was Daviþis bi sum propirte, for Daviþ was borne in þat citee, as þe Book of Kingis telliþ. And so Joseph wente wiþ Marie, þat was his wyf, in to Bedelem, to make þis professioun þat þe emperour bad make. Þei brou3ten an oxe and an asse wiþ hem, as men seien, for þis enchesoun;—Marie was greet wiþ childe; þerfore she rood upon an asse; þe oxe þei brou3ten for to selle; for Jewis haten begging. And Bedleem was fillid of men bifore þei camen to þe toun; and so þei hadden noon herborwe, but dwelten in a comune stable, and þes two beestis wiþ hem, til tyme cam to use hem.

And it felle, *while þei* weren þere, *oure Ladi bare hir child, þe which was hir firste child*, for him she bar and noon oþer. And þis is maner of Goddis lawe, to clepe sich children first born,—not for oþer was born; bifore ne after Crist she bar noon oþer. *And she wrapte Crist wiþ cloþis, and putte him in þe cratche*, for she hadde no betere place to put him in al þe hous. And so, as men singen and trowen, Crist lai bifore an oxe and an asse. And breeþ of þes two beestis kepte him hoot in þis cold tyme.

And *herdis weren in þe same contre, wakinge, and keping þe houris of þe ni3t upon þer flok.* For þis was maner in Judee, whanne þe ni3t was lengest, to kepe þer sheep and wake þat

[a] This is an interesting allusion to the enfeebled condition of the 'Holy Roman Empire' since the fall of the Hohenstaufen dynasty, which was truly brought about, as the writer says, by the popes and their adherents. The emperor at this time reigning, Wenzel or Wenceslas, whose sister, Anne of Bohemia, was married to our Richard II, was so utterly weak both in character and resources that the princes of the empire deposed him a few years later, and elected in his room his brother Sigismund.

[b] That is, market town; as in Chipping Norton, Chipping Campden, Chippenham, &c.

niȝt. And so men seien þat Crist was bore at þe myddil of þis nyȝt, for þe myddil persone in Trinite lovede myddil in many þingis. *And lo, þe aungel of þe Lord stood bi þes heerdis, and clerenesse of God shynede aboute hem, and þei dredden bi greet drede. But þe aungel seide to hem, Wole ȝe not drede, for loo, Y telle ȝou a greet joie þat shal be to al þe peple. For þis daie is born to us a Savyour, þat is Crist þe Lord, in þe citee of Daviþ. And þis shal be tokene to ȝou : ye shal fynde þe child wlappid wiþ cloþis, and put in þe cratche*, as Y shal telle ȝou. *And sudeynli, þer was maad wiþ þis aungel a multitude of hevenli knyȝtis, heryinge God and seiynge ; Glori be to God in hiȝeste hevenes, and pees be to men in erþe which ben of good wille.*

Here mai we see how Crist lovede comun povert on many maners; for he chees to be herborid in comun place, wiþouten pryde, and wiþouten worldli helpe boþe of men and of wymmen, and he chees a pore cradil þat þe child was put inne. But he hadde, passinge oþer, a pryvylegie in many þingis; for he was born wiþouten peyne or sorewe of his fadir and modir. For as he brak not Maries cloister whanne þat she was maad wiþ childe, so he brak not his modirs wombe whanne he cam out of þis cloister. And so þes just folk bifore God weren betere þan myche worldli peple, kingis or lordis and ladies, and[1] wiþ myche fare of þis world; for þis birþe was glorious, neer þe staat of innocence. Þe secounde confort of Cristis birþ was of þes many aungels; for þei weren betere þan many lordis, and her song was of greet confort. Ofte tyme, in þe olde law, apperiden aungels to men, but not in sich a multitude, ne in siche a joieful speche.

And whanne þe aungels wenten fro hem, *þes herdis spaken to hem silf, Passe we into Bedleem, and se we þis word þat is maad, þat þe Lord haþ maad, and shewid to us. And þei came hastinge, and fond þes þree persones, Marie and Joseph, and þe ȝong child putt in þe cratche. And whanne þes heerdis sawen þis þing, þei knewen of þe word þat was seid to hem of þis child* bi þe aungel. And *alle* þe men of þe contre *þat herden þis,*

[1] om. E.

wondriden, and[a] *of þes þingis, þat weren seid of þe heerdemen to hem. But Marie kepte alle þes wordis, and bare hem togidere in her herte.* And no drede she hadde greet confort, and undirstonding over oþere men. *And þes heerdis turneden aȝen, glorifiynge and heryinge God in alle þingis þat þei herden and sawen, as it was seid to hem.*

The holy company present at the Nativity.

We supposen þat aungels ledden hem to þis place in Beedleem, and confortiden hem many gatis, boþe in bodi and in soule. And þei wisten bi þes aungelis, and bi þe good will þat þei hadden, how þei shulden have pees in erþe; and herfore þei herieden God. And so, ȝif we taken hede, Crist hadde company of þre. First, of his fadir and of his modir, þat weren boþe holi folk; after, of herdemen þat lyveden symple and holi lyf. And þes weren licli mo þan two, and nyȝ þe state of innocence; for God lovede Abel betere þan Cayn þat was his broþer. And þe first was an heerde, and þe toþer a tiliyng man; and tiliyng men have more of craft þan have heerdis in þer dedis. And as God lovede Jacobes sones, þat weren alle heerdemen, so he lovede þes heerdis þat camen for to visite Crist. And so þis nativite of Crist was more þan ony oþer, ȝhe, and more þan Adames makyng, whanne he cam into þis world; for oure Ladi and Joseph passiden Adam and Eve, and þe company of aungelis passiden frendis þat weren wiþ oure firste eldris; and þes heerdis þat camen to hem passiden Adams children. And algatis þe birþ of Crist passide[1] oþer dedis þat ever God dide; for it is more to make God man, þan to make þis world of nouȝt. It is maistrie to make a virgyn bere a child, and dwelle a virgyn, more þan to make Adam of erþe, or to make Eve of Adams ribbe; but it is wiþouten mesure more to make God to be a man. For here mennis wittis moten faile. But oon ensample haþ kynde ȝovun us: as þe spirit þat is mannis soule is þe same persone wiþ him, so þe secounde persone of God is þe same persone wiþ þis man. But diversite is greet here and þere, whoso wole loke. Leeve we þis and speke we of vertues. For þis child

Reflections on the Nativity.

[1] So E; *passiden*, A.

[a] Literally rendered from the Vulgate,—'omnes qui audierant mirati sunt, et de iis quae dicta erant a pastoribus.'

is Goddis virtue, and wisdom of þe Fadir of hevene. But þis is bi his Godhede; and mo redelis[1] þan we can telle ben soþ of Crist bi his two kindis. And ȝif we taken good hede of him, Crist is þree kyndis, and o persone; for Crist is Godhede, and bodi, and soule, and ech oon of þes þree. And so, as sum men seien, Crist is sevene þingis, and ech of hem: for his spirit is þree þingis, and his bodi oþer þree þingis, and Crist is, over þis, his Godhede, but oonli oo persone of it. And so, as sevene is ful nombre of universite of þingis[a], so Crist is ful rewme of hevene, and of þis world; for al þis world bi him is betirid, and as who made a newe world. For ech creature of þis world is beterid bi his birþ. For man is beterid siþ he is bouȝt and maad Goddis sone and his eire, and þerwiþ þe broþer of Crist, which is boþe God and man; angelis in hevene be beterid, siþ þei have more felouship, and sich felouship of seintis makiþ hem more glad togidere. And þus alle þe fendis in helle ben beterid aȝens þer wille; for þer cumpany is maad lesse, and þei have harm of many felowis.

Al þis world bodili shulde serve to God and to man; and it wantide þis eende til þat Crist was maad man; for bifore, þis world fauȝte wiþ God and tormentide man, but fro þat þis pees was maad, God made þis world to serve man. And herfore aungelis in hevene, for Cristis incarnacioun, wolden not take kneling of Joon, but seiden, þat þei weren his servantis, and servantis of his breþeren; and þis þei fulfillid in dede. And so ech part of þis world shulde joie for þis nativite; but þe fendis maken sorewe, for old envie þat þei have. And for þei shulden make ioie, þei synnen in þis, and harmen hemsilf. And herfore Crist is clepid a pesible kyng in þe Chirche; for he made pees in al þis world, and lefte fiȝtinge for more pees. For man fiȝtiþ wiþ þre enemys, to have more blessid pees in hevene. And so, as many men seien, alle þingis comen for þe beste; for alle comen for Goddis ordenance, and so þei

[1] *ridelis*, E.

[a] The number *seven*, formed from the union of the triad, the 'perfect' number, with the tetractys, which Pythagoras venerated so profoundly, itself prime and masculine, marking the number of the planets, &c., &c., has been held sacred from the earliest times. See the article on 'Arithmetic' in the *Encyclopaedia Britannica*.

comen for God himsilf; and so alle þingis þat comen fallen for þe beste þing þat mai be. Moreover to anoþer witt men seien, þat þis world is beterid bi everyþing þat falliþ þerinne, where þat it be good or yvel; so moche, þat þis world is betere for synne þat is punishid in helle; for it falliþ to oure Lord to have a prisoun and prisoneris, and do his merci to hem, and savore more his seintis in hevene. And herfore seiþ Gregori[a], þat it was a blesful synne þat Adam synnede and his kynde, for bi þis þe world is beterid; but þe ground of þis goodnesse stondiþ in grace of Jesus Crist.

What is the peace which Christ sends upon the earth.

But ȝit men mai muse how Crist is pesible kyng, siþ he seiþ, he cam not to sende pees in þe erþe but swerd, and þat bitokeneþ fiȝting and noo pees. Here men seien soþeli, þat þer ben two peesis, verri pees and fals pees, and þei ben ful dyvers. Verry pees is groundid in God, whanne God loveþ a man, and to þat pees sueþ pees wiþ alle creaturis; for to men þat þus loven God done alle þingis good. And þis pees stondiþ in pacience, and mekenes, and oþer vertues; and þus was Crist pesible kyng, and he and hise hadden pees here. Fals pees is groundid in reste wiþ oure enemys, whanne we assente to hem wiþouten aȝenstonding. And swerd aȝens sich pees cam Crist to sende into erþe; for þus fouȝte Poul aȝens his fleish, aȝens þe world and þe fend; and þus dide Crist, partinge fleishli frendis fro þe love of oþer, for þe more love þat þei shulden have to Crist þat is her God. Þis fals pees is cowardise, and enemyte of God; and auctor of þis pees is þe fend of helle. And Crist contrariede þis pees, wiþ synnes þat bringiþ it in, as ben pryde, envie and bateils, ydilnes, and oþer synnes. And where verry pees techiþ pacience, þis pees techiþ fiȝting, and blasfemeþ in God, as it wolde be his maistir. And to þis undirstonding was not Crist pesible kyng. And herfore þe prophete seiþ, þat in tyme of Crist, þei shulden welle þer swerdis to sharris[1], and þer Is. ii. 4.

[1] *scbares*, E.

[a] A passage, not worded precisely as here stated, but with the same general meaning, may be found in Gregory's Commentary *In Primum Regum*, lib. iv. cap. 1. But there is a passage in the Sarum missal, in the office for Holy Saturday, containing precisely the same thought; 'O certe necessarium Adae peccatum et nostrum, quod Christi morte deletum est! O felix culpa, quae talem ac tantum meruit habere redemptorem!'

Ps. xlvi. 9; lxxvi. 3.

speris to sykelis. For of Crist seiþ anoþer prophete, þat Crist shulde do awei bateilis to þe ende of þe erþe, and instrumentis of bateilis, as bowe, and sheld, and swerd, and oþer engynes of batailis. Þus shulde it be; but þe fend reversiþ þis.

On Seint Stevenys Dai.

[SERMON XCI.]

Ecce, ego mitto ad vos prophetas.—Matt. xxiii. [34.]

The Martyrs.

Þis gospel is songen in worship of Seint Steven, þat was þe firste martir aftir Cristis assencioun; for he was oon of þe sevene dekenes chosen of þe apostlis, and stood styfli to his deeþ for bileve aȝens Jewis. And so bileve techiþ us þat he is an hooli martir. Crist seide þes wordis to two maner of folk, þat weren þe fendis capteyns in killing of martiris; and þes weren princis of preestis, and comunte of Jewis. Crist supposiþ in þis speche, þat he is boþe God and man; and so al tyme þat was, or shal be, is present to him. And he supposiþ also þat þer ben two kynredis; good kynrede, and yvel, of which ben man-sleris fro þe bigynyng of þe world to þe laste martir. And to þis kynrede shapiþ Crist his wordis:—*Lo, I sende to ȝou prophetis, and wise men, and scribis;* and al þis is for ȝour good, to teche ȝou Goddis lawe: *and of hem shal ȝe kille, and do upon þe crosse, and of hem shal ȝe tormenten in ȝour synagogis.* And here mai we see þe malis of þis kynrede, for a synagoge, as þei seien, is an holi place; and hereinne þei turmenten just men. And þe synne was[1] þe more, and blyndenesse of witt also, for þei wenden to do wel in þis. And so þei pursuen Cristene men fro cite to citee, þat shal veniaunce come on hem[2] at þe dai of jugement. And þus þei done her fadirs work, sleyinge martiris bi þer tyme, *þat al just blood come on hem, þat is shed in erþe, fro þe blood of just Abel to þe blood of Zacarie, þat was Barachies sone, slayn of hem bitwixe þe temple and þe auter.*

[1] So E; *is*, A. [2] The words *And—hem* are italicized in E.

Þis is a blessid ende ordeyned bi Goddis lawe, for no synne mai be done, but ȝif justise be þerwiþ; and so, þis justise makiþ þe world more fair þan þis synne mai mak it foul. Muse we not of þis Zacarie, how he was Barachies sone and whanne he was kild, as þis gospel telliþ; for many men have many names, and algatis in þe olde lawe; and a man is a sone of a fadir longe bifore; and many þingis ben hid to us, how þei weren speciali done [a]. And þus we taken þe word of Crist, and trowen it soþ as bileve, siþ ech word of þe gospel is trewe, siþ it is bileeve; siþ ech compleet resoun telliþ treuþe þat we shulde trowe, and ech part of þis resoun bitokeneþ þe same treuþe. Crist seiþ to þis folk:—Soþli, Y seie to ȝou, alle þes þingis shal come upon þis kynrede. Þes Jewis weren a part þerof, and so þis kynrede was þere, and herde þes wordis of Crist, for a part of it herde hem. Aftir, Crist declariþ þat þis malice was oonli in hem; for God was of good wille to do good to his kyn; but sum of hem wolde not take þis goodness of God. And þus seiþ Crist:—*Jerusalem, Jerusalem, how ofte wolde Y gadere þi children, as an henne gaderiþ her chekenes undir hir wynges, and þou woldest not*, but toke in veyn Goddis grace.

And here men douten comunli how Goddis wille was reversid, siþ þe Psalme seiþ:—þat al þat God wolde, he dide generali in hevene and in erþe. But here it semeþ þat Austin wolde seie on Ps. cxxxv. 6.
þis manere [b]:—þat Goddis wille mut nedis ever more be fulfillid; and so, as ofte as Crist wolde gadere children of Jerusaleem, as ofte weren þei gaderid undir his proteccioun; and whanne he wolde not gadere hem, her synne was in cause, and bi riȝt wisnesse of God, þei musten nedis be punishid; and so Goddis wille was fulfillid in punishing of hem. God wole sum þing uttirli, as þing þat he wole be; and þes þingis moten nedis be, siþ God is al myȝtti. And sum þing wole God upon condicioun; and telliþ men his wille, how, bi his lawe, men shal be punishid þat breken þis general wille in ony part þerof, þat is fulfillid in sum part. And so, siþ God biddiþ do þis þing, and ordeyneþ to punishe for þe trespas, God wole on þis maner þat þis dede be don. And so ever Goddis wille is ful-

[a] See p. 240.
[b] See St. Augustine's, *Enarratio in Psalmum* cxxxiv. § 10.

fillid, ouþer in dede, or penaunce. Ȝif a man do meedfulli þat God biddiþ him do, Goddis wille is riȝtli fillid in dede, as God biddiþ; ȝif a man aȝenstondiþ God and doiþ aȝens his wille, ȝit Goddis wille is fillid asideli[1] by punishinge of þis man. And God haþ ordeyned ever more siche wille to be fulfillid þus. And so, as men speken in Latyn[a], ȝif God biddiþ þee do þis dede, God wole þat þou do þis dede, al if þou doist it not; for þou art in dette to do þis dede, and in þat is Goddis wille endid. But God wole not þat þou doist þis dede, for God knowiþ not þis treuþe, but God wole þat þou do þis dede as God wole þat þou shuldist do þis[b]. And so Crist doubliþ þis citees name to telle defaute of þer unkyndenesse; *how þei sleen Goddis prophetis, and stoone Goddis servauntis sent to hem*, as was Stephen and many oþer, þe which al þis citee killide.

And after Crist telliþ þe veniaunce þat shal be taken for þis synne. *Lo, ȝour hous shal be lefte to ȝou desert*, for defaute of dwelleris. And þis þing cam after in dede, soone after þat Crist steiȝ to hevene. And so Christ seiþ to þis kinrede; *Certis, I seie to ȝou, ȝe shal not se me fro henns, til þat ȝe seien, blessid be he þat is comen in þe Lordis name.* Anoon þis kynrede diede fro Crist, and þanne þei wisten þat he was God, and how he cam to þer profit, al ȝif þei weren unkynde to him. And þis knowing was peyneful to þis kynrede þat shulde be dampned; and þis folk suffride þis peyne bifore þat þei sawen Crist. For God is redi in peyne ȝyvynge as he is redi to ȝyve blisse; for his justise nediþ boþe to þe toon and to þe toþer.

[1] *sydely*, E.

[a] *as men speken in Latyn.* The reference in the text is probably to the great work of Archbishop Bradwardine, the 'profound Doctor,' entitled *De Causa Dei contra Pelagium*, in which the whole subject of free will and predestination was exhaustively handled, and the popularity of which was very great. It appeared about the year 1340, and, as Sir Henry Savile says (pref. to edition of Bradwardine's *De Causa Dei*, 1618) was immediately on its publication 'tanto omnium doctorum exceptus applausu, ut per omnes fere bibliothecas totius Europae describeretur.' To this work Chaucer refers in the well-known passage in the Nun's Priest's tale, and reproduces some of its subtle argumentation in the fourth book of *Troylus and Cryseyde*.

[b] God does not will thee to do a particular act in obedience to his command, because he is ignorant of the truth (that thou wilt not do it); but God wills thee to do the act, *in so far as* he desires that thou shouldst obey his precepts, though thou in fact doest it not.

ON SEINT JHONES DAY.

[SERMON XCII.]

Dixit Jesus Petro.—JOHN xxi. [15.]

Saint John describes himself in his gospel in three different ways.

Þis gospel telliþ how Crist ordeynede Joon to lyve and die, and how Crist wolde þat Joon cam to blisse wiþouten killing. Joon telliþ how *Jesus seide to Petir þat he shulde sue him,*—not oonli bi paas of feet,—but in suffringe deþ as dide Crist. And Peter knew þis witt of God, and wolde fayn wite how Joon shulde die. But Joon clepiþ himsilf bi þree names and leveþ his owne propre name. For þes wordis þat Joon telliþ here sounen to excellence of him; and þanne God wole þat men be pryvy, and ȝeve þe soþe to grace of God. And þus seiþ þis gospel of Joon, *how Petir turnede him and saw Joon.* And þe firste name of þes þree sowneþ in to Goddis grace, and is seid in þis maner: *Peter, as he turnede him, saw þat disciple þat Jesus lovede, how he suede Christ,* as Peter; but ȝit he wiste not of his deeþ. And þis souneþ to grace of Crist, þat he lovede þus Joon bifore; for more grace mai not God ȝyve þan sich love bifore disertis. Þe secounde name þat Joon clepiþ him, stondiþ in familiarite of Crist: how *Joon restide* on Shir Þursdaie[1] [a] *in þe soper on Cristis brest.* Þis homlynesse was a greet grace, and meveþ men for to trowe þat þis Joon hadde witt of Crist. And al þis cam of grace of Crist. Þe þridde name þat Joon clepiþ himself, þat Peter shulde knowe bi resoun, is þis þat Joon *seide* to Crist, *Lord, who is he þat shal traye þee?* Þis word was seid on Shir Þursdai, whanne Crist was at his soper, for þanne tolde Crist, but comunli, þat oon of

[1] *Scher Thursday*, E.

[a] Shir Thursday is Maundy Thursday; 'so called,' says Nares in his *Glossary*, ed. 1859, 'from the custom of shearing or shaving the beard on that day.' He quotes from an old Homily,—'For that in old faders' days the people would on that day *shere* theyr hedes, and clyp theyr berdes, and pool theyr heedes, and so make them honest ayenst Easter day.'

hem shulde traye him; and Petir wolde wite which þat he were. For, as men seien, Petre wolde have fouȝte wiþ him. And Petre saw þat Joon was nyȝ Crist, and homly[1] wiþ him, and spake to Joon þat he shulde axe Crist which was he þat shul traye Crist, as Crist hadde seid. And al þis souneþ to Cristis worship, and to wisdoom of Crist. And þus Joon nempnede þis þridde name, and leeveþ to boste of himsilf.

The manner of Saint John's death.

Whanne Peter sawȝ þis disciple, þat was Joon Evangelist, *he axide of Jesus what shal worþe of þis* Joon. But Jesus answeride to Petir in wisdom and pacience, and seide: *Y wole þat he dwelle þus til Y come*[a]; *what is þat to þee? sue þou me.* And it is ynowȝ þee to cunne, and to do[2] at þis tyme, and axe no more. Here mai we se, how Crist wolde þat neiþer Petre ne Joon wiste þanne Judas name, whom Crist wiste þanne to traye him. And so Crist shewide togidere boþ pacience and charite. But Crist shewide after lore more to note; how men shulden not bisien hem to knowe þingis unpertinent to þe helþe of þer soule. And þus seide Crist: *What is þat to þee.* And so *þis word wente among þe apostlis, þat þis Joon shulde nevere die.* And so wordis þat ben wel seid mai liȝtli be taken amys; siþ apostlis token amys þis word of Crist so pleinli seid. And þus Joon telliþ þis defaute, and seide, þat *Jesus seide not þat Joon shulde nevere die; but Jesus seide* in þis maner: *But I wole þat Joon dwelle þus till þat Y come, what is þat to thee.* And Cristis wordis myȝten be verified on þis maner, ȝif Joon were deed; þat Crist wolde þat Joon lyvede longe, wiþouten martirdom in bodi, til Crist cam in his owne persone, and warnede Joon to come to him and ete in hevene wiþ his breþeren in Cristis feste þat he hadde ordeyned. And þus telliþ þe storie of Joon, þat was longe after; as it bifel, Crist cam to Joon, and tolde him how he shulde come to his breþeren upon Sundai next after, and so Joon diede in his grave[b]. Lord! siþ þes wordis

[1] *homely*, E. [2] *do þat*, E.

[a] So in the Vulgate, 'Sic eum volo manere donec veniam. Quid ad te?'

[b] This 'storie' is given at large in the *Legenda Aurea* of Jacobus de Voragine. 'Cum igitur esset Johannes XCIX annorum, a passione Domini secundum Ysidorum anno LXVIII, apparuit ei Dominus cum discipulis suis dicens, Veni, dilecte mi, ad me, quod tempus est ut *in mensa mea cum tuis fratribus epuleris.* Surgens autem Johannes coepit ire.

of Crist mai be wel þus undirstonden, what shulde meve ony man to take fals wite bi hem? After þese meke wordis of Joon, and comendinge of Goddis grace, telliþ Joon of himsilf: *how he is þat disciple þat beriþ witnesse of þes þingis and wroot þes þingis* in þis gospel; *and we witen þat his witnesse is soþ.* And sich a witnesse, unsuspect, shulde be trowid of trewe men and not be holden for fals, siþ it is oure bileve. Prove þou þat þis gospel is fals, and after dampne it if þou canst.

ON CHILDREN MASSE DAY.

[SERMON XCIII.]

Angelus domini apparuit.—MATT. ii. [13.]

The slaughter of the Innocents.

Þe Lordis aungel apperide in sleep to Joseph, and seide: Rise, and take þe child and his modir, and flee into Egipt, and be þou þere til Y seie to þee; for it is to come þat Eroude seke þe child for to lese him and his felowis wiþ him. *And Joseph roos up, and toke in þe nyȝt þe child and his modir, and fledde into Egipt. And Joseph was þere to þe deeþ of Heroude. And þis was done of Joseph, for to fulfille þat þat was seid by þe prophete, þat seide: Out of Egipt Y clepe my sone,* seiþ God of Crist. *And þanne Heroude sawȝ þat he was disseyved of þe kyngis, and was ful wroþ, and sente into Bedelem, and slowȝ al þe children þat weren in Bedelem, and in alle þe coostis biside, þat weren of two ȝeer and wiþinne, after þe tyme þat he souȝte out of þes kyngis,* þat Crist shulde be of age. For as men seien comunli, þe same ȝeer þat Crist was born, Eroude wente to Rome and brente þes kyngis

Cui Dominus, *Dominica die* ad me venies.' The legend goes on to describe how St. John caused his grave to be dug near the altar in his church at Ephesus, and laid himself down in it; from which point the story evaporates, as it were, in a cloud of miracles, and makes no mention of his actual death. This, however, our author might have found in St. Augustine, who, in Tract CXXIV *In Johann. Evang.*, says that it was related in an apocryphal writing that the apostle, after his grave had been dug, 'ibi se tanquam in lectulo collocasse *statimque eum esse defunctum.*'

ship[a], and dwelte þere aboute two ȝeer bifore he cam aȝen. And þerfore he slow alle þe children þat weren two ȝeer, for he dredde him of Christ þat he shulde take his kingdom; siþ þis alien[b] was kyng bi þe graunt of Romayns, and he wiste not how Crist wolde do þat was bi kynde kyng. *And þanne was fulfillid þat was seid bi Jeremye: A vois was herd in hiȝ*, which vois was a *wepinge and a greet weiling,—Rachel was weping for hir children and she wolde not be confortid, for þei weren not*, quic þus.

Þis prophecie is undirstonden on many maneres of men. Sum men undirstonden it, þat Rachel wepte in spirit þat þei weren not hir children þat weren kild in Bedleem, but hir sistris children; for þei weren kild martiris. Oþer men undirstonden by Rachel holi Chirche; and þes martiris weren hir children þat she wepte fore, not for þe martirdom þat was in hem, but for þe synne þat was done aȝens hem. And þe remenant of þe word is undirstonden[1] denyingli, þat þe Chirche wolde not be confortid of þis, þat her children weren dede. For she þouȝte it no disconfort by many enchesouns; oon, þat it mut nede be, as God himsilf haþ ordeyned,—and he ordeyneþ evere for þe beste, ȝif we coudyn perseyve it. How shulde we grutche aȝens God þat we trowen doiþ so wel? Also, we trowen

[1] So E; A has *undirstonding*.

[a] *brente þes kyngis ship*. This singular legend is not found, so far as I can discover, in any writer of earlier date than Petrus Comestor, (the Mangiadore of Dante, *Paradiso*, xii. 134), author of the *Historia Scholastica*, from whom De Lyra quotes it. Peter was a priest of Troyes in the twelfth century; the *Historia* is said to have been produced in the year 1181. In the dedication, addressed to the archbishop of Sens, Peter declares that he had written the work at the urgent entreaty of many friends, in order to 'elucidate the too brief and obscure narrative of holy scripture.' Labbe, in his *Scriptores Ecclesiastici*, thus writes of him;—'Historiam Ecclesiasticam consarcinavit camque glossis tum falsissimis tum insulsissimis refercivit, quae tamen ita tum ubique obtinuit, ut ipsi scripturae sacrae nudae ac purae pene preferretur.'

The story of the veracious Petrus is, that while Herod was on his way to Rome, whither he had been summoned by Augustus with reference to the quarrels between him and his sons, he stayed for a time at Tarsus in Cilicia, and burnt all the ships of the people of Tarsus, in revenge for their having provided the wise men with a ship to return home in. Whereby the prophecy in the forty-eighth Psalm was fulfilled, 'Thou shalt break the ships of Tarshish with an east wind,' Tarshish being of course identical with Tarsus!

[b] Herod was an alien and no Jew, being the son of Antipater the Idumaean.

þat þes seintis weren take in þer best tyme, so þat many ben betere þan þei shulden have be unmartrid. Whi shulde þe Chirche sorowe for her grete goode? Many sich resouns ben maad, þat men shulden be pacient and confourme hem to Goddis wille, and enjoie of þe more goode. And þus men seien þat þe Chirche is worshipid bi martirs. Crist is heed of martiris, and oonli bi himsilf; but his membris ben martris upon þre maneres: sum in wille and dede,—and þus was Stephen martrid; and sum in wille, and not in dede,—and þus was Joon martrid; and sum men in dede and not in wille, and þus weren þes children martrid.

But men douten comunli how alle þes weren martris, siþ circumcisioun was þanne as nedeful as now is baptym. But licly many of hem weren kild bifore þe ei3tþe dai, and, bifore þat, þei shulden not be circumcidid bi þe lawe. Here many men þenken þat þer ben many circumcisiouns, as þer ben many baptemys, as it is knowun comunli. And God is not so oblishid to sensible sacramentis þat ne he mai, wiþouten hem, 3yve a man his grace. And as God 3af martiris grace, wiþouten baptym of water, bi baptym of þe Hooli Goost and bi water of Cristis side, so mai men suppose of circumcisioun; and so alle þes Innocentis weren circumcided in soule. Þus mai men suppose bineþe bileeve.

Question raised whether all the Holy Innocents were martyrs.

And many men supposen þis more þan of þes seintis þat now ben canonisid bi þe Court of Rome, for lordship, or money, or favour of partis; for þus may þe Court be blyndid in many sich canonisingis. Also, fals witnessis proven not bifore God; whi shulden we bileve þat þes witnessis seien soþ? also, many sich signes þat ben holden myraclis mai be done bi þe fend, and many moo þan þei; what evidence is of þes, þat þis soule is in hevene? Som soulis ben in hevene bi witnesse of holi writt, and þis witnes is more worþ þan a þousand courtis; and bileve of Cristen men is þat þes ben seintis. But men supposen bineþe bileve þat oþer men ben seintis, after evidence þat þei have, ouþer more or lesse: as sum men supposen, and sum leeven levefulli; and sum men trowen treuli, þat alle sich seintis profiten not to men but 3if þei maken hem love Crist. So, 3if men wolden betere love Crist wiþouten sich feestis,

He assails the canonization of saints as practised by the Court of Rome.

it were beter to hem to wante sich seintis. But wiþ þis it is soþ, þat many ben seintis in hevene, as Laurence and Kateryne [a], alȝif Rome canonise hem nevere. But siþ þes seintis ben not expressid in þe lawe of holi writt, men ben not holden to trowe it expressli þat þes ben seintis in hevene: for after þat treuþe is in holi writt shulden men trowe þis treuþe. And so, as it is ofte seid, holi writt conteyneþ al treuþe: sum treuþe expresli,—and þat shulden men þus trowe,—and sum treuþe pryvyli,—and þat shulden men trowe in comune. And God woot of þes festis, wheþer þe Chirche ben betere for hem; for if men loven more Crist and holden betere Goddis lawe bi þis multitude of festis, and bi þe seiyng of her houris, þanne it profitiþ to sich men to kepe sich þingis wel. And ȝif þes festis, wiþ þes ymages and þes houris, weren left of men, and þanne þei loveden betere Crist, and diden betere service þat he bad hem; þanne it profitide to sich men to leve siche serymonies. And it semeþ to many men, siþ Crist, wiþ alle hise apostlis, lefte alle siche þingis and lyvede betere in charite, and kepte betere þe bidding of God, so men myȝten now do. But men shulden not here diffyne, but ȝif God tolde it hem; for boþe sich doyng and sich lyvynge myȝte do, in caas, harm or good. But algatis men shulden seie, þat þei shulden not leve þe office þat Crist bad hem expresly for sich newe ordenaunce.

The multitude of festivals of doubtful profit to the Church.

And it is knowun þat many harmes and many errours fallen bi þes festis; first, in þe purchasyng of canonisyng of seintis at Rome; after, in coveitouse occupiyng togedre moneie bi siche seintis; and algatis in mystrowyng þat men have of sich seintis. As sum men trowen þat Seint Thomas, Erchebishop of Cantirbirie, diede for dowyng of þe Chirche, and to defende goodis þerof. And it were more licli to men, and more acording to Goddis lawe, þat men shulden be seintis in hevene for to bringe holi Chirche to þe ordenance þat Crist

It is dishonouring to Saint Thomas of Canterbury to say that he died in defence of the Church's possessions.

[a] At the early period (middle of the third, and early in the fourth century) at which these saints lived, no formal rules for canonization existed. Yet St. Laurence is a strange instance to choose; for though he was not formally canonized, his feast was solemnly kept in the Roman church at least ever since the fifth century; and this was the more natural, because he was a native of Rome. See his life in Alban Butler (Aug. 10).

ordeynede; and þat was pore state of preestis. And herfore trowen many men, þat cause þat made Seint Thomas martir was, þat he spake aȝens wolves þat weren aboute to murþere lambren; and suffrede not, for defaute of preching, Goddis vyneȝerde passe to a wortȝerd. And þus bishopis and clerkis, wiþ kingis, holden stifli aȝens Thomas; and þus we redyn[1] of Seint Thomas, and trowen it betere, but lesse þan feiþ. And þus shulde we not stryve, as foolis, how hye þis Thomas is in hevene, and what seintis in hevene he passiþ; as done þes newe foundun ordris of her patrouns[a], for whom þei stryven how hie seintis þei ben in hevene. And ȝit þei can neiþer teche bi resoun ne bi bileve þat þei ben seintis in hevene, ne þat þei passe þe leste in hevene. But men mai trowe, whoso wole, þes fablis for which foolis stryven. God ȝyve us grace to love him, and kepe his lawe, and love it; for þat is betere to Cristene men, þan kepe þes festis of þes seintis. For ech preier to þese seintis moot be knytt wiþ helpe of God. For, if we loven Crist in his ordre betere for love of siche seintis, þanne þes festis profiten to us; but comunli þei done us harm. But al oure craft were for to knowe what we shulden take as bileve, and what þing we shulden suppose, and what þing forsaken as fals.

[1] *reden*, E.

[a] *as done þes newe foundun ordris of her patrouns.* This looks like a reference to the famous *Liber Conformitatum* of Bartholomew of Pisa; but if it be, this sermon was not written by Wyclif, for that work, according to Gieseler (Eccl. Hist. vol. iv. p. 155) was not written till 1385. In it is said, (I quote from Gieseler) that the brother Pacificus had seen in a vision many seats in heaven, 'inter quas vidit unam eminentiorem aliis et prae omnibus gloriosius fulgentem, et ornatam omni lapide pretioso;' of which seat it was told him,—'haec sedes fuit Luciferi, et loco ejus sedebit humilis Franciscus.' It is, however, probable that the exaltation of their founder in Paradise was a favourite theme with Franciscan preachers in all countries, long before the appearance of the *Liber Conformitatum*.

þE GOSPEL ON þE SIXTE DAY AFTER CRISTMASSE DAI.

[SERMON XCIV.]

Erat Joseph et Maria.—LUC. ii. [33.]

The writer prefers expounding Holy Writ to amusing the people with stories about the Saints.

To sum men it plesiþ for to telle þe talis þat þei fynden in seintis lyves, or wiþouten holi writt; and sich þing plesiþ ofte more þe peple. But we holden þis manere good,—to leeve sich wordis and triste in God, and telle sureli his lawe, and speciali his gospelis; for we trowen þat þei camen of Crist, and so God seiþ hem alle. And þes wordis, siþ þei ben Goddis, shulden be taken as bileve; and more wolen þei quykene men þan oþer wordis þat men knowen not. And þus þes festis of þes seintis han þis good biside oþer, þat man mai wel telle in hem þe understonding of þe gospel.

Þis gospel telliþ a treuþe to us, how *Joseph and Marie*, Cristis eldris, *weren woundringe of þes þingis þat weren seid* þanne *of Crist;* for alle þes wordis weren newe to hem, and seid of God, as we bileven. And as Austin seiþ on þe Psalm [a]: Trowe it not, for Y seie so; but, ȝif Crist seie so, wo is him þat trowiþ it not. And as we shulden have bileve þat alle Cristis wordis moten nede be trewe, so we shulden have bileve þat þis sentence was seid of Crist; which sentence is told to us bi figuris and bi mannis writing. And þis is þe leste bileve þat we shulden have in al oure feiþ. And ȝif we ben disseyved in þis, oure owne synne is in cause. We shulden not trowe in þis ynke, ne in þe skynnes þat is clepid book[1], but in þe sentence þat þei seien, which sentence is þe book of liif. For, al if þer ben many treuþis and dyverse resouns in þe gospel, neþeles ech of þes treuþis is þe substance of God himsilf.

The prophecy of Simeon.

Symeon was an oold man, and *blessid Marie and Joseph ;* for he bilevede þat Jesus hir sone was togidere God and man, and so he trowide þat bi him Marie and Joseph coulden[2] be saved.

[1] *a boke*, E. [2] *schulden*, E.

[a] I have not been able to verify this reference.

þis *Symeon seide to Marie*, þat he trowide was Goddis modir[1]: *Lo, þis child is putt here into falling doun and rysyng up of many folk þat ben in Israel, and into a signe to which it shal be aȝenseid*, of wickide men; *and þi soule, which is his, shall passe swerd* of compassioun. For Marie suffride in herte wiþ Crist and hadde myche sorewe in þis world. For to sich folk wolde Crist ȝeue blisse, and þus þer blisse savouride more; for it is seid comunli þat man may not passe fro þis joie streiȝt unto þe joie of heven, for þanne hevenli joie savouride him not. And þus ech man of worldli lust, ȝif he shal after come to hevene, mote nedis have a litil space to purge him of his worldli lyf; and þanne shal blisse savoure him, whanne he is purgid þus fro þis world. And so Crist, wiþ his modir and alle hise apostlis, hadden here sorowe; and þus þei weren disposid here to take betere þe blisse of hevene. And it is no drede to clerkes þat ne þe spirit of oure Ladi, þe which is lyf of hir, and in which Crist was wlappid, was a spirit of Crist; as alle þingis moten nedis be hise. Lord! siþ sophistris graunten þat þis[2] fadir of þe[3] hound is myn, and ȝit he is not my fadir[a], whi shulde we not graunte also þat oure Ladies soule is Cristis; and so myche more, as Cristis wille and hir wille was ever at oon? þe eende whi oure Ladi suffride þus, was herfore ordeyned of God, for she shulde be more hooli, and more disserve to Cristene men, and beter printe Cristis dedes, and telle hem hise evaungelistis.

And þus many men tellen þis cause to dyvers ententis; þat oure Ladi shulde have sorewe, *þat pouȝtis be shewid of many hertis*. Sum men construen þis þus: þat oure Ladi, bi þis sorewe, lovede more tendirli mankynde, and made hem shewe her pryvy synnes. And so, bi þis merit of oure Ladi, þouȝtis of apostlis and oþer weren shewid of many hertis to God, bi confession; or ellis, þat þus oure Ladi þouȝte betere on dedes þat Crist dide, and shewide hem to Luke and oþer, to witnesse hem of many hertis.

[1] So in E; A italicizes the words *Goddis modir*. [2] þe, E. [3] þis, E.

[a] On the fallacies arising from ambiguity of the middle term, see the chapter on Fallacies in Whately's Logic, §§ 8-12, and the collection of examples in the Appendix, Part II.

The witness of Anna.

And þer was an oold womman, Anna, þat was a prophete in þis tyme: *she was douȝter of Fanuel, of þe kynrede of Aser. Þis Anna wente wel in her daies, and she lyvede sevene ȝeer wiþ hir hosebonde* þat was weddid wiþ hir *fro her maidenhod. And þis Anna was widewe unto foure score ȝeer and foure, þat wente not out of þe temple, but servede þerinne, boþe niȝt and dai, bi fastinge and devoute preieris. And þis* Anna *cam þe same tyme, and made hir confession to God, and spake of Crist,* as[1] of God and man, *to alle oþer,* þat camen to hir and weren in bileve, *and abiden þe biyng aȝen of mankynde.* Here men douten comunli how old þis Anna was, and wheþer þes foure score ȝeer and foure ben countid in hir two eeldis bifore, as in tyme of hir maidenhood, and in tyme of hir wedlok. But leve we þis witt to God, and wite we wel þat þis Anna was an old womman; and so Crist wolde have witnesse of ages and statis of folk. Crist wolde have witnes of old folk, as weren Anna and Symeoun; and he hadde witnesse of ȝong folk, as weren Innocentis martrid for him; and he hadde witnesse of myddil folk, as weren his fadir, and modir, and herdis. But comunli Crist hadde witnesse of just folk of good name.

And whanne þei hadden do alle þingis in þe temple, þat fel to be done bi Goddis lawe, þei turneden aȝen to Galile, to þe citee Nazareth. For, siþ Crist was circumcisid, and pore offringe was maad for him, þer was no more þere to do bi Crist, of so tendir age; but whanne he was of twelfe ȝeer, he cam aȝen wiþ his eldris and enfourmede þe doctours of þe temple, as þe gospel of Luk seiþ. And in þe meene while, *þe child wexide and was confortid, ful of witt, and þe grace of God was wiþ him.*

[1] So E; A reads *and.*

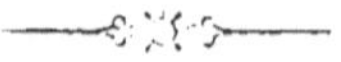

[SERMON XCV.]

Postquam consummati sunt.—Luc. ii. [21.]

Þis gospel telliþ of Cristis circumcisioun, þat was done on þe eiȝtiþe[1] daie fro þat Crist was bore. And þis religioun bigan at Abraham þe patriark; and þis religioun was done in hem longe after þer eiȝtþe daies[2][a]. But þis was kept speciali among þe Jewis; but now we kepen it not, but þing þat it figuriþ. Þe first book of Goddis lawe telliþ of Adam and Eve, how þei lyveden nakid in tyme of þer innocence. But fro þei hadden synned, þei wisten þat þei weren nakid, and þei founden in lymes of gendrure rebellioun to resoun; and þei shameden herof, and hiliden þes lymes, for man shameþ kyndeli of workes of synne. And þus God bad Abraham to þenke on þis synne, þat men shulden kitte awey þe skynne of þer ȝerde; and þis kitting awei is clepid circumcisioun. Many causes þer ben whi þis prophytid to Jewis; for, bi þis þei þouȝten betere on þe synne of Adam; bi þis þei fledden more þe foule synne of lecherie. And to þis synne weren þe Jewis ful redi; and herfore swynys fleish was forfendid Jewis[b]. And bi þis obedience þat Jewis maden to God, weren þei knowen from oþer men, whanne þei weren slayn in bataile. Siþ Crist myȝte not synne, and algatis in lecherie, Crist was circumcidid, to fulfille þe lawe, and to telle men aftir how he clensiþ þer hertis fro synnes þat þei han done, in dede, in word, and þouȝt.

The Circumcision.

[1] *eyȝtþe*, E. [2] *þe eyȝt dayes*, E.

[a] For (Gen. xvii. 10) Abraham was ninety years old, and Ishmael thirteen, when the rite was practised on them, and on all the men of the houshold.

[b] Nicholas de Lyra (*Biblia Sacra*, in Levit. cap. xi.) explains that the flesh of the camel, the hare, the Hyrax Syriacus, or choerogryllus, (translated 'coney,') and the swine, was forbidden to the Jews, because by the first is mystically signified pride, by the second timidity, by the third avarice, and by the fourth filthiness,—vices which are respectively opposed to the four cardinal virtues, prudence, courage, justice, and chastity.

And þis is þe first ernest[1] þat Crist ȝaf for mannis kynde, and seide þat he wolde save it bi blood of þis Goddis lomb. Men seien þat Crist þries shed his blood for man: first, in circumcision of þis tendir membre; þe secounde tyme, longe after, whanne Crist swette his blood whanne he praiede for man, and dredde to suffre deþ; þe þridde tyme, and moost, whanne þe blood of Cristis bodi was drawyn out in many maneris bi violence of turmentouris. Þe blood in his fleish was drawyn out bi scourging; þe blood in his veynes was drawyn out bi nailis; and þe blood of his herte, where Cristis liif was tresourid, was drawyn out bi persing of spere of a knyȝt. Lord! siþ Crist seiþ þat þe blood of just Abel shal be requyrid of Cayn, myche more þis blood of Crist. And siþ suffring bi charite is meritorie and helpyng, myche more þis suffringe of þe persone of Crist. And þus goostli circumcisioun was evermore nedeful; and it hadde vertue and ende in þe blood of Crist.

The name Jesus.

Þis gospel telliþ shortli of þis circumcisioun. Luk seiþ, *Whanne eiȝte daies weren endid, þat þe child shulde be circumcidid, his name was clepid Jesus, þat was clepid of þe aungel bifore he shulde be conceyved in wombe.* It is knowun to trewe men þat Crist was þries clepid þus; oones, whanne he was circumcidid, as we clepen children whanne þei ben baptizid[2]; þe toþer tyme, whanne Gabriel spak wiþ oure Ladi, and telde hir how she shulden conseyve Crist, and he shulde be clepid Jesus. Þe þridde tyme was Crist clepid Jesus in þe Trinite wiþinne; and þis was hiȝest cleping, and moost of vertu. For by[3] þe ordenance of þis oþer þan þer power; and bi þis seiþ Poul, þat in þe name of Jesus ech knee is bowid, of hevene, of erþe, and helle; and ech tunge confessiþ þat oure Lord Jesus Crist is in þe glorie of God his Fadir. And so þis word Jesus, seid of trewe men, is of gret vertu aȝens þe fendis. And, as sum men speken, þis name is often teld, sum tyme privyli, and sum tyme apertli, and it was ofte figurid bifore þat Crist was bore. Jesus is as myche to seie as Savyour. And so Joseph in Egipt was figure of oure Jesus. Josue, þat ledde Goddis folk, and

Phil. ii. 10.

[1] *ernes*, E. [2] *baptymed.* [3] So E; *bifore*, A.

partide þe lond of biheste, figuride oure Jesus bi many propirtees; and so dide Jesus Sidrakis sone; and Jesus Nanes[1] sone[a].

Mystical meaning of the word VIX.

And, as men seien, in þis word 'Unneþe shal þe just man be saved,' is menyd þis word Jesus, whoso coude undirstonde it. For in þis word Vix ben but þree lettris, V, and I, and X. And V bitokeneþ fyve; I bitokeneþ Jesus; and X bitokeneþ Crist. And so þis resoun seiþ þat þe just man shal be saved bi þe V woundis of Jesus Crist oure Lord.

Þe Gospel on Twelfþe Evyn.

[SERMON XCVI.]

Defuncto Herode.—Matt. ii. [19.]

The Return from Egypt.

Þis gospel telliþ how Crist cam from Egipt. For in tyme þat Crist was þere, þat is not made to us to knowe, was þe first Heroude deed, þat slouȝ þe children for Cristis sake. For in meke abiding sendiþ God remedy; and þus seiþ þe gospel þat, *Whanne Heroude was deed, lo, þe aungel of oure Lord apperide to Joseph in sleep, and bad him ryse, and take þe child and his modir, and go into þe lond of Israel, for þei ben dede þat souȝten þe childis liif.* It is seid bifore, þat God is good maistir, þat sendiþ siche messangers to conforte his disciplis, and telliþ but litil at oones, þat þei shulden not forȝete; but evere as þei han nede, þei shulden ben newe confortid. God woot al þing bifore þat it be done; and so he ordeynede his angel to come to Joseph in Egipt anoon, whanne Eroude was deed, to telle him þes tiþingis. And so Joseph dide noȝt but þat þat God tolde him. And ȝif Eve hadde do so, she hadde venquishid þe fend, and not hadde daliance wiþ him til þat she hadde ben disseyved.

And wite we wel, þat not oonli Heroude souȝte þe liif of Jesus, but many of his servauntis for love of him. And þus

[1] *mannes*, E.

[a] That is, Joshua the son of Nun.

lordis seien, we wolen þat it be so. Two maneres of sekyng þer ben of men: sum men seken men to do hem good and worship; and þus þre kingis souȝten oure Lord Jesus; and sum men seken a man to do him harm and dispit; and þus Heroude and his servantis souȝten Jesus Crist; and þei wolden have kilid Crist. And þus þei souȝten Cristis liif; for his spirit þei myȝten not dere; and his bodi þei tolden litil bi, but þei wolden not þat his spirit hadde quiked his bodi.

And Joseph roos and took þe child and his modir also, and cam in to þe lond of Israel; but warli, as þe aungel tauȝte him. And, *whanne Joseph herde þat Archelaus, Heroudis sone, rengnede in Judee for his fadir, he dredde for him to go þidir. And Joseph was amoneschid in sleep bi angel how* he shulde go; *and wente into Galile. And Joseph cam and dwelte in a citee of þat contre, þat was clepid Nazareth; for to fulfille þe prophecie þat Jesus shulde be clepid of Nazareth.* And so he was; for Pilat wroot upon his cros þis writing, as þe gospel telliþ; Jesus of Nazareth, King of Jewes. And so, as Luk telliþ, oure Ladi was grett in þe citee of Nazareth, and þer she conceyvede Crist; and þus bi many resons was Crist clepid of Nazareth.

Christ is still, and ever will be, persecuted in his members here on earth.

Beside lettre of þis gospel, mai men meeve[1] doutis of scole; but me þinkiþ now, it is bettre to touche lore of vertues. We shal bileve þat al þe gospel, be it nevir so literal, techiþ what þing shal bifalle, and how þat men shal lyve. And so, as Crist in his ȝoungþe was pursued by many men to dispise him and slee him in his owne persone; so, unto þe dai of dome is he pursued in his membres, and algatis in Goddis cause, bi resoun of Goddis lawe. We shulden not presume, but hope, þat we ben membris of Crist; but wel we witen, ȝif men haten us and pursuen us for Cristis cause, þanne þei pursuen Crist in his membris, and haten þe cause of Crist. For betere cause myȝte not Crist have þan defending of his lawe; for þis cause made Crist be deed many weies bifore oþer; and Crist, for þe beste cause, suffride here martirdome. Studie wel Goddis lawe, and þe treuþe þat sueþ ofit, and defende it booldli,—boþe to preestis and to þe world,—and þou shalt have enemyes to

[1] *move*, E.

pursue þee to þe deþ. And as Crist was pursued boþe of preestis and knyȝttis, so þou shalt be pursued of þes twoo bi diverse resouns. Sum tyme knyȝttis ben chevetaynes, as it fel of þe eemperours, and sum tyme preestis ben maistris, as it was in Cristis tyme. And so it mai falle now, boþe of popis and bishopis. For ȝif men þenken Goddis lawe sharp[1], and to lette avauntage of þis world, men of þis world, bi þe fend, wolen haten hem þat puplisshen it. And so slouþe and cowardise ben cause of þis fals pees; and so wanting of þis pees is signe to many þat God loveþ hem. Ech word of þis gospel mai be told to þis entent; but it suffisiþ to have þe roote, and go liȝtli to oþer wittis. And muse we not how þis kingdom cam from Archilaus to Heroude; for if it hadde be profitable, God wolde have tolde it in his lawe. And so many treuþis profiten more while þei ben unknowen to men þan þei shulden profite knowyn; as Goddis lawe techiþ us.

Þe Gospel on Twelfþe Dai.

[SERMON XCVII.]

Cum natus esset Jesus.—Matt. ii. [1.]

Þis gospel telliþ, how þre kyngis camen afer out of þe eest to do worship to Jesus Crist, as þei weren tauȝt bi Goddis lawe. And þus seiþ Mathew in þis gospel, þat *whanne Jesus was born in Bedeleem of þe lond of Judee*, for diversite of anoþer Bedeleem, *in þe daies of Heroude þe Kyng*. (And þis was þe first Heroude, more þan þe two after, and he was kyng of Judee bi þe eemperour of Rome; and he hadde it in pees, þat tyme þat Crist was bore. And þus seiþ þe testament of Jacob, whanne he tolde of Judas his sone: 'Þer shal not be taken aweie þe ceptre[2] fro Judas kynde, ne a duke þat shal come of him, til þat Crist come, þat is to be sent[3]; and he shal be abiding of heþene men,' þat he shal turne. And þus it bifel

The Epiphany.

Gen. xlix. 10.

[1] *to scharp*, E. [2] *septre*, E. [3] So E; *seint*, A.

of Heroude, for þe tyme þat Crist was bore; for þanne regalie of þe Jewis was taken aweie, and ȝovun to Heroude.) And þes þre kingis weren wise men, and lyveden in worship after þer astat, and tauȝten her peple Goddis lawe and resoun, as þei hadden be þree men of hevene. And fro þe tyme of Balam, þat was profete of Moab, þer weren kingis in þat contre to aspie his prophecie. For he seide þat a sterre shulde springe of þe kynde of Jacob, and Gentil folk shulde loute þat child þat shulde be bore in tyme of þis sterre. And so, whanne þis sterre apperide on Cristemasse niȝt, or bifore, þes þree kingis ordeyneden hem to come and worshipe þis child. And so þei camen upon dromedis wiþinne þe þrittenþe daie; for her weie was ordeyned redi, wiþouten letting, how þei shulden come. And, for þei wisten þat þe Child was greet, þei camen to Jerusalem, þat was þe heed citee of þe contre, and hopiden þat Crist was bore þere. And þere *þei*[1] *axiden opinli, Where is he þat is bore Kyng of Jewes*, as Balaim tolde in his prophecie, *for we sawen þe sterre of him in þe eest*, þat haþ led us, *and we ben comen wiþ ȝiftes to loute him*, as we shulden. *And whanne Heroude herde þes wordis, he was disturblid*, bi many causis, *and al þe citee of Jerusalem was disturblid wiþ him.* He þouȝte þat so grete men wolden not come so fer þidir, but ȝif þei hadden wist bi certeyn tokenes þat a kyng of Jewes were bore; and þis kyng shulde reve him þe kyngdome þat he hadde. Men seien þat þis sterre was sich þat it was bineþe þe moone in þe overmeste[2] part of þe eir, and movede as God wolde þat it movede. And so þes þree kingis weren meved bi liȝt and leding of þis sterre; and so þei myȝten in litil tyme come to Jerusaleem.

Num. xxiv. 17.

The worship of the Magi.

And Heroude gedride alle princis of preestis þat weren in Jerusalem, and alle þe scribis of þe peple, to wite where Crist shulde be bore. And þei seiden to him, þat he shulde be bore, *In Bedleem of Judee; for so was it writun bi þe prophete, þat seide þus*, of þis toun:—*And þou, Bedeleem, in þe lond of Juda, art not lest among þe princis of Juda; for of þee shal come out a duk þat shal reule my folk of Israel. Þanne Heroude made*

[1] So E: not italicized in A.

[2] *overmoste*, E.

privyli clepe þese þree kingis, and lernede of hem þe tyme of þis sterre þat apperide to hem, and sente hem into Bedelem, and seide to hem, (but falseli):—*Go ȝe, and axe bisili of þis child,* þat is bore; *and whanne ȝe hav foundun him, telle ȝe me aȝen, þat Y come and loute him. And whanne þei herden þe king* þus speke, *þei wenten out of Jerusaleem; and lo, þe sterre þat þei sawen in þe eest meevede bifore hem til þat place þat it stood, evene above where þe child Jesus was. And whanne þes kingis sawen þis sterre, þei hadden myche joie wiþal. And þei entriden in to þe hous, and foundun þe child, wiþ Marie his modir; and þei fel doun bifore þe child, and loutiden him,* devouteli. *And þei openeden þer tresouris, and offriden to him* þree ȝiftis, *gold and mirre and encense;*— as þei weren tauȝte to trowe of Crist þat he was boþe king and preest, and shulde die for mankynde. *And þei token answere in þer sleep, þat þei shulden not turne aȝen to Heroude; and so bi anoþer weie þei turneden aȝen to þer lond.*

Bi þis gospel mai we lerne, how Crist coveitide honest poverte; for he was not bore in þe kingis citee, but in pore uplondish toun,—not in þe beste place of þe toun, but in a pore comune stable. And þes kyngis weren enfourmed bi tymes what alle þes þingis menten. And so we singen in þe chirche, þat þes þree ȝiftis of þe kingis weren ȝovun of ech of hem, and bi certeyn causis ordeyned of God. Bi þe gold þei miȝten bie þingis þat was nedeful for Crist, and bi þe mirre þei myȝten strengþe þe membris of Crist, and bi þe encence þei myȝten putte awey þe stynke of þe stable. And Crist ordeynede bi his lawe, þat he shulde not þus begge, but lyve in an honest poverte lik to þe state of innocence. And þat þe þre kingis camen so fer to bringe þes goodis unto Crist, bitokeneþ Cristis lordship þat he hadde wiþ his povert. But me þinkiþ þat þe witt is betere þat þe Chirche singiþ of þis; gold is Cristis regalie, in encence his presthode, and in myrre his sepulcre[a]. And þus alle men shulden worshipe hem. Seculer lordis shulden worshipe Crist, and þat þis gold shulde teche hem; preestis also

Lessons taught by this gospel.

[a] The writer no doubt refers to the following passage in the Sequence used on the festival of the Epiphany (Sarum Missal):—

Huic Magi munera deferunt praeclara,
Aurum, simul thus cum myrrha;
Thure deum praedicant, auro regem magnum,
Hominem mortalem myrrha.

shulden worshipe Crist, bi þe lore of þis encence; and alle comunes shulden worshipe Crist, for we ben alle dedli, and in tyme of oure deþ and aftirward we haue noon helpe but him. And þis shulden we do in liȝt; for we shulden worche discretli. And, as Gregory techiþ[a], we shulden wenden fro þe fend al bi anoþer weie þan we camen into þis world. For bi synne we camen hidir, and contynneden here in synne; but we shal wende fro þe fend unto oure countre, þat is hevene, bi þe weie of vertuous[1] liif, and þanne we suen þes þree kingis.

Þe Gospel on Conversioun Dai of Seint Poul.

[SERMON XCVIII.]

Ecce reliquimus[2] *omnia.*—Matt. xix. [27.]

Leaving all things for Christ's sake.

Þis gospel telliþ of þe meede þat Crist bihiȝte to his hie knyȝtis. Petre was of greet bileve, and hardi in axing, and axiþ þus Crist:—*Lo, we hav forsaken alle þingis, and we hav sued þee; what mede shal be to us for þis suynge?* Here men douten comunli, how Petre seide soþ; siþ men forsaken not but þing þat þei have hadde, and Petre was a fishere, and hadde but litil þing. Also þer ben many þingis þat Petre þouȝte nevere on; but how shulde he forsake þing þat nevere cam in his þouȝt? Also, Petre forsoke nevere þe Holi Trinite, ne þe manheede of Crist, þat ben many þingis. How approveþ Crist þes false wordis of Petre? Here it semeþ to many men þat Petre undirstood þus,—þat þei forsoken alle þingis[3],—for alle þes worldli goodis; siþ þei helden þer bisynesse and þer wille fro þes goodis. And þis witt mente Crist, in his speche

[1] So in E; A has *vertues*. [2] So in E; A has *relinquimus*. [3] The words *þat—þingis* are om. in E.

[a] St. Gregory, *Homil. X.* 'A regione nostra superbiendo, inobediendo, visibilia sequendo, cibum vetitum gustando, discessimus: sed ad eam necesse est, ut flendo, obediendo, visibilia contemnendo, atque appetitum carnis refrenando, redeamus. Per aliam ergo viam ad regionem nostram regredimur; quoniam qui a paradisi gaudiis per delectamenta discessimus, ad haec per lamenta revocamur.'

aftir to Petre. And þus biddiþ Crist bi Luk and Joon to forsake and hate seven goodis. And þes wordis mai serve wel to þis undirstonding; and þis witt was soþ of Petre and oþer apostlis; siþ a manere of forsakyng is to leeve wille to siche goodis, and þei hadden not suyd Crist þus, but ȝif þei hadden left sich will. And it is liȝt to assoile objectis aȝens þis[a]. To þe firste we seien, þat Peter, bifore he suyd Crist, hadde in his affeccioun al manere of sich þing; and þis desire he lefte, and so alle siche þingis. To þe secounde word we seien, þat þer ben many þouȝtis and many desiris to þingis, as special or general. Petre hadde general desire to al manere of siche þingis, and general forsakyng axiþ sum mede. And clerkis seien, þat special mai not be wiþouten general, and þis forsaking makiþ hem to have þes þingis þe which þei forsoken,—ȝhe, betere þan þei hadden bifore; as, ȝif a man forsake for Crist his fadir and modir, he haþ hem þanne betere þan whanne he lovede hem fleishli.

Difficulties solved.

The þridde obiect þat here is maad goiþ not aȝens oure sentence. For ech man mai wel wite þat Petre þouȝte not to leve Crist, siþ Petre seiþ, next aftir, þat þei suen Crist; and þat is verri tokene þat þei forsaken not þus Crist, siþ þei forsaken al manere of erþeli þingis for Crist; and þis axiþ grete mede, siþ it is myche, and wilful; and mede bihiȝt to traveilours makiþ hem traveile betere. Oþer chartris he nediþ not but þe word of Crist; for wordis of þe firste treuþe passen alle oþer chartris.

Jesus seide to hem, to whom he spak þes wordis: *Soþeli I seie to ȝou, þat ȝe þat þus hav suyd me, in þe laste making of men*[1], *whanne mannis sone shal sitte in sete of his majeste, ȝe shal sitte in twelve setes and juge twelve kynredis of Israel.* Here shal we wite þat Crist spak not oonli to þes twelve, but generali to oþer seintis þat passingli suen Crist; for ȝif Crist bihiȝte þis to Scarioth, and lefte to ȝeve þis mede to Poul, what truþe were in Cristis wordis, or what mede to oþer men? It semeþ þat Crist undirstondiþ his sitting at þe dai of dome; for þis seete of juging is propre to him, boþe God and man; and þerfore it is

Final reward for such leaving.

[1] So E; A excludes *making of men* from the italics.

[a] It is easy to solve the objections raised against this text.

wel clepid, a seete of his majeste. Þis noumbre of twelve is noumbre of alle passinge seintis, þat nyȝ suen Crist in staat of apostlis, and algatis forsoken[1] þe world for the love of Crist. Þe noumbre of þes seintis shal be partid in twelve, and juge alle lesse seintis, which ben also partid in twelve. And alle þes ben Jacobis sones, and seen all clereli God. And þus seien men comunli þat þre manere of men shal come to Cristis jugement. Sum, passinge seintis þat sueden nyȝ Crist, as patriarkis, and Baptist, and oþer Cristis disciplis. And þes, for þei weren liȝt and ensample to oþer, shal juge oþer þat sueden hem to þer boþe[2] worship. And þis jugement shal not be but þis witnessinge of treuþe. Þe secounde part þat shal come to Cristis laste jugement shal be seintis þat shal sue þes grete seintis. And it is no contrariouste[3] þat þes same seintis ben of þes boþe partis, bi dyverse resouns. Þe more part of men, in þe laste jugement, shal be men þat shal be
Ps. i. 5 dampned, and þis is a greet part. Of þes men seiþ þe Psalm, þat þei risen not up in jugement; þei shal be jugid of God, and of alle hise seintis, for to go to helle for her wickid liif. And þis mede, bihiȝt of Crist, passiþ alle þes worldli goodis. Blessid be þis duke of bataile, þat þus rewardiþ his knyȝtis; for þis is more confortable, and betere bi a þousand part, þan wages ȝovun in erþeli batailis of knyȝtis or of clerkis. Lord! siþ þis suyng for[4] Crist is forsaking of worldli goodis, and profiting in poverte after þat Crist lyvede, how myche shulden we preestis drede þat we failen in þis!

And for þis myddil part þat shal come to þe jugement, bihotiþ Crist, þat *ech þat forsakiþ for him* ony of þes eiȝte þingis[5], *shal have an hundred fold here in þis lyf, and, after, pesible possessioun of þe liif of blisse.* Scorne we þes foolis þat seien, bi þes Cristis wordis, þat ech seint shal have here a hundrid wyves at þe laste, and so of oþer sevene þingis þat þe gospel rehersiþ. Here mark we alle þes eiȝte, which ben *hous and breþeren, sistren, and fadir, and modir, wif or children, or feldis,* wiþ oþer rentis. And marke we þe fruyt þat man haþ of worldli havyng of þes eiȝte, and, on þe oþer side, havyng þat just men have here; and

[1] *forsaken*, E. [2] *broþeres*, E. [3] *contrarioste*, E. [4] *of*, E.
[5] So E; om. A.

we shal wel undirstonde þat þis secounde havynge passiþ an hundrid fold þe first in fruyt and profit. And here we taken two þingis as Cristyn mennys bileve:—oon, þat sich men han al manere of þingis; anoþer, þat sich goostli havynge passiþ worldli havyng. And þanne mai we telle scorne by sich asse argumentis:—ȝif a man shal have here an hundred fold so good þing as is þis wif, þanne he shal have an hundrid wyves! Kepe we wordis of þe gospel, and witt of it þerwiþ, and alle þe fendis or false men mai not disprove a word þerof.

Þe Gospel on Candilmasse dai.

[SERMON XCIX.]

Postquam impleti sunt dies.—Luc. ii. [22.]

It is seid comunli, þat oure Ladi haþ fyve festis: Concepcioun, Nativite, Annunciacioun, Purificacioun; þe fifte is Assumpcioun, whanne oure Ladi was deed. Þe ferþe of þes festis is seid in þis gospel, and is clepid comunli þe feste of Candilmasse; for Jewis hadden a lawe,—and we kepen ȝit sumwhat þerof in purifiynge of wymmen,—þat a womman, after þat she was deliverid of a knave child, shulde, in sixe wokes after, come to þe temple and be purified þere, after þat þe law lymytide. And al ȝif oure Ladi nedede not to be þus purified, ȝit, bi counseil of God, she fulfillide þus þe lawe. For her sone seiþ after, I cam not to undo þe lawe, but to fulfille it; and so he made his modir do. And so telliþ Luke, þat, *fro þe daies weren fulfillid of purifying of Marie, after þe lawe of Moises, þei brouȝten Jesus in to Jerusalem to sette him bifore God.* For alȝif God be everywhere, ȝit we seien he is in chirchis on a special manere, as he is in juste soulis. *And so þei offriden Crist to God; as þe law axide þat every male þat openeþ wommans bodi to his issue shal be halewid to þe Lord; and offride for him* a certeyn þing,—*as a peire of turturis or two briddis of dowves.* For riche folk shulden offre for purifying of wymmen a ȝong lomb of o ȝeer, as Goddis

The Purificacion.

lawe tellip; and it sufficide to pore folk to offre a peire of turturis, or two dowve briddis, for þe child þat was born. And so we mai not denye þat ne Crist and his eldris weren pore folk, for þei chosen þe secounde.

Simeon prophesies.

And þer was a man in Jerusalem þat was clepid Symeon; and þis was a just man, and hadde drede of Goddis lawe. And þis man abood conforting of Israel; and þe Holi Goost was in þis Symeon. And þis man hadde answere of þe Holi Goost þat he shulde not se deþ, but ȝif he saw first Crist. And he cam into þe temple bi leding of þe Holi Goost. And whanne þei brouȝten þe child Jesus, his eldris, into þe temple, þat þei shulden do after þe custom of þe[1] *lawe for him, Symeon toke him in his armes, and blessid God, and seide: Now, Lord, þou levest þi servaunt after þi word in pees, for myn iȝen han seen Crist,* þat is *helþe* to þe world. And he is þi owne Sone, þe same God þat þou art. *And his helþe þou hast ordeyned bifore þe face of al manere peple, to be liȝt to shewing of folk, and glorie to þi folk of Israel.*

Lesson of the gospel,—that we should hope for heavenly bliss.

To þis feeste of oure Ladi answeriþ þe fourþe vertue, þat is, hope of hevenli blisse. And it was fulli in hir; for, as bileve lastide in hir whanne it failide in apostlis, so she hopide ever more þat she shulde come to blisse of hevene. For siþ she trowide þat hir Sone shulde rise fro deeþ to lyve, and how and whanne he shulde rise, as God himsilf hadde tauȝt hir, how myȝte þis Ladi myshope þat ne she shulde come to hevene? In þis we shulden sue þis Ladi, and þenke ever on hevenli blisse, and traveile þerfore, niȝt and dai, in hope for to gete þis blisse; and what woo þat we have here, take it in ful pacience, for þe joie þat we hopen to gete in þe blisse of hevene. Lord! siþ a tiliyng man hopiþ ofte to have his fruyt, how moche more shulden we have hope to come to blisse of hevene. And þis hope is of þis kynde, þat it mote be contynuel, and ever more meritorie, to large a mannis blisse in heven. It makiþ a man mery and glad, and suffre al þat falliþ to him; for it is groundid in riȝt bileue þat God doiþ al for þe beste. No man failiþ þis hope[2] but if he synne on oþer syde; and algatis but if he forȝete to þenke on hevenli blisse. Men

[1] So E; om. A [2] *in þis hope*, E.

þat ben stoppid wiþ worldli þou3tis, or wiþ lustis of her fleishe, failen to plese þis Ladi here, and folwe her in þer þou3t; and þus þei maken not þe[1] Lord myche, ne hir spirit is glad in God. But þus dide oure Ladi Marie, as þe gospel telliþ of hir. And þus fewe men in þis liif wanten ernes of dispeire; for þei þat ben depid in synne, and þenken not but on þes worldli goodis, wanten hope of hevenli blisse, and þus þei growen in dispeire. And on þis shulden we prestis þenken; and algatis prestis of þe world, þat suen not Crist in poverte, but þenken how þei mai be riche here. And þis synne is more in coventis þat ben groundid in her goodis, and ever ben depid in þer synne for defaute of ri3t hope.

Þe Gospel on þe chairinge of Seint Petre.

[SERMON C.]

Venit Jesus in partes Cesarie[2].—Matt. xvi. [13.]

Þis gospel telliþ how Petre apostle passide in bileve oþer apostlis, for he was more sad and hardi to trowe of Crist þat he shulde. Matheu telliþ þat *Jesus cam into þe contre* þat siche a cite was inne sett[3] þat was clepid *Cesarie of Filip*[4]. And of two men it hadde þe name. Þis citee hadde þree names; first, it was clepid Lachis; and siþ it was clepid Dan, after þe kinrede of Dan; and after of Philip, Heroudis broþir, þat hadde þe fourþe part of þis rewme, it was clepid Cesarie of Philip, in worship of þe emperour and him[a]. And þis citee was divers

The faith of Peter.

[1] *þis*, E. [2] *Cesaree*, E. [3] *sett ynne*, E [4] *Philip*, E.

[a] If the writer had consulted St. Jerome, he would have found (see Smith's *Bible Dict.*) that Dan and Cesarea-Philippi were two different places, standing about four miles apart, at two different sources of the Jordan. But perhaps his authority was F. Brocardus of Strasburg, a Dominican friar who visited the Holy Land in 1283, and whose description of his journey is given in Canisius's *Thesaurus*, vol. iv. Brocardus similarly confounds the position of Dan or Laish (he calls it Lesem), with that of Paneas or Cesarea-Philippi, to which he gives the additional appellation of Balenas.

fro Cesarie of Palestine, in which dwelte Centurio[a]. But alle þes weren worldli names; and þes men, to gete þer name lastinge here, but not in hevene, leften sich dedis here in erþe, over þe state of innocence. And þus done þes newe ordris, in cloistris and in oþer housis, and þenken to myche on hir liif here, and to litil on hevenli liif. We shulden þenken on goode workes, to make men to forsake þis world, and þenken on Crist and on his liif; for sich þouȝtis wolen lasten wiþ us.

The people's opinion of Christ.

And þus *axide* Crist here, for greet witt þat was in him, among *his disciplis, who he was,* bi his manhede. For it is seid ofte tymes, þat on foure maneris is man brouȝt forþ. Þe fourþe manere, and propre to Crist, is, þat he cam of a virgine oonli. And so to make mede in apostlis, and to teche þe Chirche after, Crist brouȝte in þis questioun, *and axide what men seide of him.* As men hadden dyverse opynyouns of Baptist, what he was,—sum men seiden þat he was Heli, and sum men þat he was Christ, and sum men þat he was anoþer prophete, as techiþ Joones gospel,—so weren many opynyons of Crist. And herfore seiden Cristis apostlis bi oon witt, how dyverse men hadden here dyverse opynyons. For *sum men* seiden þat he was *Baptist;* as Heroude, and men of his opynyon, seiden þat Joon was risen to liif, and he hadde vertue to do miraclis, as þe dedis of Crist shewiden. *Oþer* men seiden of Crist þat he was old *Heli,* þe prophete; for Heli was taken up in a chare of fire, and aftir he apperide no more. *Þe þridde* men seiden, bi Cristis workis, þat he was *Jeremye* þe prophete, *or anoþer grete prophete.* Somme seiden oon and sum anoþer. *But Crist axide his disciplis*[1], *whom þei seiden him to be.* But *Peter answeride*

Peter's confession.

gloriously, as a trewe man, for alle þe apostlis, *and seide* on þis maner, *Þou art Crist, Sone of God lyvynge.* Bi þat þat Petre clepid him Crist, he knowelichide þat he was þe greet prophete, þe which was bihiȝt bi Moises to þe folk in þe oold lawe. And so Petre knowelichide þe manheed of Crist. In þat þat Petre seide after, þat Crist was þe Sone of God lyvyng, he knowelichide Cristis Godhede fro þes fals Goddis. Imagis and

[1] *apostlis,* E.

[a] The writer seems to have mistaken the 'Centurio' of the Vulgate (Acts x. 1) for one of the names of Cornelius.

mawmetis ben falseli clepid Goddis, but þer is but oo lyvynge God, as þer is but oon þis Goddis Sone oonli.

Christ's promises to Peter.

And Crist answeringe seide unto Petre, Blessid art þou, Symount Barjona, for fleish and blood tolde þee not þis, but my Fadir þat is in hevene. Here we trowen, bi Cristis wordis, þat Petre moot needis be blessid; and so he hadde bileve wiþ charite ordeyned to blisse. And so, as Petre moste nedis synne, but he myȝte not synne deedli, so þe boot [1] of Petre, þat is holi Chirche, mote nedis suffre tribulacioun, but it mai not perishe. Petre is now clepid Symount, bi his propre name, and now clepid Barjona, or sone of Johanna, and now clepid Petre, as Crist clepid him here.

And þus *Crist seiþ to him here, þat he is Petre, and upon þis stoone shal he grounden his Chirche.* Þis corner stoone is Crist, of whom Petre haþ þis name; and on þis same stoone is hooli Chirche grounded. And þus Petre and ech man signifieþ þis stoon. And aftirward Crist telliþ þe strengþe of þe Chirche, and bihetiþ first to it, *þat þe ȝatis of helle shal not have myȝt aȝens it.* Cristis Chirche mai here be troublid bi þe fendis lymes, and þes lymes mai be clepid ȝatis of helle. For bi þes many fendis comen in and out, and þei ben ȝatis to many men to entre in to þe weie of helle. Þese ȝatis mai kille þe membris of Crist, but þei mai not harme hem, for Crist kepiþ her soule, and victorie of it is betere þan bodili deþ. And þes ȝatis in þis turmenting doen harm to hem silf, and profit to Cristis Chirche which þei weenen to distrye.

Þe secounde pryvylege of Petre stondiþ in þis; *þat Crist shal ȝeve him þe keies of þe rewme of hevene.* Þes two keies ben soþli seid witt and power, to teche men þe weie to hevene, and to opene hem þe ȝatis. And þes keies hadde Petre wiþ many oþer seintis, for alle men þat comen to hevene have þes keies of God. And so we shal not undirstonde þat þes ben keies of metal, þat oonli Petre beriþ, to opene hevene ȝatis to men; but þei ben lore and power, þat men have goostli of God. And so þis laste word seid is nede to be undirstonden wel, þat, *What kyn þing þat Petre bindiþ upon erþe shal be bounden in hevene,*

[1] *buot*, E.

and what kyn þing he unbindiþ upon erþe shal be unbounden in hevene. And þes wordis weren not oonli seid unto Petre, but comunli to þe apostlis, as þe gospel telliþ after, and, in persones of þe apostlis weren þei seid to prestis, and, as many men þenken, to alle Cristen men. For, if man have mercy on his soule, and unbinde it, or binde it, God bi his jugement in hevene jugiþ þe soule sich. For ech man þat shal be dampned is dampned for his owne gilt, and ech man þat shal be saved is saved bi his owne merit. And þus men seien comunli, þat wordis of Crist ben undirstonden, whanne þes keies erren not fro þe keies above. And so it were nede here to wite what is holi Chirche, and what ben þe keies of hevene, or whanne prestis bynden or unbynden. In þis þrefold disseit ben many men blindid; for as bi þe firste leesyng was mankynde lost, so bi þis secounde lesyng is þe Chirche disseyved. Þe first lesyng was of þe fend, whanne he reverside God, and seide to Adam and Eve þat þei shulden not die. Þe secunde lesyng is of þe fend, and of[1] Anticrist his viker; þe which lesing is poudrid wiþ ypocrisie. He seiþ þat he is next Crist bi manere of lyvyng, and so whatever he seiþ mote nede be soþ; and bi þis foule heresie is þe Chirche disseyved.

Þe Gospel on Seint Mathies Dai.

[SERMON CI.]

Confiteor tibi, Pater, Domine.—Matt. xi. [25.]

God's wisdom given to the meek.

Þis gospel telliþ how Crist answeride to feyned wordis of þe peple, and telde many hie treuþis to lore of his Chirche. And þes treuþis ben pertinent to chesyng of Mathi[2], for þis feste telliþ how Mathi was chosen in þe stede of Scarioth, aftir þat he hadde hanged himsilf. And so telliþ Matheu, how Jesus in þat tyme answeride to þe peple, and seide on þis manere:—*I confesse to þee, Fadir, Lord of hevene and of erþe, þat hiddist*

[1] So E; om. A. [2] *Mathy*, E.

þes treuþis fro worldli wise men and ware, and shewidest hem to meke men, and dispisid of þe world. And þe laste[1] cause herof is told þus of Crist: *Ʒhe, Fadir, þou didist þus, for þus it was liking to þee.* We shal undirstonde here, þat not ech confessioun is rounyng in an eere of a mannis owne synne, but graunting of treuþe wiþ graunting of God. And þus spekiþ Crist, þat is of more auctorite þan alle þes popis þat ordeyneden confessioun of rounyng. And here mai we see how God is Cristis Fadir wiþouten ende, wiþinne, bifore þat he be Lord; but he is ever Lord of þis brode world; and þis world is understonden bi hevene and bi erþe. Þis treuþe þat Crist confessiþ, falling to þe apostlis, stondiþ in þis word; þat þei cowden many trewþis þat weren hid to olde[2] wise men and war of þe world, as weren Scribis and Fariseis, and oþer worldli men. And cause of þis dede of God is open to trewe men; for God wole shewe to men how al wisdom is of him, and he wole ȝeve it freeli to meke men þat he loveþ. So þat nouȝt likiþ to God but for certein enchesoun.

Mathias chosen an apostle for his meekness.

And þus, for Mathi was meke, God chees him apostle. For it is not leveful, for vertue of bileve, to denye þat God wrouȝte in castinge of þes lottis, and in alle dedis of þes apostlis, þe whiche chosen Mathi. And, as it is seid bifore[a], þis chesing were ȝit betere, for mannis affeccioun is falsly varyed, and speciali whanne worldli wynnyng is knyttid to þe chesing. And ȝit men trowen þis heresie as if it were bileve, þat ȝif ony be chosen bi mannis lawe þanne he is treuli chosen. And ȝit boþe þe cheseris, and he þat is chosen, in þis displesen to God. And practik of þis heresie doiþ myche harm in chesing, as we mai see at eye in chesing of þes popis. Lyve þe cheseris a meke liif, and leeve þei to chese a worldli state, and kepe þei þe fourme of þis chesing, and þei shal chese wel. For, no drede, sich disturblyng cam never of chesing of þes popes, ȝif þei weren pore and meke, and lyveden as þe apostlis.

All things delivered to Christ.

And, for disciplis of Crist shulden trowe to his speche, he telliþ what falliþ to him bi vertue of his Godhede. Crist seiþ[3],

[1] So in E; *leste*, A. [2] So E; A has *boldun*. [3] So in E; A gives the words 'Crist seiþ' as part of the quotation.

[a] See p. 304.

þat alle þingis ben ȝovun him of his Fadir, and no man knewe fulli *Goddis Sone but his* owne *Fadir, and no man knewe þis Fadir but his Sone, and* oþere men *to whom he wolde shewe.* Þe firste of þes þree wordis techiþ þat Crist is God, for ellis þe Fadir myȝte not ȝeve him alle þingis. For ȝif we undirstonden bi alle þingis, alle creaturis, ȝit þe Sone is bifore þat he have alle creaturis; and in þat beyng bifore he mote nede be God. And ȝif we undirstonden al þing wiþinne in God, þat Crist haþ al þis þing ȝovun of his Fadir, ȝit Crist moot nedis be God, ȝif þis gifte be trewe; for þanne Crist haþ þe Holi Goost, and propirtees of þre persones, and þe Fadir of hevene in a manere, þe which mai oonli acorde to God. And so, for þe first word is soþ, Crist mot nedis be God. And of þis wole it sue þat Crist is almyȝty, all witti, and al wilful, as þe Trinite is; for Crist is þe same God þe which is þe Trinite. Of þis wole sue þe toþer word after, þat no resonable þing knowiþ þe Sone at þe fulle but þe Fadir of hevene; for þei ben algatis evene. And after þis speche of þe Trinite, þe whiche is even in himsilf, shulde Crist speke of þis cunnyng, þe which is þe most þat mai be. Þe þridde word sueþ of þes: þat no man knowiþ þe Fadir but þe Sone, and þes men to which þis sone wole shewe þis knowing. Þe peple myȝte se at iȝe how þat Crist was verri man. And so Crist comeþ doun to mannis speche of knowing. Þe Sone, bi his Godhede, knowiþ evenli þe Fadir; and, bi þat þat he is man, he knowiþ as myche as man may knowe; and so his knowing moot be comuned to men after þat þei ben able. Þe Holi Goost is þe same kynde þat is þe Fadir and þe Sone, and þerfore Crist, supposing þis, leeveþ to speke of þis Goost.

And of þis may men gadere how men shulde trowe here Cristis wordis, siþ he is God þat mai not lye, ne faile to man in his lore. And, for Crist is boþe God and man, and haþ breþeren of his lesse kynde, þerfore he turneþ him to his breþeren and confortiþ hem in þer travaile. *Come ȝe alle to me, seiþ Crist, þat travailen and ben chargid, and Y shall refete*[1] *ȝou. Take ȝe my ȝok upon ȝou, and lerne ȝe of me* þis lessoun,

[1] *refreesche*, E.

þat Y am mylde and meke of herte, and sue ȝe ȝoure Fadir in þes two, and þanne, *shal ȝe finde reste to ȝoure soulis*, in ȝoure traveil. *For my ȝok is swete, and my charge is liȝt.* And þes wordis of Crist, to conforte religiouse men, ben betere þan alle þes newe reulis þat ben cloutid to Cristis wordis; for, in what staat þat þou be in Cristis religioun, lerne wel þe lessoun of myldenes and mekenes of Crist, how he kepte him in al his lyf, in what troublyng þat he was inne. And ȝif þou be on Goddis half, þou shalt lyve mekeli aftir Crist.

Þe Gospel oure Lady Day in Lente.

[SERMON CII.]

Missus est Angelus Gabriel a Deo.—Luyk. i. [26.]

Þis gospel telliþ to þe Chirche how þe aungel grette oure Ladi, and how she, bi hir mekenesse, ablide hir to conseyve Crist. And þis þridde feste of oure Ladi is a wondir hiȝe feste, for in þis was Crist maad man, and Crist passiþ alle oþer seintis. And so men seien comunli, þat oure Ladi hadde fyve joies. Þe firste was at þis tyme whanne she conceyvede Crist bi mekenes. Þe secounde was whanne she bare Crist wiþouten peyne at Cristemasse; þe þridde was whanne it was shewid to hir þat Crist was risen fro deeþ to lyve; þe ferþe was whanne she saw hir sone stie in to hevene; and þe fifþe joie was whanne she was deed and take to blisse. And to þes fyve joies ben answerynge fyve vertues þat we mai have; and ȝif we wolen worshipe þis Ladi, holde we þes vertues wel. Þes fyve vertues ben in þis ordre: mekenesse and chastite, bileve and hope, and charite; and ȝif we kepen hem we plesen God. And siþ Crist and his modir moten nedis be of oo wille, þus shal we plese to Marie, þe which is Goddis modir. The Annunciation.

Luk telliþ how, *Gabriel was sent fro God to grete Marie.* And, for sum men ben clepid Gabriel, þerfore þe gospel specifieþ þat, *þe aungel* Gabriel was sent fro God *to Nazareth*, þat was, *a citee of Galilee*, in which citee oure Ladi dwelte. *And þis maiden was* The greeting of the angel.

weddid to Joseph, þe which was of Daviþis hous, and name of þe virgyn was Marie. And wel she is clepid a virgyn so ofte in þis Gospel, for she was virgyne whanne she was weddid, and a virgyn after to her deþ. And a litil before þis wedding, þis aungel grette þis maiden þus; and so was Crist conseyved of hir in verri matrimonie of Joseph. It semeþ þat Ambrose, upon Luk, seiþ [a], þat þei weren weddid bifore, and soone, bitwixe þat tyme and nyȝt, þe aungel cam and grette Marie þus. And algatis, on ech wey, oure Ladi was weddid in þe same hour, or nye þat hour þat she was greet [1]. Suppose we þat þis greting cam after, and neiþer wordis ne resoun semeþ to aȝen seie þis. Þis *aungel cam in to þis maiden, and seide to hir* on þis manere, *Hail, ful of grace, God is wiþ þee; blessid be þou among wymmen.* Þis angel clepide not now Marie bi hir propir name, þat she was clepid, for common uss [2] wiþ lordis and ladies axiþ, þat comun servauntis of hem clepen hem not bi propre name, but bi name of excellence; as men þat speken of oure Kyng leeven to clepen him Kyng Richard, but seien þat þis is þe wille of þe Kyng, or þus þe Kyng biddiþ to do [b]. And clouting of þis word Marie to þis gretinge of þe angel is not worþ ful myche pardone, but ȝif it be [c] two þousand ȝeer; as men seien þe pope haþ grauntid [d] for þe seiyng of an orisoun bitwixe þe sacryng and Agnus Dei. But many þenken þat þe Pater noster is þe bettere. And so it semeþ to many men þat God and þe pope varien, siþ God doiþ al þing upon resoun, and not but for certeyn causis.

[1] *gret*, E. [2] *use*, E.

[a] S. Ambros. *Comment. in Lucam*, Lib. II, cap. 1.

[b] This indication of date, which confines the composition of these sermons within the years 1378-1399, has been considered in the Introduction.

[c] 'but ȝif it be' appears to be used here in the sense of 'much less.' But perhaps the sentence should be punctuated thus,—'myche pardone; but ȝif it be, two þousand ȝeer, as men seien, þe pope haþ grauntid,' &c.

[d] I have searched the *Bullarium* (that of Cocquelines, Rome, 1739), which however is very meagre for the pontificate of Urban VI, and toiled through the numerous proclamations of indulgence of that pope, which are thickly strewn over the pages of Raynaldus, the continuator of Baronius, but without finding anything to support the statement in the text. The usual indulgence granted to those who took up arms against the anti-pope was a plenary indulgence, on the same conditions and with the same privileges as were customary in the case of crusaders to the Holy Land.

Oure Ladi, *whanne she herde þis greting, was troublid in þis word, and þouȝte,* as a wise maiden, *what manere shulde be þis greting.* Þis troublinge in þis gretinge puttiþ no synne or blame in Marie, siþ Crist seiþ þat his soule is troublid, bifore his deþ. *And þis angel seide to hir, Drede þe not, Marie, for þou hast foundun grace bifore þe Lord* of alle Lordis. And here þis aungel, for confort, clepide Marie bi hir propre name, to telle þat he knewe hir wel, and eke þe Lord þat sente him. For whoever haþ founden grace of a lord is loved of him. *Lo, þou shalt conseyve in wombe, and þou shalt bere a sone, and þou shalt clepe his name Jesus. And he þis* [a] *shal be greet, and he shal be clepid þe sone of þe hiȝeste Lord; and þe Lord God shal ȝeve him Daviþis seete,* þe which Daviþ is *his fadir; and he shal rengne in Jacobis*[1] *hous wiþouten ende*[2] *and of his rewme shal be noon ende.* Bi þis mai men undirstonden þat Crist was king, as Daviþ was, but more spirituali, as his kyngdom was more spiritual. For ech worldli lordship mote nedis have an ende; and þus rengnyng wiþouten eende in þe hous of Jacob, and þat of his rewme shal be noon eende, tellen how Crist rengneþ spirituali, and not contrarie to worldli lordis. Christ's spiritual Kingship.

And Marie seide to þis angel, On what manere shal þis be, for I knowe no man fleishli? *And þis angel answering seide to hir, Þe Hooli Goost shal come above in þee, and þe vertue of alþer hiȝeste* Lord *shal make umbre unto þee.* Þe vertue of God makiþ umbre, whanne in a lowe place it lettiþ heete [3] of synne, as it fel in oure Ladi; for she was lower in kinde þan aungels, and she conseyvede wiþouten synne. *And þerfore þat holi þing þat shal be born of þee shal be clepid Goddis Sone,* singulerli bifore oþer. *And lo, Eliȝabeth þi cosyn, and she haþ conseyved a sone in hir elde; and þis moneþ is þe sixte to him þat is clepid bareyne* [b].

[1] *Jacobs*, E. [2] So in E; om. A. [3] *þe bete*, E.

[a] 'He this' is the reading in this place of a single MS. (Bodl. 277) of the later Wycliffite version.

[b] *to him that is clepid bareyne.* Both A and E concur in this reading, and the expression a few lines below, 'Zacharie in reprefe was clepid bareyne,' leaves no doubt that it is correct. But it is not easy to understand why the writer adopted this most erroneous version of the original, or where he found any countenance for it. The very numerous MSS. of the two Wycliffite versions all read 'hir,' and the rendering of the Vulgate is 'illi quae vocatur sterilis.' Did the writer inadvertently read 'qui' for 'quae?'

For Zakary, Baptist fadir, hadde geten Joon sixe moneþis bifore; and so bi a litil tyme Joon was man bifore Crist. But evene bi sixe moneþis was Joon born before Crist; for Crist was man, but not Joon, fro þe[1] tyme þat he was conceyved. And Zacharie in repreef was clepid bareyne, wiþouten fruyte. *For no word þat God seiþ shal be impossible to him;* and so, siþ God wole have it þus, it mote algatis be so.

The Conception.

And Marie, as ful ripe in mekenesse, *answeride* þus *to þe aungel:* Lo, here *þe handmaiden of God; Be it done to me after þi word.* And, as men seien comunli, in þis tyme Marie conseyvede Crist. For, as Eve, for þe tyme þat she was moost proud, loste mankynde, so Marie, for þe tyme þat she was most meke, won mankynde. And here, ȝif þou wilt plese Marie, or God hir sone, be algatis meke; for mekenes wole plese to Marie, siþ she woot it plesiþ to God. And herfore she seiþ in hir song: God bihelde þe mekenesse of his maiden, and certis, herfore, lo, alle kynredis shal seie þat I am blessid. And so, ȝif þou wilt plese oure Ladi, traveile þou to growe in mekenes. Also, siþ ech hie þing mote have a good and stable ground, and ȝif þou wilt come to hevene þou moost make a tour þidir, and so, if þou wilt come to hevene, stable þee in Cristis mekenesse. And so as þe sentre is lowest of alle þingis, so Crist is þe mekeste þat mai be. Also, þe lower þat a vessel is, þe more of licour wole it take; and so þe mekere þat a man is, þe more of grace wole he take. And so, ȝif þou wilt have grace of God, meke þee wele in þi soule; for mekenes meveþ to pacience, and to al oþer manere of vertues.

The example of Mary teaches meekness.

[1] So E; *for tyme,* A.

Þe Gospel on Philippis Dai and Jacob.

[SERMON CIII.]

Non turbetur[1] *cor vestrum.*—John xiv. [1.]

Þis gospel telliþ, how Crist confortide his disciplis upon Shire Þursdaie, as he dide comunli in wordis þat he seide hem þanne. Joon telliþ in fyve capitlis wordis þat Crist spake after his soper; and, among oþer þingis, he tolde hem how he shulde be bitrayd, and how he shulde be after turmentid and deed, and how þei shulden have drede boþe wiþinne and wiþouten. And herfore he medlide wiþ al wise wordis of confort. Crist biddiþ first in þis Gospel, þat *her herte be not troublid* wiþinne, *ne drede* for perils wiþouten, for confort þat þei shal have of him. ȝif þei ben sad in þis bileve, þat alle þes þingis moten nedis falle, and for þer betere afterward, boþe here and in hevene, þei shulden not be troublid wiþinne to leese ony vertue; for þanne þei shulden falle fro vertues, for good þat God made to hem. And, bi þis same resoun, þei shulden not drede of bodili peril; for al þis shulde turne hem to good bi þis same bileve. And, for to make hem siker of þis, Crist seiþ þis word, *ȝe trowen in God, and trowe ȝe in me.* As who seiþ, ȝe moten nedis trowe in God, or ellis ȝou failiþ charite; and ȝe mai not trowe in God, but ȝif ȝe trowen in me, for Y am þe same God, þat is God þe Fadir. And so wordis þat Y telle ȝou moten nedis be soþ. ȝif God telle us a þing, who of us wolde drede þerof, siþ we ben certyn of bileve þat God mai not disseyve us? And oonhede in Godhede, wiþ Trinite in persones, is ofte seid in þis gospel, and in oþer boþe. And þus bileve shulde be ground to conforte men in þis weie.

Christ's discourses at the Last Supper.

And men shulden not muse on þis, þat ne þer ben diverse meritis. For, as þer ben in ech man diverse degrees of bileve, so þer ben in Cristis apostlis diverse degrees of meritis. And

'Many mansions,' degrees of merit and reward.

[1] So in E; A has *turbentur*.

for to quiete hem in þis Crist seiþ to his apostlis, þat *in þe hous of his Fadir ben many dwellingis;* as who seiþ, Have ȝe sum degree of feiþ and hope and charite, and laste ȝe, creessyng þerinne to ȝour lyves eende, and ȝour place is ordeyned in hevene after þat ȝe ben worþe. What man shulde herfor lette to serve God wel, but raþer he shulde enforse him to encresse in Goddis service. And þes disciplis shulden truste in þis meene persone Crist; for, as he seiþ soþli, *ȝif ony þing* in hevenli blis *were lesse*, or defauty, *he wolde have teld hem.* And in proof of þis þing, *he stieþ up* in his tyme, *to make hem a place redi þere*, as he dide aftirward. And siþ he is boþe God and man, he woot wel how it is þere; and gabbing in sich a Lord were more synne þanne ever was.

Final bliss, and the way to it.

And, for Crist mai not bigynne a þing but ȝif he make an eende þerof, þerfore he seiþ, þat *ȝif he wende þus to hevene he shal come aȝen and take þes apostlis to him.* And þis shal be verified at Cristis comyng at þe dai of dome, *þat where Crist is* evermore, boþe in stede and in blisse, *þei ben þere wiþ him* after þis dai wiþouten eende. *And ȝe witen whidir Y go, and also ȝe knowe þe weie.* And þus Crist certefiede hem þat þei witen þe ende, and þe weie how þei shulden come to blisse, over þat þe fadirs wisten in þe olde testament; and þus þei may truste in Crist as meene persone of God and man. *But Thomas seid here to Crist, Sire, we witen nere whidir þou goist, and how mai we knowe þe weie? And Jesus seide to him: I am weie, truþe, and lyf.* As ȝif he wolde meene to Crystene men: Knowe ȝe me, and love ȝe me, and ȝe knowe alle þes þingis. For Crist wole teche his disciplis bi litil and litil alle þes. And so þe liif þat Crist ledde here is þe weie to come to hevene; for but if we suen him in þis liif, we shal never come to blis. And þe trewe reule þat he ȝaf is treuþe, to teche men þat wolden ellis erre. And he is liif many weies to susteyne men yn þis traveile.

Christ's mediation.

And so Crist seiþ soþli [1], *þat no man comeþ to þe Fadir but bi him;* for his manhede is nedeful meene to make asseþ for mannis synne, and his Godhede mote nedis meeve to come þis weie, so fer fro erþe. And muse we not of þe knowing þat

[1] So E; A includes the word in the quotation.

we moten have of þis Fadir. For Crist seiþ soþli, *þat ȝif þei hadde knowen him, certis þei hadden knowe his Fadir.* For whoso knowiþ Cristis Godhede, he woot how God seiþ al þing; for þis word of God is his Sone and Crist, þat we shulden knowe þus; and þanne he knowiþ him þat seiþ, þe which is God þe Fadir. *And after ȝe shal knowe þe Fadir* beter þan ȝe ȝit done; *and ȝe have saien him*, bi bileve þat bringiþ in þis knowing.

And, for þese wordis weren woundirful, þerfore *Philip seide to Crist: Sire, shewe us þe Fadir, and it is ynowȝ to us. And Jesus seide to Philip þanne, So longe tyme I am wiþ ȝou, and ȝit ȝe knowen not me, Philip. Whoso seeþ me, he seeþ my Fadir; how seist þou, shewe us þe Fadir? Ne trowest not þou þat I am in þe Fadir, and þe Fadir is in me? þes wordis þat I speke, I speke hem not of mysilf: but, certis, þe Fadir þat dwelliþ in me is þat ilk þat doiþ þe werkes. Ne trowe ȝe not þat Y am in þe Fadir, and þe Fadir is in me? ellis, trowe ȝe my Godhede, for þe workes þat Y do. Soþeli, soþli, I seie to ȝou, þat man þat trowiþ in me shal do þe werkes þat Y do; and þe moste of hem*[a] *shal he do, for I go to my Fadir*, and my chirche, þat is my bodi, dwelliþ ȝit stille in erþe. And I shal not be idil in hevene, *for whatever ȝe axen þe Fadir in my name, þat shal Y do.*

Alle þes wordis þat Crist seiþ here axen sutil undirstonding, ȝhe, more þan we mai have while we lyven in þis liif. It is nedeful here to knowe, how þe Godhede of Crist is oþir in kynde þan his manhede, al if þei boþe ben oo persone. And þis Godhede is so sutil þat it is comune to þre persones. And so, whoso knowiþ þis Godhede in oon mote nedis knowe it in ech of hem; for þes þree persones ben not diverse, as þree men, or þree oþer substances, but ech of hem mai nowher be, ne ouȝt do, wiþouten ech oþer. And þis mannis witt mote be clene þat shulde knowe wel þis matere. The doctrine of the Trinity.

[a] 'Majora horum faciet;' Vulg.

Þe Gospel on Ascencioun Day[a].

[SERMON CIV.]

Recumbentibus undecem discipulis.—Mark xvi. [14.]

Christ's last appearance to the apostles.

Þis gospel telliþ in what form Crist toke his leve at his apostlis. Mark seiþ, þat enleven apostlis restiden after þat þei hadden eten, and Jesus apperide unto hem, and reproveden untreuþe of hem, and hardnes of þer herte, for þei trowiden not to hem þat sawen þat he was risen from deþ. And Crist seide to hem, Go ȝe into al þe world, and preche ȝe þe gospel unto alle maner of men. He þat shal trowe and be baptisid shal be saaf; and certis he þat shal not trowe shal be dampned. And þes signes shulen folowen hem þat shulen bileve in my name: Þei shulen caste out fendis, þei shulen speke wiþ newe tungis, þei shulen take awei addris, and ȝif þei drynken ony dedeli þing, it shal not noie hem; þei shulen putte þer hondis on syke men, and þes seke men shulen fare wel. And soþeli þe Lord Jesus, fro he hadde spoke þus wiþ hem, he was taken in to hevene and sittiþ on Goddis riȝt side. And þei wenten her weie, and prechiden everywhere, and þe Lord wrouȝte wiþ hem, and confermede her *wordis wiþ þes signes suing*.

His practice authorizes our breaking our fast before communion.

Here men shulden note þes wordis, for ech of hem beriþ greet witt; first, how Crist toke leve at his disciplis fro þe tyme þat þei hadden eeten. He ȝaf þe sacrament to hem after þer mete comunli, and Crist spak wiþ hem comunli after þat þei hadden sumwhat eten. And no drede to Cristene men þat ne Crist dide þus for certeyn cause. O cause was herfore, þat men shulden eten in good mesure, þat þer wittis weren more sharp, and þei more able to serve God. And Crist wiste þat men shulden ordeyne reversingeli to Cristis dede, and herfore he ordeynede þus, to telle þat þe contrarie is leveful. And þis shulden þes men note þat proven þat þe ost is not breed; for

[a] This sermon is not found in MS. E (Douce 321).

þanne, þei seien, man brake his fast, etinge þe oost whanne it is sacrid, and þanne he shulde not take aftirward Goddis blood þat is sacrid in þe chalis. Lord! whi witen not þes foolis þat þer accidentis maken men drunken whanne þei taken hem above resoun, as Poul witnessiþ? And witt proveþ where þis man be excusid of gloterie, for he is drunken of an accident. And siþ taking of þis þing in mesure was no synne in Cristis tyme, what vertue haþ mannis statute to make þis be synne more þan þanne? Þes founed wordis fordone Cristis fredom, and bileve þat men shulden have. Ȝif þis be no synne to God, it is no synne for to charge to eeten in mesure bifore þe masse, and after to synge and use. 1 Cor. xi. 21.

Aftirward we shulden wite, how Christ reprovede unbileve and hardnes of apostlis hertis, þat weren bifore, and þanne weren taken awei, for þei hadden not sorewe ynowȝ for þese errours þat þei weren inne. And þei shulden note þe wordis of Crist þat he spak þat tyme to hem. And þis is anoþer note, how Crist bad hem þanne go and preche þe gospel freli to alle manere men. And wo be to hem þat letten þis, for jurisdiccioun or oþer cause; as wo is to hem þat leven þis, and prechen dremys, fablis, and gabbingis. And it is not ynow to have nakid bileeve, but men moten have charite, þat shal fourme oþere vertues. And þis baptisiþ men wiþ baptym of þe Holi Goost.

But ȝit men douten of þes wordis þat Crist spekiþ aftir. It semeþ þat alle men þat bileven moten nede have þes fyve signes; and siþ noon of us haþ hem, noon of us haþ bileve. Here men seien comunli, þat seintis at þe first tyme hadden alle þes fyve signes betere þan we have now. But trewe men have in a manere alle þes signes now. For whanne þei delyveren hem of synnes, þei casten out fendis in þe name of Crist. And þei speken wiþ newe tunges, for alle þingis þat men done in grace be newe bi titil of grace. And Crist seiþ, in Apocalips[a], þei taken awei addris þat þei have of þer fleish; for þer will is awei to displese God bi þer lust. And dedli drynke, ȝif þei taken it, or oþer þing þat comeþ to hem, anoieþ

[a] Is the reference to Apoc. xii. 9?

hem not, but bringiþ hem to blisse þat God haþ ordeyned to hem. And ȝif þei blessen men, or what þing þat þei done, Cristene men shulen be beterid, wheþer þei be saved or dampned. And so it semeþ þat þes men oonli trowen þus, þat God haþ ordeyned to blisse; for oþer men ben in greet synne and in greet unbileve, alȝif it be florishid for a tyme.

But men noten last here, how Crist sittiþ on þe riȝt side of his Fadir, siþ his Fadir is oonli Godhede, and haþ no figure as man haþ. And here men knowen as bileve þat Christ sittiþ not on þe bodili side of his Fadir in hevene, for his Fadir haþ noo sich side; but þe Fadir haþ sum men ordeyned to dampnacioun, as ben fendis in helle and men þat shulen be dampned þere; and þes ben þe left side of þe Fadir, on which Crist shal not sitte. Sum men ben on þe riȝt side; as alle men þat shulen be saved, and ordeyned to come to blisse after Goddis firste ordenaunce. And þus Crist bi his manhede sittiþ on his Fadirs riȝt side, for no þing mai be nerre Godhede ne more blessid þan is Cristis manhede. And so he sittiþ on his Fadirs riȝt side on oþer manere þan ony oþer mai sitte.

Þe Gospel on Mydsomer Evyn.

[SERMON CV.]

Fuit in diebus Herodis.—Luc. i. [5.]

The writer denounces those who had turned the freedom of the New Law into a bondage.

Þis gospel telliþ a playen[1] storie how þat Joon Baptist cam forþ. Luk telliþ, how *þer was in daies of Heroude kyng of Jude o prest clepid Zacarie, of þe gendrure of þe preest Abia. And* loot[2] fel to þes preestis to mynistre in þe eiȝtiþe woke. *And Zacaryus wif was of Aarons douȝters, and hir name was Elizabeth. And boþe þes two weren just bifore God, going forþ in alle Goddis mandementis and in alle justifiying of þe Lord wiþouten pleint.* Fadirs of þe olde lawe weren myche chargid over men now; for þei kepten þes same ten mandementis, þat we kepen

[1] *pleyn*, E. [2] So E; *lo it*, A.

in þe newe lawe, and over, ȝif þei wolden be juste, þei mosten kepe cerymonyes, and many lawis judicialis, þat us nediþ not now to kepe. And, for þes two kepten al þis wiþouten grete blame of God or man, þerfore Luk preisiþ Baptistis eldris in keping of þe olde lawe. But woo is to hem in tyme of grace, þat þus have chargid þe newe lawe, þat we have now more to kepe þan þei hadden in þe olde lawe. For[1] þes men have distroyed freedom, and pervertid Cristis Chirche, and so, as myche as in hem is, þei have maad Crist unfree, and þis unfredom is worse þan al þe richessis of þis world.

The Angel Gabriel and Zacharias.

And þei hadden noo child ȝit, for þe womman was bareyne, and þei weren boþe olde, passid wel in tyme of her eelde. And it fel þat Zacarie dide his preestis office in þe temple, as it fel to his tyme, and custom þat þanne was. He wente herbi aloone to offre ensence in þe inner part of þe temple; and al þe peple was wiþouten preiynge in þe tyme of þis ensence. And oure Lordis aungel apperide to him stonding on þe riȝt side of þe auter. And þis preest Zacarie was disturblid, and dredde herfore. But þe aungel seide to him, Drede þee not, Zacarie, for þi preier is herd; and Elizabeth þi wyf shal bere to þee a child, and his name shal be clepid Joon, and joie and gladnes shal be to þee, and many shal enjoie in his birþe. He shal be greete bifore God, and wyn and sidir[2][a] *he shal not drynke; and he shal be fild wiþ þe Holi Goost ȝit fro his modir wombe. And he shal turne many of þes children of Israel to þe Lord God of hem. And þis Joon shal go bifore Crist, in spirit and vertue of Helye;* for Joon was Hely in figure, as Christ seiþ þat mai not lye. *And þis* Joon *shal converte þe hertis of þe* formere *fadris in to þe* love of þer *sones*, þat tellen hem þat Crist is comen; *and men out of bileve Joon shal turne to prudence of juste men.* For it was a greet prudence to trowe þe signes of Crist, þat he was þe prophete bihiȝt to þe fadirs of þe olde lawe. *And so Baptist made redi to þe Lord a perfect folk* in riȝt bileve.

[1] So E; *And for*, A, which leaves the construction incomplete.
[2] *sydre*, E.

[a] Both Wycliffite versions render the *siceram* of the Vulgate in this place by *sydir*. Ducange identifies sicera (other forms of which are sisara, cicera, and cisara) with the French *cidre*, whence comes our 'cider.'

Christ condemns both church-endowment and the celibacy of the clergy.

Here mai men douten, and trete of þe staat and liif of prestis; how þei ben dowid and wyflees aȝens Goddis autorite; for Crist forfendid dowyng boþe in him and in hise apostlis, and approvede wedding in apostlis and many oþer. And þis is þe caste of þe fend, to kyndle fir in[1] heerdis; for or þei moten boþe brenne, or þe kepere mote leeve his craft and traveile to kepe þis fir[a]. And preestis shal not do boþe wel.

Þe Gospel on Mydsomer Dai.

[SERMON CVI.]

Elizabeth impletum est tempus pariendi.—Luc. i. [57.]

The nativity of John the Baptist.

Þis gospel telliþ of þe forme þat Joon Baptist was born inne, and seiþ; *To Elizabeth was tyme fulfillid to bere child.* For þe Wise man seiþ þat alle þingis have þer tyme. And siþ al þing mote nedis come in tyme þat God haþ ordeyned it, muche more þe tyme of Joon, þat God ordeyned[2] so speciali. *And* þus Elizabeth *bare þis child. And her neiȝboris and her cosyns herden þat she was delyverid, and helden þat God hadde maad his mercy greet wiþ þis olde wiif, and joiefulli þankide God wiþ hir. And it fel in þe eiȝtiþ daie, þei camen to circumcide þe child; and þei clepiden him Zacarie after his fadirs name. And his modir answeride and seide, Nay, but he shal be clepid Joon. And þei seiden to Elizabeth, þat no man was in hir kyn þat was clepid bi þis name;* whi shulde he be clepid so? *But þei bekeneden to his fadir, what he wolde þat he were clepid, and he axide a metal pointel*[3], *and wroot, and seide, Joon is his name.*

Eccles. iii. 1.

Zacharias recovers his speech.

And so miracle was wiþ Joon Baptist, boþe bifore his birþe and aftir; for, as men taken of þe gospel, Zacarie trowide not

[1] *and*, E. [2] So E; *ordeyneþ*, A. [3] *poyntel*, E.

[a] The meaning appears to be:—it is a wile of Satan to promote the celibacy of the clergy, because thereby he kindles the fire of unlawful passion ('melius nubere quam uri') in Christian pastors, who then either continue to burn with it (and so fall into sin), or have to leave their proper pastoral work in order to take such measures as may keep this fire under control.

to þis aungel, and þerfore bi þe wille of God he was doumbe til þis tyme, and here he recoveride his speche, and tolde what þe child shulde hatte[1]. For boþe his eldris helden in þer mynde how Gabriel wolde þat he hiȝte Joon. *And herfore woundride folk al aboute. And anoon his mouþ was opened, and his tunge was unboundun, and he spak and blesside God for þe þing þat bifel þus. And drede was on alle her neiȝboris. And þes wordis weren publishid upon alle hiȝe coostis of Judee. And alle þat herden of þis þing puttiden in þeir herte and seiden, Who, trowist þou, shal þis child be? for þe hond of oure Lord was wiþ him.* Sacarie was a famous man, wiþ Elizabeth his wyf, and many myraclis weren bifallen aboute þe birþe of þis Joon; and þus þe contre preiside him muche, for many causis þat weren in him. It was a miracle þat þe aungel telde him in so holi a place; it was miracle þat Sacary was dombe, for he wolde not trowe þis aungel; it was miracle þat so oold folk brouȝten forþ þis child in her olde daies; it was miracle þat his eeldris on þis manere namyde þe child; and al þe lyf þat Joon lyvede was ful of miraclis bifore and after.

Against the patrons of new orders.

And þus his fadir profeciede, bi filling of þe Holi Goost; Blessid be þe Lord God of Israel, for he haþ visited and maad þe biyng aȝen of his peple. And so Joones fadir and his modir and he himsilf weren maad prophetis. And here mai trewe preestis touche how þis world is blyndid bi foli, when it sueþ men as patrouns þat weren foolis and ful of synne, and leven Crist and Baptist þat weren bigyneris of oure ordir. And herof pleynede Crist in þe gospel, þat þei singen neiþer wiþ him ne wipen[2] wiþ Baptist, but wiþ oþer foolis whos liif is biside bileve.

[1] *hote*, E. [2] *wepen*, E.

Þe Gospel on Petris and Poulis Evyn.

[SERMON CVII.]

Dixit Jesus Symoni[1] *Petro.*—John xxi. [15.]

The calling of St. Peter.

Þis gospel telliþ how Petre and oþir preestis shulden love God, and travailen in his chirche. And, for þis love stondiþ in þe grace of God, þerfore *Crist clepiþ Petre, Symount, Joones soone.* For whoso prechiþ to þe peple and techiþ hem Goddis lawe, he is þat ilke in whom is Goddis grace; and juste eldris may disserve grace to þer children, as it is teld bifore of eldris of Joon Baptist. Crist in his laste speche wiþ Petre apostle axide him þries where[2] he lovede him; and his bileve is aweie, þat troweþ not[3] þat Crist seide þus for to prynte his love in Petre, and his successouris.

Christ's charge to him.

And þus Christ axide first, *Symount, Joones sone, lovest þou me more þan þese? And Petre seide to Crist: Ȝhe, Lord, þou wost þat Y love þee.* Petre[4] was here curteys and temprid fro presumpcioun, for he seide not þat he lovede Crist betere þan any oþer apostle, but he seide, Crist wiste wele þat he lovede him. And here Petre confesside þat Crist knewe al þing. *But Christ seide to Petre,* in shewing of þis love, *þat he shulde fede his lambren,* bi þe lawe of Crist; as who seiþ, if þou love me, þou most do þis dede. *Þe secounde tyme axide Christ where Symount Joones sone lovede him. And Petre seide to Crist, Ȝhe, Lord, þou wost þat I love þee. And Christ seide to Petre,* to conferme þis word, *þat he shulde fede his lambren,* in lore of þer soule. For as mannis soule is betre þan is þe bodi of him, so feeding of his soule is betere þan is feding of his bodi. And siþ lambren of Crist ben oo bodi wiþ Crist, more love myȝte no man shewe þan þus for to fede his lambren. *But ȝit Christ axide þe þridde tyme, where Symount Petre lovede him. And Petre hadde sorewe þat Christ axide þis þus ofte, and seide aȝen to Crist, Lord, þou*

[1] So E; *Symony*, A. [2] *wheþer*, E. [3] So E; the words *þat troweþ not* are om. in A. [4] So E; *Petre* is italicized in A.

woost alle þingis, þou wost þat I love þee. And Crist bad him shewe þis in dede, and fede his sheep, þat is more þan þes oþer, as sheep passen lambren.

No man þat is in bileve drediþ of þis gospel, þat ne Crist chargide þes wordis ech bi resoun; and so he tauȝte apostlis to feede his sheep in pasturis of holi writt, and not in roten pasturis, as ben fablis and lesingis and lawes of men. Þe pasture everemore grene wiþ treuþis þat nevere more failen, is þe lawe of holi writt, þat lastiþ in þe toþer world. But, for a good heerde shulde kepe his sheepe fro wolves, and defende hem fro scabbis and fro rendinge, þerfore Crist bad Petre þries þat he shulde kepe his sheepe. Crist tauȝte not to his heerde to reise up a croyserie and kille his sheep, wiþ his lambren, and spoilen hem of þeir goodis; but þis is lore of Anticrist, þat þe fend haþ now brouȝt in; and bi þis it is knowen þat þes ben not Petris vikeris.

Peter was charged to feed, not to kill, Christ's sheep.

And Crist techiþ Petre, and in him alle his vikeris, how it falliþ to him to do aȝen his firste will. *Soþli, soþli, I seie to þee, whanne þou were ȝonge þou girdist þee, and wentist whidir þat þou woldist; but now, whanne þou wexist oolde, anoþer shal girde þee, and shal lede þee þe weie which þou wolt not*, of þi silf. And þis word seide Crist for to telle to þe Chirche bi what deþ Petre shulde clarifie God. For Crist seiþ bifore, in þe gospel of Joon, þat þe moste propirte þat followiþ a good herde is, þat he putte his lyf for his sheep, for þus dide Crist, and wolde þat Petre þus suede him. And þe moste contrarie condicioun, þat sueþ Anticrist, is to putte his sheepis lyves for his cursid lordship.

ON OCTAVE OF MYDSOMER.

[SERMON CVIII.]

Dixit Zacarias.—LUK i. [18.]

Þis gospel telliþ þe middil of a storie of Seint Joon Baptist. Þe vigile of Baptist telliþ how Gabriel bihiȝte him, and þis

The unbelief of Zacharias.

storie telliþ how Zacarie mistrowide. And so Luk telliþ, how *Zacharie seide to þe aungel, Wherof shal Y wite þis*, þat Y shal gete a child; *for I am an oold man, and my wif is passid in eelde?* Here þis Zacharie trowide not to þe aungel; but Marie trowide to þis aungel þat he seide her soþ, but she wolde be certefied more of þe manere. And þus sum men reden as two wordis þis axing, On what manere shal þis be, for I knowe not man. But þis Zacarie mistrowide, and maad þerto his evydence; and so boþe þes weren troublid, but Zacarie more, for þe troubling of hym refte him bileve. *But Gabriel telde him*, wherfore he shulde trowe. *For I am Gabriel, þat stonde bifore God, and I am sent of him to telle þee þes good tiþingis;* and siþ it is þus, I mote nedis seie soþ, for I mai not see but treuþe in þe book of liif, and an aungel þat is confermed mai not lye to a man. *And lo, þou shalt be domb, and þou shalt not mowe*[a] *speke unto þe dai þat þes þingis be done;* and þis penance shalt þou have, *for þou trowedist not to my wordis, which shal be fild in þes tyme*. And here mai we se, bi logik of þis aungel, how al þing mote nede be; for noþing mai ever be but þat þat[1] God haþ ordeyned to be in his tyme; for ellis hadde Gabriel seid fals, þat he myȝte not speke til þanne.

And þe peple abood Zacarie, and wondride þat he tariede in þe temple. And whanne he cam out, he myȝte not speke to þe peple; and þei wisten þat he hadde seen sum visioun in þe temple. And he was bekenynge to hem, and dwelte dombe for þe tyme. *And whanne þe daies of his office weren fulfillid, he wente hoom to his hous*, and þanne was Joon geten. *And after þes daies conseyved Elizabeth his wiif; and she hid hir* for shame *fyve moneþis* aftir. *And she seide to hirsilf; For þus haþ oure Lord do to me, in þe daies þat he caste to take awey my reprofe among men.* And þus cam Elizbeth hoom, whanne she feelide þat Joon was quike; and so he myȝte witnesse þe comyng of Crist in þe wombe of Marie, whanne she cam to Elizabeth. For Joon made þanne joie in manere of dansing in presence of

[1] So E; om. A.

[a] 'mowe' is the lost infinitive of the verb 'may;' it is the English form corresponding to the German 'mögen.' It occurs in this place in both Wycliffite versions.

Crist, as þe gospel seiþ. And so trowe not to hem þat seien, þat it is six moneþis bifore þat þe soule [a] be couplid wiþ þe bodi, and bifore it haþ plantid soule[1], and siþ soule of beeste[b]; but as we bileven þe wordis of þe gospel, þat Baptist was glad in comyng of Crist, so we supposen þat he was on lyve a litil bifore þat Jesus was conseyved, but we musen not how muche, siþ it is Goddis privyte.

Reflections on the sin of unbelief.

Of þis gospel mai we take, how it is grete synne to mystrowe to holi writt, siþ God punishide Zacarie for he trowide not to his aungel; and more ben wordis of God þan wordis of þis aungel. And þus defaute in bileve is bifore alle oþer synnes, and siþ God seiþ al treuþe, no treuþe shulde be denyed; but summe may men doute, and sum trowen wiþ drede, for God seiþ þis treuþe, or ellis God seiþ it not. O how myche ben þei to blame þat seien þat Goddis lawe is fals, for mysundirstonding of a fool or an heeretik! Certis, bi þe same skile þei myȝten seie þat God is fals, siþ God signifieþ to hem fals undirstonding, in peyne of þer former synne, bi which þei ben blindid, and þus God were þe falseste þing þat evere was in þis world. For þei seien þat falshede is no defaute in a þing, whi seien þei not þat God is fals for perfeccioun of God, siþ God meveþ fals men, for þer former falshede, to undirstonde

[1] *plauntis of soule*, E.

[a] That is, the rational or human soul.

[b] The writer appears to repudiate, with Aquinas, the doctrine which held that before the rational soul,—*anima intellectiva*,—in virtue of which man is man, was joined to the embryo, it had been animated successively by a vegetative and a sensitive soul, so as to be conformed to plants during the first, to animals during the second period of gestation. In the treatise *De Spirituali Creatione* among the *Quaest. Disputatae*, Aquinas writes (art. 4) 'Quidam vero dixerunt quod a principio inest anima vegetabilis, et illa eadem cum fuerit magis perfecta fit anima sensitiva, et tandem fit anima intellectiva.' But the Christian philosopher, holding out for the oneness and incorruptibility of the human soul, will not admit this; he looks upon the embryonic changes as indicating successive stages of the one soul, but no more. 'Sic cum in embrione primo sit anima vegetativa tantum, cum perventum fuerit ad majorem perfectionem tollitur forma imperfecta, et succedit forma perfectior, quae est anima vegetativa et sensitiva simul, et ultimo cedente, succedit ultima forma completissima, quae est anima rationalis.' To these three elementary stages St. Augustine, in the *De Quantitate Animae*, adds four more, that of moral effort, in which the soul is seeking virtue, that of moral perfection and rest, that of spiritual effort or tendency towards God, and that of the soul's union with and rest in God.

falsly? and þanne þei seien þat God is fals. And þus God shulde meve men falseli, whanne evere þey synnen[1], and þus he were a fals God in punishing of sinful men. For, siþ falshede in God is good, ȝeve we him ynowȝ þerof; for God mai not have a name, but ȝif he passe al oþer þing. Blessid be treuþe, þat made us passe alle sich fals fantasies, and wite þat alle creaturis ben trewe in þat þat þei ben of God.

ON TRANSLATION OF SEINT MARTIN[a].

[SERMON CIX.]

Nolite timere pusilus[2] *grex.*—[LUKE xii. 32.]

Christian courage.

IN þis short gospel Crist confortid his servantis, and biddiþ hem not drede; for treuþe is strengere þan alle þer enemyes. Men shulden not drede but for synne and lesing of vertues, for peyne is just and of Goddis wille; whi shulden men drede or sorewe þerfor? And þus sinful men shulden have drede and hope togidere, of diverse þingis; as þei shulden have sorowe and joie togidere of dyverse þingis. And þus synne concludiþ men moost of al þing þat mai be; for it bringiþ man[3] to fyve markis[b] more noyousli þan oþer skilis. Crist seiþ here to hise apostlis, þat *þei shulden not drede*, al ȝif þei ben *a litil flok.* For to rekene þe firste treuþe, and alle þe aungels þat ben wiþ him, þe part of a just man is betere þan fals part
2 Kings vi. 16. of a þousaund; and þus biddiþ þe prophete his child, þat he shulde not drede him, for many moo ben wiþ hem þan wiþ þe contrarie part. Stonde a man in vertu and treuþe, and al þis world overcomeþ not him. For if þei over comen him

[1] So E; *be synneþ*, A. [2] *pusillis*, E; a clerical error for *pusillus*. [3] om. E.

[a] The feast of the translation of St. Martin's relics (July 5) is not in the Roman missal, the office for the day being of the octave of SS. Peter and Paul. The gospel which the Sarum use appropriated to this festival is found in the Roman missal among the gospels for the Common of a Confessor not a Bishop.

[b] *bringiþ man to fyve markis.* This seems to be a proverbial expression, used of a person who was brought to poverty, or into any desperate strait.

wiþ þis, þei overcomen God and his aungels; and þanne þei shulden make hym[1] not God, but betere þing shulde make þis.

But here men seien comunli, þat þer þen þre manere of dredis: kindeli drede, and drede of sones, and þerwiþ drede of servantis. Kindeli drede was in Crist, whanne he dredde to suffre deeþ. But þis drede cam ȝit of synne, for ellis no man shulde have suffrid peyne. And þus peyne is unkindeli, for to loke to bigynnyng þerof. Þe secounde drede haþ many degrees, after þat men ben betere wiþ God. Sum is bigynnyng drede, whanne men dreden to wraþþe God; and þis is bigynnyng to fle synne, and rote of alle mannis wisdom. Ȝit, whanne man drediþ more for to synne aȝens his God, and his tempting is overcomen þat shulde moove him to synne, þanne haþ he chast drede; but wel is him þat haþ þis drede. Þe þridde degree is best of alle, þat men clepen holi drede; and þis dwelliþ here in erþe, and evermore wiþ man in blis. And þis drede haþ no peyne, but unpower for to synne. And þus aungels have þis drede more þan ony oþer þing. But þe Godhede mai not drede, for it bi kynde mai not synne. Boþe þes dredis bringen not in synne. But þe þridde servant dredde. Whanne a[2] man synneþ aȝens God, and mote nede be ponished of him, þis is oon[3] unkindeli drede, as it is unkindeli to synne; and þis drede forfendiþ Crist in þes wordis þat he seiþ here. And þus men seien comunli, þat man shulde not drede to fiȝte ȝif his cause and manere be good, for noȝt but synne makiþ man coward. For ȝif man fiȝte wiþout cause, to be holden an herti man, he beriþ wiþ him þe synne of pride, þat makiþ him coward aȝens God. And þus þingis þat loven pees ben moost hardi, as þingis in hevene.

Three kinds of fear.

And Crist telliþ here a cause to make his disciplis hardi, þat þei shulden not drede þus: *For it likide to þer Fadir to ȝeve hem þe rewme.* Here mai we see many treuþis in þes wordis þat Crist seiþ. First, how þe Godhede of God is Fadir of alle þat he ȝeveþ blisse. Þe secounde treuþe in Cristis wordis is nede to ȝyve þis blisse. For, as þingis þat ben passid nedli moten have be passid, so al þat God ordeyneþ nedeli moten

Motives of hopefulness.

[1] So E; *not make him*, A. [2] om. E. [3] *an*, E.

have be ordeyned. And þe þridde treuþe of þes wordis is, þat Crist shewide to þes disciplis þat þei shulde come to blisse, for he telliþ þer Fadir likede so. Here may we gadere opun resoun þat Cristis children shulden not drede; for ȝif God ȝeve a betere þing, he ȝeveþ al þat sueþ þerof; as God mai not ȝeve a bodi, but ȝif he ȝeve quantite and figure. And so, siþ pees sueþ of þis blisse, God mote ȝeve pees whanne he ȝeveþ blisse. Also, siþ God is almyȝtti, alwitti, and al wilful, no þing þat is aȝens God mai overcome him þat is wiþ God; for siþ God seþ þis fiȝting[1], or him failiþ power or wille, ȝif his servaunt be overcomen in fiȝting for Goddis cause. And þus trewe men ben confortid to putte awei þis þridde drede; for be þei never so fewe or feble, þei bileven þat þei mai not be disconfitid. And þus þe cause þat Crist here telliþ makiþ his knyȝttis to be hardi.

The possession of riches tends to make men cowardly.

And þus Crist confortid his apostlis, for to sue him in povert: *He biddiþ hem sille þat þei have and ȝeve almes* prudentli. For certis, among alle cowardisis, cowardise of richesse is þe moste. For many men þat have richessis dare neiþer seie a soþ, ne defende a soþ seid, for drede of leesing of þis richesse. And so men loven richesse more þan þei loven treuþe of þer God. And in þis cowardise ben freris and oþer ordris þat ben dowid. And unneþe ony riche man wantiþ clene þis cowardise. And þis is more þan cowardise of bodi, þat comeþ to man for drede of bodi; for a man shulde kindeli love more his bodi þan his goodis, siþ goodis of kynde ben mouche betere þan ben goodis of fortune. But Crist telliþ ofte to his martirs, þat þei mai not be his disciplis but ȝif þei loven more him þat is treuþe þan loven þer owne liif. And wiþ þis feiþ was Baptist armed, and oþer apostlis, wiþ Cristis martiris; for þei wisten wel þei myȝten not faile in victorie, to die þus. And þus, for richesse of þis world makiþ moost cowardise, Crist bad his knyȝttis be pore, and sille her possessiouns, and of þat priis ȝeve almes, or ellis of meeblis þat þei hadden. But wite wel, it is noon almes to make ypocritis more cowardis, or to ȝeve þes newe ordris þingis þat þei ben chargid bi, for þis is not work of almes[2], but work of unmercy to men.

[1] *God is fiȝting*, E. [2] *mercy*. E.

And þus Crist meeveþ to be pore bi resoun of surete. *Make ȝe to ȝou sachelis þat wolen not waxe oold, but tresour þat, failiþ not in hevene, whidir þe þef comeþ not, ne þe mouȝþe distrieþ; for, certis, where is þi tresour, þer is þi herte,* and þi wille. Tresour is clepid comunli, prescious þing þat man telliþ muche bi and hidiþ sumwhere. And so men þat shal be saved maken þer tresour in God; for þis tresour is of oþer kynde þan ben þes riche men, and it is prescious good, for it is good of grace. And siþ Crist is al þing þat seintis have nede of, þis tresour is more nedeful þan al þis erþeli tresour; for þeves mai not stele þis, as jewels or moneie, and mouȝtis mai not feble þis, as þei mai cloþis or jewelis. And so, siþ þis tresour is more prescious and more sikir, what man shulde not traveile moost for to have þis tresour? ȝif þou traveile treuli to have þe blis of hevene, þou hidist þis tresour where it mai not faile; for God shal be þi cloþing þat mai not wexe old, for he is charite; and he shal be þi peny þat mai never be rusty; and þeves mai not come to hevene, ne take of hevenes blis. Þis is eende of wisdoms, to traveile for sich a tresour. And drede we not þat ne man mai bi good liif wynne him God, þat is al maner of tresour, to make him blessid in hevene. For þis is kyndeli eende to which man is ordeyned; for man is ordeyned[1] to blisse, and to laste ever more, and have wiþout defaute al þat hem nediþ.

Treasure in heaven.

Þe Gospel on Octave dai of Petre and Paul.

[SERMON CX.]

Jussit Jesus discipulos assendere in naviclam[2].—Matt. xiv. [22.]

Þis gospel telliþ a storie that ech man shulde wite, but speciali apostlis and vikeris of hem. *Crist bad his disciplis stie into a bote, and go bifore him on þe water til þat he lefte þe peple. And Crist lefte þe puple and stiede in to þe hil, for to preie aloone*

Peter walking on the water.

[1] So E; A om. the words *for—ordeyned.*

[2] errors of the scribe for *ascendere* and *naviculam.*

for staat of his Chirche. *And so, whanne þe evenyng cam, he was þer aloone;* for his disciplis were in þe water, and þe peple hadde left him. *And þe boot, amydde þe water, was shaggid*[1] *wiþ wawis, for þe wynd was contrarie* to hem. *And þe fourþe vigile of þe nyȝt,* þat was nyȝ þe dai, *Crist cam to his disciplis walkinge on þe water. And þe disciplis, seeyng him walking upon þe water, weren troublid* among hemsilfe, *and seiden it was a fantum*[2]. *And for drede þei crieden. And anoon Jesus spak to hem and seide* to hem þus: *Have ȝe trust, I am; drede ȝe not. And Petre answeride and seide, Lord, ȝif þou be Crist, comande me to come to þee upon þe waters. And Crist seide* to Petre, *Come. And Petre wente doun out of þe boot, and walkide*[3] *on þe waters, for to come to Jesus. But Petre, seeyng þe wynd grete, dredde him* of þe peril; *and whanne he bigan to drenche, he criede and seide, Lord, mak me saaf. And anoon Crist held forþ his hond, and toke Petre, and seide to him, Þou of litil bileve, whi doutidist þou here? And whanne Crist steie in to þe boot, þe wynd cesside, and þei þat weren in þe boot camen and loutiden Crist, and seiden, Verrili þou art Goddis Sone.*

Mystical Interpretation of the Gospel.

Þis storie men tellen to þe secounde witt of Goddis word, and seien, þat þis boot traveilinge in þe water is þis Chirche here þat wandriþ to þe daie of dome. Þis wending of Crist to þe hill is his stying to hevene. Þere he preieþ aloone for mankinde here; for alȝif oþer seintis preien þere in spirit, neþeles in bodi and soule preieþ Crist ȝit aloone. And whanne þe sunne wente doun, was Crist aloone preiyng þus. But he visitide his Chirche þe fourþe vigile of nyȝt, whanne he shewiþ perilis to his Chirche þat fallen to men here in erþe. But Crist goiþ upon þe water, for worldli soris[4] noien him not. And þis boot is troublid here, but it drenchiþ not uttirli. Petre is þe moste man þat sueþ Crist in his Chirche; and he wolde sue Crist here, but he failiþ in bileve. But he mai not be drenchid, for Crist wole have his Chirche saved. Crist comeþ into þis boot whanne he haþ alle þes men to hevene, and þanne ceessen alle þe tempestis þat men suffren here in erþe, and þei knowen verrili how þat Crist is Goddis Sone.

[1] *schoggyd*, E. [2] E om. the words *and—fantum*. [3] So E; *walking*, A. [4] *sores*, E.

And þis witt applieþ þe pope, wiþ his cardinalis, to hem, and seien þat þei ben Cristis Chirche þat flooteriþ[1] þus in þis boot; and þei mai nevere be drenchid, al if þei fallen in many perilis. But þes men shulden wite, first, þat þei sue[2] Crist in lyvyng in poverte and mekenesse, and in lore of þe gospel; for ellis þei gon not bifore Crist on þis water, to make redi to him, but ben raþer drenchid in þis water, and seken after worldli goodis; or ellis ben þe peple þat Crist leeveþ, þat disturblen him and hise. Bileve techiþ trewe men þat þis Chirche goiþ not bi kyn, but bi manere of suynge of Crist in perfit weie of vertues. But as preestis weren worse til þei weren at lowest degree, as preestis of þe olde lawe þat weren fordone in Cristis tyme, so mai þis court drede for liif contrarie unto Crist, leste þei ben þe worste men þat lyven here in þis Chirche. For ypocrisie makiþ hem not good, but more stynke bifore treuþe. And þei ben not porest here, making hem tresour in hevene, for al þer breeþ and þer liif is about worldli goodis; and þus þei lasten not in þis boot, but ben drenchid in þis see. And þus þei axen not Crist helpe, as dide Petre, whanne he sank; but al þer hope and desire is in þingis þat ben bineþe. For ȝif þei lyven contrarie to Crist, in þis world ben no falser men. And neiþer kynrede ne place maken men Cristis vikeris, but suyng in weie of vertues, what manere men þat ever þei ben. Errour in sich wittis makiþ many dremeris to faile, for þei taken noon hede to good liif, but to fals opynyouns here.

How applied by the Roman Court.

This application refuted.

Þe Gospel on þe feeste of Sevene Briþeren.

[SERMON CXI.]

Loquente Jesu ad turbas.—Matt. xii. [46.]

Þis gospel telliþ a storie þat touchiþ mouche witt, and telliþ how Cristis children ben knyttid here in charite. Matheu telliþ, how *Jesus spake to þe peple; and lo, his modir and his breþeren*

Christ's true kindred.

[1] *floteþ*, E. [2] *sueden*, E.

stooden wiþouten to speke wiþ him. And sum men seien þat Cristis breþeren weren men of his kynrede. But his apostlis weren wiþ him, and herden him speke to þe peple, as þei weren in streitere place, and more hard to come to. *And oon seide to Crist, Lo, þi modir and þi breþeren stonden wiþouten, sekyng þee. And Crist answeride to him þat tolde him þis, and axide who was his modir and his breþeren. And Crist stretching his honds to his disciplis seide þes wordis* of witt: *Lo, here my modir and my breþeren. For who ever doiþ þe wille of my Fadir þat is in hevene, he is my broþer, and my sistir, and my modir also.*

This gospel misinterpreted by many.

Þes wordis of Crist ben scorned of gramariens and devynes. Gramariens and filosophris seien, þat Crist knewe not his gendris; and bastard dyvynes [1] seien algatis þat þes wordis of Crist ben false, and so no wordis of Çrist bynden, but to þe witt þat gloseris tellen. But here we seien to þes trowauntis þat þei blaiberen [2] þus for defaute of witt. Leeve we þes heretikes as foolis, and seie we sum witt þat God haþ ȝovun us. Soþli, Crist techiþ here þe preciousite of his preching, þat man shulde not, for fleishli kyn, lette to teche Goddis word. And þes wordis seiþ Crist to him þat was aboute to lette his lore. And þus telliþ Crist a sutilte þat is of goostli breþeren in God; for, be it man or be it woman þat serveþ God treuli, he is on þes þree maneres knitt to Crist in sibberide [3]. For distinccioun of kynde is litil to telle bi in þis matere. First, he is Cristis broþer bi [4] his soule, þat is his spirit; siþ, he is Cristis sistir bi his fleish, þat is worse; and after, he is Cristis modir bi þis hool kynde, made of hem two. For þis modir haþ conseyved Crist, and norisiþ Crist wiþinne hir; and þis is betere cosynnage and more sutil þan is of kynde. And make þes gramariens sorewe þat þei knowe not þes gendris, and so þes founed philosophris shulden sorowe of þer error, þat þei witen not of oo man þat he is ech of þes þree þingis; he is soule, he is bodi, he is man, maad of þes two. But to þe hool man is merit or demerit proprid. Leeve we here þese trowaunt doutis, and enforce us to lerne Cristis wordis, to preche hem to þe peple, and leeve þing þat is lesse worþ, and þanne fleishli cosynnage shulde not lette us to do þis.

The writer's interpretation.

[1] So E; *dyvenes*, A. [2] *blaberen*, E. [3] *sybred*, E. [4] *to*, E.

þE GOSPEL OF MAUDELEN DAI IS RED ON FRIDAI IN † QUARTER TENSE †[a] IN SEPTEMBRE AMONG FERIALS

ON SEYNT JAMES DAI.

[SERMON CXII.]

Accessit ad Jesum.—MATT. XX. [20.]

Þis gospel telliþ how fleishli kyn procuriþ ofte harm to þe soule, and how a womman, Cristis aunte, *Mary, James modir and Joones*, þat was *Sebedeus* wiif, *cam to Crist* for þis enchesoun. But she cam wiþ þes children and loutide Crist, *and axide him;* for it is seid comunli þat wymmens preier is wel herd. *Crist axide hir*[1] *what she wolde, and she seide to him, Comaunde þat þes two apostlis*, þat ben *my sones*, and þi cosyns, *sitte next þee in þi rewme, þe toon on þi riȝt side and þe toþer on þi left side.* Crist knewe wel þis wommans witt, and how it cam of þes apostlis; for þei herden bifore of Crist, how þat he shulde have a rewme, and þei trowiden þat Crist shulde be an erþeli kyng in þis world; and þere þei wolden be nyȝ Crist, for cosynnage and traveile here. Crist spekinge to þes apostlis, and levynge to speke wiþ þeir modir, seide how þis cam of hem, and how men shulden have ordre in speeche, everemore speking þere where þei hopen moost to profite. *Crist seide to þes* apostlis, *ȝe witen not what ȝe shulden* gladli *axe;* for þing þat profitiþ to mannis soule shulde he axe, and nouȝt ellis. The petition of the mother of James and John.

And, as Joon seiþ wiþ þe gildene[2] mouþ[b], þis word of Crist liȝtiþ þe world, and dampneþ here many men, þat coveiten hyenesse of worldli stat. For many men bi weyward witt coveiten here to be popis cardinalis or bishopis, or oþer worldli Commentary on the gospel.

[1] So E; *here*, A.

[2] *golden*, E.

[a] The MS. has two words here inexplicably contracted; but they evidently stand for 'Quatuor Tempora,' or, as it is called in Ireland, Quarter Tense; for the gospel read on St. Mary Magdalen's day (July 22) is the same as that for Ember Friday in September, on which there is a sermon (No. 112 of the Ferial Sermons) in the present collection.

[b] St. Chrysostom, *Homil. in Matth. XXXV.*

dignite, not for hele of þeir soule, but to have here worldli wynnyng. And all þis dampneþ Crist here. For þis wille is venymous; and it falliþ ofte tyme þat sich havyng of worldli worship dampneþ men ever more in helle; and so it doiþ harm to þe soule. But ȝif men wolen be hye in hevene, þei moten lerne anoþer lessoun, to profite to þe Chirche þat þei mai, and to leeve worldli worship. And þis profit nediþ ofte to suffre anoies here in þis world, þat þese prelatis fleen algatis, for þei wolden here have þe contrarie. Þerfore Crist axide of þes disciplis a questioun pertinent herto, *Mai ȝe two drynke, seiþ Crist, þe chalis þat I shal drynke?* And wiþouten drede Crist undirstood bi þis chalis his passioun. And þes two disciplis myȝten not for shame denye to drynke of þis coppe. *And* þus *þei grauntiden* to Crist, *þat þei myȝten* drynke of his coppe; for it were al aȝens skile to coveite sich a prelacie, but ȝif men have þe ende þerof wherefore þei shulden coveite it. And siþ Crist is al wiys, and drinkiþ himsilf of þis coppe, what man shulde bi resoun forsake to drynke herof? For bi þis is þe soule fed, and disposid to come to blis, but bodili fode is for þe bodi, and makiþ wormes mete redi. And þus *Crist grauntiþ þes apostlis þis betere drynke,* and leeveþ þe toþer. But ȝit Crist, of his curtasie[1], interpretiþ þer wordis to goode; and doiþ worship to his Fadir bi trewe wordis, as he shulde. Supposing þat þei undirstonden sitting in þe rewme of hevene, *Crist seiþ, þat it falliþ not to him to graunte hem sich sittinge, but sich sitting shal þo men have to whom it is ordeynid of his Fadir.* Here grutchen Anticristis disciplis and seien, þat Crist seiþ here fals; for siþ Crist is þe same God þat is þe Fadir and þe Goost, whatever þe Fadir ȝeveþ or grauntiþ, þe same þing grauntiþ Crist. But here þese foolis moten undirstonde, þat Crist spekeþ ofte bi his manhede; for þe peple knewe his manhede, and undirstood it speciali. And þus, whanne Crist biheetiþ to hem þat him falliþ not to ȝeve hem þis, he undirstood þes wordis þus, þat he shulde not, bi his manhede principali, ȝeve þem þis; but he shulde ȝeve to hem þis, to which it is ordeyned of his Fadir. And so, ȝif þei disserven þis, he sikerid hem þat þei shulden have þis.

[1] *curtesie,* E.

And þus spekiþ Ambrose[a], sayngc comun speche of Crist, þat þe sacrid oost is not breed, for it is not principali breed. And such error blindiþ many, in þe sacrament of þe auter, to seie þat it is an accident wiþouten suget, and no breed, as Ambrose seiþ. But þes foolis myȝten bettere seie þat neþer James ne Joon ben blessid for Crist seiþ þat him falliþ not to graunte hem ony degree of blisse. But þis is ful of eresie, as falshede in which it is groundid. And defaute of undirstonding þat shulde be of Goddis lawe and of þis doctour, Ambrose, blyndiþ here þes eretikis.

On Assumpcioun Evyn.

[SERMON CXIII.]

Loquente Jesu ad turbas.—Luc. xi. [27.]

Þis gospel telliþ how it is more to heere Goddis word and kepe it, þan to bere Crist bodili and norishe him, as Mary dide. And so a litil storie is told in presing[1] of our Ladi; and after is knitt a blessid sentence bi distinccioun of Crist. Þe storie telliþ *how Crist spak to þe peple* of soule helþe. *And a womman of þe puple* hadde devocioun in his wordis, and *burst out in an hyȝe vois, and seide* on þis manere to Crist: *Blessid be þe wombe þat bare þee, and þe tetis þat þou didist soke. And Crist answeride to þis womman*, and tolde a more presciouse treuþe, *and seide þat, but bi more resoun, blessid be þei þat heeren Goddis word and kepen it.*

Those truly blessed who hear the word of God and keep it.

But we shal undirstonde here, þat on two maner is Goddis word herd,—first bodili, bi eeren of bodi, and eke goostli, bi eeren of soule. Þe firste heeringe is litil worþ, but in as mouche

Two ways of doing so.

[1] *preysyng*, E.

[a] St. Ambrose, *De Sacramentis*, lib. iv. cap. 5: 'Antequam consecretur, panis est; ubi autem verba Christi accesserint, corpus est Christi.' Wyclif in his *Confessio* (*Fasciculi Zizaniorum*, p. 127) quotes a passage from the same work, differing slightly in words, but precisely to the same effect. The 'for it is not principali breed' is Wyclif's gloss upon the words of St. Ambrose.

as it helpiþ to þe toþer; siþ Scarioth herde Crist þus, and beestis and briddis myȝten also. On þe toþer manere heeriþ no man but ȝif he knowe sentence of Goddis word. And on þis wise seiþ þe Psalme[1] þat I shal heere what þe Lord God spekiþ in me; but wel Y woot þat he shal speke pees and love to his peple. And þus, on two maneris, may a man kepe Goddis word; first, to printe þe witt in his soule, and after to reule his liif þerbi. And þus shulde ech Cristen man heere and kepe þe word of God. But over þis kepyng shulde preestis kepe wiseli þe word of God, and shape hem for to preche it, for profit of þe Chirche; and þis is þe beste work þat ony man mai travaile here. And þus mai we liȝtli see how þis sentence of Crist is soþ; siþ no man mai come to blis but ȝif he heere and kepe Goddis word; but many men and wymmen ben saved þat baren not Crist bodili; ne oure Ladi myȝte not come to blisse, but ȝif she hadde herd and kepte þis word.

Ps. lxxxv. 8.

The privileges of Mary.

And herfore God ordeynede hir to be maistiresse to his apostlis, for she fel not fro þe feiþ, ne fro þe wordis of hir sone, but kepte hem wel in her herte, and caste wel what þei menten. And herfor it is no wondur ȝif she be more blessid þan oþer. Þe Chirche singiþ of oure Ladi þat she haþ distroied alle heresies[a], for she is special maistiresse to distroie þes heretikes. And siþ she is aftir þe dai of dome, whanne þei shal no more noie þe Chirche, it is soþ to þis entent þat she haþ distroied alle heresies.

Against letters of fraternity.

And siþ she was occasioun of þe wordis þat Crist seide here, se we how þes wordis helpen men to distroie þes vices. A comune heresie þat now rengneþ in þe Chirche is lettris of fraternite, generali among þes ordris[b]. And herfor se we how þes lettris stonden wiþ Goddis lawe. Heryng and kepyng of Goddis word is betere þan þe birþe of Crist; þis birþe is betere þan þes lettris; and so heeryng and kepyng of Goddis word is algatis betere þan þes lettris. But Cristis word in no place techiþ þat men shulden have þes lettris; and þerfore

[1] So E; *Salm*, A.

[a] 'Gaude Maria virgo, cunctas haereses sola interemisti.' Tract used in Masses of the B. V. M. from Christmas to Easter.

[b] See p. 67, note B.

shulden men reste in þes wordis, and traveile not aboute þes lettris. For as ful and sufficiaunt is Cristis lawe as his manhede; but his manhede is ynowȝ wiþouten oþer to come to hevene; and so his lawe is ynowȝ, to here his word and to kepe it, for to come to blisse of hevene, wiþouten ony sich lettris. And þis þing mai be confermed. For ȝif a man have a þousand of sich lettris, but ȝif he kepe Goddis word, he shal be dampned in helle. And ȝif he kepe wel Goddis word, wiþouten havyng of sich lettris, he shal be savyd in hevene, as oure bileve techiþ us. And so havyng of siche lettris is oþer impertinent to blis, or ellis it is harmful, letting men to come to blisse. Also bi siche lettris is not sibbirede[1] getun of Crist; but ȝif þei brouȝten a man to hevene, þei maden þat man Cristis broþir and sister and his modir, as þe gospel beriþ witnesse. For Crist seiþ, Whoever doiþ þe wille of his Fadir þat is in hevene, he is Cristis broþer, and his sister, and his modir. Also, ȝif sich lettris diden þis good to men, brennying or dstroiyng of hem shulden pryve þes men fro sich good, ouþer in bodi or in soule. And so, ȝif we hadden þes lettris brent, or eeten wiþ myis[2], or distroied, we shulden wante þe profite of þes lettris; ȝhe, ȝif we weren þanne betere wiþ God. Bi siche resouns þinken many men þat þes lettris mai do good for to covere mostard[3] pottis, but not þus for to wynne men blis; siþ sich men þat graunten þes lettris wyten not wheþer þei ben fendis lymes, or þat her preier shal ouȝt availe to hem silf or to oþer. And þes resouns letten many to chaffre wiþ þeir preier. For preier of men mai profite to oþer, but not þus bi chaffaring; siþ parting of meritis of men hangiþ oonli in Goddis wille, and not in shewing of sich lettris, neiþer to God ne to man; siþ we oblishen not us bi hem to þing þat is not in oure power. And þus þis help is newe feyned to injurie of God, siþ it is propre to God to graunten sich help to whom he wole. And þes lettris helpen not þerto, but raþer letten, for blasfemye. And sich broþirheed of blasfemes shulden be fled, for fendis sibreden.

[1] *sibreden*, E. [2] *mys*, E. [3] *mustard*, E.

Þe Gospel on Assumpcioun Dai.

[SERMON CXIV.]

Intravit Jesus in quoddam castellum.—Luc. x. [38.]

Jesus in the house of Martha and Mary.

Þis gospel telliþ a storie of Crist, how he tauȝte to his Chirche which is þe beste stat here. Luk seiþ, þat *Jesus entride in to a castel, and a womman þat hiȝte Martha toke Crist in hir hous*, to fede him and his apostlis. And manye men þinken here þat þis castil was a wallid toun, for ofte tymes þe gospel clepiþ sich wallid touns, castels. Men supposen over þis, þat þis Martha and hir sistir, and Lazarus þer broþir, hadden al þing in comune; and þis Martha was beste hous-wyf, and best coude ordeyne for hir hous; and þus she hadde speche to men bifore hir broþir and hir sistir. *Þis sister was Marie Mawdeleyn*, þat was a ful devout womman fro þe tyme þat she was purgid of Crist, and sett in þe weie of hevene. And so þis *Marie* Mawdeleyn, fro þe tyme þat Crist cam to hir hous, *sat mykeli at Jesus feet, to heere Goddis wordis* of him. For Jesus hadde þis maner, to speke ever Goddis wordis whanne he wiste þat þei shulden profite to ony peple þat herden hem. And so Crist prechide ofte, now at mete, and now at soper, and what time þat it was covenable ony peple to heere him. And so Martha fedde Crist bodili, but he fedde hir sistir goostli. And so he ȝaf þe beter for þe worse, as it falliþ God to ȝeve. *Martha enforside her bisili to serve Crist and his disciplis*, but Marie sat stille at Cristis feet to heere þe wordis þat he spake. *And Martha stood bifore Crist*, and playnede to him of hir sistir [1]. *Sir, she seiþ, takist þou noon heede þat* þis Marie, þat is *my sistir, haþ left me aloone to serve to þee*, and to my gueestis? I preie þee, *seie to hir, þat she rise and helpe me.* And þus Crist, þat was taken for juge to acuse Mawdeleyn, was maad avocat of þis Marie; for he holdiþ ever for trewe part [2]. And þus many trewe men, boþe aprentis

[1] So in E; A includes *of hir sistir* in the italics. [2] *þe trewe part*, E.

and avocatis[a], wolen no[1] procure in a cause bifore þat þei heeren it, and þis cause to þer witt haþ þe part of riȝtwisnes; for ellis þei maden hemsilf avocatis aȝens treuþe wiþ þe fend. And aȝens þis foule synne shulden men speke upon resoun. For al ȝif Goddis lawe teche þat procuraturis shulden have hire, and jugis shulden have noon hire of men þat þei travailen fore, neþeles þis is mys-turned, for riȝt is turned to coveitise. *Crist spak* a meene weye, and tauȝte þe Chirche in þes wymmen, and spak in *þes wordis: Martha, Martha, þou art bisie and troublid aboute ful many þingis; but certis, o þing is nedeful*, and betere þanne þes many þingis: *Marie haþ chosen þe beste part, þat shal not be taken from hir.*

The two sisters signify the active and the contemplative life.

It is seid comunli, þat þes two wymmen ben two lyves, actif and contemplatif; þe first is Martha, and þe toþer Marie. And actif liif axiþ in mesure bisynesse aboute worldli þingis; and alȝif þis liif be good, þe toþer liif is moche better. And so, for men failen ofte in þis liif fro love of God, Crist doubliþ þis word Martha, for two passen fro unyte. Crist telliþ how actif liif mut nede be troublid for many þingis; but contemplatif liif stondiþ in oo þing, þat is, God, and haþ no bisynes aboute þingis of þis world. For as a man bisieþ him not how his shadewe shal passe þe water, so men þat ben contemplatif bisie

[1] *not*, E.

[a] *aprentis and avocatis;* that is, barristers practising in the common law courts, and pleaders belonging to the church courts. By the term Apprentitius (from the French *apprendre*, to learn), as applied to the legal profession, was originally meant, according to Ducange, a law-student merely,—one who frequented the courts and universities in order to gain legal knowledge. But at an early period it became, in England at least, a more honourable appellation. In Fleta, the author of which wrote under Edward I, the Apprentitius appears as the lowest kind of legal practitioner admitted to the king's courts;—'in curia autem regiâ sunt servientes, narratores, attornati, et *apprenticii*' (lib. II. cap. 37). In the reign of Edward II. the term seems to be used much in the same way as 'barrister' is now-a-days; thus the jurist, Andrew Horn (on whom see Selden's *Dissertatio ad Fletum*), dedicates his treatise *Speculum Justitiarum* (*Justitiariorum?*) to the 'Apprentitii ad barras.' Spelman (Glossarium *in voce*), says that the Apprentitius, after a course of legal training extending over seven years, was permitted 'cancellos salutare,' i.e. to come up to the bar, and there to plead. He thus corresponded to the 'outer barrister' of modern times; and so completely is this the case, that Fortescue (quoted by Spelman), with Selden, Plowden, Sir Henry Finch, and Sir Edward Coke (quoted in Cowell's *Interpreter*), speak of Apprentitius as being only another name for barrister-at-law.

hem not aboute worldli goodis, but þei trusten and hopen in God þat alle þes þingis shal falle to hem. And oonli in swetnesse of God þei bisien hem, and taken þe toþer in mekenes and in poverte, as Crist haþ tauȝt in word and dede.

Some think that three modes of life are here approved;

But men supposen over þis, þat Crist approveþ here þree lyves. Þe first is good, as children lyven whanne þei ben cristened. Þe secound liif is þe betere; and þis is clepid actif liif, whanne men travailen for worldli goodis and kepen hem in riȝtwisnesse. And þis is hard, but it is possible; and alȝatis ȝif coveitise be left; for Crist techiþ bi Matheu þat men shulden not be besie aboute her fode and hilyng, but bisynesse shulde be for hevene, þat shulde be eende of mennis traveile. And exces of þes goodis lettiþ ofte tymes þis eende. Þe þridde liif is þe beste, as Crist seiþ þat mai not lye. And þis is sumwhat here in erþe, but fulli in þe blisse of hevene. And here douten many men wheþir of þes two lyves is betere. But men þat biholden [1] bileve of Crist witen þat þis þridde liif is best; for Crist seiþ þus þat mai not lye, and chees to lyve ever þis liif. For, alȝif Crist dide erþeli workes, neþeles he dide on sich mesure þat his soule was ever fed in contemplacioun of God. And in þis many apes weenen to sue Crist here and þei slippen into þe fendis weies for defaute of Cristis lore.

but of these the third, the contemplative life, is the highest.

Þree resouns ben comune þat þis þridde is þe beste liif. Oon, for Crist þe beste maistir seiþ þus, and mai not lye. Also, þis lif mote nedis laste in blis of hevene wiþouten ende; but þes oþer two lyves moten nedis be eendid here. And so þis liif þat makiþ men betere, and more lastiþ wiþ hem in joie, mote nede be betere þan þe toþer þat algatis moot be taken from man; and þis is þe resoun of Crist in þe laste word of þis gospel. Also, an eende þat kinde ordeyneþ to come to men, bi certeyn meenes, is alȝatis betere þan þes meenes, þat comen nevere but for þis eende; as, siþ mannis liif is eende of his eting and oþer dedis, þis liif is betere þan þis eting, or ellis kynde ordeyned amys. And so, siþ þes two firste lyves ben meenes to þis þridde liif, algatis þis þridde is þe beste, þat God ordeyned to ende þes two. And in no persone ne ony stat ben þes first [2] lyves for

[1] *holden*, E. [2] *two first*, E.

to preise, but ȝif þei ben quykened bi þis þridde, þat shal laste evere perfitli.

And ȝif þe pope haþ maad a lawe contrarie to þis sentence, or ȝif an aungel come from hevene or from helle, reversing it, trowe not to þes aungels, but trowe to Crist þat seiþ þis sentence. And resouns aȝens Crist ben not worþi to be rehersid; as sum men seien, þat[1] ellis þe pope lyvede evere a synful liif, siþ he chesiþ þe worse and þe hardere for þe betere. But here we graunten to þes men þat þis is soþ whanne þei have proved þat þe pope leeveþ þe þridde liif for[2] þe secounde. For þe Chirche shulde beter be governed ȝif alle preestis lyveden þis þridde lif; for þus it was in Cristis tyme, and in tyme of his apostlis.

and no authority is to be listened to on the other side.

Þe Gospel on Seint Bartulimew Dai.

[SERMON CXV.]

Facta est contencio inter[a].—Luk. xxii. [24.]

Men seien þat Seint Bertolomew was nobleste of þe apostlis[b]: and herfore in þis daie is þis gospel red. Men seien þat Cristis apostlis streven for a good cause; for þei wolden have a captain aftir þat Crist was deed. But I can not excuse hem of a vein wille. But however it be of þis, þis gospel semeþ to teche us þat synne of prelatis now-a-daies passiþ þis presumpcioun. For *apostles streven* þanne, not who shulde be more to God, ne more to þe world, but, *who shulde be holde more;* for ellis miȝte strif be among hem which shulde be put bifore, and decisioun of þis myȝte oonys for ever ceesse þis discord. But

The strife among the apostles.

[1] So E; *and*, A. [2] *or*, E.

[a] In the Roman Missal this gospel is assigned to the feast of St. Apollinaris (July 23); that for St. Bartholomew's day is taken from Luke vi. 12-19. The writer of these sermons, like the Prayer-book, follows the Sarum use.

[b] Referring to this legend, Cave says, in his *Antiq. Apostolicae,*—'By some [St. Bartholomew] is thought to have been a Syrian of noble extract, and to have derived his pedigree from the Ptolomies of Egypt, upon no other ground, I believe, than the mere analogy and sound of the name.'

now, among oure prelatis, we moven not who shulde be holde more, but which is more, uttirli, boþe to God and to þe world. And here we synnen doubli, deniyng þat we knowun not, and reversing Cristis sentence of morenesse þat he spake of. But oure goode maistir, Crist, determynede þis discencioun; and seiþ þat þer is double gretnes among men here in erþe,—gretenesse among knyȝttis, and gretenesse among clerkis. Cristis disciplis shulden not coveite gretnes of knyȝttis, but gretenes of clerkes is morenesse of mekenesse and morenesse[1] in service, wiþouten ony booste.

Temporal greatness withheld by Christ from his disciples.

And þus seiþ Crist, þat kyngis and gentilefolk have lordship of hem, and þo þat have power on hem ben clepid goode doeris. But ȝe shal not þus lyve, in noon of þes þre pointis. For worldli lordshipis shal not be among ȝou; ne power to prisoune shal be in oon upon oþir; ne ȝour goode dedis shal not stonde in ȝyvynge of worldli goodis; *but he þat is more amonge ȝou be maad as ȝonger, and he þat goiþ bifore, be he as a servere.* Þat is to seie, þe mekere of ȝou is more of ȝou, and oon shal go bifore anoþir, not for worldli worship, but to serve more mekeli to oþir of his felouship. And þis mai ȝe se, seiþ Crist, bi my lyf among ȝou: *Wheþir holde ȝe more him þat settiþ, or him þat serveþ?* Certein ȝe holde more *him þat sittiþ at þe mete. But Crist is among hem as a good servere.* On þe day bifore, Crist washide her feet and wipte hem wiþ a cloiþ, as þe gospel of Joon telliþ; and þanne he putte in dede soilyng of þis questioun. *And siþ apostlis ben þo ilke þat weren wiþ Crist whanne he was temptid*, and Crist ordeynede siche meenes to aȝenstonde pryde, preestis shulden þenke on þis lore, and traveile aboute mekenes. And þis lyf is not wiþoute mede, bi witnesse of Crist. And herfore he ordeynede hem þe kingdom of hevene, as his Fadir ordeynede hym, for mekenesse þat Crist hadde.

Their superiority is in meekness,

And þanne shal þei ete and drynke upon Cristis bord in his rewme; and þis is mede wiþouten eende, more þan ony worldly mede. For þanne shal þei sitte upon troones and juge kynredis of Israel; whiche kynredis ben seintis in hevene, þat shal knowe bi apostlis þat more mekenesse in þis world axiþ more hyenesse in hevene.

[1] So E; *moresse*, A.

And wel were him þat coude þis lore, ȝif þe gospel tauȝte him no more. And reversing of þis lore now, bi dowyng of þis Chirche, haþ maad al newe preestis and oþer ordir fro Cristis Chirche [a]. For more worldli lordship axiþ þe more service to preestis, and lettiþ hem to be more servauntis, and more hie in Cristis rewme. And þus, whanne Crist biddiþ þat his preestis shulden not lyve þus, þat preest is now holden betere þat lyveþ more lordli. And þis pride of þe fend distrieþ myche of þe Chirche; and Y can see no more mede þan to distrie þis[1] preestis pride. Take awei þes brondis ȝif þou wole quenche þe fier.

though the lives of the clergy set aside this truth.

Þe decollacioun dai of Seint John Baptist in Hervest, þe gospel.

[SERMON CXVI.]

Misit Herodes.—Mark vi. [17.]

Þis gospel telliþ þe cause and forme whi þat Baptist was do to deþ, and seiþ, how þat *Heroude þe kyng sente and held Joon Baptist, and bonde hym in prysoun for a womman, Herodias, which was wiif and weddid to Philip, Heroudis broþir. For Joon seide to þis Heroude, It is not leeveful to þee for to have þi broþeris wiif*, while ȝe boþe ben on lyve. And herfore þis *Herodias aspiede Joon many gatis, how he myȝte be do to deþ.* But alȝif she wolde do þis, *ȝit she myȝte not come þerto.* Þe cause of envie to Joon was his tellinge of treuþe, þat shulde be profitable to Heroude and eke to þis wickide womman. And þis cause shulde glorifie martirdome of a man; for it touchiþ Goddis riȝt, and profit of þe yvel part, and charite of þe martir þat telliþ þis for Goddis sake. And beter cause haþ no man in suffringe of martirdome. *Þis Heroude dredde Joon Baptist, for*

The beheading of John the Baptist.

[1] þes, E.

[a] That is, — church-endowment, practised in defiance of the teaching of Christ, has separated the modern clergy, as well as the cloistered orders, from the true Church of Christ.

he wiste þat he was a just man, and þerto an hooly man, and kepte him more tenderli. For men have kyndely drede of God and of his lawe. *And* þerfore Heroude *herde Joon, and aftir him dide many þingis, and herde Joon wiþ good wille,* in þingis þat touchide conscience. *And whan a covenable day fell* to Heroude and þis wickide womman, *Heroude, in þe daie þat he was born inne, made a feste to tribunes and to princis* of þe temple, *and to þe gretteste* maistris *þat dwelten in Galile.* And þus many men þenken þat Heroude was an ypocrite; for he caste to slee þis Seint Joon, and florishide it wiþ falshede. And as men supposen, al þis cast cam first of þis false womman. For as wymmen, where þei ben goode, passen oþer creaturis, so, where þei ben turned to yvel, þei passen many oþer fendis.

And whanne þe douȝter of þis womman *was entrid in to þe halle, and pleside to Heroude and his gestis bi tumbleris lepyng*[a], *þis kyng seide to þis wenche þat she shulde axe what she wolde. And he swore to þis wenche þat whatever she axide him he shulde ȝeve it to hir, if it were half his rewme.* And bi þes wordis it semeþ þat þis fraude was cast bi þis womman and Heroude; or ellis he were to greet a fool, to ȝyve half his rewme for lepyng of a strumpet. *And þis wenche wente forþ and axide at hir modir, what she shulde aske* of þis kyng Heroude. *And hir modir bad hir axe þe heed of Joon Baptist. And whanne þis wenche cam in anoon wiþ haste to þe kyng, she axide and seide, I wole anoon þat þou ȝeve me þe heed of Joon Baptist in a dishe. And þe kyng was sori; for his grete ooþ and for his gestis he wolde not make þis wenche sorowful, but sente for a man-sleere, and bad brynge to him þe heed of Joon Baptist. And he girde of his heed in prisoun, and brouȝte his heed in a dishe and ȝaf it to þis wenche, and she ȝaf it to hir modir. And whanne þis þing was herd, þe disciplis of Joon camen and token his bodi and putten it in a sepulcre.*

[a] The ὀρχησαμένης of the original is rendered in the Vulgate 'quum saltasset,' which the first Wycliffite version naturally translates, 'whanne the douȝter . . . . hadde lepte,' and the present writer understands of a tumbler or female acrobat. Such displays were common in the middle ages. Chaucer, in describing a festive meeting (*Romaunt of the Rose*, near the beginning), speaks of 'saillouris:'—

> 'There was many a tymbester,
> And saillouris that I dar wel swere
> Couthe her craft ful parfitly.

What man wolde not suppose, þat ne al þis þing was done bi fraude of þis fals womman, for treuþe of Joon displeside hir? And doyng of Heroude was not wiþouten blame, for he shulde not swere þus to a ȝong strumpet; and ȝif þis fool hadde swore þus, he shulde not fulfille þis ooþ; for folie hepid upon folie greveþ God more. She axide þis heed in a dishe bi feyned addicioun, for so she myȝte more liȝtli brynge þis heed in to þe kyng, and wite more sikirli bi þe siȝte of many men þat it was Baptistis heed þat she hadde in þe dishe. And men þat sawun þis done shulden not rebelle aȝens þe kyng, for it was done in þe prisoun pryvyly fer from men.

And feyned treuþe of þe kyng semeþ to foolis to excuse þis deed, and so it semede no help[1] to venge þe dede þat was done. And sich a cautil of þe fend is in many grete synnes. For men feynen bi ypocrisie þat þis þing moste nede be done, and goodnesse wiþ treuþe of hem excusiþ hem of þe dede. And, for wymmen ben of short witt, þei ben meenes to siche dedis. But folie and lustis of men ben often more to blame þan wymmen. As, ȝif wymmen knewun not Goddis lawe in dowyng of preestis, and it semeþ to wymmens witt boþe almes and merci, and þei meeven lordis herto,—as þes wymmen diden Eroude,—þis synne is in þes proctours, but more in þes lordis. And þus fendis wilis of freris aqueynten hem wiþ ladies, and þei ben meenes to lordis to have þat þes fendis axen. And þus is fiȝting brouȝt in, and Goddis lawe reversid. For who may denye þat ne lordis done aftir ladies, or þat freris conseilen wiþ ladies, or myche synne is now up bi workes of lordis? And knytte alle þes togidere, and freris ben ground þerof, more sutil and sinful þan þis lepynge strumpet. But unknowynge of Goddis lawe excusiþ hem not here, for þat shulden lordis trowe, and not þes fals meenes. For fendis and þer giles shulden be put bihinde God, and treuþis of Goddis lawe shulden be taken in worshipe.

Application of the conduct of Herod and Herodias to modern times.

[1] So in E, which has the word *boote*, crossed out, before *help*; A reads *no but to venge*.

Þe Gospel on Nativyte and Consepcioun daies of oure Ladi; and on Cristemasse Nyȝt bifore Te Deum.

[SERMON CXVII.]

Liber generacionis.—Matt. i. [1.]

The genealogy of Christ.

Þis gospel telliþ *þe gendrure bi which Crist cam* of Jewes. For he cam of his modir, and she and Joseph weren of oo kynne. Matheu[1] was tauȝt of God to write þus þis booke, and in þre fourtenes to eende þus þis gendrure. He takiþ two *bigynneris, Daviþ* and *Abraham;* for to þes two was speciali Jesus Goddis Sone bihiȝt. Daviþ was putt bifore for worshipe and acordaunce, alȝif Abraham was bifore and brouȝte forþ holi kynredis. *Abraham gat Isaac, and Isaac gat Jacob; Jacob gat Judas and his oþer breþeren,* And þes þre patriarchis weren þree holi men. Of þes twelve Jacobis sones Judas was þe beste; neiþer þe firste, ne þe last, but cam of his first wyf. And of him tolde Jacob þat Crist shulde come. *Judas gat Phares and Zaram of Thamar.* Þis Phares and Zaram weren boþe getun togidere; and þis Thamar was not þe firste wyf of Judas. *Phares gat Esrom, and Esrom gat Aram; Aram gat Amynadab, and Amynadab gat Nasoun; Naasoun gat Salomoun, and Salomoun gat Booz,* of a wonmman þat was *Raab*[2], þe which was an alien, and helpide mouche Jewes; *Booz gat Obeth of Ruth,* þat was an alien; *Obeþ gat Gesse, and Gesse gat Daviþ þe king.* And in þis firste fourtene ben aliens and synful folk, for Crist wolde save aliens and oþer synful men. Daviþ þe laste of þes fourtene is clepid a kyng; for God made him kyng; and bifore þis Daviþ weren patriarkes and jugis, and no kyngis of Jewis, as Goddis lawe telliþ. Saul was þe firste kyng of Jewis bifore Daviþ, but he was a wickide man, and Crist cam not of him.

Daviþ gat Salomon of hir þat was Uryus[3] *wyf; Salomon gat Roboam, and Roboam gat Abias; Abias gat Asa, and Aza gat*

[1] So E: *Mathu*, A. [2] *þat hiȝte Raab*, E. [3] *Uries*, E.

Josephat; Josephat gat Joram, and Joram gat Osias; Josias[1] *gat Joathan, and Joathan gat Achaz; Achaz gat Ezechie, and Ezechie gat Manassas; Manasses gat Amon, and Amon gat Jose; Jose*[2] *gat Jeconie, and oþir breþeren whanne þei weren taken to Babiloyne*, bi werre of þe kyng. Þis is þe toþir fourtene þat Matheu telliþ, and leeveþ here foure kyngis wiþouten liynge. For he þat bigetiþ a sone bigetiþ his sones sone; and so foure kingis weren left[a], soþli for greet cause.

And whanne þes kyngis weren ceessid of worship of þer kyngdom, but not of þer gendrure, *Jeconie gat Salatiel; Salatiel gat Sorobabel; Sorobabel gat Abyut; Abyut gat Eliachym; Eliachym gat Azor; Azor gat Sadoc; Sadok gat Achym; Achym gat Elyut; Elyut gat Eliazar; Eliazar gat Mathan; Mathan gat Jacob, and Jacob gat Joseph, Maries housebonde; of which* Marie *is Jesus born, þe which is clepid Crist.* And so, to counte Joseph Marie and Crist, is þis þridde fourtene fillid þat þe gospel spekiþ of. And alȝif we have not þis þridde gendrure in holi writt, ȝit we trowen þat it is soþ[3] bi autorite of Mathew, as we trowun þe firste gendruris boþe bi autorite of Genesis. Mathew comeþ dounward in rekenynge of Cristis eldris, and Luk goiþ upward, rekenyng of more fadris. For it sufficide to Mathew to telle how Crist bicam man bi þes þree fourtenes, biginnynge at Abraham. But Luk, figure of preestis[b], telliþ more diffuseli how man stieþ up to God, from Adam to þe Trinite. And variyng of names, wiþ leevyng of sum fadris, techiþ how Matheu and Luk varien not in sentence[c]. Explanation of the differences in the two genealogies.

[1] *Osias*, E. [2] *Josy*, E. [3] So E; A has *soiþ*.

[a] The four kings left out are—Ahaziah, Joash, Amaziah, and Eliakim. See the note on the subject in Dean Alford's Greek Testament.

[b] *Luk, figure of preestis.* The figure of the calf in the Apocalypse (ch. iv.) was very early associated with St. Luke, who was thought to treat more fully than the other Evangelists of the priestly office of Christ. See Cave's *Antiq. Apost.*, p. 169. In the *Legenda Aurea*, it is said, 'Lucas figuratur in vitulo, agens de Christi sacerdotio;' and it is shown at great length how this evangelist was 'recte ordinatus,' in relation to God, to his neighbour, to himself, and to his office of writing the gospel.

[c] Dean Alford (in his notes on Matt. i. and Luke iii.) thinks that no attempt to reconcile the two genealogies has succeeded, laying stress at the same time on the fact that both give the line of Joseph, not that of Mary.

And þis text moten preestis knowe, to undirstonde Goddis lawe, and to defende it from false men þat arguen aȝens it. For siþ it is our bileve, we trowun fulli þat it is soþ[1]; and many helpis þer ben to undirstonde þis gendrure. For we may wite how Crist cam of aliens, and how þis comyng was figurid in oþir dedis þat Crist dide; as þe gospel of Luk telliþ how Crist cam to Jerusalem, boþe þourȝ Samarie and þe cuntre of Galile; and siþ Samarie was þanne in þe hondis of gentile men, and Galile was þanne in þe hondis of Jewis, þis comyng bitokeneþ þe gendrure of Crist, how he cam boþe of Jewis and gentil folk. And þis bitokeneþ over, how he wolde save hem boþe. Crist cam not evere of þe firste sone, but ofte of þe toþer sone; to teche us þe lore þat spiritual gendrure is figurid by Cristis comyng, and God telliþ more þerof þan of kyndeli gendrure. And þus ech word of þe gospel were lore to Cristene men, to travaile and to undirstonde þe privytees of God. And þus shulden preestis ȝyve hem to contemplacioun, and leve worldli occupacioun, wiþ vanytees of þe world. For wordis of Poul techen us þat what kyn þingis ben writun ben writun to oure lore, and to confort of us. And so bi suche confort we shal growe in hope.

Romans xv. 4.

On Hooli roode Day in hervest.

[SERMON CXVIII.]

Nunc judicium est mundi.—John xii. [31.]

Christ contending against Satan and judging the world,

Þis gospel telliþ how þat Crist in al his liif was aȝens þe fend, and speciali in his passioun þat he suffride of so greet love. And þus seiþ Crist of greet witt; *Now is jugement of þe world, now þe prince of þis world shal be cast out.*—Here men undirstonden þe world, þo men þat lyven worldli, and mesuren hem not bi Cristis lawe, for to go þe weie to hevene. Al þe folk of þis soort is a world þat shal be dampned. Al þe liif þat

[1] So E; A has *soiþ*.

Crist lyvede here was a jugement of þis world, for it was an open mater to juge it at þe dai of dome. For no man may excuse þis, siþ God and man lyvede þus to teche men þe weye to hevene and fle þe falsnesse of þe fend, and ȝit man leveþ Cristis lore, and goiþ þe weie þat þe fend techiþ, þat ne þei leden[1] a liif here to make hem dampned aftirward. And so dampnacioun is taken now for dampnyng executid. And now, for cause of þis dampnyng, as þis gospel spekiþ here, þis world þat þus shal be dampned haþ a capteyn, þat is þe fend, þe which is clepid kyng and prince; for he is kyng of alle þe children of pryde, and he is prince of þis world, for he lediþ his lymes þis weie. But Crist seiþ here þat þis prince shal be cast out bi him. For Crist overcam þis fend, and tauȝte anoþer good lore, how þat men shulden come to hevene, and leeve þe fendis weie þat he tauȝte. For alȝif þe fend have children þe whiche he bigiliþ þus, neþeles þe ground is Goddis, siþ þei have her[2] kynde of God. And so þe fend, in al his werkes, is a tirant and a þeef.

But here shal we undirstonde þat al þat God haþ ordeyned to peyne moten nedis be dampned in helle; but many, bigilid bi þe fend, weren ordeyned to turne to Crist; and þes weren ever ordeyned to blis, and nevere to be dampned in helle. And to þis entent spekiþ Crist in þe word þat comeþ aftir, þat *ȝif he be hiȝed fro þe erþe, he shal drawe alle þingis to him silf.* No doute Crist spekiþ here of his passioun of þe crosse; for þanne Crist is hiȝed fro þe erþe to many undirstondingis. And ȝif Crist semede þanne faile power to do ouȝt, ȝit he was þanne almyȝti, and his drawing was ful strong, for þanne he drowȝ bi his vertue alle men þat he shoop to blis. And so he drowȝ fro þe fend many þat he wenede to have, and so þes þat leeven undrawun wanten þe eende þat þei shulden have, and so þei ben clepid nouȝt oftetymes in holi writt. And þus spekiþ Crist here, þat þei ben alle þingis þat he drawiþ. Defaute is not in þis drawer whi þes fendis lymes ben not drawun, but defaute is in hem, þat þei fasten not on þis drawere, siþ noon is drawun but wilfulli, and he wantiþ good will; þei ben so slipre and so hard þat Goddis word takiþ not in hem.

drawing all men and things to himself.

[1] *and þus þey leden*, E. [2] *þe*, E.

Þis same gospel expowneþ to what entent Crist seide þes wordis. *Certis Crist seide þis, to telle what deeþ he shulde die. But þe puple answeride to Crist, and seide þat þei have herd of þe lawe þat Crist dwelliþ wiþouten ende, and how seist þou þat mannis Sone mote be hiȝed? who is he þis mannis Sone*, and how shulde he suffre þis deþ? But Jesus saw how þis peple undirstood sumwhat bileve, and þei faileden on oþer side of þingis þat þei shulden undirstonde. And þerfore *seiþ Crist* þus: *Ȝit a litil liȝt is in ȝou. Walke ȝe while ȝe have liȝt, þat derknesse take ȝou not.* It semeþ þat þis peple wiste how Crist tolde þat he shulde die upon þe crosse for mankynde, and þerbi drawe his children to him; but it semeþ þei wisten not now þat Crist was boþe God and man, and bi his soule he mai not die, as he dieþ not bi his Godhede; but whanne he is deed bi his fleish, his soule passiþ and drawiþ from helle. And þus Crist seiþ þei have a litil liȝt, for þei have but litil bileve. But þei shulden walken in þis bileve, and so come to more liȝt; for ȝif þei walkyn in
Rom. xiv. 23. derkenesse of unbileve, þei gone amys, siþ al þat is not of bileve mote algatis be synne. *For Crist seiþ* afterward, þat, *He þat walkiþ in derknes, he woot not whidir he goiþ.* And so it is in goostli walking; he þat wantiþ bileve of Crist woot not for þat tyme wheþer he goiþ to hevene or helle, for liȝt of feiþ wantiþ him.

And, for Crist is bileve, þe which þat men shulden trowe here and se aftir clerli in blisse whanne þei ben clene come to hevene, *Þerfore, seiþ Crist* aftirward, *þe while ȝe have liȝt, bileve ȝe in liȝt, þat ȝe ben children of liȝt;* þe which liȝt is God himsilf. Here mai we se, in bileve, how feiþ is nedeful for to have, and how fleishli lif here is contrarie to Cristis crosse, and how þat worldli liif is dirk and makiþ men go from God.

Þe Gospel on Seynt Matheu Evyn.

[SERMON CXIX.]

Vidit Jesus publicanum[1].—Luc. v. [27.]

Þis gospel telliþ how Matheu was chosen, and how heretikes grutchiden herfore; for treuþe haþ evere adversaries, þat beren hevy þat it shulde shyne. Þe gospel telliþ þat *Jesus saw a puplican þat hiȝte Levy*. And þis Levy was Mathew[2], as many men have diverse names,—as þis Mathew[2], Petre, and Poul, varieden þer names whanne þei weren apostlis. And þis manere have þe popis, whanne þei ben newe maad popis. But God wolde þat þei changiden to vertues as dide apostlis of Crist. But sum men seien þei changen to synnes, for her chesyng is not of God; þei ben not clepid of Crist to mekenesse, but to pride and worldli liif. And þus al is ypocrisie, and no fruyt to þe Chirche þat þei done, in þis chesing bi ordenance of mannis lawe; and þis envenymeþ myche of þe Chirche bi process of tyme. Jesus siȝ þis Levy *sitting at þe tol-boþe, and seide to him, Sue me*. And wiþ þis word he ȝaf him vertue.

The call of Matthew.

And here þe fend blyndiþ men whanne þei proven bi Goddis lawe þat þei shulden make siche chesing, for Crist clepide his apostlis. But certis an ape is not so blynd in knowing of diversite. It semeþ þat bi Goddis lawe men shulden purge first þe popis state, and algatis þat he were pore and witti, and willi[3] for to profite to þe Chirche after Goddis lawe; and þanne chese him, as Mathi[4] was chosen. And þis were sum similitude to sue here Crist and his apostlis. For wel Y woot þat alle þes cheseris witen not wher þei chesen a fend; as þei witen not wher þei lawe be evene aȝens Goddis wille[5]. And þes two ben to dirke weies to lede alle Cristyndoom to hevene.

Popes should be chosen in the same way that St. Matthias was chosen.

Þe storie telliþ how þat *Mathew*[6] *forsok al þat he hadde, and*

Gospel continued.

[1] So E; *Vidit Jhesus puplicanum*, A. [2] So E; *Mathu*, A. [3] *willy*, E. [4] *Mathi*, i.e. Mathias, is the reading of E, and seems preferable; A has *Mathu*. Compare Sermon CI. [5] *lawe*, E. [6] So E; *Mathu*, A.

suede Jesus, boþe in place and in vertues. *Þis Leevy made Crist a greet feeste in his hous*, wiþ mouche folk; for, as þe gospel telliþ, *þer was moche puple of puplicans, and of oþer men*, his aqueintis, *þat weren come to ete wiþ him. And Phariseis and scribis of hem grutchiden aȝens Crist, seiyng to his disciplis, Whi etin ȝe and drynken boþ wiþ puplicans and sinful men?* Sich men ben puplicans þat traveilen aboute comune work, to gadere tollis and comyne rentis, to þe use of þe emperour. And þis travail dampneden Jewis, as traveile of sinful men; and for using of þis work þei dampnyden[1] men þat comuneden wiþ hem. *And Jesus answeryng seide to hem, Hool men have noo nede of leche, but seke men* in þer bodi. And so, siþ Crist cam to heele men, and seþ þat sich men mai be hool, he moot bi resoun comune wiþ hem, and maken hem hool as he disposiþ. *For Crist cam not to clepe just men, but sinful men to do penaunce.*

The modern Pharisees, from covetousness, hinder poor priests from communing with the poor and sinful.

Here mai we see þat it is good to sum men to comune wiþ sinful men; but þei moten be as Crist was, not to be worsid wiþ þes men. But whanne þei mai do hem good, it were synne to lette þis good. But þes scribis and Phariseis magnefieden þer owne stat, þat no man shulde take from hem, but encreese in worldli goodis. And þus seien now oure Phariseis, boþe religiouse and preestis. But Crist telliþ not bi þis sentence, for it is nest of coveitise. For stat þat Crist ȝaf to his apostlis is now to generali dispisid, þat men shulden be apaied wiþ foode and wiþ hiliyng to her bodi. And al mennis bisynesse shulde[2] be sett to gete vertues to þe soule, for þanne þei seken þe rewme of God, and riȝtwisnesse of þis rewme. And wiþ þis God mai not faile of þes two þingis to mannis bodi; as Crist proveþ bi Matheus gospel, boþe bi foulis and bi lilies. For if men failen in foode or hilyng, þat is for her synne bifore. And þat is more for þer profit, ȝif þei ben wise and pacient; for a betere wey to hevene is algatis more profitable, and he is an overmyche fool þat wole have al his goodis here.

[1] So E; *dampnen*, A. [2] So E; *shul*, A.

Þe Gospel on Seint Matheus Day.

[SERMON CXX.]

Cum transiret Jesus.—Matt. ix. [9.]

Þis gospel þat Mathew seiþ here is nyȝ al oon wiþ þe laste; but ȝit oo gospelere[1] expowneþ anoþer, and varieþ sumwhat to oure lore. Matheu[2] telliþ, *þat Jesus passinge saw a man þat was clepid Matheu*[2]. And þis he meneþ bi himsilf, for it sowneþ to Goddis worship and to repreef of himsilf. What worship shulde þis Mathew have, þat he sat in þe tol boþe, occupied wiþ þe worldli workes, and þus fer fro þe liif of Crist? Grace and mercy is in Crist þat he wolde clepe þus siche a man, boþe bi vois and bi wille, to leeve siche worldli workis, and to go riȝt þe weie to hevene *in suynge þis good duke.* Matheu leeveþ of his feeste, for it sowneþ to worldli fame, and telliþ *how, Jesus eet in þe hous, and puplicans and many sinful wiþ him.* And þis word sowneþ not to boost of Matheu[2], but to mercy of Jesus Crist. But *Fariseis* of Cristis tyme *hadden desdeyn* of þis dede, *and seide to Cristis disciplis,* in repreef of him and hise, *Whi etiþ your Maistir wiþ puplicans and sinful men,* þat is unleeveful? For who shulde comune wiþ cursid men, lest þat he were foulid wiþ hem? And þis word wolde be liȝtli seid now of men þat we feynen cursid; for we holden a more synne to ete and drynke wiþ sich men þan us[3] to do a cursid dede þat were aȝens Goddis worship. For Phariseis coveiten þer owne wynnyng, and leeven þe worship of God. But *Jesus herde þes* blynde wordis, *and seide* to þes Phariseis, *A leche is not nedeful unto men þat faren wel, but to syke men þat faren yvel;* and so it is goostli. *And Crist bad þese men go forþ and telle folk what it is, þat he wolde mercy and not sacrifice.*

Humility of St. Matthew exemplified in his account of his own conversion.

And who so cam þis dai in þe Chirche, and tolde þis ordre

The modern clergy perse-

[1] *gospeller,* E. [2] So E; *Mathu,* A. [3] *þus,* E.

cute those who, like Christ, preach mercy before sacrifice.

wiþ þis[1] sentence, preestis wolden clepe him eretike, and moven oþer men to holden him siche, for þei tellen more bi þer wynnyng þan bi treuþe of Goddis lawe. Ȝif þou wolt asaie þis now, preche opinli to þe peple þat God telliþ more bi workes of mercy, þe which ben in a mannis soule, þan bi offring, or by dymes, or oþer goodis ȝovun to freris, and þou shalt have enemyes anoon to bere heresie on þee. For þei holden as bileve þat ȝif þe ordre þat Crist ordeynede were holden streitli, as he bad, holi Chirche were distroied. But Crist seiþ þat he cam not to clepe just men from þer weie, but to clepe sinful men from þer errour þat þei ben inne. Here mai we wel witen þat Crist moveþ alle good men; sum yvel men Crist clepiþ from wrong weie þat þei ben inne; and sum good men Crist mooveþ to go gladlier her riȝt weie. And so Crist moveþ ever to good, and from errour þat men ben ynne.

On Myȝhelmasse Dai.

[SERMON CXXI.]

Accesserunt discipuli ad Jesum.—Matt. xviii. [1.]

Who is the greatest in the kingdom of heaven.

Þis gospel telliþ how Crist loveþ men þat dwellen in þis world. And we shulen take as bileeve þat Crist loveþ more vertuous men, whiche he haþ ordeynede to blisse, þan all þe men þat shal be dampned, for Crist loveþ ech þing aftir þat it is good. And þus seiþ þe storie of Matheu, how, *Disciplis cam to Jesus and axiden him, who, he hopiþ, is more in þe rewme of hevene?* Leeve we gramariens doutis[a] wher 'quis putas' be two wordis or oo word, and of what part, and what is þe witt þerof; for here us þinkiþ it is o word and þis is þe witt þerof; What is þi jugement, which man is more here; for hope of Crist, þat

[1] So E; *þese*, A.

[a] De Lyra mentions no such doubts, and it is difficult to realize the state of mind of that 'gramarien,' who should speculate on the possibility of 'quis putas' being one word. Both Wycliffite versions translate, 'Who, gessist thou.'

mai not erre, is his riȝt jugement, and þis word wantiþ noumbre and persone and [1] witt of wordis bi hemsilf.

Christ's answer to the question.

And Jesus tauȝte his answere in dede, for it is profitable to men; siþ whomever Crist jugiþ more is more algatis, siþ jugement of þe world and of men failliþ ofte. *Jesus toke a litil child*, in quantite and in soule, for he was litil in bodi, and þerwiþ he was meke. Rekke we not who þis man was, ne trowe we not to mennis talis þat þis was Marcial, or Joon, or anoþer apostle[a]; for ȝif Crist wolde þat we couden þis, he wolde have tolde þis in his gospel. But kepe we us in mekenesse þat Crist wolde put us inne. For ignorance of þis doute doiþ noon harm to Cristen men, and knowyng þerof shulde do no good to geting of þe blisse of hevene. Crist toke þis litil man, *and putte him in myddil of apostlis, and seide to hem, Soþli, but ȝif ȝe ben convertid, and be maad as litil children, ȝe shal not entre into þe rewme of hevenes*, for ȝour pride. For, ever as a man is more meke, evere þe betere man he is. And so, as Crist is beste man, so is he þe mekeste man. And as nouȝt mai be lowere þan centre, so noon mai be mekere þan Crist. And it is oon to suppose þat þis is þe mekeste man and þat þis man is Crist, ouþer on o manere or oþer. Alle men of þe rewme of hevene drawun to þis centre, to make þis rewme. And þis centre holdiþ up al þing, and put [2] it in his degree. But þis centre is everywhere, and not only in oo point.

Þis word of Crist may wel be proved undirstonding sadnesse in vertues; for no man mai have ony vertue but ȝif he have mekenesse, ground of alle. And siþ no man mai come to hevene, but ȝif he be cloþid in vertues, it is open to trewe men þat no man mai come to hevene, but ȝif he have mekenes to grounde his toure up to hevene. And siþ bileve techiþ us þat holi Chirche is a bodi, and þis noble bodi is ordeyned of Crist, bi every part and joynture þerof, it semeþ to many men

[1] *as*, E. [2] *putteþ*, E.

[a] St. Jerome, in his commentary on this passage, is silent respecting the identity of the little child. But Petrus Comestor in the *Historia Scholastica* (cap. xc.), and Nicholas de Lyra, both give the tradition referred to in the text, namely, that this little child grew up to be a certain St. Marcialis, who was sent into Gaul by St. Peter, and preached the faith to the people of the Limousin

þat alle þes newe ordris ben rotyn postumes, and tatered cloutis. Lord! siþ freris blamen wel tatring of mennis cloþis, how myche were it to blame tatring of þe Chirche cloutis. But þat þat þes newe ordris leeven in mannis siȝte, þei fulfillen in oure modir, þat is a betere persone. For alle þes ordris ben cloutid bi Cristis religioun wiþouten his autorite, and departid among hem silf. And it semeþ to many men þat þei ben þe charge[1] of þe chirche, and enpeiren Cristis ordre his lawe and his ordenaunce. And þus þenken many men þat þei shulden be suspect, bifore þat þei hadden groundid her liif in Cristis lawe. And many men have conscience to forþere þes ordris, in word and in dede, bifore þat þei ben tauȝte þat Crist approveþ þes ordris; for ellis þei reversiden Crist and weren wiþ Anticrist. And so alle þes novelries, þat ben not groundid in Cristis lawe, men supposen as heresies til þat þei ben tauȝte þe contrarie. And dymes, and offringis, and defending of þis persone þat doiþ aȝens Goddis lawe, semen bi lawe of conscience to be aȝens Goddis wille, and so shulden men leeven hem. But leeve we þis matere, and trowe to Cristis word, *þat whoso mekiþ him, as þis ȝong man, he is þe more in þe rewme of hevenes. And whoso takiþ sich a litil oon in þe name of Crist, he takiþ Crist;* at þe leste in his membre. For we supposen þat Crist preiseþ not þe fend in þis ȝong man. *And whoso slaundriþ oon of þes litil þat trowen in me, it spediþ to him þat a mylne stoon be tied in his nekke, and þat he be dreint*[2] *in þe depenes of þe see.* And, as Gregori seiþ [a], it spediþ to þis man þat he have hevy worldis charge to depe him in worldli traveile; for þanne he shulde mekelier in caas be dampned in helle þan he now shulde. *Woo be to þe world of sclaundris! For it is nedeful þat slaundris comen, but neþeles woo be þat man bi whom slaundre come.*

[1] *grete charge*, E.

[2] *dreynt*, E.

[a] Commenting on this passage of St. Matthew in his *Moralia* (lib. vi. § 57) St. Gregory says that by the sea we must understand this world,—by the mill-stone, worldly business,—and that there are some who, forsaking the common life of the world, and betaking themselves to spiritual contemplation, not only go astray themselves, but mislead the little ones of Christ. 'Qui ergo unum de minimis scandalizat, melius illi fuerat, alligata collo mola asinaria, in mare projici; quia nimirum perversae menti expeditius esse potuisset, ut occupata mundo terrena negotia ageret, quam per contemplationis studia ad multorum perniciem vacaret.'

Slandre is wrong dede, þat makiþ man falle in synne. And þis falliþ boþe in worldli men and oþer, and speciali in ypocritis of þes newe religiouns; for þei done woo to oþer[1] ordris, and jugement of oþir men for her ypocrisie makiþ many men be sclandrid. For novelries in oure lawe maken errours in jugement, and so þei harmen þe Chirche boþe in soule and bodi. Crist biddiþ aftirward, *ȝif þi hond or þi foot sclaundir þee, kitte it of, and caste it fro þee.* Here men seien soþli, þat bi her bodili lymes ben undirstonden mennis workes and mennis affeccions; and þes ben kittid fro men whanne þe vertue of þeir soule wantiþ sich workes, and occasioun to do þus. *It is beter to þee to be here feble or crokid, and, wiþ þis, come to hevenli liif, þan to have here þes lymes and after be sent to helle.* Þis word is ful dredeful to men þat wolen here be greet, and have many servantis, or many of her ordre, and after, for parting of her synne, ben dampned to helle. And þus was Joon Baptiste wiþouten hondis or feete here[a], and so he was myȝty in hevene for his symple meeknesse. And to þis entent seiþ Crist, *Ȝif þin iȝe sclaundre þee, pyke it out, and caste it fro þee.* Bi þis iȝe we undirstonden yvel siȝte of a mannis eye; as leecherous and coveitous have ofte wickid iȝen. Caste awei þes wickide workis, and turne þee to medeful siȝte. And ȝif þou be a greet maistir, as bishop or erchedekene, and þou have a wickide servaunt þat turneþ þee to coveitise, putte him out of his office and remeeve him fer awey. *It is betere to þee to come wiþ oon iȝe to þe liif, þan here have two iȝen and after be sent to þe fier of helle*, as it is betere to men to lyve here a simple liif, and come after to hevene for mekenesse of þe herte, þan after myche myrþe here be dampned in helle.

Be ȝe war þat ȝe dispise not oon þat is litil here; for soþli I seie to ȝou, þat her aungels seen evere þe face of my Fadir which is in hevene. Alȝif men seien comunli þat ech man haþ two aungels, a good and an yvel, to do him good and traveile him, — The poor and simple of Christ ought not to be despised.

[1] So E; *ber*, A.

[a] The words must not be taken literally, for no such astounding legend was ever afloat concerning John the Baptist or his martyrdom, so far at least as I can discover,—but simply as meaning, 'in this sense John the Baptist, after he was thrown into prison, was helpless and resourceless, reaping thereby a greater reward in heaven.'

neþeles men þat shal be saaf have algatis blessid angels which in al her worching seen evere God clereli, for God is everywhere, and seeþ syche gode werkis [1]. And þis meeveþ many men to dispise not þes pore men [2] and of simple state here; for we witen not how God loveþ hem. And among evidence þat shulde meeve men to mekenes, bileve of þis gospel shulde meeve men to flee dispite. For ȝif a man were ayre aparant [3] of Englond or of France, many men wolden do him worship for þis worldli titil; myche more ȝif a man be eire of þe blisse of hevene. And apparaunce of þis heritage is more licli to trewe men, bi good lyf of men after þe lawe of Crist, þan apparaunce of worldli lordship bi dissence of heritage. And so wickid liif of men makiþ hem serve þe fendis children; as it is seid þat a bishop haþ a þousand iȝen to noie, but he haþ not half an iȝe to profit after Goddis lawe. And þus many men supposen þat þes ben blynde fendis children. For many men have molworpis [4] izen, þat þinken evere of worldli goodis, and þes ben no good lederis to teche men þe weie to hevene.

Þe Gospel on Alle Halwen Evyn.

[SERMON CXXII.]

Respiciens Jesus in discipulos.—John xvii. [11.] [a]

The unity of believers.

Þis gospel telliþ how Crist preied for his apostlis upon þe Þursdai þat he shulde die on þe morewe. And so he medliþ many treuþis, boþe hiȝe and sutil. Joon seiþ *þat, Jesus lokynge upon hise disciplis seide: Holi Fadir, kepe hem in þi name which þou hast ȝovun me, þat þei ben oon, as we two ben oon.* And here it is seid comunli, þat ech oonhede is of sum fourme. And so þer ben foure oonhedis þat men speken of comunli.

[1] So E; A reads *seen wiþ sicbe workes*, which makes no sense. [2] So E; om. A. [3] *beyr apparaunt*, E. [4] *moldwarpis* or *mollis*, E.

[a] In the modern Roman missal this gospel belongs to the mass 'for the removal of Schism;' the gospel for All Hallows eve is taken from Luke vi. 17-23.

Þe leste oonhede is in peple[1], þe which ben oon in kynde; and ȝif þei ben oon in vertues þan þei ben more oon. Þe secounde oonheede is of man; þat many partis of him ben knitt in oo soule and governed bi þe vertue of it. Leeve we oþer oonhedis of oþer bodies bi her fourmes. Þe þridde onhede is of þe Chirche and of her partis, oon in God; and þis is more woundirful þan ony man can her[2] telle. Þe ferþe oonhede and þe moste, þat is rote of alle oþir, is oonhede of þe Trinite, in þe fourme of oo Godhede. And þus þree persoones ben oon, and noon oþer mai þus be oon. Neþeles Crist preieþ þat hise apostlis ben oon, as þe Trinyte is oon; but not in þe same manere; but as þe Trinite is oon in oonhede of substaunce, so Cristis apostlis ben oon in þe same Godhede, and mai nevere after be severid, as þes þree persoones mai nevere be severid. And þis is sum similitude, al ȝif it be fer fro God. And betere preier miȝte no man preie to God for synful men. *Crist seiþ* of his apostlis: *Whanne he dwelte wiþ hem, he kepte hem in his Fadirs name, and noon of hem perishide but þe child of lesyng*, þat moste nedis be lost, for he was a quyk fend, *to fulfille Holi Writt.* And here men douten comunli whi Crist chees Judas, siþ Crist wiste þat he shulde be dampned. But here we seien þat[a] for helpe of þe Chirche þat Crist wiste þat he shulde do, and, as Crist himsilf seiþ here, to fulfille holi writt. And þe same questioun maist þou axe, whi God made men þat shulde be dampned, siþ þat God wiste of þese men al þat shulde befalle of hem? siþ God ordeyneþ good for hem, and good þat falliþ to his Chirche; for þei have levere þus to be dampned þan nevere to have be; but þei wolen not þis expresli, alȝif þei wolen þis pryvyli. And myche good cam of Judas, wherefore we shulde þanke God, and dampne þis traitour to Crist, and flee siche bi ensaumple of him. Lord! siþ Scarioth was ordeyned to be in Cristis religioun, þe which is þe beste þat mai be, and Crist suffride him to go out þerof, whi shulden not þes newe ordris suffre men to go from hem, and speciali whanne þei synnen

[1] *þe puple*, E. [2] *here*, E.

[a] Understand, after *þat*, the words 'Christ chose him.'

and men wolden go out for vertues? And many of þes newe ordris passen Scarioth in coveitise, and for averise of goodis þei ben traitours to treuþe.

Many þingis telliþ þe gospel of Crist and of Scarioth, þe which ben liȝt to men after, ȝif þei wolden take hem. Crist telliþ bifore of traiterie of Scarioth, and how he shal be dampned to helle, notwiþstonding his ordre. *Crist seiþ* aftirward, *þat he comeþ to his Fadir, and spekiþ þes þingis to his disciplis, þat þei have his joie fulfillid in hem.* And, as Crist myȝte not faile of þis, so þei myȝten not faile of þis ende. And alȝif Crist was evermore in wending to his Fadir,—for he myȝte not gon abak, ne erre in his weye bi synne,—neþeles, in tyme of his deþ, he wente out of þis worldli lyf. *Crist ȝaf to his disciplis Goddis word* for to preche, *and þe world hatide hem, for þei ben not of þe world,* as Crist is not of þis world; and þerfore weren þei goode prechours. He þat loveþ worldli goodis and worldli dwelling, as propre to him, is lettid to seie þe treuþe, as we mai se in þes ordris. *Crist preieþ not to take hem ȝit out of þe world, but to kepe hem* here *fro þe greet yvel,* and þat þei profite to þe Chirche in þe name of þe Trinite. Crist seiþ of hise apostlis, *þat þei ben not of þe world as he is not of þe world.* And þis men undirstonden þus; þis world is alle þo men þat ben dampned for love of þe world. And þanne þis word of Crist is open, for þei loven heven and litil þis world. For sich as is þis fadir and priour of þe ordre of Cristyn men, sich ben his children of his covent, and haten þe welþe of þis world. And bi þis mai men knowen which ben disciplis of Crist.

And Crist preieþ to þis ende, *þat his Fadir stable hem in treuþe,* and þanne he stabliþ hem in *his word; for his word is þe firste treuþe.* He biddiþ not stable hem in worldli wordis, as ben fablis and feyned lesingis, but in treuþe of Jesus Crist, which þei shulden trowe and teche. And, to conferme þis preier, Crist spekiþ to his Fadir, *As þou sentist me in to þis world, so Y sente hem in*[1] *þis world*[2]. Crist cam in to þis world to witnesse treuþe, and to liȝte þis world; and as Crist boþe God and man cam hidir to þis entent, so alle his disciplis

[1] *into*, E. [2] So E; in A the words *As—world* are not italicized.

traveilen þus unto her deeþ. How shulde treuþe not kepe hem þat stonden þus to defenden treuþe? Crist, and Baptist, and oþer moo hadden not here reward for þis, but in hevene blis, hid fro men, for þe world is unworthi to take it. And trowe we not þat clepid miraclis þat ben maad at þe tumbis of seintis maken hem more blessid in hevene þan oþer þat done not here sich miraclis. And to conferme þis word of seintis, seiþ Crist of himsilf: *For hem I conferme mysilf, þat þei ben confermed in truþe.* Alle þe dedis þat Crist dide here weren so stabled in God, þat boþe þei and manere of hem moten nedis come as þei camen. And þes dedis of Cristis liif weren maad ensaumple to his disciplis, þat þei shulden sadli do Goddis workes, and take þerto ensaumple of Crist.

Comfort for Christians who have believed without having seen.

Crist ȝeveþ us after a confort and seiþ, *He preieþ not oonli* for hem, *but for alle þat comen after and bileve in Crist bi her word.* And þes wordis seid of Crist shulden quykene men þat ben dede, and, ȝif bileve stood in hem, make hem do as apostlis diden. For alle men þat shal be saf, riȝt to þe dai of dome, moten nedis in þis sue Crist, and ellis þei shal not make oo Chirche.

Christ's prayer for unity.

And þus seiþ Crist, þat his preier moot nedis make alle seintis oon; for o bodi, þat is holi Chirche, drawiþ[1] to Crist, as erþe to þe centre. For as it is seid bifore, *holi Chirche moot nedis be oon, as þe Fadir is in þe Sone, and þe Sone is in þe Fadir;* and so, bi stabilnes of Cristis membris, *þat þe world trowe þat God sente him*[2]. And now prelatis traveilen to litil to maken men trowe þis bileve, for þei gon not in Cristis weie, neiþer bi word ne bi dede. And Crist seiþ of þes membris, *þat he ȝaf hem þe clarite*[3] *þat his Fadir ȝaf hem; þat þei ben oon after oonhede of Persones;* and so þis oonhede be þus maad,—*þat Crist be in his lymes, as þe Fadir is in Crist. And so þei ben endid in oon,* be fillid[4] in þe blisse of hevene, *for þus shal þe Chirche wite how þe Fadir sente his Sone and lovede membris of þe Chirche, as he haþ loved Crist. Fadir, þo þat þou ȝavest me, Y wole þat þei be þere þat Y am, þat þei see my clarite*[5] *which*

[1] So E; *þat drawiþ*, A. [2] So E; the clause is not italicized in A. [3] *charite*, E; *clerenesse* in both Wycliffite versions. [4] *and so þey ben in one, and þis endyng in one schal be fulfillyng*, E. [5] *charite*, E.

þou hast ȝovun me. And confermyng of þis preier is treuþe of þes wordis, *þat þe Fadir lovede Crist bifore þe making of þe world. Juste Fadir, þis world haþ not knowun þee, but Y have knowun þee, and þes knewen þat þou sentist me. And Y have maad knowun þi name to hem, and I shal make it knowun, þat þe love þat þou hast loved me be in hem and Y in hem.* And in þis hiȝe unite is endid þe blisse of þe Chirche.

Þe Gospel on alle Halewen Day.

[SERMON CXXIII.]

Videns Jesus turbas ascendit.—Matt. v. [1.]

On the eight beatitudes.

Þis gospel telliþ of eiȝte blessis þat answeren to eiȝte vertues in þe weie, and bi þes shulden Cristyne men dispose hem to come to blis. *Jesus seying þe puple stiede in to an hil, and whanne he was sett his disciplis camen to him. And he openede his mouþ and tauȝte hem and seide, Blessid be pore men in spirit, for hern is þe rewme of hevene.* Ech word of þis gospel is of greet wisdoom. For it is ful notable þat Jesus saw þis peple able to be lerned, and hadde mercy on hem, and ȝaf hem so plentenously þes ȝiftis of goostli mercy, for þes ȝiftis ben betere þan ȝiftis of bodili mercy. Crist wente into an hil, and his disciplis wenten wiþ him, to teche þat þei shulden be nyȝ hevene þat shulde teche or lerne þis lore. And þus molde-worpis[1] þat wroten þe erþe ben unable to þis loore. Sitting of Crist in þe hil bitokeneþ stabilnes in þis lessoun. And herfore seintis writen mouche of þis sermoun of oure Lord in þe hil, for auctorite of þe doctour, and many circumstanciis of him, makiþ þis lore notable to alle Cristene men aftir. For what man of bileve trowiþ þat Crist openede þus his mouþ, (and he is wisdom of þe Fadir and þe same God wiþ him, and as he openede his mouþ to speke, so he openede hertis of men to heere and undirstonde þes wordis, and teche hem men þat camen aftir), þat ne

Immense significance of the Sermon on the Mount.

[1] *mollis*, E.

he wolde forse[1] him to knowe hem, boþe for worshipe and for profit?

The first beatitude.

Crist seiþ first, Blessid ben þo þat ben pore in spirit; and here Crist techiþ mekenesse, aȝens pride of worldli men. And here men seien soþli, þat Crist clepide povert in spirit, for bodili poverte is noȝt, but ȝif it have þis poverte. For boþe vertues and synnes ben first in þe spirit. And wanting of goodis standiþ wiþ a dampned man; as beggeris and þeves ben ofte porer þan Joob was; but poverte in spirit stondiþ in mekenes,—whanne a man knowiþ þe makere above, how he is riche wiþouten eende, and we ben pore beggeris,—and puttiþ hem[2] mekeli in þe ordenaunce of God. How þat God wole ordeyne for his servaunt ouþer do or suffre, he holdiþ him wel paied; siþ God is a ferour[3] and he is Goddis instrument, redi wher God wole make him hamer, or tongis, or a stiþie, to suffre howevere þat God wole. And certis noon comeþ to hevene but ȝif he be þus pliable; for a ferrour formeþ not his metal, but ȝif it wole be temperid, and þis vertue lastiþ boþe here and in hevene. And þerfore seiþ Crist, þat sich pore men have þe rewme of hevene. For þe blisse of hevene falliþ not to a creature but ȝif he be þus pore; as Crist, and aungels, and oþer blessid seintis have fulli þis poverte, and þerfore þei ben blessid. And no man myȝte here lerne more nedeful lessoun þan bigynne at þis poverte, and grounden him wel þerinne. And so shulden men note þe firste proude noumbre[a], and aȝen ech part of it grounden hem in mekenesse. Sum men ben proud for holynesse þat þei feynen; and þes men ben ypocritis moost perilous of alle oþere. Sum men ben proud for cunnyng þat þei have; as þe laste frend of Joob seide, his beli was ful as

Job xxxii. 19.

[1] *bisyen*, E. [2] *putten hym*, E. [3] *ferrour*, E.

[a] The number 2 is probably meant by the 'firste proude noumbre.' The Pythagoreans called it τόλμη among other things, and assigned to it various revolutionary attributes. But no author that I have consulted speaks of the number 6 otherwise than as synonymous with perfection, as symbolizing matrimony, creation, and a hundred other excellent things. The number 9 on the other hand was treated with great indignity; Peter Bungus says that it denotes the ruin of the angels, who fell through pride, and of whom there were *nine* orders, that it embraces all heretics, and characterizes infidels and idolaters, &c., &c. See the *Denarius Pythagoricus* of Meursius in Gronovius' *Thesaurus*, vol. IX, and the *Numerorum Mysteria* of Petrus Bungus.

a toune fillid wiþ must þat wantide aventing. And þus seien wise men, þat Crist, in þe firste word, undirstondiþ bi spirit þe wynd þat a man haþ, for it falliþ to meke men to be wiþouten bostyng, for sich proude bostours hav to mouche of sich wynd. But ȝit oþer proude men bosten of bodili strengþe; and summe of beute of bodi, as Roboam and Absolon. Þe fifþe pride, and þe laste, is pride of worldli richesse,—as þe gospel telliþ of bosting of a proude man, how he wolde reste in his goodis and alarge his bernes. And as many ȝiftis as man haþ of God may he be proud of but oonli of vertues. And so sum men tellen sixe þe secound proude [1] noumbre [a], how sum men ben proud for nobley of her kyn. But povert of spirit is medecine for alle sich. Bigynne here þis poverte and ende it in hevene. For ȝif þou be þus pore, þou dispisist þis world.

The second. Þe secounde vertue in þis weie nedeful to us here, *is myldenes in beryng*, þat sueþ of þe firste; for whoever is pore in spirit is mylde to his neiȝbore, boþe in word and in dede, and not fel as a lioun. And as pride is quenchid bi poverte of spirit, so bi þes two vertues ben quenchid envie and ire. And Crist seiþ wiseli þat mede of þis vertue *shal after be, havyng of þe lond of lyf.* And þis is for to come, as þis myldenes is here; for in hevene mai no man be austerne to oþer. And alȝif sich myldenes makiþ men here lordis, neþeles bi þis lond Crist undirstondiþ þe lond of blisse. For alle þes eiȝte vertues have for her mede þe blisse of hevene by diverse resouns.

The third. Þe þridde word of þis eiȝte is seid in þis maner: *Blessid be þei þat weilen, for þei shal be confortid.* Ȝif a man avise him how Goddis wille is reversid by synne þat rengneþ in þe world, in persones and comynetees, he shal have mater to morne, and litil to be glad. For, siþ ech man is holden to confourme his wille to Goddis, he is not on Goddis side þat is glad of sich synne. For alȝif God sorew not as men maken sorowe, neþeles, bi Goddis lawe, God is seid to be ireful, and algatis wiþ sovereyne joie God ordeyneþ for peyne; and þis is mater to morne to men þat ben in charite. And ȝif a man be glad for

[1] So E; om. A.

[a] See note on preceding page.

sich synne, wiþ oþer men of his lond, for him þinkiþ þat hardynesse or worldli profite comeþ þerof, he assentiþ on two maners to þe synne of hem. And for sich assenting God poneshiþ juste men wiþ shrewis, boþe in pestilence and werris, and oþer comyne veniauncis. For fewe or noon ben in þe[1] rewmes þat ne þei assenten þus, ouþer faillinge in helpe to distrye siche synnes, or faillinge in repreef of men þat synnen þus. But in blisse, where we shal see þat God doiþ al for þe beste, and men shal be confortid boþe of joie and peyne, men shal be fulli confortid for sich weiling here. And þis mooveþ many men to seien her Pater nosters, and preie in þe þrid[2] word þat Goddis wille be done. And so of þe same þing men mornen and have joie. And so, ȝif we þenken of weiling of oure owne synne, and mournyng of oure neiȝboris synne þat we dwellen wiþ, and tariyng of oure blisse þat we shal have in hevene, we have litil mater for to lauȝhe, but raþer for to morne. For companies and castelis maken us not syker here.

Crist seiþ in þe ferþe word: *Blessid be þei þat hungren and þirsten riȝtwisnesse, for þei shal be fullid* in þe blisse of hevene. And as þe nexte, mornyng, lettiþ slouþe in Goddis service[3], so þis fourþe, hungring, lettiþ men fro coveitise. For ȝif we þenken on Goddis lawe, and speciali of preestis, how þei defoulen Cristis ordenaunce, turnynge aȝen to synne of fleishe þe world and þe fend, a just man shulde hungre and þirste þe riȝtwisnesse of sich men. And more desire þat man shulde have to perfourme þis riȝtwisnesse can Y not see here, þan wille þat Cristis ordenaunce were fillid in mesure and noumbre and weiȝte þat Crist haþ ordeyned for his Chirche; and algatis in poverte of spirit þat his prestis[4] shulden have. For ȝif þe state of preestis be more worldli þan knyȝtis state, who drediþ þat ne pride wole sue, wiþ averice and lecherie, and leevyng of þe office þat Crist bad his preestis do? And so, in stede of heerdis þat shulden teche þe weie to hevene, þe Chirche is ful of wolves þat sinken and drawun men to helle. For Cristis ordenaunce was riȝtwise, and speciali of preestis poverte; alȝif newe sectis seien now þat Cristis ordenaunce were now ful of venym. Þis

The fourth.

[1] om. E. [2] *þridde*, E. [3] *servauntis*, E. [4] So E; *prest*. A.

shulden lordis þenken on, and traveilen to amende þis; for ellis þei shal not be fillid in hevene bi blisse of þe lymes of Crist. For whoso seiþ þat þei consenten not to þis synne, þat is rote of oþir, he disseyveþ þes lordis in lore þat schulde[1] be her soulis helþe. But alȝif sum men mornen, and crien of þis defaute in þe Chirche, ȝit þe fendis part is so strong þat grete and harde gobetis wolen laste to þe tyme of þe laste dome. And so we shal hungir here and after drynke softeli riȝtwisnesse. For after domes dai, we witen wel þat þe fendis part shal not be þus strong.

The fifth.

Þe fifþe word of Crist is þis: *Blessid be merciful men, for þei shal sue[2] mercy*, þat shal be comyn to al þe Chirche. And here þe fend bindiþ men, and telliþ hem þat mercy axiþ ȝyving of riches and of worldli þingis þat mooven men to do aȝens God. Þese heretikes þenken not how Crist ponishiþ here his children, which he wole be pore here, to be riche after in hevene. And þis vertue serveþ aȝens al synne, but alȝatis aȝens averise.

The sixth.

Þe sixte word þat Crist seide stondiþ in þis forme: *Blessid be men of clene herte, for þei shal see God.* And þis vertue is bridil aȝens fleishli synnes, and alȝatis aȝens leccherie. For love of sich men, which ben as beestis, is fer from þe love of God. And alȝif men changen her willis after her eldis, neþeles þree willis ben here to oure purpos. Sum men have childis wille, þat feden her wittis wiþ sensible þingis and ȝaping[3] [a] of childis gamen, as ȝif þei weren foolis, and after þis comen to mannis witt þat holdiþ al þis foli. But þei ȝyven hem to justing and sheeting[4] and wrastling[b]; and þes suen ofte more foli þan doiþ

[1] So F.; *shulden*, A. [2] *have*, E. [3] *japing*, E. [4] *scheting*, E.

[a] *ȝaping* or *japing* is trickery. Chaucer says of his Pardoner (Prologue to Canterbury Tales),—

'And thus with fained flattering and japes,
He made the persone and the peple his apes.'

And we read in Gower (*Confessio Amantis*, lib. II),—

'This Geta forth bejaped went,
And yet ne wist he what it ment.'

[b] *to justing, sheeting, and wrastling;* in other words, to the favourite pastimes of the upper, the middle, and the lower class respectively. With regard to the first, it must be remembered that our author wrote but a few years after the death of Edward III, the reviver of the Round Table, and the founder of the order of the Garter, whose reign was the culminating period in England of the spirit of Chivalry. Justing was then, and continued to be for a century and a half afterwards, the favourite amusement of persons of condition. It was usually practised with 'arms of courtesy,'

þe firste elde. In þe þridde eelde men have fleishli willis, and wille of worldli goodis to maynteyne hem longe. And þis lastiþ in worldeli men wel nyȝ to her eende. But sum men, after þes þre, have good wille or yvel, as men þat delitin hem in riȝtwisnes of God, or ellis in þe fendis synne, þat ben calendis[1] to þe toþer liif. And peril in þis liif is moost for to flee. For whanne fleishli likyngis passen from a man, ȝif he shulde be dampned, he haþ pride, envie, and ire, and coveitise of worldli goodis lastiþ ever wiþ him; and þis he beriþ in his soule aftir þat he be deed. And men of sich unclene hert ben leed[2] in to tempting. And liif þat men shulde lede evere is begunne in þis eelde; and þus it were ful nedeful to lyve wel in þis laste elde. For as worldli lustis ben fer from aungels, so worldli desiris ben passid fro þis eelde. Lovynge of clenenesse and riȝtwisnesse for þis tyme shulde occupie mannis soule, as it doiþ in hevene: for ellis he haþ a fendis liif, and occupieþ him in þes foure,—in pride, envie, and ire, and coveitise, þat never is fillid.

Þe sevenþe vertue þat man haþ is for to make pees, or to procure pees, or ellis to preie for pees, or to lyve riȝtli for to procure men[3] to pees. And of þes *pesible men*, Crist *seiþ, þat þei ben blessid, for þei shal be clepid* aftir *Goddis children*. And meede of alle þes sixe is markid for to come, for eende of hem

The seventh.

[1] *kalendis*, E. [2] *led*, E. [3] *riȝtwisly for to stire men*, E.

that is, headless lances, and blunted swords without points; but sometimes, as when certain knights undertook to maintain the honour of their country in a foreign land, weapons *à l'outrance* were, though under regulations, employed, and most often with deadly effect. Chaucer gives us the whole order and regulation of a tournament in the Knight's Tale. (See Scott's *Essay on Chivalry* among his Miscellaneous Prose Works.)

Shooting with the bow was an out-door occupation which was well-nigh universal among the middle and lower classes in the fourteenth and fifteenth centuries. The men exercised in shooting regularly, to keep their hands in as archers. Even ladies, as the illustrations of old MSS. shew, were much given to the use of the bow, both with the sharp-headed arrow in the pursuit of deer, and with the blunt arrow in bird-bolting.

Wrestling was a popular amusement with our forefathers as far back as the Saxon times; in the Middle Ages it is mentioned along with bull and bear baiting, putting the stone, throwing the bar, football, and the like. It does not appear that they were sufficiently brutalized at that time to enjoy boxing. See Wright's *Domestic Manners in England during the Middle Ages*.

alle is first in þe toþer world. But it is ful myche to be clepid þanne Goddis child; for þanne a man is eire of Crist, and so confermed in blis; for alle þes vertues ben not fulle, but ȝif blisse sue hem.

The eighth. Þe eiȝtiþe word and þe laste þat Crist spekiþ in þis mater is seid, *þat þei ben blessid þat suffren pursuyng for riȝt, for hern is þe rewme of hevene,* as it is of þe first men. For he þat is pursuid to deþ for defence of riȝtwisnesse haþ here sum siȝt of blis, and sum telling of sikirnesse, and so he haþ here in eernes[1] oþer wise blisse þan þes oþer; and as men seien comunli, þei passen to hevene wiþouten peyne. And, for þis is a nedeful vertue, and more hard þan þes oþer, þerfore mede of þis vertue is wel þus joyned to it. For certis, ȝif men wolden stifli stonde, and many togidir, for riȝtwisnesse, þe fendis part shulde be ful feble, and pees, wiþ welfare, shulde men have. And so it were ful nedeful to moove many to þis vertue. And siþ wanting of þis vertue bringiþ in contrarie synne, drede of cowardise hereof shulde meeve men to þis vertue. For many ben traitours to God, and proctours to þe fend,—ouþer privy or apert,—þat wolen not stonde for Goddis lawe. And þus Crist applieþ his wordis speciali to hise apostlis, and techiþ hem how pursuyng þat men dreden here moost, shulde be confortable to hem þat stonden for Cristis lawe. *Blessid shal ȝe be, seiþ Crist, whanne þat men shal curse ȝou, and whanne men shal pursue ȝou, and shal seie al maner of yvel aȝens ȝou; lying, for me. Joie ȝee and be glad; for ȝour hire is mouche in hevenes.* And þis word confortiþ men to stonde aȝens Anticrist, for he wole faste curse men and pursue hem as eretikis; but he is cursid þat leveþ herfore to telle Goddis lawe and his wille.

[1] *ernes*, E.

www.ingramcontent.com/pod-product-compliance
Lightning Source LLC
Chambersburg PA
CBHW030936110726
47900CB00004B/1025

* 9 7 8 3 3 3 7 2 8 2 1 3 4 *